My thanks go to the following people who so gener-ously gave me valuable information during the writing of this book:

To the members of the Gaiety Theatre, Ayr, in particular Alan Davies, Theatre Manager; Kirstie McDougall, Facilities Manager; Gordon Taylor, Arts Officer; Alistair Green, Assistant Stage Supervisor.

To Janet and Ian (The Krankies) who welcomed me backstage during a performance and found time to talk to me between appearances.

To all the members of their wonderful company.

To Karen Hunter, the beautiful and gifted violin-ist and singer, who gave me an insight into her life as a performer.

To Betty Fischer, USA, who sailed on the great Atlantic liners between the wars, and to her Scottish cousin Betty Case, who organised our meeting.

To Lilian Bernard Levi, who remembers when she journeyed by rail to the South of France in the 20s and 30s.

To my faithful correspondents among Bristol's Senior Citizens, and in particular to Reginald Tippett.

And to John, who never grumbles and gives me unfailing support.

# Chapter One

When Tessa Morland met her cousin, Eve Brook, for the first time she disliked her.

The day began as usual at seven when her mother called her, putting a match to the gas-light against the early morning January darkness. 'Come on, Tessa, time to get up.' It never varied.

She obeyed and dressed, shivering in the cold, her movements restricted in her bedroom under the eaves which was little bigger than a cupboard. But it was her own and had been for three years since the day she was fourteen and had reluctantly left school to go to work.

'You're almost a woman, now,' Mum had said. 'You need privacy.'

It seemed strange to be putting on her Sunday best for a weekday, but today was Great-grandmother Brook's funeral. She had never met her late relative so could be excited without feeling sad at the idea of meeting relatives who were, Mum said, rich folk.

Tessa had never managed quite to believe Mum's stories of how Dad was descended from a wealthy family who had cast off their daughter, Tessa's grandmother, because she had run away to marry a carpenter. Dad was silent on the matter. He was silent a great deal of the time, deferring to his wife, partly for the sake of peace, but mostly because she ran his life evenly, without fuss. He had always been quiet, said Mum, but more so after the Great War which had ended eleven years ago in 1918, when the terrible slaughter had stopped and, his duty as a soldier finished, he had returned. Joey sometimes asked him questions about the war, but Dad always frowned and shook his head.

When Tessa was small she had asked her mother, 'Why don't we ever meet our rich relations? Are they wicked?' She had heard the word so often in chapel that it came easily to her lips.

Mum had pursed her mouth disapprovingly. 'Their money's come down to them from their parents, not like ours that your father has to work hard for. Idle rich!'

'We're connected to the idle rich,' Tessa had told Ruff the dog who had licked her hand. Not the same dog they had now because he had died. They always called their current dog Ruff.

She fed him and the cat and called Susan, her sister, and Joey, who slept in one of the two first-floor bedrooms, their beds divided by a tall screen. Susan had the half with the window. Tessa would have hated to sleep in Joey's dark corner, but he didn't seem to mind. He was eleven and phlegmatic. He groaned, rolled over and slid out of bed, and Tessa returned to Susan who was, as she had known she would be, asleep again. Susan was ten and lazy. Tessa yanked off the bedclothes and left, ignoring her sister's squeals of protest.

The family sat down to breakfast.

'A proper breakfast' Mum called it, which meant that plates would be well stacked with bacon, sausages and tomatoes, with a fry-up of any leftover potatoes or stale bread on the side. Mrs Morland watched her family closely at all times, a short, plump guardian in a floral wrap-around pinafore, determined to force plenty of what she considered the right amount of nourishment into her brood. This, for such a purpose, included her elder daughter even though she was no longer a child.

As the family ate, Mrs Morland chivvied them. 'Dad, finish up those potatoes. And you, Joey and Susan – you can both get more off those bacon rinds if you try. Tessa! You've left the fat and you've hardly put any butter on your toast. How many times must I tell you that you'll never be healthy if you don't eat? Look at our Joey and

2

Susan. Nice, plump children both.'

Tessa didn't need to look to know that her brother and sister resembled a couple of suet puddings and she'd had to let out the seams of their clothes more than once. When Mum wasn't looking she scoffed her bread with its scraping of butter and slipped the remainder of her bacon to the dog, who lay quietly at her feet, a tail-wagging receptacle of the tidbits she frequently dropped for him. She washed the dishes while Susan wiped.

Dad, wearing his slightly rusty black suit and a black tie, saw the younger children off to school, reminding them that they were to eat their midday meal with a neighbour.

They protested loudly as a matter of form. Neither expected to be taken to the funeral; the invitation hadn't included them. Dad silenced them by slipping them toffees.

Tessa was enlisted for the inevitable dusting, polishing and sweeping, before she went to her room where she put on her Sunday coat and hat. They were beginning to show signs of wear and with altered hems would soon be relegated to every-day. Mum insisted on modest hems, outraged by the fashion for skirts above the knees. A new decorous trimming would be allowed on the hat which 'cheered it up', as Mum put it. It wouldn't look out of date, being the helmet shape which had dominated millinery since 1922.

'We can't afford black things just for one occasion,' Mum had said and Tessa agreed. She didn't want a new outfit in black. In fact, she was hoping to persuade Mum to let her have something much brighter next time it was her turn for new clothes.

Seeing the black-edged funeral card printed in beautiful letters in coal-black ink, and the invitation to a house in Frenchay for lunch afterwards, Tessa realised that Mum had been telling the truth all along. Not that she ever told lies, of course. A pillar of the chapel she was, and so was Dad, but Tessa had noticed that people tended to glorify their antecedents in an attempt to thrust their heads above those of their neighbours. Now it was proved that Great-grandmother Brook had actually existed and she was quite sorry she had never met her. She had never seen anyone of so great an age as ninety-one, almost a hundred.

She leaned forward, peering into her small mirror, gazing malevolently at a spot on her chin which had erupted during the night. Surreptitiously, although she was alone, she extracted a box of Rachel face-powder from a small space behind her handkerchief drawer, licked the tip of her finger and made a concealing paste which she patted on the pimple.

Mum surveyed her elder daughter. 'You're growing out of that coat too fast,' she said accusingly. 'It'll need a lot of alteration.'

'Sorry, Mum,' said Tessa, then felt mutinous. Why did she apologise for things which weren't her fault? She couldn't help being five foot eight. Perhaps it had something to do with the humility of her parents. They knew their place in life and stayed in it. Tessa wasn't quite sure of hers. There must be something better than her daily work in a grocer's shop. This sense of being shut out of something beyond her experience tormented her.

'Mr Grice the Grocer,' she had said once. 'He sounds like someone from the Happy Family cards.'

Dad had actually lifted his head from his *Western Daily Press* and reproved her. 'He's a respectable man, Tessa, and not one to be mocked, especially when he's offering you a safe job where you won't get dirty, not like you would in a factory.'

Neither Mum nor Dad had a strong sense of humour. Mum didn't laugh much even during the family visit to the pantomime at Christmas, though Tessa had to admit that some of the humour was beyond her, too. Other people collapsed with mirth. Every year, Mum came out stiff with indignation. 'We're never going to the panto again! Never! I don't know why they have to be so rude!' But everyone, including many of the chapel members, went and the women discussed it in their Bright Hour. Mum couldn't bear to be left out so each 27 December found them in their seats in the back of the circle in the Princes Theatre, Mum with a half-pound box of Fry's Assorted Chocolate Varieties, Dad with his toffees and the three children clutching bags of liquorice allsorts.

Mum and Dad's steadfast wish was to live quietly, unnoticed, in their cottage just beyond the suburbs of Bristol. Their garden brushed the edges of the country-side and consisted of a large fruit and vegetable patch with a chicken coop in one corner, all of which they tended meticulously. Mum also had a tiny flower bed by the rarely opened front door and a herbal one at the back. Their ambitions reached no further than for Dad to grow better vegetables than his friends and for Mum to encourage her hens to bring forth larger eggs than any other member of their nonconformist chapel. Dad was a carpenter working for a small builder and content with his job.

'You're definitely growing,' pronounced Mum. 'It's to be expected of course at seventeen, but I'm not planning on getting you a new coat until spring. Your Sunday one will have to do, funeral or no funeral. It's a good job it's a nice dark brown. You'd better move a couple of but-tons. Your top half's being squashed.'

'If I ate all you try to make me,' said Tessa, 'I'd grow even bigger, then where would we be? Anyway, it's the fashion to have a squashed chest.'

Mrs Morland stared at her daughter for a moment, trying to decide if she was making fun, then Dad came in and talk of bodies ceased. Bodies were private, to be hidden beneath layers of clothes, their intimate functions confined to a single, once-a-week investigation by Mum: 'Have you been?' If the answer was 'no' the unlucky one would receive a dose of Syrup of Figs on Friday night. She carefully measured the amount, then added more 'just in case', and the recipient was left to deal with the uncomfortable results as best they might. It was useless to try to fool her. If she thought that any family member's all-important bowel was non-functioning she was relentless in her watchful pursuit.

Mum had let the chickens out earlier, the cockerel chasing his wives and impregnating as many as possible during the race for food, crowing his victories, a process Mum pretended never to see. Now they were trying to scratch in the frost-hard dirt. Ruff was chained to his kennel outside and Stripey the cat was turned loose. The big jug of milk was placed on the marble slab in the north-facing pantry and covered with a damp cloth weighted with beads and Mr and Mrs Morland with their elder daughter went outside to wait for the taxi. Dad had ventured to suggest that they stay in by the fire until it arrived, but Mum refused. 'We must be ready as soon as it gets here,' she insisted. So Dad locked the door and they stood in the cold until the car drew up which was to carry them to Frenchay where Great-grandmother had lived all her life. The discussion regarding hiring a taxi or embarking on a convoluted journey on trams and buses from their nearest depot in Kingswood had continued through the whole day and part of an evening.

In the end Mum settled it. 'If we turn up at your posh relative's funeral in a bus they'll look down on us. I shouldn't be surprised if all the other guests had cars.'

'Won't they have proper funeral cars?' Tessa asked.

'I shouldn't wonder,' said Mum, 'though they've not sent one for us.'

'They don't know us,' said Dad in his mild way.

'Then how have we got the invitation, answer me that if you can?' demanded Mum, and Dad subsided.

In the taxi Tessa folded herself between her parents in the back. 'You must take after someone from the past,' said Mum. 'Our Joey and Susan aren't like a couple of bean poles. I hope you won't grow much more. It's such an expense.'

The taxi drew up at the end of a line of large limousines which was moving slowly to the church door. Mum tutted. 'This'll cost us more. We could get out and pay him off and walk.'

'That wouldn't look right,' said Dad. 'We've got a taxi and we'll stay in it till we reach the church door.'

He so seldom asserted himself that Mum agreed, if huffily, and contented herself with watching critically as he paid the fare, frowning at the threepenny tip. They were conducted to seats at the back of the church which was icy in the winter gloom and Mum slid her umbrella, from which she would not be parted, beneath the seat. Tessa shivered, but only partly from the chill. She was fascinated by the number of obviously rich people who were there, overwhelmed by the vista of black, wondering if the wealthy kept special clothes for funerals or simply bought new. Most of the women were swathed in fur and the men wore expensive-looking overcoats or morning coats and discarded their top hats on the seat beside them. Dad had his usual Sunday bowler. An organ was playing softly and the mood was lugubriously respectful, fitting for the last rites of a woman who had almost reached her century.

Mum nudged Tessa. *'They're* not so posh,' she whispered.

Tessa looked at the group of men and women in plain suits and hats. 'I expect they're servants.'

Before Mum could reply the coffin was carried in, followed by the chief mourners, and the congregation stood and obliterated the view of Dad and Mum, though Tessa was able to follow its progress to the trestles in front of the altar. The service seemed to go on for ever. Was it the great age of her late relative which made it necessary to put her to rest with so much hymn-singing, preaching, praying and pomp, or her importance? She wondered about the woman who lay in her coffin. She must have been very wrinkled and shrivelled. There had been an old lady who was brought to chapel every Sunday by her relatives who practically had to carry her and she'd been a mass of wrinkles. Her mouth had sunken in because she had no teeth, and she was nowhere near a hundred.

Afterwards the mourners stood in the churchyard in

the wicked January wind which whined and rattled the bare branches as if they were old bones, lifting the men's hair, causing the women to clutch their hats, as they waited to see Great-grandmother Brook's heavy oak casket lowered into its final resting place. It was during the graveside prayers that Tessa opened her eyes and saw a girl of about her own age watching her. She was everything Tessa would have liked to be. She held herself gracefully, she was very pretty, and peeping from beneath her cloche hat in wings which brushed her perfect skin, striking a brilliant, irreverent note in the gloom, was rich auburn hair. It was exactly the colour Tessa had always coveted. Around the girl's shoulders was a sable stole.

Tessa was shaken with envious dislike. In spite of her endeavours to circumvent Mum's efforts and eat less she knew herself to be somewhat plump and her hair, though thick, was a nondescript colour between fair and brown. The girl's eyes held hers forcefully and Tessa looked away first and realised that an elderly woman was frowning at her. She hastily closed her eyes, then felt indignant. The woman herself could not have been praying.

Curiosity nagged her and she lifted her head and peered again through half-closed lids to see that the red-haired girl was still watching her, as was a tall young man by her side. He gave her the merest hint of a wink which brought quick, embarrassed colour to Tessa's face. But maybe he hadn't winked at all. Maybe he was blinking away a tear. The thought of her own mortification if she had winked back at a man who was struggling with tears unnerved her.

At last the ceremonies were over and the mourners waited for their cars, the men stamping their feet, the women drawing their furs closer around themselves. The servants were already being hurried away.

'How are we going to get to the house from here?' muttered Mum.

The young man who had winked at Tessa approached them. 'Mr and Mrs Morland and Miss Tessa Morland, I believe?' He had an American accent which Tessa recognised from films which she sometimes daringly crept in to watch. She loved the new talkies.

'Who are you?' asked Mum.

Tessa shrank from the hectoring tone which Mum used when she was unsure of herself.

The man appeared not to have noticed. He smiled and held out his hand. 'I'm Paul Jefferson, one of the many descendants of Great-grandmother Brook. I've been asked to see you safely to the house.'

Mum bestowed one of her tight smiles on him as he shook first her hand, then Dad's. 'We didn't bring a car,' she said.

'No. Places were left for you to accompany the cortège. We expected you at the house before the service.'

Tessa could sense Mum bridling with indignation. Dad would get it in the neck later for not knowing the proper form. Paul Jefferson took Tessa's outstretched hand in his and enveloped it, concealing her glove with the darned fingers, allowing it to lie there a few seconds. She knew she was blushing. She hated this visible sign of her vulnerability even more than she hated the pimples which always arrived when she least wanted them.

'Nice to meet you, Mr Jefferson,' she said.

'Do please call me Paul, and may I call you Tessa? After all, we are distant cousins. Kissing cousins, as we Americans say. There are quite a number among the mourners.'

Tessa's blush grew more fiery, but her curiosity overcame her diffidence. 'Are the people you stood with American?'

He looked around. 'Eve seems to have disappeared. Typical. She does exactly as she pleases. The chap over there, the very tall one, is her father. His wife is next to him.'

'Has Eve got red hair?'

Paul's smile widened. 'She would hate to hear her hair described as red. Auburn, or titian, are the terms she uses.'

'Titian?' asked Mum.

'An artist who painted women with red hair,' explained Dad. He sometimes came out with bits of knowledge in a way which surprised his family.

Tessa liked Paul. He towered over her and that was a nice change. The few boys her parents had so far allowed her to be friendly with, strictly under supervision, were often no taller than she and sometimes shorter.

'Looks have nothing to do with anything,' Mum always said. 'You can't choose a husband by the way he looks or how big he is. What a girl wants is a good provider who can pay the rent every week and look after her and his children properly.'

Tessa had never dared express her belief that a husband and babies need not be the sole aim in a girl's life. She wanted to live a little before she settled down, though she had no idea of how. Mum and Dad wouldn't let her go out even with boys they approved of. As for accompanying her friends to the local church dances, it was out of the question. When Tessa asked why, she was met by a long stare from her mother and the statement, 'I know what's best for you.' Sometimes Mum added, 'Little do you know the dangers out there!'

The panto, an annual trip to Bristol Zoo, a week or two at the seaside in August in Weston Super Mare and rambles organised by the chapel were considered quite enough excitement for anyone.

Paul looked to be in his early twenties. Not strictly handsome, his face broke into deep laughter lines between his nose and the corners of his mouth when he smiled. There were laughter lines, too, around his eyes, which didn't disappear even when he was serious. At the moment his eyes were slightly reddened, perhaps from the wind, perhaps from suppressed emotion.

Paul handed Mrs Morland into a long, black chauffeur-driven limousine and was waiting to assist Tessa. He looked at her so searchingly she wondered if he had guessed her thoughts and climbed into the car so fast she almost tripped over her own feet. Mum's lips were pursed in the expression she used when she was determined not to be impressed. Dad followed Tessa, placing his hat on his knees, while Paul climbed in beside the driver. The car slid smoothly on its way to Great-grandmother's house.

It was very large, a grey stone monument to wealth, reached by a long gravelled drive running between an avenue of trees. Mum's mouth dropped open then she frowned as she hung on to her sense of her own importance. Another of her sayings ran: 'Keep yourself respectable and you're as good as anyone.'

'Fancy your relatives living here,' she addressed her husband. 'It's quite close to us as the crow flies, and you never knew.'

Dad mumbled a little.

'What's that you say, Walter?' snapped Mum, still determined to prove her unimpressed state.

He gestured towards the front. 'Hush up, Lily.'

Mum gave him an indignant look but his assumption of authority quelled her. The car drew up at the large double doors. Her equilibrium wasn't proof against a black-coated footman and for a moment it looked as if she might try to shake his hand. Tessa felt so nervous by now that she stumbled again as she got out of the car and might have fallen, but for Paul's steadying arm. 'Easy does it,' he said.

'Sorry,' she muttered. Damn! She'd done it again. Apologised. She'd also thought a bad word which she'd picked up from one of Mr Grice's customers. She liked the sound of it, the emphasis which gave vent to her feelings, but pray God she never forgot herself enough to say it aloud, especially not here.

Inside the warm, tiled hall the footman took their coats and Mum's umbrella which she relinquished reluctantly and Dad's hat. Tessa was thankful she was wearing her Sunday hat and a smart burgundy marocain dress she had made herself from a free paper pattern in Mum's *Home Chat*. She'd wanted to make cami-knickers too, but Mum had ordered her to throw that 'disgraceful

11

thing on the fire', referring to the tissue paper pattern. Tessa had pretended to do so, but had hidden it with her box of face powder. However she'd had no chance yet to use it and was wearing her usual knitted wool vest and knickers, itchy, but useful for their cottage where the family lived mostly in the kitchen, the only permanently warm place. Even there the door opened directly on to the garden. The only other fire ever permitted was in the best room, and that seldom. Her underclothes were clingingly hot here where not only were there great fires in the hall and drawing room, but radiators, too.

The Morlands followed a parlour maid with black ribbons flowing from her cap through one of the doors leading from the hall into a room which Mum described afterwards to her neighbours as 'Big as a hotel, but not much furniture and not a stick of it new. All old stuff, though, mind you, it had been well looked after.' Tessa's feet sank into the deep pile carpet as she advanced to meet the lady who was acting as hostess.

'Tessa, this is my aunt, Mrs Rose Brook,' said Paul.

Mrs Brook held out a long white hand. 'How do you do? I don't think we have met.'

Tessa was daunted not only by Mrs Brook's haughty demeanour, but by the fact that her dress of tiered crêpe was breathtakingly beautiful and made Tessa's own appear exceptionally cheap. She took the proffered hand. 'No,' she said baldly. 'It's nice to meet you.'

Mrs Brook's severely plucked brows rose a little. 'I cannot place you. From which branch of the family do you come?'

'Miss Morland's grandmother was Henrietta Brook,' explained Paul, though Tessa was mystified as to how he knew.

'Ah!' Mrs Brook gave her a searching look down her long Roman nose. Like most of the family she was tall and so thin Tessa wondered if she ever ate a good meal. 'The carpenter's wife.'

Tessa was shaken by anger. How dare this snooty

woman speak of Grandma Morland so contemptuously? And, by implication, her own mother, also a carpenter's wife.

'Did you ever meet my grandma?' she asked aggressively.

Mrs Brook's smooth forehead creased into a frown. 'I did not.'

'She was lovely, very kind and gentle.' Tessa had begun to stumble over her words and Mrs Brook turned to Mum and Dad and, in her contemplation of this undersized (to her) plump couple who were also part of the extended family, forgot Tessa.

Paul took her elbow and guided her towards a large table set with a white cloth and colourful dishes of food. 'Aunt Rose didn't mean to annoy you. Let's have something to eat,' he suggested. 'What do you fancy? Sausage rolls? Lobster patties? Sandwiches? There's chicken, tongue, and various other bits and pieces thought up by Cook.'

Tessa was flustered by her exchange with his aunt and daunted by the enormous length and breadth of the table and the quantity and variety of dishes, few of which she had seen even in Mr Grice's shop. Most of the guests were ignoring it, drinking wine and smoking, including many of the women who held long cigarette-holders between fingers with painted nails.

Paul identified the food and Tessa, hungry now, said, 'I'll try the lobster. I've never had it before. And what are those black things?'

'Caviare,' said Paul, smiling. 'You spoon it on to the little round crackers.'

By the time she had finished choosing small portions of several of the unfamiliar delicacies, Tessa's plate was piled unexpectedly high and Mum was glaring across the room at her for breaking another of her home-grown rules. 'Nice ladies don't ever eat too much when they're out. It makes them look greedy and bad-mannered.'

Tessa sat in a corner as far away from Mum as she could get, her plate on her knee, while Paul placed a glass of golden wine on a small table at her elbow before circulating.

Mrs Morland edged her way to her daughter. 'You're eating a lot, aren't you? And I hope you won't be drinking that wine.'

'But, Mum, the food is there to be eaten and there isn't anything else to drink. And they've got lovely puddings, things I've never seen before. I promise I won't be a pig.'

'Well, you'll just have to manage without a drink. Fancy only having alcohol. Disgraceful, I call it.'

As if Paul knew exactly when Tessa needed help he appeared beside her mother. 'Mrs Morland, you really should sample the cream meringues, and the madeleines are altogether perfect, one of Cook's specialities. It was so cold in the churchyard and plenty of food will warm you. Isn't it amazing how hungry one becomes at funerals?'

Mrs Morland gave him a suspicious look and hesitated, giving him the opportunity to serve her the sweetmeats he suggested. Then he piled another plate with puddings for Tessa, and Mrs Morland, after one last scathing glance, found a seat nearer the fire.

'Is your mother still cross?' Paul asked.

Tessa glanced across the room. Her mother was sitting with her chest thrust out, looking like a pouter pigeon. She said, 'I'm afraid so. We're teetotallers so she doesn't like to see the wine.'

Paul was astonished. 'Teetotallers? Really! Don't tell me you are members of the Band of Hope?'

'What do you know about the Band of Hope?'

'Not much. I was astonished when I learned that there was an organisation existing solely to ban liquor. In America most of the population are trying to circumvent Prohibition. That's a law which was passed actually banning drink.'

'I read about it. What's wrong with being teetotal?'

He put out a placating hand. 'Nothing, of course.'

Mum was hidden now and Tessa said, relenting and

14

smiling a little, 'I'll try the wine.'

'That's the girl,' said Paul.

Servants, a man and two women, moved about, offering food and drink, emptying ash trays, quietly directed by another man in black.

'Who is he?' she asked.

'Who? Oh, that's Partridge the butler. Nice chap. Looked after Great-grandmother perfectly, even when she was a bit, well, forgetful. Actually, her wits were none too sharp by the end.'

'Who else lived here besides Great-grandmother?'

Paul smiled at her. 'No one, except the servants.'

Tessa was astonished. 'Do you mean to say she had this huge place and all these people working for her, just her, by herself?'

'She certainly did, and many more below stairs, as well as three nurses in constant attendance in her later years.'

'Didn't she want the company of her family?'

'Not at all. She was a great old girl, but grew rather suspicious, afraid that someone might try to influence her in the matter of her will.'

Tessa drank deeply of the wine which was replenished almost immediately by the butler. She felt confident now, daring even.

'Did you discuss her will with her? That's so morbid!'

'She didn't find it so. She brought up the subject constantly, threatening to cut out this one, then that one. But she was well served by her solicitor who's pretty ancient himself and little has been altered or added for several years, except a few codicils as various babies were born. If you'll excuse me, Cousin Tessa, I see my aunt signalling rather frantically.'

Tessa was sorry to see him go. She liked him and his conversation was fascinating. She wondered if Dad and Mum were enjoying themselves. She caught sight of Dad standing with a group of men. He was looking up into their faces, intently following their conversation of which snatches reached Tessa. 'America . . . the share market . . . plenty of money to be made . . . courage needed.' He, too, was sipping wine and when the crowd of chattering people parted for a moment, Tessa saw Mum give him a basilisk glare. Dad nodded at intervals as if he knew what the men meant. Perhaps he did, but they talked over his head as if he were not there and when he ventured to speak Tessa caught the quick look of derisive amusement which flashed between two of them. Abruptly she wanted to go home. What were they doing here, anyway, mixing with these people who thought themselves better than the rest of humanity, being looked upon almost as freaks? She felt protective and made her way towards her mother who was seated with three ladies discussing hats.

'I am becoming weary of the cloche,' said one. 'Do you recall what gorgeous embellishments we once wore? Feathers and fruit and ribbons, even birds.'

'So pretty!' exclaimed the second lady.

The third sighed, 'I'm sure that the fashion must change soon.'

Mum spoke a little too loudly in her determination to join in. 'I've kept all the lovely feathers from the cockerels we've killed over the past few years. One day perhaps I'll be able to decorate my hats like I used to.'

After a pause the first woman said, 'How sweet!'

'Perfectly delicious,' agreed the second.

The third looked bored. They were mocking Mum and Tessa grew angrier and wondered how she could get her parents to leave.

'Don't frown,' murmured Paul into her ear.

She turned and said urgently, 'They're making fun of my mum! And my dad, too.'

'Are they? Oh dear, I'm afraid they are.' His reply irritated her, but at least it was candid. 'Don't mind them,' he said. 'The men like to have someone to display their worldly wisdom to and the women have to sharpen their claws several times a day.'

'Well, I don't think much of them. Are they all your relations?' asked Tessa.

'Yes. Great-grandmother left a lot of descendants.

Mrs Morland doesn't seem to mind their silly talk.'

'That's because she doesn't realise—' began Tessa, and stopped.

'Of course she doesn't. She isn't used to society bitches.'

Tessa gasped. 'If she heard you swear she'd tell you to wash out your mouth with soap.'

'Swear? Oh, sorry, but that's what they are. And by the way, don't forget that they're all related to you, too.'

Tessa stared around the crowded room. The idea staggered her. All these people in their expensive clothes with their upper-class voices were members of *her* family. There they were, munching and drinking while their cigarettes and cigars lay on ash trays, still alight, sending thin spirals of blue smoke into the warm air. 'Fancy being related to them all! How did you find out about us?'

'I didn't. It was the solicitor. I believe he employed a company which investigates such matters.'

'*Detectives*?'

'Respectable ones.'

Tessa wondered if he was teasing her, but found she didn't mind. 'There must have been lots of times when no one thought of us. Weddings, christenings, funerals—'

'Yes, but this is different.'

'Is it? Why?'

'Your family is mentioned in Great-grandmother's will.'

'Is it? I don't think Mum and Dad know that. They were puzzled by the invitation.'

'They should have had a letter. If they didn't, they have a pleasant surprise coming.'

'Did she have a lot of money?' asked Tessa.

'A lot.'

'I suppose it's divided equally among all these people?'

'I shouldn't think so.'

'I thought you said you knew all about her will.'

Paul's brows went up. 'Snappy little thing, aren't you?'

But his grin tempered his words. 'I know only what Great-grandmother and the solicitor chose to tell me. She and I were good friends. I shall miss her,' he added, sounding bleak.

This brought home to Tessa that a woman had died and left a gap in some lives. She wanted to say something soothing, but no words came. How could she console a man anyway who until today had been a stranger to her, by mouthing platitudes about a dead person she had never known? Would he want her to? She didn't think so.

Their attention was taken by the entrance of the red-haired girl who strolled in chatting amiably to a man who couldn't hide his admiration. Tessa glanced at Paul who was smiling in the girl's direction and felt another surge of jealousy. Boys had complimented her on her own looks but they weren't a patch on this girl's, and further-more she was wearing a silk and lace frock which was utterly ravishing.

'There's Eve at last,' exclaimed Paul.

'She's very pretty,' said Tessa, the words forcing them-selves out grudgingly.

'And you hate her!' His voice was filled with mirth.

'No, I don't! Don't be silly!'

Paul laughed outright and Eve walked across the room towards him, greeting people on the way in an easy manner, closely followed by the man. She made a care-less gesture towards him and said something. He left her and attached himself to a group.

'Where have you been?' asked Paul.

'None of your business! Why were you laughing?' She didn't wait for an answer but turned her attention to Tessa. 'I saw you at the funeral, but I don't remember meeting you before.'

Close up Eve was even lovelier, her white skin perfec-tion, her hazel eyes luminous, and when she smiled her teeth were white and even. Tessa's were just a little bit crooked even though the dentist had pulled a couple to make more room in her mouth.

'This is Tessa Morland, a long-lost cousin,' said Paul.

'Oh! I thought I knew them all. Which branch of the family are you?' Eve opened her small bag and took out an amber cigarette holder, fitting a gold-tipped cigarette into it. Paul obliged her with a light and she drew smoke down into her lungs then allowed it to wreathe her face, like a movie heroine.

'My gran was Henrietta Brook.'

'Oh? I don't recall the name.' Eve inhaled again. Tessa had never seen anyone smoke with such style. Not that she was familiar with women who smoked. None of Mum's friends would dream of indulging in such an unladylike habit. Dad's friends held their Woodbine or home-rolled tobacco between brown-stained fingers until they were down to the very last bit of stub, and Mr Grice smoked a pipe and that only in his living room. Eve's voice was clear, its accent no more intrusive than Paul's.

'Henrietta married Grandpa Morland for love,' said Tessa proudly.

'Really?' Eve stubbed out her cigarette. 'Paul, get me a glass of wine and a sandwich, for God's sake. I'm hungry and parched. Funerals!'

'Yes, really,' said Tessa vigorously.

'Oh, yes, we were talking of your family. I do remember something. Didn't Henrietta run off with a workman who was doing a job in the house? I believe she lived on a very small scale for the rest of her life.'

Piqued by her off-hand manner, Tessa said, 'I only half believed what I heard about you all, and she was *very* happy with Grandpa. I'm surprised that Great-grandmother refused to forgive her. Fancy keeping a grudge against her own daughter for the rest of her life.'

Eve shrugged. 'Great-grandmother might have taken her back, but Great-grandfather must have been a frightful disciplinarian. He crossed out Henrietta's name in the family Bible. Silly old josser! He nearly put the pennib through the paper in his temper. My mother showed me. I think she hoped it would put me off a most unsuitable guy she believed I had fallen for. But I told her I was only amusing myself. I was, too.'

'A guy?'

'American for man,' explained Paul, returning with a glass of wine which Eve tossed down her throat with no regard for what Mrs Morland would call manners, following it with a small sandwich which she pushed whole into her mouth.

'My grandpa was a master carpenter,' said Tessa. ·

Eve swallowed her sandwich and said, 'Hardly what Henrietta's mother wanted in the family.'

'My father is a carpenter, too,' said Tessa.

Eve gave her a baffled look. 'Indeed!'

Her tone stung Tessa further. 'Jesus was a carpenter,' she said, so loudly that several conversations stopped and she was regarded with astonishment by some of the guests and amusement by others. She couldn't think why. After all, they had just been to church and laid Great-grandmother to rest with lots of prayers so presumably they were Christians. Conversation broke out again and Eve began to give Paul a rapid stream of news about people of whom Tessa had never heard. To her pleasure he stopped his cousin in mid-flow. 'Tessa doesn't want to hear a load of chatter about our crowd.'

Eve shrugged and walked away and the man who had escorted her rejoined her.

'Who is he?' Tessa asked Paul.

'Just another relative. Jack Padbury. Nice chap.'

'Is he engaged to Eve?'

'Good lord, no. I can't imagine her settling for him. He's not quite rich enough and far too diffident to push his interest. He's always afraid he might annoy her. Eve will need a strong hand to control her.'

'He looks as if he'd like to marry her.'

Paul smiled. 'Do you always analyse people?'

Tessa gave the question her full attention. 'I suppose I do.'

'I see. And how do I come out?'

Tessa looked sideways at him from beneath her lashes

in a way that sent the chapel boys into stammering, blushing embarrassment. 'I'm not obliged to tell you.' To her chagrin Paul laughed at her and she wasn't sure she liked him after all.

'You're very sweet,' he said.

Sweet! She hated the word. It was patronising and insipid. 'I think I'll see if my mother needs me.'

Paul detained her by putting his hand lightly on her arm. 'If I have offended you I'm really sorry. Won't you forgive me?'

She looked up into his face. His clear blue eyes were studying her in a way which disconcerted her. 'You haven't offended me,' she lied.

'You didn't like me calling you "sweet", did you?'

Once more the mortifying colour flooded her face.

'I meant it in the nicest possible way. You're like a breath of fresh spring air after most of the girls I know. Sweet like a flower.'

Tessa was overcome by his compliments and the way he was looking at her, but also by the wine which was beginning to make her feel slightly out of control. She should be cautious. She might be an innocent, but she wasn't stupid. This man was a practised flirt, leaving her side and returning when it suited him. He was trying his tricks on her, treating her exactly as Mum and Dad were being treated by the others. Later, this toffee-nosed lot would laugh at the funny provincials who had turned up at the funeral. Eve would laugh, too. 'I shall see if Mum wants me,' she said abruptly, and left him.

# Chapter Two

As Tessa had anticipated she and Dad were berated for drinking wine.

'I was just being polite,' said Dad, pleadingly.

'Being polite! I hope *I* was polite and I didn't need to touch alcohol. You'd have thought someone would have made a pot of tea, but I managed without any drink at all.'

'You're good, Lily,' said Mr Morland, 'and she sets us a fine example, doesn't she, Tessa?'

She agreed, but her mother continued to chide them. 'It's a great pity they haven't banned drink here like they have in America.'

Mr Morland ventured, 'But look what that's led to. Gangsters—'

'I know all about that!' Mum did, too. She was morbidly fascinated by the accounts of gang-land wars, the mobs and Feds. 'It's all brought about by the wicked people who go on making the demon drink,' she always said, 'and that kind of thing could never happen here.'

Once Joey had asked innocently, 'Why do you read about it, Mum, if you hate it so much?'

'It's a Christian duty to acquaint yourself with sin so you can fight it,' she had snapped.

'Don't be angry, Mum,' begged Tessa now. 'Dad and I can sign the Pledge again.'

'What! You'll do no such thing. I don't want everyone in chapel talking about you!'

Tessa was glad. Now she had broken the Pledge she wouldn't feel bound by it. She had enjoyed the wine and the pleasantly woozy state it had engendered in her. In fact, looking back she had enjoyed the day, even if her final moments in the Brook house had been soured. She had not had a chance to speak to Paul again and she was sorry. Tease or not, she couldn't help liking him.

Dad had gone to see Great-grandmother Brook's solicitor and Mum had been grousing to Tessa. 'I've not been able to settle properly to a thing all morning. I dropped my shortcrust pastry on the floor and had to throw it out and make another batch. The hens will eat it, but it's a wicked waste. And my Victoria sponges only rose to half their usual size. I'll have to make more for the Bright Hour, it's my turn to do the teas and I can't let anyone see these. We'll have them hot with jam and custard for tea. And your father's lost a morning's pay so I just hope he's got some good news when he gets back. Now the dinner's nearly ready and he's still not here.'

Dad arrived at last. 'What's happened?' demanded Mum, not waiting for him to take off his coat.

'We'll talk in the best room,' he said solemnly.

Joey and Susan were given their meal in the kitchen and watched Tessa enviously as she followed their parents to the sitting room. Dad sat in his chair by the fireplace which held crumpled newspaper, sticks and small lumps of coal. It was never lit on a weekday except for a special occasion, like Christmas. The room was spotlessly clean and very cold; the linoleum around the edge of the carpet shone like polished ice. Mum sat down opposite him and Tessa was waved to a wicker-work stool.

'I went to the solicitor's office,' said Dad, drawing out his moment, making Mum frown impatiently. 'I was treated like a toff, a proper toff. It was Mr Morland this and Mr Morland that. I tell you, Lily, when someone knows you belong to a posh family, they respect you.'

'Such nonsense,' muttered Mum. 'Worldly goods, don't forget. Worldly goods.'

'That's how life is lived by many,' said Dad in the

pontificating way he sometimes adopted. Although so quiet at home, he was quite in demand as a speaker in the local chapels.

Tessa wanted to shake them both. 'Dad,' she begged, 'I'll have to go back to work without my dinner if you don't hurry.'

'You're right, Tessa, and I'm hungry for mine too.' Mr Morland drew a deep breath, reached for his cigarettes, replaced them when he caught Mum's eye and remembered that smoking was forbidden in the best room, and said, 'The upshot of it all is that we've been left two hundred pounds.'

'*Two hundred*?' Astonishment robbed Mum of further speech.

'Two hundred,' repeated Dad triumphantly. 'A real nest egg for our old age.'

Tessa didn't know what she had been expecting, but judging by the house in Frenchay Great-grandmother must have been worth thousands. Two hundred pounds was a lot of money, but she wasn't foolish enough to imagine it would make much of a difference to their daily lives.

'That's wonderful, Dad . . .' she began.

'It's going straight into our savings, of course,' said Mum. 'You agree, don't you, Walter?' She was pink with excitement.

'Couldn't we use a bit of it for a holiday?' Tessa asked tentatively.

She was regarded by two pairs of astonished eyes.

'A holiday?' said Mum. 'What do you mean? You've always had a holiday, ever since you were born. Unlike some. We're booked up for August as usual in the boarding house in Weston.'

'I mean a different holiday,' persisted Tessa. 'There are seasides where the tide never goes out and you can paddle and swim all day.'

'What nonsense!' said Mr Morland crossly. His news was having an irritating effect on his daughter. 'Tides have to go out. They're controlled by the moon.'

'I mean it doesn't go out miles and miles like Weston, it's just a bit further away, and it's always nice and sandy all over, not with acres of thick mud. At the funeral people were talking about going to France, or Italy, or even America for holidays.'

'They'd have done better to spend their money on a decent funeral meal,' snapped Mrs Morland. 'Bits of this and that instead of a proper sit-down dinner. Stingy, I call it.'

'Now, Lily,' said Dad, 'you can't say they're stingy, not now we've got a fortune to tuck away.'

'That's no thanks to them. Your grandmother must have repented. I bet if the lot we saw today had their way we wouldn't have got a thing. Who else was in the office?'

'No one. Only me.'

Mum snorted. 'The others went somewhere else to divide the money between them. I didn't take to them at all, not at all.'

'Well, it wasn't up to them,' said Mr Morland mildly. 'It seems that old Mrs Brook put us in her will after her husband died. My mother had already passed on or things might have been different. And she remembered her servants, too, every one, down to the scullery maid. In fact, the old ones got pensions for life.'

'She must have been nice at any rate,' admitted Mum.

'Yes, she must,' said Tessa. 'I'm sure she'd understand if you spent some of the money now. We could really enjoy it.'

'I have enough enjoyment out of life already, thank you very much,' said Mrs Morland, 'and so does your dad. And I thought *you* were contented. I'm surprised at you, wanting to be such a spendthrift. If we were like that you wouldn't have such a comfortable home.'

The Westminster chiming clock on the mantelpiece, one of their cherished wedding presents, proclaimed the half hour and Mrs Morland got to her feet. 'Walter, you'll have to eat your dinner fast to get back to work on time. You, too, Tessa. You'll need to run.'

She stemmed the torrent of rebellion which was churning her insides and obeyed.

Eve Brook climbed from her bath and grabbed at the towel which was warm from the radiator. She wrapped it round herself and stalked into her adjoining bedroom, leaving a trail of wet footprints on the carpet, and stood by the fire where she dripped on to the Oriental rug. She was bored, bored, bored. For three weeks, ever since Great-grandmother's funeral, she had been living with her mother in Padding House, a barn of a place in Frenchay. Paul had his own flat in Clifton and no wish to leave his comfortable bachelor quarters. She did not blame him. She found Frenchay in the winter utterly dreary. She had not minded it at first, imagining herself driving into Bristol to theatres and night clubs until, amazingly, Mother had put her foot down and forbidden such frivolities so soon after Great-grandmother's decease.

It was ridiculous. Her parents felt no grief at the old lady's death. On the contrary, they were irritated because, although they had received a share of her money, out of her extensive and costly collection of jewellery all she had left Mother were a few minor pieces which needed resetting and cleaning.

Father had escaped back to the States where he was no doubt enjoying himself in his usual way. She suspected that he chased after other women. Mother was knuckling under to convention, concerned that someone might pass critical remarks about lack of respect for the dead. 'It's a lot of damned nonsense!' Eve said aloud now, though she would not dare to say so to her mother. She had a way of looking at one, wordlessly, that was totally daunting.

Eve's experience of Great-grandmother had been on one occasion in her early childhood when she had been lifted on to the knee of a wrinkled crone who smelled of peppermints and wintergreen oil, and who kissed her with dry lips over a chin bristling with whiskers. The second time she saw her had been in her coffin, her skin as yellow as old carved ivory. Someone had clothed her in heavy white satin and she looked incongruously bride-like. The only jewel she wore was her thick gold wedding ring. She had lost the bristles and Eve wondered if some-one had shaved them after death. Or maybe one of the nurses had done it while she lay dying. Eve grimaced. She was getting morbid and no wonder.

She wandered over to the window and looked down at the garden streaked with cold winter sunshine, at the shrubs and trees, dripping with melting frost, and the sight made her shiver. Dark clouds were massed in the distance and probably held snow. God, she'd really be holed up here if there was a deep fall. She had to get out, do something to relieve the monotony.

She dried herself quickly in front of the fire and pulled on the brassiere which flattened her breasts in the cur-rent style, fastened the hooks and eyes on her suspender belt, stepped into her cami-knickers and dragged on a pair of new, flesh-coloured silk stockings. When in her irritable haste she snagged one and had to match up another, she swore. At times like this she missed having her own maid. Because of her hasty temper she had never kept one for long and after the latest had left in tears, Mother had told her coldly that she could in future enlist the services of a housemaid. Eve had not minded. Maids could be a damned nuisance, prying and spying when she wanted to pursue her life unobserved. Now if she laddered a stocking, or tore a garment, she simply threw it away. Of course, if it was the kind of frock Mother labelled 'important', a housemaid had to be coaxed to mend it before someone suggested that Eve herself might benefit from a little sewing.

She hurled the stocking on the fire and watched it flare in the flames. Money was no problem. Father had oodles of it and her allowance was generous. He was making a lot more by dealing on the New York Stock Exchange. He had left for the States only two days after the funeral because he was ostensibly unwilling to trust business entirely to his partners. In the end, Eve had been relieved to see him go. She had wondered if a funeral might have softened his attitude to her, caused him to show her a little humanity, even love. It hadn't.

She descended the wide staircase as her mother crossed the hall from the library on her way to the small sitting room which had been Great-grandmother's favourite. Mrs Brook looked up at her daughter, her eyes cool as they took in the bottle green coat and skirt with astrakhan trimming, the pale green blouse and dark green hat adorned only with an encircling ribbon.

'Not in black, Eve? I thought I made my wishes clear.'

'For heaven's sake, Mother!' Eve spoke without heat. Calmness impressed Mother so much more. She strolled on down the stairs. 'I didn't know the old lady and you hardly met her, so why the fuss?'

'She was a relative – a distinguished one. And once I knew her quite well.'

Eve's temper overcame her. 'You cared nothing for her.'

Mrs Brook's brow creased in a frown. 'I respected her.'

'Careful, Mother,' said Eve. 'You tell me never to frown, remember? Wrinkles?'

'You had better watch your tongue. No man likes a sharp woman.'

Eve smiled. If Mother knew the half of it! Men cared for bodies, not tongues. Well, not in the way she meant. 'I'll try to remember,' she said.

'Please do. You are going out?'

'Observant of you.'

Mrs Brook lifted her eyebrows. There was anger in her eyes and Eve knew she was going too far. She said quickly, 'Sorry, Mother, being cooped up has made me cross. I need air and exercise.'

'Both may be had by walking round the garden. It is extensive enough. Put on a coat.'

Eve sighed and her mother said, 'Perhaps you would prefer to walk on the common.'

29

'It might be – different,' said Eve. She had been about to say 'more fun', but that would have earned another reproof.

Mrs Brook nodded. 'Very well. Enjoy your outing.' She continued on her way across the hall. Her figure was as trim as a girl's, her legs long and slender. She was beautiful, too, in a composed, ice-maiden kind of way. A hairline crack manifested itself in Eve's composure, a door in her mind opened for a second, and she slammed it shut before pain could escape and surface, as it did in dreams.

She collected her silky sleek ponyskin coat, her leather driving gauntlets, and left the house by the back door, the nearest way to the common. Mother might be watching and listening, though she doubted it. It was Mother's way, and always had been, to issue a command and expect it to be obeyed without question. It was this which had enabled Eve to break so many rules.

She hurried to the big stable-house where the cars were garaged. She checked that the front gate was open, then slid behind the wheel of her little red two-seater, started it up and roared out into the road. Mother's quick ears must have caught the noise, but too late to stop her. 'To hell with the common,' Eve shouted, then began to sing: 'Only a rose I bri-i-ing you-o-o . . .' Her voice wasn't equal to the demands of the tune and she swung into a jazzy version of 'I Can't Give You Anythin' But Love, Baaaby'. She liked to sing. She was as good as many show girls she had heard and better than some. She was sure she could sing professionally if it weren't for her parents' stuffy outlook. But they would cut off her money instantly if she ever sang in public. By 'public' they meant outside their circle, or for a fee. They smiled indulgently, in front of others at any rate, when she joined the band at private dances. One day, she promised herself, she would break away and do as she pleased, but if she did she would need to get money from somewhere other than Father.

She had been driving aimlessly and saw a signpost

pointing the way to Kingswood and recalled the name from somewhere. Oh, yes, Paul had mentioned it. Tessa lived there. She pulled up by a field gate. Fat cows were cropping grass, their feet crackling on the frosty turf, their breath steaming like smoke. She tried to light a cigarette. She was clumsy in her gauntlets and pulled them off. The cold bit into her fingers. She threw the unlit cigarette into the field, wondering idly if a cow would eat it and if she did would she produce milk tasting of tobacco?

What could she do next? Her boredom was unendurable. In normal circumstances she could have driven to Bristol and shopped in Park Street or Whiteladies Road, but what was the use of buying clothes if Mother insisted on black? She could have bought colours for later, but when Eve had something fresh she had to wear it immediately, before she grew tired of it.

Then she hit upon a splendid idea. She would visit Tessa. That, at least, might amuse her. Tessa's parents were such funny little fat people and Tessa herself, trying to hide a nasty pimple with a blob of powder, was amusing. The solicitor would know their address, but not having listened to anything anyone told her about Great-grandmother's will, since no money was coming directly to her, she had no idea even of his name. Paul might know. She wondered where she could telephone and drove back to a small public house she had noticed. She pushed open the door. The bar floor was covered in sawdust which gave off a pleasing woody scent and a log fire glowed with hot ash. At the sight of a woman several pairs of disapproving eyes were turned on her.

The barman was elderly and regarded her grimly. 'Yes?'

Eve's mood changed. She was made suddenly aware that a lady was not welcome in a public bar. Far from being daunted she was enchanted, hugely enjoying this instant rural rejection. She smiled. No man could resist Eve when she turned on her considerable charm; it illuminated her beauty.

'Can I help you, miss?' asked the barman. He did not return her smile, but was no longer hostile.

'I'm being very silly, I know,' she said sweetly, 'but I am on my way to visit a cousin and have left her address at home. I wondered if I might use your telephone?'

At this the men laughed, indulgently, as one might at a child. 'Lor', miss,' he said, 'I haven't got a telephone. What would I be wantin' with one?'

Eve looked disappointed. She did it well. She had often thought she might make a serious actress. 'Oh, dear. Whatever shall I do?'

'What's your cousin's name, miss?' asked a man wearing thick trousers and huge black boots.

'Tessa Morland. Her parents are Walter and Lily.'

The men shook their heads. 'Sorry, miss. Is that all you've got to go on?'

'Well, I know that she lives somewhere around Kingswood.'

'Kingswood way?' The barman spoke first, half resenting the intervention of his customers. 'I can tell you how to get to Kingswood. When you're there you could ask at the post office. They've got all the addresses.'

'Unless the party in question never gets a letter,' interposed the man in black boots.

The barman ignored him and led Eve outside to direct her. He had been right and Eve obtained Tessa's address from Kingswood post office. As soon as she had it she wondered whether to bother after all. Her dull mood was wearing off and she was hungry. But having come so far she would go on. She rather wanted to meet Tessa again. At the funeral she had seen the way her cousin stared at her and had known with the confidence of a girl who has always been beautiful that Tessa both admired and envied her.

When she came to the Morlands' cottage she was astonished. It was so tiny. Grey stone, with a tiled roof and a lean-to built on the side; not even picturesque, with the garden a winter wasteland of frozen cabbage stalks. Fowls were clucking and pecking right up to the

32

door. As she watched, Mrs Morland came out and threw some rubbish into a dustbin. Just before she went back inside she turned and looked around and caught sight of the red car parked at the end of the rutted lane. Eve waved, but Mrs Morland did not see her. Eve got out and made her way up a brick path. She knocked at the front door and heard Mrs Morland call, 'Go round the back.' She opened the back door.

'Yes, miss?'

'I am Eve Brook.'

'Oh?'

'I am a relative of the late Mrs Brook.'

'The late—?' Then Mrs Morland's face reddened. 'I see. We were at the funeral.'

'So was I.'

'I don't remember you.'

Eve was suddenly tired of standing in the cold. 'May I come in? I hoped I might see Tessa.'

Mrs Morland stepped back. 'Yes, come in. Our Tessa's still at work, but she'll be home for her dinner. If you like you can have a bit with us.' The concession was enormous, although Eve did not realise it. Invitations to the Morlands' home were few and given formally beforehand.

'Oh dear, that would have been nice, but I must be back home by dinner time.'

Mrs Morland looked at a clock on the mantelpiece. 'It's nearly half-past twelve. That's our dinner time. But if you have to go . . .'

The room fascinated Eve. It was so incredibly small. Along one wall was a range, black-leaded until it shone like steel. A pot of something which smelled good bubbled on it. In fact, the kitchen was redolent with mingled scents which made Eve's mouth water.

'We're having stew with dumplings,' said Mrs Morland.

'Dumplings?'

'Don't you like them?'

33

'I don't know. I've never tried them. But I'm sure I would.'

Mrs Morland was putting a yellow mixture studded with currants into a metal tin.

'What are you doing?' asked Eve.

'Making a cake, of course.' Mrs Morland's aggressive attitude was giving way to friendly scorn. 'Fancy not knowing what I'm doing. Where were you brought up?'

Eve didn't reply. She took in the scrubbed deal table and the five plain chairs set under it. On either side of the fireplace were two small easy chairs.

'Take your coat off or you won't feel the benefit when you go out,' said Mrs Morland. 'And sit down.' Eve hung her ponyskin on a hook behind the door and sat down, placing her feet on a rug which was made of rags sewn together in a haphazard way.

Opposite the range an entire wall was taken up by a dresser which held blue and white china with matching cups hanging from hooks. Two chocolate cakes and a number of small buns were cooling on wire racks.

'This is my baking day,' said Mrs Morland.

'Do you bake on the same day every week?'

'Of course. I always do things the same day every week. If I didn't they wouldn't get done. Stands to reason. You have to have a routine.'

'Don't you ever get bored? I know I should if every week was the same.'

'Bored? I don't know the meaning of the word.'

'I do,' sighed Eve.

Before Mrs Morland could reply the kitchen door opened and Mr Morland came in, bringing a rush of cold air with him.

'There's a nippy-looking red two-seater bottom of the lane,' he said.

'Shut the door carefully,' ordered his wife. 'I've got cakes in the oven.' She turned to Eve. 'I don't suppose you'd know but if a door slams a cake can sink in the middle.'

'No, I didn't know.'

34

'I remember you,' said Mr Morland, holding out his hand. 'You were at the funeral.' His hand was cold and as rough as sandpaper. Perhaps she had reacted to this for he suddenly withdrew it hastily. 'Hands get rough at the carpentry.' He hung his coat and cap over Eve's fur.

'Miss Brook's come to see us, Walter,' said Mrs Morland.

'So I see.' He washed his hands at the kitchen sink and dried them on a towel hanging over the range.

'Get out of my way, do,' said Mrs Morland.

Her husband smiled faintly and seated himself opposite Eve who waited for him to speak. He remained silent, content apparently to lean back in the warmth of the fire and relax. No one she knew would allow a guest just to sit and be neglected. Actually, it was quite pleasant. Perhaps she would try it some time. But she wished they would offer her a pre-lunch sherry.

Again the door opened and Tessa came in. A wind was getting up and a sudden gust of air caught the door and shut it violently.

'Tessa!' cried Mrs Morland.

'Sorry, Mum, the wind caught it. Gosh, the morning's been busy. We had that Mrs Milton in again, the one with eight kids, she wanted something on tick and Mr Grice wouldn't give it to her. You should have heard her language. There's a red motor car by the gate. I wonder—' While she spoke she had removed her hat, hung up her coat and gone to the sink to wash her hands. Now she turned, still using the towel, and saw Eve.

'What—?'

Eve said, 'It is nice to see you again, Cousin Tessa. We had so little chance to speak on the sad occasion of Great-grandmother's funeral that I decided to pay you a visit. I should have telephoned – written – before I came, but I drove here on the spur of the moment.'

'That's your car by the gate?'

'Yes.'

'I thought it must belong to one of the local boys, a fellow called Frank Anderson. He buys old crocks, does

35

them up and sells them. They're always breaking down when he's first testing them.'

Eve's eyebrows rose slightly as she wondered what Father would say if he had heard her new Alvis described as a crock.

Mrs Morland spread a white cloth on the table and Tessa arranged knives, forks and spoons, with side plates and glasses of water, while Mr Morland went out and returned with a plush-seated chair ornately carved.

'It's from the best room,' explained Mrs Morland.

Tessa called from the door and two children came racing in, then stopped dead at the sight of the visitor. Mrs Morland dished out portions of stew, filling plates, not asking anyone how much they wanted, while Tessa cut slices from a crusty loaf which she placed in the centre of the table. The stew was even better than its aroma and Eve ate greedily, dunking bread into the gravy so that nothing could be wasted.

Mrs Morland regarded her quite benevolently. 'You'll have tasted nothing like that anywhere else,' she said.

Eve glanced up. 'No, I haven't. It's simply delicious. Perhaps you could give me the recipe and I could get Cook to follow it.'

Mr Morland shook his head and Mrs Morland said, 'Cook, eh? Well, cook or no cook, I never show my recipes to anyone. They're all made up by me. When our Tessa and Susan get wed I'll pass them on, and to Joey's wife too – if I like her well enough – but that's all.' She sent a stern look to Joey who squirmed at the idea of marriage to a *girl*.

Eve bent to the task of wiping her plate completely clean, a move which was echoed by the others. Funny that a French way of eating heartily and leaving nothing should apply also to these cottagers. Pudding was served. Sponge as light as air with golden syrup pouring down the sides from a small crater at the top. They ate it with custard, creamy with best Jersey milk, Mrs Morland informed Eve. The meal ended with cups of tea and home-made biscuits and Eve was replete and looking forward to talking to her cousin. This glimpse of a world so different from hers had whetted her appetite and she could not wait to find out more. When Tessa wiped her mouth, asked to leave the table and picked up her coat, Eve said, 'You're not going, are you?'

'I must,' said Tessa, looking surprised. 'The shop opens again at half-past one and I have to be there ready and waiting. You'd be amazed how often there's a queue at dinner time.'

'You'd think they'd get their groceries in once a week on a Saturday,' said Mrs Morland.

'Not everyone's got the money,' said Mr Morland, shrugging into his coat and ramming his bowler on his head. 'Unemployment's going up all the time. Some have to live from day to day.'

'Well, it wouldn't suit me,' said his wife.

Eve watched as everyone kissed Mrs Morland before they left. Family kisses were rare in her life and even then they only extended to faces brushed lightly while lips made a *moue* into the empty air.

'Does Tessa have to work very hard, Mrs Morland?' asked Eve in her best manner.

'She does, but she doesn't mind. She was the same at school and she's always got her nose in a book. I'm flummoxed at some of the things she reads. Really hard stuff. She spends a lot of her money on books at jumble sales.'

'She is clever then?'

'I reckon so.' Mrs Morland tipped flour into her scale and placed a brass weight on the other side. 'I've got more baking to do,' she said pointedly.

'May I go upstairs to tidy myself?' asked Eve.

'Go to the top to Tessa's room. The lav's out the back.'

Eve used the outside lavatory which nearly froze her then climbed the stairs and combed her hair. Everything in the cottage fascinated and astonished her. She looked round Tessa's room, absorbing as much detail as she could.

Downstairs she said, 'What interesting books Tessa has.'

'Did you notice the shelves? Mr Morland made them. He's a very good carpenter. Everything he does is beautifully finished.'

Eve left the warmth of the Morland kitchen and returned home reluctantly, prepared to meet her mother's reproaches. 'You abused my leniency, Eve.' Mother's voice was glacial. She couldn't recall a time when it wasn't. But when had Mother ever shown warmth to her? 'I gave you permission only to walk on the common.'

Eve threw herself into a deep, velvet-upholstered armchair. It smelled slightly of dust and she wrinkled her nose. 'Couldn't Great-grandmother afford a vacuum cleaner? You'd think with all her money she would have.'

'She was old-fashioned. Eve, you are trying to change the subject.'

Fat chance, thought Eve. 'No, Mother.'

'Why did you drive out when I had expressly forbidden you to leave the vicinity of the house?'

Eve decided to play it cool. 'I am sorry, Mother. The thing is, I decided to call on our relatives.'

Mrs Brook re-seated herself. 'I see,' she said sounding relieved. 'Whom did you visit?' She picked up a linen cloth and bent to her embroidery.

'The Morlands.'

'Who?' Mrs Brook looked up sharply.

'You know, the funny little plump couple and their rather spotty daughter.'

Mrs Morland laid her work in her lap. 'Eve, how could you? Those people! Absolute outsiders! If Great-grandmother had not been eccentric enough to include them in her will we should never have known of their existence.'

'No, Mother, but now we do.'

'There was absolutely no need to continue the acquaintance.'

'I suppose not.'

Mrs Brook resumed sewing. 'What kind of place do they have?' she asked and Eve smiled. Mother was not entirely free from curiosity.

She described the kitchen and its occupants exactly as they had struck her and her mother listened intently. 'How many rooms have they?'

'I couldn't tell, but not many. Two only on the ground floor, I think, and a kind of lean-to for a scullery and, I guess, a couple of bedrooms and an attic room.'

'I suppose it is big enough for three – if you are accustomed to that sort of thing.'

'There are two children younger than Tessa.'

'And all five of them live in such cramped quarters?'

'Yes, plus a large dog and a cat.'

'Incredible! Of course, I am not so foolish as to be unaware of poverty, but to think that we are actually blood relatives . . . It is very odd.'

'I agree, Mother, but when you get to know them they are nice people. Mrs Morland keeps the place spotlessly clean and she cooks like a dream.'

'That is something, I suppose.'

Eve grinned, then composed her face as her mother glanced up at her. She wanted to shock Rose more. 'They don't have a bathroom, only a lavatory outside.'

'Good God! In this day! Surely – but you say they have little room and I dare say nowhere to put a lavatory inside.'

'Mr Morland has built a glass-covered way to it from the back door. It's rather sweet, you know, plants grow there in pots in the spring.' She hesitated then said supplicatingly, 'I do think that Tessa has possibilities. I wondered if I might make a friend of her. Not a close one, of course,' she said hastily, as her mother's needle paused, 'but someone to whom I could talk and perhaps invite here for tea. Or, if not here, to one of the restaurants in the town.'

'I am not sure. Why should you wish to? You have had several invitations from Bristol girls of your own social standing.'

'To balls and dinners, but I can't accept them.'

'Perhaps I have been too strict. You may telephone and ask one or two nice girls to tea tomorrow.'

'Thank you, Mother. I have been feeling a little lonely.'

Eve injected just the right amount of pathos into her tone and Mrs Brook sighed. 'You are still young.'

'I'm nineteen.'

'Yes.'

'May I see Tessa again?'

'Really, when you get a notion into your head you become so stubborn.'

'But her life fascinates me. And she is well behaved.'

'I do not think so. She has no social graces at all and neither have her parents.' Mrs Brook was silent for a moment. 'However, perhaps it would do you good to see something of how the poor live.' Mother engaged, as did other ladies of her acquaintance, in good works devoted to the welfare of the poverty-stricken lower classes.

'Surely Tessa is deserving of our attention,' said Eve. 'After all, her relationship to Great-grandmother was exactly the same as mine.'

'That may be an argument against pursuing the acquaintance. They might presume upon it. That could become embarrassing.'

'I will not allow that,' said Eve. 'Tessa and I will never meet once we return home.'

Mrs Brook said, 'True. I will consider the matter.'

Eve knew better than to pursue the argument further.

At dinner that night Mrs Brook said, 'I have given the matter of your friendship with Tessa Morland some thought and have decided that you may see her sometimes.'

'Thank you, Mother,' said Eve decorously. 'I think Tessa could become quite acceptable with a little tuition. She seems different from her parents.'

Eve had made a tactical error. Her mother frowned. 'That odd little couple! Fortunately your acquaintance will be a short one. In what way is Tessa different?'

'She is more lively, much more clever. Her mother seems quite astonished by her. I wonder why she left school so young? She reads a lot, not just novels but books about all sorts of things. I tidied myself in her bedroom – such a darling little place tucked under the eaves, though so cold – and she has a set of bookshelves over her bed.' Eve had been about to tell her mother that Tessa's father had made them, but stopped herself. No sense in reminding her that Mr Morland was a carpenter. That had been the root of the trouble created by Henrietta so many years ago. 'I saw some quite learned books there. Her mother says she buys them in jumble sales.'

'I see. Perhaps you may benefit one another.'

'Yes, Mother. Thank you very much,' said Eve demurely. 'May I go into the town tomorrow? I should like to visit the Museum and Art Gallery.' She kept her composure when Mother gave her a sceptical look.

'You may, and you have my permission to look round a department store.'

'Thank you.' Eve took a step nearer, prepared to kiss her mother's cheek, but Mrs Brook had already bent her head over her work.

On the following morning, when Eve had left, Rose Brook sat in the small sitting room with her hands idle in her lap, thinking of her daughter. Eve was beautiful in every physical way. Rose had doubts about the state of her spirit. The sooner she was married the better. She was not clever, but that was an advantage. Few men wanted brainy wives. In the modern idiom they might claim they did, they might protest that their women should be liberal free-thinkers, but it was an undeniable fact that pretty women got married first. Of course, if a woman could be beautiful and clever enough to hide her brains, that was best. That's what she had done to capture Ralph.

Thinking of her husband caused her heart to beat faster. She felt too perturbed to continue sewing and wrapped her needlework in a white cloth and placed it in the Regency work stand. It was a lovely piece, one of the few delicate objects in this house of gloomy Victorian grandeur, and she had been wondering if she could get Paul to sell or even better give it to her. She picked her way through the jungle of small tables and stools and went to her bedroom where she sat at the carved mahogany toilet table and gazed at her reflection. She twisted this way and that in an effort to check on her profile, as she did every day at home, using her three-way mirror.

Home . . . Ralph was at home. What was he doing? Poring over his endless calculations? Conferring with his partners, speculating on which shares bought and sold would bring the fastest profit? At present, in the New York Stock Exchange, money was changing hands so rapidly that men scarcely knew in which commodity they were dealing. Perhaps he was with yet another woman? His new secretary? Rose had seen her on a rare visit to Ralph's office, blonde, curvaceous, lush, one who probably performed well in bed. She caught her breath sharply. Push it from your mind, do not think of it, do not give it the importance which clarity of thought would bestow on it. She picked up the silver-backed hand-mirror and held it so that her profile was visible.

Was her neck beginning to sag, just a little? She patted it with the backs of her hands. That was the recognised beauty procedure which she had learned in her twice-weekly trips to her beautician. She stared at herself again. The curtains were drawn back allowing the cold harsh January light to fall mercilessly upon her. Lines had begun to appear round her eyes and across her forehead, barely noticeable but definitely there. She leaned forward on her elbow and peered closely. 'I am growing old,' she said aloud, and bit her knuckles savagely. Just before she had left America for the funeral she had heard several of her women friends discussing their looks.

Martha Ruscoe had asked, 'Have you heard about treatment with glands? They're supposed to make you look younger.'

The others had surveyed her. She was attractively smart, her dark suit topped by a black straw hat trimmed with a black silk rose. Her skin and teeth were good, evidence of the latter given by her somewhat sheepish smile. 'Well, I'm thinking of giving the treatment a try,' she said defensively.

'What happens?' asked Carrie Murfitt.

'I don't really know, but they couldn't do anything to me without asking me first, could they? I should want to be sure it was all right. Anyway, if I suddenly appear looking like an ape, you'll know why.'

'An ape?' gasped Carrie. Her prettiness was fading rapidly, her face growing plump and rather dough-like, her dark hair showing streaks of grey. And she was ineffably dumb. It was a combination which apparently held her husband captive and still clean-living after twenty years. At least, no one had ever been able to pin a rumour on him. Herbert was a handsome man whose figure had not thickened an inch since he was at college.

Miriam Talbot had laughed, then lowered her voice. 'She's talking about monkey glands.'

'*Monkey* glands! What do they do with them?'

'I think they must extract something and inject it.'

'Inject it in you, do you mean?' Carrie was horrified.

'That's what I've heard,' said Miriam. Her black hair made a surprising contrast to her clear blue eyes. Her beautician kept the grey from her hair by the constant use of dye. Her attitude to life was amused, quizzical, and her forehead was delicately lined.

Carrie shuddered. 'I shouldn't care for that.'

Martha had chucked her under the chin affectionately. 'You don't need them, darling. Herbert sees you with the eyes of love.'

Carrie had laughed delightedly, not appreciating Martha's underlying bitchiness. The four of them had been together through the same exclusive school and the same Swiss finishing school and were held together only by shared memories.

'What do you think, Rose?' asked Carrie.

She had shrugged as if the matter of looks bored her.

'If Martha wants to try something new, why shouldn't she?'

Rose wondered if Martha had received the gland treatment yet and if it had made a difference. If so, she would consider it. She would try anything to hold on to Ralph, however precarious that hold might be.

She got up and paced her room. She desperately wanted to go home, but there were some points of law over Great-grandmother's will which had to be cleared up. Ralph had given her the power to sign the necessary documents and left with obvious relief. A daily sight of her husband, if only for a few moments, was a terrifying need. Without it she would wither and die. Knowing it, she had remained silent about his infidelities. She had allowed Eve to be raised by servants so that Ralph would not come to regard her as a mother-figure, so as to be accessible to him at all times.

It had entailed no real sacrifice. She had not wanted a child and neither had he and she still damned the night she had been careless enough to conceive. Her efforts to rid herself of the baby had failed, and then her mother had discovered her condition and informed her grand-mother. They were delighted, and plans to find herself an unscrupulous doctor and rid her body of this physical invasion had had to be forgotten. Her mother was aware of Rose's distaste for her pregnancy and had watched her closely. Rose even suspected her of collusion with her maid. Ralph had not approached her bed during her entire pregnancy and for some time afterwards. There were days when he had seemed almost amused by her predicament, at others disgusted. He had absented himself from all contact with the birth, and had always treated Eve with distant carelessness. Rose could not remember him ever holding his child in his arms.

At first she tried to care about her child. According to the German psychoanalyst, Sigmund Freud, human frailty was the result of deprivation in early childhood. Could that be why Eve was so wilful? Rose knew that she often lied about her activities, but her flirtations were harmless – all girls flirted these days. Carrie's son, Elliot, was deeply attracted to her and both families believed they would make an excellent match. Eve went along with their hopes and expectations. At least, she seemed to. Elliot was in love so perhaps he could persuade her burdensome daughter into an early marriage.

# *Chapter Three*

For the first time Tessa found her job with Mr Grice boring. She had always previously enjoyed working in the shop: measuring and counting, gauging the wants of the customers before they spoke as they became familiar to her, listening to their small confidences. It was astonishing how many women told her quite intimate details of their lives, in spite of her youth, as if her white-aproned state transported her from the ordinary sphere of life.

She put a bowl of withered apples left over from Christmas on the counter with a reduced ticket. She became quite excited when thrifty housewives began preparations for Christmas, giving them full measures of dried fruit scooped from the great sacks especially ordered by Mr Grice. (He and Mrs Grice tended to pour goods onto the scales and bag them fast, thus gaining an ounce or two.) She sniffed the aromas of cloves and allspice and nutmeg which pervaded the shop and mingled with the tangy scent of the extra apples and oranges. There were the long boxes of dates with their gaudy pictures of desert arabs mounted on camels standing on top of vast sand dunes. Inside were neat rows of dates, still on the stem, and a little wooden fork to prise them out.

Then there were the improvident wives, or those stricken by the bitterness of unemployment, who hurried in at the last minute, hoping to find a bargain in a piece of bacon just on the turn, or potatoes lightly touched with frost, looking distraught as they tried to cope with

47

the extent of their poverty. Mr Grice, with all the superiority of an independent shop-owner, treated them disdainfully, as if poverty was a crime. If he wasn't there, Tessa diligently searched out slightly damaged cans and boxes which would have been marked down later and allowed them to go at sale prices, juggling the till. Mum would have called that dishonest, but Tessa didn't care. More than once, where she knew there would be disappointed children, she had dropped in a couple of balloons or whistles and paid for them from her own purse.

Now as she dusted and cleaned the shelves and counters she thought constantly of Eve Brook and the extraordinary style of living affected by her kind and was shot through by pangs of envy. She was also angry. Why should some people have to struggle for food to put into the mouths of their family while others squandered money on so much that was unnecessary?

She ventured to say so at home. Mrs Morland stared at her in amazement. 'People get what they deserve in this life,' she stated.

'But what makes the Brooks and their friends deserve so much and others so little?'

'It's not for us to question the ways of the Lord,' Mrs Morland said firmly. 'The poor are always with us. That's just the way of things.'

'Then it's a way that should be changed,' said Tessa hotly.

Her parents ignored such retorts, telling each other that she would 'grow out of such nonsense'.

Today, Mr Grice had refused to drop the price of the Christmas apples even a farthing for a woman who wanted one for her toddler.

'I've already knocked a halfpenny off,' he said firmly.

'The poor mite left the shop crying,' Tessa told the family at supper. 'He's a mean man. I wanted to give her the extra out of my own pocket, but he was watching and—'

'What! Give your hard-earned money to a woman who could probably manage fine if she didn't smoke cigarettes and roll home from the pub every night, drunk as a lord?'

'She didn't look that sort,' said Tessa. 'And her husband's out of work.'

'Then they'll have the dole and she should manage on that!'

Mr Morland said mildly, 'The dole doesn't amount to much, Lily. Some of the boys go barefoot even in this weather, poor little souls.'

Mrs Morland plunged her hands into hot, soda-laced water and began to wash dishes. 'There's plenty of boots to be had at jumble sales for coppers. When we had ours at the Bright Hour everything went really cheap. Don't tell me that a woman can't afford a couple of pence.'

Tessa, who had automatically picked up a tea-towel, said, 'The woman in the shop today hadn't an extra farthing, Mum, and her little girl's toes were showing through her boots.'

'Then she should be trying to buy boots, not apples,' snapped Mrs Morland.

Susan, who had been sitting at the table with a drawing book and crayons, spoke up. 'Mum, if the lady didn't have an extra farthing for an apple, how could she have a penny to buy boots?'

Mrs Morland bristled with indignation. 'Get on with your colouring!' She rattled the cutlery angrily, sending splashes of water on to the wall. 'Now look what you've made me do. I wish you'd all give over arguing.'

Mr Morland subsided behind his *Western Daily Press*, but Joey who had a mischievous streak said, 'Our Susan's right, Mum. We do sums every day at school and you can't take away more than you start with.'

Susan giggled. 'A girl I know told me that if you go to the grammar school you can. You do something called algebra and that means you can take things away from nothing. You use letters for figures.'

Joey gave a shout of deliberately irritating mirth. 'She's having you on and you're daft enough to believe her!'

Mrs Morland turned and glared at them all. 'Am I to

have no peace? Walter, stop them!'

Dad lowered his paper. 'Now, now, children. Enough's enough. No more noise or you'll give Mum a headache.'

Mrs Morland was far from pleased by his intervention. 'Headache? I never have a headache! I never have a thing wrong with me and neither do the rest of you. Anyone who has a good clear-out once a week stays healthy. It stands to reason, if you get rid of all the germs there's none left to make you ill.'

Joey and Susan collapsed into giggles, Tessa had to turn away to hide her smiles and Dad's newspaper was trembling.

Mum made one of her quick turnabouts. 'You can laugh,' she said complacently, 'but you've got to admit I'm right.'

When the washing up was done Dad lifted a length of chenille cloth from their latest acquisition, a wireless. Without consulting anyone, he had actually saved for it and presented it as a group Christmas present. Mrs Morland had been astonished and cross at such a waste of money, but beneath the watchful eyes of members of her family who had travelled to share Christmas Day, had forced herself to smile. Later she'd grumbled, but hadn't been able to hide her pride at being the first in the whole family to own a wireless and had made sure that everyone at chapel knew about it – in a roundabout, deprecatory way, of course. Only Dad was allowed to touch it.

Now, as he tuned it, it gave out a strange cacophony of whines and shrieks at which Mum tutted, then the sound of a dance band filled the room.

She laid down her knitting. 'My word! I have to say it's amazing. I can't get over it. Where's that coming from, Walter?'

'London. Probably from some big hotel where folk are dancing.'

Mrs Morland shook her head. 'Dancing! Drinking, too, I shouldn't wonder.'

Tessa began to sing along. 'Blue Skies smiling at me, nothing but blue skies do I see—'

'Save your voice for the choir,' said Mrs Morland.

'But it's good practice, Mum. And the tune is very pretty.'

'It's not half as good as proper music.'

'Hymns, you mean,' said Joey.

'Of course.'

'What about posh music?' he asked. 'My teacher told us about a man called Mozart. She said he was the best musician the world's ever known.'

'A foreigner!' snapped Mum. 'And where did you learn the words of that song, Tessa, if I might be so bold as to ask?'

'From the wireless,' she said meekly. As if to prove her words a male voice filled the room with his mellifluous tones and Mrs Morland shot her husband an indignant look. 'Heathen music,' she said. 'That thing will have to go.'

There was a concerted howl of protest and Dad said reasonably, 'The programmes are getting better all the time and you enjoy the religious services.'

'People would do better to go to chapel.'

'But what if they're invalids and can't?'

Mum thought for a moment, then nodded, glad to extricate herself from the argument with grace. 'Yes, I dare say a wireless does do good to some.'

The frost succumbed to heavy rain and the weather became unseasonably mild.

'It isn't natural,' said Mum. 'We ought to have cold weather this time of year. It kills the germs.'

She could be right, thought Tessa, but there were early buds in the garden, Dad was honing the blade of his spade and she was feeling as restless as if spring was already here.

She waited until Mum was in a good mood after a successful baking day and was seated by the range with a cup of tea and a home-made ginger nut, then said

51

tentatively, 'Mum, I think I'd like to look for another job.'

'What!' All Mum's placidity disappeared. 'Have you done something to upset Mr Grice? You haven't been pandering to slutty women, have you, selling things cheap that you'd no right to?'

'Mum!'

Mrs Morland frowned, then picked up her tea. 'No, you wouldn't do that. You're too good a chapel-goer to be dishonest.'

'Thank you.' Tessa just failed to keep a touch of sarcasm out of her voice.

Her mother frowned again. 'I don't know what's come over you. Mr Grice is pleased with you, everyone says how nice and polite you are, and you've been in that job for over three years—'

'But that's the trouble! I'm tired of it.'

'You weren't tired of it before you met Eve Brook,' snapped Mum.

'That's got nothing to do with it. I'd just like a change.'

'Nonsense! That girl has upset you with her foolish ways. You'll stay where you are until some nice boy comes along and you can get engaged. You'll find how right I am when you begin to share things with the right fellow. Dad and me spent hours in the shops deciding what furniture we could afford, and I bought plain table-cloths and chair-backs and embroidered them. The years of our engagement flew past.'

Tessa had heard it all before and it sounded as dreary now as it always had. She thought of wandering round the shops with one of the local boys.

'Frank Anderson likes you,' said Mrs Morland.

'Mum! Can you see him going round stores with a girl, even if he ever manages to wash all the oil and grime from his face and hands? He spends most of his life crawling about under cars. I shouldn't wonder if his whole body was filthy. Fancy having to go to bed with a man with a dirty body!'

'That's enough, Tessa! Frank's a good boy. His

mother tells me he's got his eyes fixed on owning his own garage some day. Then he'll be able to order other men about and dress in nice clothes. He's not a bad-looking lad, either, when he washes. He looks smart in chapel.'

'His nails are still black, though, and I can always smell petrol on him.' However, Tessa conceded one of Mum's points. Frank was pleasant. He was also tall.

'He's never given me a second glance,' she said.

Mrs Morland glanced at her daughter speculatively. 'He may not seem to, but I've noticed him watching you when he thinks you aren't looking. He's too sensible to tie himself down until he's got something good to offer a woman.'

'He'd better not wait too long, then, or he'll find all the women snapped up by boys who aren't quite so careful.'

'He's worth waiting for and some girl will see it, even if you don't.'

Tessa took another ginger biscuit and chewed, looking pensively into the glowing fire, wondering what marriage to Frank Anderson would be like. No, it wasn't for her. What was? She wished she knew.

Eve was bored, too. The legal complications over the will kept her mother in England and Rose was becoming increasingly nervous and irritable, especially when her daughter lounged around the house doing nothing. In spite of all her mother's exhortations, Eve did not read or sew or knit. Her chief interest lay in the gramophone and then only if she was allowed jazzy dance records. In the end, Rose had given way and Eve spent hours winding up the gramophone and playing records, throwing herself round the room in one of the latest travesties of dance. Or hammering away on the piano singing cheap songs with ridiculous words. In the end, to Rose's relief, this palled too.

Eve attended a few tea parties and went to the Colston Hall and sighed her way through a programme of religious music. She decided to visit Tessa again. Surely that would afford her some amusement, and if she timed her visit well she could enjoy some of Mrs Morland's undeniably good cooking.

February had turned cold and she was glad to be admitted to the Morland kitchen.

'I thought we'd seen the last of you,' said Mrs Morland.

'I am so sorry, Cousin Lily. Mother preferred me to remain with her after the recent bereavement.'

Mrs Morland was thrown off balance by being addressed as 'Cousin Lily' by a chit of a girl and merely muttered, 'Quite right too.'

'Yes, indeed. But she has given me permission to go out and about a little and I decided to come here. I do hope you don't mind?'

'No. No, of course not. Don't you have anywhere else to go?'

It was Eve's turn to be disconcerted. 'Er, yes, I guess. I mean, I've had invitations.'

'Why don't you accept them?'

'I have. A few. But I thought – I like Tessa. I always wanted a sister.' She assumed a sad look. 'But I have none, nor brothers.'

Mrs Morland said complacently, 'I've got a son and two daughters.'

'Yes.'

'Daughters are a great comfort to a woman, especially when they've grown up. I suppose you're a comfort to your mother.'

Eve blinked. The notion of being a comfort to Rose almost made her laugh.

Mrs Morland talked of her beloved chapel. 'You ought to come along and see what it's like for yourself.'

Eve was astonished, irritated, then amused, but she answered seriously, 'I am not sure if Mother will allow it. Our church is different from yours.'

'Most churches are different from ours,' Lily said proudly. 'Our preacher is an evangelist. He saves souls. This year alone he's already saved seven.'

Eve was fascinated. 'How? What does he do?'

Mrs Morland's eyes gleamed. Here was a chance to take another candidate to the altar.

'Sit down, Eve, and we'll have a cup of tea and I'll explain.'

She sat willingly by the fire. Tessa was not due home for another half hour and she wanted some amusement. She sipped the tea and ate a cheese biscuit. 'Cousin Lily, these are so delicious. You must have made them!'

Mrs Morland recognised flattery when she met it but appreciated it all the same. 'Of course I did.'

'Why do you work so hard when it would be easy to buy things at Tessa's shop? She could even carry them home for you.'

'Huh! Shop stuff. I'd rather make my own, thank you very much.'

'Well, I for one am delighted that you do. You were going to tell me how to save a soul,' she prodded gravely.

Mrs Morland seated herself opposite. With her plump cheeks rosy from baking and a few tendrils of curling hair escaping from her mob cap, she looked like a baby doll Eve had once owned. 'It's all a matter of explaining things properly,' she said. 'Some ministers don't do it as well as others, but the one we've got now is a real marvel – Mr Stratton. I could listen to him preach for hours. By the time he's finished explaining to sinners how to give their lives to the Lord, he's usually got penitents waiting for him to give them God's blessing.'

'And that means they're saved?'

'Well, they still need a lot of talking to before they understand properly. Mr Morland is good at that,' Lily finished proudly.

'Your whole family is busy – so different from mine.'

Mrs Morland got up to stir the stock pot simmering on the range. 'What line of work is your father in?' she asked as she sat down again. 'Or doesn't he work at all?'

'Oh, yes, he works very hard. He's a member of the New York Stock Exchange.'

'A what?'

55

Eve enlarged and Mrs Morland stared at her. 'Do you mean to tell me he just buys and sells things standing among a lot of other men? How can he? How can people buy something they've never even seen?'

Eve smiled and shrugged her shoulders deprecatingly. 'I'm not really sure, Cousin Lily. I don't understand it very well myself. But he makes a lot of money doing it.'

Mrs Morland shook her head. 'To each his own. Give me a man who does a proper job and comes home with good honest dirt on his hands.'

The door opened and Tessa entered with a rush. 'Eve, I saw your car. I'm ever so glad you came. I wish I hadn't to go back to work.'

'Can't you stay home for once?'

Mrs Morland snorted. 'Stay home!'

'Yes, she could say she wasn't well. I would take the message.'

Mrs Morland glared at her and Eve realised she had made a bad mistake. 'Tell lies, you mean?'

Eve sighed theatrically. 'You are right, of course, Cousin Lily. I am learning a lot from you.'

Mrs Morland wasn't quite satisfied and Eve waited, feeling unexpectedly nervous as she realised that she did not want to be cut off from this little cottage and her newfound relatives.

'You need to learn a lot more by the sound of things. Tessa, lay up the table. I can hear Dad and the children. I've got behind talking.'

Eve jumped up. 'Please let me help.' She grabbed a handful of cutlery and filled glasses of water, and afterwards sat down to a meal of sausages and fried bubble and squeak, a mash of leftover potatoes and cabbage, as tasty as everything cooked by Mrs Morland.

'Eve's been asking me questions about the chapel,' said Lily to the table at large.

Eve felt warmed by Mr Morland's smile. 'That's good news. You should come along one night. Why not next Sunday? Our Tessa's going to sing.'

'Sing? Oh, I adore singing. I didn't know you could, Tessa.'

'The Lord's given her a good voice and she uses it to His glory,' said Lily.

Back in Frenchay Eve said to her mother, 'May I go to the Morlands' church next Sunday?'

Rose shot her daughter a suspicious look. 'I don't understand. You have never shown the least inclination towards religion.'

'I attend church with you, Mother.'

'Reluctantly,' said Rose coldly.

Eve avoided an argument. 'Tessa is going to sing. I should very much like to hear her.'

'You are spending altogether too much time with that family.'

'But you gave your permission. And I have been good.'

Rose did not smile at Eve's semi-humorous tone. 'We shall be returning home soon. My business here is all but finished.'

'I don't want to go home. I would prefer to stay here!'

Eve's outburst surprised herself as much as Rose. She said more gently, 'I would like to remain here, Mother.'

'What nonsense. You will accompany me.'

Eve was furious at her mother's autocratic attitude, but hung on to her temper. 'Why should I not stay in England for a time?'

Rose thought of Elliot Murfitt. She was sure that if she took Eve home he would pursue his interest in her, perhaps propose marriage. Moving restlessly, she watched her daughter as she got up and sauntered across the room. Eve was beautiful enough to turn any man's head and she needed wealth to keep her content. As content as she ever was. And the Murfitts were exceedingly rich.

'There are those in America who are missing you,' she said.

Eve said without turning from the window, 'Oh? Who?'

'You are popular among the young men of our acquaintance.'

Eve shrugged and Rose clenched her fists, digging her nails into her palms. 'Is there no one whom you favour above the rest?'

Again Eve shrugged and Rose's anger overcame her. 'Do not shrug your shoulders at me! Speak to me, and face me when you do.'

Eve turned slowly and gave her mother a prolonged stare. 'Yes?'

'I asked you a question.'

'Oh, about lovers? No, I don't favour anyone. Though,' she said speculatively, 'I do like Paul. I always have. Why does he live in England?'

'I suppose he prefers it here, though how anyone can is beyond me! Inconvenient houses, hardly ever any ice for drinks, such inefficiency!'

'I should enjoy getting to know him better and you can't object to my wanting to learn more about your own sister's son.'

'You really care for Paul?'

'I like him very much and I believe he likes me.'

Rose hoped this was true. To have Eve married and living so far away from New York would suit her very well.

Eve obtained permission to visit the Morlands on Sunday. She dressed with care, but even her plainest clothes stood out among the unimaginative, dingy garments worn by the rest of the congregation. The small chapel was unadorned, its brightest note being the flowers on the altar. She would have preferred to sit at the back, but accompanied Tessa's parents and her small sister and brother, scrubbed to a shine, to the third row from the front. Tessa was with the choir in a gallery behind the pulpit.

Eve barely listened to the tedious readings and prayers but when Tessa's name was announced her attention was captured.

'Our sister in the Lord will give us a solo taken from *Ruth*,' intoned Mr Stratton.

The organ played and Tessa began to sing and Eve was astonished. The power of her voice sent it soaring to the high ceiling and its beauty was undeniable. 'The blessing of the Lord be upon Thee,' she sang, 'and the light of His countenance shine upon thee . . .' The words pierced Eve's consciousness and brought a lump to her throat. I'm going to cry, she thought. I don't believe it, I'm going to cry. She struggled with an emotion too foreign for understanding, clamping down as she always did on any turbulent feelings. Tessa sang on. '. . . And bring thee prosperity.' That was better. So even in chapel they put prosperity high on the list of their requirements. That was something Eve understood.

Later, she listened to the preacher's long, over-emotional sermon and was embarrassed as two adults and three children stumbled to the front in floods of penitential tears, the children watched by their moist-eyed parents. The reformed sinners were whisked into an inner room and the service was over at last. Eve walked back to the Morlands' cottage.

'I don't suppose you've ever seen anything like that before,' said Mrs Morland complacently.

'Never!'

'Did you feel the call yourself?'

'In a way,' said Eve.

Mrs Morland shook her head. 'You can't feel the call "in a way". You'll know when it comes.'

'Did you like my singing?' asked Tessa.

Eve looked at her cousin who was regarding her with some anxiety. Did it matter to her what Eve thought? Apparently it did.

'It's not for you to ask her such a question,' snapped Mrs Morland. 'What you did you did for the Lord. It doesn't need to be talked about.'

She had relieved Eve of the need to answer for which she was grateful as she realised that she was jealous and resentful that Tessa's voice was so much better than her own when she had received tuition from professionals.

\* \* \*

Later, Eve returned home.

'Did you enjoy your little outing?' asked Rose.

She said as calmly as she could in the face of her mother's acerbity, 'It was certainly different.'

'How exactly?'

Eve did not want to talk about it. Although she had done her best to disengage herself from the happenings in chapel the raw emotion openly displayed there had opened up wounds she had no wish to explore.

'Is Tessa's voice any good?' asked Rose.

'Excellent.' Eve suddenly felt like giving her the praise she had ungenerously withheld.

'Has she taken lessons?'

'I don't know. The Morlands don't discuss it. They say it's all for the Lord.'

'Really? How odd they are. If you remain in England, will you continue to cultivate their acquaintance?'

This was the first sign Rose had given that she might allow Eve to stay and she answered demurely, 'Not if you don't wish it, Mother, though they are very good people.' In fact she had every intention of seeing her odd, newfound relatives where she found the kindly warmth her life lacked.

Rose picked up her embroidery and Eve saw that her hands were shaking a little. 'I have decided that you may stay, but only for a short while. While you were out Paul called and said he would be delighted to have you live here for as long as you like. He does not intend to sell the house. I suppose one day he will bring a wife home.'

'Thank you.' In her relief Eve almost got up to embrace her mother, but held back. Rose had capitulated without grace and had kept up the barrier she maintained between herself and her daughter. 'How kind of Paul. Although I hope he does something about the decor before he asks a modern girl to share it with him.'

'I have no doubt he will. He is not a fool.'

'No, Mother.'

* * *

In the event Rose Brook was unable to leave England until spring when she sailed thankfully to New York. Her sister met her on the quayside and greeted her with a kiss which Rose turned her head aside to receive on her cheek. Betsy Jefferson was like her sister only in height. In all other ways they differed.

'Welcome home, Rose,' she said. 'I've missed you.'

'I cannot think why,' said Rose coolly.

'Neither can I. Don't be a grouch.'

'How is Ralph?'

'He telephoned asking me to apologise for not being here. I've hardly seen him while you were away. He's caught up in his business affairs.'

'I see.'

'I'm not sure you do, darling.' Betsy's face, as rounded and plump as her body, had a concerned look. 'There was a collapse in stock prices in February and thousands were ruined before the banks came to the rescue. Reginald says they will not always be able to step in.'

'Ralph will be safe,' said Rose. 'He is far too astute to be caught.'

'I hope so,' said Betsy doubtfully. Her husband's wealth lay in land out of which his family had built up a considerable fortune. He was not interested in stocks and shares.

'Ralph will manage as he always does,' said Rose, irritably. 'So far he has stayed ahead.'

'I hope you're right. That things will go well, I mean. It's a pity he's not at home. I'm lucky to see quite a lot of Reginald.'

Rose said nothing. Her brother-in-law spent much of his life on the golf course and, in Rose's opinion, was a bore.

The two women climbed into Betsy's chauffeur-driven car and the luggage was loaded on to the back.

'Come and have dinner with us,' said Betsy.

'No, thank you. It's kind of you to ask—'

'Kind be damned! You're my sister. Can't you ever unbend, Rose?'

She glanced at Betsy. Her face was as pink as her unbecoming hat and her skin, innocent of any beauty treatment, was dry with tiny wrinkles around her eyes and mouth. Rose thought, She's only a little older than I am but she looks a lot more.

'Have you seen enough?'

'Sorry. Was I staring?'

'Yes, and if you're about to tell me to waste my time in beauty parlours, you can save your breath. I've better things to do.'

Betsy's good humour was almost impossible to dent and Rose relaxed and smiled. 'I will have a meal with you. Thank you for asking.'

Reginald welcomed her by hugging her, impervious to her rigid stance. Others kept their distance from the Brooks but Betsy and Reginald had no hesitation in touching and kissing. Ralph loathed it even more than Rose, but the Jeffersons had so much love it continually spilled over to embrace others.

When Rose returned home it was almost ten o'clock and Ralph was still out. The stately butler who doubled as valet welcomed her. 'Your luggage arrived safely and has been unpacked by the housekeeper, madam. Mr Brook is still at his office.'

Rose nodded. 'Mrs Jefferson told me how busy he was.'

'Yes, madam.'

Rose went straight up to her bedroom. Its muted shades of ivory and ordered precision failed to soothe her tonight. She was sure that if Ralph did not come home it was because he was with another woman. She ached with wanting him. Her maid had been given a holiday and was not expected back until the following day so she ran her own bath and brushed her own hair. In defiance of the prevailing bobbed fashion she had kept hers almost shoulder-length. It was glossy and fair still, grey hairs being kept at bay with discreet use of dye. She massaged skin cream into her face and neck. First thing tomorrow she would make an appointment at the beauty shop. She wondered if Martha had given the monkey gland treatment a try.

She climbed into bed, her narrow figure making scarcely a bump beneath the bedclothes, and lay awake until she heard Ralph's car. She got up and put on her prettiest dressing gown, wondering if after her long absence he would want to make love to her. She hoped he would.

He was in the dining room pouring himself a whisky.

'Ralph,' she said, unable to control her shaking voice, desperately aware that she was betraying her need, fearful of his rejection. She was not surprised when his reaction was cool. On the few occasions when there was intimacy between them, he preferred to initiate it.

'Rose, you have come home.'

'As you see. I cleared up the rest of Great-grandmother's business affairs. Paul was a help to me.'

'Good. Pity the young fool chooses to live abroad. I suppose he does not work. He has the makings of a fine stock-broker. Calm in a crisis, willing to take risks, plenty of money. Did he say anything about returning?'

'Not a word. In fact, he's keeping on the house at Frenchay.'

'I see. It puzzles me that Great-grandmother chose to leave it to Paul. It should have gone to an older member of the family.'

'I believe they were very fond of one another.'

'Were they? Or did Paul flatter her vanity?'

'I don't know,' sighed Rose, who cared nothing for the house.

'Is Eve in bed?'

'She preferred to remain in England for a while. She has made friends.'

Ralph shrugged. 'I hope she behaves herself.'

'I am sure she will. Have you behaved yourself?' The words escaped Rose's vigilance and she went hot as Ralph surveyed her icily.

'I must assume that is meant to be a joke?'

'Of course, darling.'

63

Perhaps it was her compliance, perhaps he needed comfort after a long day, perhaps he even found her attractive, but that night Ralph made love to her and, in the face of his almost clinical approach, she contrived to contain her rapture.

Eve felt like a prisoner released from jail. When her mother had departed she ran from room to room. She put music on the gramophone, playing it as loudly as possible, whirling about in a frenzy of pleasure, singing breathlessly: 'Blue skies, smiling at me, Nothing but blue skies, do I see . . .'

She had visited the Morlands several times and heard Tessa sing again and had conceived a wonderful, daring plan.

She sank into a chair, opened the evening paper and began to make a list of theatres and night clubs.

Tessa's discontent increased as she saw more of Eve. She was prepared to listen endlessly to her cousin's account of her life. She had had many boyfriends. 'As long as I see boys of my own—' Eve had stopped. She had been about to say 'class' ' – type,' she said, 'Mother and Father are quite happy about it.'

'You're lucky. Mine won't let me go out with a boy at all.'

'Don't forget you're two years younger than me.'

Tessa had sighed. 'I know. Were you forbidden to see boys when you were seventeen?'

'I was sent to a finishing school at sixteen. We used to climb out of the windows at night and meet them.'

Tessa's eyes had widened. 'What a wonderfully adventurous life you've led.'

Eve smiled. The time was not yet right to tell Tessa the extent of her adventures.

The day was spring-like, the sun warm and the breeze soft when the two girls walked along the lanes near Tessa's house.

Eve said, 'How would you like to sing with me?'

'I should love it. Do you mean you want to join our choir?'

Eve smothered a laugh and waved an imperious hand. 'No, no, I mean modern singing with a dance band, and later on the stage.' She had taken Tessa's breath away. Her cousin gazed at her open-mouthed. 'It isn't such an outrageous suggestion. I don't suppose you know, but quite a lot of performers sing duets.'

'But surely that means a man and a woman together.'

'It just means two, silly.'

Tessa said crossly, 'I know what duet means. But it's usually a man and a woman.'

'Yes, darling, but we could sing in a female duet. Wouldn't you like that?'

Tessa said, 'I expect I should. How would we begin?'

'At parties – things like that.'

'Things like what?' asked Tessa suspiciously.

'Goodness, you are being stubborn. Do you dislike the idea so much? If so . . .'

'No, of course not. I should love to partner you.'

'That's better. For a long time I've performed with dance bands . . .'

'Dance bands! Did your parents allow that? Mine never would.'

'Stop interrupting! The bands were playing at private parties.'

'I see. But I only go to family parties. I've never been to one that had its own dance band.'

'I have. And I can get us into houses here. I've had plenty of invitations since I arrived in Bristol.'

Tessa gazed at Eve who said, 'Well?'

'Well, what?'

'Tessa, you are being deliberately obtuse. If I can organise it, will you sing with me at parties?'

'Mum and Dad would never give their permission.'

Eve picked up a stick and slashed at the hedge, disturbing a pair of birds which rose twittering into the sky.

'You shouldn't do that,' said Tessa.

Eve threw down the stick in disgust. 'I can always ask someone else.'

'Oh? Who?'

Eve was nonplussed. 'Several people, I'm sure.'

'Would they get their parents' permission?'

'Of course. Not everyone is as stuffy as Cousins Lily and Walter.'

'I thought you liked them!'

'I do. Very much. But they are rather old-fashioned, aren't they?'

Tessa admitted it, then said calmly, 'If you can get someone with no restrictions, why ask me?'

Eve realised that she would need to handle this carefully. She had underestimated both Tessa's intelligence and will. 'My dear girl,' she cried, 'you are family.'

Her words made an impression. Tessa gave her a warm smile. 'I hadn't thought of that. I didn't know of your existence before this year. Yes, we are family.'

'So you'll do it?'

'Sing with you? I don't hold out much hope.'

The girls returned to the Morland cottage. Mrs Morland was in the garden wearing a large flowered mob-cap. The clothes line was hung with rugs at which she was thumping with a cane carpet beater. She was almost lost in clouds of dust.

'Hurry into the house,' she cried. 'It's amazing how much dust rugs will pick up. Give me linoleum any time.'

'Why is she doing that?' asked Eve as they removed their coats.

Tessa put the kettle on. 'She's begun the spring cleaning. Usually I help but she let me off today.'

'Because I'm here?'

'Of course.'

Eve's heart soared. As far back as she could remember no one had ever altered their routine to accommodate her. She felt a pang of guilt at the way she was trying to inveigle Tessa into something she knew her parents would utterly condemn.

Tessa put biscuits on a plate and Eve grabbed one and

ate it greedily, so fast that the flavour scarcely had time to register before she took another.

'I wonder you stay slim when you eat so much,' said Tessa.

'That's another thing. You'll have to lose a bit of weight when we begin our singing.'

'I didn't say I would.'

The door opened and Mrs Morland came in. She removed her mob-cap and apron and took them through to the scullery for washing. 'Oh, you're making tea. Good. My mouth's that full of dust, you'd never believe! Are you enjoying the biscuit, Eve?'

'How could I not enjoy something made by you?'

Mrs Morland smiled complacently. 'My mother handed down that recipe and she got it from her mother.'

Tessa lay awake, unable for once to sleep. As she had walked Eve to her car, her cousin had pressed her to make a decision.

'I've got to know, Tessa, so that I can arrange something.'

'But I'll never be allowed out at night, not for anything except chapel, and especially not to sing at parties.'

Eve had simulated indignation. 'I hope you're not suggesting that my friends' parties are irregular in some way?'

'Of course not. I just mean that Mum and Dad are very strict with me.'

An odd expression had crossed Eve's face, one which gave Tessa an urge to throw her arms around her. Then Eve had said, 'Couldn't you arrange to creep out after they think you've gone to bed?'

'But what if they should come into my room?

'Do they usually?'

'Mum often does.'

'What time do you go to bed?'

'About half-past nine.'

'What? What time do they go?'

'At ten o'clock.'

'Every night?' Eve had been astonished.

'Every night,' said Tessa solemnly. 'They do everything to a routine.' Then she had broken into giggles, setting her cousin off.

The laughter broke a barrier and Tessa had ended by agreeing that it might be possible to get out after ten. Now she was worried and wished she had been firmer. Eve was so determined. She wouldn't let her off.

'I rely on you,' were her last words before she had driven away.

Tessa lay worrying for a long time, but the spark of rebellion which dwelt deep inside her was being fanned to a small flame. Life with Eve was holding out excitement, and that was exactly what she wanted.

# Chapter Four

Eve's first summons arrived. The girls had rehearsed a couple of times in Padding House when Tessa had ostensibly gone there to tea. She had begun to enjoy closer contact with her cousin, but was still anxious at the idea of singing to the general public. Especially as it involved deceiving her parents. It couldn't be in the least like chapel.

Eve had written her a letter in a manner which demanded her obedience, careless as always of her cousin's dilemma. Of course Mum had asked who her letter was from and what it was about.

'It's from Eve, Mum.'

'Good gracious! She was here only a few days ago. What can she have to say she couldn't say then?'

'Nothing much. She's going to a party.'

Tessa prayed that her mother wouldn't hold out her hand for the letter. If she did she had wild ideas of dropping it accidentally on purpose into the fire.

She sighed with relief when Mum was content to allow her to read it out with quick expurgations. 'Always parties! I'm surprised Mrs Brook allows her so much freedom. Fancy going back to America and leaving her here on her own. In that great house, too. I would never do a thing like that.'

'Another cousin has come to stay there,' said Tessa. 'She's a spinster, Eve says, and very strict.'

'How old?' asked Mum, getting straight to the point.

'About fifty, Eve says.'

'That's all right then.'

What Eve had actually said was, 'Cousin Tildy is a small-minded, po-faced, skinny old cow! I met her at the funeral and hated her on sight.'

'How will you get away without her seeing?' Tessa asked.

Eve had laughed. 'Don't worry about that. You look after your own escape.'

Tessa lay in bed fully clothed listening for the sound of her parents retiring for the night. She heard their footsteps pause at Joey's and Susan's door, then Mum climbed the attic stair. Tessa shut her eyes as Mum opened her door, peeped inside and listened for a moment, then closed the door quietly. She did this sometimes to order Tessa to stop reading and put out the light. 'You'll ruin your eyes and have to wear glasses and you won't like that!'

These nocturnal visits revealed a gentleness in her, a warmth, that was never permitted to show during her busy day and Tessa felt guilty and mean at the way she was deceiving her. But she had promised Eve and couldn't deny the flicker of excitement that kept her fully awake. She waited another half hour then climbed out of bed and, carrying her shoes, tiptoed down the stairs, avoiding the ones which creaked. She put on her shoes, not stopping to tie the laces, and eased back the bolts on the back door. It struck her for the first time that having no key she would have to leave her family asleep, unprotected by locks or bolts. She dithered, feeling like a criminal, then the tug of adventure decided her and she stepped through the door and raced along the garden path, her shoe-laces flying, down to where Eve was waiting in her car.

'You've been an age,' was her reproachful greeting.

Her nerves jangled, Tessa's immediate response was to snap. 'I came as soon as I could get away.'

'Well, get in now you're here.'

Tessa moved quickly and tripped over a shoelace.

'For heaven's sake! Will you get in!'

Tessa climbed into the car, muttering an apology, and Eve revved the engine noisily then pulled away from the kerb.

Tessa tried to reach her feet but it was impossible in the confined space. The hood of the car was up and Eve's perfume permeated every corner.

'You smell lovely,' said Tessa.

'Chanel,' said Eve carelessly. 'What are you wearing?'

'My best dress.'

'Idiot! I mean what scent?'

Her voice was only half-humorous and Tessa gave a nervous laugh. 'I haven't any. Mum doesn't think it's necessary.'

What Mum said was: 'No good, clean girl needs scent, except decent soap and perhaps a bit of talc now and then. If she keeps herself properly washed, she'll always smell nice.'

'Did you say you are wearing your best dress? That's good. It's a pretty one, is it?'

'I don't think you could call it pretty. In fact, you've seen it.'

'Not that ghastly rag you wore to the funeral?'

'That's my best dress,' cried Tessa hotly.

'I should have known. You can't go on stage in that.'

'I'll have to, or in my petticoat.'

Eve laughed and so did Tessa, though she was feeling far from amused.

Eve drove to Stoke Bishop and turned into a curving drive. A large house had light spilling from every room and the sound of a dance band reached them.

Eve began to hum and her excitement communicated itself to Tessa and mingled with her fear until it was impossible to tell which emotion was uppermost.

Eve greeted the butler with careless ease. 'Where are the ladies' cloaks tonight?'

'Good evening, Miss Brook.' He snapped his fingers and a maid came hurrying. 'Show Miss Brook and—' He stopped and waited.

'Miss Morland,' said Eve.

'—and Miss Morland upstairs.'

The large bedroom being used as a cloakroom was warmed by a roaring fire which was reflected in the extra mirrors which had been utilised. The bed and chairs were covered in evening wraps, mingling satin, brocade and fur.

'Good,' said Eve. 'There's no one here.' In her usual way she disregarded the presence of the maid detailed to attend the ladies.

Tessa began to remove her coat and Eve dragged at it and threw it on top of the stuff on the bed. 'Good lord, it's even worse than I remember.'

'My family isn't rich like yours!'

'All right, don't lose your rag. We'll have to do something to jazz it up.'

She herself looked hauntingly lovely in an apple green frock, simply but beautifully cut, which revealed her knees. A pale lemon belt was tied round her hips, ending in a bow. Round her neck she wore a pearl necklace long enough to be wound several times round her throat before descending to her hips. Her long eardrops were jade; her slender legs were enhanced by flesh-coloured silk stockings which ended in apple green silk shoes.

Beside her, Tessa looked frumpish and the realisation brought a rush of jealousy and irritation. 'I could never dress like you,' she cried. 'I knew I shouldn't have come.'

Eve's frown vanished. 'It's all right, darling, I'm not cross. I was frowning because I was thinking. I don't often do it.' She gave another laugh, though it was rather strained, before she grabbed a hairbrush from the dressing table. 'Here, brush your hair until it shines.' She removed her pearl necklace and wound it around Tessa's throat. 'Your stockings – they're lisle, aren't they? They're very wrinkled.'

'Lisle stockings always wrinkle. They're more practical for my kind of life, and anyway I can't afford better ones.'

'They won't do.' Eve turned to the maid. 'Please bring us some wine.'

The girl gave a small curtsey and left and Eve began pulling out the dressing-table drawers.

'Eve, stop it! What are you doing? Those are somebody's private belongings.'

Eve turned round holding up a pair of black silk stockings. 'Put these on, quick, before the maid gets back. For heaven's sake, stop being so bourgeois! One pair won't be missed. There are dozens here. I'm sure Mother's maid steals ours all the time.'

Her furious urgency mesmerised Tessa into removing her own stockings and pulling on the black silk. The feel of them on her skin was such an exquisite pleasure she almost forgot her reservations. Eve had dragged open more drawers and found some ribbons. 'Take your shoe laces out. Do as I say. Come on, hurry!'

She threaded red ribbon through the eyelets and tied it in two large bows. 'Keep brushing your hair. It's already looking better. Don't you brush it every night? I suppose not. You'll have to take better care of yourself if we're to be partners.'

Tessa opened her mouth to say they would be no such thing but felt suddenly uplifted and carried along by the illicit thrill. She could not have imagined anything like this. She looked at her reflection. Her hair was longer than fashion dictated, but it fell in gleaming waves and curls. The pearls enlivened her dress wonderfully and the silk stockings emphasised the slimness of her legs. Even her serviceable shoes looked more exotic with the ribbons.

'Sit down,' commanded Eve. She applied cream to Tessa's face, followed by powder, then handed her a lipstick. 'Put this on.'

'But I've never . . .'

'Never used it before. I know. Put it on!'

Tessa obeyed, then was drenched in scent as Eve pumped vigorously at a scent spray she had found on the dressing table. She pulled her cousin to her side and they stood looking at themselves in a cheval glass. 'You see,' said Eve triumphantly, 'you can look pretty when you try. Wait until we get you into some decent frocks and shoes and things. You'll be a stunner.'

The maid returned with a tray which held two glasses of pale amber wine.

She sniffed suspiciously at the scent as Eve seized a glass and handed it to Tessa. 'Drink this. It'll give you some Dutch courage.'

She gulped the wine down, enjoying the fruity taste. Lifted by the glow it gave her, and carried higher by her sudden awareness that she really could look pretty, she followed Eve downstairs. When they entered, a ballroom music enveloped them in a veil of melodic sound and Tessa was startled by the number of guests, although afterwards she realised that there must have been fewer than a hundred. Their appearance was hailed by shouts of greeting from Eve's acquaintances and Tessa hesitated nervously. Eve's eyes glistened like jewels and her body was taut with expectation. She seized Tessa's hand and pulled her round the outside of the dancers performing the frenzied steps of the Shimmy, until they reached the bandstand.

The band leader was young. He wore a white tie and tails and if his hair had been any slicker it could have been used as a mirror. His face was narrow, his eyes calculating. He looked the girls up and down. 'You must be the singers.'

Eve nodded, giving him a brilliant smile, then he turned his attention to the band which reached a crescendo of saxophones and drums then died away.

'Sit there,' he said to the girls, pointing to two chairs.

'He doesn't look very pleased to see us,' whispered Tessa.

'Who cares?' was Eve's careless reply. 'If we take any notice of people like him we'll never get anywhere.'

'Well, it's not much of a welcome,' she said, suddenly wary. 'He did ask us to sing, didn't he?'

'Mmm, not exactly. I persuaded my friend . . . Here she is.'

A young woman climbed on to the bandstand. 'Hello, Eve. I thought you were to be alone.' She stared curiously at Tessa, her eyes roaming over the dark dress and the newly decorated shoes, seeming to assess their worth. Tessa felt cheap and tawdry then annoyed. Who was this rich woman to criticise her? She returned the look with one of haughty disregard borrowed from Eve. 'Kitty, this is my cousin, Tessa Morland,' said Eve, carelessly. 'Tessa, Kitty Bamford, our hostess. Tessa's a professional. I thought she would give the act some class.'

Kitty smiled. 'Good. Keep it short, won't you, darling? We're here to dance. We like our music quite loud and it would never do to drown your songs.'

Tessa watched her departure, trying to hang on to her nerve. 'Why did you have to tell a lie about me?' she hissed.

'Keep calm, ducky,' said Eve. 'A little lie never hurt anyone. And in any case, you sing all the time.'

'In chapel! It's hardly the same.'

'Good lord, I should say not!'

Tessa should have known that Eve would be impervious to anything but her own desires. She looked at the prospective audience. Small tables had been set up around the dance area and men in evening suits and girls in glittering, silken dresses were drinking and smoking, filling the ballroom with a blue haze.

The band leader, whose name was Cliff Carter, announced the next dance and finished the announcement with the information that he had been lucky enough to engage the services of that well-known duo, the Kissing Cousins. Tessa looked at Eve who was smiling. 'Get up, Tessa, that's us.'

Kissing Cousins! The term brought the memory of Paul back to Tessa vividly, and the realisation that he had made an unforgettable impression on her so flustered her that she had to search her mind for words she knew well. The band struck up, and what looked to Tessa like a thousand faces were turned towards the stage. When the music reached the cue for the song she almost missed it and her voice came out semi-strangled. Eve began the words to 'Shakin' the Blues Away' and gave her partner a dig in the ribs. Tessa took a deep breath and her voice grew stronger. 'Shakin' the blues away, Unhappy news away . . . Shake off your cares and troubles . . . shake them away.' Couples whirled around the floor and when the music stopped their applause was clearly directed towards the singers. Eve bowed delightedly and so did Tessa. The clapping had surprised her. No one clapped in chapel where every talent was reckoned to be God-given and unemotionally accepted as such.

'They like us,' said Eve from the corner of her mouth. 'Ready?'

The band began to play a slow version of 'Whispering' and Eve began, as arranged, 'Honey, I have something to tell you . . .' Then Tessa joined in. 'Whispering while you cuddle near me, Whispering so no one else can hear me . . . there is no one like you . . . Whispering that I love you . . .' The sentimental words got under her defences and gave her voice a husky break. Then they were taking their bows again and the band swung into a leisurely version of 'She's Funny That Way'.

'That's it for now,' said Eve. 'I'm going to get a drink.'

She left the platform and Tessa followed her down the steps to the dance floor. She felt hazy from the delayed action of the wine on her nerves and wished she hadn't drunk it. Her brief elation had died, allowing guilt to surface. What if Mum had needed her? Supposing someone had been taken ill? She longed with all her heart to be at home lying in her own bed, safe in her own room. A hand was held out to her and she looked up to see a smiling Paul. 'Care to dance?'

Immediately the world changed for her. 'Yes, please,' she breathed, then wished she hadn't sounded so grateful.

'Kitty told me she had engaged a singing act,' said Paul as he guided her with a gentle, but compelling hand on her back. 'I had no idea you were a member of Kissing Cousins.'

'Neither had I!'

'What? But Eve told Kitty . . .'

'Eve said nothing about it to me. The title, I mean. In fact, I thought . . .' Tessa stopped, feeling disloyal to Eve.

'Go on. You thought what? Tell me, I won't be shocked. I know my cousin.'

'Well, I thought that we were going to sing at a small private party.'

'Is that what she told you?'

Tessa tried to cast her mind back to Eve's actual words. 'I don't know now. Maybe she didn't. I may have just assumed it.'

'This *is* a private party.'

'Yes, but not small. Not to me, anyway.'

'Eve probably thinks it is. Small in importance, that is. She's attended some pretty grand affairs in America.' He smiled. 'You have a pretty voice.'

'Thank you.'

'And you use it to good effect. The small break was a touch of genius.'

Tessa opened her mouth to explain that it had been caused by anxiety, then stopped. If it had created such a good impression she should leave well alone.

As the plaintive alto saxophone and the solo clarinet wailed their individual sounds, Paul's arms were around her, sending her into a state of euphoria where nothing mattered but the music and the movement of the dance. Then it ended and he led her off the floor to a group at one of the tables. She murmured greetings when she was introduced to a couple of heavily made-up young women. One was named Poppy and she could have sworn the other was called Tiddles, though it seemed unlikely. Poppy stared at her, half smiling, as if she were an amusing specimen of another species. A thick-set man rose and bowed, a look of admiration in his eyes which helped to heal Tessa's bruised feelings. Then Jack Padbury hurried up, his mind as usual on one track.

'Good evening, Miss Morland. Have you any idea where Eve could be?'

'I'm sorry. I assumed she was dancing.'

'The band is taking an interval.'

'Oh.' Tessa felt foolish. She hadn't noticed that the music had stopped, and the girls shrieked with laughter.

'She must be in love,' said Poppy. This brought a fiery blush to Tessa's cheeks which made them laugh even more.

She was pleased to see the irritated look which Paul shot at them. 'Would you like some refreshment, Tessa?' he asked. 'A cocktail, perhaps.'

'I would, darling,' said Poppy. 'Dinner seems ages ago and supper won't be served until eleven-thirty and I'm *ravenous*.' She pouted, turning her brilliantly painted lips into a red funnel.

'A cocktail won't fill you,' remarked Paul.

'No, darling, but it will stave off the pangs.'

Paul called a waiter who fetched a tray of drinks and tiny savoury biscuits. Poppy stirred her glass, sending the cherry spinning, and Paul handed a drink to Tessa. 'Do you like cocktails?'

'Of course she does,' cried Tiddles.

'I don't know,' said Tessa, 'I've never tasted any.'

This brought more shrill laughter and Paul frowned.

Jack said, 'So you don't know what's happened to Eve?'

Poppy blew cigarette smoke in his direction. 'I thought I saw her talking to the band leader.' There was no mistaking the innuendo in her voice.

Jack flushed. 'I'll see if I can find her. She may want refreshments.'

'Unless I miss my guess, she's already taking the kind of refreshment she needs,' murmured Poppy, which made some of the others giggle.

Paul appeared not to notice the remark and seated himself by Tessa's side. 'Will you be singing again tonight?'

'I don't know. Eve didn't tell me.'

'She doesn't tell you much, does she?'

'I have to leave everything to her. I know nothing

about this kind of thing.' She swept her hand round, including the entire room in her confession.

Paul frowned again. 'Let's hope that Jack finds her and you can ask her.'

He smiled at Tessa's doubtful look. 'Doesn't she like you asking questions? You must stand up to her. She's always had an outrageous will and a quick temper, too, if she's crossed. You mustn't allow yourself to be intimidated.'

Eve appeared, looking flushed. 'There you are!' she said to Tessa.

'And there you are,' said Tessa, nettled at her accusatory tone. 'Jack Padbury is looking for you. He seemed to think I should know where you are.'

'He's such an idiot. Is that a champagne cocktail? Delicious.' She picked up Tessa's glass which had hardly been touched and downed the contents. 'Mmm, lovely.'

Poppy and her friends had greeted Eve with loud and largely false exclamations of pleasure which she returned with interest.

Jack arrived and Eve said lazily, 'Hello there.'

'Where have you been?'

She gave him a look which caused him to take a step back. 'I should like a cocktail,' she said. 'And so would Tessa. I've just drunk hers. And bring more of those little savoury things. Lots.' She lit a cigarette as Jack hurried away to do her bidding.

The girls were to sing once more after supper and when it was announced Eve declared her intention of accompanying the guests to the supper room. Tessa hovered, not sure of what she should do.

'Come along, my dear,' said Paul's voice in her ear, 'you must be hungry, too.'

She turned on him a look of gratitude that made her eyes shine and lit up her face.

'You're very pretty,' he said. 'But I dare say you know. Girls do, don't they? Though, of course, they can't admit it.'

Tessa blushed and Paul laughed softly. 'Perhaps you

don't think about yourself that much. No, I don't believe you do. You are so different from these others.' He waved a hand in the direction of the tail-end of the guests as they surged to the supper room. The band left for their own food below stairs and Paul said, 'Let me look at you properly. I haven't had a chance before.' She held herself still beneath his intense gaze. Then he sighed.

'Is there something wrong with me?' She was worried and prepared to be indignant.

'I suppose Eve made you wear make-up and tied your shoes with red ribbon. And I dare say those pearls are hers.'

Tessa's hand went protectively to her neck. 'Why should they be?' she demanded hotly.

'Don't be cross with me, Tessa. I assure you I mean nothing detrimental.'

She melted in the warmth of his voice, yet she was wary. He was a welcome guest in this house, a member of a society whose ways were unfamiliar to her. Flirting was a pastime to him and his kind. Knowing this she still could not bring herself to pull away when he bent and kissed her softly on the lips. It was all she could do not to put her arms round him and pull him close and she went hot with embarrassment. Eve would have known what to do, but no man would dare take such a liberty with her.

Then Paul smiled at her and she smiled back and the moment passed and he was guiding her towards the room where supper was being served.

There were tables and chairs and he led her to the largest. 'Meet our host and hostess, Tessa,' he said.

She was surprised. She had expected older people to be in charge. Instead, Kitty Bamford, who looked about twenty, turned and looked at Tessa. 'We've already met,' she said. She held out a languid hand adorned by large rings and touched Tessa's lightly.

'Tessa,' continued Paul, 'this is Kitty's brother, Rupert.'

He sprang to his feet. 'I say, you were splendid. Simply splendid.'

Tessa thanked him shyly.

Kitty asked, 'Are you a regular employee of the band? They are taking their supper elsewhere.'

Tessa flushed but Paul reminded her quickly, 'Tessa is here with Eve.'

'Oh, yes, Eve Brook.'

Kitty frowned but Rupert, who was still on his feet, cried, 'Eve is simply splendid, isn't she? So unconventional. I suppose it comes from being half-American.'

Kitty leaned forward and sniffed. 'I do believe you use the same perfume as I do.' The appraising look she gave to Tessa's clothes, which seemed to their wearer to be growing more dreary by the minute, seemed to express her amazement that a girl so garbed could afford so expensive a scent.

Tessa squirmed inwardly, sure that Kitty had guessed she had purloined her scent. When she sat on the chair Rupert held for her she tucked her legs beneath it, trying to hide the black stockings and ribbons. She made a vow that never again would she allow Eve to lead her into such a scrape.

Kitty looked past her. 'Eve! How kind of you to sing for us. And to bring Miss Morland with you.'

Eve threw herself into Rupert's vacant chair and helped herself to an oyster pattie. 'Mmm, delicious.'

'Cook has given us a very good spread,' said Rupert. 'But of course, she always does.'

'Tessa borrowed your perfume, Kitty,' said Eve carelessly. 'I knew you wouldn't mind. She had nothing like it of her own, poor dear.'

Rupert said sympathetically, 'I know my sister will forgive you, Tessa. She is kind at heart.'

He became the recipient of a frosty stare from Kitty and Tessa felt like slapping Eve for laying the blame on her. She wondered what time it was. She wondered when this torment of anxiety would end.

Eve helped herself to another of the patties and said gaily, 'Lovely food, darlings. I shall eat simply tons! Come on, Tessa, you're not doing it justice. Let's make pigs of ourselves.'

In its plenitude the supper reminded Tessa of the

funeral meats except that many of the dishes were hot. She allowed Paul to fill her plate, just as he had done in Padding House, and refill it as she tucked into the unaccustomed luxuries. Her wine glass was replenished by attentive waiters and by the time supper was over and couples began to drift back to the ballroom, their cigarettes leaving a smoky trail, Tessa was in a very relaxed state.

Eve gave her a curious look as she stumbled slightly climbing the steps to the stage where the band was tuning up.

'You're drunk,' she hissed, but not malevolently. In fact, she was amused. 'I hope you can sing when you're pie-eyed.'

'Pie-eyed?' Tessa hadn't heard the term before and repeated it a couple of times. Then Cliff launched into a charleston and Tessa found herself tapping her feet to the catchy music. She had heard similar rhythms on the wireless but not seen it danced and was amazed at the sheer physical effort put into it as the dancers leapt and kicked, bent and stretched.

Eve was scowling and hissed, 'That Kitty Bamford is such a snob. If she had any decency she would have asked us to join in.'

'Doesn't she want us to dance?'

'She didn't suggest it,' snapped Eve.

'But I already did. With Paul.'

'No wonder she was so irritated.'

'You didn't tell me anything about how I should behave.'

'Oh, shut up!' retorted Eve. 'And if you can dance, so can I.' She leapt down the steps on to the ballroom floor and within moments was jumping like a grasshopper while Jack Padbury tried to keep up with her.

I'll never go through this again, thought Tessa.

The Kissing Cousins sang several more numbers, then were given their cue for the last one.

'Shepherd of the hill, I hear you calling . . . I miss the fold and my poor heart is yearning . . .'

Tessa was reminded irresistibly of chapel. The shepherd, to her, was Jesus. They were jazzing up a sacred song. It had seemed different when she and Eve had rehearsed it, but now, blared out by the band, swung into by her and Eve, the words seemed sacrilegious. Many of the dancers joined in the chorus, most of them tipsy, several quite drunk, others smoking while they danced. She felt a tumultuous onrush of guilt that made her falter and earned her black looks from Eve and Cliff. What was she doing here, making a mockery of God? She would be punished. Mum and the pastor promised punishment for sinful behaviour. By the time the song ended she had convinced herself she was a sure candidate for hell-fire.

Then Paul asked her to share the last waltz with him and once more her fears melted in a glow of pleasure as they moved to the gentle melody of 'Russian Lullaby'. His arms round her made her feel secure. No, more than that. They made her happy. She looked up at him, her eyes shining, and his embrace tightened.

'You're a darling. Don't let Eve spoil you.'

'She's been kind to me,' Tessa managed, overcome by delight.

Paul frowned and began to say something, then the dance ended and he thanked her with a small courtly bow before he escorted her to the stairs. Tessa longed to stay with him, to make him understand that she wanted to see him again. In her fear that she might give herself away she just mumbled a thank you and hurried up to collect her coat. The room was filled with a chattering, laughing throng of young women who acted as if she was invisible. She went downstairs to the front hall where she was to meet Eve. Her cousin appeared. 'I'll just dash up for my wrap and be with you,' she said. She was breathless as if she had been running.

Paul came up to Tessa. 'Is my scatter-brained cousin taking you home?'

'Oh, yes, she said she'd only be a minute.'

His brows went up. 'Did she, though? I'd better wait.

Eve's minutes are rather elastic at times.'

But she appeared quickly. ''Night, Paul. Come on, Tessa.'

She drove fast, swerving round bends, obviously the worse for drink, and Tessa was relieved to arrive safely at the end of her lane. Eve held out her hand. 'Better give me my pearls, darling.' Just before she drove away she said, 'It went well, didn't it? We make a good team. I'll let you know about the next rehearsal. I've got something lined up. You're a game kid.'

Tessa knew she was an idiot for allowing Eve's praise to flatter her. Her cousin was clearly a practised flirt and liar, but she couldn't conquer her glow of satisfaction. It upheld her as she tiptoed through the kitchen door and locked it. She stood listening. Dad was snoring. The familiar homely sound destroyed all her pleasure and filled her with sickening remorse. She crept up to her room and went to bed, hoping she could shake off her depression and sleep. It was three o'clock and in four hours she would have to get up ready to go to work.

Her mother had to shake her to awaken her. She was drowsy until Mum said, 'What's that smell? Have you been wasting your money on scent?'

'No, Mum.' Tessa's heart beat hard and her conscience sprang into painful action. 'A customer came in the shop with a bottle and dabbed some on me,' she said. A blatant lie. Another step on the road to hell!

'I didn't notice it last night, but I was frying onions.' Mum added coal to the fire of guilt by saying, 'It's not like you to sleep so heavy, love. You're not ill, are you?'

'No, Mum. I'll be up in a jiffy.'

Mercifully her Sunday shoes, with the red ribbons still threaded through the lace-holes, were hidden beneath the bed. She dragged the ribbon out and shoved the shoes in the wardrobe. Today she must buy new laces with her few remaining pence.

Tessa ate her breakfast beneath Mum's watchful eyes. 'Are you sure you're not sickening for something? You look heavy about the eyes and you're a bit pale, too.'

'I'm all right, honest, Mum.'

'If you say so, but it's an early night for you tonight. There'll be no choir practice. I'll send a message.'

Tessa had forgotten the practice anyway and had promised to see Eve to discuss their first engagement and rehearse for the next. 'I promised Eve I'd see her,' she said.

'When did you promise?' asked Mrs Morland sharply. 'I don't remember you saying anything about it before. Dad and I told you you weren't to see her except on weekends unless she comes here. Is she coming here?'

'No. I forgot. I'll telephone her.'

All morning in the shop Tessa had to push herself to keep up with her work and twice she almost gave the wrong change, causing Mr Grice to send severe glances her way. Just before lunch she got a second wind and energy surged back into her and with it precious memories of the previous evening. During her lunch hour she walked to a telephone box.

'Hello. Is that Miss Brook?'

Eve's voice: 'Tessa? You have no need to shout. The telephone does it all.'

'Sorry.' She dropped her voice. 'I'm not used to telephones.'

'That's perfectly obvious. What do you want?'

Tessa felt repulsed. 'Isn't it convenient to talk now?'

'For heaven's sake, say what you want to say. I am in the middle of lunch.'

'Sorry. I'm wondering if you could visit me at home tonight.'

'Why?' snapped Eve.

'Because Mum reminded me I'm not supposed to go out during the week.'

'You did last night.'

Tessa was furious. 'Yes, I did, and I feel dreadful about it. I wish I hadn't and I won't again!'

'Now, now, darling.' Eve sounded alarmed, placating. 'I was only teasing. I'll visit you and we can have a nice talk. We can go for a walk or a drive.'

'No, we can't. Mum thinks I look too unwell for choir practice and she says I've to go to bed early.'

Eve sighed loudly. 'We'll talk in your room. I'll bring along some songs and you can look at them.'

Eve replaced the telephone receiver and returned to her bedroom. She had actually been asleep when the call came. She sat on her bed and yawned, stretching her arms high. Then crossing her hands behind her head, she leaned back on the pillows. The first engagement of the Kissing Cousins had proved even more successful than she had hoped. She had been asked by several people to sing at their forthcoming dances and parties and Cliff Carter had hinted at professional engagements. She laughed softly. No, that wasn't strictly true. She had been the one who brought the subject up. His reply had been given with a wink.

'You be good to me and I'll be good to you,' he had said.

The implication had been clear. She frowned a little. She found him physically unattractive and wondered how long she could keep him at bay with a few kisses. His mouth was wide and altogether too damp and his wandering hands had been difficult to repel. He had smelt sweaty, too. It was almost impossible not to get sweaty dressed in full evening dress in a hot ballroom, working such long hours. Nevertheless, the guests did not smell.

She pushed the thought of Cliff to one side and allowed her mind to dwell on Tessa. Her cousin had performed creditably. She was still too diffident to give of her best, but she would get over that, especially when she began to earn money. Meanwhile there was the Anderson party to prepare for and this time Eve had made sure that she and Tessa were to be guests as well as performers. Last night she had behaved as if she was unaware of Kitty's hostility, but all the same it had made her smart painfully.

She rang the bell and asked for coffee and toast and

sat up in bed surrounded by song sheets, reading the words aloud, humming the tunes, discarding, choosing. 'I Can't Give You Anything But Love, Baby'. That could be sung with a swing. Cliff said he preferred jazzed up numbers to sentimental ones, but couples liked to hold one another occasionally while someone sent a soothing melody over their heads.

Rose Brook sat among her friends as they chattered about Martha Ruscoe's brush with monkey glands. Apparently the whole thing had fallen through.

'It seems that the best treatment is to be got in Germany,' explained Martha, 'and I couldn't go off on a trip like that without telling Carl. He wormed the whole thing out of me and I'm glad that he did. He said that a man called Niehans is the doctor concerned and it seems he injects patients with a mixture of—' she lowered her voice conspiratorially '—placenta and testicular cells.'

'God, how ghastly!' said Miriam.

'That's what I thought. I should not care for it *at all*. However, I didn't give up entirely. When I told you I was visiting a friend in the south, I'm afraid I was not being honest with you. Carl encouraged me to spend time in a clinic where I learned all kinds of things about diet and vitamins. I already feel years younger.'

Rose's eyes flickered over Martha. She did look more alert, but that could be excitement. Nothing about her had changed dramatically.

'And I got some marvellous beauty tips. White of egg rejuvenates the skin, yolk of egg in shampoo helps the hair. Oh, and lots of information. I tell you, girls, it's worth having a try. Each woman is given her own regime. And exercises. Of course, I couldn't manage them all, but I can do some.'

'Show us,' clamoured the other two.

Martha gave a coy giggle. 'No fear! They make me look so undignified. I wouldn't dream of allowing even Carl to see them. Some of them—' she giggled again '—the pelvic ones, are positively naughty.'

Miriam and Carrie laughed.

Rose stood abruptly. They were in the Murfitts' drawing room whose colour combination of flame and bottle green set her teeth on edge. 'I have to go,' she said.

'Oh, must you?' Carrie was genuinely sorry. She loved having people about her. In fact, thought Rose, her life held nothing but activities to do with people: card games of all kinds, At Homes, tea parties, dinners, anything to avoid her own company.

Rose found it difficult sometimes even to be civil to her. 'Please excuse me, Carrie. Ralph will be home by now. He's been so busy of late I have hardly seen him.'

Not by a flicker of an eyelid did she betray the fact that she had caught the derisive glance exchanged by Miriam and Martha. All the same as she made her way to the front door, accompanied by the Murfitt butler, she burned with impotent fury. She had absolutely no idea of when she would see her husband again and they guessed as much. Since arriving home she had discovered that the busty blonde had been quickly superseded by a dark-haired girl – slim, intelligent and clever. Rose had met her once only when she brought some papers to the house, but had been instantly certain that she would know exactly how to plan a campaign to attract a man like Ralph.

A frisson of fear made Rose feel cold. Her solitary consolation had always been that her husband would stay with her. Now she was terrified that this young woman might cause him to forget his wife entirely, perhaps even risk the censure of society and leave her. If he did, she knew the humiliation and loss would destroy her.

At home she sat in her bedroom. It was decorated in cool blues against grey, reminding Ralph, he had said, of an iceberg. The implication that it suited her personality had been obvious. He came home unexpectedly early. For 'him, that was. It was nine o'clock and Rose had eaten dinner alone. He bent and brushed his lips against her cool cheek.

'Have you had an interesting day?' he asked.

'I visited Carrie.'

'Good, good.' He had already seated himself in an easy chair and picked up a newspaper, turning at once to the financial page.

'Martha told us she had been thinking of trying monkey glands to bring back her youth.'

'Good God!' Ralph lowered his paper. 'What a disgusting subject for ladies.'

'I thought so. I left quite early.'

'I should think so. Did Carrie mention Elliot? Did you see him?'

'His name was not brought up.'

'I think you should tell Eve to return home,' said Ralph. 'We do not want Elliot to look elsewhere for company.'

Rose sighed softly. She was fully in agreement with his sentiments, but the idea of having Eve around to disrupt her life was disagreeable. She supposed, however, she would have to write and order her home.

Ralph studied his wife for a moment. 'You look smart.'

'Thank you. I purchased the gown in London.'

Ralph nodded. 'It is still the best place to shop.'

Rose remained as still as an ivory statue beneath his gaze. She sensed, rather than saw, the way his pale blue eyes travelled over her.

Ralph studied her. He liked the gown and the modest adornments of a string of small garnets with eardrops to match. She had boxes of good jewellery but thought it vulgar to display it except on grand occasions, a point of view he shared.

He thought of his new secretary, Irene Martinez. In some ways she and Rose were alike. They both had pale complexions and slender physiques, but Irene's presence was a constant challenge to him. She was impervious to flattery and rejected his advances while appearing to beckon him on. He knew he was being skilfully played by a woman expert in flirtation and the novel experience was titillating, even while it annoyed him. And her wicked eyes promised bedroom delights . . . He wondered how long and what it would take to get her into bed. Maybe, for once, he would find a woman who could satisfy him for more than a few weeks. He never had yet and was constantly seeking a fulfilment he never managed to grasp. His former secretary with her ample curves had disgusted him almost at once and had been bought off. Men who knew him, men who envied his success with women, would be amazed to learn that he was desperately looking for the ultimate love and would keep trying until he found it.

Rose stood and wished him goodnight, and he said, 'May I come to you tonight?'

She could not prevent the flicker of anticipation in her eyes and it both amused him and increased his appetite. She never let go beneath his caresses, never gave way to wanton cries of pleasure, and he found that preferable. And she would relieve the irritation which Irene's unavailability had caused him.

# Chapter Five

Tessa's work in the grocer's shop became more bearable, not because she enjoyed it in the old way but because she could balance it against the excitement which Eve brought into her life. She had been persuaded to sing at more parties, creeping out at night fearfully, afterwards feeling wicked in chapel, but more and more addicted to the thrill of singing and being applauded. The twinges of conscience became less sharp as the weeks passed, thus proving that the minister's warning about the road to hell being a slippery slope was true. Not that she thought she was doing anything so terribly wrong. Mum and Dad were too strict. Even when she passed her eighteenth birthday they still insisted on choosing where she should go and that she be home and ready for bed by ten. Her naturally eager impulses had for years been stifled by their narrow principles; Eve had simply been the catalyst precipitating her into a bid to escape.

The services of the Kissing Cousins were quite sought after, though Tessa, still troubled in spite of her resolve, had agreed to appear on fewer occasions than Eve demanded. On-stage, she suffered less from nerves, especially as she realised that her voice possessed the quality to provoke genuine admiration.

She still had to hang on to her equilibrium when Paul appeared at a party or dance. His eyes, which she had believed so lazy, were nothing of the sort. In fact, they seemed to see deeper than most. He quite often paid her attention, dancing with her, talking to her, escorting her to supper, and she was forced to acknowledge that the hope of seeing him again was the factor which enabled her to smother her feelings of guilt. She dared not dwell on the way she felt about him. Paul was attentive when he was with her, but never made the slightest effort to see her outside her engagements. Any notion that he might turn permanently to a girl from such a home as hers when he had the pick of the rich and beautiful was just a foolish fantasy.

Sometimes it seemed that Mum or Dad must find out what she was doing. She never returned home without wondering if Mum had discovered that the mound in the bed was merely a bolster. She half expected Susan, who was losing her puppy fat and getting very bright as she grew taller, to discover something that would reveal her sister's secret. In a way she protected Tessa because Mum's attention was riveted on the fact that Susan threatened to grow faster and taller than her elder sister and consequently even more expensive to clothe. Money, too, caused Tessa pangs of conscience. Hostesses insisted on paying the Kissing Cousins for their services, even when they arrived as part entertainers, part guests, and Tessa had cash hidden with her box of face powder. She could have helped Mum with it.

One night, when Eve was driving her home from a dance in Clifton, Tessa asked, 'Does Paul have a special girl friend?'

Eve laughed softly. 'Interested, darling?'

'Just curious.' She was picking up a few tips on dissembling.

'As far as I know he's never liked one girl above another.'

'Do you think he ever will?'

'You *are* interested.'

'Of course I am. Why not? He's an attractive man.'

'But difficult to pin down?'

Tessa, objecting to Eve's mockery, fell silent. Then Eve said, 'He'll get married one day, and when he does it will be to someone of impeccable lineage without a stain on her character.' She laughed raucously. 'So that lets me out.'

'Why? What do you do that's so bad?'

Eve reached for her cigarette case. 'Light me a fag, I'm gasping.'

She drove the rest of the way with a cigarette in the corner of her mouth, mumbling non-committal answers so that conversation died.

When spring gave way to a warm summer the number of parties dwindled. Eve assured Tessa that this was quite usual. 'So many of them are doing the season. London, you know.'

'Yes, I do know. I'm not a complete ignoramus. Anyone can read the papers and magazines.'

'That's true.' Eve was quiet for a moment then said, 'Have you ever wondered what it would be like to stand on a real stage, in a theatre, and get paid for singing?'

'We get paid now.'

'Peanuts!' scoffed Eve. 'I mean real money. Professional money.'

'Never!' Tessa was horrified. 'That would mean being out every single evening with you. Shows begin about seven and end late. It's impossible.'

'Why? Is it because you're deceiving Lily and Walter? Is that your only objection?'

'Deceiving my parents, isn't that enough?'

'You haven't cared before. Why now?'

'I *have* cared. Anyway, it's different singing at private parties. If I appeared in a theatre someone would be sure to see me and tell Mum or the pastor.' Tessa shuddered at the idea.

'We don't need to be obtrusive, Tessa,' Eve explained earnestly. 'We should be only a small part of a much larger show. We'd probably perform in front of the curtain while the scenery was being changed. And if you use theatre make-up, no one will know it's you. After all, they won't be expecting to see a choir-girl on a stage. They'll just think you look like Tessa Morland.'

Eve always managed to sweep her along in a rush of enthusiasm, but when they were apart and Tessa lay wakeful in her narrow bed in the attic room, doubts invaded her. She recalled the pantomimes, the only criterion she had, and tried to imagine herself in a spangled costume in front of a dark auditorium. She couldn't do it and told Eve so.

Eve laughed and leaned back in her deck chair. It was Wednesday afternoon, Tessa's half day from the shop, the weather was fine and the girls were in the Morlands' garden. Not on a velvet lawn, but a small patch of unproductive scrub. 'I'm not surprised the idea makes you nervous. It rather frightens me.'

'You? I thought nothing frightened you.'

'Now you know you were wrong.'

Her admission made Tessa feel better. 'Actually,' said Eve, 'I came to tell you of an engagement I've accepted with Cliff's band.'

'Without consulting me?'

'Certainly. Why not? You've not objected before.'

'But this is different.'

'Of course it is. It's a good chance for us. Our first professional appearance. We'll get paid properly. Some of my friends seem to think we should work for them just for fun.'

'I can't possibly come!'

Eve scowled. 'I see. Our first true professional chance and you're afraid to take it.'

'It's not that! You won't understand.'

Eve shrugged, looking dejected. 'All right, I'll say we can't come. I'll have to let the band down and it won't do our reputation any good, but if that's what you want . . .'

'It isn't a question of want.'

Mr Morland, who was weeding the vegetable bed, looked up at them.

'We're attracting Dad's attention,' said Tessa. 'Next thing he'll be asking if we're quarrelling, then Mum will want to know why.'

'I don't want to quarrel. I want us to be friends and partners.'

'When is the dance to be? Where?'

'When? Next Friday. Where? In a dance hall the other

94

side of Bath.' Eve smiled, all her charm blossoming.

Tessa turned a startled look on her cousin. 'You know Friday is late night at the shop and I hardly have time for tea before choir practice.'

'Skip practice for once.'

'I can't possibly, you know I can't. I've got a solo to rehearse for Sunday. I have to be ill before I'm allowed to stay away from chapel. And the other side of Bath! That's about ten miles. That's stupid.'

'Stupid, am I?' said Eve sharply.

'No, I didn't say that, but you are being very thoughtless. You won't try to understand that I have to work and Saturday is our busiest time. The women get their husbands' wages on a Friday night.'

Eve sighed. 'I admit I do tend to forget the details of your hopelessly plebian life, but honestly, I don't see how we're going to turn our act into a professional one if you put chapel first. Or work.'

'I've always put chapel first, and you don't have to sound so sarcastic. That's the way I've been brought up and you've known it from the beginning.'

'So you're happy to go on in your own boring way? I suppose you'll end up with that greasy mechanic – what's his name, Frank something – who hangs around you?'

'Anderson,' supplied Tessa. 'He doesn't hang around me. He gets greasy, but he does his best to keep clean on Sundays and he's got a way with engines. He's walked home with us from chapel several times and Mum has asked him in for a cup of tea.'

Tessa didn't try to explain because Eve would never understand the serious implications of Mum's action which, in their society, meant that she and Dad would approve of Frank as a possible suitor for their daughter.

And of course Eve didn't. 'Walked home with us from chapel! Got a way with engines!' she mocked.

'It's a good trade to be in, Dad says. There are lots of motor cars and I'm sure that the girl who marries Frank will have a good life.'

'Is that your secret ambition? To marry a man who

spends most of his time lying under motors? I thought there was more to you than that!'

Tessa flushed. 'Who said anything about marrying?' she cried.

'You did, darling.'

'I meant it in a general way. And if it comes to that, you seem pretty friendly with your precious Cliff.'

'Cliff? What a cheek! As if I'd consider him seriously. I see him as a way to fulfilling our ambitions.'

'*Your* ambitions! Before I met you I had no thought of singing anywhere but chapel.'

Eve sprang to her feet. 'All right! If that's all you want out of life, I've been helping the wrong person. I can find another partner. The world's full of girls who want to go on the stage. Or I might go solo.'

'Your voice isn't powerful enough,' said Tessa.

Eve looked as if she wanted to strike her. 'So you despise my voice as well as my ideas?'

'Sorry,' said Tessa quickly. 'I didn't mean to be nasty. Do sit down again. It's too warm to quarrel. And Dad's looking at us again.'

Eve wavered, then sat in the deck chair and lolled back. 'Do you think your mother would have a fit if I lit a cigarette?'

'Yes,' said Tessa.

Eve opened her bag and took out her cigarette case and lighter, paused, and put them back. Antagonising Tessa's mother wasn't going to help. She liked coming to the Morlands' house, she enjoyed the homely, delicious food, took an odd comfort from the inevitable routine, and most of all she enjoyed Mrs Morland's fussing. When she'd had a cold Cousin Lily had insisted on dosing her with some obnoxious home-brewed mixture which had nevertheless eased her sore throat. She gave advice freely and unasked, some of it good, all well-meant.

Tessa smiled warmly at her when she didn't light up and perversely that irritated Eve. 'Your parents should get into the twentieth century,' she said. 'They're still buried in Victorian times.'

Tessa was indignant again. 'Don't bother to come here if you think so little of them. I'm going in. I've got some mending to do. Some of us have to look after our clothes.'

She stormed into the house, past her surprised mother who was taking a batch of scones from the oven, and up the stairs to her room where she sat fuming.

Mum called up, 'Come down, Tessa. Tea's ready. Hot buttered scones and honey.'

She got up and went slowly downstairs where Eve was seated at the kitchen table lavishly spreading a scone with butter which melted into the warm dough. She spread a thick dollop of honey and took a large mouthful.

'Delicious, Cousin Lily,' she mumbled through the food. 'Absolutely delicious.'

Tessa drank a cup of tea, but refused a scone and her mother frowned. 'Look at her, Eve, she's getting quite thin. She's been refusing puddings for weeks. I like to see a girl with flesh on her. You could do with more.'

Eve smiled. It was at her insistence that Tessa had been losing weight. Deliberately, Tessa took a scone and ladled butter and honey on to it, ate it and took another.

Mrs Morland beamed. 'That's more like it.'

Tessa, having accustomed her stomach to sparser fare, felt a little sick.

On Friday, Tessa just managed to get to choir practice on time. It was a long and stringent one, the choirmaster being meticulously demanding, especially with her solo, and after it she felt tired, dreading what was left of the evening. Eventually Eve had persuaded her that she must attend the dance. She had resorted to pathos.

'I promised Cliff,' she had wailed. 'Surely you won't let me down? Please, Tessa, as a personal favour. It won't matter how late we arrive as long as we make an appearance. Tessa, darling, you must come. I can't be a Kissing Cousin on my own.'

Tessa had yielded and ever since wished she hadn't. There was something about Eve, a quality which weakened her resolve. But her capitulation wasn't only from weakness. Although her cousin seemed to have everything, she never seemed really happy. Tessa often felt sorry for her.

Eve drove her to Bath after she had slipped from the house. The girls arrived at eleven-thirty and went straight to work. Eve had organised a more suitable wardrobe for Tessa from her own collection of clothes. 'When we become real professionals we'll wear the same colours,' she had said. Tessa had made a mental note to take up this bland assumption with her later. Tonight she wore Eve's pale blue chiffon frock and a long necklace of pink beads. Her feet were larger than Eve's so her cousin had bought her a pair of silver shoes with tiny heels which would match anything. In the small, frowsty ladies' cloakroom, Tessa peered at herself in the full-length mirror, pleased at the way the chiffon flowed over her newly slender shape. The colour suited her, too. She applied make-up with a now skilled hand, patting in cream, powdering and painting her face, and giving her hair an extra brush.

She felt she owed a lot to Eve. The attention she had paid to her looks, at her cousin's prompting since their career began, along with her diet, had worked wonders. Her hair was glossy, the fine bones of her face accentuated, and her skin now free from spots.

She and Eve sang several numbers. Tessa still had butterflies before she began, but when she launched into song they disappeared. Sometimes the girls harmonised, Tessa taking the lower key and Eve's clear, thready soprano lifting the notes to a higher register.

She returned home that night, creeping in as usual, fell into an exhausted sleep and coped in the shop as well as she could the following day, stifling her yawns. She wondered how long Kissing Cousins could continue. She couldn't keep up this double life. Apparently Mrs Brook was agitating for Eve to return to America and Tessa didn't know whether she was relieved or not.

Last time she had met Paul he had asked, 'Will you make the stage your career?'

'I don't know. I should like to.'

'From what you've told me, your family wouldn't approve.'

'No.'

He had laughed. 'You don't waste conversation, do you?'

She had laughed with him. 'I can't think of anything more to say.'

'That doesn't stop most women from talking.'

Tessa had felt stricken. He was classing her with other women which she took to mean he had no particular preference for her. She had kept her feelings well under control. No girl, Mum said, ever let on to a man how she felt about him. He must be the first to speak.

She changed the subject. 'Why do you live in England when your parents are in America?'

'I like it here.'

'Don't they mind?'

'My parents are easy-going. We write quite often and I shall see them in the fall. Autumn to you.'

'You're going away?'

Tessa tried to keep the disappointment out of her voice, but Paul had turned a searching look on her and frowned. 'I shall be back,' he said.

'When?' She wished the word unsaid immediately.

He had shrugged. 'When I'm ready.'

'Eve's parents want her to go home,' she said, changing the focus of attention.

'Eve will do what she likes.'

'She's very strong-willed,' agreed Tessa.

'Very. Don't let her lead you into any scrapes.'

'I can take care of myself.'

'I wonder.'

They had been interrupted there by the hostess and Tessa was left to consider the implications of his words.

The time for the annual visit to Weston came round. Joey and Susan were wild with excitement, reminding Tessa of the days when a visit to the seaside meant nothing but happiness at the prospect of two weeks on the sand or climbing the rocks at Anchor Head; listening to the band; walking the length of the pier and putting pennies in the automatic machines which showed gruesome enactments of executions using tiny mechanical dolls; bathing in the blue-grey water; eating icecream every day and taking meals in someone else's house, served by the landlady's daughters. Sometimes it rained. In fact, there had been holidays when it rained for a week and blew cold the rest of the time, but somehow it hadn't mattered. If it was dry Mum and Dad had sat imperturbably in their deck chairs while their brood played beside them. If it rained they visited the local amusements which included concert parties. Two whole happy weeks when the usual rules were bent, if not quite broken. Sundays always saw them in chapel.

Tessa had actually forgotten her holiday this year until reminded of it by Mr Grice.

Mrs Grice had given her a suspicious look. 'Are you all right?'

'Yes, of course I am.'

'You've got thin.'

'So Mum keeps saying. I'm just following the fashion.'

'Fashion!' If Mrs Grice's words had not proved her contempt, her own ample figure did. 'You'll make yourself ill. There's plenty who've got too thin and caught TB.'

'I don't think I shall. Mum gives us good food all the time. Some people never get enough.'

'That's true. Shiftless lot they are, too, sitting around waiting for someone to give them something for nothing instead of going out to look for work. And *that lot* haven't kept their promises to help the working man – as if anyone ever thought they would.'

By 'that lot' Tessa knew she referred to the Labour Party which had won a victory in the spring election. Mr Grice and Dad always voted Conservative but neither Mrs Grice nor Mum had exercised their hard-won vote at all. So much for the suffragettes.

'There are more than a million out of work,' Tessa

said. 'There just don't seem to be enough jobs to go round.'

'I hope you're not siding with *that lot!*' said Mrs Grice, hands on large hips.

Tessa was thankful to be interrupted by a customer and her noisy children.

In the evening Eve arrived. 'Tessa, I've had a marvellous idea!'

She was wary. 'Oh, yes? What?'

'I'm going to France for a holiday. Will you come with me?'

'What?' Tessa looked at her cousin as if she had suggested a trip to the moon, as she might as well have done for all the chance Tessa would have of going abroad. 'France?'

'Don't look so dumbfounded. It's quite easy. You simply get on a boat and sail over the Channel, and before you know it you're basking in the sun and swimming in water which is a good few degrees warmer than the icy stuff surrounding Britain.'

Eve was gay and voluble and at her most likeable. It frustrated Tessa to refuse her. 'I can't possibly. We're going to Weston. It's all arranged.'

'I am going abroad and you are coming with me,' Eve said dogmatically.

'No, it isn't possible.'

'Yes, it is. I shall speak to Cousin Lily at once.' She ignored Tessa's protests and confronted Mrs Morland.

As Tessa had expected, her mother was astonished, shocked.

Eve was undaunted. 'Please, Cousin Lily, darling, I'm so fond of Tessa.'

Mrs Morland said gently, 'I know you are, my dear, but she must take her holiday with her family. That's the proper way to do things.'

'Surely not for *ever*!'

'No, of course not. When she meets the right young man and gets married, they'll make their own arrangements.'

Eve stared at Mrs Morland, then making a huge effort, concealed her exasperation. She said softly, 'I understand. Of course you want Tessa with you. She's so sweet, isn't she? And so lucky. I haven't any sisters or brothers like her and I am often lonely.' She managed to squeeze out a couple of tears which she allowed to roll down her face.

Mrs Morland said, 'There, there, my love, don't cry. Sit down and we'll have a nice cup of tea and one of my little currant cakes. You'd like that, wouldn't you?'

Eve sat obediently at the kitchen table. 'I'll take the tea,' she said mournfully, 'but not the cakes. I couldn't swallow them. I can never eat when I'm upset.'

Mum tutted and looked at Tessa. 'Your cousin wants you to go on holiday with her. Abroad,' she added.

'Yes, I know. I've told her I can't.'

Instantly Mum was indignant. 'Without asking me first?'

'Well, yes, I said we always go to Weston.'

Eve covered her face with her hands and gave a convincing sob.

Mrs Morland patted her back. 'Where exactly are you going? Will your mum and dad be with you?'

'To a villa in France. Not with my parents. They don't have much time for me,' said Eve in a muffled voice.

Mrs Morland tutted again. 'I'm sure you must be mistaken. Parents love their children. Some don't show it like others.'

'I'm not mistaken.'

Mum shook her head. 'Are you going with relations then?'

'No.'

'Well, who will you be with?'

'Friends.'

'Whereabouts exactly?'

'Cap d'Antibes in the south, right by the sea. It's beautiful.'

Mrs Morland didn't look reassured. 'Do you know them well, these people?'

'Of course. They are very respectable. Back home we always go to Palm Springs, but even there I don't have a really close friend, not the way I am with Tessa. She's family.' Eve paused. 'She's really like a sister.' She paused again. 'Just as you and Cousin Walter are like parents.'

She looked down at her hands, blinking hard, and Tessa almost applauded.

'Now, that's going too far,' said Mrs Morland, though Tessa could tell she was pleased. 'That's not saying much for your mum and dad.'

'They're not like you,' muttered Eve.

Mr Morland came in from the garden and washed his hands at the sink. 'Hello, what's up? What's upsetting our Eve?'

His use of the word 'our' was startlingly new and yet seemed suddenly right. 'She wants Tessa to go on holiday with her, Walter.'

He turned and wiped his hands in his slow deliberate way. 'We always go to Weston.' He hung the towel over the rail by the range. 'Do you want to come with us, Eve?'

For an instant she was in danger of losing her mournful façade. She had driven once to Weston and viewed the expanse of sand and the horizon of water way beyond the mud flats with utter disdain.

'That would be simply delightful, Cousin Walter, but I have already accepted an invitation. I can't let my hostess down.'

'Quite right.' Mr Morland nodded his head approvingly.

'Who exactly is your hostess?' asked Mrs Morland.

'Kitty Bamford. Her brother Rupert will be there too. Mother and Father met them when they were over here for the funeral. They are older than me and my English grandparents knew their family.'

'It sounds all right,' admitted Mum, 'though I wonder your parents haven't told you to come home by now.'

'They've given their permission for the holiday.

Europe is so far from America. I may not get a chance like this for ages.'

'That's true,' said Mr Morland. 'America's a long distance off.'

Tessa moved restlessly. In spite of her certainty that her parents would refuse, a vision of golden sand, blue sea, and young, carefree company had taken hold of her.

Then her father asked, 'What do you feel about it, Tessa? Would you like to go?'

Believing the question to be simply rhetorical she said cautiously, 'It would be different.'

Eve lifted her head and gazed appealingly at Mr Morland who said, 'I've been abroad. During the war, that was. I saw some lovely places, though lots of them were ruined by the shelling. What do you say, Mum?'

'I was waiting for you to say first.'

There was a brief pause then she asked, 'What about the lady who looks after you – what's her name?'

'Miss Coleman,' said Eve.

'Is she going to France?'

'No, she has to visit her sisters in the north. One of them is very old and frail.'

Every word she uttered added a subtle touch of poignancy.

Mrs Morland said, 'Poor thing. Our Tessa means a lot to you, doesn't she, Eve? I don't like to refuse . . .' She got no further as Eve jumped up and threw her arms around her. 'Thank you, thank you, Cousin Lily. Oh, I'm so happy.' Mrs Morland smiled weakly. 'We'll get a passport sorted out. Tessa can borrow some of my clothes.'

'She's got seaside things of her own,' said Mrs Morland.

Eve calmed down. 'Of course she has. How silly of me. Thank you a thousand times, Cousin Lily and Cousin Walter.' She kissed both of them, bending her tall, ⎣raceful figure to their short, stout ones.

Later, Eve climbed into her car. It was hot and the hood was folded back. 'Tomorrow,' she said to Tessa, 'we'll get everything moving. I'm terribly glad they said yes.'

Tessa was suddenly irritated. 'They never really did. You performed your act well. You should go on the stage.'

Eve was not in the least disconcerted. 'Isn't that what I've been saying? I am going on the stage, and you'll be with me when I do.'

'Kitty Bamford isn't old.'

'I didn't say she was. I said she was older. She's twenty-four.'

'She doesn't strike me as being particularly responsible.'

'You are making judgements on a girl you hardly know.'

'Will she be the eldest there?'

'Shouldn't think so. Her party will be a mixture of all sorts.'

'I thought she disliked us when we sang at her dance. I was sure she thought I'd taken her scent.'

'She did, but we've met several times since and she's forgiven me.'

'Is it true your grandparents knew her family?'

'They met.' Eve laughed. 'Goodnight, darling. See you tomorrow.'

She drove off, waving a hand above her head, her auburn hair blowing in the breeze.

Mrs Morland had bought Tessa two summer frocks. When Eve saw them and the black sand shoes, commonly known in Bristol as 'daps', she could scarcely contain her amusement. The advent of a black sateen bathing dress with a skirt reaching part-way down the thighs was a dreadful threat to her composure until Tessa, readily reading her cousin's expressions, led her upstairs and took her to task.

'Stop mocking Mum and Dad. She used some of her holiday money to buy the dresses.'

Eve, recognising Tessa's real distress, said no more.

Tessa grew more excited as the day for departure grew nearer, expecting Mum and Dad to change their minds at any minute. But eventually she and Eve set off. They travelled south and boarded the boat. Everything was marvellously novel to Tessa and an overnight stop in Paris had her gasping. Eve permitted her no time for sight-seeing but instead whisked her to several exclusive shops and paid for evening and beach wear, including a jersey swimsuit, the attenuated bodice striped and belted, the bottom so skimpy Tessa thought she would never have the nerve to put it on.

Eve was amused. 'The others will wear much briefer outfits. They would only laugh at that black satin thing.'

'How do you know they'd laugh? You don't know them all that well.'

'I know the type. It's the same the world over. People like us go around in packs. We always need others for protection.'

'From what?'

'From the plebs. They're getting uppity.'

Tessa ignored the provocative reply. If she reacted Eve would simply grow more outrageous.

Berths were booked on the wagon-lit and when Tessa discovered that she was to sleep overnight on a train she was overcome with pleasure. She lay listening to the sound of the wheels on the tracks, the hiss and hoot of steam, until the swaying motion lulled her to sleep. She awoke with a start, then remembered where she was and laughed aloud at the difference between this and the short trip to Weston. Tentatively, she raised the leather blind. The sun had risen and shone brilliantly on the rich red earth of the south of France where already people were at work in the fields.

They left the train at Nice where Jack Padbury waited for them with an enormous yellow open car. He shook Tessa's hand, then looked as if he was going to kiss Eve before she held out her hand to him. He took it and held it for a moment. She jerked it away irritably. Tessa wished he wouldn't show his disappointment so obviously. It only encouraged Eve.

Tessa was thrilled by the spacious villa built in gold-coloured stone with its irregular pink-tiled roof and furniture which was unusual and intriguing. Kitty met them in the wide, cool hall.

'What a pleasant surprise it was to learn from Eve that you were coming,' she said to Tessa who was instantly embarrassed and left with nothing to say except, 'Thank you.'

In the living room, Poppy reclined on a white beechwood chaise-longue which was upholstered in cream silk, a perfect foil for her black beach trousers, white silk shirt and long floral coat. The inevitable cocktail stood on a small table beside her, the inevitable cigarette dangled between her reddened lips. Tiddles was seated in a tub-shaped chair of pale wood with yellow upholstery. The rest of the company, about ten Tessa thought at first glance, lounged on couches and chairs of tubular steel and canvas. Paul was not among them. The girls stared inquisitively as Eve introduced Tessa and the men sprang to their feet, offering the newcomers their seats.

'I dare say some of you recognise Tessa from her singing with Eve,' said Kitty. 'Such a charming voice. Rupert, darling, do give the girls a cocktail.' She glanced at her watch. 'I expect you are hungry. It will be lunch-time soon.'

In the dining room Tessa was seated on one of a set of grey-silk-upholstered chairs, feeling as if she had strayed by mistake into a moving picture. Everything she saw was exotic, almost every word these glamorous people uttered, alien to her. No one spoke of anything as simple as housekeeping, or the price of food, or the financial situation over which Dad had lately been shaking his head. Their talk ranged over clothes designers, movies, books, artists and the latest gossip, some of which was amusing, some innocuous, but much to Tessa's way of thinking, unkind or even vicious. She scarcely dared take her attention away from the unfamiliar dishes and the array of silver in case she made mistakes.

'Tessa likes reading,' said Eve.

'Do you?' Tiddles said eagerly. 'Have you brought any books with you? No? Oh, well, never mind. I've asked Harrods to send some. You can borrow mine if you like. I brought an Agatha Christie, *The Mystery of the Blue Train*. Do you like her writing?'

'I haven't read any of it,' confessed Tessa.

'Perhaps your taste runs to higher things? I've a Virginia Woolf, and *Death in Venice* – that's a Thomas Mann.'

Tessa was overwhelmed by the rapt attention she was being given by the others. 'Thank you,' she said quickly. 'I don't mind what I read.'

'Heavens!' exclaimed a girl in a pink dress which was almost backless. 'How quaint!'

'Tessa is wise to read anything. She will form her taste that way.' That was Jack and Tessa threw him a grateful look. Eve scowled. She didn't care to hear any of her admirers praising another woman, however obliquely, however badly she treated them.

Tessa learned that Paul was expected the next day and couldn't hide her relief and pleasure.

'You'd better not fall for him,' said Eve in the room they shared.

'I won't!' declared Tessa.

'You're blushing.'

'You know I blush easily. I wish you wouldn't make such suggestions. I don't like it.'

Eve shrugged. 'I'll take my bath now,' she said, disappearing through a white door.

Someone had unpacked the girls' luggage. Eve's clothes hung in profusion in the wardrobe and filled most of the drawers in the matching lowboys. Tessa wondered what the maid had thought of her scanty supply. She had shoved the stuff Mum had bought to the bottom of her case and was mortified to see that the maid had hung it with the rest. When Eve left the bathroom Tessa carried her towel through and discovered she needn't have bothered to bring it.

The bathroom reminded her of a palace in a pantomime, everything in gleaming marble and glass and chrome. Her body looked pink and very naked, reflected from every angle. There were six towels, three of which Eve had used and dropped on the floor. Tessa bathed in deep water she scented with bath salts and dried herself on a hugh fluffy towel, then hung it carefully on a chrome rail. She powdered herself with talcum, hung up Eve's towels, pulled on her nightdress and returned to the bedroom.

'What a wonderful place,' she said. 'I've never seen such a bathroom.'

Eve was in bed, leaning against the black satin headboard, a gold quilt covering her. She was smoking, tapping out the ash into a glass ashtray, the crystal lamp on her bedside table picking out fiery gleams from her hair. She looked beautiful. 'I don't suppose you have,' she said. 'Of course, it's rather small—'

'*Small*!'

Eve laughed. 'In America we concentrate on our bathrooms. And just before dinner Kitty showed me round the villa and hers is over twice as big as ours.'

'How many bathrooms are there?'

Eve lifted her brows. 'I don't know. I wasn't counting. I should think there must be one to a room.'

'Is this Kitty's house?'

'It's a villa, and yes, it's Kitty's. Her parents gave it to her for her twenty-first birthday. They paid for all the improvements but she chose the decor. All the stuff is *Arts Décoratif*.'

'French.'

'Yes, very up-to-date French.'

Tessa climbed into bed, sure she wouldn't sleep, wishing she had taken advantage of Tiddles' offer and had something to read. She said, 'I like to read before I sleep. I saw some books in the sitting room. Would anyone mind if I borrowed one?'

'I shouldn't think so,' said Eve. 'But beware of the midnight creepers.'

'The what?' Tessa envisaged some kind of insect or small furry creature. 'What are they?'

Eve laughed. 'You're so ignorant.'

Tessa understood. 'People visit one another at night, do they? By the sound of things my ignorance will soon be cured.'

'That's the girl!'

Tessa tried to rest, then gave it up. 'It's no good. I must read. I'll chance it.'

Eve yawned. 'I'm exhausted.' She switched off her light and settled down. Tessa stared at her cousin and decided to try once more to sleep, but she was far too exhilarated. Paul was expected tomorrow. Her heart thumped harder. Even so, she thought nostalgically of her room at home where she could light an illicit candle and snuggle down with one of her precious books.

Eve's heavy breathing proved that she slept. Tessa thought back over the intervening weeks between her parents' permission and her actual departure for France. She had faced several heart-stopping crises. And the more difficult it seemed the more she wanted to go, especially when she learned that Paul Jefferson was to be one of the party.

First, Mr Grice had grumbled at the disruption of his routine. 'I've got you booked to go on holiday the first and second weeks in August and you want to change it right at the last minute,' he grumbled. 'You'll be away for the whole two weeks, I suppose.'

'Oh, yes,' said Tessa. No one would travel all the way to France for one week, would they?

'Well, I just hope my sister-in-law can change her arrangements and step in for you.' That hurdle had been cleared, but the Grices still groused. They were as much sticklers for order as Mum and Dad. Mum kept having doubts which she expressed volubly. Dad had come to Tessa's rescue here, pointing out that Eve was a member of his family and as such entitled to be trusted. Then the

110

awkward subject of money had been raised. Eve had assured the Morlands that her father had sent a special sum to pay for Tessa because he considered her such a good influence, all due to her home life. Mrs Morland had looked doubtful, remembering their reception at the funeral.

'They were rather uppity then,' said Eve, beguilingly, 'but now I have told them so much about you, they realise how perfectly splendid you are.'

Mrs Morland absorbed the flattery and as Dad said, 'You can't offend a relative by refusing a gift and that's what this holiday is.'

Eve was amused at the furore caused by so simple a thing as a vacation in Cap d'Antibes. In her world people said they were going somewhere, ordered a maid or valet to pack, then went.

After what seemed like an eternity, Tessa climbed carefully out of bed. She had not brought a dressing gown. In fact, she had never owned one because Mum declared that only sluts came downstairs without dressing first, so she borrowed Eve's kimono. It was scarlet satin with embroidered blue and gold dragons and she slipped her arms through the wide sleeves which were draped almost to the floor. Wrapping it round herself she crept out and made her way to the drawing room. The blue-white light of the moon shone through the long French windows. She tried them and found they were not locked and slipped through them and on to the balcony.

She caught her breath at the beauty of the night with the moonbeams reflected in the rippling sea. Lamps twinkled like stars from boats and there were a few from the exotic villas half hidden by the lush vegetation. She took deep breaths of the warm, scented air, then jumped and cried out when a pair of arms went round her and a man's voice murmured, 'Darling, you came! I've been waiting and hoping.'

'Who are you?' she asked, her voice quavering in her panic.

111

'What? Damn! Sorry. It's Tessa, isn't it?'

She turned. 'Jack!'

'Sorry,' he said again. 'I thought you were Eve.'

'Oh. Were you expecting her?'

'I was hoping. She said she might spend a little time with me. I thought she – it's the dressing gown.'

'I see. At least, I think I do.'

Jack laughed. 'Eve uses the gown as a house-coat sometimes. I've seen it only in the most respectable way. Unfortunately.'

'Sorry,' Tessa said.

He laughed again, softly. 'Let's stop apologising, shall we? You couldn't sleep either?'

'No. This is all so new to me. Actually I was going to look for a book, but the lovely night tempted me out here.'

Jack motioned to the chairs and they sat down. He took a packet of cigarettes from his dressing-gown pocket. 'Smoke?'

'I don't. But I think I would like to try.'

'It might make you sick.'

'I'll have to begin some time. Everybody does it.' She had unwittingly given a very good imitation of the girl in the pink dress. To her relief he chuckled.

'You're a talented kid.'

'I'm not a kid.'

'Just an expression.' He blew out smoke which mingled with the scent of the abundant flowers.

Tessa took a tentative puff, then another, and found she liked the taste of tobacco. She wouldn't be able to indulge at home, of course, but while she was here she would do as the others did.

Jack was silent, staring out across the bay, and she said impulsively, 'You are very fond of Eve, aren't you?'

It was gauche and she deserved to be snubbed but Jack said quietly, 'Very fond.'

No one in the villa had so far permitted a hiatus to develop and she racked her brain for something interesting to say.

Then Jack said, 'You're a restful girl, Tessa.'

He meant it as a compliment but she wasn't sure she liked it. It made her sound like an old shawl or a feather cushion. No one would ever call Eve restful, or Poppy or Kitty or Tiddles. Or, indeed, any of the women staying here.

# Chapter Six

Breakfast the following morning was served on the terrace overlooking the sea and Tessa revelled in the sun and the view while she ate croissants and preserves and drank fruit juice and coffee.

'Did you sleep well?' asked Kitty.

'Very well, once I got off.' Tessa smiled nervously, realising too late that her answer could be construed as criticism.

Kitty raised her brows. 'Do you find the bed uncomfortable?'

'Oh, no, not at all. It's a fine bed. I think it was the excitement of being here. Everything is so lovely and so different.'

'It's certainly different from the cold grey shores of Britain,' said Eve as she strolled in wearing her kimono. She poured coffee, threw herself into a chair, and lit a cigarette. She stared at Tessa in a way which made her feel uncomfortable.

'What do you know about Britain?' demanded Poppy. 'You've hardly ever been there.'

'Enough to know I don't want to live there always,' drawled Eve. She was clearly in a foul mood and the others left her alone, except Jack who hovered round her like a bee over a flower.

It was decided that they would swim.

Eve and Tessa went for their bathing costumes and towels. 'Surely you aren't going to bring that skimpy towel to the beach,' jeered Eve.

'It's the only one I've got and you've no need to be so

nasty to me. I've done nothing to deserve it.'

'Is that so? You call creeping out to meet Jack in the night "nothing"?'

'How do you know?'

'Is that all you care? "How do you know?" My God, it's the quiet ones who are the worst!'

Tessa was angry. 'I couldn't sleep and went to look at the moon, that's all.'

'It isn't what I heard. You were seen with his arms round you.'

Tessa's anger deepened. 'Who said that?'

'I shan't tell you.'

'I see. Anonymous gossip. Fine friends you have!'

'If you don't like them you needn't come again. In fact, I don't know that I should want you to if this is the way you behave as soon as you're away from home.'

'It isn't! And what if I had arranged to meet Jack? He isn't yours! You don't want him!'

'So you admit it?'

'Admit what? You sound like someone in a melodrama.'

Eve stared at her. 'Good lord, you've got claws. I never would have guessed it.' She took a long drag at her cigarette.

Tessa, seeing her wonderful holiday about to disintegrate into a bickering disaster, said impulsively, 'Sorry, Eve. The truth is he thought I was you.' Her cousin looked blank and she explained. 'I have no dressing gown so I borrowed yours. Don't be cross.'

'Oh, I see. Just remember, though, Jack isn't available.' She picked up her bathing costume. 'You can swim, I suppose?'

'Yes. A woman at our boarding house in Weston taught me.'

Even pulled out a drawer. 'Here, use this.' It was a huge red and white striped towel.

'Oh, thank you. You can be so nice when you—' Tessa stopped. She was being gauche again, but it was such an easy trap among these people whose lives were so

116

fantastically different from her own.

They were not the only sun worshippers this morning and Kitty's guests were on speaking or nodding terms with everyone they met. In spite of their declared enthusiasm for swimming no one in her party went into the water. They lay on white or orange mattresses, or towels laid on warm, flat rocks, massaging themselves until they were slippery with Patou's latest suntan oil, smoking and chatting in a desultory way, all intent on acquiring the fashionable tan. When Tessa saw their outfits she was thankful that she wasn't wearing black sateen.

The sun grew hotter until the rocks looked as if they were shimmering and the sky was pale with heat. To Tessa the water looked more and more inviting. She got up and said tentatively, 'I think I'll swim.'

'Must you be so athletic?' murmured Kitty. 'All right, swim away.'

'Are you coming, Eve?'

There was no reply. Perhaps she was asleep.

Tessa slid gratefully into the sea, breaking its blue-green calm. The sun's rays warmed the water to a depth of at least three feet and her white legs seemed to ripple with the motion of the sea. Even where the sun didn't penetrate she could see the seabed. It was the first time she had known that the sea could be so clear. She struck out in a strong breast stroke until she reached a large raft where several people sunned themselves. A man opened his eyes and held out his hand. 'Need a lift aboard?'

Tessa could have managed, but politely allowed him to help her. She took off her white bathing cap, brushed her fingers through her damp hair and sat on the edge of the raft, her knees under her chin, gazing out to sea. It seemed incredible that she should be here. Two whole weeks of pleasure lay before her, and soon she would see Paul.

'Your first day?' enquired the man who had helped her.

'How do you know? Oh, I see, I'm not sunburned.'

117

'You soon will be. Best take care, though. You don't want to end up with blisters.'

'No. You're very brown. How long have you been here?'

'Oh, only a few days, but I've been in Deauville as well as St Moritz in February. It all helps.'

'St Moritz is a ski resort, isn't it?' Tessa was rather proud of her knowledge.

The man raised his brows. 'That's right.'

But Tessa had stopped listening. On shore she saw that two figures had joined Kitty's party, one of them a man with tall, lissom grace. Paul. As she watched he dived into the sea and began to swim to the raft. When he reached it he lifted himself easily to sit beside her, shaking water from his hair, causing the other occupants to exclaim as the droplets splattered their warm, dry skin.

'They said you were out here, Tessa. How splendid that you could come to the villa. Eve said you might.'

She felt exhilarated. He had actually swum to her. She felt very conscious of the amount of flesh she was displaying and had to stop herself from crossing concealing arms over her breasts whose cleavage was evident.

'You look very pretty,' said Paul.

'My hair's tangled.' She was behaving self-consciously and wished she could have thought of a smart answer. Eve and her friends always had smart answers and never apologised for their appearance.

Paul smiled and his face broke into the laughter lines she found so beguiling. 'I'm surprised it's wet at all. Most of the girls I know either flap around in the water with their heads well up to protect their latest hairdo or don't go in at all.'

'I like swimming.'

'So do I.'

He lay back, his hands beneath his head, squinting at the sky, while she searched her mind for something intelligent to say.

'Relax,' said Paul, as if he understood her dilemma.

118

'I'd better go back. Eve may want me.'

It wasn't at all what she had meant to say or what she wanted to do. She cursed her idiocy and was glad when Paul said, 'Let her want. In any case, I don't suppose she does. She'll have landed another fish by now. I arrived with a chap called David Selby. He's been in Australia and Eve's never met him. She immediately appointed him her new flirt.'

'That's nice for her. What about him?'

'He seemed only too content to oblige and he can take care of himself.'

'Jack won't like it.'

'Jack? He's a fool.'

'I thought you liked him.'

'I do. The best I can hope for him is that he meets someone who can take his mind off Eve.'

'Maybe David will be the man she really wants.'

'Eve wants every man she sees. This definitely won't be serious. His family estates are mortgaged. The Australian visit was to spy out the land to see if they should emigrate.'

'But Eve has plenty of money.'

'She won't marry a poor man.'

'If she loved him she would.'

Paul laughed loudly, causing the sun-seekers on the raft to frown at this man who so determinedly disturbed their peace. 'She will make certain she falls for a rich man. If she ever loved someone without money she would enjoy him for a while, but that's all. The only one who won't be put off is Jack. He's rich, but he's too easy a prey for her. And I suppose she likes to keep him dangling in case she ever needs him.'

'She's been very kind to me,' said Tessa, suddenly feeling disloyal. 'I'm going back.' She slid into the water, hoping that Paul would follow her, and after a few moments he did.

If Tessa had hoped that the holiday would give her a chance to be alone with Paul she was disappointed. Eve had been right when she said that her kind of society moved around in packs. Tessa thought they were more like a flock of birds: the girls dressed in their beach wear or evening gowns which, with their low-cut bodices and bare backs, were even skimpier; the men in white or cream shorts or trousers and casual shirts; and all of them always chattering, drinking and smoking. She tried to imagine Dad or any man she knew dressed or behaving in such a way, but her imagination wouldn't stretch that far. Dad's only concession to the seaside was to exchange his bowler hat for a panama, Mum's to wear a dress with no sleeves which revealed her plump arms.

Tessa soon tanned and like the other girls daringly went about in the evenings without stockings. Beneath her frocks she wore wisps of silk and lace, insubstantial undergarments with hardly anything between the legs. They were teddies, Eve had explained, and all the rage. She had bought her cousin four in different colours, white, black, ecru and ivory. Tessa felt at first as if her lower half was naked until she became used to the freedom. Then she wondered how she would ever return to normal clothes. She pushed the doubt aside, just as she did all thoughts of the future. She meant to enjoy this brief, crazy interlude.

Then came the joyful day when Paul decided she should learn to drive and began to teach her. She was entirely happy, not so much because of the new skill, but because of the hours she now spent alone with him. Once she had conquered her nervousness she handled the Hispano-Suiza or the Bugatti with comparative ease.

'You'll do,' he said, after a few lessons. 'You're a natural born driver. If you can drive these monsters you'll manage anything.' It was a compliment which brightened her day and as if that wasn't enough he took her along the coast for lunch, to celebrate her new accomplishment, he told her.

They sat at a table for two eating sole served with a brandy, lemon and cream sauce, washing the delicious concoction down with wine. Tessa felt frighteningly happy and a little drunk.

Paul smiled. 'It's different from the Bristol Channel, isn't it?'

He decided to drive them back to the villa and Tessa was content to sit by his side. When they were nearly there he stopped the car. They looked down the hillside, past the yellowing grass and shrubs to the azure blue of the sea.

'It's all so beautiful,' sighed Tessa.

'Are you sad?' Paul sounded as if he cared.

'I am rather. I don't suppose I shall ever see such a place again.'

'Why not?'

'People in my kind of life don't take holidays abroad.'

'Why not?'

'It never crosses their minds. Britain is good enough for them. It's cheaper, too. I suppose I'll eventually settle for the same things as my parents.'

'But you like it here so much, Tessa, and if you want something badly enough you'll get it.'

She turned her head to look at him. He had leaned over to gaze down the hillside and his face was close to hers. It seemed quite natural that he should kiss her. The intoxicating mixture of sun, good food and wine drowned her in pleasure and she clung to him. The kiss deepened and she shivered and murmured his name. When they broke away she stayed quite still, looking up into his eyes.

'Tessa, you are so—' he stopped and smiled '—no, I won't say sweet. What can I call you? Delightfully, refreshingly innocent. You don't mind innocent, do you?'

'I suppose not.'

'You don't sound very sure.'

'No.' How could she tell him that the touch of his mouth fired her body with new sensations which begged her to hold him close, to allow him to take any kind of liberty he liked? It was shaming and she said stonily, 'I think we had better return. They'll be wondering about us.'

Paul began to speak, thought better, and started the car.

Tessa couldn't maintain a silence that she found uncomfortable. She said, 'Since meeting Eve and the others, to be called innocent sounds practically insulting.'

He glanced sideways at her. 'Don't think that. Never think that. Don't change, Tessa.'

She wanted to tell him that she would do anything, be anything, if it would please him. She held her tongue, fearful that it would run away with words best left unsaid.

Their drives continued.

'Good lord,' said Poppy one day, 'can't she drive yet? There's really nothing to it.'

'Besides, when she gets back to England she'll have to learn to drive on the left side,' said Tiddles.

'She'll be fine,' said Paul.

Tessa stayed silent and Eve gave her a swift mocking glance. 'Yes, she's a quick learner in every way, isn't she?'

'Meaning what, darling?' asked Poppy.

'Singing. What did you think I meant?'

Poppy raised her brows and returned to her magazine.

Paul took Tessa to explore the town of Antibes. 'It used to be a Greek trading post back in the fourth century BC,' he told her.

'So long ago? There must be so many memories caught up in the stones.'

'That's almost poetry. Do you write poetry?'

'Not really. I used to scribble verses and lately I've been trying to think of a song lyric. I've jotted down a few words. I suppose you could call it poetry, if you were being kind. Very kind,' she added after a moment's reflection.

Paul laughed. They were seated in the green shade of a vine-covered awning drinking the local red wine. 'Will you compose your own music and sing your songs in public?'

'I shouldn't think so. I couldn't compete with proper composers. Eve and I stick to the well-known songs. I know a little about music. I took piano lessons and Eve plays, as I'm sure you know. Actually,' she confessed, 'I have tried to do a little composing.'

'Sing something of yours to me,' he said.

'Here? I couldn't possibly. Besides, I haven't yet written any music down. Nothing's been good enough.'

'What about the lyric?'

'I told you, I've scarcely begun it.'

'Tell me what you've done so far.'

She said, dissembling, 'Popular songs can sound sentimental or trite, but when they're set to good music can become wonderful.'

'Such as?'

Tessa looked round. A cat sat cleaning its face, a woman in black carrying a bundle of washing along the heat-baked street disappeared into one of the villas. There was no one to listen. She drew a deep breath and sang softly, 'She's got eyes of blue, I've never cared for eyes of blue, But she's got eyes of blue, And that's my weakness now.'

To her surprise Paul joined in. 'She's got dimpled cheeks, I never cared for dimpled cheeks—'

Tessa gained confidence and increased the power of her rich voice and they finished the song, laughing. There was applause and they turned to see the patron and his wife beaming and clapping.

Paul got up and executed an elaborate bow which delighted them.

Tessa smiled at them shyly. 'You see what I mean,' she said to Paul, 'the words come to life with the music.'

Another bottle of wine was opened and he said, 'I heard Sam Browne sing that with Jack Hylton and his orchestra.'

'Oh, how marvellous. I should so love to see him in person. I've listened to him on Eve's records.'

'Sing again.'

'Bossy, aren't you?'

123

'I like your voice.'

'Do you honestly?'

'Now you're fishing for compliments.'

'Am I? I hadn't realised. I'm not used to compliments. In our chapel everyone uses the talents they're gifted with. We don't give praise and we aren't supposed to admire ourselves.'

'Not very helpful to the talented,' said Paul.

'And you believe I'm talented? All right, I won't fish! Do you like dance music?'

'I like all music. Well, almost all. Is it your ambition to be a professional singer?'

She was silent for a moment, then said, 'Yes,' and it was as if the answer had come from a long way off where, unrealised by her, it had been forming. 'Yes, I would like that.'

'Please, let me hear what you've written.'

'I would much rather not.'

'How can you hope to become professional if you're too nervous to let anyone hear your work?'

Tessa could have told him he wasn't just anyone. He was special to her and he made her shy. 'All right. I'll recite something I've just begun. This is it: "Remember me? I'm the girl you left; I'm the girl who promised to be true, To you. Remember me?" '

Paul waited then said, 'Go on.'

'That's as far as I've got. It isn't much, is it?'

'It's a beginning. What will you rhyme with left?'

'I don't yet know.'

'Bereft? Deft?'

'They're not very romantic words.'

'Heft?'

'I don't think any of those will do.'

'Use a different ending. How about "I'm the girl you love?" '

'Oh, yes,' said Tessa, 'and I could say "stars above"—'

'Or "hand in glove".'

They both dissolved into laughter.

'You're a good sport, Tessa,' said Paul. 'Not many

124

girls would allow their poetic efforts to be laughed at.'

'I don't know that I'm partial to being mocked. But you're different.'

'Am I?' Paul smiled and glanced at his watch. 'Time we were returning or the others will rise to new heights of sarcasm.'

Tessa burned with embarrassment. His reaction to her impetuous words was clear. He didn't wish to be regarded as different. They drove back in a silence which she no longer found so companionable.

The end of the fortnight began to loom horribly near. Eve was often missing from their room when Tessa went to sleep. Tessa supposed she was with David who seemed smitten. Jack made valiant efforts to be sociable though he looked strained and unhappy. Sometimes Tessa didn't go straight to sleep but lay wondering what it would be like to walk in the warm moonlight with a man who admired her. Not any man. For her it would have to be Paul. The idea scared her. Did she love him? How could she tell? The room seemed empty if he wasn't in it. Today he had gone off to visit nearby friends and the day had turned dismal for her. The driving practice had stopped and she missed it horribly. Did that add up to love? She tried not to think of the end of the holiday when she would return to Bristol and maybe never see him again.

With three days to go she asked Eve where their cases had been stowed away.

'Whatever for?'

'We need to be ready. My fortnight away from work is over. I have to be back on Monday.'

Eve laughed. 'You idiot! Surely you didn't think we were staying for only two weeks!'

'But of course I did! You know I only get a fortnight off and that's generous of my employer. Most people only get a week. And I don't get paid for holidays.'

'Good God, Tessa, stop being so idiotic.'

'What do you mean?'

'I have no intention of cutting short my vacation.'

'But I must go back or I'll lose my job! Mum and Dad will go crazy!'

'You can find another job. And you can phone your parents – oh, no, I forgot you don't have a telephone. Well, write to them, telegraph them. I'm sure they will understand.'

When Tessa remonstrated further Eve said, 'That's gratitude for you. I bring you here, buy you lovely things and all you can think about is some piddling little job. You don't care about me at all. You are so ungrateful.'

'Oh, Eve, no, I'm not. It's just that I need my job. I don't have money the way you and the others do—'

Eve gave an exclamation of annoyance and walked out of the room. 'Don't be such a bore!' The words floated back over her shoulder.

Tessa followed her to their bedroom. 'You can stay, but I must go back. Please help me.'

'I shall do no such thing.'

'Give me my tickets then and I'll make my own way home.'

'No. I want you to stay. I brought you along for company.'

'You have your friends!'

'I want to travel back with you.'

Tessa stared at her cousin whose expression was implacable. 'Eve, try to understand. Jobs aren't so easy to come by and my family need my wages.'

Eve allowed a cloud of smoke to drift from her mouth and nostrils. 'Do you want me to write to them?'

'I want my tickets home.'

'Then want must be your master.' Eve flounced off again and demanded that Jack take her for a drive, a move which delighted him and irritated David.

Tessa went to Paul and his sympathy was like a healing balm, but he entirely misunderstood her dilemma, believing that she needed help just to communicate with her parents.

'It's not that.' She explained and finished, 'Eve had to

persuade them to let me come. I had no idea she meant to stay away longer than two weeks.'

'Surely your employer will be amenable? After all, it is the first time you have been abroad. I should write to him.'

Tessa was deeply disappointed. He could no more comprehend her dilemma than Eve. 'I simply have to get home.'

Paul frowned. 'You could travel alone, though I would far rather you didn't.'

She looked at him in surprise. 'Why not? Do you think I'm so helpless?'

'Not at all. You strike me as being very determined, but you might find it difficult to undertake such a journey unaccompanied. Do you speak French at all?'

'I've picked up a few phrases.'

Paul smiled. 'It really won't do, you know. Besides, I should like you to stay.'

'Do you mean that?'

'Yes. You're by far the most interesting girl here and what's more you have a sense of humour, a very rare quality among the women I know.'

His words lifted her. He liked her. Perhaps more than liked her. Under his direction she telegraphed Mum and Dad and followed it up with a letter. She didn't write to the Grices.

Having committed herself, she was still worried and Paul said, 'Don't look so downcast, Tessa.'

Her name on his lips was like a caress and as usual his charm engulfed her. 'There is so much more to see and do,' he said, 'we haven't even been to the Baccarat Rooms.'

'That's gambling, isn't it? I can't gamble.'

'You must. Everybody does.'

'Not where I come from.'

'Doesn't anyone have a flutter on the Derby or Grand National?'

'Some do, but not Mum and Dad.'

'You needn't tell them.'

'I can't afford it.'

'Do stop frowning at me. I'll stake you.'

'No!' She was shocked. Never take money from a man, Mum always said. They'll take liberties if you do.

'No strings,' said Paul. He was smiling, his teeth very white in his tanned face. Unable to resist, she smiled back.

It was decided that they would motor to Juan-les-Pins. The casino there was smaller than the new one in Cannes. There were some protests, but Kitty was adamant. 'It's more exclusive and we shall meet lots of our chums there.'

Tessa wore her favourite dress, a pale rose georgette with handkerchief points, loosely belted round her hips. She took a long look at herself in the bathroom mirror. The sun had tanned her skin to a pale gold, her complexion was perfect, her hair burnished. She looked pretty and confident and as if she belonged here. The realisation pleased yet frightened her when she thought of returning to her humdrum existence.

She found the casino hot and overcrowded but the excitement of the play soon got to her. Paul pointed out various celebrities including the beautiful Lady Ashley and the wife of Harpo Marx. Very few of the men had changed from their daytime wear, but the women had emptied their jewel cases and their diamonds caught the overhead lights and sparkled against their brown skin. Tessa won and at the end of the play was able to repay Paul and have some money left over.

Eve congratulated her. 'I dare say that's more than you earn in a week.'

'It's more than I earn in a month,' cried Tessa exultantly.

'You see, I was right to make you stay.'

They danced at Caravelles and later ate bacon and eggs at Maxime's where Lady Inverclyde was entertaining some of her yachting friends.

Tessa sat in the back of the Bugatti and was driven to the villa in the early hours of the morning, drowsy from sun, sea, food and cocktails, reliving the hours of enjoyment which had been doubled by Paul who had hovered over her during the gaming like a guardian angel.

Rose and Ralph Brook were breakfasting, though Rose ate very little. Often lately she and Ralph met only first thing in the morning. Occasionally he accepted invitations to dinner parties given by his business associates and Rose dutifully talked to the wives who bored her while he discussed business and money with the men. He made love to her infrequently and dispassionately. It satisfied her for a short time, then left her empty and miserable.

Ralph lifted his eyes from the financial page of his newspaper. 'It is time Eve returned.'

'I have written to her several times urging her to do so.'

'You cannot have put it strongly enough.'

Rose was irritated. 'Exactly what would you like me to say? I can hardly threaten her.'

'Why not? If we cut off her allowance she would have to come back.'

Rose was startled. 'That is rather a Draconian measure.'

'Eve needs such measures. She is far too wilful.'

Rose did not fail to catch the implication that Eve's unsatisfactory behaviour was due to her mother's influence. After a moment she said, 'I had not realised how much you wished her to return.'

'I have no personal preference in the matter. I am thinking of the Murfitts and especially Elliot. They are in Palm Springs where you and Eve should be. You should have her under your supervision, furthering her opportunity for marriage. It is your duty to make sure that she sees the boy as much as possible. I cannot understand why you did not insist on bringing her back with you. She is far too young to be left alone.'

'She is nineteen and she has a chaperon.'

'Tildy Coleman did not impress me as being the kind

of woman suited to control Eve.'

'You said nothing about this when I came home.'

'I expected Eve to follow you almost immediately. When I understood that she was staying on, you had already engaged the woman. You must write again and insist on Eve's return.'

'Perhaps you should write.'

'I cannot think why she should take notice of me when she ignores her mother.'

'She might. She cares for your opinion.'

'Nonsense! Eve cares for nobody's opinion but her own.'

'This is getting us nowhere, Ralph.'

'Exactly. It would be best if you fetched her.'

'Do you mean travel over and bring her back as if I were her jailer?'

'It is sometimes a mother's duty to act as jailer.'

'What about a father's duty?'

'You know full well that I cannot leave New York. The market is fluctuating from day to day. Inflation is rising.'

'I thought the banks' intervention had steadied things.'

'It did last year. Prices soared, but at present there is no telling exactly what may happen next. People are such fools and panic easily.'

'So you will not accompany me to England?'

Ralph glared at her. 'Have you heard a word I have been saying?'

'Of course I have. You do not appear to be unduly pessimistic about our finances. Surely you can take a couple of weeks off.'

'I never took you for a fool. Yes, the market has steadied but one cannot tell if it will last. I have told you, this past year figures have fluctuated wildly.'

'To hear you and other men talk, that seems to be normal on the stock market.'

'It is up to a point, but last year people got scared and when that happens they sell. And when too many investors sell—'

Rose was abruptly weary of discussing money which bored her anyway. 'Your partners can take care of things. Ralph, why can't we go to England together? It would do you good to have a vacation.' She tried to keep emotion from her voice.

Ralph said loudly, 'I don't want a damned vacation! You seem to have no comprehension of my business, no care at all.'

'How can I? It takes you from the house so much more nowadays yet not so long ago you told me you had made millions. Haven't you enough money? Why try to make more?'

'I enjoy working, pitting my brain against others. I enjoy making money and I do not intend to lose it. I suppose the miserable day will come when I have to retire, but when it does I intend to be among the millionaires.'

'You can only spend so much at a time.'

Ralph said coldly, 'Scarcely a remark I'd expect from an intelligent woman.'

Rose fell silent. She wanted to pour herself a cup of coffee but her hands were shaking too much. Ralph returned to his paper and soon afterwards got up to leave. 'May I assume that you will be going to England?'

'Eve is in Cap d'Antibes with a party of friends. You will hardly wish me to go there and take her away as if she were a naughty child.'

'I suppose not.' Ralph paused at the door. 'I take it her companion is with her?'

'I imagine so. Eve did not mention her in her letter.'

'Write to her at once. Who is she staying with in France?'

'Kitty and Rupert Bamford.'

'A good family, but who knows how young people turn out these days?'

'It may not prove simple to bring her back. As you remarked, she can be very wilful.'

Ralph stared at her, hostility radiating from him.

'Must you always be so negative? You are her mother. That should be enough.'

Tessa received a letter from her mother which was filled with reproaches. 'You should be home now. I suppose you think a letter saying you're stopping on is enough? Mr Grice is very angry. So is Mrs Grice. Tell that cousin of yours you're to come back at once.'

Tessa sighed and showed the letter to Eve who laughed. 'I've got a similar one from my mother. She says that as soon as I return to Bristol I must pack for the States.'

'Will you?'

'I am not even going to think about it. I intend to enjoy my stay here.'

'I suppose you'll answer your mother.'

'I shall send her a postcard. I advise you to send your mother one, too.'

'You'll have to go back to America now, won't you?'

'Do I detect a note of regret?' Eve grinned. 'Got used to seeing the bright lights with me, have you?'

She was in a sarcastic mood and Tessa declined to answer. Then Eve made one of her quick changes and said, 'Sorry, Tessa, very sorry. I'm being horrible to you and you don't deserve it.'

Sighing with relief, Tessa said, 'It's all right. Don't give it another thought.' When Eve was repentant Tessa realised how fond she was of her.

Kitty decided they would have a special dinner on their last night, invite friends and dance in the villa. The evening was crowded with glittering people and the air was dense with smoke and saturated with the fumes of alcohol. Jack had designated himself barman and seemed to know all the combinations for any cocktail demanded. Tessa had grown to like them, but had not seen them mixed before and was surprised to discover that they were all spirit-based. No wonder they were so potent. She drank sparingly. She wanted to remember every second. She danced through the night, several times with Paul, and when he held her in his arms and they swayed to a dreamy slow waltz she wished that the party would go on forever.

Eve enjoyed the party, too. Someone had brought along a man whom she hadn't met before. Charles Ware was older than the others, somewhere in his thirties, she guessed, tall and spare, his dark hair just tinged with grey. He looked experienced and was certainly suave, exactly the kind of man she liked best. She sat with him on the veranda and talked and his eyes told her clearly that he found her attractive. She wondered what kind of lover he would make and the very idea filled her with excitement. She enjoyed David's love-making, but he was young and not very skilled. Jack never entered her bed. He never had. She found endless amusement in keeping him at a safe distance yet promising more, using all her powers of seduction. It was useful to have a man ready to bend to her will. She wondered if she could somehow manoeuvre Charles into making love to her.

She convinced herself she could, but at the end of the evening he came to say goodnight, bowing a little over her hand. 'Thank you for your company,' he said. 'I hope we meet again.' Then he left her, smiling a knowing smile, as if he were well aware of her efforts and amused by them. The evening went sour and she snapped at Tessa when she wanted to talk over the good time they had had.

When Tessa gave that up and asked if she had much packing left to do, Eve told her to shut up. Tessa was no longer so easily put down by her. In fact, Eve thought she had even given a slight shrug and that infuriated her. She lay in bed, fulminating against Charles Ware and men in general. Some had professed to love her, and then when she allowed them to explore the pleasures of her body they had drifted away and probably chalked her up as another conquest. Couldn't the fools see that she was the victor and they the pawns? All the same, it was galling to watch them latch on to another girl and often get engaged to someone Eve considered insipid.

Eventually she fell asleep and drifted into her recurring nightmare. As soon as it began she knew, with a neutral part of her mind which floated above, watching, that it would end horribly. It happened every time, and no matter how she struggled to wake up it continued inexorably to its end. Tonight she dreamt she lay in Charles Ware's arms. She couldn't see his face, but knew it was Charles. He was holding her close, touching her, caressing her, until her whole body writhed with desire. He began to enter her then his face became shockingly clear. The man who held her was her father. In her dream she struggled to scream her horrific outrage until she awoke, sweating and crying aloud. Someone stood over her, a figure who was only a shadowy outline. Frantically she pushed it away, before she became aware of her cousin's voice.

'Eve, wake up. You've been having a nightmare.'

She stopped fighting and threw herself at Tessa, clutching her convulsively, sobbing helplessly. Tessa sat on her bed and held her, swaying like a mother trying to comfort a child. 'What was it?' she asked. 'Tell me, then you'll forget.'

'I can't! I can't!'

'Try. I get nightmares too. Everyone does.'

'Not like mine!'

'No, we've all got our secret fears.'

Her words brought Eve back to full awareness. Her sobs and cries died away and she pushed her hair from her face. 'I'm all right now. Go back to bed.'

'Can I get you a drink?'

'No.'

'If you're sure.'

'Absolutely!'

Tessa's even breathing soon showed that she slept. But Eve lay wakeful. Sometimes if she fell asleep again the same night the dream returned to plunge her once more into shame.

'So you thought you'd come back!' Mrs Morland faced

Tessa, her chest puffed out like an indignant pigeon.

'Sorry, Mum, I did try to leave.'

'You couldn't have tried very hard.'

'Honestly, I did. Eve had the tickets.'

'You could have asked her for yours.'

'I did, but she didn't want to stay on alone.'

'Why not? What was wrong with the place?'

'Nothing. She just wanted me. And Paul said—'

'Paul? Paul who?'

'Paul Jefferson. You remember? The man at the funeral who was so kind. He said it wouldn't be wise for me to travel on the Continent alone.'

'You wouldn't have been alone if Eve had come with you. Well, your dad is angry and it takes a lot to get him that way, and so are Mr and Mrs Grice. They say they don't know if they'll take you back.'

Tessa couldn't suppress the quick leap of excitement at the prospect of freedom, before she said, 'Surely not? I've worked for them for so long.'

'You've let them down. It would be different if you'd been ill, but you just stayed away enjoying yourself.'

Tessa put down her case and travelling bag that Eve had bought her to take her new clothes. 'What's that?' demanded Mrs Morland.

'A present from Eve. She bought me a few things and I had nothing to carry them in.'

'What things?'

'Just something suitable for the weather. Mum, you've no idea what it's like. The sun shines all day and every day and it's never cold, not even in the night.'

'We had good weather at Weston, thank you very much.'

'I'm so glad. I thought about you.'

'Not enough it seems. It was the shock of our lives to read your letter.'

Tessa didn't want to listen to her mother's recriminations. She wanted nothing to spoil her memory of such a perfect holiday. 'Is there any tea in the pot?' she asked. 'I'm parched.'

'Is that all you've got to say? You drive Dad and me

out of our senses with worry and you want tea. How can you be so selfish?'

'I'm sorry, Mum. I didn't mean to be.'

Tessa sounded near to tears. The contrast between what she had left and what lay ahead seemed too much to bear. All the others had plans and prospects of more sun, more parties, more of everything amusing. She was ashamed of needing to struggle against resentment.

Mrs Morland studied her daughter then said, albeit a little grudgingly, 'Sit down. I'll pour. I've made a batch of currant buns. Would you like one?'

'Yes, please. No one cooks like you, Mum.'

Mrs Morland said complacently, 'So you say. I suppose you've been eating lots of fancy foreign muck.'

'I didn't like all of it.'

'I should think not. Why folk have to go gallivanting abroad when there's so much in England I don't know. It's downright unpatriotic.'

Tessa sipped her tea and munched the bun which was light and full of luscious currants. Her mother sat opposite her, frowning. She broke her silence by saying, 'What was the place like?'

'The villa?' Mum's insatiable curiosity couldn't be kept in abeyance for long. 'It had lots of modern furniture and big rooms. Polished floors and rugs. And a bathroom to every bedroom.'

'What?' Mum's eyes were like saucers. 'How many were there?'

'I never found out. They weren't the sort of people you could ask.'

'That's ridiculous!' pronounced Mum. 'We've managed all our married life without even one and no one could say we weren't clean! Whoever needs so many bathrooms?'

'People like Eve and her friends just take it for granted, though she did say that there are only two in Padding House. She says that it's different in America.'

'Don't they have any poor people there?'

'I suppose so but Eve didn't mention them.' Tessa

finished her tea. 'Shall I unpack now?'

'You'd better. After dinner we'll go and see the Grices.'

Tessa lifted the case and the bag then Mum said, 'Stop a minute. Let's see the stuff Eve bought you.'

Tessa handed her the bag and waited for the explosion. Mum didn't fail her. She drew out the frocks, exclaiming, 'You can see through this one! This couldn't cover your knees! There's hardly a back to this one! This is worse, it must have showed part of your bosom! Well, we'd better not let Dad see them. What are these?' Inevitably she drew out the teddies. 'What are they for?'

'That's modern underwear, Mum.'

'Do they go over your vest and knickers, or under?'

'That's all I needed under my frocks. It was so hot,' Tessa added, pleadingly.

'They're downright disgusting! Men must have been able to see your body through bits of stuff like this and a flimsy dress.'

'No, they couldn't, honestly.'

'And what's this supposed to be?'

'A nightdress.'

'It's more like a party frock. Satin and lace and ribbons. I've never seen such a thing. If I'd known that Eve was going to let you walk round half naked I'd never have let you go. Fancy buying you stuff like this!'

'She wore the same kind of clothes. So did all the others. Eve didn't want me to be different. You know she looks on me as a sister.'

Her words calmed Mrs Morland a little, though she still threw dark glances at the garments she had dropped back into the bag. 'Go on up. Leave the bag. We'll get rid of this stuff later, though it can't go into any of the chapel jumble sales. Perhaps the Salvation Army would like them, though I can't think what for. Your Dad would say put them on the fire.'

Tessa flinched. The idea of her beautiful silks and satins and gossamer georgettes dissolving in flames made her feel quite ill.

Mrs Morland called her back. 'On second thoughts, best take this bag up to your room. I'd rather Dad didn't see those things, and there's Joey. They'll be in for their dinner soon.'

# Chapter Seven

Tessa's interview with the Grices upset her and tarnished her memories of pleasure and happiness, of sunny sea and sky, of exotic food and wine and cocktails. Not of Paul. Nothing could intrude there. Certainly not these mundane people with their bourgeois ways. 'Bourgeois' was a word often used by Eve and her friends. Even thinking it made Tessa feel sophisticated.

Mrs Grice was the more reproachful but instead of making Tessa feel apologetic, her plump well-nourished face and rigidly waved hair, her air of complacent sanctity, only added to the girl's irritation. 'We've always done our best for you, Tessa,' she said, 'and you repay us by breaking our trust.'

Mr Grice said, 'Mrs Grice's sister altered all her plans to give us help. It was very good of her.'

Tessa thought, I've earned every penny you paid me and more. 'Please thank her for me,' she said, trying to keep her voice meek. She and Mum were in the Grices' back parlour where Mrs Grice had been polishing her veneered sideboard on which lay a lace runner and, placed at precise intervals, two vases, a candelabrum and a bowl of fruit. In the cream-tiled fireplace was a large vase of dried flowers. When Tessa had first described to Mum the glory of the Grices' living quarters she had longed to see it all, but she had never until now been invited inside and the fact that she was here as a miscreant completely spoiled her enjoyment.

Even here the familiar smell of the shop permeated the air. It could hardly be said to disgust Tessa but today it couldn't thrill her when only two days before, her nostrils had been filled with the scents of flowers and expensive perfume.

Mrs Grice snapped, 'I've already thanked her!'

'And we paid her,' said Mr Grice. 'You'll have to forgo another two weeks' wages on top of the ones you've lost already.'

'That's fair,' said Mrs Morland. She would accept anything to ensure that Tessa wasn't sacked, and continued eagerly but with the correct humility, 'Does that mean you're willing to take her back?' Tessa felt like yelling, 'Keep your stupid job!' But she wouldn't, of course. She must earn money to take home.

Mr Grice pondered, rubbing his chin. 'If she promises never to do such a thing again, she can come back.'

Mrs Grice nodded. 'We couldn't overlook such behaviour twice.'

'She promises,' said Mum, smiling her relief. 'Thank you ever so much. Tessa, thank Mr and Mrs Grice.'

She did so.

'She can start back on Monday,' said Mr Grice.

Tessa walked home, listening to her mother's mingled recriminations on her thoughtless behaviour and instructions for the future.

As they neared the cottage Tessa asked, 'Are you angry with Eve?'

Mrs Morland hesitated. 'I suppose I am, but it wouldn't be fair to blame her for what you did. You've got a will of your own – far too strong, Dad and me think sometimes. Besides, it's not easy to be angry with her. Her parents don't seem to care that much about her and I can't say I took to them. I know she can be annoying, but she's not had proper guidance. Underneath I'm sure she's a sweet girl with a biddable nature. She couldn't be expected to understand how important your job is. You couldn't have explained it properly. I suppose it's better that she didn't have to travel on her own. She's so pretty. Anything might have happened to her.'

Tessa felt a sharp stab of anger. 'But you wouldn't

have minded if I'd travelled home alone?'

'I never said that. I can't say I'd have liked it, but you haven't lived the same kind of life as Eve. You're more used to the world.'

Tessa held back a retort, though it infuriated her to have her mother make such a claim when she had never been allowed out on her own except to work or chapel while Eve had almost complete freedom. She wondered how long Mum would keep her blinkered vision of Eve. However, she wanted to retain her cousin's friendship and only said mildly, 'I'm glad you think I was right to stay on.'

Mrs Morland frowned and avoided a direct answer. 'You'll have to do without pocket money for the next two weeks. Of course, if you'd been satisfied with a perfectly good holiday in Weston, none of this would have happened.'

'I know. Will you be able to manage without my money?'

Tessa hoped that the question would focus her mother's mind on her domestic skills and it did. 'Manage? Of course I can. My store cupboard is always properly stocked, you know that, and I can bake just the same as if you were bringing home your share. It would be a bad day for this family if I couldn't manage the money.'

Tessa settled back into her job and to onlookers it was as if the holiday had never been. Her only outward legacy was a fading suntan and the blonde sheen of her hair which took longer to go. Mum had been indignant about its colour, accusing her of using peroxide, but Tessa managed to convince her that the sun alone could bleach hair. Inwardly she went over and over the events of the holiday. She almost gave the wrong weight to customers and once allowed at least a pound of sugar to spill as she was transferring it from a large sack to the small blue bags it was sold in. Fortunately she managed to hide these near disasters from the Grices.

September was proving fine and warm but it suddenly

141

produced a stormy, sticky day which made her yearn for Cap d'Antibes where she had been assured the weather would remain hot and dry for some time yet. Eve had not visited or written since the holiday and Tessa decided to telephone her after work. She raced to the nearest call box on her way to choir-practice to ask her why.

Eve was laconic. 'I hadn't realised how time was slipping by, and it hasn't been so very long. Actually, I don't want your parents telling me how wicked I was. Did they create an awful stink over your extended holiday? Did you get the sack?'

'Are you sure you're interested?'

'Of course I am. No need to lose your rag.'

'No, I didn't get sacked and Mum and Dad were quite kind in the end. I've had to forfeit my pocket money for two weeks because the Grices gave my wages to someone else.'

Eve giggled. 'Poor you. Pocket money! They treat you like a child. I'll come over soon. I've been frightfully busy.'

'Doing what?'

'Seeing friends. I've got quite a number of engagements.'

'I see.' Envy flowed over Tessa like a cold wave. 'Have you seen Paul lately?' she blurted.

Eve laughed lightly. 'Once. He was at a dance in a house near the Downs, enjoying himself greatly. If I see him shall I tell him you asked after him?'

'Yes. No! Yes, if you like.'

'It's what you like, not what I like.'

Eve was in one of her most tormenting moods and Tessa said, 'I have to go. It's time for choir-practice,' and replaced the receiver.

Her mind wasn't on her singing and she kept losing her place until the choir-master, a small, dark-haired Welsh deacon, reprimanded her severely. Where once she would have curled up in embarrassment, tonight she scarcely noticed. All she saw and thought of was Paul holding some girl in his arms, dancing with her, making her laugh, enjoying her company as he had professed to enjoy hers. Last night she had taken out her notepad and glanced at the song lyric she had begun, to which she had added their amusing rhymes, but somehow now they didn't seemed funny at all.

Eve turned up the following Saturday afternoon at teatime. She came into the kitchen on a waft of expensive perfume, wearing a sleeveless two-piece in striped jersey and four rows of pearls. The belt was so high on her hips it almost reached her waist and her hair had been newly cut and styled. She looked exactly what she was: an expensively dressed, beautifully coiffured member of the wealthy set.

'So there you are,' said Mrs Morland, determined not to be impressed. 'I was wondering what had become of you.'

Eve cried, 'Dear Cousin Lily, don't be cross with me. I know I was very naughty to keep Tessa away for so long, but I did so need her.'

Mrs Morland's plump face was screwed up in a frown. 'You don't seem to have needed her much lately.'

'Didn't Tessa tell you?'

'Tell me what?'

'I've been visiting friends. Mother wished me to.'

'How would Tessa know?'

'She telephoned me. Oh!' Eve's hand went to her lips in a childish gesture. 'Shouldn't I have said so, Tessa?'

'Why not?' The revelation was unimportant but she was irritated by Eve's idiotic behaviour.

'Would you like a cup of tea and a slice of cake?' asked Mrs Morland.

'Not if Tessa is going to be cross with me. I couldn't bear it.'

Mum glanced up in time to catch Tessa's frown. 'Of course she's not cross with you,' she soothed.

Tessa was amazed at how quickly her mother fell under Eve's spell. But who could blame her? Tessa, too, was susceptible even while she was aware of Eve's duplicity.

143

After tea she walked her cousin to her car. She wanted to fire questions at her, but knew that to do so would only encourage her cousin's sharp humour.

'Aren't you going to ask me anything?' demanded Eve.

'Aren't you going to tell me anything?' countered Tessa.

Eve stopped and looked at her. 'You definitely do have claws. When I met you I thought you were rather dim and hopelessly obedient.'

'Did you really?'

'But you are neither.' With one of her unexpected, expansive gestures, Eve threw her arms round Tessa and kissed her cheek. 'I've missed you.'

Tessa tried to stop feeling ridiculously glad, but it was hopeless. She laughed happily. 'I've missed you too.'

'Are you game for more singing? I can get us some lovely engagements now I know more people.'

'I'm game.' Tessa's heart thumped. 'At least I think I am. But I worry terribly about being found out. I can't do it often.'

'I don't know why you don't just tell your people. I'm sure they wouldn't really mind. They're a pair of pets.'

Tessa was angry. 'You needn't make them sound like guinea pigs or puppies!'

'Snappy, aren't we?' taunted Eve.

'Oh, go to hell!'

Eve grabbed Tessa's arm and prevented her from walking away. 'Don't flare up! I meant it as a compliment. I only wish I could call my father and mother a pair of pets.' A sudden bleakness in her voice cooled Tessa's temper.

'I can't help it. I get so nervous.'

'All the more reason to tell them and get it over with.'

'Can you imagine their reaction? No, I don't suppose you can.'

'Would they be very angry?'

'Probably, but more likely they'd be sad and reproachful and that's much worse. I'd get a lecture on dishonesty and riotous living and anything else they could think of, and believe me if you went to our chapel you'd know they'd think of plenty.'

Eve laughed, then sighed. 'All right, I'll just find us a couple of spots. Actually, I've met Cliff Carter several times. He always asks me if we'll sing at his public dances.'

'What did you say?' asked Tessa, alarmed.

'Naturally, I told him I would have to consult my partner. What do you feel about it?'

'You already know.'

Eve climbed into her car and said, 'Shall I write to you with a date for rehearsals?'

'No, better not. Mum doesn't necessarily read my letters but she might ask to see one.'

'Heavens! It's like being back in the nursery.'

'I wouldn't know. We didn't have a nursery in our house. Can't you come here? Mum likes having you.'

'Your Mum *is* a pet.' Eve drove away fast, leaving Tessa pondering on her cousin's abruptly harsh tone.


Rose had managed to put off her visit to England, using the sudden illness of her sister as an excuse which was not wholly spurious.

'You are being ridiculous,' was Ralph's comment when she told him she did not wish to leave Betsy. 'She will have the best medical care available, Reginald will never leave her side and Paul has come over to be with her. What is wrong with her, by the way?'

'That's the problem, the doctors don't seem sure. It's all very alarming. She has had attacks of abdominal pain. Lost weight, too.'

'Is that important? She was too heavy for a woman of her height.'

'Maybe so, but she was always healthy.'

'Most likely she is merely indulging in one of the ridiculous diets you women follow.'

'She is not. She doesn't feel like eating,' said Rose, 'and she used to enjoy her food.'

'If she doesn't eat it's no wonder she's getting thin.'

'Well, I shall not leave her at present. She is my sister, not yours, so you might reconsider going over to bring Eve back.'

'Damn it, I shall do no such thing! It's imperative that I stay here and conduct my business affairs. Can't you understand?'

'No, I can't! Nowadays you think of nothing but money.'

'Do you care for the idea of living without it?'

'We are hardly likely to do that.'

'I sincerely hope not.'

Alarmed by his tone, Rose asked, 'Have you had losses?'

'One expects occasional losses, but an astute man can soon make them up. The *Broad Street Gossip* believes that the country is far too rich to be influenced unduly by stock-market fluctuations. Even so, I prefer to keep my eye on things.' When she made no answer Ralph said, 'It would not take you long to fetch Eve. I feel sure that nothing is likely to happen to your sister. And why this sudden concern? You have never been close.'

'It's not a sudden concern and I'm extremely fond of her. As girls we were great friends.'

'That was a long time ago.'

'I will not leave her.'

Ralph threw down his paper in disgust. 'You're using your sister as an excuse. You don't want to go.'

'No, I damn well don't!' cried Rose.

She so rarely allowed herself the luxury of anger that Ralph was surprised. He said after a moment, 'I suppose I can't blame you. It's not an edifying prospect.'

'It's a ghastly prospect,' said Rose quietly. 'I loathe having arguments with Eve.'

'All the more reason for bringing her back and encouraging Elliot. Once they are married your responsibility will cease.'

He got up and she watched him walk across the room to the door. His figure was as straight and spare as the day they had met, his hair still a thick dark mane. He looked at least ten years younger than he was and still fired her with the familiar ache of desire. At the door he hesitated, then returned. 'By the way, I may need more money to shore up my financial position. Just a temporary loan. Will you give me the necessary authority to use yours?'

Rose agreed readily, pleased that he had asked her for help. To her the money was merely a token, given readily out of love.

She thought reluctantly of Eve. During the past weeks she had written to her several times, first casually, then almost supplicatingly, then more and more angrily. Eve didn't even bother to reply. Rose had threatened to come and fetch her and received an answer filled with apologies, followed by an account of how busy she had been, the friends she had made, the visits she had undertaken, the hospitality she had organised. 'Honestly, Mother,' her latest letter had run, 'you would be so proud of me if you could see how expert a hostess I have become.'

Rose showed the letter to Ralph, but he proved adamant. 'I suppose it's possible that she's behaving herself, but she must come home.'

Rose had resigned herself to going when Betsy haemorrhaged. A stomach ailment was diagnosed and a specialist in the field operated on her, but would not give a hopeful prognosis. Reginald and Paul scarcely left her side. Rose was genuinely worried. Betsy's illness rekindled Rose's girlhood affection for her and she took her turn at watching by the sick bed, allowing Paul and Reginald a chance to rest, setting Betsy's mind at ease, for even in her pain she studied the welfare of her menfolk. She slept a lot, aided by drugs, and as Rose watched her deathly pale face she wondered what it was about her that had attracted Reginald. Her sister's looks had always been homely to the point of plainness while her husband, although not handsome, was most attractive. He was wealthy too and in Betsy's year could have chosen from the pick of the crop of debutantes. He must have seen through her outward appearance to the warm, loving woman beneath.

It was not until the beginning of October that Betsy had begun to fight her way back to health and Rose decided she could travel.

In the first-class compartment of the boat train on her way to London she sat fulminating against her daughter. She arrived at Padding House in the late evening. The trees were losing the last of their foliage and the brown and gold and red leaves were tossed around in miniature whirlwinds. The shrubs were already bare though the evergreens slightly redeemed the dismal state of the garden with their splashes of dark colour. As her taxi turned into the drive she remembered how much she hated the place and resented Eve's defiance even more.

Partridge opened the door to her and called for someone to help Grace, Rose's maid, to deal with her luggage. 'Mr Paul hasn't kept many of the staff on,' he said. 'There's just the cook, a couple of maids and me. Oh, and the gardener-handyman.'

Rose nodded. The house felt as oppressive as she remembered. If Paul kept it when he married, his wife would surely insist he do something about the dark enveloping gloom, the Victorian genre pictures depicting women in the throes of some species of grovelling guilt while a man looked straight ahead, grim and unforgiving. Or the studies of animals and birds gazing at the viewer, their eyes humanised, creating a worrying effect. The others were paintings of churches and cathedrals. If he married Eve she would certainly insist on changing everything, though Rose did not believe that Paul was in the least attracted to her daughter.

She changed from her travelling clothes into a grey flannel costume and white blouse. Partridge had told her that Miss Eve was at a party and Rose had expected Tildy Coleman to come running to her to tell her exactly where her charge had gone. Tildy Coleman was exactly the wishy-washy kind of female she despised, but so anxious had she been to get back home that when Tildy had offered her services Rose had accepted readily. After all, she was a member of the family. She told Partridge to ask Miss Coleman to come and see her.

Partridge, his face impassive, said, 'Miss Coleman is indisposed, madam. She has kept to her bed and a maid has been attending her.'

'I see. Send the maid to me.'

The parlourmaid dropped a small curtsey and said that Miss Coleman had a severe headache. 'She gets them a lot, madam, and sometimes they last an age.'

'How long has this one lasted?'

'About two weeks.'

'Two *weeks*! Has a doctor been called?'

'No, madam. I believe Mr Partridge suggested it, but Miss Coleman had a fit of hysterics and said she didn't want a doctor. Actually, madam, she screamed quite a lot.'

'With pain?'

'No, madam. Because she didn't want a doctor. Poor lady, she gets these headaches when she's worried. This one came on after she got a letter. From America, I think Mr Partridge said.'

Rose said, 'You may go. No, wait. I have forgotten which room she occupies.'

'It's along the end of the first-floor corridor, madam. The last room on the left.'

Rose's feet made no noise on the strip of carpet. She knocked on Miss Coleman's door, tentatively at first, then harder until a weak voice called, 'Come in.'

Tildy Coleman, always a pathetic creature, shrank back into her pillows when she saw the identity of her visitor. She began to throw off the bedclothes, got her feet tangled in a sheet and began apologising.

'Don't get up,' said Rose. 'I am sorry to see you laid low. I shall send for a doctor first thing tomorrow.'

'No, Rose, please, I don't need one. I am quite accustomed to these little upsets.'

'I do not call two weeks with a severe headache a "little upset".'

'Believe me, I am used to them. I feel better today. I shall get up tomorrow.'

'Very well,' said Rose. 'Just tell me where my daughter is tonight and I can leave you in peace.'

Miss Coleman seemed to shrink even more. Her lips moved soundlessly for a few seconds before she said, 'I am afraid I cannot tell you.'

'Why not?'

'I do not know.' Rose frowned and Miss Coleman quavered, 'She did not tell me. She is a dear girl. She would not for worlds worry me when I am unwell.'

'I do not regard her coming to see you and mentioning an engagement a worry. Why should it be?'

'No reason, no reason at all. Eve shows me great consideration.'

'Does she? How many times has she been out without giving you her intended address?'

'Sometimes.'

'How many times? Surely you have some idea.'

Miss Coleman put a hand to her head and looked wildly around the room. 'Not many. I have trusted her.'

'In other words, you have not chaperoned her properly.'

'I have done my best.'

Rose stared at Tildy for a moment then said, 'We will discuss this tomorrow when you are more the thing. I am tired, though I shall now have to wait up for Eve's return.' She cut short Tildy's apologies and left, seating herself in the small drawing room in front of the fire with her embroidery. Gradually her spirits calmed. At ten o'clock she expected Eve in at any moment, at eleven she began to be annoyed, at one in the morning she was anxious. She had ordered the servants to bed but Partridge entered, coughing discreetly.

'May I bring you refreshment, madam?'

'I thought I told you – well, never mind. I should like a glass of warm milk.'

150

As Partridge turned to go Rose said, 'Wait. You have been with the family for many years.'

'Since I was an under footman, madam. I have never worked anywhere else.'

She nodded. 'You are almost like one of the family.'

'Thank you, madam.'

'I spoke to Miss Coleman earlier.' She paused as a look of distaste crossed the butler's face. 'You do not care for her?'

He said impassively, 'It's not my place to criticise Miss Coleman, madam.'

'But you do have criticisms?'

'I'm sure she is a very kind lady, but she is far too easily manipulated.'

Rose hesitated, knowing that Ralph's reaction to such questioning of a servant, no matter how long he had been in the service of the family, would be furious. 'By Miss Eve?'

'I fear so, madam.'

'Miss Eve has cultivated a large circle of friends?'

'She has indeed. A very popular young lady.'

'Has she held any parties here?'

'No, madam.'

'I find that odd. She should return hospitality.'

Partridge did not reply.

Rose looked at him thoughtfully for a moment then said, 'I get the impression that you are holding something back.'

'Madam, you place me in a difficult position. It is not my place to criticise a member of the family I have given my life to.'

'In this case it may be, to help Miss Eve.'

'When you put it like that, madam . . . there is always a certain amount of gossip among servants. One tries to prevent it but . . .' He coughed. 'Miss Eve has been taking singing engagements.'

Rose sighed. 'Is that all? It can scarcely be called gossip when I already know it.'

'Not quite all, madam. I was aware that you had given

151

permission for Miss Eve to perform privately, but she and her cousin, Miss Morland, have sung in a public dance hall, engaged by someone referred to as "Cliff".'

Rose was outraged. 'A *public* engagement? For money?'

'As to that I cannot say, madam. The maids attend an occasional dance and returned one night very excited at having seen Miss Eve and Miss Morland performing.'

'Has this occurred more than once?'

'I'm afraid I don't know. The maids only get a free evening once a week and more often than not go to the moving picture houses.'

'I see. Thank you, Partridge.'

'I will bring your milk, madam.'

He returned with a glass of hot milk and two pieces of wafer-thin bread and butter. 'I thought you might feel a little hungry.'

'Thank you. It was thoughtful of you.'

'Not at all, madam.'

'Now you really must retire.'

'I would rather not, madam. Mr Paul left me in charge and it is up to me to make sure that all doors and windows are secured.'

Eve returned at three o'clock. Rose was exhausted but the desire to sleep had been ousted by nervous anger. She heard the car pull up, followed by a key in the front door. She could hear Eve singing quietly, 'Three o'clock in the morning, I've sung the whole night through—'

She got no further. Rose walked out into the hall and Eve saw her in the hall light which had been left on. She stopped, taken aback, then she advanced.

'Mother! What a surprise. Why didn't you let me know you were coming?'

'If I had, I dare say you would not have come home at this hour.'

Eve glanced carelessly at her watch though Rose saw that her hand was not quite steady. 'I am rather late. I've been to a party. You needn't have stayed up.' She took a

152

quick step forward. 'Is something wrong? Is Father—?'

'Your father is concerned by the unsteadiness of business.'

'Does he have cause to be concerned?'

'I have been so worried by Aunt Betsy's health I have not had time to talk much to him. I believe some traders have lost money. Come into the sitting room.'

'Oh, Mother, not now, please. I want to go to bed.'

'Do you care so little for your aunt that you do not ask after her?'

'I'm sorry. How is she?'

'Mending well her doctors say.' Rose walked back into the room and Eve, after hesitating, followed her. Rose wasted no time. 'Exactly where have you been?'

'I told you. To a party.'

'Whose?'

'A new friend. You won't know her.'

'Nevertheless I should like her name.'

Eve sighed. 'Well, she's not exactly a friend. Just an acquaintance. She held a dance.'

'Was Tessa Morland with you?'

'Tessa? What an idea. Why should she have been? She would hardly be invited to a society dance.'

'It is no use lying to me, Eve. I know what you and that girl have been up to. You have sung together in a cheap public place.'

Eve's head snapped up. 'Not so cheap!'

'How could you? Oh, how could you? To make a vulgar exhibition of yourself.'

'Oh, Mother, girls do all kinds of things nowadays. It's all perfectly innocent.'

'If that is so, why did you not ask my permission?'

'Because I knew you'd make a fuss just like this.'

'It is your deceit which angers me most.'

'No, it isn't. Well, all right, maybe it is.' Eve took a cigarette from her bag, inserted it into a holder and lit it, breathing in the smoke as if it were incense and letting it trickle down her nose and through her lips. 'Anyone would think I had committed a crime.'

'That is exactly what you have done. A crime against the society we live in. Have you any idea what would happen to you if this got out? You could be ostracised.'

'Come, Mother, don't exaggerate. I've been singing, that's all.'

'You think you know the world, Eve, but you do not.'

Rose sounded weary and quite miserable and Eve dropped her flippancy. 'I think perhaps you don't realise just how much everything has changed since your day.'

'I know that standards have fallen lamentably. That is no excuse for you to behave badly. You belong to a society which keeps to certain tenets of behaviour. Do you wish to be cut off from decent people, ignored by the young men of our acquaintance?'

Eve shrugged.

'Elliot Murfitt is conventional.'

'Don't I know it! One would think he was an old man.'

Rose came so near to losing her temper she almost slapped her daughter. 'I must assume,' she said, her voice quivering in her effort to keep it under control, 'that you care nothing for breaking rules. You think only of your own doubtful pleasure.'

Eve smiled, her eyes narrowed, catlike. 'That and money.'

'So you take money for making a spectacle of yourself?'

'A spectacle? No, really, Mother, that's going too far. Tessa and I give good value. Why shouldn't we be paid?'

'You do not need money.' Rose said the word as if it had been 'manure'.

'It's fun to earn something and Tessa finds it useful.'

'I knew I should have nipped that acquaintanceship in the bud. Such vulgarity!'

'Tessa isn't vulgar.'

'That is a matter of opinion. I take it that she instigated this behaviour?'

Eve looked at her mother calculatingly. 'Actually, it was my idea. Tessa loves to sing. She would like to be a professional.'

'On the stage, do you mean?'

'Yes, and there's no need to look like that. The stage isn't the well of vice you seem to think.'

'Is it not?' Rose's voice expressed pure disdain. 'How do you know? Or have you been performing in some music hall?'

'They call them variety theatres in Britain now, Mother. Music hall's quite déclassé.'

Rose dug her nails into her palms in her efforts to stay calm. 'Have you sung in such places?'

'Good lord, no, but I've met some stage people. They seem nice enough. I would quite like to tread the boards.'

'You are brazen! You get an allowance from your father, a generous one. Why have you done this?'

Eve shrugged. 'Excitement, chiefly. I get quite a kick out of spending something I've earned.'

'What arrant nonsense! Tomorrow you will begin packing to return to America.'

'I will not!'

'Your father wishes it.'

Eve gave her a measured look. 'Does he? Did he say he missed me? Is he longing to give me a great big fatherly hug?'

'Don't be ridiculous! He thinks your place is with us and he is right.'

'Would Elliot's name have come into the conversation?'

'Go to bed. I shall speak to Tessa Morland's parents tomorrow and tell them exactly what I think.'

'Don't do that!'

'Do you dare to tell me what I should or should not do?'

'I'm sorry, Mother, I didn't mean to be so abrupt. The Morlands won't understand. They are religious. They would be dreadfully shocked if they knew—' Eve stopped, too late.

'Are you telling me that the Morlands do not know that Tessa has been out singing? No, that isn't possible.

155

She couldn't stay out half the night without their finding out.'

Eve kept her eyes fixed on her mother who continued slowly, 'Why, I do believe you are telling the truth. What a ghastly, deceiving sort of girl she must be. And to think I believed her respectable, if a little commonplace.'

'She *is* respectable and far from commonplace, especially her voice. That is beautiful, better than mine.'

Rose paused for a moment. It was unlike Eve to praise someone above herself.

Eve said, 'Mother, please leave Tessa alone. Her parents will try to stop us meeting if they find out.'

All Rose's anger returned, but remembering that Partridge was probably hovering about the hall, she kept her voice low. 'I forbid you to meet her again. How do you think I feel? How would your father feel? Would he find this edifying? You seem to forget that he is English. Have you been shaming him in front of his friends?'

'Has he got any?'

Eve's voice was so bitter that Rose was taken aback. 'Why,' she stammered, 'of course he has. And he has us. He wants only for you to have a good life.'

'To marry Elliot?'

'Would that be so bad? Father thinks of your future.'

'What a pity he has never thought of my present. He has never left off work except to follow some pursuit of his own. I have scarcely ever seen him.'

'That's what men's lives are like. They tend to huddle together.'

'It doesn't work like that in Tessa's family.'

'Those people!'

'It isn't like that in Aunt Betsy's family either. Are Paul and Uncle Reginald still sitting by her bed?'

Rose took a deep breath. 'Probably. And I have kept watch, too. I should have travelled before this if she had not been so sick. Your father wished me to fetch you earlier.'

'Fetch me? He makes you sound like a gun dog.'

'This conversation is becoming trivial,' said Rose. 'I am going to retire.'

'So am I,' snapped Eve, and walked out of the room and up the stairs.

In the hall Rose met Partridge. 'Miss Eve has returned. I need not have worried. She was at a friend's party.'

'Yes, madam. Good night, madam.'

Rose ascended the stairway, knowing that Partridge did not believe her.


Tessa was on her way home from work to her mid-day meal when Eve's car stopped beside her.

'My mother's arrived,' said Eve rapidly. 'She says she's coming to see your parents. She's found out about our singing and she's furious with both of us.'

'She's coming here to tell Mum and Dad?'

'Yes, so if you can I should get your oar in first. They'll both be there now, won't they?'

'But what can I say? This is dreadful. What am I going to do?'

Tessa was appalled and Eve felt sorry for her. 'Shall I come with you and explain?'

'Thank you, but no matter who explains or how they do it, they're going to be upset and I shall be punished. We'd might as well say goodbye now because we shan't be allowed to meet again.'

'That's what my mother said.'

'Yet you're here.'

'Yes, and I'm not going to let them spoil our friendship. You must stand up for yourself, too. Get in the car,' she commanded and Tessa obeyed. 'They can tell us what to do but we don't have to listen. We'll let this die down a bit then begin again.'

'We won't be able to. It'll be easy for them to watch me.'

'You've got away with it up to now.'

'Only by deceiving them. Oh, lord, this is going to be awful.'

Eve offered Tessa a cigarette but she shook her head. 'They'll smell smoke on me. Eve, I'm terrified!'

157

'You can't be terrified of Cousin Walter and Cousin Lily. They're sweet.'

Tessa said goodbye to her at the end of the lane and for days waited for the moment when Rose Brook would arrive and she would be confronted with her sins. She was a bundle of nerves by the time a smug-looking Eve came to see her again. She was waiting in her car.

'We're saved!' she cried. 'Mother has forgotten about us and our singing. Have you read the news?'

Tessa, faint with relief, barely heard her.

'Are you listening, Tessa? Have you read the news?'

'What news?'

'The New York Stock Market has collapsed.'

'Has it? What does that mean? I don't really know what a Stock Market is.'

'A large building where men yell at one another and make money.'

'By yelling at one another?'

'There's more to it than that. Mother is worried about Father. She's gone back to America to be with him. She tried to make me go but I put up a fight and she gave in. She always puts Father before me, so now I'm free to do as I like.'

That was not quite true. Before she left Rose had given Eve hurried instructions. 'Don't make any big purchases. I've had a letter from your Uncle Reginald. He says that your father looks ghastly. I'm afraid he may have lost quite a lot of money. I shall not know until I can talk to him. I'm surprised that you refuse to accompany me at such a time.'

'He won't even notice,' Eve had said. 'He never does.' Before her mother could reply she added, 'Fortunes as large as his aren't affected that easily. I'm sure you'll find Uncle Reginald is exaggerating.'

Now Eve smiled at Tessa. 'So we can go ahead with our plans.'

'Didn't your mother forbid you to take any more singing engagements?'

'She said she'd prefer me not to, but her mind was full

158

of Father's problems. From the way she spoke, I might end up needing money!' Eve laughed.

Tessa didn't know whether to be glad or sorry. Much as she loved the bright lights, the excitement of dressing in wonderful clothes, using make-up, and above all holding an audience with her voice, she had to contend with her ever-present guilt. 'I suppose the parties are beginning again?'

'Yes, but we must enlarge our audience, make a real name for ourselves. There's an audition for girls for the next show at the Empire. We must be there.'

Tessa was astonished. 'Are you crazy? Audition for the *Empire*?'

'Yes, why not?'

'Because it's a variety theatre. Because it has comics who make vulgar jokes and girls who dance in next to nothing—'

'Have you ever seen their shows?'

'Of course not! Mum would never—'

'Then how do you know?'

'I see their adverts in the newspapers and sometimes I've looked at the photographs outside the theatre. It's a wonder to me the police don't tear them down.'

Eve gave her a quizzical look and Tessa smiled. 'I wouldn't mind appearing on the stage, really, though I don't see myself in that particular theatre.'

'That's rather a snobby attitude, isn't it? In any case, we have to get through the audition first.'

'There's no hope of my getting through an audition because I shan't be there. Are you coming home with me?'

Mrs Morland said crossly, 'You're late, Tessa.'

'Sorry.'

'It's my fault,' said Eve. 'I stopped her.'

'I didn't see you there.' Mrs Morland's irritation subsided. She could never be really annoyed with Eve.

'Dear, dear Cousin Lily, it was my fault that Tessa's late. You will forgive me, won't you? You're so sweet and kind.'

Tessa watched her mother's indignation melt beneath the warmth of Eve's flattery.

In spite of Tessa's protests the next engagement Eve obtained for them was in a public dance hall. 'It's at the Glen at the top of Blackboy Hill,' she explained.

Tessa had heard of it and often wondered what it could be like. It was such a pretty name. She pictured it hung with diaphanous draperies with lots of silver and gold, like a scene in a pantomime. Perhaps the orchestra would be dressed in green like elves. She was again confronted by the grim battle between desire and deception. In the end her longing to taste the exhilaration of singing won and she crept out of the house and down the lane where Eve waited for her. Together they drove into Bristol.

The Glen turned out to be quite a small and ordinary dance hall at the bottom of what seemed like a quarry, with the usual frolicking young men and women and a band. Quickly the rhythm of the music took over her senses and she tapped her feet to its beat as she waited for their cue.

They swung into a fast number and Tessa stood up, exhilaration washing over her, making her heart beat faster, holding her in an irresistible wave of pleasure as she swayed to the music before beginning to sing: 'You're the cream in my coffee, You're the salt in my stew, You will always be my necessity, I'd be lost without you . . . You're the sail in my love-boat, You're the captain and crew . . .' Paul would laugh at the words. They would laugh together. She had to fight off the memories as she kept singing.

They performed three more times during the evening before the band struck up for a number which almost floored her. As she sang, 'He's got eyes of blue, I've never cared for eyes of blue, But he's got eyes of blue And that's my weakness now . . .' she was carried back to the shady leaf awning, laughter and wine sweet on her lips, hot sunshine and Paul's mouth caressing hers.

It was all she could do to finish.

As Eve drove her home she said, 'Why did you suddenly fade in that last song? I thought for a minute you were going to stop altogether.'

'Sorry.'

'Did it remind you of someone?'

'I said I was sorry. I won't let it happen again.'

'It did remind you of someone! Was it a man?'

Tessa said nothing and Eve smiled. 'So you will be singing again?'

'Will we be going to any more of your friends' houses?'

'Why don't you ask what you really want to know? Will you be seeing Paul soon?'

Tessa denied it, but Eve said, 'I've warned you. He's only interested in girls with family and money behind them.'

Tessa said angrily, 'I may not be rich but surely you're doing yourself a disservice when you say I don't have family background. We *are* related!'

'Don't be ridiculous,' snapped Eve. They were on the brink of a quarrel and both girls realised it and drew back.

'We mustn't fall out,' said Eve as Tessa left the car. 'We must always be friends.'

# Chapter Eight

Rose arrived home in a fever of worried speculation. The voyage had been a nightmare with information constantly coming through on the ship's ticker tape of horrific falls in share prices. Many of the men looked increasingly ill as they waited for the next cable. Their spirits rallied when they learned that prominent bankers and heads of trust companies had put up forty million dollars apiece to shore up the market. 'A two hundred and forty million dollar pool is bound to turn things around,' they assured one another. When, later that day, it was discovered that Richard Whitney, vice-president of the Exchange, had put in a bid for ten thousand shares of steel, then offered to purchase twenty or thirty million dollars worth of stock, a measure of reassurance returned and the men relaxed a little and managed to smile.

The ship docked on 28 October and Rose left Grace to supervise her luggage and raced home to find that Ralph was not there. This was no surprise, but when she enquired of Belper she learned that he had not been home for two days.

She telephoned Reginald. 'Calm down, my dear,' he said, 'I have seen him. He's scarcely left the Exchange and has been eating here because we're nearer his office.'

'Has he lost much money? On the boat it seemed as if fortunes were simply melting. Then things picked up. I don't know what to expect.'

Reginald paused then said, 'I had best be honest with

163

you, Rose. Things are looking grave.'

'For Ralph?'

Reginald said carefully, 'I believe he has had some losses. It's inevitable at the moment, but you know your husband. He's clever and quick-witted, I'm sure he'll come about.'

'Will he be home today?'

'I can't tell. Shall I send word that you've returned?'

She hesitated, an ache to see him throbbing through her, then said, 'No, best not. I have no wish to distract him.' She was about to replace the receiver when she remembered her sister. 'Oh, God, I'm sorry. How is Betsy?'

'In reasonable health. She's eating properly, obeying the doctors, and has been allowed to sit out of bed for several days.'

'Thank God.'

Rose went into the library and wandered around touching Ralph's books, sitting briefly in his big leather armchair. She could not settle. Worry gnawed at her like a broken tooth. On the boat there had been rumours flying around. It was said that men had committed suicide rather than face the prospect of poverty. The thought made her heart race. She longed to go to Ralph, to tell him that money didn't matter, that he was all she wanted in life, that without him she would wither and die. Of course, she could not. Such an emotional outburst would embarrass and anger him. Whatever he needed she would give him; she would be whatever he wanted. She despised herself for her own submission, but to her he was life.

That night at eleven she telephoned Reginald again. 'Have you heard from him?'

'No, my dear, if I had I would have called you.'

'Yes. Of course. Do you think he will be with you tonight?'

'I don't know.'

'Where does he go? The Exchange has been closed for hours.'

'He is probably with his friends.'

Rose almost blurted, He has no real friends. 'Yes, I'm sure you are right.'

'I should get some sleep.'

Rose went to her room. Grace had unpacked and a fire leapt in the grate. Ralph insisted on fires though the house was efficiently heated. Odd, thought Rose. A fire is a living thing and his nature is so cold. Perhaps that's why he needs the flames? She was so weary that her thoughts began to spin, making no sense at all. Grace helped her to bed and she slept. In the morning the maid brought tea.

'Did your master return last night?' Rose asked.

'No, madam.' She hesitated. 'Madam, I can't help knowing that the stock market is in trouble and I've got money tied up in shares myself. I think everyone in the house has. Are they safe?'

'Of course. Why should they not be? I shall get up.' Her lids were heavy and a throbbing behind her eyes warned that a headache threatened.

When the telephone rang she raced to it. Her disappointment seemed unbearable when she did not hear her husband's voice. Reginald said, 'Ralph came here very early, at six the servants say. He ate, then left.'

'What did he say? Does he know I am home? How is he?'

'I'm sorry, no one saw him except Cook and a kitchen maid.'

Rose felt sick with frustration.

'Are you there?' asked Reginald anxiously.

'Yes.'

'At least we know he's still functioning.' He tried to be jocular and failed.

'Thank you. Reginald, you're being so kind,' she said, suddenly ashamed of the cavalier way she was treating her brother-in-law.

'Anything I can do . . .'

'I don't know. I must just go on waiting.'

'Spend the day with us. It would do you good to have company.'

'I think I would prefer to wait here. I know you'll

telephone me if you have any news. And it would not do Betsy any good to have me around her just now. Give her my love and say I shall visit soon.'

'If you're sure . . .'

Rose read the papers where the news was a confusing picture of good and bad. That evening the phone rang. It was Carrie Murfitt. Empty-headed, fluttery, the last person she would have chosen to speak to.

'Hello, Rose. How are you?' Carrie sounded as if she were enquiring about the health of a very sick friend.

'Hello, Carrie. I am well, thank you. How did you know I was here?'

'Reginald rang me. He said you sounded a bit down in the dumps and thought I could cheer you up.'

Rose silently cursed her brother-in-law. 'How kind, but I don't need cheering. I have plenty to do while I wait for Ralph.'

Carrie's voice became as hushed as if she were speaking across someone's grave. 'It's all so dreadful, isn't it? So many of one's friends . . . society will never be the same again.'

'What are you talking about?' asked Rose irritably.

'Of the collapse of the stock market. My dear, you must know . . .'

'Of course I do. It seems to dominate the news and all the way over on the boat it intruded. I've also been reading about it and listening to the wireless. It is so very tedious. We have had scares like this before. Why, only last year . . .'

Carrie interrupted her excitedly, 'Not like this, dear. Herbert says that millions of people are ruined. Ordinary people who have sunk their life savings into the market have lost the lot. And people we actually know are reduced to poverty. I am so thankful that Herbert has never been interested in the stock market. We had shares, of course, and now they are worthless, but there were never enough for their loss to change our lives.' Her voice became a sibilant whisper. 'And have you heard of the suicides? Men are leaping from the tops of sky-scrapers.'

166

Rose's fear made her furious. 'Are you suggesting that Ralph . . . ?'

'Oh, no, my dear, of course not! I shouldn't have said so much.' She gave a little laugh. 'I'm supposed to be reassuring you.'

'Well, you are not!'

'I'm so sorry. Shall I come over? I would be happy to keep you company.'

'No, thank you!' Modifying her tone Rose said, 'I really do have things to attend to. I shall see you some time soon.'

'Miriam is giving a cocktail party for everyone who has lost money. I'll see you there.'

Rose muttered something before she rang off. Miriam's cocktail party sounded like dancing on people's graves. She certainly would not attend.

The evening dragged. Rose told Belper to say she was 'not at home' to any callers except family. She could not settle to reading but ran her eyes over her accumulated correspondence without taking in its meaning. She threw the letters to one side. In the end she took up her sewing and eventually the slow, measured stitching began to soothe her nerves.

Late that night Ralph returned. She heard his footsteps in the hall, his short greeting to Belper, before he came into the drawing room. He looked terrible, his face pasty, his eyes blood-shot and dark-ringed. He had been drinking. He nodded to her and walked swiftly to the sideboard where he poured himself a large whisky and drank it, immediately pouring another.

She got up. 'Ralph?'

'Have you heard?'

'About the problems on the stock market? Yes.'

'How much have you heard?'

'Apparently it has collapsed.'

'Do you know what that means?'

'Ralph, do sit down.' She patted the easy chair by the fire. 'You look positively ill.'

He obeyed her like an automaton. 'Do you know what it means?' he asked again.

'Some are ruined. Is it being exaggerated? People love disasters that don't concern them directly.'

'This is no exaggeration and it concerns us very directly indeed. The market is almost completely dead. I can't see the way ahead. No one can. It is the ruination of America.'

Rose stood facing him. She ached to touch him, to hold him and drive the desperate look from his face. 'Have you lost money?'

'Yes.'

'Much?'

'A very great deal.'

'How much?'

'Everything! Well, virtually everything.'

'Do you mean—'

'I mean exactly that. When this is over, I have every reason to think I shall be a pauper.'

Rose suppressed a gasp. 'Darling! Oh, I am so sorry.'

He looked up at her, grinning like a death's head. 'Are you? Yes, I am sure you are, though I doubt if you know what it means.'

'We can retrench,' she said eagerly. 'We will save so that you can begin again.'

'I've used your money, too. You will probably never see it again.'

Rose was taken aback. The fact that she had signed over her disposable assets to him had been so unimportant to her that it had slipped her mind.

'Every last cent.' He sounded determinedly jaunty.

'Don't,' she begged.

'You have never lived without money, have you?'

'No, and neither have you.'

'True. What an interesting fate lies ahead of us. By the way, where's Eve?'

Rose had forgotten her daughter. 'Eve? In England. I came back as soon as I heard of the financial crises.'

'Leaving her again?'

She was angry at his implied criticism. 'She refused to accompany me and I put you first. Isn't that a wife's duty?'

'You are strong on duty, aren't you?'

And love. For you, she longed to say.

'Well, Eve may have to stay in England. I doubt if we have the fare for her return.'

Rose sat down. 'Surely it cannot be that bad?'

'You see? You do not understand.'

'Maybe not. Perhaps you can explain it to me.'

Ralph held out his glass and Rose took it automatically and refilled it. He put his hands over his face, rubbing his eyes, then took the glass from her. 'Sit down. You make me nervous, hovering over me like some damned nanny.'

After all these years he still possessed the power to hurt her in small ways as well as large. She sat and waited.

'We shall have to leave this house. Not immediately. I shall go to the Exchange as usual in the hopes that there may be a miracle. I still hold shares in American Can, Radio and United States Steel, all once reckoned to be cast-iron certainties. Unfortunately I bought high and now they are low and there's no one buying anyway.'

Rose tried to imagine losing the house. It had been in her family for generations and she loved every stone of it. She said, 'There is still the trust fund.'

Ralph stared at her. 'Your trust fund? So there is. You actually have some money. Your trust fund!' His laugh lacked humour. 'You have allowed the interest to accumulate, haven't you? How exciting.'

The bitterness in his voice hurt her. 'We shall not starve and we may be able to keep the house. I hope so. I shall see my lawyers.'

On the following day Ralph set off for business as usual. He had lain with her last night. Rose had hoped to comfort him, but if he had meant to make love to her he had changed his mind. Her longing had got the better of her and she had reached out to caress him. He had jerked away from her, obviously unable to bear even the touch of her hand, and the searing pain of his rejection pained her even more than usual. Soon after, he had gone to his own room. This morning he had eaten scarcely a thing before leaving.

She wandered around, moving from room to room, touching the furniture with a caressing hand. Much of it had been bought by her forebears, but she had added to the collection, taking immense care that the nineteenth-century American John Jeliff rosewood armchairs went well with the English Regency sofa table, that mahogany Maher chairs were complemented by a Chippendale bookcase, and that delicately engraved Dorflinger glass-ware sat comfortably side by side with eighteenth-century Bristol. She had used her own money and much of her unreciprocated passion had been directed into furnishing the house, creating a beautiful and harmoni-ous whole. Never had she considered it might be lost to her.

Ralph looked less distraught when he returned. Some businesses, including American Can, had declared an extra dividend and when Vice-President Whitney had announced that the market would close at one-forty and not open until twelve noon on the day after, then remain closed on Friday and Saturday, the news was received hopefully by those still struggling to stay on the success ladder.

But it was only the extreme panic that was over. Forced liquidation completed the ruin of many who had managed to stay afloat, however precariously, and on 13 November the bottom prices for the year were reached.

Ralph broke the news to Rose. 'Now I really do have nothing. No money in the bank, nothing with which to meet bills, pay the servants, run the car, keep up this house, buy food and clothes. No money. Nothing! How do you fancy a walk-up cold water apartment in Lower East Side? Or maybe it would be better to move to the country? A small cottage somewhere. We could keep a cow and a pig and a few hens. I could hire myself out as a labourer, though I doubt if I'd get any work. So many farmers have lost everything too. Nothing to say?'

Rose kept cool. 'I have seen my lawyers and have

been examining the household books. We need not leave here although we cannot afford all the servants. There will be money enough for clothes as long as we are circumspect. No holidays will be possible, but that will not worry you. You have never wanted one.'

Ralph smiled thinly. 'So not all the news is bad. We can stay here and manage on your money. Which servants will you dismiss?'

'I have not decided. I thought you would like to talk it over.'

Ralph shrugged. 'It's your house, your money. You do as you please.'

'Very well.' Rose refused to allow his ungraciousness to affect her, outwardly at least. 'I must have the housekeeper and Belper cannot go. He has been with the family for years. We can do with fewer maids and keep only one car. I must learn to drive myself which will dispense with the need for a chauffeur.'

Ralph sat down and for the first time relaxed his guard. He looked exhausted, vulnerable, and the familiar longing to close the space between them seized her. She took a step towards him and almost imperceptibly he drew back. She turned away. 'Shall I pour you a drink?'

He nodded. 'I wonder how I shall cope with idleness,' he said.

'Are you no longer a member of the Stock Exchange?'

'I've not been thrown out, if that is what's worrying you. But I cannot trade without good money behind me.'

'If I could break the trust I would. You should have it all.'

He looked at her. 'My God, I believe you. Why? I am not much of a husband to you.'

It was the first time he had ever admitted that he might in any way be inadequate and hope flowered in her. Was this a pattern for the future? From now on Ralph would be dependent on her for everything. The idea filled her mind and heart. Other women would not be interested in a man without a cent to call his own. To hell with them! To hell with the Stock Exchange! To hell with wealth!

The disaster which had destroyed so many was like a breath of life to her. He was hers.

'I can sell my jewellery,' she said. 'And there are pictures I have bought and various artifacts—'

'No! I will never permit it.'

She drew back. She had been too eager. She must guard his pride. Money was one thing; her personal possessions quite another. And she would never be able to deceive him. He knew exactly what she owned.

Ralph decided they should go to Miriam's cocktail party and Rose, secure in her newfound domination, did not argue. He dressed with his usual care, filling his gold case with expensive cigars and his hip-flask, a necessary adjunct to every man's accessories since Prohibition, with whisky.

Grace assisted Rose into a gown of ivory georgette with which she wore plain gold jewellery. She placed her narrow, silk-stockinged feet into ivory satin shoes and Grace draped a cape of ivory velvet and white fur around her shoulders.

Ralph scrutinised her. An outsider might believe he took an intense interest in her appearance because he cared for her but Rose was not deceived. She must look well dressed and wealthy to bolster his consequence in the world, especially now.

Miriam and her husband Oliver had a large house in Sutton Place. Ralph and Rose were admitted by the butler and announced with customary solemnity. At first glance the party seemed like any other. It took Rose only a few moments to realise that the atmosphere was unduly frenetic.

Miriam greeted them. 'Hello, darlings, so glad you could come.' She pressed her cheek against Rose's then Ralph's. 'Drinks in the usual place.' She peered over their shoulders at more arriving guests whom she greeted as effusively. Cocktails were being mixed with bootleg gin and dispensed by a solemn-faced barman assisted by a maid. Everyone was swallowing them as if they were perishing of thirst, the air was blue with smoke and the

172

sultry voice of a black singer borrowed from the Cotton Club fought for ascendancy through the chatter.

Voices rose and fell, people laughed loudly. Rose smiled until her face felt stretched. Then, very gradually, the men began drifting together and their talk was of money. No matter how hard Miriam tried to break it up she was unsuccessful, and when Oliver became one of the group she smiled thinly and began to discuss her new winter wardrobe in an excessively loud voice which drew her husband's attention from time to time.

Rose sank into one of the few chairs in the room which was furnished with stylish sparseness and watched the men. They had dropped their guards, their attitudes were gloomy and she wondered how many of them were staring ruin in the face.

Martha Ruscoe drifted over and looked down at her friend. 'Had enough of the jolly party?'

'Yes,' said Rose shortly. She modified her tone. 'I think I am tired.'

'Aren't we all, darling? I gather Ralph has been hit hard.'

Rose's expression remained serene. 'He has sustained some losses.'

'Come off it, dear, he's dropped a packet. Carl says so.'

Rose seethed at Martha's vulgarity. 'He has lost some money.'

Martha said bitterly, 'Carl will not be able to go on trading. He followed Ralph's tips as if they were the tablets from the mountain.'

'I trust you are not blaming Ralph for your husband's failure?'

'No, I don't suppose I am. They were all in it together. Fortunately Carl did not touch any of my money.'

'I am pleased for you,' said Rose. 'As it happens Ralph did not use any of mine, either.' The defensive lie slipped out smoothly and Rose's mind raced ahead to the extra difficulties she had created for herself.

She held her hand before her mouth, hiding a small,

simulated yawn. 'I think I shall have to leave soon. The trip to England was enervating.'

'You've brought back Eve?' The words were more of a statement than a question.

Rose said casually, 'No, the dear child was having such a marvellous time with her British relatives and friends I decided to leave her there.' She did not look to see how her answer had been received.

On the way home Ralph said, 'It was like a damned speakeasy. Well, you can look upon that as a farewell party. They cannot possibly keep up their standards. They'll have to give up the house.'

'Oh, poor Miriam. It's all so awful.'

'Save your pity for yourself. You're going to need it.'

The next day Rose tackled the question of the servants. She explained as much of the circumstances as she considered warrantable and set out which of them would have to go. They looked sick but not surprised. 'Servants are losing their positions all over the place,' explained Belper later, 'and lots of them have been investing. It seems as if everyone in America took a chance on the stock market.'

Only one of the housemaids protested tearfully. 'I've lost money too,' she wailed. 'I've been saving against my old age and now I've got nothing. Please, Mrs Brook, I'm fifty-five, I'll never find another decent place. Can't you keep me on?'

Rose wavered then remembered her budget which was now too tight to allow any sympathy. She shook her head. 'I'm sorry.' The woman left, sobbing.

Rose had visited Betsy once and was kept informed of her progress by Reginald. She went to see her again. Her sister was seated in a comfortable armchair by a fire in her bedroom. She was much thinner, still pale, but contentment flowed from her.

'There you are,' she said when Rose entered.

She felt irritated. 'I've been frightfully busy.'

Betsy lifted her plain face for a kiss. 'I was not being reproachful, darling. Your poor nerves must be so fragile. I believe Ralph has been hit badly. Reginald says he is ruined.'

Rose seated herself opposite her sister and held out her hands to the fire, keeping her face averted. 'An exaggeration. I cannot deny that Ralph has suffered in the collapse, but we are still solvent. We can keep the house and live in a civilised manner.'

'Of course. You have your own money.' Betsy was so truly happy for her that Rose warmed to her.

Betsy asked, 'Will Eve be arriving soon? Carrie says Elliot would like to know. He has never been interested in stocks and shares and his personal fortune is intact. I know for a fact that he offered his parents money, but they won't take it. Carrie will have to retrench.'

Rose was startled. 'I understood that the Murfitts had lost little.'

'Carrie insists on saying so but it is not quite true.'

Rose was thoughtful. Who would have guessed that beneath Carrie Murfitt's scatty exterior lay so much pride?

She said nonchalantly, 'Eve is rather naughty to stay away so long. I shall have to demand her return. The dear girl is having so much fun in England, but it is time she faced up to her responsibilities.'

'You can hardly call Elliot her responsibility,' said Betsy in her straightforward way. 'Not yet, anyway. I would have thought if Eve cared for him she would be worried to leave him for so long. There are plenty of girls who would willingly have him, especially now.'

Rose sighed theatrically. 'Young people these days! There is no telling how they behave. How is Paul?'

'As marvellous as always.' Betsy forgot Eve completely in favour of her beloved son. 'When I was so sick he hardly ever left my side. Such a dear, sweet boy.'

'Will he stay in Bristol? In my opinion the Frenchay house is a white elephant. I cannot understand why he doesn't get rid of it.'

Her mild criticism did what she had hoped. It completed the task of taking Betsy's mind from any other issues. 'He will do what is best,' she said. 'I am quite willing to abide by his decisions. However, he says he will stay with me until I am able to walk at least two hundred yards without losing my breath.'

As soon as Tessa arrived home on Saturday after work she knew that something bad had happened. She and Eve had sung the night before between films at the Regal in Staple Hill. Tessa hadn't wanted to go. 'It's too near home,' she had protested, 'and I'll have to tell a whopper to get out in the evening.'

'Say you're coming to Padding House with me. Tell them I need advice about altering a gown. Surely you can think of something.'

Eve had managed to persuade her. She had used the sewing excuse, her fingers crossed behind her back. Now Mum and Dad were obviously waiting for her and the table wasn't even laid for tea.

'There she is,' declared Mum. 'Tell her, Walter.'

Dad said, 'Your mother's friend, Mrs Millington, was at the Regal last night and said you were singing on the stage. Of course, we told her she must be mistaken, but she said she'd known you since you were born and she hadn't made a mistake—'

Mum could keep silent no longer. 'She says you were with another girl and when she described her we knew it was Eve.'

'She's made a mistake, hasn't she, Tessa?' pleaded Dad.

'Let her speak for herself,' said Mum.

Tessa walked slowly into the room and hung up her coat. Her mind was racing, seeking a way out, but there was none. She couldn't keep up the deception. She turned to face her parents. 'It's true. Oh, Mum, Dad,' she begged, 'please, don't be cross. There was no harm in it.'

Mum was outraged. 'No harm! You, a girl brought up in chapel and shown the ways of righteousness, have gone to a place where they show sinful pictures and sung to the people who watch them? And you say there was no harm in it? You made a spectacle of yourself at a picture house! You've shamed me in front of everybody. By now the whole chapel will know.'

'It isn't very Christian of them to gossip,' said Tessa. 'And what was Mrs Millington doing in the Regal? I thought she disapproved of films.'

'That's for her conscience. You've certainly no room to criticise anybody. And as for Eve, well, I would never have thought it of her. Such a biddable girl. Though considering the way her parents leave her alone it isn't so surprising. She gets no guidance. But I thought she was respectable.'

'She is,' said Tessa, 'and so am I. Singing doesn't make us bad.'

'Of course it doesn't as long as you yield your talent to the Lord, but to make a show of yourself at a picture house! What did you sing?'

The sudden question took Tessa off her guard so much that for a moment she couldn't recall what they had sung.

'Was it something too bad to talk about?' demanded Mum.

'No, of course not. We did "When You're Smiling".'

'That's got nice words and a pretty tune,' said Dad.

Mrs Morland frowned at him. In her opinion, since the advent of the wireless, Walter was coming under some unfortunate influences.

'There was another song, Mrs Millington said.'

'Didn't she tell you what it was?' asked Tessa, silently cursing Mum's friend.

'No, she didn't.'

'I can't think why not.'

'What was the other one, my love?' Dad spoke softly, earning himself a glare from his wife.

' "Let's Do It",' said Tessa.

The expected storm broke. 'That's a nasty song,' said Mum. 'I heard it on the wireless one day. It's got suggestive words.'

177

'Why did you listen then?'

'Cheek! I won't have cheek!' Mum's face was bright red with indignation. 'You know full well I always face up to Satan's mischief so I know how to combat it. And it's a good thing I do because now I know that you sang a bad song.'

Tessa said, 'I'm tired. Can I sit down?'

'You stand there until I'm finished.'

'Let her sit,' said Dad. 'Let's all sit down. We could do with a cup of tea.'

Tessa's knees were wobbling and she seated herself thankfully at the table and since Mum made no move Dad slid the kettle over the fire. It began to sing at once. 'Mum was about to get the tea when Mrs Millington called,' he said.

Mrs Morland continued to stand and glare, then reluctantly sat down and sipped at the tea Dad poured. She began to fire questions at Tessa. 'Have you sung away from chapel before?'

'A few times.'

'A *few* times? How many?'

'Just a few.'

'Where?'

'At private parties at Eve's friends' houses.'

'I don't understand. When? You've been home where you ought to be by ten o'clock and when you're out we always know where you are. Except last night. Such lies!'

Tessa swallowed. Having her behaviour brought out into the open like this made it seem unbelievably deceitful. 'Sorry, Mum. I really am sorry. I crept out after you and Dad were in bed.'

This shocked even Dad. 'Tessa!'

'You bad girl!' cried Mum. 'You abominable sinner! How could you do such a wicked thing?' She was badly shaken and Tessa put her cup down. 'Mum,' she said, 'I really am sorry. I know I shouldn't have done it, but I do love the modern songs. To tell you the truth,' she continued, deciding to get it all out into the open at once, 'I should like to go on the stage.'

'The stage? *The stage*!' Mum was scandalised. 'Never!

178

Never will I allow a child of mine to work in a den of iniquity.'

'But, Mum, there are good and bad stage people like everyone else. You don't have to mix with the bad ones.'

'How do you know what they're like? Have you ever sung on a proper stage? And I don't mean in Eve's friends' houses.'

Tessa drew a deep breath. 'Yes, sort of. We sang one night with a band at a dance. Over in Bath. Eve drove us there.'

Mrs Morland was bereft of words, a state so rare that Dad looked at her anxiously. 'Are you all right, my love?'

She fanned herself with a newspaper. 'I'm certainly not all right! To think that a daughter of mine . . . the evil . . . sneaking out at nights . . . singing evil songs . . .'

'They're not, Mum. "Let's Do It" is supposed to be funny.'

'Funny! I don't think it's at all funny. I couldn't bring myself to say the words even to myself. And to think we let you go to France with Eve and her friends! What you got up to there, heaven only knows.'

'I behaved myself,' said Tessa. 'Honestly I did.' She pushed the memory of Paul's kisses and the gambling casino to the back of her mind.

'I dare say she was good,' said Dad anxiously. 'With an example like you've always given her, Lily, she knows what's right.'

'Knowing it and doing it are evidently two different things to her. Tessa, you've hurt me, really you have.'

She hated herself. 'I never meant to. I am sorry. Please, please, forgive me.'

Mum stopped fanning herself and leaned forward, her plump face solemn. 'Dad and I will forgive you because that's the Christian way, but you have to repent and that means you give us your solemn promise that you will never ever sing again except at home, in holy services and at socials.'

Tessa was silent. Her ambition held her fast. She must

179

seek success on the stage. 'I can't. I wouldn't be able to keep it.'

'What? I never heard such brazen-faced wickedness.'

'It's better to tell you the truth.'

'You should obey your mum,' said Dad. 'She's got your welfare at heart.' He looked at her hopefully. She wanted to please him but couldn't surrender. Then, when his eyes wandered to the plates of ham and egg sandwiches and cakes waiting on the dresser, she wanted to laugh. The poor dear! He loathed scenes, and he was hungry.

'Shall we have our tea?' she suggested. 'We'll all feel better afterwards and can talk about this calmly.'

'Tea?' snapped Mum. 'You can think of tea at a time like this?'

'I'm hungry,' said Dad. 'And the children are waiting to be called. We won't be able to discuss this in front of them,' he finished hopefully.

'Very well, we'll eat,' said Mum, 'but I'll never give in over this.'

Susan and Joey were called from upstairs where they had been listening with their ears pressed to the floor and cast many glances of amazement, admiration and envy at their big sister.

Tessa retired that night feeling fraught. The argument had been abandoned then resumed when the children went to bed. They had argued until eleven o'clock and Mum only stopped because it was so long past their usual bedtime and Dad had to be early for work.

'I suppose you won't be sneaking off tonight?' was her parting shot.

Tessa went straight up, but in spite of her weariness she was wakeful. She heard her parents come upstairs and waited for Mum to open her door. She did not do so and Tessa felt bleak.

Tessa tried to reach Eve on the telephone, but she seemed always to be out. She wrote, but before her

180

letter could have reached her cousin she arrived unexpectedly at the Morlands' just before Sunday tea. She was extremely agitated, so much so that she didn't notice the frigid atmosphere. 'I had to come, I've had bad news.'

Mrs Morland forgot her spleen. 'My dear girl, whatever's the matter?'

Mr Morland came down from the bedroom where he had been enjoying a nap between chapel services and Joey and Susan kept still and quiet, hoping that for once they weren't going to be turned out of the adult world. When Mrs Morland began to shoo them away Eve said miserably, 'No, let them stay. They might as well know. It's dreadful. I had a letter from my mother yesterday. I've got no money.'

The Morlands were puzzled. 'Hasn't your dad sent you any?' asked Mrs Morland.

'Oh, it's much worse than that. It's too awful. He hasn't any to send me! Mother says that Father has lost his fortune and my allowance is to be cut to almost nothing. It looks as if I shall have to work and I don't know how! I've never done any.'

Mrs Morland actually smiled. 'My dear girl, is that all? You'll manage.'

Eve didn't seem to hear. 'I've got nothing at all until my next cheque arrives and that will be ridiculously small. And what work could I do? I'm not trained for a thing.'

Mr Morland said, 'I'll be glad to help out until your cheque gets here.'

The Morlands hadn't gauged the depth of Eve's distress and she was irritated. 'You don't understand! Haven't you heard of the collapse of the American Stock Market?'

'Of course,' said Mr Morland portentously. 'It's been in the newspapers.'

'Not much has been said about how dreadful it is for people like me. I've never wanted for anything. Now I'm going to be beastly poor.'

181

In view of the humble circumstances of the Morlands Tessa thought her remarks lacking in tact, but that was typical of Eve. She was selfish, inconsiderate, egotistical . . . yet Tessa couldn't help feeling sorry for her.

'If there's anything your Cousin Walter and me can do to help—' said Mrs Morland.

Tessa caught the derisive impatience which flashed across her cousin's face before she said, 'How *sweet* of you. You are so kind to me, but I couldn't pay you back so I mustn't borrow.'

Mr Morland nodded approvingly. 'I suppose your dad will be wanting a job. Why doesn't he come back to Britain? There's unemployment here and it's getting worse, but I'm sure a fine man like him could find work. He was born British, wasn't he?'

'He isn't trained to do anything but buying and selling shares,' said Eve. 'Besides, he would think that was giving in. No, he'll stay in the States and try to rebuild his business.'

'Tea's ready,' announced Mrs Morland as the kettle boiled. 'Sit yourself down, Eve. A cup of tea and bite to eat will put roses back in your cheeks. You look quite washed out.'

'I slept badly,' she said. She ate a scone and some cake, but refused tinned pears and condensed milk with an inward shudder. The children's eyes gleamed. All the more for them. They tucked into the Sunday treat, soaking bread and butter in the juice, behaviour which astonished Eve. The thought of bread soggy with pear juice revolted her.

Susan and Joey were sent for a walk. 'Keep clean, mind,' their mother admonished. 'Don't forget chapel tonight.' They left with reproachful looks. Interesting things were happening again and they were to be excluded.

Eve took another cup of tea and said carefully, 'Cousin Lily, Cousin Walter, I must earn now and I need Tessa's help more than anything.'

'She'll be glad to do what she can, won't you, Tessa?'

'Of course, Mum.'

'You said you'll still have an allowance. Might I ask how much?' asked Dad.

Eve said, 'It won't be enough to live on. In future I'm to have only two pounds a week.'

Mrs Morland's eyes opened wide. 'But that's the equivalent of some men's wages! Surely you'll be able to manage.'

'Not after I've paid board and lodging.' Eve assumed her most pathetic expression. She wasn't wholly acting.

'Can't you stay in Paul's house?' Tessa asked.

'Of course, but I must pay my way.'

'Has Paul lost his money, too?'

'No, he isn't affected by the crash, but I won't sponge off him.'

Tessa's sympathy began to wilt. Eve had not paid a penny for her keep since moving into Padding House. Eve took a deep breath and spoke softly, keeping her eyes fixed on Mrs Morland. 'The only way I have of making money is by singing.' Her voice grew softer and persuasive. 'It's the only talent I have. That, and playing the piano. To be successful I need Tessa. Please, will you allow her to come on singing engagements with me?'

For a moment there was silence in the kitchen except for the faint hiss of the steaming kettle and the tick of the kitchen clock. Tessa waited, holding her breath.

Mum said, 'You made me forget how angry we are with Tessa. We've found out that she's been singing with you in public—'

Eve's eyes opened wide. 'Didn't you know anything about it?'

Tessa's temper boiled at her ready treachery, but she kept silent.

'No,' said Mum. 'Do you mean to sit there and tell me you didn't know she was creeping out behind our backs?'

Tessa was scrutinised by three pairs of eyes. She sat still and silent, her face expressionless. Justice demanded that she defended herself, but instinct kept her quiet. Maybe her cousin would get round her parents where she had failed.

Eve said, 'It's all my fault. I wanted her to sing with me so much. She has such a beautiful voice. I shall never forget hearing her for the first time in chapel. "The blessing of the Lord be upon you". Marvellous words.'

Tessa wasn't surprised to see her mother's face soften. 'It's a shame about your dad,' she said.

Eve nodded, swallowing hard.

Mrs Morland said, 'You know, my dear, you could come and live here with us and get yourself a nice little job. I know Tessa's room's a bit cramped but we could manage a camp bed. There are lots of factories quite close making boots or corsets. No, perhaps not. You've never been used to rough work. Well, shopkeepers often want assistants and there are always women who want mother's helpers. Do you like children?'

Eve couldn't trust herself to answer and Mrs Morland said, 'Why not come to the evening service with us? You can pray about it and for your poor dad and your mum, and we will too. Tessa will be singing,' she added, tempting her further.

Eve said, 'What a good idea. I'm so glad I came. I should have known you would help. May I use your room to tidy myself, Tessa? I rushed out so fast I scarcely stopped to comb my hair.'

Tessa looked at the perfectly groomed waves and said, 'Come on up.'

In her room Eve said, 'Sorry, Tessa. I know I was awful, but I had to keep on their good side.'

'How easily lies come to you!'

'You haven't done badly in that direction yourself lately,' said Eve huffily.

'Goodness me! I thought you didn't know about my wicked deceit. The mirror's there. You can use my comb if you wish. I scrubbed it this morning.'

'I've got my own, thank you.' Eve was petulant. 'I don't see why you have to behave so nastily to me.'

'Don't you really. My parents are barely on speaking

184

terms with me. A neighbour saw us at the Regal . . . I told you it was too risky.'

'Well, at least it's brought it all into the open. I'll have another go at them after chapel.'

'And that's another thing, I don't like the way you mock them about their religion. They're too fond of you to realise what you're doing, but I know. Chapel means everything to them and you use their faith and trust to get your own way. You don't care tuppence about them or their beliefs.'

Eve cried passionately, 'That's not true! All right, I can't get excited about a bunch of people going on about God, but I do care for Lily and Walter. I do! I do!'

Eve's eyes met Tessa's in the mirror and she was shaken by the intensity of the emotion they expressed. 'You really are fond of them?'

'I am. And of you. Honestly.'

They all walked to chapel together and Eve was once more delighted by the power and intensity of Tessa's voice when she gave it full rein. 'I absolutely must have you as a partner,' she murmured to her as they filed out behind the others towards the minister waiting to shake their hands.

Back at the cottage, Mum made cocoa and served it with biscuits, then Joey and Susan went to bed. The others moved to the best room and Eve wandered to the upright piano and examined the photographs displayed on the lid. She lifted them one by one and asked who they depicted. Mum needed no prompting. She adored discussing them, especially after Eve told her that they made her feel so much a part of the family. She found some sheet music and played and sang a hymn and Mum was fired with ambition to convert her. She saw it as merely a matter of time, a short time, plus some gentle persuasion, after which Eve would forget all this non-sense about public performances and so would Tessa. The fire was dying down when Mum looked at the clock as the Westminster chimes sounded half-past nine.

Eve sighed. 'I must leave soon and let you get to bed.

It's so cosy here.' She sighed again and Mrs Morland's face softened.

Eve seized her chance. 'Cousin Lily, are you sure you won't allow Tessa to sing with me? I do so want her.'

'My dear,' said Mrs Morland, 'you should go home to your parents. Of course we'd miss you, but they must need you at a time like this.'

Eve gave her a desperate look and burst into tears. 'They don't need me! They don't want me. They never have. I want to stay near you. I want Tessa and Joey and Susan. Don't refuse me, please?'

Mrs Morland was horrified. She folded Eve in her arms. 'There, there, my dear. You're wrong about your parents. Mothers and fathers always love their children, but if you really want to stay . . .'

'I do, I do!' Eve lifted her tear-stained face.

Mrs Morland took a handkerchief from her pocket and wiped away the tears. 'I want to help you. I just wish you would turn to the Lord and see how He solves all our problems.' Eve clutched her convulsively and Mrs Morland said slowly, 'I'll prove it to you. We'll make a bargain. I'll let Tessa sing with you on Saturday evenings if you'll promise to spend every Sunday evening with us and come to chapel.' The idea took Eve's breath away and prevented her from expressing the sardonic reply which Tessa was sure had almost burst from her.

'In the end,' went on Mrs Morland, 'you'll discover that you want to offer your gift only to the Lord.'

Eve finally said in a small voice, 'It's a deal, Cousin Lily. And bless you for helping me.'

'Not on the stage, mind,' warned Mum. 'It's all right at friends' dances and parties, but not on the stage.'

Eve gave a faint smile. 'We're not professionals, though I'll make sure we get paid. It'll be useful for Tessa to earn something.'

'Tessa makes good money already,' said Mum, 'but she can add the extra to her savings for her bottom drawer. I have to trust you to make sure that everything is respectable and above board.'

'Thank you, thank you, Cousin Lily,' cried Eve. She kissed Mrs Morland noisily, making her laugh.

Mr Morland escorted Eve to her car while Tessa helped her mother clear the dishes. When he came back he was smiling. 'She's a nice little puss. She was ever so pleased about the singing and of course she knows all about rich people's ways. Even though she was so upset I could tell she's sophisticated, yet she's as sweet as honey with it.'

# Chapter Nine

The arrangement seemed to work well. The Kissing Cousins received invitations and Eve dutifully showed up on Sundays for chapel.

One day she said, 'Paul's back in Britain. I was beginning to think he had decided to stay in the States for good.'

That had been Tessa's secret anxiety, though she was ambivalent about her feelings for him. Perhaps the man who gave you your first kiss would always hold a place in your life.

Mrs Morland insisted on Eve coming to spend Christmas Day with them and bringing Miss Coleman. Susan and Joey had made paper chains which were hung from corner to corner and there was a sweet-smelling tree decorated with baubles fashioned from cones dipped in silver and gold paint, and little painted wooden shapes which Joey had made in school woodwork and which resembled nothing much but were supposed to be reindeer. The cottage was warm, inviting, and the food delicious though heavy. After dinner which they ate at mid-day Eve felt like a grounded balloon, her stomach distended by meat, savoury stuffing and sausages, rich pudding and mince pies.

They sat in the best room and listened to records. This year Dad had come home with a gramophone and even Mum had no quarrel with this. 'You can choose what you want to hear,' she said placidly, folding her hands over her plump stomach. She wore a new outfit of tweed skirt with a burgundy jumper she had knitted herself and over which, for much of the day, she hung the new apron given her by Susan. There was little choice of music which consisted of innocuous, tinkling tunes, and allowed Eve's attention to wander.

Lately, she decided, she had behaved quite well, even without proper chaperonage. There hadn't been a man in her life for quite a while. Perhaps the constant hammering her morals received in chapel each Sunday was improving them, but honesty compelled her to admit that she hadn't really met anyone she fancied. Even Jack Padbury didn't call so often. She frowned as she remembered his latest proposal. He had heard of her family's lost fortune and had been so sure she would accept him. Perhaps that was what made her reject him so fiercely. She had surprised even herself by her sudden surge of pride and it had obviously demoralised Jack.

Miss Coleman was deeply happy and her usually sallow face glowed with food and warmth. 'A Christmas fire' Mr Morland called the one roaring up the chimney in the best room, while Mum kept the kitchen range red hot.

They ended the day playing word games. Eve thought them rather silly at first, then began to enjoy them. Mum insisted on giving her Ovaltine and a mince pie before she left. 'It's a cold night. You need something inside you to keep you warm.' Eve had eaten more that day than in the previous two. She laughed but took the refreshment in the spirit in which it was offered.

She drove home through the icy streets which had taken on a festive air as party revellers made their way home on foot. Some children were carried on their fathers' shoulders where they swayed, with heads nodding. Mothers held small hands or carried a baby wrapped in a shawl, while other little ones clung to their skirts. Some pushed prams filled with sleepy children.

Miss Coleman tutted. 'Fancy keeping tinies up so late.'

Eve hardly heard her. She wondered what it was like

to be hoisted to the strong shoulders of a father who loved you.

The Kissing Cousins had an engagement at a party and Tessa's eyes wandered over the guests, wondering if Paul would be there, telling herself that it didn't really matter to her. When he arrived, escorting a very pretty girl, she knew that it mattered very much and that he had become frighteningly special to her. She wondered if he remembered their days in the sun and their gentle kisses. When she and Eve sang he watched them and seemed to be paying them complete attention until the girl came back from somewhere and he bent his head to make a remark which brought a smile to her face. Tessa was so thrown by this she almost lost the song. Almost. She was learning fast to control her feelings when performing.

When they had finished Eve hissed, 'Did you see the girl with Paul? I can't stand her. Her name is Andrea Talbot and she's rich in her own right and heiress to millions. That's a model gown she's wearing. Cut by Madeleine Vionnet, I'm sure. Look at the way it hangs.'

Tessa said, holding grimly on to her feelings, 'That's no reason for disliking her.'

Eve gave her a sideways glance and showed her teeth in a smile which was more of a grimace. 'You're jealous, aren't you? Did you honestly suppose he would care about you? You looked as if you'd been given a million in gold when you got back from those driving practices in France. Everyone was amused.'

Tessa came near to striking Eve and walking off the stage. So she had been an object of derision at the villa, had she? Paul had probably laughed at her too. She felt sick. 'I dare say we both amuse people,' she said. 'You with your lost fortune and me coming from the lower orders.'

'Lower orders be damned,' muttered Eve. 'We're cousins, don't forget, kissing cousins.'

That went a long way to wiping out Tessa's anger with her.

They were being treated well tonight. The party was thrown by the Henleys, Tiddles' parents. They were plain-looking folk, and there were a number of younger brothers and sisters who welcomed Eve and Tessa as warmly as they had welcomed their guests, insisting that they should eat in the supper room and dance if they wished.

'The Henleys are kind,' said Eve, 'but be careful not to presume too far. You can't expect them to want paupers clinging to them.'

'I wouldn't dream of clinging to them,' said Tessa crossly. 'And I'm not a pauper.'

'And I am?' Another of Eve's quick spats of temper flared. There were times when Tessa thought their friendship would never last and this was one of them.

'*You* a pauper? You! I wouldn't dream of calling you that,' she said indignantly. 'You've got more money coming in than many working men. And we may not be rich, but I've been brought up to value my independence.'

Eve was astonished. Did Tessa really believe that? From the time she had been born she had been cocooned by her parents, cushioned in caring love which she apparently took for granted. She felt the familiar stirring of envy and went off on another tack, determined to establish her own superiority by having the last word.

'There's another thing I've been meaning to warn you about,' she said. 'You must learn the difference between genuine people and the *nouveau riche* who think they are quality but who are really upstarts who made their money in the war.'

Tessa stared at her cousin. She had been about to make a sharp retort, but caught an expression on Eve's face which troubled her. She said pacifically, 'Dad goes on about them. He says they were war profiteers who benefited by others' misery.'

'Your dad talks sense,' said Eve. She was as relieved as Tessa to get out of their argument.

Tessa liked hearing Eve praise Dad. She was nice

about Mum too, and although she still had a tendency sometimes to laugh at them, seemed to feel genuine affection for them.

Eve was often confused by her own feelings. She still lived in Paul's house with Tildy Coleman who, plagued by headaches and an easy prey to colds, had almost ceased even a half-hearted attempt to supervise her and crept about making as little fuss as possible so that no one would notice her and ask her to leave. Eve was glad she didn't interfere yet at the same time angry with her and with her own parents who no longer seemed to care what happened to her. They were entirely bound up in their own problems and Eve resented it.

The few letters she received from her mother spoke only of Father's distress, his struggles. If she asked about Eve it was as an afterthought. Eve was coldly furious with her father for what she saw as his gullibility. She blamed him for the steep drop in their living standards, for the times she made plans only to remember, sickeningly, that there was nothing with which to execute them.

Padding House had become like a prison which she both hated and enjoyed. Then, when she exchanged its luxury for the Morlands' small cottage and was enfolded in the warmth of a true family, she found herself resenting their cosy placidity and vowed she would shake off the tentacles of their affection before they weakened her. At other times she was overtaken by pity and love for her father and decided that she must return to America to be with him. The impulse died as quickly as it was born, killed by his years of indifference.

At supper Tessa was invited to sit at Tiddles's table. 'How pretty you look,' said Tiddles in her kind way. She called a maid who brought some smoked salmon, a delicacy Tessa had never tasted and hoped she would taste often in the future. 'Your singing is becoming well known,' said Tiddles. 'I often hear of you. It's a pity you can't sing more than one night a week. Why is that?'

'My parents' decree,' smiled Tessa, wondering nervously if she was to be subjected to teasing banter, perhaps not from Tiddles but from others who were listening.

'Quite right,' said Jack Padbury who had joined the table. 'A young lady shouldn't have to work too hard.'

There was good-humoured laughter and Tessa drew a deep breath. 'It isn't that,' she said, gently but firmly. 'My family isn't well off and I work during the week. And on Sundays I sing in our chapel choir. I have done so since I was quite small.'

She had felt compelled to speak and hoped the conversation would end there, but Jack Padbury, who was likeable but undiscerning said, 'How jolly. What work do you do?'

'I'm an assistant in a grocer's shop.'

There was a small silence and Jack said again, 'How jolly.' He sounded unsure.

'It's jolly hard work,' said Tessa and the others laughed, appreciatively this time.

'Well done,' said Tiddles. 'Now, what would you like to eat next?'

'Lamb cutlets, please.'

As supper progressed Tiddles asked Tessa, 'Have you read the latest Dornford Yates? It's a mystery novel. Different from his humorous books but very satisfying.'

'I don't know his work at all,' confessed Tessa.

'No one can know all the authors. I enjoy hearing you sing. Your voice is so beautiful. Have you had it trained?'

'In a way. Our choir-master is very clever. He says I'm a mezzo-soprano. He's Welsh and knows about singing.'

'How fascinating.'

She was genuinely intrigued and Tessa said impulsively, 'Why are you called Tiddles? I mean, you're not like a cat or a kitten. You're not fluffy like some of the girls, or always showing claws—' She stopped. She was floundering and couldn't think how to continue without maligning someone. 'I mean,' she said desperately, 'you

194

like reading proper stuff, not rubbish.' She stopped again and waited for some scathing remark which would put her back in her place, especially as she had once more caught the attention of the others, including Poppy.

Tiddles said, 'It is rather a silly name, isn't it? But better than Cuddles.'

'What?'

'I'm the eldest in the family and my mother and father had waited for a long time before I made my appearance.'

Poppy shrieked with mirth. 'They made up for the delay afterwards. Once begun they couldn't stop.'

A grimace of distaste crossed Tiddles's face, but she kept cool. 'I do have several adorable brothers and sisters, Tessa, but when I was born Daddy thought I would be the only one. He called me lots of pet names including Cuddles until I went to school and begged him not to. He did stop but then I became Tiddles. Just as silly, isn't it, but it's stuck.'

Supper over, the dancing began again and Eve and Tessa sang 'The Varsity Rag', a quick number which demanded a joyous tone, something which Tessa found exceedingly difficult when Paul was swinging to it with Andrea who, with her waving brown hair and dark eyes, was enough to turn any man's head, even without the advantage of her model gown whose bias cut swirled around her pretty body, showing every one of its curves to advantage. Then the band went into a slow number.

'Lover come back to me . . .' Tessa sang, her eyes on Paul. But a lover had to be there in the first place before he could come back and Paul had shown her no more – well, perhaps a little more – than friendship. At least, that was what she had believed at the time, but now she knew that these people exchanged endearments and kisses without thought. She feared she had built their acquaintance into something he had never intended. They finished with a rousing song. 'If it's naughty to rouge your lips; Shake your shoulders and twist your hips, Let a lady confess, I wanna be bad . . .' The words bit deep. Tessa wanted to be bad in so many ways she was bewildered. She would like to rip the Vionnet gown from Andrea Talbot's back and tear it to shreds, she wanted to grab Paul, to make him hold her, kiss her . . . She wanted to demand the truth from him. Did he kiss all his girl friends? Did he go further? Her body burned at the idea. She wrested her thoughts away from their unhallowed path. She meant nothing to him.

To Tessa's surprise Jack Padbury asked her for the last waltz. He was preoccupied and appeared to be gaining little pleasure from the dance, a situation which irritated her. He looked down at her and said, 'Sorry, I was neglecting you. Forgive me. You have a lovely voice.'

'Thanks.' Surely he hadn't asked her to dance only to pay her a compliment?

He said, 'I want to ask you something. Do you think we could sit this one out?'

Tessa would have preferred to dance, but she agreed and he seated himself beside her on a small sofa.

He said nothing, staring at the dancers, watching Eve. 'You wanted to say something?' she prompted.

'Eve likes you. She trusts you. If you gave her advice she would take it, wouldn't she?'

'Good heavens, I shouldn't think so. She follows her own bent.'

'Oh. She does have a strong will, I know that.' He sounded bleak. 'I'm really gone on her,' he said desperately, 'and she will hardly give me the time of day. Would you have a word with her? Perhaps you could ask her what she's got against me? I really thought she'd take me when her father lost his money.'

'She isn't up for sale,' said Tessa, indignant on Eve's behalf.

'Oh, no!' Jack flushed. 'I didn't mean it the way it sounded. I care for her, I really do. I would look after her on her own terms and be content to wait for her to care for me.' Tessa said nothing and Jack went on, 'You must think me awfully wet. It's just that . . .'

196

'I understand, but I don't think Eve will ever marry someone who can't dominate her.'

Jack sighed. 'I could never be a bully.'

'That's very clear, but there's a difference between bullying and sensible authority.'

Jack shook his head sadly and Tessa thought, I wouldn't want to marry him either. He's far too weak. He stood and held out his arms. 'Let's finish the dance.'

As she and Eve were getting ready to leave Tessa said, 'Jack asked me to try to find out why you won't accept him.'

Eve turned furiously and glared at her. 'How dare he! How dare you discuss me!'

Tessa slipped off her dancing shoes and laced up her brogues. 'I didn't start it. I had to answer the poor man. He dares because he says he's gone on you.'

'I know. What of it? It's none of your business.'

'I never said it was. I'm passing on a message.'

'Well, don't bother in future.'

'I shall do what I damned well please!' snapped Tessa. 'If someone asks me to tell you something, I shall do it.'

Eve snatched up her hat and jammed it on her head. 'Go to hell!' she shouted and stalked out of the room.

Tessa couldn't believe at first that her cousin had actually left her stranded. She waited outside the house as the downstairs lights were replaced by those in the bedrooms. The night air was chilly after the Henleys' house and she shivered. Was Eve punishing her by keeping her waiting? Perhaps she should call a taxi? This meant going back into the Henleys' to ask to use the telephone and it would be inconvenient for everyone. And the taxi would eat up some of tonight's money. Eve was the limit.

She had turned back to the wrought-iron gates when a car pulled up. She swung round in relief. 'Eve, I thought you'd gone—'

She stopped. Paul was smiling at her from the driving seat. 'You look bereft. What's happened? Eve passed me, driving like the devil.'

'I was supposed to get a lift home with her. There's been a mix-up.'

Paul climbed out and opened the passenger door for her. 'I suppose you mean she's taken offence at something and left you flat?'

Tessa said nothing.

'Loyal, aren't you? But I know my cousin only too well.' He tucked a fur rug round her knees.

'I shouldn't have tried to interfere in her affairs, but Jack—'

'Yes?'

'Nothing. I mean, it's nothing I can discuss.'

'I can guess what he wanted. I wonder when the poor sap will see Eve for what she is.'

'Never, by the looks of it,' said Tessa gloomily. 'And by the way, she isn't so much bad as miserable. She's unhappy a lot of the time.'

The car slid smoothly from the kerb. 'Perceptive little thing, aren't you? She's always had a sad streak. If she was wise she'd take Jack's offer. He's not a fool and would make her secure and content if she'd let him.'

'Secure maybe, but not content. She needs a stronger man.'

'He could be strong if he wasn't so tormented by his passion for her. That won't last for ever. Sooner or later he's sure to meet a girl who'll be kind to him. Someone like you, for instance.'

'You think I would make a good partner for him?'

'I think you'd make a good partner for any man.'

'Have I so little personality that I could sink it into any man's?'

'Now you are annoyed with me. No, I don't mean that at all.'

She waited, but he said no more and soon they were at the end of Tessa's lane.

Paul leapt out and opened her door. 'Sorry if I upset you.'

'You haven't,' she replied coolly. 'Your opinion of me isn't particularly important.'

198

'I don't think I care for that. I thought we were friends.'

The sudden warmth in his voice held her fast. 'I hope we are,' she said quietly.

'So you forgive me? Tell me so. You can't leave me without setting my mind at rest.'

'What exactly did you mean when you said I'd make a good partner for any man?'

'I meant that with your clear-thinking intelligence you would adapt yourself to make your relationship work.'

'That sounds like friendship, not marriage. For that you should be in love.'

'Do you really think so? George Bernard Shaw said: "When two people are under the influence of the most violent, most insane, most delusive, and most transient of passions, they are required to swear that they will remain in that excited, abnormal, and exhausting condition until death do them part." '

'Do you believe that?' asked Tessa.

'Why shouldn't I?'

'Because it's a cynical attitude. Love and marriage need strong emotions.'

'A typical woman's viewpoint.'

'I should find it difficult to offer any other.'

Paul laughed. 'I always forget what good company you are.' Am I easy to forget? Tessa wondered. He continued, 'That was a bit crass of me, wasn't it? Do you forgive me?'

She simulated a yawn. 'For what?'

'You're learning new ways. A pity. Your lack of sophistication was charming.'

'If I didn't learn new ways as I grew older, I should be in a sorry state.'

'I know, but it's still a pity. Isn't there a loving boy-friend longing to marry you?'

'I'm in no hurry. I have ambitions.'

'Let them go, Tessa. Settle down with your innocence unimpaired.'

'My ignorance, don't you mean? A woman can maintain her innocence no matter what.'

'I don't think so, especially one who makes a close friend of Eve.'

'That's putting it rather strongly, isn't it? Her behaviour isn't exemplary, I know, but it's just high spirits with her.'

'Perhaps. I'm very fond of her.'

She shivered.

Paul exclaimed, 'How thoughtless of me to keep you standing here! I'll walk you to your door.'

'No need,' she said abruptly. 'Goodnight. And thank you for the lift.'

'My pleasure,' said Paul. She had gone a few yards when he caught up with her. 'How about a goodnight kiss?'

'No.'

'You kissed me before.'

'That seems a long time ago when we were in a holiday mood.' She walked away.

'True,' he said to her unresponsive back as he watched her progress to the cottage. She heard his car start up and drive away. He couldn't know how severely she had been tempted.

Eve arrived on Sunday morning and came upstairs full of apologies. 'Did you tell your parents I abandoned you? How did you get home? I'm really sorry, Tessa. I shouldn't have driven off like that.'

'No, you shouldn't. Paul brought me home.'

'Did he? That must have made you happy.'

Tessa said coolly, 'It certainly did. I was about to call for a taxi.'

'You still like him a lot, don't you?'

'He's quite nice.'

'Quite nice! You should hear the way your voice alters when you say his name. You should see the look on your face.'

'If all you've come to do is annoy me, you had better talk to Mum and Dad. In any case, I'm studying my solo for tonight.'

'Nonsense. You must know it by heart. You're so talented.' Tessa shot her cousin an angry glance. Eve grinned. 'All right, all right. I'll talk to Cousin Lily.' She left and Tessa heard the rise and fall of her voice from downstairs.

Tessa sat down heavily on her bed. Did she give herself away over Paul? How shaming. She must put up her guard.

Ralph finished winding up his business. Irene Martinez did not break off contact with him when he had to let her go from his office along with his other employees. She actually seemed quite sorry for him, an attitude which he didn't appreciate. She had wanted to continue working for him.

'I have money of my own,' she said. 'Surely you could afford to keep me in some capacity on a lower salary? Or maybe your wife could use me as her personal secretary. She does so much charity work and sits on so many committees.'

Ralph said coldly, 'You above all others are conversant with my financial position. What is left of Rose's money will barely cover the upkeep of the house and the remaining servants.'

Irene's full lips curved in a smile. Contrary to fashion she wore her black hair plaited and twisted in a convoluted pattern about her boyish head. It was always a surprise to see that her eyes were green when one was expecting the darkest brown.

'You find something amusing in all this?' asked Ralph.

'Is that how you read me? As being amused by you? How wrong you are.'

Ralph was surprised by the languor in her voice. After keeping him at bay for so long she was now displaying distinct signs of invitation. He put out a tentative hand and laid it on her shoulder, then pulled her towards him. She accepted his kiss, before returning it with passion. The familiar ache of desire seized him. They were paying a final visit to his office, one of many in the large building, and at any moment they could be interrupted.

'Come,' said Ralph. 'We'll find somewhere.'

He drove to a small hotel he had used before. Irene did not speak. In the small sparsely furnished room she began to undress without haste, then stopped to unwind her hair which fell in gleaming strands around her shoulders. Then she removed the remainder of her clothes. She was tranquil and Ralph wondered as he watched her how many times she had done this.

She was slim, but Ralph had not expected her naked body to look so thin. Her bones seemed almost to protrude through her white skin. She was as bony as a boy. He touched the hollows in her shoulders, smoothed his hand over her tiny breasts down to the ridges of her hips. She excited him as no one had before. He undressed rapidly, eagerly. Usually he took his women with a minimum of heat, using them as a means merely to gratify his own sexual needs. The chief thrill lay in the chase and final capture.

With Irene it was different. When she began to caress him, to move sinuously beneath him, denying him entry, keeping him waiting, instead of making him angry she increased his desire until, when she did stay still and he slid into her, he could barely hold back until she cried out in her own fulfilment.

Afterwards he lay with her and looked up at the rather dingy ceiling. 'This room isn't suitable for you,' he said.

'Have you used the place before?' she asked.

'Why do you want to know?'

'I see. You have?'

'Yes.'

She smiled. She was aware that he took women then discarded them as unemotionally as he discarded cards in a game of poker. 'Where would be suitable for me?'

Ralph twisted round to look at her and desire stirred again. This time she used no tricks, but allowed him full rein. 'My God,' he said, as he fell back on to the bed. 'You're a witch, do you know that?'

She smiled, a tight, closed smile, then said, 'Where

would I fit in? Where do you see me?'

Marvelling at a tenacity which was as powerful as his own, he said, 'In an apartment in a decent part of town, with pictures and books around you. Do you like reading? Do you care for paintings?'

'Oh, yes,' she said.

Ralph pulled the covers over them. He lay quietly, amusing himself with visions of where he would instal her until he remembered with a jab of shock that he no longer had money.

His sharp intake of breath made Irene turn to him. 'What's the matter?'

'Everything!' He got out of bed and sat on the side with his head in his hands. 'Every goddam thing! You know I've nothing left?'

She held out her arms. 'Come back,' she said softly. 'Let's not discuss money.'

'These days I think of little else.'

'You were thinking of something else just now.' She lit cigarettes for them both. 'Your wife has the money now,' she said casually.

Ralph coloured. 'I could hardly use that to set up a—'

'Say it,' said Irene coolly, 'a mistress.'

'I cannot think of you that way. You are much more than that.'

'Already? You don't know enough about me.'

'I know enough to realise that I cannot let you go.'

'Then surely you must find a way for us to be together?'

'I cannot use her money,' he said. 'It would be despicable.'

Irene laughed softly and the sound brought him round to face her. She stubbed out their cigarettes and drew him back to her with her long, thin arms and again he lost himself in a depth of pleasure entirely new to him. He drove back alone, leaving Irene to take a taxi, and half way home it occurred to him that if she was willing to become his mistress in his present circumstances, she must care for him. He found the idea pleasant, reassuring. She is passionate when I want her, he thought, cool when I do not. Her contrasts fascinated him.

Eve faced Tessa angrily. 'Why do you want to go out with him?'

'Why not?' countered Tessa, trying to be reasonable.

Mrs Morland's continual efforts to bring Tessa to Frank Anderson's notice had borne fruit and he had asked her to go to a theatre with him. She had hesitated. She liked him but didn't want him to get serious. She fell back on the excuse that she would have to ask her parents' permission.

Frank had smiled. 'I've already got it,' he said triumphantly.

'You mean you asked them before me?'

'Well, yes. It seemed the right thing to do.'

Tessa had used one of Eve's mocking expressions. 'How quaintly old-fashioned of you.' She had nearly added 'darling' before she remembered that the word carried very different connotations in Frank's world. She could barely admit even to herself that part of the reason for her acceptance was that it would provoke Eve who so often provoked her. Eve autocratically demanded her presence when someone called upon the services of the Kissing Cousins, which these days was practically every Saturday night, but dropped her during the week and was occasionally unavailable at weekends when she had met a new man who interested her. Twice Tessa had turned up to find herself singing alone.

She had chided, 'You'll get us a reputation for irresponsibility. Soon we shan't be asked to sing at all.'

Eve only laughed. 'Of course we will, darling. Where else would they find anyone so cheap?'

She was annoyingly right. The disastrous fall of the American Stock market had begun to have world-wide repercussions and many people had to cut back on expenses.

'What happened to your plans for us to go professional?' asked Tessa.

'Fat lot of chance we have with your mother for ever watching you.'

Again Eve was right. Mrs Morland had repented giving her permission but felt she couldn't withdraw it. If she could get Tessa married, or even engaged to a decent young man like Frank, she would forget nonsense like singing with dance bands. After all, reasoned Mrs Morland, every girl longed for marriage, a home of her own and babies. It was only natural. Since their first date Tessa had gone out with Frank several times. Her parents were delighted and so were Frank's.

'He's a good lad,' said Mr Morland. 'In spite of these difficult times, he's expanded his garage and tells me he's looking for another mechanic.'

Tessa smiled obligingly as her parents tried hard to slide her into marriage. The Kissing Cousins were an undoubted success, though sometimes she did wonder if she would be happier relying on her own ability to make a success of entertaining without Eve's unreliability to handicap her.

Occasionally she was subject to doubt, wondering if she was doing wrong, if she should use her God-given voice only for her religion. It wasn't surprising since the message was drummed into her from all sides. Mum and Dad, the minister, the choir-master, and now Frank. The pact which Mrs Morland had made so hopefully with Eve was still valid but her cousin had begun to make excuses for not visiting on some Sunday nights and, as weeks went by without the girls meeting, Mrs Morland was thankful. She invited Frank to tea on several Sundays and this week had asked his parents to come to supper after chapel. Tessa had sighed when she heard this. The next step would make her a welcome guest in the Anderson house after which everyone would begin looking for the announcement of an engagement. She felt herself being spirited towards domesticity. In spite of Eve's casual attitude, Tessa's happiest times were still those she spent singing with her.

Then one day Eve arrived unexpectedly at the Morlands' and held out her left hand. On the third finger a large solitaire diamond glinted sharply. 'I've got myself engaged,' she announced.

Mrs Morland jumped up to embrace her. 'Congratulations! Look at the size of her ring, Walter. Isn't this good news?'

'Who is it?' asked Tessa, struggling with disappointment at this abrupt cessation of her career.

'Jack.'

'Jack Padbury? But you always said—'

'I know what I said,' snapped Eve. 'I can change my mind, can't I?'

'Don't rile your cousin,' said Mum to Tessa. 'This is good news.'

Dad poured some of Mum's home-made blackcurrant juice and they toasted Eve.

'You must bring your young man here and let us meet him,' said Mrs Morland.

'Of course,' said Eve in a tone which told Tessa she would do no such thing. She doubted if she would see much of her cousin in future and her job at Grice's seemed more onerous than ever.

Rose Brook looked up from her letter. 'Ralph! Eve writes that she is engaged.'

He tore himself from the financial pages. 'Without a word to us? Who is he?'

'Jack Padbury.'

Ralph looked blank and Rose said impatiently, 'He was at the funeral. He's related to you in some way.'

'I don't remember him. Has he any money?'

'The family is wealthy and Eve says he has given her an enormous diamond ring. One assumes that they were not victims of the crash.'

'Do you have to mention the bloody crash all the time?'

Rose disliked him swearing and he knew it. She said, 'I don't mention it all the time. You brought up the subject of money.'

'I know, I know.' Ralph had no real wish to talk about Eve. The idea of her marrying a rich man was attractive, but he was far more concerned over his affair with Irene. It had been a surprise to him to learn that many old houses in the cross streets on the East Side had been converted to respectable apartments with fairly steep rents. Irene's was furnished in an elegant mix of Georgian and modern. Wine red velvet curtains hung at the high windows. She sat at a charming writing desk to write letters and pay her accounts. At the foot of her large mahogany bed was a heavily carved Spanish chest. The dining-room furniture was early American. The polished floors were rich with antique rugs faded to soft colours.

On his first visit Ralph looked round, astonished. 'I paid you a good salary but not enough to cover this style of living.'

'I got it honestly, sir,' whined Irene, making him smile. 'My family have dealt in antique furniture for years,' she said in normal tones. 'I've only an uncle alive now and he's retired. All the furnishings came to me through my father and he left me enough money to live comfortably on.'

'Why do you work?'

Irene indicated a deep couch into which Ralph sank and accepted a large whisky and soda.

She seated herself beside him with her drink. 'I said I could live comfortably. I didn't say I could live excitingly, interestingly. I'm lucky. I've been able to choose my employers, and I wanted to work for you ever since I saw you about two years ago. I was taking shorthand notes for one of your colleagues at a business meeting.'

'I didn't notice you.'

Ralph wished the words unsaid. They would have provoked an indignant response from most women, but Irene only laughed. 'You've never had your nose off the grindstone. You've noticed nothing.'

He said bitterly, 'There's no grindstone left now. How much did you lose in the crash?'

'Not much. Dabbling in stocks and shares is of little interest to me. Now,' she took his empty glass and pulled him to his feet, 'let's do something that interests us both.'

He followed her into her bedroom.

# Chapter Ten

Eve was pleased. That morning Charles Ware had telephoned and asked if he might take her out to lunch. She hadn't heard from him since the holiday and had given up on him. Now she decided to tease him by pretending to have forgotten who he was. 'Who did you say?'

He was unperturbed. 'Of course, it was months ago. Charles Ware. We met in Kitty Bamford's villa in Cap d'Antibes.'

'Oh, yes, I believe I do recall you now.'

'It's quite understandable that you should forget me. A popular girl like you will have so many invitations, it must be difficult to remember every one.'

Eve thought she detected mockery in his tone. She asked coolly, 'Where have you been? It's – how long did you say? – almost nine months.'

'As long as that? Time enough for the seeds we sowed to germinate.'

He was definitely having fun at her expense.

'Are you still there, Eve?'

'Yes.'

'May I take you to lunch?'

'Hang on a minute, will you?' She rustled the leaves of her newspaper. 'Yes, my diary is clear.'

'Marvellous. I'll pick you up around twelve-thirty.'

Eve dressed carefully, thanking God for her grey Chanel suit which would always look smart. With it she wore a white blouse and a jet and silver twisted necklace and earrings, cursing the day when costume jewellery had been brought into vogue. If she'd been able to get her hands on some of the family jewels she could have sold them and bought new outfits. She gazed thoughtfully at her engagement ring, then removed it and hung it on a porcelain ring tree. She teased some strands of her bright hair over her forehead and put on a pale green hat with a grey feather. She hesitated over her last pair of silk stockings. She needed them for evenings. But for a date with a man like Charles Ware she must look her best. She took a last glance at herself in the cheval glass. Black suede pumps and gloves, a grey handbag . . . she looked good. At the last minute she remembered that Jack was expected for lunch and phoned him.

'Sorry, dear, but I have a crashing headache. I shall have to stay in bed.'

Jack was sympathetic. 'Poor darling. I'll come anyway. I could read to you, cheer you up.'

She nearly screamed her frustration. 'No, thank you,' she managed. 'I have my wireless. There's sure to be music and that will soothe me.'

'Do you think you'll be well enough to come to the dance tonight?'

Eve cursed silently. She had forgotten the Talbots' ball to which she had looked forward.

'Are you still there, Eve?' asked Jack, anxiety roughening his voice.

He had used the same words as Charles and Eve felt a small sting of guilt. 'Yes, I'm still here. I was just thinking. If I'm allowed to have peace and quiet through the day, I guess I'll get to the dance. You may call at nine and we'll see.'

'Thank you, darling. I do hope you'll soon feel better.'

'Thanks. How will you pass your time?'

'Without you? Not very happily. I'll probably go for a spin. I've bought a new car. A beauty. A Bugatti. She's French and—'

Talk of cars bored Eve at the best of times. 'I can wait for the eulogy,' she said.

'Of course, darling. I'm being thoughtless. Do you have something for the pain?'

210

'The pain? Oh, my headache. Yes, thanks. Where will you go?'

'The weather's fine, the sun is quite warm for spring. I'll have lunch in a hotel in the hills.'

'Enjoy it,' she said and replaced the receiver. It was useful to know where he would be today.

Eve checked her handbag. Powder compact, lipstick, rouge, cigarette case, lighter, handkerchief . . .

There was a knock on her door and she said impatiently, 'Come in.'

Tildy Coleman poked her head round the door. 'Ah, there you are, Eve.'

'That's clear enough.'

Tildy flushed. 'Yes, indeed. You're going out?'

'What does it look like?'

'Who will you be meeting?'

'A friend.'

'A man or a woman?'

'That's my business.'

Tildy's flush grew deeper and Eve realised that besides being hurt, she was annoyed. That wouldn't do. She was unlikely to do anything to jeopardise her position in Padding House, but she might have a sudden rush of conscience and decide to write a warning letter to America. Eve couldn't risk that.

'Sorry I snapped,' she said. 'I've a bit of a headache.'

'Oh, I am so sorry. But shouldn't you lie down? When I have one of my headaches I cannot stand upright without feeling nauseous.'

'It's nothing like that. A lunch with friends will do me good.'

'If you say so, my dear. You will be attending the Talbots' dance tonight, I believe?'

'Would I miss it?'

'No, of course not. But you must conserve your energy.' Eve frowned and Tildy said quickly, 'How pretty you look.'

'Thanks.'

Tildy waited a moment then left.

Charles Ware was waiting for her on Frenchay Common where Eve had asked him to stop.

He was lounging in his car, a dark green Bentley, smoking. When he heard the sharp tap of her heels on the road he jumped out, grinding his cigarette into the ground. He took her hand and executed a slight bow. In any other man she might have found it ridiculous but somehow one didn't think of such a word in connection with Charles. He looked her up and down. 'Very pretty. What's all the mystery about? Why couldn't I come to the house?'

'Mother appointed a tiresome companion for me. I don't want her to know where I go and who I am with.'

Charles's eyebrows rose slightly. They were dark and on the heavy side. He said only, 'We can't have your finery ruffled. I shall raise the wind-shield.'

Eve seated herself in the passenger seat and he covered her with a rug. 'Where are we going?' she asked.

'I thought we might drive up into the hills.'

'No!'

'No need to be so vehement. I'm at your command.'

She laughed unconvincingly. 'Sorry. I don't feel like driving far. I have a slight headache.'

'Oh, have you? Poor you. How fortunate I am that you feel fit enough to come out with me.'

'Lunch in a quiet nearby place would suit me very well.'

Charles started the car. 'I like a girl who's gallant about pain.'

He sounded anything but sympathetic and Eve was sure he was trying to ruffle her.

'When I see the die-away airs my chaperon puts on whenever her head aches, I'm glad I'm not a martyr.'

'Is she the same as your companion, or are there two dragons guarding you?'

Eve laughed. 'The same. My parents are in the States. Mother appointed Tildy before she left.'

Charles negotiated the narrow lane leading to the main road. 'Such attractive scenery,' he said. 'The river and overhanging trees. Some are beginning to bud.'

'Very pretty,' she said.

'You must enjoy good walks?'

'Yes.' She had never walked far.

'Don't worry, I won't give you a lecture on horticulture.'

Eve just smiled.

He glanced at her. 'You must smile more often. You look far lovelier when you smile. And I'm told it keeps wrinkles at bay.'

'I don't think I'm quite old enough to worry about wrinkles.'

'Not yet, I agree, but one day—' He swerved to avoid a small boy on a bicycle. 'I sometimes wonder if parents deliberately try to rid themselves of their offspring. I would never let a son of mine out on the roads at so young an age.'

Eve was startled. 'Are you married?'

'Certainly not! If ever I marry, I shan't cheat on my wife.'

'Perhaps you are an eternal bachelor?'

'No. I just haven't met the right girl.'

'What's your idea of the right girl?'

'I'll know her when I meet her. Just as Jack knew when he met you. Congratulations, by the way. I'm told you have a fabulous ring. You will have to show me when we reach the restaurant.'

He drove into Bristol and stopped outside the Grand Hotel. 'I'm well known here. I'm sure we can get lunch without booking. Oh! Will it be quiet enough for your headache?'

'I hope so.'

'So do I. We'll try, shall we? I'm sure the hushed, reverential atmosphere will not make it worse.'

Eve thought it might have been better had she chosen to drive to the hills where she would have been less likely to meet anyone she knew.

He opened the door for her. 'You don't look very pleased. Do you dislike the Grand?'

She smiled. 'Of course not.'

'Because if you do,' he said in a solicitous tone which she was sure was assumed, 'we can go elsewhere.'

'This is fine, thank you.' If someone mentioned to Jack that they had seen her she would simply say they had made a mistake. She would think up some excuse. He would never dare doubt her.

When she removed her gloves Charles said, 'Why, Eve, where is your ring? I was looking forward to seeing it.'

'I can't get my glove over it.'

'Good lord, that's going to cause you endless problems in the future. You may even have to wear a different-sized glove.'

'Perhaps.'

'You will have to buy two pairs and use one of each.'

'Perhaps.'

'You do not wish to discuss it? And why should you. Such a trivial matter.' Eve almost ground her teeth. 'I'll call for menus,' he said.

Lunch was delicious. Clear soup, delicately steamed sole, and braised beef. Charles ended with a cheese savoury. Eve chose fruit.

'I like to see a girl with a good appetite,' he said.

Eve smiled thinly. Having had a chance to look at the other women lunching today she realised that although her Chanel suit looked as good and expensive as it undoubtedly was, it was very slightly out of date. And when a girl she knew drifted past wearing an ensemble of a red and white crêpe dress with accordion pleating under a draped coat of matching red and a tiny hat of the same colour, all of the very latest style, she felt angry and envious.

'A pretty outfit,' said Charles.

Eve was startled. His eyes were moving between the girl and herself and she had the unpleasant sensation that he could read her mind. Damn the man! That was an indecent insight into a woman. 'I couldn't possibly wear that shade of red,' she said casually. 'I think I shall have a cigarette.'

'Please, take one of mine.'

She smoked and drank several cups of coffee, then Charles looked at his watch.

'Oh, I am so sorry,' said Eve drily. 'I do hope I'm not keeping you from a more important engagement?'

Charles spread his hands. 'Would I be so crass? No, I was simply thinking of your indisposition and wondering if you were allowing yourself enough time to rest before the dance.'

'You're right.' She stubbed out her partly smoked cigarette which was Turkish, especially blended for him, and expensive. She took perverse pleasure in wasting it.

In the car Charles tucked the rug back around her. 'Will you save some dances for me tonight? If your headache permits you to attend, of course.'

'You are to be at the Talbots'?'

'Yes. You sound surprised.'

'I haven't seen you around lately.'

'I arrived in Bristol a few days ago. I travel between my places to check on this and that.'

'How many?'

'Miles or places?'

'Places.'

'I have an apartment in Paris and one in London, a house in Bristol and the family seat in Somerset.'

'What? No hunting lodge?'

It was a foolish remark and Eve waited for him to demolish her. He only said gently, 'I have many invitations and can choose where to hunt and fish. Actually, I don't go in much for either. They involve physical discomfort, the end result is scarcely ever satisfying, and I have never seen the attraction in killing for the sake of it.' He flipped open his gold case. 'Cigarette?'

Eve took one and he brought out his lighter. It was gold too.

'Is there no sport you care for?' she asked.

'I play golf and tennis and swim where the water's warm. My chief sport lies in laying siege to beautiful women.'

For a moment she was breathless, then said, 'How absolutely brazen!'

'It's honest.'

'How far do you carry your siege?'

'Until the – shall we say? – edifice is conquered.'

'You can't be including me in your plans!'

'Why not?'

'Because I'm engaged to be married.'

'Ah, yes, but not yet irrevocably tied. And you removed your engagement ring.'

'I told you why.'

'Yes, you did, and I didn't believe a word of it. You are very beautiful, Eve.'

His voice was low and attractive. She fell silent. Was this the beginning of a campaign? She didn't know if she was flattered or outraged. When he left her on the common she walked back to the house slowly, trying to come to terms with the fact that she found him exceedingly attractive. He held out a promise of danger and excitement.

Eve took a long time over her evening toilette. She took a hot scented bath and her hair was washed and brushed until it gleamed. She studied her naked body in the mirror. Long slender limbs, high breasts, a narrow waist, good skin. She was lucky. As she stared the image of Charles Ware came to mind and suddenly she felt idiotically shy and hurried into her silk teddy and petticoat.

She studied her face before she began her make-up. When she had shopped for Tessa in Paris she had also picked up a few things for herself. Good job I did, she reflected, I couldn't afford this stuff now. She finished by dabbing a little scent behind her ears, on her knees French style, and between her breasts.

Her frock was powder blue crêpe de Chine, sleeveless and with the low back that suited her well. Her long necklace of blue and cream beads and drop earrings added the finishing touches. She hadn't worn this ensemble in England so no one would remember it. When a

216

maid tapped on the door to say that Mr Padbury was waiting, Eve picked up her fur wrap and went downstairs.

Jack was in the library being fussed over by Tildy Coleman.

He beamed at her. 'Darling, you look absolutely spiffing.' Eve managed not to look bored. Spiffing! Charles would never use such a word to describe her. 'Has your headache quite disappeared?'

'I'm sure it must have,' said Tildy, 'as she went out for lunch after all.'

'You went out?'

'My headache got better.'

'I could have taken you for lunch.' Jack looked disappointed.

'Yes, of course. I tried to telephone you, but got no reply.'

'No reply?'

Eve hurried to rectify her slip. 'I mean, I couldn't reach you. Of course I had a reply.'

'That's odd. The servants didn't mention it.'

Eve frowned. 'Are we going to stand here all night discussing your domestics' failings?'

Jack was immediately contrite. 'Of course not.'

Tildy had scurried off at the first sign of dispute and Jack took Eve in his arms.

'Careful, you'll crush my dress.'

He held her gingerly and kissed her gently. 'I wouldn't want to spoil your appearance. I couldn't. No one could! Oh, Eve, I wish you would set the date for our wedding. It's terrible having to wait.'

'Wait for what?' She held her eyes wide open.

Jack went red and said jerkily, 'You know what. I want to make you my wife. I want to make love to you.'

Eve glanced at him. He was blushing deeply. 'My dear man, you make it sound about as romantic as plum duff.'

'I'm sorry.' She saw that she had really upset him. 'I'm a plain speaking man. I can only say what I mean.'

She had no wish to spend the evening with a sulking

partner and so smiled placatingly. 'Dear fellow, I'm only teasing.'

Jack stopped the car at the entrance to the Talbots' country house to allow her to alight before he parked further on.

As Eve walked into the hall a girl in a floaty outfit shrieked, 'Darling! Who was that superb man I saw you with at lunch today? What an absolute sweetie.'

'He is just a friend,' said Eve coldly.

'It isn't fair,' cried the girl. 'You've captured one male. Why should you have another?'

'He's an old acquaintance.'

'I say, don't lose your rag. I was only teasing.'

'I think you've said enough,' said her partner as he steered her away.

Eve hadn't realised that Jack had heard part of the exchange. 'What was that about? What man does she mean?'

She sighed. 'I was with Charles Ware, but I wasn't going to tell that nosy female. You remember? He was a guest of Kitty Bamford's in France. I felt better quite quickly, but I couldn't get hold of you to tell you. Then he telephoned and asked me if I would care to lunch with him. Should I have refused? It might have sounded awfully rude. Did I do wrong?'

'Of course not, darling. He's older, isn't he? Could be pushing forty.'

'I have no idea.'

'The music has begun. Shall we dance?'

They jigged around the dance floor to a hotted up version of a song. Eve knew the words. 'There's a rainbow round my shoulder . . .' she sang in a voice made breathless by the athletic movement required by the Black Bottom. Jack looked ridiculously happy, and even more so when he held her in his arms as the band played a slow foxtrot. Eve relaxed a little. Jack was a nice man. He would make a kind and caring husband. She could do a lot worse and she was utterly fed up with having to watch what she spent.

'What are you thinking?' he murmured.

'How nice it is to be here with you,' she said dreamily.

His arms tightened round her and his eyes grew dark. Perhaps there was more to Jack than she had suspected. In fact, it might be a good idea to find out how much more before they got married. Her loins tingled. She wondered what her chances were. He'd probably be shocked.

Then she herself was shocked as a voice she knew began to float over the heads of the dancers. 'I'll get by, as long as I have you; though there be rain and darkness too . . .'

'Tessa!' She whirled round, missing her step and would have lost her balance completely if Jack had not steadied her.

'So it is,' he said. 'She's got a splendid voice. She's wearing a pretty frock too, isn't she?'

That fact hadn't escaped Eve. How did Tessa come by such clothes?

Tessa sang on: 'I'll not complain, I'll see it through . . .'

Eve's eyes devoured her cousin. The frock was a dark blue, pale pink-flowered chiffon. The waist was higher in accordance with the up-to-the-minute style, the skirt flowed to a couple of inches below her silk-clad knees. Her shoes were dark blue with a few diamantes sparkling here and there. Her hair – if Eve wasn't so sure that Tessa knew nothing about the art of beauty, she could swear her cousin had used a coloured wash. It gleamed bright and sleek.

'Poverty may come to me, it's true . . .' sang Tessa.

'Steady on, old thing,' said Jack as Eve stumbled again. 'I think she's seen us.' He waved to Tessa who sent him a tiny smile.

'She's seen us all right. That last line was directed straight at me.'

Jack was embarrassed. He knew of the Brooks' straitened circumstances but to talk of money, even indirectly, was simply not done. 'Surely not? She seemed like a nice girl to me.'

'You know nothing about her!'

Tessa sang: 'But what care I? Say, I'll get by, as long as I have you.'

Eve wrenched her attention back to the dance steps with difficulty. Jack tried a couple of times to talk to her, but she ignored him and he gave up.

The music stopped and Eve felt like marching straight from the floor to the band-stand and demanding the answers to a few questions. Such as, what was one half of the Kissing Cousins doing up there on her own? And how had she got to know a dance-band leader who was a stranger to Eve? And where in hell had she got that frock when her cousin was wearing one of last year's models?

She sat down at one of the small tables, fanning herself. 'Shall I bring you something to drink?' asked Jack.

'Champagne. And while you're away, I'll have a word with Tessa.'

'Good girl,' said Jack. His approval annoyed her. 'Shall I escort you to the band-stand?'

'Don't be such a silly ass! I'm perfectly capable of walking there myself. Meanwhile, I'm perishing with thirst.'

'Of course. Sorry.'

Jack hurried away and Eve walked to the band-stand, trying to look nonchalant. As she got closer to her cousin she saw how the colour of Tessa's dress deepened the blue of her eyes. She was wearing make-up too. Discreet and clever. Eve almost quivered with fury.

Tessa had seen Eve and Jack as soon as she stood up to sing and, as Eve suspected, had directed the line about poverty straight to her.

Eve climbed the three steps to the band-stand and several of the musicians looked curiously at her. 'Just what are you doing here?' she demanded.

'Singing.'

'I can see that. But without me? I thought we were a team. I thought we only went out together.'

'You haven't been near me for two months. If I waited for you to contact me I should never get any work – and I need it.'

'It's Friday, too. I thought Saturday was your night for singing.'

'It was, but now it's Friday as well. Mum lets me have a lie-in on Sunday.'

'No chapel?'

Tessa's chin went up. 'I don't neglect my duties.'

'I'm surprised your mother allows you out alone.'

'If you'd bothered to visit us you would know that things have changed. And I don't suppose Jack will let you sing.'

'I shall do as I please. Jack won't stop me.'

'He's a nice fellow,' said Tessa.

'How are you getting on with Frank?' asked Eve.

'I see him at chapel.'

'Does he still walk you home?'

'Sometimes.'

Eve was even more annoyed. She seemed to be making no impression at all upon Tessa. 'I shall visit you soon,' she said.

'That will be pleasant. Mum and Dad often speak of you. *They* think you're a really nice girl. Jack's returned, by the way. He's brought your drink.'

'He can wait. I wanted to ask you where you bought that frock.'

Before Tessa could reply they were interrupted. Charles Ware said smoothly from behind Eve, 'Good evening, Tessa. Mrs Talbot says I may ask you to dance. Will you?'

She smilingly agreed. Eve was transfixed with anger. She excused herself quickly and made her way back to Jack, trying to conquer a rage which she realised was compounded chiefly of jealousy, mixed with regret. She had forgotten the thrill of performing in public.


Tessa permitted Charles to drive her home. If she couldn't catch the last tram she had to take a taxi, an expensive necessity.

'You sang very well,' he said. 'You have a lovely voice.'

'Thank you.'

'And you look so well.'

'Do I?'

'Are you well?'

'Perfectly, thank you.'

'You have also grown a lot prettier since last we met.'

'Have I?'

'You have one bad fault, though.'

'What is that?'

'You don't talk to me properly.'

Tessa laughed softly. 'I don't wish to say something which could be wrongly construed.'

'Really? How interesting. What can you mean?'

'You have a reputation for being a lady-killer. I don't want to discover for myself whether or not it's true so it's safer to say nothing.'

'Ouch! I wish I had left you in silence.'

'It might have been wiser.'

'Your worry over my reputation didn't stop you from accepting my lift.'

'Beggars can't be choosers and I'm sure you are enough of a gentleman not to force yourself on a woman who has no interest in you.'

'Thank you so much!'

'Have I made you angry? I meant to compliment you.'

'I have had better compliments.'

'I'm sure you have. Would you like me to give you some?'

Charles' hand tightened on the steering wheel. 'I can manage without.'

'Of course you can. You don't need a poor songstress to flatter you.'

Charles laughed unwillingly. 'You've changed. When we first met you were like a little mouse. Eve dominated you. She tries to dominate everyone.'

'I would prefer you not to insult my cousin.'

'You really are cousins?'

'We share a great-grandmother.'

'I see. Eve is different from you. She's a hard little nut.'

222

'I've already asked you not to insult her.'

'Sorry. That was just a glancing reference. I'm much more interested in you. What's happened to give you—' He paused.

'To give me what?'

'Polish? Sophistication? I should like to find out. May I call one day and take you out?'

'No, thank you.'

'Good God! You don't believe in softening the blow, do you?'

'Not in this case. I'm positive you have plenty of protection against blows and mine was not severe.'

'I wouldn't be too sure of that. I really like you, Tessa.' He slowed before turning into a main road, then drove on. 'You live on the other side of town, you said.'

'That's right.'

'I know the way to Kingswood, but you'll need to direct me from there. Why won't you come out with me?'

'Because you're only amusing yourself. I suppose you live an idle life and want me as a diversion.'

Charles was silent for a moment. 'Tessa, I don't just want to amuse myself. I like you. You have spirit.'

'And that's almost all I have at present.'

'You sound angry. Bitter. Except that you are not the kind of girl to resent things.'

'Perhaps not for myself.'

'Has something happened to someone you care for?'

'My father. He's been put on short time. Employers are beginning to cut back on staff. They say there's a recession.'

'That's hard luck on him.'

'It's hard luck on the whole family, but particularly him. He's always been proud of being a good provider.'

'A good provider,' said Charles thoughtfully. 'I've not heard that phrase before.'

'Of course you haven't. It probably couldn't exist in your world.'

'My world? We all live in the same one, Tessa.'

'No,' she said shortly, 'we don't.'

'And I suppose your singing means more money coming in.'

'Yes. Mum doesn't really like it but she allows it when it's someone like the Talbots. Tiddles Henley put in a good word for me with them. I met her quite by chance when she was out shopping and she insisted on taking me to Bright's for tea. Somehow I found myself telling her of our problems. She's been an absolute brick, helping me all she can.'

'I remember Tiddles. Such a stupid name for a girl with so much character.'

'Yes. I like her a lot.'

'Eve doesn't sing with you any more?'

'Not lately. I can hardly blame her for losing interest now she's engaged. I expect her fiancé takes up all her time.'

'Jack Padbury's tenacity finally paid off.'

'He loves her.'

'And she loves him?'

'She must do or she wouldn't have accepted his proposal.'

'Come, now, Tessa, you are not that naïve.'

'Turn down this road, please,' she said. Charles obeyed her and stopped at the end of her lane when she said, 'This is where I live.'

He looked round. 'Where exactly?'

'Up there in the cottage with a light burning. Mum always leaves a light in the window for me.'

'How motherly of her.' He sounded genuinely pleased. He jumped out and opened her door. 'Go safely home, Tessa.'

'Thank you.'

She had turned from him when Charles said, 'Won't you say goodnight properly?'

She didn't turn round. 'In what way?'

He was silent for a moment. 'I should like a kiss, but a handshake will do. For now.'

They solemnly shook hands. Charles said, 'One day you will kiss me.'

'I think not.'

'I shan't give up.'

'That's entirely up to you. Lay siege if you wish, but remember, I'm not Eve. Persistence won't wear me down. I intend to be a success without any man's backing. At the moment I obey Mum because she's had enough upsets, but one day it'll be different.'

Charles laughed. 'I don't doubt it! But remember, I'm not Jack Padbury to follow you round like a little dog. Those are not my tactics.'

'Goodnight.' Tessa walked up the lane and into the house. He didn't drive away until she had closed the door behind her.

She hung up her coat, picked up a saucepan of milk left ready by Mum and put it on the range. The tin of home-made biscuits stood on the table but she wasn't hungry.

The door opened and Mum came in. 'Hello, love, are you tired?'

'Mum! I didn't wake you, did I?'

'No. I couldn't sleep. Add a drop more milk to that pan, will you? I could do with a drink as well.'

'What kept you awake?'

'I think I ate too much at supper.'

Tessa made no answer. The reason was far more likely to be worry over Dad. He was ashamed of being put on short time and no matter how often he was assured that it wasn't his fault he couldn't shake off the feeling. As his pride sank Mum's seemed to grow. She had cut down on house-keeping, not easy where money had always been allotted meticulously, but suet pudding tended to appear more often on the menu than fruit pie and scrag end of mutton made good broth and cost little. Perhaps Mum really had indigestion after the heavy food she served, but her economies enabled her to save money in her blue metal cash box where every slot was labelled: chapel collections, Bright Hour, rent, rates, gas, clothes, extras – though not much went into the latter these days.

'Was it a nice evening?' Mum asked as she sat down with her cup of cocoa.

'Very good. The Talbots are kind people. They allowed me to dance.'

Mum looked at her sharply. They might be glad of the extra money, but if Tessa showed any signs of becoming enamoured of the wanton life lived by some the singing would stop. 'Who did you dance with?'

'A man called Charles Ware. He brought me home.'

'I thought I heard a car. What's he like, this Charles Ware?'

'He's an older man. He was at Kitty Bamford's villa in France. He's always a perfect gentleman.'

'All right, but you be careful, Tessa. These people aren't our sort. Was your cousin Paul there?'

She sipped her milk carefully. 'No. I haven't seen him for a while. Maybe he's in America.'

'I got the impression that you were a bit sweet on him.'

'Oh, Mum, he's nothing to me. I dare say he'll marry an American.'

'Maybe.' Mum got up. 'Come on, my girl, up to bed with you. You don't want to be tired for the choir.'

In her room Tessa slipped off her dress. She knew that it had made Eve furious and couldn't help smiling at the memory. Evening frocks had become a problem, then she had heard of a second-hand shop where ladies sold their unwanted clothes. The recession was hitting many who had never before considered money and there were bargains to be had. And Mum had remembered an ancient aunty who lived in Kingswood who used to do dressmaking.

Mum and Tessa had gone to call on Aunty May. Her tiny house was dingy and smelt of cats and cabbage but it was her own, and with her widow's pension and her way with her needle she managed. She pored over fashion pictures and she and Tessa made subtle alterations to the frocks. Tessa nipped off silk flowers and substituted belts for sashes until in the end their original owners would have had to look closely to recognise their discarded garments.

* * *

Sunday passed with its usual soothing effect. Dad and Mum forgot their worries in the pleasures of worship and the special food served by Mum. She had managed to keep up that tradition so far.

On Monday Tessa went to work as usual. She hadn't told her mother that for some time now during the early part of the week the shop was almost devoid of customers and the ones who did come in were either poor managers who had run out of food, or those who were too poverty-stricken to buy more than a little at a time as they pawned their possessions throughout the week to be retrieved at weekends. Today the blow she had feared fell.

After lunch, Mr Grice called her into the family room behind the shop. He looked nervous as he asked her to sit down. 'Tessa, I'm really sorry about this but I'm going to have to put you on short time. From the end of this week it'll be Thursday, Friday and Saturday only.'

For a moment she could say nothing for the lump in her throat. Although she had found the job tedious she had been proud to make a significant contribution to the family finances.

'I'm sorry too,' she managed. 'And my money?'

'Well, it'll have to go down, of course. You must have realised what was happening?' he added pleadingly.

She had expected it but was still shocked. 'Yes, I've realised. It's happening to more and more people. Dad's never been short of work before, but he—'

'The shop's just not paying like it should. The long and short of it is we can't afford you.'

Tessa got up. 'Thank you for being so frank with me.' She finished the day's work trying to think of ways of breaking the news gently to her mother. There was no gentle way.

She hung up her things behind the kitchen door and walked over to the range. Last night after a week of mild weather there had been a frost and the wind was keen, but the gleaming range was comfortingly hot.

Mrs Morland carried a chair to her. 'Sit down. You

look all in. It's those late nights singing. They'll have to stop.'

'No, Mum. I can't stop now.'

Mrs Morland's hand was stayed as she was about to pour tea. She stared at Tessa, then resumed pouring. 'Here, get this down you. You're shivering.'

'I know.' She sipped the tea gratefully. 'Mum, Mr Grice called me in to their back room today. I've been put on short time. I shall be working only three days a week.'

Mrs Morland sat down heavily. 'So it's come. I was afraid of it.'

'Were you, Mum? You never said.'

'No. I kept hoping. I heard that Grice's Grocery was doing hardly any business at the beginning of the week. They're not the only ones and things are getting worse. Too many men are earning less and soon it'll be bankruptcies for the bosses and the sack for the men. And the dole.' She whispered the last word. It was the final humiliation to have a man on the dole.

'I'll get more singing jobs,' promised Tessa.

'No, it mustn't come to that. We can't expect you to wear yourself out.'

'But I can make up the short fall easily. I get lots of offers.'

'To sing in rowdy dance halls? No.'

'I don't have to take any notice of rowdiness. I can just do my songs then come home.'

'Those who touch filth are bound to be contaminated by it.'

'Mum! That's not a nice thing to say. As if I would! I'm sure I'd be perfectly safe.'

Mrs Morland looked hard at her daughter. 'Maybe, maybe not. You wouldn't mean to forget your religion, but in the end you'd back-slide. I've read about show girls. Lots of them are gangsters' girl friends and get up to all kinds of wickedness.'

Tessa couldn't help laughing. 'Mum, you're talking of America. We don't have gangsters here. Not in Bristol.'

'Just because we don't hear of them doesn't mean they

aren't there. Bad people are everywhere. You have to keep a watch for those that try to get you on the slippery road to hell.'

Tessa held out her cup for more tea. It sounded as if the latest prayer meeting had been led by an evangelist with promises of eternal death for gangsters, crooks and possibly dance band leaders, and everlasting life for the white-souled. There was no use arguing with Mum until the effect wore off, but she made up her mind that she was going to get more performing work.

After their encounter at the Talbots' she was not surprised when Eve arrived unexpectedly later that evening.

Mum welcomed her. 'You're a naughty girl, aren't you?' she said with a smile that showed she was joking. 'We haven't seen you for ages.'

'I'm sorry, Cousin Lily.' Eve bent and kissed Mrs Morland. 'My fiancé is so demanding.'

'Just like Mr Morland when we were courting. He wanted me to go out with him every night, but my mother was wise and said no. She believed that if you gave too much of your company to a man before marriage he might just get fed up and go wandering. Make him wait, was her motto.'

'*Cousin Lily!*' Eve pretended to be shocked. 'How teasing of you.'

'Teasing or not, I reckon she spoke the truth. Sit down now you're here. You'll have tea and eat with us later?'

'I'd like to. What have you got? Something smells nice.'

'A meat and vegetable pudding,' said Mrs Morland. 'A bit heavy, but satisfying.'

Mr Morland came in. 'It sticks to the ribs,' he said. 'Hello, our Eve. I saw you arrive. I was down the garden.' He washed his hands at the kitchen sink. 'Are you staying a while?'

'She is,' said Mum. 'I've just used the last of the gooseberry jam and there's tarts and custard to follow. I hope we get a good crop this year.'

'We shall need it,' muttered Mr Morland.

Joe and Susan came bounding in. 'Hello, Eve. We saw your car.'

She was glad to see them, glad to see them all. They welcomed her without question, warmly and lovingly. Later she followed Tessa upstairs to her cold little bedroom. 'Now then, tell me. Where did you get that frock you were wearing at the dance?'

'I knew that's why you'd come,' said Tessa angrily.

'Not at all. I like it here.'

Her voice held the ring of truth and Tessa calmed down. She told her of the second-hand clothing shop and her great-aunt's skill. 'You should try it,' advised Tessa. 'Aunty May would do any alterations you wanted.'

'Wear clothes some other woman has owned?' said Eve aghast. 'She might even recognise it and she'd know I was buying her cast-offs. Tessa, how could you?'

She was angry again. 'How could I not? Where do you expect me to get money for different frocks? I can't wear the same one all the time. I've got three now.'

'Let's see them.'

Tessa opened her wardrobe door.

'They're lovely.' Eve touched them gently. 'Lovely. But I couldn't. I really couldn't.'

'Please yourself.' Tessa shut the door with a bang.

'What about underwear to go with them?'

'I've still got the stuff you bought me. Mum was going to destroy it but she couldn't bring herself to do it and now she never mentions it. I've got two pairs of silk stockings which I treat like cobwebs. And a velvet cape. That was easy. Aunty May cut up an old curtain and took out the best bits. Incidentally, I shall be singing more in future. I've been put on short time.'

Eve felt restless and dissatisfied. Tessa faced life as a working girl, dedicated to helping support her family, while she was engaged to a wealthy man who adored her and was able to buy her anything she wanted. Yet Tessa seemed happy, while she had to keep a firm hold on herself to hide her discontent.

'Won't you join up with me?' asked Tessa. 'You used

to think that the Kissing Cousins had a great future. What happened to your dreams?'

'They went the way of all dreams once you wake up,' muttered Eve.

'Mine are still as bright as ever. Still, I suppose Jack wouldn't let his fiancée work.'

'He doesn't control what I do.'

'No?' Tessa said softly.

Eve glared at her, then laughed. 'You rotten pig. You're deliberately tormenting me. As for Jack – I'll sing with you again, any time I like. When's the next engagement? And by the way, how did you get to meet that band leader? And who is he?'

'Josh Raven? I buy *The Era*, a stage newspaper. It's got everything. Jobs and digs and shows and acts. Everything. He was calling for singers to audition and I went along.'

'Will I have to audition?'

'I don't know. Are we partners again?'

'You bet we are,' said Eve, suddenly enthusiastic.

# Chapter Eleven

'Don't you trust me, Mum?' asked Tessa.

Mrs Morland flushed angrily. 'Of course I do.'

'Then why not let me take more singing engagements? I can sleep late on Tuesdays and Wednesdays. If I don't work, what else can I do? I'll just be hanging round you all day and you won't like that.'

'That's enough of your cheek. There's plenty you can do here.' Mum smacked her rolling pin so hard on to her pastry that flour flew in the air and landed on the kitchen floor in white drifts. 'Now look what you've made me do! And it'll probably turn out heavy.'

Tessa fetched a floor cloth and carefully wiped up the flour. 'Your pastry could never be heavy. Mum, please, I'm not stupid and I'm old enough to take care of myself. And Eve will be with me. You like Eve, don't you?'

'You know I do. Poor neglected lamb. Though I think that an engaged girl ought be making wedding plans not gallivanting round dance halls with the likes of that man, Cliff Carter.'

'What do you know about him?'

'Nothing first-hand, but Mrs Millington said her niece saw him and Eve having dinner together in a cafe. She said he's a very nasty man.'

'Does she know Eve and Cliff?' Tessa was intrigued, but Mum took the question as being cheeky and said so.

'Mrs Millington's niece recognised Eve from chapel and she goes dancing a lot. That family aren't really God's chosen. She says that he's married with children and from all accounts has got more than one girl in trouble.'

233

'It doesn't surprise me. I couldn't stand him. If I promise not to work for him, will you give your permission?'

Mrs Morland placed a pastry top on an apple pie, cut off the excess and fluted the edges. She opened the oven door and took out the crusts she used to test the temperature. 'Just right.' She put the pie in the oven. Then she sat down looking defeated.

It was as if the Rock of Gibraltar had turned to marshmallow. 'Mum! Are you ill?'

'No. Tessa, my love, I know you want to help, but I don't know if Dad would like you to be a dance hall singer. Don't you understand what all this has done to your father? Have you looked at him properly since he was put on short time?'

Tessa had. Dad was beginning to stoop. 'I'm just trying to help.'

'I know.'

'Has he said anything about my singing?'

'It was all right when it was a bit of fun, but lately he's said things about having to be kept by his daughter. He feels the shame of it.'

'He's not kept by me! And there's no shame in being under-employed! It isn't his fault and it's happening to more and more people. It's happened to me and I'm not ashamed. It isn't my fault, either.'

'I know that, but it doesn't help your father. And he sees some men losing their jobs altogether and is terrified of it happening to him. It would kill his spirit to have to go on the dole.'

'Should I ask him about my singing?'

'No, such talk would upset him. Couldn't you do a bit of dress-making? Dad wouldn't mind that. It's woman's work and done quietly. You're handy with your needle and Aunty May would help. You could borrow her sewing machine. People wouldn't notice you the way they do when you sing.'

'I'm not that much enamoured with sewing. I do it when I must, that's all. And there's Eve to consider. She wants to bring back Kissing Cousins.'

'Kissing Cousins! What a name! It's hardly decent.'

234

'It's just an American term.'

'American!' snapped Mum.

'What's wrong with America?'

'I've told you. It's full of gangsters and mobsters. No place to live.'

Tessa laughed. 'They don't inhabit every part.'

'Well, if you think I'm funny, there's no more to be said.' Mum jumped up and attacked her baking.

Tessa went to see Josh Raven and as a consequence told Mum she had invited a friend for Sunday tea.

'Who is she?'

'Not a girl, Mum, a man.'

'But Frank will be here. You can't have two men friends at the same table. And you've no business asking him without coming to me first.'

'I don't look on Frank as my boy friend, not yet, and I didn't think you'd mind me asking someone to tea. I want you to meet him. He's really nice and he wants me to work for him.'

'Doing what?'

'He's in the entertainment business. He could give me hours which would still let me go on working for the Grices.'

'On the *stage*?'

'No, the same as I've been doing. Just working with a band.'

Mum set her lips, but said no more.

Josh drove up the bumpy lane in a low green two-seater and parked in front of the cottage.

Frank, who had been looking sulky since Tessa told him that a man friend was coming to tea, glanced out of the window and forgot his annoyance. 'Look at that,' he breathed. 'A Brooklands Nine 1928 model – and it's perfect!'

He hurried outside and joined Josh in mutual admiration of the car. They entered the kitchen together talking animatedly.

Tessa stepped forward. 'Have you two met before?

You seem to be getting along well.'

Josh smiled and Frank grinned sheepishly. 'We've not met before,' he said. 'It's the car. A beauty!'

Tessa introduced them and took them into the best room where Mum was sitting in her Sunday dress waiting to serve tea from a tea-trolley the shelves of which were crammed with sandwiches and home-made cakes. Joey and Susan, well scrubbed, also clothed in their Sunday best, were seated on the fender stools. A fire glowed in the hearth. Tessa smiled gratefully at her mother. Everyone sat down while Mum conducted tea in an elaborate ceremony. She asked each person what he or she would like, then put it on to a small plate, one of her cherished set, and Dad bore it to the person concerned. The solemnity of the process awed Susan and even affected Joey who had managed to eat very little when Mum decided that the trolley should be removed. His eyes followed it as Tessa wheeled it away.

It would have been better if Mum had laid the kitchen table and let everyone eat heartily, instead of trying to impress Josh with her notion of high living. Joey and Susan were sent out and whispered, 'Tessa, could we have some more?'

'I'm starving,' said Joey.

'You're far from that,' grinned Tessa. 'Go ahead. Eat.'

Back in the other room the men were smoking and Tessa could almost see Mum's nose twitching. When they had gone the windows would be opened and a thorough polishing undertaken to rid the room of tobacco fumes.

Josh offered his packet to Tessa who shook her head. She could do with one but hadn't told Mum yet that she smoked.

'What line of business are you in?' asked Dad.

Josh was surprised. 'Hasn't Tessa told you? I'm a dance band leader.'

'She told me,' said Mum defensively. She had taken a liking to Josh.

'I see,' said Dad, frowning.

Mum said, 'He could give our Tessa some work.'

'She's a shop assistant by trade,' said Dad.

'She's also a singer,' said Josh.

'She already does too much of that.'

'Many people would like her to do a lot more.'

'Shops are respectable places,' said Dad.

There was silence for a moment then Frank said loudly, 'I don't like Tessa making a show of herself.'

Mr Morland frowned. Frank might be a possible son-in-law, but that didn't give him rights over what Tessa should do. Not yet. That was a father's concern.

'Tessa has a superb voice,' said Josh. 'She tells me she sings in the chapel choir. I used to.'

'Church or chapel?' demanded Dad.

'Chapel. My people are all Baptists.'

This was a surprise to Tessa. It raised Josh several notches in her parents' eyes.

'Then you'll know that we don't like her meeting—' Mum paused, then said, ' – the wrong type of people.'

'I understand perfectly, Mrs Morland. If you'll allow her to work for me I'll watch where she sings and who she meets and I'll make sure she gets home safely afterwards.'

Mum considered. 'I suppose your work keeps you out late at nights.'

'Yes. Very late. Sometimes nearly all night. Society dances often end by serving breakfast.'

'The idea!' said Mum. 'Your wife can't see much of you.'

Josh smiled. 'I'm not married.'

'Anyone in mind?' asked Dad.

'No one serious. I don't think it would be fair to a girl to expect her to put up with my kind of life.'

'Why not?' demanded Frank belligerently.

'I keep such irregular hours. I keep hoping to meet a singer or actress whose working hours will match mine.'

Frank stared at him suspiciously.

'That sounds sensible,' said Mum.

237

'What ambitions have you got?' asked Dad.

'I've got an engagement to play on the wireless,' said Josh. 'We – that's the band and I – will be going to London for that. I'm hoping we'll get more broadcasting.'

The Morlands were deeply impressed. 'The wireless!' said Dad.

'Fancy that,' said Mum.

Frank looked stormier than ever.

Tessa's heart thumped. To sing on the wireless would be a first step to fame.

'Tessa couldn't go to London and stay on her own,' said Mum.

Josh said gently, 'She wouldn't be on her own. I would take care of her.'

Dad frowned. 'That won't do. That won't do at all.'

'It certainly won't,' agreed Mum.

'I could drive you there to supervise her lodging, if you wish, Mrs Morland. You can make sure she gets a landlady who keeps a decent house.'

'She's never been to London,' said Dad. 'What do you think, Mum?'

She considered. 'I think I trust Josh to make sure everything's above board.'

He smiled. 'So you'll let Tessa sing for me?'

'Locally. We'll think a bit more about her going to London,' said Dad.

'Can she sing on more nights?'

'I might let her go out on Mondays and Tuesdays,' said Dad. 'I'll give it some thought.' He rose to his feet and looked pointedly at the clock which obligingly chimed six. 'We're due back in chapel by half-past.'

Josh got up at once. 'Shall I see him out?' asked Frank, annoying Mr Morland again.

'No. I shall do that.'


Primed by Tessa, Eve arrived soon after Josh had left. She wore her grey suit with a modest brooch in one lapel and an unobtrusive hat. Now the idea of singing again had been put into her head she was wild to begin. She hadn't told Jack because it could have started an argument. Not that he exercised much control over her.

She wanted, needed, money for her car, for clothes, for all the good things in life. Some singers made big sums on the stage and she had been reading about the film world where fabulous salaries were given to the stars who had surmounted the difficulties of switching from the silent movies to the talkies. There were huge opportunities in Hollywood, the place in California where movies were made and where stars lived in sumptuous houses. If she tried to explain her need for money to Jack he would pester her again to marry him soon. The thought bothered her; in fact, more than bothered her, it repelled her. Jack's money beckoned insidiously, but he had always bored her and now she was in his company so often she discovered just how tedious she found him.

'Hello, our Eve,' said Mr Morland.

'You look really nice,' said Mrs Morland. 'Aren't you cold with no coat?'

'It's cooler than I thought, but I'll be all right in chapel.'

'Is that why you're here?' Mrs Morland beamed.

'Of course. I'm very sorry, Cousin Lily. I've neglected you lately.'

'You should have come to tea,' cried Joey. 'We had it in the best room and there were tons of lovely things to eat.'

'Have you had tea, Eve?'

'Yes, thank you.' She had drunk a cup of tea with Jack before getting rid of him. He hadn't believed her when she said she was going to visit Tessa, but hadn't dared say as much outright. 'You haven't bothered with her for ages,' he'd said.

'No, that's why I'm going now. I promised my cousins I would attend chapel and I've not kept my word lately.'

'You're going to chapel?'

'Yes.'

Jack looked at her searchingly. 'Why tonight?'

Eve shrugged carelessly. 'I just feel like it.'

'I could come with you.'

Eve nearly swore at him. 'No. Maybe you can come another time. Not tonight.'

Tessa had counted on Josh softening her parents' attitude and on Eve for continuing the process. From her seat in the choir, who sat in tiers behind the preacher, she had a clear view of Eve's face and had a job not to laugh as her cousin struggled to keep boredom at bay. Tonight they had a visiting minister who took a single text which he thundered at them repeatedly and on which he enlarged and elaborated until even she lost the point at which he had begun.

Eve sang the final hymn with the gusto of relief and the Morlands escorted her to their home which they reached at eight o'clock. Supper was taken in the kitchen. Eve tried to imagine her parents listening to a preacher for a whole hour. She said as much to Tessa when they went up to her room to tidy their hair.

'He does go on a bit,' agreed Tessa with a grin. 'Now, Eve, it's up to you to win my parents round. They liked Josh and I really want to sing on the BBC.'

'I'll do my best.'

'How's Jack?'

'Jack? He's fine. A bit bossy, but I can cope with that most of the time.'

'Are you sure you ought to be marrying him?'

'Why shouldn't I?'

Tessa shrugged. 'You don't sound very loving when you talk about him.'

'What would you know about it? Have you ever been in love? Oh, I suppose you're still mooning over Paul.'

'I am not!'

'Good job. He's practically engaged to Andrea Talbot. It was so sickening at the Talbots'! She positively draped herself over him and if he danced with anyone else she was watching him the whole time. Her partners must have felt they were with a zombie. Debutantes are expected to be gay and full of fun. But who knows? She

240

may meet someone she likes better than Paul and then he'll be free again. Unless he meets another girl *he* likes.' Eve patted her waves into perfection. 'Charles Ware left early the other night. Someone said he was seen outside with you.'

'He gave me a lift home. I missed the last tram.'

'How did he find that out?'

'I don't know. He just drove up and I was glad to see him.'

'I bet you were. You must have given him a hint.'

'Eve, I did no such thing! And what business is it of yours anyway? He's a single man and you're an engaged girl.'

A quarrel hovered between them, they both decided to cool down and when they went downstairs they were on friendly terms.

As Tessa had hoped, Eve's cajoling ways worked their magic on Mr and Mrs Morland and the girls were given permission to accept engagements for Monday and Tuesday nights.

'It's still rather tiresome that they won't let you sing full-time,' complained Eve as Tessa walked her back down the lane to her car. Tessa was remembering that Josh had driven his to the door regardless of the potholes and that pleased her. 'I don't blame Mum and Dad for wanting me to keep a safe job.'

'It doesn't sound all that safe lately.'

'No. Have you seen much of that nasty dance band leader, Cliff Carter?'

Eve stopped walking. 'What exactly does that mean?'

Tessa felt a secret pleasure that she had for once dug under Eve's skin. It made a nice change.

'Nothing,' she said nonchalantly. 'A girl I know said she saw you out together.'

'I was asking him for engagements for us.'

They walked on. 'Do you know Josh Raven?' asked Tessa.

'His band is good, isn't it? And he's a swell-looking guy.'

'It sounds funny to call a man a guy.'

'Does it? Did you know that Josh was born in America? Yes, you must have known by his accent. His parents were angry because he insisted on starting a band. They thought it very down-grade so he came to England out of their way. They were rich, but his father invested everything in the American Stock Market. When it crashed his father jumped out of a sky-scraper.'

'Oh, no! That's dreadful. Dreadful!'

'He wasn't the only one. Personally I think it was cowardly of men to kill themselves and leave their wives and families to cope. Josh's mother died soon after. Apparently she couldn't manage at all. It's not easy to go straight from wealth to poverty and women like her have never done a hand's turn in their lives.'

'I dare say the poor men were out of their minds with worry. That's why people commit suicide. The balance of their mind is disturbed.'

'My father would never do a thing like that. He's too brave.'

Tessa was astonished. There was a ring of loving pride in Eve's voice. It was bewildering. She refused to go back to the States and hadn't seen him for ages, yet she quite clearly admired and loved him. Questions raced around Tessa's mind, but something warned her not to ask them.

As Eve drove away and Tessa walked slowly back up the lane she thought about her own father. His pride was dented, but the idea of him taking his own life had never occurred to her.

On Monday morning Eve woke in an odd mood. She wanted Jack's money, yet craved to be free. Would he prove a good lover? It might make up for anything he lacked. She decided it was time to find out.

That evening she drove to Brislington and turned into the drive leading to Jack's house. The door was opened by the butler.

He smiled at her. 'Miss Eve.'

'Is Mr Jack at home?'

'Yes, indeed. Will you wait in the drawing room. There's a good fire.'

'Thanks. Are Mr and Mrs Padbury at home?'

'No, miss.'

Eve was thankful. Jack's parents strongly disapproved of her and allowed it to show. She poured herself a stiff whisky and added a little soda. She drank it fast and it added its fire to the devilment that was in her mind.

Jack hurried in. 'Darling! What a marvellous surprise.'

'What were you doing?'

'Reading, or rather trying to. Your face kept coming between me and the book.'

'What are you reading?' Eve sounded bored. She *was* bored. She didn't give a damn what he was reading, but having brought herself to a certain point she was now nervous.

'I've got E. M. Delafield's new book, *Turn Back the Leaves*. I don't care for it as much as her others. It—' Jack stopped as Eve sank into a chair by the fire and held out her glass.

'More.'

'What are you drinking? Whisky? Strong stuff for a little girl.'

She kept her tongue between her teeth. She loathed it when he called her 'little girl'. It was so bloody patronising. If he considered the matter at all he would say it was meant to be protective.

'Did you go to the Morlands' service?' Jack asked.

Eve resented the suggestion of amusement in his voice. 'I did.'

'I hope you feel better for it.'

'It's difficult to tell. I feel better for having seen them, especially Tessa. Jack, I've made up my mind about something.'

He handed her the whisky. His eyes brightened. 'Oh. What's that?'

Eve knew full well that he had jumped to the conclusion that she had decided to get married. She seemed disinclined to answer and after a few moments he asked, 'How are the Morlands?'

'Well, but worried. Cousin Walter has been put on short time.'

'What?'

'Short time. Fewer hours of work. He's a carpenter, paid by the hour.'

'I see.' Eve seemed to be expecting more so he said, 'Are they short of money?'

'What do you think?'

Jack flushed at her sarcastic tone. 'I think they probably are. Is that why Tessa has begun singing without you?'

'Oh, you noticed.'

'I'm not entirely unobservant, you know.'

'Of course you're not.' Eve felt quite drunk and put down her empty glass on the table with a bang.

Jack picked it up hastily and examined the table for marks.

'For God's sake, Jack!'

'One of the maids could get fired for damaging an antique.'

'Have I damaged it? Are you going to fire me?'

'Must we argue?'

Eve stood up unsteadily. 'Of course not, darling, that was the last thing on my mind when I came here. The first thing was this.' She put her arms round him. Surprise held him still for a second or two then he pulled her close. He bent his head and she put her lips to his, gently at first, then her mouth opened and her tongue slid out and caressed his lips before she slipped it into his mouth.

He broke away. 'Eve! For heaven's sake!'

'Don't you like that?'

'Of course I do. But, darling girl, you can't possibly know what that does to a man.'

'Oh dear.' Eve looked down at the carpet.

'Where did you learn such a trick?' he asked gently.

She said. 'There are books about it. I read one or two.'

'I've never read a book like that.'

'You talk too much.' Eve held him so tight that her breasts strained against him. 'Kiss me again,' she breathed.

He hesitated. His cheeks were flushed, his eyes dark with desire. 'Kiss me,' she ordered.

This time when she caressed him with her tongue he didn't try to stop her. She felt him hardening against her thighs. He was easy to arouse, as easy as any other man. She could almost admire him for his past restraint.

'Eve,' he said. 'Eve, my love, my darling. Let's get married soon. Please.'

'Maybe.' She kissed him and touched him and stroked him with all the finesse of which she was capable.

'We've got to stop this,' he gasped. 'You don't realise—'

'What?' She held her eyes wide open.

'You make me want to do more than kiss you.'

'Do I, darling? Do I? What time will your parents be back?'

'What?'

'Your parents. When will they return?'

'Very late.'

'Can we get to your room discreetly?'

'Eve—'

'Well, can we?'

'I'm going to take you home. Right now.'

She refused to release him, holding him against her, moving gently upon him. 'I don't want to leave you, darling. Please don't make me.'

Jack stared down at her. She knew she was giving conflicting signals, behaving one moment like a shy virgin, the next like a tart, and Jack couldn't make sense of her. 'I shall take you home,' he said, but there was less conviction in his voice.

'No, please,' she murmured. 'I can't bear to go.'

She looked up at him briefly and saw with satisfaction his inner turmoil reflected in his eyes. 'Let's get to know one another properly, Jack. After all, we're going to be married.'

'I suppose there would be no harm in getting closer,' he said, as if to himself. 'A cuddle, that's all.'

She wondered what he considered a cuddle.

'So we'll go up to your room? We've never really been alone together, have we?'

'Upstairs, then,' he murmured and led her by the hand to his bedroom.

Jack's bedroom was obtrusively masculine. 'A real man lives here,' she murmured huskily.

'God knows why I brought you here,' he said. 'This is all wrong.'

'How can anything be wrong between an engaged couple? We're practically married.'

He locked the doors leading to his dressing room and the corridor and pulled her to him. His mouth on hers was hot and demanding and aroused Eve. Maybe after all he would prove a good lover. He stroked her body through her clothes which she found devastatingly frustrating. Then his hand slid easily into her white lace teddy and she gasped. There had to be more now.

Her reaction triggered Jack off. He lost his gentlemanly calm. Without finesse he removed her clothes and his eyes devoured her nakedness with intense concentration. 'Beautiful,' he said. 'And mine.'

She had begun this in a spirit of recklessness and had raised her own desire to a high pitch of intensity. She watched through lowered lids as he removed his clothes, pretending not to see him, as if she was too bashful to stare.

He came to her and she held out her arms, savouring the moment, looking forward to the pleasure of his caresses, revelling in the way she would drive him to madness before she allowed him to enter her. Then he was lying on her, his weight pinning her down. He was in her before she was ready, his hips thrusting hard and fast. He reached his climax quickly, not satisfying her, and finished by jerking himself out of her and lying back, panting for breath. She lay there, quivering with frustration. 'What about me?' she gasped. 'For God's sake, what about me?'

246

'You!' Jack raised himself on his elbow and stared down at her, his face filled with anger. 'You? You want more? I'm not the first with you, am I?'

'No, damn it, no!' she yelled.

'I expected to marry a girl who was a virgin. Unsullied . . .'

Eve leapt out of bed and began to dress. 'Did you indeed! How unsullied? In what way?' She dragged on her stockings, laddering them in her haste. 'If I had been unsullied before I certainly wouldn't be now!'

'You seduced me.'

'You bloody prig!'

'I thought you did everything in innocence.'

He ran his hands through his hair making it spiky and that, his white nakedness and the unfulfilled state in which he had left her, made Eve begin to laugh hysterically. She couldn't stop. She laughed with tears raining down her face, more and more of them, tears of fury and frustration. She tried to put her blouse on back to front and laughed more. Through the haze of whisky and tears she saw the anger building in Jack. He got off the bed and looked as if he might strike her. She slipped on her shoes. 'Goodbye,' she said breathlessly. 'I'll be going now.'

Her laughter echoed down the corridor, the stairs and the large empty hall. As she closed the front door behind her she saw the startled face of the butler. She climbed into her car. It wouldn't start and her tears died and she felt cold and empty. The engine fired on the third try and she drove home, her hands tight on the steering wheel. She had left her gloves somewhere and her fingers were white with pressure and cold and her engagement ring stood out and flashed fire in the street lamps.

'You've finished with Jack?' Tessa was startled. Eve had a feverish look. 'Did you quarrel?'

'Sort of.'

Tessa decided to let the matter drop. Eve was still wearing her ring so she assumed it was only a lovers' tiff. Josh had sent a message that morning to ask if the Kissing Cousins could sing with the band tonight. Tessa had sent back an enthusiastic 'yes' and had been on the point of going out to telephone Eve.

'Come into the house,' she said. 'I'll make you a cup of tea.'

'Could you make it coffee?'

'Of course.' Tessa spooned Camp Coffee into a cup. Eve watched as Tessa added water and milk to the thick liquid. It was very sweet and she disliked it but she drank it. It was hot and comforting. She had hardly slept the night before. What had driven her to do such a crazy thing with Jack? She had yielded to an urge which reason told her was stupid. Trust him to be so prissy, and his love-making was crude. He would end the engagement, or if he didn't she would.

She had lain down and fallen asleep and the dream began. She had tried to run from it. In her dream she was running from the terror but was captured easily, then gave her body eagerly only to wake with the familiar horror at seeing the face of her lover. Her father. It was obscene. And to make matters worse her frustration had spilled into her dream, and in her half-waking state she had reached sexual fulfilment which had made her feel dirty.

'Hadn't you better visit Jack and make up your quarrel?' suggested Tessa.

'No. We're finished.'

'Will you send his ring back?'

'Why?'

'You can't keep your engagement ring unless you intend to marry him.'

Eve held out her hand and twisted it, watching the brilliant sparkle. 'I shall keep it,' she said. 'He can afford it and I may need to sell it. I'm so damned hard-up. And I've earned it spending endless hours with him.'

'Won't he ask for it?'

'Probably not. He wouldn't consider it a gentlemanly thing to do.'

'You'll be glad we're singing tonight,' said Tessa. 'More money.'

'Where?'

'At a private function. Josh is sending a car and I suggested we pick you up from Padding House.'

'I'll go back and change later. May I stay a while? Will Cousin Lily mind?'

Tessa raised her brows at her cousin's little girl voice. 'You don't fool me, Eve, so don't bother trying.'

'All right, I won't. You are a cow, Tessa.'

'Because I see through your tricks?'

'No, because you tell me you do.'

'Well, that's honest.'

'If we're honest with each other we'll get along fine.'

'I hope you're right.'

When Eve left she bent and kissed Mrs Morland. 'You're so sweet,' she said and for a moment looked as if she might cry.

Josh sent a car to Tessa's house at the exact time he had promised. Mum gazed at the closed black vehicle which awaited her. 'Now that's what I call a respectable car. Not like Eve's. Off you go. Don't forget you've to be home no later than twelve.'

The dance was held in a country house a half hour's drive from Kingswood. The place was ablaze with light and the sounds of the band floated through the night. Tessa felt the familiar tightening of her stomach as her eagerness to perform warred with her nervousness.

The girls touched up their make-up in a small downstairs room. Tessa had on the frock she had worn for the Talbots' dance. Eve wore yellow chiffon and looked exquisite, though she remarked angrily that her dress was over a year old. Tessa ignored the grumbles. She felt she was beginning to get Eve's measure.

Neither girl knew the family they entertained so there were no invitations to join the dancers or to eat with the guests. Indeed, they were relegated to the back room with the band when they stopped for refreshments during the supper interval. Eve forgot her annoyance under Josh's soothing influence. He was a gentleman who had been educated at the right schools and actually done the New York and the London season. Tessa watched dispassionately as her cousin set out to captivate him. As far as she could tell, Josh was amused by Eve's advances. Tessa's equilibrium was more sorely tested when Paul arrived late at the dance. She saw him at once. It was as if there were some kind of electric signal which told her when he entered a room.

The Kissing Cousins began their next number. 'I may be wrong but I think you're wonderful . . .' Tessa directed her words to Paul. Not that he would know, or care. He seemed to have forgotten the joyous days they had spent in France and she wished she could forget them too. Eve managed to indicate by an occasional glance at the band leader that she was singing to him. Josh was definitely amused.

They followed with, 'I must have that man . . . maybe he's cooled off or maybe I'm crossed off his list.' Their voices blended well which was amazing considering they had only been able to rehearse for an hour and that without the band.

Their last song of the night was 'Broadway Melody'. Then the Kissing Cousins were finished in time for Tessa to be home by twelve.

Eve sat back in the luxury of the car. 'This is how a star should live.'

'A star?' jeered Tessa. 'You can't call yourself a star.'

'I know,' said Eve impatiently. 'But one day I will be. I'll have men lining up just for a kiss.'

'Is that your ambition?'

'That plus a few other things, like money and clothes and jewels.'

'Anything else?'

'Sure. Houses, cars, servants, a swimming pool in the backyard.'

'Modest, aren't you?'

'No, and why should I be? There's money in entertainment for those who can grab it.'

'Why did you throw Jack over? He's nice and he's crazy about you. And he's rich.'

'I know. My parents will be so mad when I write and

tell them it's off.' She spoke dreamily and began to sing. 'Don't bring a frown to old Broadway . . . You've got to clown on Broadway . . . Broadway always wears a smile . . .' She turned to Tessa. 'That's true. I've always loved the Broadway shows. One day I'll be up on a stage wowing the audience.'

'I'm happy for you. Where will I be?'

'I don't know. Maybe you'll sing with me, but if you can't I'll go solo.'

'Then you'll have all the money.'

Eve grinned. 'Yes, and I should like to have famous people at my feet.'

'Knowing you, you'd probably step on them,' said Tessa.

Eve laughed. 'Talking of money,' she said, 'where's my share of tonight's? Did he pay you?'

'Of course. He gives me an envelope during the supper break.'

'Different from Cliff. That swine made us wait. How much do I get?'

'Half. That's ten shillings each.'

'Is that all?'

'If we make ten shillings three times a week we shall have three-quarters of your allowance.'

'That's true. But I want more.'

'You always want more.' Tessa was tired and suddenly irritated and it showed. Eve went into a sulk.

Just before they reached the cottage she said, 'I suppose you're peeved because Paul ignored you.'

'He did not.'

'He only waved at you.'

'Goodnight,' said Tessa and slammed the car door, a reaction she immediately regretted. Her family had done nothing to deserve being awakened from their sleep. It was also a wasted gesture because then she had to open the door again to tell Eve that Josh expected them to rehearse with the band on the afternoon before their next engagement.

The Kissing Cousins always had work, sometimes with

251

Josh, sometimes with other bands. Their act was good and kept up to scratch by Tessa's insistence on regular rehearsals and her determination to reach as high a standard as possible.

One night they turned up at a dance to find that Cliff Carter's band was playing in place of the one they'd expected.

'Why are you here?' demanded Tessa.

Cliff grinned. 'The other blokes have been hit by flu. Over half the band has gone down with it.'

During the interval, when the entertainers took refreshments in a side room, Cliff watched Eve leave for the cloakroom. Tessa got up to follow her and he caught at her arm. 'Wait a minute, kid.'

'Let me go!'

'I've got a proposition.'

'I'm not interested.'

'You might be if you'd listen.'

Tessa glanced at her watch. 'Make it quick. The interval's nearly over.'

'I'll leave time for your titivating, never fear, though you don't need much. You're real pretty, Tessa. All right, I'll get on with it. You could earn as much as you both do singing on your own.'

Tessa tried to free herself. 'I'm not interested,' she said again.

'You might be if you thought about it. Times are hard and getting worse. You're the one with the good voice. Eve's nothing up to you.'

'I'll trouble you to let go of me.'

'OK! If you don't want to be told.'

'I don't.' Tessa hurried after her cousin and stood at the mirror to touch up her make-up. Her hand was shaking so much she had to remove her lipstick and begin again. Cliff Carter gave her the shudders.

She outlined her mouth. Her complexion was clear now except for the odd spot at certain times of the month, but they no longer bothered her. She had soon discovered how to use stage make-up to conceal imperfections. She was learning also how to pick her way through the social niceties of behaviour, accepting invitations to join guests, feeling no resentment when treated with indifference. And she knew, deep down, that come what may, she meant to be a full-time professional entertainer.

Sometimes she went to a music hall, always a matinee so that her parents wouldn't know. She hated deceiving them again, but they went their way and she must go hers. She bought the best seat she could afford at the time, usually in the gallery, and sat enthralled by the acts. Once, Eve accompanied her and complained so bitterly about not being in the stalls or a box that Tessa decided not to ask her again. Eve didn't mind. She was going out quite often with Charles Ware.

'He's a great guy,' she said, 'and so skilful at everything he does.'

Tessa was able these days to pick up correctly the not-so-subtle inflections in Eve's voice and assumed she was having another affair. She wondered if the Kissing Cousins would survive. Eve's ambition seemed ephemeral and Cliff Carter wasn't the only one to suggest that Tessa should branch out on her own. Then Eve would say something, or get an expression on her face which saddened Tessa who would have comforted her if she had known how. Once when a sharp frost turned everything crisply white and made ice rinks of the road Eve had stayed with the Morlands and Tessa had been awakened by her anguished moans. She had shaken her out of her nightmare and held her close until she stopped trembling. They had spent the rest of the night in Tessa's bed, cuddled together, but Eve refused to describe the dream which upset her so badly.

# Chapter Twelve

The number of people out of work increased daily. In 1931 a National Government consisting of all three political parties, Conservative, Labour and Liberal, was formed to try to deal with the increasing financial depression. Unemployment benefit was cut and at the shop Tessa saw the effect on the women. Many who had made sacrifices to pay their grocery bill regularly were in debt. Others, tightlipped and angry, bought smaller quantities of cheaper food and watched their children's health deteriorate.

All the same, it was a shock to her when she arrived home one Thursday evening and opened the door to find no tempting smells of cooking wafting out. Dad sat at the kitchen table and Mum, white-faced, was offering him a cup of tea and talking to him in soft, soothing tones.

Mrs Morland turned at her entrance. 'Good, you're home.'

'What's up? Is Dad ill?'

'I wish it was only that,' he muttered.

'Now, then, Walter, that won't get us anywhere. We have to think. We must keep our spirits up and trust in the Lord.'

'I do trust in the Lord,' said Dad angrily, before he lapsed back into gloom, muttering, 'I've always been a good-living Christian. What have I done to deserve this?'

Tessa hated to hear him sound so defeated, so bitter. 'Will someone please tell me what's happened?'

'He's lost his job,' said Mum flatly.

'Dad? But he can't have! He's the best workman they've got.'

'I'm the last to go,' he said. 'The firm's been going downhill for a long while. Today the boss told me there's only enough work for him and his son. I've seen it coming, but I kept hoping . . .'

Mum poured Tessa a cup of tea. 'Here, drink this. It's supposed to help shock.'

Dad gave a bitter laugh. 'It won't help me. It won't stop the shame of having to beg for money.'

'What do you mean, beg?' asked Tessa.

Her father didn't reply and her mother said, 'Unemployment benefit. The dole.'

'But, Dad, you've paid the insurance to get it. It's only what they owe you. It's not begging.'

'I've never taken a penny I didn't earn. I won't do it. I won't sign on.'

Tessa began to protest again, but Mum shook her head. 'I'm just going out to get a lettuce for tea. Come and give me a hand, Tessa. We need radishes and onions too.'

The day was sunny and dry, a rarity in this wet year. Outside in the garden the vegetable beds with their ranks of plants, as strictly lined up as guardsmen, promised future nourishment.

'Look at that,' said Mum, her voice wavering slightly. 'Dad does everything well. He uses markers and string to plant seeds properly. He's a good man, Tessa.'

'I know that, Mum.'

'But in some ways he's not strong.'

'Do you mean he's ill?'

'No, not ill, just that he needs someone to boost him when he gets down in the dumps. I put it down to the blood he got from his posh relatives. They've never been used to hard toil.'

Tessa thought, The same blood is in me and I won't give up, not ever.

'He's not weak,' continued Mum, 'don't take me wrong, but his nerves are a bit on the delicate side.' She cut off a lettuce head, then straightened her back. 'We shall have to work hard to help him keep his pride.'

'What will you do if he won't sign on the dole?'

'He will. He knows he will, but he has to make a protest.'

Tessa pulled a few radishes, bright red and juicy, while Mum dug up an onion.

'He'll be all right in the end, won't he, Mum?'

She was silent for a while. 'I expect so, but I've been worried for ages.'

'You knew he might lose his job?'

'I knew the orders weren't coming in and that people owe his boss a lot of money.'

'Can't he get it from them?'

'They've run out of money themselves. And small businesses he's contracted to have failed. It's a terrible chain and Dad's entangled in it.'

Tessa felt disgusted with herself. Her life had been so full she had scarcely looked at her parents. Now she saw that Mum looked careworn and there were tiny lines round her eyes. 'I can help,' she said eagerly.

'I know, love, and you do. You don't keep much back for yourself and you work hard. I'm proud of you.'

'Even of my singing with bands?'

Mum smiled. 'Even that, now I've got used to it. In fact, I don't mind telling you I get quite a thrill when I see the Kissing Cousins advertised.'

Impetuously, Tessa kissed her mother who looked pleased but said, 'Get along with you. I'm going to lay tea. Fetch Joey and Susan, will you? They're down in the field fishing in the old pond.'

Tessa lingered. 'Mum, you've still got the money Great-grandmother left you. That should help for a while.'

Mum stopped. 'There's something I haven't told anyone. Yesterday the landlord came round. You know he usually sends an agent and when I saw him it gave me a nasty turn.'

'But he's a nice man. You've always said so.'

'That's why he came himself. He's in financial trouble and is selling off his rented property.'

'What happens if you can't buy?'

'Eviction!'

'No, he couldn't!' Tessa remembered the Millers who had lived in Kingswood. Only last week she had seen them, poor and uneducated, the father unemployed for two years, turned out for not paying their rent. They stood on the pavement, a small group of desperate human beings with pitifully few possessions. They had been surrounded by neighbours, a few jeering, mostly sympathising, some recognising the possibility of finding themselves in the same humiliating, terrifying position.

'I tell you, Tessa, at first I couldn't think straight, but when he'd gone I remembered Great-grandmother Brook's money. We can use it to buy our home.'

'Will it be enough?'

'It will. I went to see the landlord this morning. He's asking a hundred pounds. It would be worth more empty, but we've been here since we got married and as sitting tenants he says we can buy cheaper. We get the freehold of the land as well. It's a fair bargain. When all the bills are paid, solicitors and people like that, there will still be some left. Dad might even go into business for himself.'

Tessa walked along the lane to call the children, not noticing for once the sweetness of the flower-filled hedges. She could think only of Dad. To make a living in the construction industry he would need transport, ladders, paint brushes, all the paraphernalia of a repair man, and if his boss couldn't make a go of it what chance had Dad? He would be kind where he should be firm. He'd let people off debts because they were poor.

She saw her brother and sister before they saw her. They were both muddy and wet. 'Catch anything?' she asked.

Joey grinned. 'Fish weren't biting.' He held up a jam jar filled with moss and water weed. 'Snails.'

'Tip them out,' she said. 'You know Mum won't have them in the house. And you as well, Susan.'

Her sister giggled and obeyed.

She hurried the children home, washed their hands and faces under the garden tap and cleaned their clothes with a brush she found in Dad's shed.

'Why can't we go inside and get ready for tea?' demanded Joey.

'Because, my dear little brother, Mum isn't herself and I don't want her to see the state you're in.'

'Who is she if she's not herself?' asked Joey cheekily.

'Less of your sauce.'

'Dad's been grumpy for ages,' said Susan.

'And Mum smacked me yesterday for nothing,' said Joey.

'I doubt it was for nothing,' said Tessa drily. 'Come on, you look presentable. Just.'

'Dad's lost his job,' said Joey.

'How do you know?'

'I overheard him telling Mum.'

'You shouldn't listen at keyholes.'

'I wasn't, was I, Susan? She heard too. We were looking for caterpillars and the window was open.'

'You should have let them know you were there.'

'We couldn't,' said Joey. 'They were too unhappy.'

The children's faces fell when they saw the bowl of salad. Even on hot days they wanted stew and dumplings or something equally substantial, but they were subdued by the atmosphere and ate their share with a good helping of potatoes. The afters made up for the salad. Bread and butter pudding, rich with eggs and milk and currants.

Eve turned up on the following Sunday and was welcomed with the usual pleasure. She had sold her engagement ring. With the proceeds plus earnings and her allowance she kept her car on the road. She saw it as existing at subsistence level and was lugubrious. Nothing the Morlands said seemed to cheer her. She attended chapel with them and from the choir Tessa could see her during the sermon, consulting her watch every few minutes.

Frank walked home with them. His presence at Sunday supper had become routine. So had his proposals of marriage. Tessa had told him repeatedly that she intended to remain single for years, but he was convinced that he could persuade her to change her mind.

'You'll soon feel the need for settling down in your own home with your children about you,' he said confidently. His brown eyes, wide open like a child's, gave him an air of vulnerability which, instead of enlisting her sympathy, irritated her. He was handsome, though. Paul wasn't really good-looking at all.

'Does he have to come?' whispered Eve to Tessa.

'It looks like it.'

'He's a nice-looking guy. He's quite big too.' For a moment Eve sounded lively, then she settled back into gloom.

After supper she said quietly, 'I must talk to you, Tessa.'

Tessa led the way upstairs feeling apprehensive. Their singing career was going well. They performed mostly with Josh Raven whose popularity was growing along with the Kissing Cousins'. Eve's voice was still the weaker of the two, but her high soprano made a pleasing contrast to Tessa's lower-toned mezzo-soprano.

She could be sweet and Tessa made allowances for her swings of mood. There were times when she seemed to be driven by some dark, inner force. In the bedroom it was hot and Tessa opened the window and breathed in a lungful of air. 'When the rain stops it's warm.'

'It's been a ghastly summer so far,' said Eve. 'God, I wish someone had invited me to go on holiday.'

'You'd have gone?'

'Wouldn't you? If Kitty had sent us both an invitation you would have accepted like a shot.'

'Not if it meant letting Josh down.'

Eve was annoyed. 'You're so damn goody-goody.'

'I'm not. I just keep my word.'

'And I don't?'

'Eve,' said Tessa gently, 'what's up?'

'Oh, everything! I've got to leave Paul's house. That means I'll have to live in digs, or go back to the States and live at home. It's a ghastly prospect. I can't afford a decent apartment.'

Tessa hid her dismay. 'Your parents would be glad to see you.'

'And that would suit you fine, wouldn't it? You could take a solo spot and make good on your own. At least, you think you could.'

'Don't judge me by yourself!' Tessa snapped.

'What's that supposed to mean?' The fire went out of Eve again. 'Oh, hell, I'm sorry. My parents wouldn't care tuppence if they never saw me again.'

'I can't believe that.'

'Well, you should. They never wanted me to be born and they haven't forgiven me for jilting Jack.'

Tessa had often wondered why she had, but had never asked and Eve had kept silent.

'Are you sorry you did?'

Eve sighed. 'He's boring.'

'Lately he's got much more lively.'

This had not been lost on Eve. It was as if, released from bondage to her, he had become another person.

'Would you marry him if he asked you now?'

'Why are we talking about him?' said Eve. 'It's past and done with. I have to deal with the present.'

'Of course. I can't understand Paul turning you out, though. Is he going to sell the house?'

'On the contrary, he's going to live in it. With his blushing bride, Andrea.'

Tessa saw the blow coming too late to deflect the anguish it caused her. She leaned out of the window pretending to look into the garden, but she saw nothing.

Eve was still speaking and Tessa realised she hadn't heard a word for several minutes.

Eve realised it too. 'For goodness' sake! What's so fascinating about the garden?' Tessa turned and Eve said, 'You can't still be hankering after Paul? After all this time? He's scarcely given you the time of day for

261

ages. My God, you're still in love with him!'

'I'm not! It's the heat. It makes me feel quite sick at times and this room is so small.' The words had been formed somewhere even though Tessa had felt incapable of putting together a coherent sentence.

Eve said, 'I may as well go.'

Tessa didn't try to stop her and heard her tapping down the stairs, heard her goodbyes, the sound of the Alvis starting up, then dying away into the distance. She sat on her bed, staring into space. She thought she had destroyed her dream of love for Paul, but she hadn't. It had been there all the time, waiting to crush her with this weight of sorrow.

The Morlands didn't see Eve for some time after that, though she turned up for the Kissing Cousins' engagements. Tessa's questions were parried.

Finally, she handed Tessa a card. 'That's where I live now. It doesn't have a telephone which is inconvenient. People will have to send telegrams if I'm wanted in a hurry and they won't bother and I shall miss everything.'

Tessa was irritated by her self-pity. 'Surely they can send invitations through the ordinary post? Other people manage.'

The address was a respectable one in Clifton. 'Have you found lodgings with a friend?'

'No. I've got a room in an old house that's come down in the world. It's a boarding house now. I have to share a bathroom with another girl who has no manners.'

'Why? What does she do?'

'I forgot I wasn't in Padding House and left a tiny rim round the bath. I bathe every day, twice sometimes, and it wasn't much of a rim, but she yelled at me. She called me a slut. The impudence!'

'I'm sorry. You could come here, you know. We'd make room for you.'

Eve frowned ferociously and Tessa waited for a sharp retort which didn't come. 'I know,' said Eve, and her voice was an odd mixture of anger and regret. 'I know.'

'It's not too late. You can still move in.'

'No. I'm sorry, Tessa, I simply couldn't bear to live in such a tiny cottage with no bathroom and an outside lavatory, so squashed in with other people, no matter how fond I am of them. And now your father's at home so much, I just wouldn't be comfortable.'

Mr Morland had obtained only one small job of papering a room. After that, nothing. Fortunately he had invested only in a hand cart and ladder. He signed on at the Labour Exchange, and was in receipt of the dole, a sum far lower than his former wages and payable for only twenty-six weeks. If he failed to take a job offered, any job, the money would be withdrawn for six weeks. Mrs Morland performed miracles of managing and never failed to display complete loyalty to and admiration for her husband.

Then Mr Grice called Tessa into the parlour and told her sadly that they had to dispense with her services altogether. 'The shop's barely making a living for us,' he said. 'I'm really sorry, Tessa.'

Mum received the news with resignation. 'I knew it would happen. The shop's always half empty and there isn't half the amount of stuff on the shelves there used to be. Well, never mind, love, we'll manage. But I'm afraid it's the dole for you too.'

'Not while I can earn by singing,' said Tessa.

'That's true.' Mum was in a dilemma. She certainly didn't want another of her family to join the dole queue, yet deep down she still felt that singing with a band was not quite a nice way of earning a living. At present at the Bright Hour she could mention Tessa's popular singing with a smile of indulgence. 'Just a little hobby and she's helping out a cousin.' She said, 'I like Josh Raven, but I'd feel happier if he was married.'

'Mum!' Tessa kissed her mother's cheek. 'You'll never be any different, will you? To you, marriage is the most important thing in life.'

'Well, it is, isn't it? That's what we were put on earth

for, to marry and have children. It says so in the bible. And I think it makes a person look respectable. A married man would be fatherly to you.'

On the Saturday on which Tessa left the shop for good, Mrs Grice handed her a large bag of groceries. 'A parting gift, Tessa. I wish you could have stayed.'

Mum greeted the appearance of the groceries with indignation. 'We're not paupers!'

'She knows that, Mum, it was just the kindness of a friend. Don't be cross.'

Mrs Morland glowered for a moment longer before admitting, 'No, she's not a bad sort.'

Tessa stood the cans and packages on the pantry shelf where they remained for weeks before Mum could bring herself to open them.

Her dismissal sent Dad into a rage. He stamped out and went straight to the Labour Exchange where he was offered work as a casual labourer on a building site, work so filthy that the regularly employed men refused to tackle it. He spent days up to his knees in mud digging out a foundation and ruined his trousers and boots. The work was far too strenuous for him, but he didn't grumble, which made it worse for those who loved him. He gave up only when a sharp attack of bronchitis laid him low. Then it was back on the dole.

Tessa vowed that somehow she would make a success on the stage. Somehow, she would earn enough to relieve her family's distress.

Josh Raven looked particularly handsome one night.

'He's practically incandescent,' said Eve. 'I wonder what's happened?'

They discovered in the interval. 'I've got an offer to play in a London hotel, probably for six months,' he announced. 'And an invitation from the British Broadcasting Corporation for regular work.'

His words created a sensation.

'From Savoy Hill?' asked the drummer.

'Where else? And if we're successful the BBC will

record us from the hotel itself. We're going to be famous, boys.'

'Where do we come in?' demanded Eve.

'You'll come in with us, I hope. The money will be better and you'll get famous too. People will talk about the Kissing Cousins. Who knows, there might even be film work?'

'Don't lose your head, boy,' advised the pianist, Sammy Jacobs, a man older than the others who had been playing piano to any audience he could muster since he was twelve and turned professional at fourteen. 'Keep your feet on the ground.'

Josh grinned. 'I don't know if I can. I feel I'm flying!'

Eve glowed with happiness. As the girls freshened up in the cloakroom she said, 'We're sure to be famous, Tessa. Anyone who appears on the wireless gets famous.'

'You can't appear on wireless,' she said. She couldn't imagine Mum and Dad letting her go to London.

'Oh, you know what I mean. I wonder when we have to leave Bristol?'

Tessa fell silent. In Mum's eyes London was as sinful as America, even without Prohibition and gangsters.

'They will let you come, won't they?' asked Eve.

Tessa shrugged. 'Shouldn't think so.'

'But they must, they absolutely must! I can't go on as a duet on my own. Even your parents will realise that.'

'*Even* my parents?'

'Oh, stop being so annoying. You know I adore them but they aren't exactly sophisticated, are they?'

'No, they're not that,' agreed Tessa.

They returned to the stage where the band was settling down for the next stint. The idea of London was so unexpected, so thrilling, that Tessa could hardly keep her mind on the songs. She'd never be permitted to go.

'If I were you, I should do what you want, no matter what they say,' advised Eve. 'Good lord, you'll be twenty soon.'

'It's easy for you to talk. You're twenty-one and

nobody tries to stop you doing anything.'

'You think that makes me happy?' flashed Eve in one of her outbursts.

'Are you ready, girls?' Josh was waiting to begin and Eve and Tessa sat on the stage on two chairs and looked as decorative as possible, small smiles pinned to their faces. Eve was still angry and Tessa could feel it directed towards her. She sensed her pain and wished she knew what drove her cousin.

But they were professionals now and when their turn came they were ready, singing in a harmony they didn't feel. 'Embrace me, my sweet embraceable you; Embrace me, you irreplaceable you . . .' Tessa had to fight hard to go on. She had struggled to destroy her feelings for Paul, yet during rehearsals these words had tormented her. It was silly because the song hadn't even been heard until after the golden summer she had fallen in love with him.

'What in hell's up with you?' demanded Eve as they took their seats while the band swung into their version of 'Happy Feet'.

'Nothing.'

'You looked weepy at rehearsal. Is it that song?' Tessa remained silent and Eve probed further. 'Have you been seeing Paul lately? Did he hold you while it was played? Did he—?'

'Shut up!' snarled Tessa so loudly that Josh frowned at her.

The twelve o'clock curfew had been lifted. Mrs Morland, practical, resigned, had persuaded Dad. Tessa had no longer to get up early and she earned more money by staying. Josh promised to see that she arrived home safely. As she climbed into a taxi, leaving Eve to use another, she felt desperately tired, a weariness that had little to do with the late nights, and everything to do with emotional upheaval. 'Damn Paul!' she whispered. 'Damn him!'

'Did you speak, miss?' asked the driver.

'No, I was just going over a song.'

'I've heard you and the other girl. I took the missus dancing one night. You're better than her.'

'Eve is good. We harmonise well.'

'But you're better,' said the driver stubbornly and Tessa felt too tired to continue the conversation.

As Tessa had known, her request to accompany the band to London caused a tremendous upheaval in the family. 'No!' Mum said emphatically when the subject was first brought up.

'I won't have a job when the others leave,' pointed out Tessa. 'I'll have to sign on the dole.'

Mrs Morland said sadly, 'Better on the dole than exposed to temptations in London.'

'Don't you trust me?'

'Yes. It's other people I don't trust.'

Dad looked on. He hadn't spoken and it worried Tessa. He usually had firm opinions on important family matters.

'I promise not to do anything you couldn't watch,' said Tessa.

'You say that and you mean it, but it's easy to get led astray. Look at that time we went to the funeral. You drank wine. The very first time you were offered wine you broke the Pledge and drank it.'

'Fancy bringing that up now! I had to be polite, didn't I?'

'What if you're offered strong drink again? Will you take it?'

Tessa enjoyed cocktails and wine and cigarettes. 'I'll be very careful.'

'It isn't enough—'

'Let her go,' said Dad. They stared at him. 'Let her go. What is there for her here? The dole or some job she'll hate.'

Mum succumbed, though with an ill grace. By the time she had thought it over and resumed her battle stance it was too late. Josh had drawn up a contract and signed up the Kissing Cousins. As a minor-in-law she should have

267

got written permission from her parents, but almost without a twinge she gave her age as the same as Eve's. She was on her way to London, to sing on the wireless. She would be a star. She and Eve travelled up together and took a small flat as near Savoy Hill as they could get. 'It'll do for now,' said Eve, 'though there's not enough room to swing a cat.'

'I don't suppose we shall need to swing a cat,' said Tessa a little tetchily. She was tired, emotionally rather than physically.

At the last minute Mum had again voiced her doubts about London. The worst was when she said, 'What shall I do without you? There's Dad getting more and more miserable and Joey and Susan growing up. They need a lot of looking after and I have to do it all. And when they leave school they might not get jobs either the way the country is going.'

'All the more reason for my earning money, Mum. There'll be enough to send some home.'

'There's no need for that. You'll have to buy good clothes and I can manage.'

Eve had asked Paul if she might continue to garage her car with him. 'Of course you may,' he had said. 'I'll drive you to the station.'

'He thinks we shall be famous,' Eve told Tessa in the train. 'He's going to listen in.'

'Good,' said Tessa.

'I've got a copy of the *Radio Times*.' She turned over the pages rapidly, then frowned. 'It's got us down as the Kissing Cousins. Not a word about our real names.'

Tessa stared down at the closely printed page. 'It only mentions Josh's name.' She turned to gaze from the window.

'Paul said he'll bring Andrea to hear us. She'll be visiting London to buy something extra special for her going away outfit.'

Number Two, Savoy Hill turned out to be a building on the Embankment behind the Savoy Hotel. From outside it looked like an office with its friendly commissionaire sitting at a little desk in the hall. They were shown round by a big dinner-jacketed man with white hair and a large matching moustache who introduced himself as Colonel Brand.

Even Eve was awed by the actual studios. They were shrouded on every wall by draperies and curtains to deaden unwanted sound. Waiting for each broadcaster was a four-legged box on wheels which, explained the colonel, contained the microphone. On a side table surrounded by chairs was a notice which the girls read: 'If you cough or rustle your papers, you will deafen millions of listeners.'

'Millions?' breathed Tessa.

'Millions?' echoed Eve.

'Would that really happen?' asked Tessa in a whisper.

The colonel smiled. 'It isn't to be taken absolutely literally, but it makes us realise that all movement and extraneous sound must be muted.'

The colonel wheeled the microphone experimentally across the room. It emitted a loud squeak. 'We always test them,' he explained, 'because often we need to move them about. That one needs oiling before you go on the air.'

'Is this where we'll be?' asked Eve.

'It is, indeed.'

'How will the band fit in?' asked Eve. 'It's not a very big room.'

'It's proved big enough for some of the most famous bands,' said the colonel in a voice which made her laugh nervously.

'I'm sorry,' said Eve. 'I've never been here before. I didn't know.'

The colonel regarded her benevolently. She was looking particularly fetching today in a pale green frock and small matching hat with a feather. 'I quite understand. I can see that you young ladies have a proper respect for the medium of broadcasting.'

He looked at his watch and handed them over to a young man in a dark brown suit who escorted them to the front door.

'He must be terribly busy,' said Tessa.

'He works hard,' said the young man, 'but at the moment he's anxious to get back to his game of bridge. He always plays when he has nothing special to do. By the way, my name's Tony Hapgood. I'm a general dogsbody.'

Eve held out her hand. 'How do you do, Mr Hapgood. I'm Eve Brook and this is Tessa Morland.'

'Nice to meet you, and you can call me Tony. Everybody does.'

He left and the girls stood for a moment looking back at the building. 'Millions,' said Tessa again.

Josh Raven and his band, newly christened 'Josh Raven and His Melody Men', were in place in the studio, all in immaculate evening dress as insisted upon.

'Nobody will see us,' Tessa had said.

Josh said, 'Mr Reith – he's the overall boss – says everyone must wear evening dress at night and his word is law.'

So the girls sat in their flimsy gowns and in the end were thankful that they had worn something light. The only cooling system in the padded room were two fans which merely moved the air lazily. Sweat poured down the musicians' faces as they played. When it was time for the Kissing Cousins to sing they crept to the microphone, standing close together, remembering that they must sing in a muted way, not as if they were trying to send their voices over a chattering concourse on a dance floor. The chosen songs were decorous as befitted a programme which reached into homes where children might hear them. Mr Reith was rigid in his ideas of what was or was not suitable for home listening. 'Painting the Clouds with Sunshine' and 'With a Song in my Heart' were both innocuous. Tessa found it difficult to keep a check on her powerful voice, but she managed it and at the end of the broadcast the station manager congratulated everyone. 'You'll be hearing from us,' he promised.

The musicians were thankful to get out of the steaming room and moved silently along the corridors past other studios where entertainers were awaiting their turn. Outside, Eve and Tessa shivered, huddling into warm wraps.

As they prepared for bed Tessa said, smiling at the absurdity of the notion, 'It's a pity we can't hear ourselves on the wireless.'

Eve said, 'Josh said we might be able to make a gramophone record. We could hear ourselves then.'

'A gramophone record!' Tessa sat up in bed hugging her knees. 'I never dreamt that could happen to me. I could never have imagined all this.'

'Glad you came?'

'Oh, yes, though in the end Mum wasn't very happy about it.'

'I know. What about Cousin Walter?'

'Dad?' Tessa thought about him, about his defeated look and the way his shoulders had begun to hunch. 'I don't think he minds. I'm tired, Eve. I think I'll settle down. Goodnight.'

Eve climbed into her bed. 'It's no good ignoring facts, Tessa. I've seen Cousin Walter getting more and more disheartened.'

'If you know that, why ask?'

'I shall start looking for a place of my own tomorrow,' said Eve.

Tessa didn't answer. Eve wanted her own place because she had made a hit with Buzzy Lewis, one of the trumpeters in the band, having given up trying to ensnare Josh who had proved impervious to her charms. He seemed to like Tessa better.

She wouldn't mind having her room to herself and at her present wage of five pounds a week could well afford it and send some money home if she was careful. Eve, at close quarters, was a disturbing presence. She was candid about her enjoyment of men and sometimes mocked Tessa for her virgin purity. Tessa let her mockery slide over her. She wondered what would have happened if Paul . . . But she mustn't think of Paul. He would soon be married.

She enjoyed her new life which was so different. She

271

received a short letter from Mum. 'We heard you on the wireless last night. It was very funny to have your voice coming out of the horn. It cheered Dad up no end for a while. The hens aren't laying well. We are all well and hope you are.'

Tessa laughed and sent a cheerful answer enclosing a ten shilling note for which Mum thanked her in a dignified way, saying it would be spent on new shoes for the children.

Their work lay mostly in the great London hotels, in particular the Dorchester. Tessa's description of its size and grandeur brought dire warnings from Mum. 'Just do your job then go straight home. Don't forget you're a Christian girl and there are always people with wicked ways waiting to trap you.'

Tessa had no intention of being trapped by wicked ways, interesting though they sometimes appeared. This taste of life near the top was acting on her like a drug, one to which she was now totally addicted, and nothing and no one would get in the way of her progress as a singer. Maybe, one day, she would be a star in a musical play, just like Jessie Matthews whose singing and dancing were the sensation of London and who had performed in New York and been courted by Hollywood. They were making movie pictures in Britain, too.

Her dreams soared, then were brought back to earth with a crash as Josh had yet another row with Eve who could not, or would not, behave. Often they began rehearsals without her, Tessa singing solo, and more than one member of the band muttered that they preferred it that way.

The one band member who never complained was Buzzy Lewis. He was having the time of his life with Eve who was not only a willing but an enterprising lover. No one mentioned his wife and children back home in Manchester and Tessa was sure Eve wouldn't care if they did.

By day Tessa wandered round the great stores, marvelling at the beautiful clothes on sale, breathless at some of the prices and wondering at the way every expensive store and small exclusive shop simultaneously offered frocks with hems seven inches from the ground. How did they know simultaneously about the change in fashion? She found her way to art galleries, and above all visited theatres and cinemas whenever she could. At a talkie she saw 'The Smiling Lieutenant' and adored the broken English of Maurice Chevalier and the pert prettiness of Claudette Colbert, then was indignant at the way the critics ran the film down.

When she said as much to Josh, he laughed. 'Some of what they say is true. Oh, not because of Miss Colbert or Chevalier – they're really great – but the way Hollywood handled them. The producers will have to do a lot better than that.'

'Would you go to Hollywood?' asked Tessa.

'Yes, I would.'

'Even if you think they produce bad films there?'

'Some good ones have come out, and even if the band was in a bad film we should be noticed and that's important for a future in show business.'

'Do you think we'd have a future there?'

'You and Eve? Probably. If she ever learns to behave herself.'

Tessa coloured and Josh said, 'You are very fond of her, aren't you?'

'Yes, I am. She really is my cousin, you know, though not a first one. That's why we call ourselves the Kissing Cousins. Eve says it's an American term. But, of course, you'll know that.'

'Eve worries me sometimes.'

'I know,' said Tessa quickly. 'She'll be all right.'

Josh eyed her quizzically, then nodded. 'If you say so.'

Tess loved her family but was too buoyed up by excitement really to miss them. Nothing could spoil her joy in this new world. As long as she kept her commitment to Josh she was free. She read in bed for as long as she liked, and as well as books pored over the magazine *Melody Maker* and the stage newspaper *The Era*, revelling in the feeling that she was now part of this glamorous life; knowing that there wasn't a soul to disturb her till early the next morning. She bought an alarm clock so that she would always wake in good time for rehearsals.

Yet nothing came up to the intense thrill of singing for a living, and even an insight into the immense hard work and monumental disappointments that often made up the life of a performer didn't dampen her passion.

One morning when she answered the call for rehearsal she turned up at the large, rather draughty rehearsal rooms to discover that neither Eve nor Buzzy was there. Josh waited for twenty minutes, discussing what tonight's Dorchester Hotel programme was to be, until his good humour vanished.

'They'll both have to go,' he said, grim-faced.

'Perhaps they're ill?' begged Tessa. She disliked Buzzy though couldn't tell if her judgement was clouded by the knowledge that he was cheating on his family. Then he arrived pale and unshaven.

'You're bloody late and you look like death! Where's Eve?' demanded Josh.

'Isn't she here?' Buzzy sounded too casual and Tessa glared into his bloodshot eyes.

'Where is my cousin?'

He shrugged and Tessa, furious, lifted her hand to him. Josh leapt to her side and held her. 'Come on, love, that won't help.'

'Where's Eve?' she cried. 'She was with him, I know she was.'

Sammy Jacobs put a fatherly arm round her. 'You can't live your cousin's life for her.'

'I know, I know, but that slimy worm's done something, I know he has.'

Josh spoke to Buzzy in low tones and came over to the piano. 'It seems,' he said grimly, 'that Buzzy took a whole bottle of whisky to Eve's apartment last night and encouraged her to drink at least half of it. God knows why she did. She's too sick to come in, and from what he said, I do mean sick.'

Tessa jumped up. 'I must go to her! She'll need looking after. She's hopeless on her own. Oh, the rehearsal!'

Josh hesitated, then said, 'You're a real professional and you know the programme for tonight. Alcohol poisoning can be serious. You'd better go.'

Tessa was frightened. Mum had been right all along about the demon drink. It actually could poison you. She hailed a passing taxi.

Eve's room was unbelievably squalid and stank so heavily of whisky and vomit that Tessa gasped. The landlady who had shown her up and unlocked the door with her master key tried to peer past and Tessa moved forward quickly and shut the door behind her. Not before she heard the woman say, 'Bloody disgustin'. She'll have to go.'

Tessa kicked aside newspapers, magazines, discarded garments, even a plate of sandwiches growing mould, and walked to the bed. Eve, white-faced, looked up at her defiantly.

'If you've come here to preach . . .'

'I haven't.'

'Or to tell me I'm sacked . . .'

'Nor that. Josh let me come to you. This place stinks.'

'Nothing if not direct,' said Eve, then began to retch and heave and groan. Remembering what Josh had said about alcohol poisoning, Tessa said, 'I'm going to call a doctor.'

'I don't need a bloody doctor! I only drank too much. I'm better than I was. A lot better.'

'Well, I'll find a chemist. There must be something to help.'

'Bring some aspirin. I've got a filthy headache. Take the keys.' Eve sank back on to her soiled pillow, pointing to the cluttered mantel over a small fireplace filled with ash and half-smoked cigarettes. Tessa found the keys and went out.

On hearing her explanation the chemist looked disapproving at Tessa who remembered another of Mum's warnings: 'People who mix with sinners get tarred with the same brush.' Back in Eve's room she mixed the bicarbonate of soda, sugar and water he'd suggested and fed it to Eve in teaspoonfuls in between cleaning the room.

Eve groaned. 'Must you be so damned efficient?'

'Must you live in such a pig-sty? And I'm maligning pigs here!'

Eve managed a grin. She was still very white but had begun to feel better. Tessa collected a large cardboard box of rubbish. The box had contained bottles of wine and Tessa wondered how much of it had been drunk by Eve. She stacked the magazines and newspapers, swept and dusted. There was no polish. Eve's spasms of nausea gradually stopped and she was able to tolerate weak tea and a couple of aspirin. When she got up to stagger to the lavatory Tessa whipped off her soiled bed linen and made the bed up with sheets and pillow slips she found at the back of a tumbled cupboard.

'You're an angel,' said Eve as she crawled back into bed. 'An absolute angel.'

'I doubt if angels would feel as irritated with you as I am,' said Tessa.

'You have every right. What did Josh say? Did Buzzy turn up? He was very drunk when he left.'

'Josh is angry and, yes, Buzzy did turn up.'

'You don't like him . . .'

'Leave it. You'll feel ill again if you talk too much.'

'You're right not to like him. He knew how ill I was feeling and he left me, the bastard.'

'Does that mean you're finished with him?'

'Yes. Besides, the saxophonist is much better looking. I think he's got his eye on me.'

'Shut up,' said Tessa wearily. 'Try to sleep. I'll come back later to check on you.'

'Are you going to rehearsal?'

'It's too late now.'

'Will Josh be annoyed with you?'

'I don't think so.'

'He's a nice guy,' said Eve, and closed her eyes.

276

# Chapter Thirteen

Rose Brook read Eve's letter again, scrunched it up angrily, then smoothed it out. Ralph would have to read it or be told of his daughter's latest folly. She heard the distant ring of the doorbell then Belper announced: 'Mr and Mrs Jefferson,' and Rose greeted her sister and her husband without enthusiasm.

'We're here to make one last appeal,' said Reginald with forced jocularity. 'Please say that you and Ralph will come to Palm Springs with us?'

The Jeffersons were going on vacation later than usual because Betsy was still unwell and her doctor had wanted to keep an eye on her. She was feeling better now and for several days they had nagged at Rose to accompany them, with or without Ralph.

She held her temper in check and turned her cool gaze upon them. 'I've told you, I won't leave Ralph, and he refuses to leave New York, therefore it is not possible for me to come with you.'

Reginald's bombast was conquered quite easily but Betsy, used from childhood to her sister's ways, said, 'I happen to know that Ralph wants you to come with us.'

'How do you know any such thing?'

Betsy looked a little apprehensive. 'Darling, forgive me, but I approached him and asked. He said . . .'

'You had no right! Being my sister does not give you the right to scheme with my husband behind my back.'

Betsy subsided, close to tears, and Reginald sprang to her defence. 'What do you mean, scheme? Betsy did what she thought was right. She cares about you!'

His wife held out a restraining hand. 'I'm sorry if I've hurt you, Rose,' she stammered. 'It's true, I do care about you. Lately, since the collapse of Ralph's business, you look quite haggard at times.'

'How sweet of you to tell me.'

To forestall Reginald's indignant reply Betsy said quickly, 'I know that yours is not such a disaster as some have suffered – you still have your fortune – Ralph will find employment.'

Rose said, 'It's true that Ralph is looking around at present to find employment which suits him, but our financial position has nothing to do with you.'

Betsy's eyes filled with tears and Reginald said angrily, 'I know why he won't leave town! It's that damned secretary of his . . .' He did not see, or else disregarded, the danger signals from both women. 'Ex-secretary, I should say. What is she? A puff of wind, a skinny, undeveloped creature . . . positively ugly in my view. How he can . . .'

The atmosphere finally got to him and he stopped, appalled at what he had said.

Rose rang the bell. 'I'm sure you have appointments. No, Reginald, I will not hear another word.'

Betsy burst into sobs and when Belper made his appearance Rose sent him away quickly. 'Pull yourself together, Betsy. You demean us all when you give way to such emotion. In front of a servant, too.'

'I'm sorry, I really am. Reginald, you didn't mean what you said, did you? We never listen to rumour. Not really. Oh, damn, I don't know what to say!'

Rose stared for a moment at her sister. She was not as plump as formerly and had begun to show her age. She had always been a prey to her emotions, quixotically generous and loving without discrimination. 'You had better have something to drink,' she said.

'The doctor says no alcohol at present,' said Reginald, subdued.

Rose said coldly, 'I would not be so foolish as to offer her any. Betsy, my dear, do dry your eyes and I will send for tea.'

'Perhaps we should just return home,' said Reginald.

'No, dear.' Betsy was firm. 'I cannot leave Rose with such a cloud hanging between us.' She wiped her eyes and took out a powder compact. Her face was not quite dry and the powder clogged in small islands. But she drank tea and stayed until she felt calmer and the sisters embraced before she left. Rose even managed to endure a peck on the cheek from Reginald. He was ready to say more, to apologise further, but Betsy said she felt weak and wished to go immediately and he meekly obeyed.

When Ralph came home late that night his face was dark with fury. 'Your sister's bloody husband called me and said he had found employment for me!' he burst out.

Rose was seated in her own small drawing room working on her tapestry. The walls were hung with grey silk which held a tinge of mauve, the furniture was sparse and plain, the chief beauty being the Regency work stand which Paul had generously given her. She sat on a velvet-upholstered nursing chair so as to leave room for arm movement while sewing. The tapestry firescreen which she had designed was in muted shades. A radio and a phonograph, gifts from Betsy, stood side by side on a console table, seldom used. Rose considered the radio with its announcers constantly pounding out advertisements to be vulgar and preferred to hear music in a concert hall.

Ralph looked as if he'd had a particularly hard day. There were times when he seemed vulnerable and now Rose ached to comfort him, but she knew from humiliating experience that to make any such attempt would be to risk a cruel rebuff. Yet in the midst of her own pain she felt the spark of satisfaction that he was dependent on her.

He stood still for a moment and stared at her. She was wearing a dark blue sleeveless silk dress which emphasised her slender figure. Her fair hair was straight and shiny as a satin cap; her eyes, when she regarded him, a cool ice blue. For a moment he could say nothing as he realised that she and Irene were similar in build and in their choice of decor. The knowledge made him extremely uneasy.

'He had the impudence to offer you employment?' she said.

He had known she would be indignant on his behalf, yet perversely wanted to annoy her. 'He did it out of the goodness of his heart,' he said.

Rose lifted her thin brows but did not reply and that irritated him. He threw himself into the easy chair and looked around though the room never changed. He wondered idly where she kept the phonograph records.

'He is such a fool,' she said.

Ralph took out his cigarettes and offered her one. She refused but got up and placed a cut glass ashtray on a small table by his elbow. 'Yet he is not such a fool as I. He still has his fortune.'

Rose could not think of a reply which would not earn a rebuff. She picked up her sewing and tried to thread a needle, but her hands trembled and she relinquished the attempt.

'I must find employment of some kind,' said Ralph.

'There's no pressing need. My money covers all our expenses at present.'

'You don't need to remind me that I am now totally dependent on your charity.'

Rose managed to say calmly, 'I've never considered the money you once paid into my account as charity. Why should you feel that way now our positions are reversed? Anything I have has always been yours. You know that.'

He did know it. She had placed a reasonable allowance at his disposal and would never question the way he used it. Today he had bought Irene a pretty bracelet which had taken a large part of his monthly income. She had merely opened the box, smiled, said a polite thank you, and placed it in a drawer with others.

'Don't you like it, Irene?' he'd asked.

'It's very pretty. Now, let's have lunch. I've made poached salmon with capons to follow, just the way you like them.'

'You cooked lunch yourself?'

'You know I always do.'

'You could afford a maid.'

'We've been through this before,' she said. 'I have a cleaning woman and I enjoy cooking. It's creative.'

He had eaten a little of each dish and afterwards they had made love. For Ralph the first thrill of possessing her was fading, and although Irene still displayed intense enjoyment, he wondered if he was about to be cursed again with waning interest. Rose was holding out a sheet of crumpled paper. 'What is it?'

'A letter from Eve. I'm sorry, but I screwed it up, then had to unfold it. I thought of asking Grace to iron it, but did not wish her to read it.'

Ralph read it and swore. 'She intends to stay in England.'

'You should cut her allowance, then she would have to return. I wonder how much longer Elliot will wait. He's been dating other girls, but I believe she could still attract him.'

'Damn it!' Ralph crashed his fist into the palm of his hand. 'Damn the stupid little fool! Fortunes in her grasp and she lets them go. First Elliot and now Jack Padbury. Or maybe he tired of her. Maybe he got sick of being shoved around.'

'You don't know that Eve behaved badly towards him.'

'Rose, we're not children to be fooled by her. She treats everyone abominably, men especially. What is the attraction in England?'

Rose shrugged slightly. 'She mentions the Morlands.'

'Who?'

'Walter and Lily Morland. Those vulgar relatives of yours. They were invited to the funeral and got two hundred pounds as a legacy.'

'Oh, them. I can barely recall what they looked like. Surely you are mistaken? Eve would never mix with such people.'

'That's what I thought, but it seems that the daughter, Tessa, and Eve sing together on a regular basis.'

281

'Eve likes to sing.'

'I wonder you know that much about her,' said Rose with a rare flash of anger. 'From what Eve says it appears that they sing at dances.'

'For money?'

Rose turned aside from his frown. 'She doesn't say, but it wouldn't surprise me. The Morlands must be glad of every penny they can get and Eve's allowance is minute compared with what we gave her formerly.'

Ralph stubbed out his cigarette. 'Damn the girl! I refuse to quarrel about her. Get her back here and married off.'

Tessa was worried. Eve was discontented and growing more so every day. The saxophonist had amused her for a while, then that had fallen through and, to Eve's fury, the break had come from his side. She wasn't used to being dropped and the advent upon the scene of a girl from the musician's home town who had turned out to be his fiancée was an unpleasant surprise. The new arrival had taken one look at the Kissing Cousins and demanded that the wedding date be set early. The saxophonist had obliged and had then joined an orchestra which played permanently in their local hotel.

The loss of a good musician had annoyed Josh who had been forced to hold auditions when he should have been arranging music. The new man was older and not interested in women.

Tessa loved her new life and was terrified that Eve might spoil it for them both. Despite their differences she was growing fonder of her cousin. She was exasperating, thoughtless, infuriating, but Tessa couldn't help caring about her. She seemed to have no proper grasp on life, no yardstick by which to measure herself.

'I'm sick of singing with Josh and his merry men,' said Eve one night as she and Tessa ate supper in a small restaurant.

'Well, I'm not,' said Tessa, spearing a piece of fish. 'I think it's great and I love it.'

'You're so damned unsophisticated! I would have thought London might have put you wise to a few things.'

'It has. I really can earn a good living.'

'You've seen some of the stage shows. Wouldn't you like to be part of one of them?'

'Of course.'

'Well, then . . .'

'I'm not ready for that.'

'When will you be? We've had months with Josh and we still sing in the same places, almost the same songs.'

'Except on the wireless. We're a success there and we always have to have new material.'

'The wireless! No one can see us and no one even knows our names. I asked Josh if he could tell people who we were and he said if he did he'd have to name all the members of the band.'

'I know all this. Why are you telling me again?'

Eve flicked her fingers imperiously and a waiter wandered over and took her order for more coffee. 'What a ghastly place this is,' she said, watching his slow progress.

'You didn't think so at first. You were as pleased as I was at finding somewhere that stayed open almost all night with prices we could afford.'

'I used to eat at the Savoy or the Café de Paris. The waiters there just added more tables and chairs as people arrived.' Eve smiled reminiscently. 'Of course it's impossible to do dances like the charleston without space and sometimes the dancing area grew so small that one almost landed in a chocolate mousse or a plate of soup. And there was always a cabaret. Comedians and singers and others.'

'Shall I get up and sing for you here? We could have a small dance if you like. There are a couple of gents over there who've been eyeing us.'

The two men were shabby and down-at-heel and Eve scowled. 'Go on, make fun of me.'

'Somebody has to keep your feet on the ground.'

She lit a cigarette. 'You've an answer for everything.'

Tessa leaned back and took a cigarette offered by her cousin. 'It's just as well or you'd trample me into the ground.'

Eve smiled reluctantly, then laughed. 'Who would have thought that we'd end up like this?'

'End up? I thought this was only a beginning.'

'True.'

'And Josh has raised our money.'

'To six pounds. Some rise!'

'It's a lot to me. And you still have your two pounds from your mother.'

'I used to spend twice eight pounds in a morning's shopping for stockings and bits and pieces. And stop frowning at me! I know about the unemployed and the hunger marches and all the other gruesome things that are happening. They aren't my fault and I don't see why I should worry. I've had to adapt. Why can't they?'

'It isn't so easy to adapt if you have a wife and children hungry, and no prospect of work.'

Eve sighed. 'God, Tessa, don't start. I wish I'd never mentioned money. I suppose you still send some of yours to your mother?'

Tessa nodded. It sounded as if things were in a bad way at home. The dole had ended for Dad and all that was left was an appeal for charity from the Guardians. She knew he'd sink with shame if he tried that and, in any case, the fact he now owned the house would probably go against him. Those without income had to be reduced to the dregs before they received handouts. She had gone home for a few days between Christmas Day and New Year and had to suffer reproaches because she has absented herself from such important religious and family occasions.

'I'm an entertainer now,' she'd explained, 'and they're expected to work harder at holiday times.'

Mum had said stubbornly, 'Heathens! It's chapel they should be in when we celebrate the birth of our Lord, not dance halls.'

Tessa moved restlessly at the memories of home.

'Come on,' she said to Eve, stubbing out her cigarette. 'Let's go.'

'Can I stay with you tonight?' Eve looked pale and was shivering.

'Are you ill? Or just cold?'

'Neither. I'm nervous. I haven't slept well for ages.'

'Have you been dreaming?'

'Sometimes.'

They reached Tessa's room which she had made attractive with small touches of her own: a blue and gold vase, brass candlesticks holding red candles, a couple of prints on the wall, and books.

'There's only one bed,' said Eve.

'I had the other taken out when you left.'

'Well, I wouldn't have done that. You never know when you'll need an extra bed.'

'That isn't likely to happen.'

'It's happened now.'

Eve was in an argumentative mood and Tessa said, 'If you're not feeling well you can have the bed. I shall be comfortable enough on the sofa.' This wasn't strictly true. The sofa had been bought second-hand in a junk shop and its springs were somewhat erratic. However, Tessa was weary and soon began to drift off to sleep when she was awakened by Eve who shot up in bed and cried out.

Tessa rolled off the sofa and darted to her cousin. 'Is it the nightmare?'

'No,' said Eve impatiently, 'it's an idea. Why don't we try to get a cabaret spot in a good London club? I'm sure we could. And it would look so much better to my friends.'

Tessa sat down on Eve's bed. 'What do you mean?'

'I had to watch them enjoying Christmas while I was stuck on a stage singing with a band without even a mention of my name. And it's even more humiliating to be working during the season in houses where I've been a guest. People are so scornful. It's easy to see what they're thinking.'

'You did it before.'

'That was when it was only for fun and we were free to join in. Now they look on me as a professional and it's very different.'

'You *are* a professional.'

'I know. But I'm still a member of society.'

'Did they pour scorn on me?'

'Of course not! Why should they? Nobody really knows you and you've worked in a grocer's shop and didn't mind telling them that.'

'That makes me sound really vital to your scheme!'

Eve said exasperatedly, 'You know what I mean. If we appeared as an act we could have our names printed on the programmes. We would be there in our own right. Successful showbusiness folk are accepted nearly everywhere these days.'

'I have no intention of letting Josh down. Anyway, he'd probably sue us. He renewed our contract, remember?'

'I'm sure he'd let us go. I don't think he likes me.'

'I like him. I want to stay with him, and apart from that I feel I've a great deal to learn before I branch out on my own.'

'You wouldn't be on your own. I should be with you.'

Tessa yawned. 'Fancy waking me up for this.'

'You don't think we'd be successful, do you? You've no faith in yourself.'

'I've already told you, I need experience. Besides . . .'

'Yes? Besides?'

'I never know what you'll do next. You're late at rehearsals and twice you've arrived at the last minute at the broadcasting studio. Josh has let you get away with it so far, but someone else might not be so kind.'

'You pay far too much attention to such trivial details. Josh understands. He comes from a background similar to mine.'

'I wonder if you realise just how damned insulting you are at times? I'm going back to bed.'

Tessa wriggled her way between the sheets and blankets, but now her first sleep was spoilt and every sofa spring seemed to be finding tender places in her body. She lay silently wishing that Eve wasn't there so that she could turn on a light, make herself a cup of tea, read. But if Eve hadn't been there she'd be comfortable in her own bed.

'Can't you sleep?' Eve asked in a small voice.

'No!'

'It's all my fault. I'm sorry, honestly I am. Tell you what, I'll make us some tea. Or better still, some hot milk.'

Tessa drank the milk and Eve bent to kiss her forehead before she tucked her up. 'I hope you sleep now, Tessa. I shouldn't rile you. You're a brick.'

Tessa drifted off, all anger towards her cousin fading as it always did in the end.

The society season began and Eve sang with Tessa from many bandstands in hotels and private houses and watched her friends dancing the night away. Eve now had the clarinetist in thrall. He hadn't tried to hide the fact that not only was he married, but that his wife was all-important to him. 'At least I know where I am with him,' Eve said.

Tessa had given up worrying about her cousin's affairs, sordid though she felt them to be. Oddly enough, the new man, Ben Raddon, seemed actually to care for her and treated her quite tenderly at times.

The band worked through the summer months. 'Summer!' snarled Eve. 'It's been cold and rainy most of the time. What I wouldn't give for a month in Antibes!'

'You could go home,' said Tessa absentmindedly. 'You told me your aunt and uncle were in Palm Springs.' She was trying to decide which dress to wear for the evening, having flatly refused to wear the same clothes as Eve. Their colouring was different.

'I don't want to go home, and Palm Springs isn't home!' Eve shrilled. She was lying on Tessa's bed waiting to go on a shopping expedition. Not that Tessa had much to spare for shopping. The latest news from home had shocked her and she had increased her donation to the family exchequer. Mum had taken a job five mornings a week cleaning somebody's house.

'Your Dad hates it,' she had written, 'but we're hard up. We have to find the money for rates and the bad summer means the gas and coal bills are bigger than usual.'

Eve said loudly, 'I suppose you wouldn't care if I went back to the States?'

Tessa sighed, but wouldn't react.

'We're an act,' she said. 'We began together and that's how we must go on. The Kissing Cousins, remember?'

'Hell and damnation!'

'Now what's the trouble?'

'I've laddered my stocking.'

'Where?'

'Above the knee.'

'Dab a bit of soap on it,' advised Tessa. 'That'll hold it.'

She walked round the shops with Eve and watched her cousin fritter her money away. No wonder she never had any. She had talked of bringing her car to London but that idea had petered out. Cars cost money to run and garage.

When they turned up for rehearsal one October morning Josh said, 'How would you like a trip to Bristol?'

'What for?' asked Eve suspiciously.

'For something nice for you, though sad for the Bristol Hippodrome. They aren't going to put on variety any more. I telephoned and suggested that they might like a couple of Bristol girls on the stage for their last night. All right, Eve, I know you're not a Bristolian, but Tessa is and you're a double act. They said OK. What do you say?'

'Wonderful,' exclaimed Tessa.

'On the stage?' breathed Eve. 'Really on the stage?'

That brought Tessa down with a bump. 'I promised Mum I wouldn't.'

Eve was furious. 'Trust you to put a damper on things.'

'Perhaps Mum and Dad would forgive me in the circumstances, and I shall be able to visit them.'

'You miss your family, don't you?' said Josh gently.

'Very much. What will happen to the Hippodrome?'

'Since the talkies it's been going through a rough time like so many others. The London Coliseum is struggling and the Stoll gave up variety and put on "The White Horse Inn", remember? The Hippodrome's tried several ways to beat the slump. Opera, musical plays, and last Christmas *two* pantomimes, but things are bad for them. You girls may have to adapt, too. There's always the legitimate stage.'

Neither looked happy at the idea and he laughed. 'Musical comedy, perhaps. Or maybe you'll stay with the band. People will always want to dance. And there's always pantomime. That takes care of part of the year.'

Tessa brightened, though Eve looked annoyed.

Tessa and Eve travelled to Bristol by train. Tessa hadn't had time to tell her family that she was coming. When the Kissing Cousins found they were to appear with some of the great names of showbusiness who had returned for a last night at a theatre that had served them well, even Eve was impressed. Josh had booked them a room in a small hotel near the theatre and she didn't grouse once about its limitations. The rehearsal seemed a shambles, but that was fairly standard. 'It'll be all right on the night,' everyone said.

Behind the scenes there was a great deal of bustle and there were trunks and baskets, almost fully packed, ready to travel with their owners to the next engagement. Eve and Tessa stood in the wings, ready long before their act was due to go on. Most of the artistes were there with them, watching this swan song. The chorus girls opened the show with a high-kicking number then danced their way off stage. They had to make a lightning change and their circular satin skirts were spread out in the wings, shining pools of colour. Without embarrassment, they pulled off short black kilts, revealing their tights, then slid into the fresh outfits. Dressers tied tapes and grappled with hooks and eyes and the girls were back on stage, looking cool and beautiful as they performed, their pretty faces smiling out at the packed audience, and no one could have guessed that they hadn't yet been able to find further work.

The management had brought some of the very oldest performers out of retirement for a night and the girls watched entranced as one of them did his old patter and performed a monologue. The audience acclaimed him with whistles, cheers and stamping feet.

Tessa was intrigued, and moved, then realised that the third spot in the first house was upon her and the orchestra had launched into the Kissing Cousins' introduction music. The stage manager gave her a dig in the back and she and Eve were on, centre stage, standing in a spotlight. The moment approached when they must sing and Tessa was suddenly shaking with nerves. Eve actually took her hand and she realised that her cousin too was trembling.

But on cue Tessa sang, 'Listen to my tale of woe, It's terribly sad but true . . .' They were down-stage and could hear the soft sounds made by the stage hands behind the curtain as they shifted scenery for an act which needed props.

Eve was supposed to be singing and recovered enough of her senses to realise that, having let Tessa begin alone, it was better to allow her to finish the verse and so she waited to join in the refrain. 'Oh, sweet and lovely, lady be good. Oh, lady, be good to me!' The audience oohed and aahed at words which could be considered suggestive, but they were good-natured and impressed and the Kissing Cousins completed their song in comparative silence. The applause was stupendous, and although the girls knew that almost anything tonight would be received with acclaim, it exhilarated them.

The next act went on, a comedian in baggy trousers and a top hat with the lid standing up. 'I'm going to give you a biographical dictionary,' he announced. He waited for the catcalls at the long words to die away then said, 'Adam. The first man born on the longest day – it had no Eve.'

The girls hurried to their shared dressing room where a soubrette was putting the finishing touches to her spangled cap. 'How are they? Sounds rowdy.'

'They're cheering everything,' said Eve.

'Well, that's a comfort, I suppose.' The callboy knocked and shouted. 'That's me,' she said.

When she had gone Eve and Tessa stared at one another, then hugged each other. 'We did it,' said Tessa. 'We did it. But, oh, I was terrified!'

'I was speechless,' said Eve.

They laughed. 'It didn't matter,' said Tessa. 'You came through.'

'You were great.'

'We both were.'

'I won't let you down ever again,' promised Eve.

They had another spot near the end of the first act and sang 'Nice Work If You Can Get It', which brought roars of approval, especially from the men.

As they joined the others for the grand finale, some of the performers who remembered the old days of the Hippodrome were in tears and so was a large part of the audience. Tessa and Eve shed tears too. It wasn't difficult to feel emotional when a fine variety theatre had to change. The manager made a speech and the performers and audience joined in singing 'Auld Land Syne'. As it ended there were noisy yells and protests from people who were angry at the decision to alter the Hippodrome's traditions and some had to be forcibly removed. Gradually the theatre emptied and the auditorium fell silent, except for the cleaners with their buckets, mops and dusters, their hair tied up in scarves. No matter what happened next week they would still be needed.

As they removed their make-up, Eve grumbled, 'You'd think they'd have had a party for us. After all, it's a special occasion.'

The soubrette who had mostly ignored them said

scornfully, 'A party! What's to celebrate? Another theatre going over to talkies. Besides, most of the performers have to get back to the theatres they're supposed to be playing in. They've had special permission to be here tonight.'

'So have we,' snapped Eve. '*We* happen to have a very good job in London.'

Feelings were very near the surface and a quarrel could have erupted but the call-boy knocked at that moment. 'A message for the Kissing Cousins. Miss Brook, Miss Morland.'

Eve grabbed a wrapper and opened the door and the boy handed her a note. She read it and said excitedly, 'Charles Ware is outside. He wants to take us to supper.'

'Both of you?' asked the soubrette.

'Why not?' flashed Eve.

The girl shrugged. 'No reason, I suppose. My boy friends usually only want me.'

'Well, we're different,' said Eve. 'We're an act.'

'Fancy! Do you two do everything in twos?' She got up and left. 'See you in some other theatre, some other time. Perhaps!' she called back.

'I don't like her at all,' said Eve. 'She's got a nasty mind.'

Tessa laughed. 'You have to admit it looks odd for a man to be taking out both of us.'

'He's my friend, really, of course,' said Eve, 'but he's far too polite to leave you stranded.'

'I'm not stranded,' said Tessa, irritated. 'I can go to the hotel. In fact, I think I should. I'm getting up early tomorrow to visit the family.'

'I thought you told me they didn't know you'd be in Bristol?'

'They don't. I'm going to surprise them.' Tessa's belligerence died. She'd have to tell Mum and Dad that she had broken her promise and sung on a stage.

'Well, you can't visit tonight,' said Eve. 'It's long past their bedtime.'

Her mockery was affectionate and Tessa laughed. She

put on her new tweed coat with the draped curly lamb collar and smoothed it appreciatively. It was the most expensive thing she had ever bought and she felt guilty every time she wore it, knowing that she could have sent more money home. Her hat, a simple beret to be worn slanting to one side, was in matching tweed and sported a narrow silver brooch over one ear.

Eve had sold many of her things, but still kept some from the old days and Tessa tried not to feel envious of her soft, dark fur coat. Her cousin's hat was in suede and looked exclusive.

Outside the stage door Charles Ware waited, not standing with the other men, but sitting in the front seat of his car, smoking. He got out to greet them, throwing down his cigarette and grinding it with his heel. He could never look clean-shaven, thought Tessa. He probably had to use a razor twice a day, and his hair was almost black. He resembled a buccaneer and from what Eve said behaved as autocratically as one. She hung back a little, waiting for Eve to greet him first. He kissed her cheek and turned at once to Tessa, smiling. 'Congratulations to both of you. I think your act is brilliant.'

Eve, somewhat peeved at being so quickly passed over, said, 'I suppose you mean Tessa was brilliant? I dried.'

'Do you mean at the beginning? I thought you had planned it that way. Were you dreadfully nervous?'

Eve smiled. 'Dreadfully, wasn't I, Tessa? You were, too, weren't you?'

'Quaking,' she said.

'Would you like supper?' asked Charles, and on being assured that they were both starving he opened the front passenger door of his car. Eve immediately took it and Tessa sat alone in the back where she was perfectly happy to relax in its leather comfort.

'Where are you taking us?' asked Eve.

'To the Grand.'

'You'll never get a table this late.'

'I booked one,' said Charles.

'But you didn't know if we'd come with you.'

'I booked it anyway.'

Tessa decided he was arrogant to have taken their acceptance for granted, but she was too comfortable to care. The drive was short and soon she was being ushered into the warm luxury of a hotel and her coat was being taken from her by an attendant. She was thankful she had decided to wear a flowered voile frock, actually in expectation of the party which Eve had assured her would definitely be held after the show. Her cousin wore midnight blue silk with a pale blue scarf knotted in apparent carelessness at her neck.

Charles held out a chair for Eve and a waiter held one for Tessa. Charles seated himself. 'I must be the most fortunate man in Bristol tonight. Two beauties at my table and no competition.'

Tessa glanced around quickly. It took only a moment to see that her frock would never compete with the other women's. Since she had come into contact with couture fashion her taste in clothes far outstripped her ability to purchase them and she had no easy access now to Aunty May. However good the big stores, they could not attain the touch of a Patou or a Chanel. The names of the couture houses ran through her mind like a refrain: Vionnet, Schiaparelli, Lelong. Then everything was driven from her mind as she saw Paul.

He was on the far side of the room and her view was constantly interrupted by waiters and diners as they moved to and fro. Andrea, looking stunning in white, sat next to him and Tessa saw Tiddles, Poppy, Kitty and Rupert, and other men. It was a large party and she wondered what they were celebrating.

She turned away, her heart thudding. Every time she was sure she had recovered from her useless passion for Paul it was disturbingly reactivated.

Mrs Morland greeted Tessa with a mixture of pleasure and discontent. She didn't like surprises. When she had guests she always cooked something extra and gave the

294

place a special shine. She kissed her daughter. 'You should have said you were coming. I'd have got something special in to eat.'

'Mum!' Tessa hugged her. 'I'm not a visitor. I just want some of your home cooking. I'll be glad of anything you've made. I haven't tasted cooking as good as yours since I left home. Where's Dad?'

'Out looking for work.' Mum looked grim. 'Every morning he dresses in his Sunday best and goes round asking for a job.'

'Is there nothing?'

'Oh, there are jobs now and then, but there are so many young men wanting them and they always get taken in preference. Your Dad says that some of them have never served a proper apprenticeship like he did, but employers don't want old men.'

'He isn't old!'

'They think he is and they've got the last say.'

'Is he well?'

'Physically.' Mum paused and Tessa stared at her in horrified silence. 'Don't look like that, Tessa. His mind is clear, it's his spirit that's going. Nothing I can say seems to help. The minister visits him a lot and tries to uplift him. Dad's better for a time, then he sinks back.'

'Poor Dad. Does he ever think of trying in another town?'

'Leave us, do you mean? Go away somewhere where we'd never see him? I should hope not! Let the unmarried men travel. It won't do them any harm. Trouble is, most of them won't leave Bristol. They want everything handed to them on a plate these days. Here, take this.' She handed Tessa a cup of hot tea and a buttered scone. Tessa hadn't felt hungry after the late supper and had eaten no breakfast, but the ride on top of the tram had sharpened her appetite and she ate hungrily.

'Don't they feed you in London? You look skinny to me.'

'I have lost weight. I think it's all the rushing about. Actually, Mum, I was in Bristol last night.' She went on

295

to explain the circumstances and watched apprehensively as her mother's face grew grim. 'So you see, I had no time to tell you or ask your permission,' she finished.

'You promised.'

'I know. I am sorry, really I am . . .'

'Not sorry enough to withstand the devil's temptation.'

'It wasn't the devil. It was the management of the Hippodrome.' The facetious words slipped out.

Mrs Morland was scandalised. 'Mocking the Lord! What kind of people are you mixing with?'

'I'm not mocking the Lord, Mum. Please, don't go on at me. I've missed you all. I've only got this morning in Bristol. We're due back tonight to sing with Josh.'

'What chapel do you go to nowadays?'

Mum's question was barked at her, reminding her of school.

'I haven't found one yet. I've tried a couple.' This at least was true.

'What denomination?'

'A Baptist and a Methodist.'

'I see. They don't seem to have done you much good. Maybe they don't get to the root of things the way we do. Find a good chapel that follows our way to God.'

Further conversation was cut short by the entry of Dad. He smiled when he saw Tessa, but surely his shoulders were drooping even more? To her relief Mum didn't burden him with her misdemeanours. Tessa embraced him. 'It's lovely to see you, Dad.'

'And you, my love. How long can you stay?'

'Only until lunch time.'

'She means dinner time,' said Mum. 'I suppose you'll eat with us, Tessa?'

'That's not long,' said Dad.

'I know, but I have to get back to work.'

'Where's Eve? Is she in Bristol?'

'She went to Padding House.'

'Quite right,' said Mum. 'I dare say she's gone to see that nice Miss Coleman. Have Eve's parents been to

England lately? No? She must miss them. You'd think they would.'

'She writes to them,' said Tessa. 'It's a long way to America.'

'I know that. You're home early,' she said to Dad.

'Yes. I heard of a job that might suit me this afternoon so I went there and had to wait to see the boss. I've got it, Lily.'

Mum's face brightened. 'A job? God be praised. Where?'

'In the fruit market.'

'What carpentry do they need there?'

'I'm a general helper. Mostly I'm to sweep up the rubbish.'

Mrs Morland was aghast. 'But you're a skilled man. You can't do it.'

'It's all I can get.'

'I can't bear to think of it.'

'And I can't bear to think of my wife keeping me. No work is shameful and our Tessa won't have to send money to us any more. She needs it for herself.'

Mum said, resentment at the way Dad was humbling himself making her voice sharp, 'I hope you'll save your money for the future, Tessa. One day when you've finished with all that singing stuff you'll need things for your bottom drawer.'

Tessa didn't answer. Mum obviously still looked upon her singing as a temporary aberration.

Joey had been listening intently. 'You're both cleaners now,' he remarked.

His mother's eyes flashed. 'Let me see your hands. As I thought – filthy. Go and wash. And your face as well, and your neck. And tell Susan to come in to her dinner.'

'And we won't both be cleaners,' Dad called after him, 'because your mother will be staying home in future.'

The meal was eaten in an atmosphere of somewhat strained gaiety. Tessa was sure it would be far less wearing on their nerves if they brought all their worries and anger out into the open and discussed them, but that had never been her parents' way. Joey and Susan saved them from total gloom by asking dozens of questions about London and what it was like to sing on the wireless.

'Everyone at school, those that have got a wireless, that is, listen in to you, Tessa,' said Susan excitedly.

'And they do in my class,' said Joey. 'It's like having a film star for a sister.'

Mum's frowns didn't deter them and Dad seemed to accept everything. Tessa left her family sadly, but was ashamed to realise on the train journey back to London that she was thankful to be out of the gloomy, inhibiting atmosphere. Mum hadn't referred again to her appearing in a theatre, perhaps unwilling to upset her husband further, possibly resigned.

Tessa settled back in her seat, cast a look at Eve who was in one of her furious, silent moods, and tried to relax and allow the heavy meat pudding and spotted dick with syrup to digest. Her stomach, in keeping with the rest of her, could no longer accommodate her former way of life.

# Chapter Fourteen

Appearing on the stage in what she called 'a proper variety show' unsettled Eve. 'We *could* branch out on our own,' she insisted. 'We could have a proper act. Look at the way we were applauded at the Hippodrome and we only had minor spots.'

'The audience was so emotional they'd have cheered anything that moved,' said Tessa.

'Are you implying that we're not good enough?'

'I'm not implying it, I'm saying it,' said Tessa. 'We know nothing about the stage. We need more experience and we'll get it with a good boss. You know that Josh is going on tour and wants us to go with him so we'll soon be performing on stage, not only from band stands. Besides, we're still contracted to him.'

'I know, I know,' said Eve angrily. 'But he'd let us off if we asked him.'

'I doubt it. He's kind, but no fool. We're part of his show and advertised that way. And I intend to get a reputation for dependability. I'm not going to ask him so if you do, you'll go it alone.'

'You'd split us up?'

'Yes, in the circumstances, I would, but if you leave it'll be you who's doing the splitting.'

Eve said angrily, 'I suppose you'd be glad to go on alone? People have told you you're better than me, haven't they?'

'What are you talking about?'

'When I didn't turn up because I was ill some of the band said it.'

'What kind of friend let that cat out of the bag? Your latest lover, I suppose?'

'Ben? Yes, he did.'

'I'm surprised. I thought he was a nice man, apart from the fact that he's deceiving his wife, of course.'

'I think he was trying to warn me.'

'Against me?'

'I suppose so,' said Eve sulkily.

'I don't think much of that.'

'You wouldn't! You're jealous because you don't have a lover and you're still hankering after Paul. You'll never get him, you know.'

Tessa stared at her cousin. She was angrier than she had ever been in her life. Words were begging to be said: cruel, wounding words about Eve's promiscuity and her parents' neglect. Tessa curbed them and the effort held her speechless long enough for other memories to surface. Eve's vulnerability, the impression she sometimes gave of a dark and desperate need, and that dreadful dream which she would never reveal.

'We shouldn't quarrel,' she said, after a silence which Eve hadn't made any attempt to break.

'No, we shouldn't,' said her cousin, tears suddenly near the surface. 'Do you really think we're not experienced enough to start on our own?'

'I honestly do.'

Eve sighed. 'I'll let myself be guided by you. But, Tessa, one day we'll have to make the plunge, unless you just want to be known as a dance-band singer.'

'There's nothing terrible about that, but I'm vain enough to want to shine on a stage some day.'

'Well, thank goodness you've got one weakness,' said Eve.

'You make me sound like a prig. I'm only trying—'

'To do the best for us, I know. I'll be good. At least,' she finished, forestalling any comment by Tessa, 'I'll try. By the way, Ben was only giving me a lecture on making sure I was on time for rehearsals and that kind of thing.'

'He didn't warn you against me?'

'Not directly. He said that you were a true professional.'

Tessa couldn't help feeling pleased.


The winter tour began in the autumn of 1933 and would take in a dozen towns, travelling west and north. Bristol was first. They were to appear on stage at the Empire for three weeks, and everyone was happy at the idea of spending so long in one place. Tessa greeted the news about the Empire with dismay. 'Mum and Dad will hate it.'

'You've already broken your stupid promise about not appearing on a stage.'

'It isn't stupid from their point of view, and the Hippodrome was a special occasion.'

'You'll never reach the top if you refuse work.'

'I know. If only it weren't the Empire . . . The shows there are often near the knuckle.'

'Will that make little Goody Two Shoes uncomfortable?'

'I shouldn't think so,' said Tessa calmly, 'but her parents might have something to say about that! So might your guardian.'

'Who?'

'Miss Coleman.'

'She is not my guardian and, anyway, she's gone. The house is filled with workmen.'

'Gone? Where did she go?'

'How the hell should I know? Paul saw her off.'

'Did he make sure she had another job to go to? She's not well-off, is she?'

'I shouldn't think so. Has your idol got feet of clay?'

'He isn't my idol. I am surprised though.'

Eve relented. 'As a matter of fact, he didn't make her leave. When she heard about the renovations and the new bride, she just packed up and went.'

'Didn't anyone ask her for her address?'

'Partridge has it. I can't think why. She never got letters.'

'Poor thing. Where is she?'

'Why are you so interested?'

'Because she's poor and elderly and lonely and probably out of work.'

'And what can you do about it?' jeered Eve.

'I could write her a friendly letter.'

'My God, you're a sucker for punishment.'

But Eve got the address and Tessa wrote to Tildy Coleman and received a reply. She was able to tell Eve that her former companion was managing by taking in dress-making.'

'She'll starve on money like that,' was Eve's only comment.

Tessa was more concerned about Mum whose letters had been less than cheerful of late.

Before they left London Eve and Tessa bought seats at the Palladium and watched Max Rivers' Palladium Girls dancing, all looking as tanned as if they had spent the summer on the Côte d'Azur. They were followed by a trapeze artiste, and a thin giant and a stout dwarf whose routine contained rude innuendo directed chiefly at the gallery. Incongruously, it seemed to Tessa, performing sea-lions also appeared.

Eve whispered, 'How disgusting. I bet backstage stinks of fish.'

Miss Marie MacQuarrie and four other women performed on harps and there was a mimic. On the same rich bill were Robb Wilton and Will Hay whose crazily humorous routines had both girls laughing. The show was packed with talent, but everyone waited for the star of the night, Miss Gracie Fields. They chuckled at her comedy numbers, then listened entranced to her powerfully high, sweet voice as she closed her act.

On their way home, Eve said, 'I'm sure variety will never die. It can't with people like them. Besides, I want it to stay until I can be part of it. Oh, Tessa, don't let's wait too long.'

\* \* \*

On a cold, foggy Sunday morning they gathered with the band at the railway station and the whole party waited almost in silence for their train.

Eve shivered and pulled her fur coat around her, snuggling into the high collar. 'God, this is ghastly.'

Tessa nudged her. 'Stop it. The others will hear. Some of them have been travelling on the road for years.'

'And they bloody look like it,' snarled Eve.

Tessa moved away, settled herself on the corner of a props basket and took out her book.

'What are you reading?' asked Sammy Jacobs.

Tessa smiled. 'It's light stuff. *Happy Ever After* it's called.'

'My wife likes romances. Somehow I imagined you reading something sterner.'

'I do, but not at times like these. I look for something not needing concentration. I mean—'

'I know what you mean!' Sammy laughed.

He was nice and Tessa asked impulsively, 'Doesn't your wife get tired of waiting for you to come home?'

It was a cheeky question which slipped out, but Sammy smiled. 'She takes it all in her stride. She used to travel with me. She was a singer, still got a very good voice. She's not strong enough now to put up with the hardships.'

'Is it a hard life?'

Sammy looked thoughtful as he lit a cigarette. He offered Tessa one, but she refused. She enjoyed smoking, but women who did it in public were still considered fast. 'It's physically demanding, but more than that – it takes it out of you in other ways. I suppose it sounds a bit daft, but it can weaken your spirit.'

'It doesn't sound daft. I think I know what you mean.'

'Yes, you probably do. You've got imagination. Eve, now . . .' He coughed and continued hastily, 'You never really know how the public will react. I've been in bands that were good, yet folk never took to them. And I've played with ramshackle affairs that seemed to please them. There's never any way of telling with the public.

And stars have it much harder, especially single acts. Even the greatest have wobbly knees before their appearances – some are even physically sick – and it's easy to shake their self-confidence.' He glanced at Tessa's serious face and laughed ruefully. 'I should be encouraging you, not telling you the drawbacks.'

'It's as well to know them,' she said, 'but they won't beat me.'

'Attagirl!' said Sammy. Tessa smiled. Since the talkies got so popular, Americanisms were creeping more and more into the language. Tessa liked them, appreciating the sharp way they had of emphasising things.

Travelling on Sunday proved a distinct hardship when the train seemed to dawdle and spend time in sidings. 'It's always the same,' said Sammy laconically, settling himself to sleep, his hat over his eyes.

The girls had heard a few horror stories about theatrical digs and landladies, though some were the motherly sort dreamed of by the constant traveller. One would have plenty of hot water, good beds and clean blankets, a blazing fire in the sitting room and well-cooked, plentiful food. Another would offer only some of these blessings. If they had good food the beds were lumpy; if a fire blazed in the grate, the food was poor.

In Bristol Josh, Sammy and a couple of other members of the band, and the girls found ideal accommodation which Sammy had used before with a cheerful landlady, Mrs Biggs, all that performers on tour could ask for. Mrs Biggs actually suggested that they use the wash-house whenever they wished and when the clothes were clean and squeezed in the ringer, she hauled them up on a clothes rack that was situated over the kitchen range.

'It looks dangerous to me,' said Tessa. 'What if something should fall on to the fire?'

'For goodness' sake,' snapped Eve who had been looking peaky for days, 'you're so damned pessimistic.'

'Are you all right?' asked Tessa, ignoring her cousin's rudeness.

'What do you mean, all right?'

'Are you feeling unwell?'

'No. Why should you think so?'

'You felt faint as we got off the train.'

'I told you, it was just the moving about after hours of sitting.'

'When we travelled to Cap d'Antibes you were perfectly all right.'

'I didn't have the worries I've got now!'

'You've had worries for quite a time and managed to stay healthy.'

'Leave me alone.'

'I think you should see a doctor.'

'Oh, do you?'

'You're obviously not well.'

'Oh, hell! I don't need a doctor! I know what's the matter with me.'

'If you tell me I could get you some medicine. There's always a chemist who stays open in the evening.'

Eve's eyes filled with tears. 'A chemist won't help. Tessa, I'm pregnant.'

'What!'

'Hush, don't let the others hear.'

'They're all downstairs listening to the wireless. Eve, how did it happen? Damn, I know how it happened. I mean, when? Are you getting married?'

'For God's sake! Trust you to come up with such a stupid solution.'

'It's a natural one in the circumstances.'

'Maybe to you, but not to me. I've no intention of letting a kid spoil my life.'

Tessa looked at her cousin helplessly, shocked by her reaction. Even more shocked by her own, discovering that she, too, was worried that a child could spoil their lives, certainly at this juncture. 'How far are you?'

'Only about seven weeks. It'll be easy.'

'What will?'

'Getting rid of it.'

'You'll kill it?'

'Don't be ridiculous. It isn't anything yet. Not a baby. Not anything. Only a nuisance.'

'What will you do?'

'There are ways. Look, Tessa, don't ask any more questions. I wish I hadn't told you, but—' Her voice broke. 'I'm frightened. Will you come with me?'

'Where?'

'To the woman who'll take care of it for me.'

'Eve, you can't. Women die from having abortions.'

'Some die, most don't.'

'Can't you find a doctor?'

'How?'

'Perhaps Paul or Charles . . . they're both men of the world. I'm sure they'd help you. A proper doctor would know what to do.'

'Are you *crazy*? I'd rather die than tell them, and how do I know there's a doctor who would do it? Most likely they'd tell me to go on with it. And, Tessa, I *can't*. I just can't. I must get rid of it.'

'The way you're going on you probably will! Calm down. It's your own fault.' Tessa stopped, aghast. 'I'm sorry. That was unkind. I didn't mean it.'

'You're right, it *is* my own fault.'

'Who's the father?'

'Does it matter?'

'He should help you to pay for the operation.'

'I think I can manage. Just about.'

'I'll give you some if you need it.'

'Your money is saved for your parents.'

'I'll think of an excuse.'

'You'll have to tell more lies.'

'Do you want me to help you or not?'

'I may, but I feel guilty about it.'

'So do I. I've always been taught that a pregnancy is sacred. That God—'

'Stop preaching, damn it! I meant I'd feel guilty about the money.' Eve clutched Tessa's hand. 'I know I don't deserve it, but please be kind to me. You will come with me, won't you?'

'Yes,' said Tessa, feeling queasy at the idea. 'Of course. Where will it be?'

'I've got the address of a woman. I'm told she's thorough. She'll see me tomorrow morning. It's all fixed.'

'Where did you get it? The address, I mean?'

'My fellow.'

'Has he had this experience before?'

'If you're going to dig at me I'd better go alone.'

'I won't say another thing. Oh, hell, Josh has called a rehearsal for the morning.'

'You'll just have to choose, then, won't you?' cried Eve. 'Josh or me.'

'Keep calm,' said Tessa. 'There's no choice, you should know that.' She glanced at her watch. It was new and the first she'd owned. 'I've still time to get to Kingswood and see Mum and Dad.'

'No! Please don't leave me. Not tonight. I'll crack up if you do.'

Tessa sighed. Eve looked so desperate she was afraid. What if she did something to herself? Girls in her position sometimes did. 'I'll stay,' she said.

She slept badly that night and in the morning told Josh that she and Eve were ill. 'I think it must be something we've eaten.'

'We all ate here last night. What else have you had?'

'Ham sandwiches on the train. I thought the ham was a bit off, but it was all we had and the journey took so long we were starving.'

Josh frowned, then nodded. 'OK. Our first engagement is tomorrow night at the Hippodrome between the talkies and the audience probably won't care much what we do, though I hope you'll feel well enough to be there.'

'With rest we should be.'

'Eve's looked off-colour for a while now.'

'She's just tired.'

'Just tired, is she?' Josh was annoyed. 'She should let up a little. No one can be active by day and night.'

Tessa flushed. Clearly, he referred to Eve's sexual

307

exploits. 'She's not robust,' she managed to stammer.

'Who are you trying to kid? She's got a constitution like a horse.'

Tessa remembered Eve's car and tried to think of ways she could get out to fetch it without Josh knowing, but the wide downstairs hall was used as an extra room and she could hear his voice quite clearly.

In the morning Eve retched and heaved so much that Tessa thought she'd be unable to keep the appointment. And they had to wait until Josh and the others left and sneak out without meeting Mrs Biggs. For a while it looked hopeless, but the sickness passed and the girls caught a bus. The journey seemed long before they reached the edge of a small town where they found their way to the address on the piece of paper that Eve clutched. White-faced and shaking, she gave herself over to a tall, bony woman. Tessa looked at her fearfully. Her wide smile didn't reach her eyes and she wondered about the standard of cleanliness for the woman's hands were quite grubby and hens clucked their way in and out of the kitchen.

'I sell eggs and honey,' said the woman. 'It gives women a good excuse to call on me. Before I touch the young lady I have to have your word of honour that no matter what happens you don't mention me to anyone at all.'

The girls gave their promises, but her words terrified Tessa. She wanted to beg Eve not to proceed, but knew it would simply add to her fear. She forced herself to ask if she should stay with her while the operation was performed and was relieved when Eve managed to summon a weak smile. 'You look worse than I feel,' she said. 'Wait for me.'

The woman showed Eve into a back room and said to Tessa, 'You can sit here by the fire. This won't take long. I just have to scrub up.'

'Were you once a nurse?' asked Tessa.

'What do you want to know for?' The woman's eyes became dark and hostile.

'It was just your use of words,' explained Tessa.
' "Scrub up" is what our doctor always says.'

'Does he, indeed?' She turned and followed Eve.

Tessa picked up a newspaper and tried to read, but the words wouldn't stay in her head. She hoped that the woman really had been a nurse and knew what she was doing. Then Eve let out a cry, followed by eerie moans like an animal in pain, and she dropped the paper and clenched her fists and began to pray, wondering if God took an interest in those who destroyed babies.

The woman appeared. 'It's over. I've left her to rest a while. Later she'll bleed and have pain.'

'Much?'

'Could be. Some girls do. Give her a couple of aspirin every three hours and keep an eye on her. If she bleeds too much you'll have to call a doctor. If you need medical help, keep saying that the abortion just happened and none of us will get into trouble. She's got a bit of flannel between her legs, but you'll need cloth to soak up the blood. Towelling's the best.'

Eve appeared soon after, looking deathly pale, and Tessa wondered how she would get her back to their digs.

Eve paid the fee which took all the money they had apart from their bus fares and on the way back Eve sat with teeth clenched. Tessa took her to the digs in a taxi. She had to ask the driver to wait while she fetched money, praying she wouldn't meet Mrs Biggs.

Eve collapsed on her bed. It had seemed as if she couldn't get whiter but she did. Her lips and cheeks were bloodless. She refused anything but water. Tessa used their own towels to soak up the blood which began to flow terrifyingly fast. She had to wash them as best she could and dry them inadequately in front of the metered gas fire, praying she wouldn't run out of pennies. She used newspapers to protect the mattress.

When Josh returned he knocked on their door. Tessa answered, blocking his view of Eve's bed. 'I'm a lot better, but Eve isn't,' she said.

'I see. Shouldn't you call a doctor?'

'No,' called Eve. Tessa couldn't imagine how she summoned up the strength of will to sound almost natural. 'Sorry, Josh. It's nothing much and I'll be all right soon, but tomorrow it'll have to be just Tessa.'

'As long as you're well for the Empire on Tuesday. They've advertised you as a couple of Bristol girls.'

Tessa shut the door and said, 'Lord, I didn't think they'd do that. I wanted to tell Mum and Dad first. What will they say? I'd better go out tomorrow and let them know.'

Eve groaned. 'God, won't this pain ever stop?'

'I'm sorry,' said Tessa. 'Is it really dreadful?'

'Diabolical!' Eve grabbed a handkerchief and clamped her teeth down on it hard until the spasm passed. 'I'm losing so fast. Spread more papers under me. Hurry!'

Tessa watched in impotent horror as Eve endured hours of suffering during which she continued to bleed. 'It looks worse than it is,' she gasped. 'It's really no more than a heavy period.'

She held back her groans when Mrs Biggs called them for supper. 'We don't feel like eating,' explained Tessa. 'We'll have an early night.'

'Could you do with bicarbonate of soda?' asked Mrs Biggs. 'Couldn't you take a drop of milk?'

Tessa accepted the milk and drank some. She needed it. Eve seemed to be taking an inordinately long time to finish what the woman had begun. She reached the stage where she had to smother her cries with her pillow as with agonising slowness she aborted. Sometimes she ground out words between her teeth. 'Take this as a warning, Tessa. I did it just the once without protection. Just the once. Never take chances. I never will again. Just the once, that's all.'

It was hardly the time to tell Eve that she had no intention of embarking on illicit love affairs, but while she watched and waited by Eve's bed well into the night her tired mind let images slip through. Images of Paul on the raft at Cap d'Antibes, of how gently he had taught her to drive, of their singing together beneath a leafy green awning. She wondered if she would have been strong enough to resist him if he had wanted to make love to her. Damn him! she thought wearily. Damn all men who captivate women then leave them stranded.

At last it was over and Eve slept while Tessa moved quietly about the room, stuffing soiled towels and papers into a large travelling bag, washing the sheets, feeling rather sick, wondering if childbirth was this ghastly. But at least you got a baby at the end of it, not this clandestine mess.

Eve declared herself ready for the Empire. She even insisted on attending rehearsals though Josh was shocked at her appearance.

'Are you sure you shouldn't see a doctor, Eve?'

'Sure,' she said shortly. 'It was nothing. I'm over it.'

Of course she wasn't and the rehearsal left her with shaking legs and a bad headache.

'You'll have to go back to bed,' said Tessa. 'Josh will understand.'

But Eve was stubborn. 'No damned man will stop me from going on stage.'

'What if you faint or begin to bleed again?'

'I'm still bleeding,' said Eve. 'God, you're so innocent it's no wonder your parents are afraid to let you out of their sight.'

The remark was unfair, but Tessa wouldn't argue.

'Sorry,' said Eve. 'Don't worry. I'll use plenty of rouge and I promise not to bleed publicly or faint.'

'Will you be all right on your own if I go to see Mum and Dad this afternoon? They must know about the Empire by now.'

'It's all my fault if you get into hot water. Every damned thing that goes wrong is my fault.'

'Don't be maudlin.'

'Maudlin, am I? Bloody cheek!'

Tessa smiled. 'That's more like the cousin of my bosom.'

Eve had to laugh, though it turned to a groan. 'Give

them my love. Tell them I'll be out soon to see them.'

Tessa took the tram along the familiar route, got off at Kingswood Depot and walked the rest of the way.

As she feared, Mum greeted her with a grim face. 'I've read the papers,' she said as Tessa walked in. 'I suppose you've come home to explain why you keep telling me lies.'

'It's wonderful to see you, Mum.'

'You needn't think to get round me with soft words.'

'A soft answer turneth away wrath,' quoted Tessa.

'So now you bring the Good Book to your aid? Shame on you! You don't seem to have learned a thing in all the years we took you to chapel. We tried to bring you up decent. As if it wasn't enough to have a daughter singing with a dance band and going on the wireless, now you've taken to the stage. And the Empire, of all places. This afternoon the whole Band of Hope was talking about it. I got there a bit late because your dad came home late from work and I had to give him his dinner.'

'Doesn't he take sandwiches? The fruit market's right in town.'

'He does usually, but he came home early today because he's got to work tonight. What's that got to do with our temperance meeting?'

Tessa advanced into the kitchen. 'What did they say?'

'I can only guess. They didn't say it to me.'

'How do you know they said anything?'

'Sauce, as well as deceit!'

'I don't mean to be saucy, Mum.'

Mum sat down heavily on a kitchen chair. 'When I was getting near the hall I heard their voices, all going hammer and tongs, then as soon as I walked in they stopped, stared at me like I was something out of a pantomime, then all began talking again, talking about the weather. It was my turn to take a cake but I was that upset I forgot and Mrs Millington ran home to get something. I would have gone back for the cake, but she was out of the door before I got my breath back. Interfering busybody! Then she only brought biscuits, and plain

312

ones at that. Well, I could see they all blamed me.'

Tessa put her arms round her mother. Mrs Morland moved as if she would push her away, then stopped. 'Mum, I came because I don't want to fall out with you. Eve was ill and I couldn't leave her.'

'Bad, was she?' asked Mum sharply.

'Pretty bad. A stomach upset.'

'Is she better now? Did you catch it?'

'She's much better, but she's resting before the show.'

'The show put on in that place of sin, you mean?'

'The Empire? Yes. It isn't a place of sin, Mum.'

'How do you know? Have you ever been inside?'

'This morning we rehearsed there.'

'What's it like?'

Tessa had a job not to laugh as Mum's curiosity got the better of her. 'It's much bigger than I expected, lots of red plush and gilt paint. Very pretty. When I got there for rehearsal it looked strange to see the rows of empty seat waiting for people. It made me quite nervous.'

'You've no need to be nervous,' said Mum indignantly. 'Not with your voice.'

'Well, I was, a bit.'

'But you sang at the Hippodrome. Were you nervous then?'

'Yes, but it all happened so fast and it was all new and everybody was ready to cheer because of its being the last variety show.'

'You've sung at many a Christian Mission. Last time the tent must have held three hundred people.'

'The Empire holds more than that. And it's not the same.'

'It certainly isn't,' said Mum. 'I don't know what the choir-master thinks after he trained you to sing for the Lord. Does the Empire have a so-called joy plank so that chorus girls with practically nothing on can walk along it right into the audience, showing themselves off to men?'

'*Mum!* How do you know?'

'If I've told you once I've told you a thousand times – I learn all I can about the evil one's wicked ways so I can

313

combat them in the name of the Lord. Did you see any chorus girls? Were they nearly naked?'

'I saw them and I have to admit their costumes are a bit on the scanty side. But Eve and I will be wearing proper clothes.'

'You did promise not to go on the stage.'

'I know. Please forgive me, but I love everything about the entertainment world. And I must earn money and it's what I do best. And who knows? Someone might be the better for hearing me sing. I behave properly.'

'I should hope so.'

Tessa thought for a moment of the recent horror she had gone through with Eve. Was that behaving properly?

Mum looked at her shrewdly. 'You'll be in contact with sin, morning, noon and night. You've already seen that, haven't you?'

'I can't avoid it and surely it would be the same wherever I went? I don't have to copy it. You've met Josh. You like him. He takes an interest in the welfare of his people. And, Mum, I'll be twenty-one next birthday.'

'Is that to remind me that I'll have no say in what you do afterwards?'

'You'll always have your say.' Tessa hugged her mother again. 'I could never forget your advice, your goodness.'

'Not mine, Tessa. It all comes from the Lord. Always remember that.'

'Yes, Mum. Where's Dad? Is he resting?'

'Not him. He's gone to visit a sick chapel member.'

When Dad arrived, he greeted Tessa with a kiss and a reproachful gaze. 'You'll have spoken to her, Lily?'

'I have. She's going on with the stage, but I think we can trust her.'

He said nothing for a while. 'I'm sure we can,' he said, looking relieved. He dreaded discord. Tessa was glad to see that his shoulders no longer drooped. His job might be humble, but it was work.

They sat down to tea when Joey and Susan arrived.

They plied their sister with dozens of questions and she tried her best to answer them without saying anything which would offend her parents. Susan was pretty and looked quite grown-up, Tessa noted. She had lost her plumpness and was now slender and almost as tall as her sister, with a piquant, heart-shaped face, grey-blue eyes and a delectable mouth. Her hair had been bobbed and framed her face in soft fair waves and curls.

Joey was the same height with a bony, boy's face and an infectious grin.

'You've both grown up when I wasn't looking,' she said.

Susan preened herself and Joey laughed, but Mrs Morland frowned. 'They're children still,' she declared.

Susan said, 'Frank Anderson doesn't come here any more. He's courting another girl.'

Mrs Morland frowned again. 'It's not your place to talk of such things.'

'Is it true, Mum?' asked Tessa.

'It is. She's a local farmer's daughter and it's said her father's going to give her a thousand pounds when she marries as well as a cottage on his land. She'll be a good catch.' Mrs Morland sighed wistfully. 'It must be nice when you can set your children up that way.'

'We may not have worldly goods,' said Mr Morland, 'but we equip our children to wrestle with the devil. That's much better.'

'It is, Dad, it is,' said Tessa so fervently that she earned a suspicious look from her mother.

'Have you been beset by evil?' asked Mr Morland.

Tessa hedged. 'I turn aside from it. I can't forget the lessons you've both taught me.'

Dad leaned back replete and gave a sigh of pleasure. 'Your mother is a wonder. She always provides good food. That brawn was done to a turn and the currant cake was beautiful.' He got up and stretched. 'Now it's back to work. I'll see you in the morning, Lily.'

'Don't all the tram fares take a lot of your money?' asked Tessa.

315

'Bless you, I don't spend on trams. I cycle to work.'

'So far?'

'It's good for me.' Dad gave kisses all round and left.

'I kept a newspaper for you,' announced Mum. 'It's got the notice of Paul Jefferson's marriage in it.'

Tessa held herself rigid. She forced a smile. 'When was it?'

'Not yet. It was just telling folk it'll take place in two weeks. Why, Tessa, you'll be here for it. I'm sure if you contacted him you'd get an invitation. After all, you are related and he likes you. A big society wedding would be interesting. Of course, he's bound to invite Eve.'

Tessa was glad when Joey said, 'I'm staying on at school, Tessa.'

'Mum wrote to tell me. I'm very glad. Jobs are hard to come by and a well-educated man stands a better chance.'

'That's true,' said Mum. 'If Dad had been able to stay on he might be in better work now.'

'There are plenty of white-collars who can't get jobs,' said Tessa. 'The time will come when the country will be crying out for good carpenters.'

Susan said, 'I'll soon be fourteen and I might stay on at school, too.' She gave her mother a defiant glance.

'Is that true?' asked Tessa.

'Girls are still wanted in jobs,' said Mum. 'The laundry advertises quite often and so do the boot factories—'

'And the corsets,' chimed in Susan. She sounded angry. 'Will I still be a child if I go to work in a horrible factory?'

'You'll be a child for as long as I say so,' her mother replied.

'Joey's older than me and he'll still be a schoolboy.'

This was clearly an argument which had been conducted over a period of time. Tessa sympathised with Susan, but in Mum's view girls worked until they married while boys had a living to make all through their lives. She wished there was a way to give Susan a better chance, but the slump was now biting deep and millions

316

were unemployed. Marxism was taking a hold on angry men. There was even a newspaper called *The Daily Worker* which was subsidised by moneyed people. There were rallies to protest against the Means Test and Bristol had witnessed unrest and violence with the spikes of railings and bottles used as weapons and windows smashed.

As Tessa made her way back to her digs the thoughts of Paul which she had been holding back crowded into her mind. The clatter of the tram wheels over the tracks seemed to sound his name. It went round in her head in a perpetual jingle. Andrea was so beautiful and so rich. She was sure to have a huge white wedding with lots of guests in fashionable clothes and lovely hats. The food and drink would be special. Probably they'd drink only champagne. Then she and Paul would go away together to a secluded honeymoon spot. The Cap d'Antibes, perhaps? Would it be warm there at this time of year? Tessa couldn't stop torturing herself.

Eve was asleep when she reached their room so Tessa went back downstairs and sat by the fire, trying to read until it was time for a light meal before departing for the Hippodrome. Eve slept on while she changed, only stirring when Tessa was ready to go.

'Break a leg,' she murmured.

Tessa and the band performed for an audience which, as Josh had predicted, was not really interested as they waited restlessly for the next talkie to begin. A few of them sang to a couple of numbers and most joined in with Tessa in a well-known chorus from a British film. She sang the favourite number from 'That's a Good Girl'. 'Fancy our meeting, for just one more greeting, When days are so fleeting and few . . . A dream worth the dreaming come true . . .' The audience faded from her consciousness as she put her heart into the words. The dream she'd so foolishly had about Paul would never come true and she could blame no one but herself for her unhappiness. She should have understood that in his world endearments and kisses were taken lightly. Her second number was 'A Garden of Lies' and her voice broke on the words, 'We met there, and danced there, Our feet were light as air . . .' and even the rowdiest member of the audience was silenced.

Back at the digs Mrs Biggs provided cocoa or tea and biscuits for anyone who needed them. Tessa sipped her cocoa which was rich and chocolatey, just like Mum's.

Josh came to sit beside her. 'That break in your voice, Tessa—'

'Yes?' She was wary.

'It's brilliant. You know, you're a natural performer. You don't use it often so when you do it has an immediate effect. Keep it up. And thanks for going on without Eve.'

'How was it?' asked her cousin who was sitting up in bed eating soup kindly brought to her by Mrs Biggs.

'I don't think they'd have noticed or cared if I wasn't there,' said Tessa.

Eve smiled in an annoyingly satisfied way. 'Bad luck,' she said.

'I don't think live entertainers will be wanted in cinemas for much longer,' said Tessa.

'Hark at you. The great theatre seer.'

'I'm glad you're feeling well enough to be sarcastic.'

Eve's mood changed abruptly. 'Tessa, thank you for helping me. I don't know what I would have done without you. You've been a brick. I'll do the same for you one day. Oh, dear, I could have phrased that better. But I owe you one. Will that do?'

'You owe me nothing. Mum and Dad taught me to give without wanting to take.'

Ignoring this rather pretentious little speech, Eve asked how they were.

On the following day at rehearsal, Sammy congratulated Tessa on the way her singing had quietened the cinema crowd and Eve scowled, giving her cousin a hard look. They watched the chorus, pretty girls who appeared in next to nothing without a trace of self-consciousness,

318

going through their routines, parading along the joy-plank smiling and cavorting just as if the seats were already full. The comics told their jokes to the echoing auditorium, getting discouragingly few laughs from artistes and stage personnel who had heard them before. The others' professionalism made the Kissing Cousins nervous, but they got through their songs and the artistic director declared himself satisfied.

Eve tired quickly and went to sit in the dressing-room but Tessa stayed to watch the juggler and realised for the first time what intense concentration such an act needed to keep going and at the same time sustain an amusing patter. She forestalled the call-boy who was about to fetch Eve for their final song, afraid that she might be feeling too ill to go on. Eve was ready, but sitting with her eyes closed, her face drawn.

'Are you all right?' asked Tessa anxiously.

'I'm ready to sing, if that's what you mean. You know, we could easily go on as an independent act. Any band would do.'

'Any band would not do,' said Tessa, hanging on to her patience. 'Josh is as much part of our act as we are. He accommodates us.'

'Oh? How?'

'When you had your solo bit your voice was weaker than usual – quite understandably in the circumstances. He hushed the musicians so that they didn't drown you. He cares about you, Eve.'

'Weak, was I?'

Tessa side-stepped. 'They'll be waiting for us. Are you ready?'

'Of course I am.' Eve jumped up quickly, swayed and might have fallen if Tessa hadn't steadied her.

'You're not strong enough,' she protested. 'Let me tell Josh you haven't fully recovered.'

'So that you can do another solo spot? No!'

Eve kept going, though back at the digs she went straight to bed. She was up and ready to leave for the show on time. In the dressing-room which they shared

319

with a comedienne and a soubrette she was almost silent as she put on her make-up. Tessa saw Cissie Barnes, the comedienne, give a quick, amused glance at the make-up boxes which the Kissing Cousins had splashed out and bought themselves. She used an old cigar box. So did Dolly Driver, the soubrette, and Tessa resolved that at the earliest opportunity she would change her case for a cigar box. This was evidently more professional.

Eve used a wet make-up which would be more effective on her pallid complexion and stay on longer. She creamed her face, working it into the pores until she attained complete coverage, then carefully wiped off the excess. She followed with the foundation, choosing a pinker tint than she would normally use, mixed with a touch of chrome. Then with finger tips she applied rouge, again using more than usual, keeping the colour fullest on her cheekbones, blending it so that it faded into the foundation. She then worked on her eyes. Chrome and blue on her lids and a line of brown on the edges, extended beyond the corners. The powder was placed in a patting motion so as not to disturb the paint, then the surplus brushed off with a hare's foot. Eyelashes received a generous coating with a camel hair brush, each hair painted separately under and over and the brows outlined. Last, the lips. Eve had no need to try to alter the shape of her perfect mouth and simply applied colour. When she had finished whitening her neck and arms no one could have told she looked sick beneath the paint. In fact, she appeared almost indecently healthy and Tessa silently applauded her cousin.

She applied her own make-up which was quite different from Eve's. The comedienne and the soubrette finished before the Kissing Cousins and sat and watched them, Cissie with a superior smile, Dolly sympathetically.

'We haven't been in the business long,' said Tessa.

'I can tell,' said Cissie. 'But you're learning fast. Miss Brook has done wonders. Are you not too well, dear?'

'Not too well,' said Eve.

'Is it the time of the month? Men have it easier than us. They don't have tiresome bodily functions to contend with.'

Tessa felt a little shocked. Theatre people were pretty outspoken, but this was going too far.

The comedienne was on before them and when she had gone Dolly Driver said, 'Miss Barnes is rather coarse. I've shared with her before. But she's right, Miss Brook, you don't look well. You're a real trouper, though. We can never give up. Our public expects us to go on.'

Dolly was older than her make-up revealed, but she was short and had kept her figure superbly well so that seen on stage with her dancing and singing act she seemed young and got plenty of catcalls from the men in the gallery.

Tessa watched Eve anxiously, but when their call came, she was ready and they went into their act. The applause was generous and Eve forgot her weakness for a while. Then the excitement died.

'You can't do the second house,' said Tessa.

'Who says so?'

Both girls went to bed that night exhausted. Eve from physical distress, Tessa from lack of sleep and mental anguish caused by worry over her cousin and her own nervousness on this first night on-stage in a theatre which, not so very long ago, she had never thought she would enter even as a spectator.

# Chapter Fifteen

Rose Brook sat alone and wondered why her love for her husband was so persistent when it had nothing to thrive upon. Since he had become involved with Irene Martinez his sexual needs had apparently been completely satisfied and he made no demands upon his wife.

Rose thought about the latest cocktail party they'd attended. Ralph had escorted her because he insisted on keeping up appearances. The gathering was noisily jolly, thanks to the repeal of Prohibition. After thirteen years which had provoked the rise of bootleggers and gangster mobs, one could openly serve alcohol and know it to be safe to drink. But Rose could not unbend. An out-of-town friend of Martha's had asserted that when a husband's attentions were directed elsewhere a woman should be grateful that the perpetual demands of marriage were lessened. The other women present laughed at the joke, but Rose could only smile and hold her rage in check. Her body still craved for Ralph's love. She still possessed beauty, unlike, she thought viciously, the ruddy-skinned woman who thought herself so amusing. There might be a few fine lines on her face, but other men found her attractive and if she had given them encouragement she could have taken lovers. But her aching need remained fixed on Ralph.

There were times, during the long lonely nights, when she shed tears, but he would never know. She despised herself for her weakness both in caring for him and in crying for him. How many years had this latest affair lasted? Good God! It must be three at least. No woman had ever interested him for so long before. She felt a stab of fear. In the past, Ralph had been true to convention, valuing respectability in his private life and his standing in the business world. Now he was employed by a man he despised as a nouveau riche. If his sense of the fitness of things deserted him there was nothing to hold him.

She wondered what Irene Martinez gave him that she could not. She had soon discovered that Miss Martinez possessed an income which could keep her in comfort. Nowadays she probably had more to offer Ralph than had his wife who was struggling to keep up the house, pay the few remaining servants, maintain a car on the road and dress herself attractively. She writhed at the memory of a recent humiliation. On a visit to a jeweller to have a loose diamond reset in a ring, a new assistant had presented her with a bill to be passed on to her husband. It was for an emerald pendant. The store manager had seen what was happening too late to prevent it and had been profuse in his assertions that the bill was meant for a woman with the same name. Rose knew he was lying. The emeralds were exactly right for a woman with an olive complexion, black hair and green eyes. Irene Martinez, in fact. She had lain awake all that night, fighting shame and anger.

Her thoughts were interrupted by the entrance of Carrie who smiled at her sympathetically, irritating her. 'All alone?' she said, in a would-be merry tone which added to the irritation.

'As you see.'

'I was passing and wondered how you were.'

'Belper did not announce you.'

'No, that was my fault. I assured him that an old friend like me needed no introduction.'

'I see. I am well, thank you. Would you like tea?'

'I would adore a cup. And some of those little fancy cookies your Selina makes so well. You do still have her working for you, don't you?'

'Why should I not?' Rose stretched out a hand to ring the bell.

324

Carrie flushed. 'Well, you know, your changed fortunes.' At Rose's coolly uplifted brows she said quickly, 'Sorry. I do put my foot in it, don't I?'

Rose thought of cutting replies she could make, but Carrie was too easy a target and she and Herbert had had to retrench, though not drastically. Belper brought tea which Rose poured from a silver pot into porcelain cups. Carrie helped herself to two spoonfuls of sugar before reaching out for the cookies. 'Mmm,' she murmured, 'these are so good. You are lucky to still have Selina.' Rose continued to sip her tea, and Carrie blundered on, 'Of course, you wouldn't have trouble keeping your servants. You handle them so well. I dare say you get more work out of them than I do mine. This house is so beautiful, so serene. I mean, well, mine gets in muddles. The servants forget things and I haven't the heart to chide them properly.' Rose managed a faint smile and Carrie said, 'I suppose you think that very weak of me.'

'I would not tolerate lax service.'

'No, but you are more forceful than I. Do you know,' Carrie confided, 'I have always been a little in awe of servants. When I was a girl Mama always took care of that side. Herbert sometimes gets a trifle cross with me, but he always forgives me.'

'After you've shed floods of tears, I suppose?'

Carrie laughed shakily and helped herself to more cookies. 'I do cry rather easily, but Herbert hardly ever grumbles and he is so nice to me afterwards it's worth the reprimand. He buys me presents. He used to give me jewellery, but I seldom wear it and now he sends flowers. So much more romantic, don't you think?' She took more cookies. 'I really shouldn't. I'm getting quite stout.'

Rose looked at her friend. Quite stout was an understatement. Carrie was most definitely stout. Rose watched her as she finished a chocolate cookie and washed it down with tea. Her face was rounded and fleshy like her body and she perspired easily. Yet presumably Herbert loved her and as far as anyone knew he was faithful to her. How could an outsider judge what a man might need from his wife? To think that this over-weight woman dressed in a hideous pink floral frock whose colours clashed with her complexion, while a pale violet hat with two pink quills perched on the side of her head adding to the awful mismatch, should hold her husband's devotion so completely. And Herbert was quite handsome and good at business. Carrie glanced up and caught her look.

She touched her hat. 'Do you like it? I only bought it yesterday. It blends so well with my frock.'

She reminded Rose of a small girl asking for approval and she was unexpectedly moved. Carrie had never been known to malign a soul and absorbed any catty remarks about herself without a hint of a reaction. Rose had always believed her ineffably stupid, but perhaps she was the cleverest of them all. 'Your hat is very pretty,' she said, 'and so is your gown.' Both statements were true. The problem was that they were wrong for Carrie and wrong for each other.

'Have you heard from Eve lately?'

Rose did not want to contemplate the life of her daughter. 'I received a letter this morning.'

'What is the dear girl doing?'

The dear girl is set on ruining her life, thought Rose. 'She is amusing herself. She and her cousin sing.'

'Eve always had a pretty voice. Where do they sing? At parties, I suppose? I'm sure she is much in demand.'

'I believe so.'

'Is this an English cousin?'

'Yes. The girls met at old Mrs Brook's funeral and struck up a friendship.'

'She has not been home for an age, has she?'

'It does seem a long time, but when young people are busy time does slip by and the best of them can be thoughtless.'

'That's true, though Elliot—' Carrie hesitated, then continued, 'He has given us no real problems. He's courting a very nice girl. So suitable. From a branch of the Crowthers, you know.'

'I see. Which one?'

'The Washington Crowthers. Penelope is her name.'

'I know them slightly,' said Rose. 'They claim to have come over on the *Mayflower*, or at least not long after. No money.'

'That won't bother Elliot,' said Carrie. 'He has his grandmother's fortune. Eve would have had a comfortable life with him.' She stopped, coughed, and continued, 'I mean, if she had loved him, of course. No one would expect her to marry where she had no feeling.'

Rose sighed. One simply could not take umbrage at Carrie. She was like an ingenuous child. 'I am sure he will be happy with Penelope Crowther. As you say, where there is no feeling there should be no marriage.'

'I respect Eve for her decision to make her own way,' said Carrie.

'Yes. Eve is twenty-two, an independent woman. Very independent—' she smiled '—and naturally we make her an allowance. She might not have suited Elliot at all and I am sure that Miss Crowther will be ideal for him.' Rose had met Penelope Crowther a couple of times. She was gauche and rather dowdy and would undoubtedly fulfil her marriage promises and obey her husband. She wondered if the man lived whom Eve would obey.

'Her people like Elliot a great deal,' said Carrie.

'Are we to expect wedding bells soon?' Rose heard her own whimsical expression with some amusement. Somehow, with Carrie, one could so easily lapse into schoolgirl phrases.

'I believe so. Of course, if dear Eve had not chosen to stay in England – Elliot was so very fond of her.'

'Yes.'

There was an awkward silence and Carrie said, 'Betsy tells me that Paul is also planning his wedding. She and Reginald are sailing soon for England. Will you be attending?'

'I? Why should I?'

'He's family, isn't he?'

'Yes, he's my nephew it's true, but I don't think his

327

marriage necessitates my travelling so far. Betsy will take our gift with her.'

'The young lady is fortunate. Paul is a darling boy and will make a good husband.'

'I dare say. Like Eve, he is old enough to know his own mind.'

'Betsy tells me he has had his house completely refurbished and redecorated. It was full of heavy Victorian stuff, she says. Oh, but you already know that. You stayed there, didn't you?'

'I'm sure Paul has improved it.'

'Where's Eve living now?'

Rose swore silently. 'She has a place of her own. As soon as she knew that Paul would be bringing his bride to Padding House, she left. She did not need telling that a young bride would not want another girl living in the house.'

'Is she in London, or Bristol?'

'She had an apartment in Bristol before she moved to London.'

Actually Eve had no permanent address and her mail was sent collect at whatever town she was about to grace with her talents. She seldom wrote, though she had sent her mother a list of places and dates.

Carrie said, 'I think Betsy looks unwell.'

'She still suffers internally.'

'Does she diet properly and get enough rest?'

'I suppose so. Oh dear, I should know these things, but since the crash . . .'

Carrie jumped in to fill the silence left by Rose. 'We don't see much of Ralph any more. Is his health holding up?'

'Why should it not?' Rose had not meant her voice to sound quite so acerbic.

Carrie's ready blush stained her cheeks. 'No reason, I suppose, except that many men seem to have ulcers, heart attacks, all kinds of ailments since that dreadful time. Before, too, of course, but more so now.'

'Ralph is well, thank you.' Too damn well, Rose

328

thought. Well enough to chase after the Martinez woman who must be twenty years younger. 'He has to work hard to regain his lost position in business.'

'Of course.' Carrie got up. 'I must go. I have other calls to make. I'm so glad to have found you at home. We see so little of you nowadays. When I say "we", I mean all your friends. I'm holding a cocktail party tomorrow evening. Do say that you and Ralph will be there. Betsy and Reginald have promised to attend.'

'I will ask Ralph if he would like to go,' said Rose, hoping that he would not.


Tessa had asked Josh to tea at her home and suggested that Sammy Jacobs should come too. Mum greeted them with her usual politeness and she and Dad and the two men sat in the best room while Tessa bustled about with the tea things, enjoying the men's conversation.

'So you play the piano, do you?' asked Dad.

'I do,' said Sammy.

'It sounds a funny life for a man. Not like work at all.'

'It must seem strange to you, Mr Morland, but it's what I do best.'

'You travel about a lot, don't you?'

Sammy smiled. 'Showbusiness people have to travel. I suppose I'm a musical gypsy.' Dad stared and Tessa nearly laughed as he tried to make out if Sammy was serious. After all, his features were quite swarthy and his hair was black and curly, tinged now with grey. 'I'm not really a gypsy,' said Sammy. 'I'm a Jew.'

'Oh,' Mum said. 'A lot of your people play music, don't they, or act, or dance? And they seem to be successful in other ways.'

'We were granted a good measure of talent, Mrs Morland.'

To Mum and Dad, Roman Catholics and members of the Church of England (they lumped them together), especially the high church, embraced a false brand of Christianity and Jews didn't believe that Jesus was the son of God, so Sammy was a real challenge to Mum's desire to gain converts for her chapel.

'Have you ever been to an evangelist chapel?' Mum asked.

Sammy shook his head. 'Never.'

'Would you like to go to one?'

'I would have no objection,' said Sammy, his eyes mischievous.

Mum looked as if she had just won a major victory for God. She didn't understand that Sammy saw Mum's beloved chapel as entertainment, though he was too kind to let her know. Tessa caught his eye for a moment then turned hastily away. Perhaps she should be indignant, but she wanted to laugh. Mum was glowing. Here was a real sinner she could gather into the fold.

'Where's Eve today?' asked Dad.

'Resting,' said Tessa quickly. Eve was still recovering from the abortion and tired quickly. After such a bad time she had gone back to work far too soon.

'She had a nasty illness,' said Josh. 'She looks too pale to me.'

'Parrish's Chemical Food,' said Mum decisively. 'That's the stuff to get her back on her feet. Tessa, you must buy her some as soon as the shops open.'

'I'll do that,' said Josh. 'After all, she's my employee and I have her welfare at heart.'

'That's good of you,' said Dad. 'Do you belong to a union?'

Josh was startled. 'Why, yes.'

'I'm asking,' said Dad, 'because the subject is on my mind these days. If I get back into my trade I'm thinking of joining one. I used not to think like that—'

'You certainly didn't,' said Mum, scandalised. According to her, unions were for socialists, not good Tories or Liberals.

Dad was impervious to the frosty atmosphere. 'If I'd joined the union from the beginning I might not have found myself sweeping up for a fruit market. Not that there's any shame in it, but I wish I could get back to my trade. Some hopes with nearly three million out of work.' He drew breath and handed his cup and saucer to Mum who refilled it and handed it back, looking at him as if she'd never seen him before.

Susan and Joey arrived home from school. Susan had managed to persuade Mum to let her continue with her education a little longer, using the lack of jobs these days as a telling argument. They were delighted to find visitors and a special tea and sat down and tucked in, letting the conversation flow over their heads.

Tessa left with Sammy and Josh. 'What a lovely family you've got,' said Sammy as the tram lurched its way towards Old Market. He sounded so sad it worried her.

'Do you have children?' she asked.

'We were blessed with a son who died in infancy.'

'I'm very sorry.'

'Thank you.'

'Do you have other relatives, brothers and sisters?'

'I have only my cousins in Germany. Nice families both of them. I go out to see them every year and sometimes they come here.'

'Have you ever seen Herr Hitler?'

Sammy said nothing for a moment. 'I've seen him from a distance.'

'Are the things they say about him true?'

'It depends on what you've heard.'

'He hates Jews among others. He believes that people with deformities, even the blind and deaf, should be sterilised. He tells people not to spend their money with Jews. He burns books he doesn't like.'

'True.'

'All of it?'

'All of it.'

'Is it true, too, that he has built camps to imprison Jews and political prisoners? That they are ill-treated, even tortured?'

'Yes, it's true. When the Nazis took over they established so-called "wild camps", make-shift prisons where people were held in what the Nazis call "protective custody". Since then, permanent camps have been erected

331

to imprison people on almost any excuse.'

'Why does Hitler do it?'

'Only he can answer that.'

'Why is he allowed to be so terrible?'

'He's Chancellor. His word is obeyed blindly by those who follow him.'

'Doesn't anyone oppose him?'

'Yes, and it's those who are arrested. Even if they remain at liberty their lives are made unendurable. Some get imprisoned, others just disappear, leaving their families wondering what has become of them. I worry about my cousins. They are outspoken men. Rueben has no children, but Jacob is teaching his to defy Hitler. I warned them the last time I was in Germany; I tried to make them leave, but they refused to listen.'

'Hitler should be stopped,' said Tessa indignantly.

Sammy smiled and laid his hand over hers. 'If everyone thought the way you do it might be possible. At least, it might once have been possible. Governments are afraid now that if they tried to interfere they could be plunged into war.'

'Surely not?' said Tessa. 'The last war only ended fifteen years ago. I can just remember Mum grumbling about rations. Dad was in it and he won't talk about it. If it's even mentioned he gets a look in his eyes that's quite frightening.'

Josh had listened in silence to this exchange. He said, 'Sammy's right. If everyone felt the way you do, the world might be a happier place.'

'You don't honestly think we could go to war again?' asked Tessa.

'Things have never settled properly in Germany since 1918,' said Sammy.

Eve was sitting up in bed reading a magazine. The gas fire was lit giving out a cosy glow, she had her feet on a hot water bottle and was wearing a white fluffy bedjacket and altogether looked very pretty and very comfortable. She held a cigarette, an ashtray by the bed contained several butts and the room was dense with smoke.

'Is there anything you need?' asked Tessa a trifle sarcastically.

Eve grinned. 'A cup of tea when you make one?'

'I'll do it now.' Tessa put the kettle on the single gas ring in the grate, but when she turned the gas tap it failed to ignite and the fire went out.

'It needs more money in the meter,' said Eve.

Tessa produced sixpence worth of pennies and fed the meter.

'Did you have a nice time?' Eve asked absentmindedly.

'Lovely, thanks. Mum and Dad asked after you and sent good wishes. They would like to see you.'

'I'll visit soon.' Eve turned her attention back to *Picturegoer*, which she had recently discovered and whose every issue she devoured. Mrs Biggs had produced a pile of back numbers and was delighted to meet someone whose enthusiasm for moving pictures matched hers.

'Do you mind if I open the window a little before someone looks in and calls the fire brigade?' Tessa asked.

'Don't leave it open too long. The air is pretty raw.'

'No, ma'am,' said Tessa, but Eve was too deep into the dream-magazine to hear.

'Do you know,' she asked, 'that there were a thousand applicants for the chorus of Radio's new picture, *Maiden Cruise*, and only forty got chosen?'

'It wasn't brought to my attention,' said Tessa, 'but it doesn't surprise me. After all, they might not have room for a thousand beautiful dancing girls.'

Eve remained closeted in the film star world. 'Here's a photograph of Carl Brisson. Gosh, he's handsome. And his voice is beautiful. I don't see any reason why I shouldn't sing one day in a film, perhaps with him. And here's Jean Harlow – is her hair really that platinum blonde colour? She's reclining half upright between shots because her frock is too tight for her to sit down.

333

Oh, look, Joan Crawford with Franchot Tone. What I wouldn't give to act with him!'

'Aren't they in Hollywood? Why don't you be more realistic and dream about British films? After all, it wouldn't be so far to travel to Shepherd's Bush.'

'I know. I might go there first, but Hollywood is so glamorous and it's easy enough to get to. A boat to New York, a train trip and you're there.'

Tessa held out a cup of tea. 'What about the cost?'

Eve dismissed this with an airy wave which nearly caught the tea. 'Sorry.' She took it and put it on the bedside table. 'Josh has raised our money to eight pounds. I could save my allowance and I'd have enough for my fare.'

'I look forward to the day when you stop spending all your money as soon as it arrives.'

'Don't be unkind,' pouted Eve.

'You should get up soon. We have to eat before the theatre.'

'Ah, yes, the show must go on.'

'And you mustn't be late.'

'I won't. Here's Joan Crawford again. It says she uses vinegar and oil to get a good tan. The upholstery on her outdoor chairs is pure white leather. Oh, and look, Ramon Navarro in *The Pagan*.' Eve sighed. 'I wish he'd make love to me!'

'So do a million other women,' said Tessa. 'Eve, you must get up if you want supper.'

'Mrs Biggs says she'll bring it to me.'

'Don't you feel well?'

'Not very. Not yet.'

Tessa looked at her cousin who still looked pale and strained. 'Mum recommended a tonic. Josh says he'll buy it for you.'

'He's a good sort,' said Eve. 'Oh, look, here's Robert Young. Do you remember him in *Today We Live*? He's so handsome.'

'More handsome than Carl or Ramon?'

'All right, I know I go on a bit.' Eve sighed. 'One day

I'll get to Hollywood, I swear it.'

'Meanwhile,' said Tessa drily, 'you had better prepare yourself for tonight's humble appearance.'

Eve pouted, then laughed. 'You always have your feet firmly planted on the ground. One day it might go mushy and you'll sink.'

'Maybe. But I shan't go down without a struggle.'

When they left the theatre that night, Partridge, Paul's butler, was waiting for them. He handed an envelope to Eve who glanced at the inscription and stuffed it into her handbag. Back at the digs, Mrs Biggs was waiting with refreshments, eager to hear how the performance had gone.

'Very well, Josh said,' Tessa replied. 'I can never tell. I'm so nervous beforehand then when I get on the stage I can only concentrate on singing.'

'Experience will teach you,' said Mrs Biggs.

'You were on the stage, weren't you?' said Eve.

'I was that. I was a soubrette and a good one, though I say it myself. I was earning eight pounds a week when I left the business to get married.'

'We earn that, too,' said Eve. 'Both of us.'

'Yes, but I got eight pounds many years ago when it was really good money. Not that it's bad today, of course.'

'Did you never want to go back?' asked Tessa.

Mrs Biggs laughed. 'I gave it up to marry and never regretted it. I had a good man, but after twenty years and seven kids I wasn't quite the right shape.' She patted her stomach. 'I enjoy my food too much. But I missed the people and when my husband died I set up as a theatrical landlady and I've loved every minute of that, too.'

The girls said goodnight and went to their room where Eve lit the gas fire. 'She ought to come up and light it for us before we get here,' she said. 'It's freezing.'

'You're still not well,' said Tessa soothingly. 'I'll fill a hot water bottle and tuck you up in bed. You need rest.'

'You don't have to patronise me!'

'I'm just trying to care for you.'

'Well, stop talking to me as if I were a baby!'

'Stop acting like one!'

Eve glared at Tessa. Her eyes were bloodshot and her face looked all the more pallid after the brilliance of her make-up. Tessa said, 'Do get undressed.'

'I'm sorry,' said Eve. 'I'm beastly to you sometimes. I don't know why you put up with me. Why do you?'

'I can hardly be a Kissing Cousin on my own.'

'You could soon find another singer. You don't really have to be related to her.'

Tessa looked anxiously at Eve. 'I'll give you your dose of Parrish's,' she said.

'Ugh!'

'I'll fetch some milk to swill it down with.'

'I don't want any, thank you. I'm sloshing with cocoa. Mrs Biggs says it's good for me. She brought some up twice this morning.' She sat up in bed creaming her face, peered at herself, then reached into her bag for eyebrow tweezers. As she did so her unopened letter slid out and when Tessa carried the hot water bottle to the bed she saw that the large envelope bore her name as well as Eve's.

She picked it up. 'Why didn't you tell me this was for both of us?'

'What? Oh, that. I forgot. It's sure to be an invitation to Paul's wedding.'

An actual pain shot through Tessa. She picked up the envelope, fingered it for a moment, then opened it. Eve was right. There were two cards with the words printed clearly in black ink on pure white board embellished discreetly with silver leaf. Tessa looked at hers. Her name had been written in an unfamiliar hand. 'I suppose this is Andrea's writing?'

'More likely to be her mother's secretary. At least we'll get a good feed and plenty of champagne. It's on Tuesday so we won't have a matinee.'

'Why did Partridge have to deliver it?'

'I don't know. Perhaps Paul sent him. He probably thought it would seem more personal.'

It would be more than she could bear, thought Tessa, to watch Paul marry another woman. She scrabbled around for an excuse, but in her panic could think of nothing viable. She realised that Eve was watching her closely and all her defences came into play as she said carefully, 'It'll be a grand affair. We'll have to wear suitable clothes.'

'Will you mind being there?'

'Why should I?'

'You're sweet on him, aren't you?'

'Sweet on him! What would your mother say if she heard you using slang?'

'You haven't answered me.'

'Will I mind watching Paul get married? No, of course not. I hope he'll be happy.'

No one would ever know what it cost her to say it.

Tessa awoke with a feeling of oppression. Then she remembered. Today was Paul's wedding day and she would be there to watch him marry Andrea. She climbed out of bed and opened the curtains, shivering in the icy morning air. The sky was clear blue, the sun shining through a rapidly clearing mist.

'Shut the curtains,' mumbled Eve.

'They've got a lovely day for it,' said Tessa, rubbing salt into her own wounds.

Eve sat up so suddenly she felt giddy and clapped a hand to her forehead. 'The wedding! What time is it? We have to be at the church for twelve, don't we? Oh, it's only ten. Why on earth are you up? You disturbed me. God, it's cold.' She slid beneath the bedclothes once more. 'Any chance of some coffee?'

'We've only got tea.'

'Mrs Biggs has some coffee.'

'I'll fetch some for madam.'

'Don't take your misery out on me.'

Tessa swung round. 'What's that supposed to mean?'

'I just know you're dippy about Paul. You are, aren't you?'

'Not at all. And if I were, I wouldn't tell you.'

Tessa put on her dressing gown and slippers and padded downstairs. The house was quiet. The band had played the usual two houses last night and Mrs Biggs was quite content to allow her showbusiness people to sleep late. As Tessa approached the kitchen she heard the muted sound of the wireless. Mrs Biggs was seated at the kitchen table reading her newspaper.

'Hello, love, you're early. Tea's made. It's on the hob. Coffee's over there.'

Tessa poured herself a cup and measured out Camp coffee.

'Does her ladyship want coffee brought up?' Mrs Biggs indulgent smile removed any sting from her words.

Tessa hoped that Mrs Biggs never heard the insults Eve handed out to the sweet liquid which went by the name of coffee in many households. She made a face when she drank it and declared it to be disgusting.

'How do you think Eve is looking?' asked Mrs Biggs.

'Much better. You've been very kind to her.'

'It isn't difficult to be kind to her, she's so sweetly pretty and appreciative. Does she never lose her temper?' She didn't wait for an answer. 'You must be looking forward to the grand wedding. They've got a lovely day for it. I wonder what the bride will wear? Fur, I shouldn't wonder.'

As Tessa carried the cups of coffee and tea upstairs she thought of Mrs Biggs's words. Fur! Not a silk or satin gown in which the bride would shake with the cold while keeping her face in a fixed smile and trying to stop her teeth from chattering. Andrea would have comfort with style.

In fact, Andrea wore both silk and fur. Her ivory silk gown which reached her ankles was embroidered with hundreds of tiny pearls. Her white ermine wrap touched the floor; panels of white velvet let into the fur were decorated with ermine flowers. Her head-dress was a coronet of white roses and orange flowers and she carried a bouquet of the same flowers with delicate green tendrils of ivy. Everything was in unimpeachably good taste and she looked stunningly beautiful.

Paul waited at the altar with Rupert Bamford, his best man. Tessa clenched her fists. She should have stayed away. She felt as if she was suffocating in the heavy scents of the hot-house flowers, but if she had refused the invitation she would have admitted her stupid weakness. She would also have handed Eve a weapon with which to torment her.

The organ soared into bridal music and Andrea's father escorted her up the aisle while Tessa cursed the day she had met Dad's family. And when Paul turned and smiled at his bride she had to hang on to herself to refrain from crying out. She concentrated on the flowers and the bridesmaids, four of them, three adults in shades of pink and a small girl in lemon. A page in black velvet and white lace fidgeted, which kept Tessa interested for a moment. But in spite of her efforts the words uttered by bride and groom came to her as clear as trumpet calls.

Then it was over and Andrea swept down the aisle again, this time on her husband's arm, to where her maid waited with her fur wrap. Photographs were taken and the couple were transported to the Frenchay house, Andrea having chosen to entertain the guests in her new home.

Tessa and Eve were driven to Padding House. They passed along the receiving line where they were welcomed by the bride and groom, her parents, and Mr and Mrs Jefferson senior, Paul's father smart, his mother unexpectedly dowdy, both beaming out their happiness.

Dowdy Mrs Jefferson might be, but she was gentle and kind, quite different from Mrs Rose Brook, and kissed Eve and told her she should return to America soon.

'Why?' she asked flatly.

Mrs Jefferson was taken aback. 'Why? Your parents both need you. They are having a difficult time.'

'Who isn't?' said Eve.

Mrs Jefferson coloured and her husband looked cross. They shook hands with Tessa. 'You're a cousin, too, aren't you, my dear?' said Mrs Jefferson.

'A distant one.'

'A kissing one,' said Eve.

Apart from the new paintwork the house looked much the same from the outside, but inside it had been transformed. Oppressive, gloomy furniture had been replaced by delicate pieces which blended with the few Victorian pieces retained. The paint was light, as were the wall-paper and fabrics in abstract designs, and there were bright corners where there had been shadows. In the wrong hands it could all have clashed horribly, but it was clear that whoever had selected everything had an expert eye for style and colour.

Looking at the set of Andrea's firm mouth, the rather haughty bearing of her figure, knowing her dress sense, Tessa guessed that all the inspiration had come from her. She seemed to be perfect in all that she did. She would make Paul an admirable wife, a gracious hostess and a splendid mother to his children. The last thought almost caused her to drop her glass of wine.

They were in the drawing room, where the reception had been held after Great-grandmother Brook's funeral. This time she knew quite a few of the guests. Poppy was here and Tiddles who gave her a particularly warm greeting, Jack Padbury, the Bamfords, and David Selby and Charles Ware. They seemed pleased to see her. Then someone suggested that the Kissing Cousins might sing for them and Eve, smiling as always when she was the centre of attention, moved to the piano and Tessa had to follow. Only her newly acquired professionalism helped her to look serene.

'You'll have to play,' said Eve. 'I'm too tipsy.' She giggled and Tessa looked around for some music.

Paul came to her side and opened the piano stool. 'Here you are,' he said. 'Here's a good one.'

Tessa took the music sheet from him. ' "Yes, Yes, My Baby Says Yes". Very appropriate.'

340

Paul laughed. 'Do you know it?'

'Of course,' said Tessa matter-of-factly, amazed that he couldn't hear the pounding of her heartbeats. The song caused some amusement and Paul took Andrea in his arms and seemed to be trying to persuade her to dance. She shook her head, smiling at first, then frowning as he persisted. He gave up, looking disappointed.

There was applause at the end of the song and cries of: 'More! Encore!' Tessa placed another piece of music on the stand and the girls began to sing, 'The One I Love Belongs to Somebody Else'. She immediately regretted her choice. She had no problem in getting the break in her voice as she sang the poignant words, playing the most difficult act of her life. When the song ended there was silence for a moment, followed by more enthusiastic applause and murmurs of appreciation.

Paul came over to thank them. 'The Kissing Cousins sound better every time I hear them. You must sing at parties for us when you return from your tour. We shall open up the London house for part of the year. Good luck.'

Eve smiled and lifted a hand in a salute before she wandered back among the guests.

'She doesn't look well,' said Paul.

'I'm surprised you have eyes for anyone but your wife today,' said Tessa. She hoped he hadn't notice the slight bitterness which had crept into her voice.

'You're quite right and I haven't really. Isn't she lovely?' He looked over at Andrea who was laughing at something Rupert was telling her. 'She is so beautiful and very sweet and gentle.'

Tessa was surprised. Sweet and gentle? Maybe there was more to Andrea than first appeared.

Eve was flirting madly with David Selby and Charles Ware, and Paul laughed. 'She doesn't change, does she? Is there a special man friend on the scene?'

'For Eve or for me?'

Paul smiled. 'I meant for her. Have you met someone, Tessa?'

'Eve is still heart-whole as far as I know and so am I.'

'That's good. You don't need distractions when you're building a career. Did you ever finish your song? "Remember?", wasn't it?'

'That's right. Fancy you remembering "Remember?".' They laughed and she recalled the way they had laughed at foolish things before. 'No, I haven't worked on it since.'

'You really should. You are a superb singer and if you were able to use your own compositions you'd have a strong act.'

'Eve and I believe we already have a strong act.'

'Ouch! Sorry. But you should go on with your composing. Besides, if Eve really falls for someone she'll be off like a shot and you'll be stranded.'

Tessa recognised the truth of his words. Before she could reply Andrea beckoned and Paul went swiftly to her side. Then they left the guests to change into their going-away clothes.

When Andrea reappeared she was wearing a green and white tweed ensemble which was Paris-inspired. Her hat was of the same tweed with a green band, tilted over one eye. It suited her chestnut hair to perfection. As she said her farewells she looked as cool as if she were married every day. Paul watched her with an expression of tender worship which twisted the steel in Tessa's wounds, then drove her away in their large new Humber Pullman. It was majestic and expensive, an entirely suitable vehicle for Andrea, thought Tessa, as she struggled with overwhelming grief and longing. She would give years of her life to be where Andrea sat now.

A voice said softly in her ear, 'Don't let everyone see how you feel, my dear.'

The words sent a cold chill over her as she whirled round to see Charles Ware bending over her. There was no mockery in his face, no pity either, for which she was thankful, but a wealth of understanding which astonished her. When he held out his arm it seemed natural to put her hand on it.

He led her back to the drawing room. 'The show has

gone flat,' said Charles. 'It always does when the chief performers have left.'

Tessa managed a smile.

'That's better. You have a pretty smile. Shall I get you a drink? Medicinal champagne perhaps?'

'Please.'

He returned with two fluted glasses holding the sparkling liquid. Handing her one, he toasted her. 'To you and your future.'

'Shouldn't you be toasting the Kissing Cousins?'

'No. When you get to know me better you will understand that I seldom do anything I don't want to do.' He was serious again, his eyes searching her face. She had thought they were black; now she realised that they were deep blue. What made him think she would ever get to know him better?

'I've never seen anyone with navy blue eyes before,' she said. 'Hell, the wine's giving me a loose tongue . . .'

He laughed. 'May I take you to dinner?'

She was surprised then said, 'Can't. The first house begins at six-forty.'

'Yes, of course, your profession. That does put a bit of a damper on dinner. A drive then? Tea somewhere in the country?'

Tessa's mind slipped back to the days when she and Paul had driven about a very different countryside. A place where the hot sun brought out unfamiliar scents, where wine had tasted sweet beneath a living awning.

'Stop it,' said Charles sharply.

'What!'

'Stop thinking of him. He's never going to be yours. He's married.'

'I wasn't . . .'

'Yes, you were. Be honest with me, Tessa, or our friendship's off.'

He had stung her. 'In the first place we don't have a friendship, not a real one.'

'We shall.'

'And I wasn't thinking of anything in particular.'

343

'Liar! Your face said it all.'

'Heavens, I shall have to wear a mask,' she cried, managing to produce a scathing laugh.

He said seriously, 'You must learn how to present a mask to others, to control your feelings, inwardly, and develop an outer shell. Eve has one. Sometimes I think she was born with one.'

Tessa remembered Eve sobbing in her arms after her secret nightmare. 'No! I don't agree with you.'

'About what?'

'Eve.'

'You sound positive.'

'I won't discuss my cousin with you.'

'I keep forgetting you really are cousins. Amazing. You're so different.'

'As you don't know either of us very well I don't see how you can make such an assumption.'

'May I take you for a drive?'

'You don't give up easily, do you?'

'I never give up on something I want.'

'Heavens, is a drive so important to you?'

'Yes. With you.'

Tessa felt flustered. Charles was different from any other man she had met. She sensed turbulent emotions, a powerful magnetism. It was because he was older, she decided. She wondered why he had never married. She thought of returning to her digs to chatter with Eve about the wedding reception. Her cousin would dig under her skin, not as Charles had done, but with an angry malice she couldn't seem to help.

'I might come with you,' Tessa said abruptly. 'But I can't just walk out on Eve.'

'You won't need to. She left half an hour ago with David Selby. Of course, he hasn't any money, but she's probably just looking for an amusement to distract her.'

'Stop running Eve down to me.'

'I wasn't. I was just accepting her. And so should you. Come along, Tessa, let's say goodbye and be on our way.'

# *Chapter Sixteen*

Charles's car was a dark red saloon. Tessa had heard that
he had bought a new one and was surprised to find it so
understated.

He was watching her. 'Did you think I would turn up
in a snappy two-seater sports car?'

'It had crossed my mind.'

Charles opened the passenger seat door, helped her
in, and tucked a fur robe around her knees, before walking round to the driving seat. 'There's a time in most
men's lives when a sports model is what they crave. I
have passed that stage.'

'I see.'

'I don't think you do, but you will.'

He started the engine and Tessa became conscious of
the power it generated. 'What kind of car is it?' she
asked.

'I forgot. You drive, don't you? Paul taught you in
France.'

'How do you know?'

'Eve told me.'

'You talked about me?'

'I certainly did.'

The conversation seemed to have assumed some significance. He seemed to be hinting at something deeper
and she glanced at him quickly. His expression gave
nothing away. He was undoubtedly handsome, without
appearing over-conscious of his good looks. His hands
on the wheel were large and strong. Tessa had learned a
lot since she had left home and had met all kinds of men,

many of whom were anxious to pursue her acquaintance. Some she had felt genuinely liked her; others enjoyed the glamour surrounding a girl in showbusiness. None of them had emanated the particular quality of Charles Ware.

'It's made by a German company. Bayerische Motoren Werke, BMW for short.'

'What?'

'You asked me the name of my car.'

'Oh, yes. I've never heard of them.'

'They're a good, reliable company. The Germans are excellent engineers.'

'Are they? I've been hearing some very unpleasant things about them.'

'I dare say you have, though their political upheavals haven't done their car industry any harm. In fact, it will probably benefit in the end.'

'Surely you don't approve of what's happening in Germany?'

'You're referring to their Chancellor's unpleasant habit of removing those who oppose him? I must say I find Herr Hitler and his cronies a bit much to stomach. Germany is virtually a one-party state.'

'How has he gained such power?'

'Through fear, and the necessity of the people. The country had never really recovered from the war and its aftermath. On top of that, people were terrified by the street fighting between Nazis and Communists and, as they are scared witless of Russia, they chose the Nazis. The great middle class is largely responsible for his rise to power. He promises all kinds of reforms, but is an evil man.'

'You sound like our pianist, Sammy Jacobs. He's Jewish.'

'If Hitler gets his way and drives all the Jews from Germany they'll lose many of their best scientists. Some of their top business men and entertainers will go too. You'd think he'd at least keep the men and women with scientific knowledge. If he does go to war he'll probably need them.'

'Sammy says they put innocent people into camps where they are cruelly treated. Why should anyone do that?'

'Why? Power. Revenge. Hitler has a grievance. In 1924 he took part in an attempt to overthrow the elected government. It failed and he was sent to Landsberg prison for five years. He wrote a book there, *Mein Kampf*, and it's being used almost as a bible by many. It's all in our newspapers, though often one has to read between the lines. It's clear to me that Hitler is thriving on power. It can be a heady feeling.'

'Do you crave power?'

'God, no.'

'Don't you? Not at all?'

Charles laughed. 'Persistent, aren't you? It has a certain attraction, but I'm too lazy to be a dictator.'

'What work do you do?'

'I'm afraid I'm a dilettante. I ride, hunt, swim, play polo and golf, travel, read. And take out beautiful women.'

Tessa said, 'I'm just one of many, then?'

'No, that you aren't!'

She realised that she had assumed a mantle of beauty and was embarrassed. She had the impression that Charles was playing a game he played often. All right, she would play her end. 'You mean I'm not beautiful?'

'I didn't, but you're not. Not always.'

She gasped. 'That's a very unkind thing to say.'

'Who said I was kind? You've got something better than mere beauty. Eve has that, but I find her rather vacuous.'

'She is not!'

Charles smiled. 'She's lucky to have found such a loyal friend. Perhaps I used the wrong word. She veers from one way of behaving to another. Just as she veers between her men.'

This was shaky ground and Tessa had no wish anyway to discuss Eve with anyone.

When she didn't speak, Charles said, 'You have a quality, an air, which will always attract men.'

'Do I? Is it this mysterious quality of mine which attracts you?' She realised that in her determination to beat him she had again spoken without thought, but continued doggedly, 'Oh, but perhaps you're not attracted at all? You just wanted to take me for a drive so you could annoy me.'

'Do I annoy you? I'm sorry. I find you very engaging. I did when we met at the villa in France.'

'You said nothing then.'

'Of course not. You were besotted by Paul Jefferson. You still are.'

Tessa controlled the sharp stab of anguish his words gave her. 'I am *not*. Anyway, you still asked me out.'

'True.'

Town houses and shops were beginning to give way to bigger dwellings with gardens. 'Look at it,' said Charles. 'Suburbia. Rows of houses all looking exactly the same with their porches and bay windows, their little gardens and family cars. It's eating up the countryside. Soon we'll be just one big town.'

Tessa was still annoyed with him, but tried to sound rational. 'If you had lived in some cramped street without decent facilities, wouldn't you take the chance of buying a nice house where you could have all the modern conveniences?'

Charles was silent for a moment. 'You're right, but why do the houses all have to look the same?'

'Something to do with money?'

'Ah, yes, money. I tend to forget.'

'As people with large incomes easily acquired often do.'

'Oh! I was sure you possessed a sting!'

'You think you know everything about me?'

'No, I certainly don't. That's what makes you so interesting. Now, do you have a particular drive in mind? It's three o'clock and you have to be in the theatre by six-forty.'

'Heavens, no,' cried Tessa, alarmed. 'That's curtain-up. I must be there by five past six at the latest.'

'It sounds like school.'

'It's nothing like school, but in the theatre time-keeping is vital. If you are on the bill you must be ready to go on stage.'

'What happens if you fail? I mean, surely anyone could be delayed?'

'Allowances are made, but most actors don't ask for favours.'

'Do you get punished for being late?'

His semi-humorous tone annoyed her. 'There are severe penalties. If you're late too often you can be sacked.'

Charles whistled. 'As severe as that. Then I must make sure you get back. But we have time to visit Severn Beach, enjoy a breath of air and have tea. Would you like that?'

'It sounds wonderful.' Tessa settled herself beneath the fur ready to enjoy the drive in this most comfortable car, pushing the memory of Paul away whenever it threatened.

They strolled along the wide sea-wall. The wind coming off the water was strong and keen and whipped their faces to bright colour. It took Tessa's hat and Charles raced after and saved it just as it was about to land in the cloying grey mud.

She took it from him, laughing. He was laughing too. 'Tessa, today you are beautiful.'

That drove all laughter from her. 'I don't like your constant comments on my looks.'

'Don't you? Good lord, you are unusual. Of course, I already knew that, but every woman I've known loves being complimented. Are you sure you don't?'

Tessa was fuming with annoyance and frustration. Of course she enjoyed compliments. It was simply that Charles' presence, his clever manipulation of the conversation, disconcerted her. She couldn't think what to say.

'Let's find some tea,' he said. 'The last thing I want to do is irritate you.'

She poured tea from a brown china pot as they sat in a

café by a window that looked out upon the swirling waters of the rising tide.

'The Bristol Channel,' said Charles. 'It's the reason for the town. It's always been a trading port.' He helped himself to a slice of bread and butter. 'This is excellent. Do eat some more, Tessa. You could do with some extra weight. You need strength for your performance. I think I'll try to get a ticket for tonight.'

'We were sold out by last night,' said Tessa. 'I don't want to get plump,' she added crossly. 'I had enough of that as a child. Mum thinks that being fat goes with good health.'

'I'm sure she was only trying to do her best for you.'

'I know that!' Tessa stopped, frustrated again. He always managed to make her arguments sound trivial. She changed the subject. 'You've already seen the Kissing Cousins perform, haven't you?'

'Of course. I'm watching your career with interest. You improve all the time.'

'Eve will be pleased to hear it. She's been unwell. She needs cheering up.'

'I didn't say she was improving. She has stayed much the same. Just acquired a little professional polish, that's all. And a trifle more power to her voice.'

'If you're going to keep running Eve down, I won't ever come out with you again.' Charles's eyebrows climbed and Tessa blushed. 'Even if you meant to ask me,' she finished weakly.

'I intend to take you out again. As often as possible.'

'I see. We're leaving Bristol soon.'

'Yes. For Weston. A short drive away.'

'We go further afield after that.'

'As you see, I have an excellent car and there are plenty of trains and taxis.'

'You aren't serious, are you?'

'Never more so.'

He was imperturbable. Tessa didn't believe he meant what he said. He was like so many men, trying to impress. After tea she went to the ladies' room where

350

she stared at herself in the mirror. Her face was red and shiny, the result of the cold wind and hot tea. Her hair was tangled and resisted her efforts with a comb. Could Charles really see beauty in her? It was true she had never lacked male admirers, but compared with Eve she was very ordinary.

Charles took her to the theatre in good time. Eve was already in the dressing room. 'Where have you been?' she demanded.

'Where have *you* been?' Tessa retorted. 'At least I checked to see where you were before I left.'

'Oh. I went out with David Selby. He's very nice. It's a pity he's poor.'

'And I've been out with Charles Ware. It's a pity he's rich.'

Eve laughed disbelievingly. 'Charles Ware? He is interested in me, not you.'

'He seems to have changed his mind.'

'I suppose he realised I'd already left and felt like company.' This arrogant assumption staggered Tessa. 'And why is it a pity he's rich?'

'He doesn't have to think about making a living so he can concentrate on—'

'On what? Tell!'

'On people. He has time to analyse them.'

'Oh, really! Did he analyse you?'

Tessa wished she hadn't begun this line of conversation. 'Sort of.' She sat at the mirror beside Eve and began to make up. 'You seem to have enjoyed your outing with David,' she said, her face contorted as she smoothed in foundation.

'I did,' answered Eve. 'He's a nice man.' She rubbed off cold cream with a soft cloth. 'A *very* nice man.'

The girls worked in silence for a few moments, before they were joined by Dolly Driver. 'God, I'm tired,' were her first words. 'I've been out all day with my fellow. He wants me to leave the stage and get married.'

Tessa smiled. 'Congratulations.'

'Not in order, dear, I'm going on longer. I'm salting

away a nice little bank balance. I've no intention of beginning married life in a bed-sit. I want a house and garden and a car.'

There was a tap on the door. 'Are you decent?'

'It's the stage manager,' hissed Dolly. 'He's doing the half hour call himself. Come in,' she yelled.

The stage manager looked round the room. 'Miss Barnes not here yet?'

'Not unless she's hiding in a cupboard,' said Dolly cheekily, 'and that would be difficult. The whole room's only a cupboard.'

'You've got more space than the chorus,' he said and left.

There was silence as the three girls applied their make-up then Dolly said with an air of satisfaction, 'She's not arrived yet. Trouble for Miss Barnes.'

Tessa said crossly, 'You needn't have asked him in. You could have said we weren't dressed.'

'Do you mean deceive him?' Dolly's eyes opened wide with simulated horror. 'Deceive the SM? Tell him that Cissie was here?'

'No, not exactly.'

'Well, what then? And why in hell should I care anything about Miss bloody Barnes? She never cares for anyone else.'

Tessa was saved from replying by Cissie who raced in with only ten minutes to spare. She grabbed her clothes and dragged them on, then slapped on her make-up and was ready when the five-minute call came.

'You cut that fine, dear,' said Dolly.

'I was with my boy friend. He didn't want me to leave him. He's dreadful.' Cissie giggled. 'Today he turns up with a car, gets me out into the country and stops, saying he's run out of petrol. I didn't believe him. He's like an octopus. Hands everywhere.'

Dolly cast her eyes heavenwards.

It was time for the first appearance of the Kissing Cousins. Eve's colour had begun to return, though her skin was naturally quite pale and she used rouge liberally to combat the draining effect of the foot-lights. Josh and the band were in their places and they waited for the curtain to rise. It did so to quite a storm of applause. During their short time at the Empire they had become popular. Tessa, nerves gradually coming under control, was supremely happy. She loved everything about the stage. The rituals of make-up, dressing in flamboyant clothes, the camaraderie of the other performers, the smells, the sounds, the way the audience suddenly became hushed by expectancy as the huge curtains swept away. Even the bad-tempered spats which broke out, triggered often by the precariousness of their profession.

Josh, like other dance band leaders, had chosen a theme tune, 'Ain't We Got Fun', a catchy number which caught the fancy of the gallery, some of whom bawled out the words.

Eve and Tessa stepped forward and began to sing, and for Tessa that was the best moment of all. Almost better than the applause. Any trace of lingering nervousness was sublimated in the music. She sang with all her heart, sending the words out to the people on the other side of the footlights, her voice soaring to the gallery, emphasising their meaning, smiling happily when they were humorous, smiling a little wistfully when they were sad, acting out the songs so that she became a part of the words and music.

Eve, too, was learning. Her sweet soprano was growing stronger and was a perfect complement to her partner's voice.

Afterwards, Josh and the band played 'Tiger Rag', an instrumental piece, while the girls sat tapping their feet to the rhythm, their bodies swaying a little, still part of the whole act, then it was time for their second song. This was a novelty, 'I Scream Icecream, We All Scream for Icecream'. There was one more to be sung before the act went off until the second house. The orchestra began the gentle introduction and the Kissing Cousins' voices blended. 'Love is the sweetest thing; What else on earth could ever bring; A happiness to everything, As love's old story? Love is the strangest thing . . .'

Tessa singing with all her being was very conscious of the words. Love really was strange. What was it about one person that could so enslave another that life became meaningless without them? Images of Paul and Andrea on honeymoon invaded her senses and her voice broke. Josh shot her a pleased look. She kept a sweet-sad smile on her face for the audience who hadn't paid out good money on a ticket to a music hall to watch a singer looking miserable. During the interval she and Eve adjourned with Sammy and some of the others to a nearby pub where the men downed beer, Eve drank wine and Tessa a glass of lemonade. She wished she could take something stronger, something that would tame her wayward emotions which remained aroused by thoughts of Paul and his wife, but didn't dare. It went to her head too quickly and there was the second house to consider.

'You've got that break in your voice perfectly timed,' congratulated the bass player.

'Thanks,' Tessa said shortly. She felt hypocritical.

Sammy came to sit with her. 'You weren't faking the break. You're not happy.'

'How can you tell?'

'I know your moods.'

'Do you?' She thought of Charles's words. 'I must seem very easy to read. I wish . . .'

'You wish what?' asked Sammy gently.

'Nothing,' she snapped. Did she wish that Paul could have read her correctly? No, not that. To love without being loved was humiliating.

Sammy said, 'My apologies. I was only guessing. I dare say you aren't unhappy at all. Perhaps you have to think of something sad to get the pathos into your act.'

'It helps,' said Tessa.

She sipped her lemonade and Sammy got up to return to the others at the bar. She put her hand on his arm. 'Sorry I was short with you.'

'It's OK, Tessa. You can be any way you like with your Uncle Sammy.'

When Eve and Tessa left the theatre that night they found Charles Ware waiting.

Tessa was exhausted. Performing while at the same time controlling her turbulent emotions drained her. 'You again,' she said.

He seemed impervious to the rebuff and said blandly, 'Yes, me again.'

'Good,' said Eve. 'You can give us a lift home.'

'Eve—' began Tessa.

'Delighted,' said Charles, opening the passenger seat door. Eve surprised him by climbing into the front seat. He let Tessa into the back then went round to the driver's side, started the engine and drove the short distance to their digs.

Eve muttered a goodnight and walked straight through the front door which Mrs Biggs was holding open. Charles opened the rear door and, holding out his hand, assisted Tessa to the pavement. She leaned against the car, weary and sick at heart. Mrs Biggs quietly closed the front door.

'Your landlady believes we have something private to say to one another.'

'She's wrong then, isn't she?'

'Would you like a drive before bed?'

'I'm tired.' Feeling that was ungracious, she said, 'I've already had one drive today.'

'Didn't you enjoy it?'

'Yes.'

'Perhaps it's my conversation you dislike.'

'I didn't say I disliked anything.'

'Please let me take you somewhere. After all, it isn't very late.'

'I suppose not. Where could we go? I won't be much company for you.'

'We'll go wherever fancy takes you, and if you don't want to talk you needn't.'

'I can't think.'

'Then allow me to think for you.'

They drove up Park Street, along Whiteladies Road, on to the broad Downs and across the suspension bridge.

Charles drew up in front of a house set in woodland on the other side of the river.

'Where are we?' asked Tessa. 'Is this a night club?'

'No, it's my place.'

Indignation rose in her then died away. She felt so lethargic and Charles would hardly stoop to lead her into some kind of trap. She had only to speak and she had no doubt at all that he would take her straight back to the digs.

'Will you come inside?'

'I might as well.'

The house was not the largest in the area, but it must certainly have been one of the most luxurious. It was carpeted from the front door, on down the main corridor where there were other doors, up the stairs which curved gracefully to an upper landing. Charles led her into the drawing room where a fire was blazing.

'Who made up the fire?' asked Tessa. 'But I suppose you have plenty of servants.'

'My manservant tended the fire. I hoped you might come here with me.'

'This can hardly be called taking me for a drive.'

'Won't you sit down? I'll get some refreshment.'

'Mrs Biggs always supplies us with cocoa at bedtime.'

Charles wrinkled his nose. 'There may be some in the kitchen. The cook and maids probably drink it. I'll go and look, shall I?'

Tessa half rose to her feet. 'Are the servants here now? What will they think of me?'

'The women work by the day. Travers, my personal servant, lives in, but I told him he could have the night off. He piled on the coal before he left.'

'Then we're here alone.'

'Quite alone.'

'I see.'

Charles waited for a moment, watching her as she perched awkwardly on the edge of her seat. 'Er, forgive me, Tessa, but I am not sure if you prefer to be here with the servants or without?'

She laughed reluctantly. 'I don't know.' She sank back into the cushions. 'God knows why, but I trust you.'

'Not the most flattering thing I've had said to me, but it will do. For now. Are you sure you want cocoa?'

'I never said I did! I said that Mrs Biggs makes it for us.'

Charles seemed impervious to fractious retorts. He simply waited until she felt impelled to speak again.

'I think I would like something cold.'

'A drink with ice. We progress. Alcoholic?'

'No. Yes. I think so.'

Charles waited.

'I'll have a cocktail.'

'What kind would you like?'

'What kind have you got?'

He walked to a large carved sideboard on which stood many bottles, a jug, an ice pail and a shaker. 'Let me see. We have gin, orange, lemon and grapefruit juice, French and Italian vermouth, angostura bitters, rum, liqueurs, sugar, crème de menthe—'

'For heaven's sake!' Tessa laughed. 'You must hold some wild parties here.'

'Not lately. My wild party days passed away without regret.'

'Do you enjoy making yourself cocktails?'

'I prefer straight whisky or a good wine.'

'Oh.' Tessa gave this some thought. 'So are all those ingredients for girls you bring here?'

Charles said smoothly, 'I have brought a few girls here. I still do, though not often. And I give you my word, not one of them has interested me as much as you do.'

Tessa gazed around at the signs of wealth. She knew little of antiques, but everything here shrieked of money. Then she looked at Charles. He was smiling at her, assessing her responses. He was handsome, probably the best-looking man she had ever met, and his body was strong and lithe. Her own surprised her with its urgent response. She wanted to be kissed. Maybe even more

357

than kissed. She should get out of here as fast as possible. Fatigue and her yearning for Paul were undermining her will.

'I'll have a cocktail,' she said. 'Not very strong, mind.'

'I'll make you a Parisian Blonde. That's French vermouth, Curaçao and sweet cream.'

'It sounds nice.'

'If you'll excuse me for a moment I'll fetch cream from the kitchen.'

The room was silent except for the shifting of a coal. Charles' footsteps, muffled by the carpets, receded then returned. He tipped the ingredients into the shaker and shook it vigorously. The resultant drink was quite delicious and seemed harmless so Tessa accepted another. Gradually her tension eased. She had been right to come. She felt so much better.

'I'd like another,' she said.

'I don't think—'

'I didn't ask you to think. I asked you for another drink.'

He shrugged lightly. 'If you insist. Who am I to disobey the commands of a lady?'

The third cocktail seemed to have a great deal more impact than the first two. Tessa tried to get up and her legs wobbled. 'I think I should go home,' she said.

'Of course. Tessa, you're delightful.'

'I'm not sure you should say things like that to me. Not when we're here alone. I'm not sure I should be here at all. In fact,' she staggered and he steadied her, 'in fact, I know I shouldn't be here.'

'Damn right you shouldn't,' he muttered. 'Damn right.'

'You brought me.'

'Yes. Bloody stupid thing to do.'

'You wish you hadn't? You d-don't like me.'

'I like you,' he said grimly. He put an arm around her to assist her and they moved to the drawing-room door. Arriving there, Tessa stopped. Her body was sending out a crescendo of messages more demanding than any she had known before.

She looked up at Charles. 'Kiss me.'

'Not now, my love. Another time, perhaps.'

'Now! You said "my love". You do like me.'

'Tessa, for God's sake, those cocktails are strong. You—'

'Now!'

He sighed. 'A kiss then.' His lips came down on hers, gently, caressingly, then as her mouth clung insistently to his, with greater force. Her arms slid round his neck. 'Tessa, I hope you know what you're doing.'

'Of course I know. What do you take me for?'

'I don't know. I thought I did.'

Did she sense disappointment? Why should that be? Men liked making love, didn't they? He wanted her, didn't he? Men always wanted Eve. Eve was always telling her about the wonderful pleasures of sexual love. So many girls seemed to understand while she was still an infant in such matters. She pressed herself against Charles and found herself lifted and carried up the stairs and placed none too gently on a bed. He stood and looked down at her. 'Tessa, you must rest. Sleep a little and then I'll take you home.'

She giggled. 'Mrs Biggs will have a long wait.'

'Don't you have a key?'

'No. She sees us all into bed, just like a mother.'

He held out a hand. 'I didn't realise . . . Come along, we shouldn't keep the good soul waiting any longer.'

She held out both hands and when he took them she pulled him towards her. He was taken off guard and half fell on the bed. 'Tessa, for God's sake.'

'I won't go home. You can't make me.'

'I can, you know.' Once more he reached for her and this time dragged her to her feet. She sagged like a rag doll, forcing him to hold on to her. 'Go on, then. Take me to the car. Spurn me. Reject me.'

'Stop talking like a tragedy queen! Will you straighten up?'

'Make me.'

He allowed her to fall back on to the bed and stood looking down at her. She was fascinated by his stare. She writhed with wanting his caresses.

He said slowly. 'You know, you had me fooled. I thought—'

She only half listened. 'You thought? You think too much.'

He was removing her clothes. She lay naked, unbelievably unashamed. Her body was good to look at so why should she fear a man's gaze? Charles was still fully dressed and she pouted in Eve's best style. 'It's not fair. You should let me see you.'

He took a step back. 'Tessa! My God, you're lovely. You're enough to drive a man to madness, but I won't take advantage of you when you're in this state. Please dress.'

'If you mean I'm drunk, you're wrong. Well, I am a bit tiddly, but I know what I'm doing. Believe me, I know.'

His eyes travelled over her until her senses were on fire with yearning. Then he undressed, fast, dropping his clothes to the floor. 'A man can only stand so much. Tessa, I've wanted you from the moment we met.'

She twisted and turned, moaning beneath his experienced hands and mouth, her passion swelling into uncontrollable need. She said his name over and over again. Then he entered her, there was pain which was dimmed by her aching longing, and after that only sensation, wave after wave of pure joy rising to a crescendo which made her cry her release. His voice blended with hers, then his muscles relaxed.

He stayed inside her for a while, looking down into her face with an expression she couldn't define, then he lay back and lit cigarettes. They smoked for a while in silence. Tessa felt absolutely happy and fulfilled. If this was what Eve had been enjoying for years she understood why she sought it so often. What perfect bliss was to be found with a man. And there were so many men apparently willing to give it. She frowned. No, that wouldn't do. She didn't want casual love. She wanted – Her mind flinched from the memory of Paul.

'You were a virgin,' said Charles evenly.

'Yes. You are my very first lover. But not the last. I had no idea what it was like.'

'You made me believe that you were experienced.'

'Did I?'

'You did. You're a damn fine actress.'

'I'm a singer, not an actress.'

'Yes, that's true. You weren't playing a part tonight, were you?'

'No. I wanted your love.'

'If I'd known you were innocent, I should not have laid a finger on you.'

'Are you *sorry* we made love?'

'No. I would be lying if I said so. It was wonderful. But all the same, I shouldn't have done it. I've never been one for despoiling virgins.'

Tessa laughed. 'Despoiling? Is that what it was? I thought it was marvellous.'

Charles laughed unwillingly. 'Tessa, my sweet, you are adorable. I assume that Eve taught you the facts of love-making.'

'Eve? No, I've known them for ages.'

'Then I assume you took precautions.'

'What? Oh, my God!' Tessa sat up, remembering Eve's ghastly experience. 'Oh, no! Do you mean I could be—'

'You didn't? Then you certainly could be.'

'But it's my first time.'

'That won't protect you.'

'What shall I do?'

'All you can do is wait and see.'

'It's ghastly.' Tessa leaned back on the velvet padded headboard. 'Dreadful! I saw a friend of mine after she'd tried to get rid of a baby.'

'You're jumping ahead of yourself. It might not have happened.' He took a drag on his cigarette and blew out the smoke in a steady stream. 'If there are consequences would you rid yourself of an unwanted encumbrance, as your friend did?'

'I don't know if I could.'

'Because you are afraid?'

'I would be afraid, but more than that I'd feel wicked. "Thou shalt not kill", the Bible says.'

Charles sat up beside her. 'The Bible? This seems an odd time to quote the Bible to me.'

'You needn't sound so surprised. I was brought up as a Christian.'

'So was I.'

'Were you?'

'Now *you* sound surprised. All right, I confess that religion never interested me much. Does it you?'

'I'm a bit of a back-slider.'

'You're a hell of a back-slider!'

'My parents would die of shame if anything happened to me.'

'Tessa, my dear, if you should need me I shall be there. You need have no fears on that score.'

She looked into his face and believed he was sincere. 'You'd take care of me and – any encumbrance?'

'I like to think I'm a gentleman.'

'I suppose you take care of all the women who have fallen from grace?'

'So far I've had no reason to.'

'Why have you never married?'

He smiled. 'I have not married because I've never met a woman who could interest me for more than a few weeks. Occasionally months, but not often.'

Including me, she thought dismally. If I have an affair with him he'll tire of me, too. Tessa pictured herself installed in a love-nest somewhere with a child born out of wedlock, her career in ruins. She knew that that was an unworthy way of regarding the matter but she couldn't help it. 'Have there been a lot of women in your life?'

'I'm thirty-four and a normal man.'

'And a normal man must make love?'

'Unfortunately it's never been love with me. Some-times I've thought it might be, but it's always fizzled out.'

'Did you feel any love for me?' She wished the ques-

362

tion back and waited for his answer in an agony of embarrassment and apprehension.

'Just now I did. At this moment I believe I do.'

'I see. You would stand by me even without love?'

'It would be the act of a cad to abandon you.'

She felt suddenly drained of emotion. She shivered, in spite of the warmth of the room. She got up and began to dress. 'What time is it?'

'One-thirty.'

'Oh, no! Mrs Biggs must surely have gone to bed by now.'

'You can stay here. We'll think of an excuse. I'll get you a hotel bill.'

'Just take me back, please.'

Mrs Biggs was waiting and opened the front door, nodding a goodnight to Charles before she led Tessa to the kitchen. There was cocoa ready, but she sniffed and said, 'How many cocktails have you drunk? You'd better not have cocoa. Did you have a good time with your young man?'

'He isn't my young man. He just offered to take me for a drive.'

'I guess there were a few stolen kisses on the way.' Mrs Biggs sometimes slipped into picturesque prose.

'A few,' admitted Tessa, managing to smile. She felt slightly sick and after the house was quiet lay miserably wakeful before staggering to the lavatory and vomiting. Then she slept and awoke early with a headache.

In the cool grey morning the events of the night before looked very different. She had behaved in a wanton, totally irresponsible fashion. She had given away what a girl should value beyond price, a gift only to be offered to a husband. That's what girls were always taught. But when she thought of last night a delicious thrill ran through her and she realised that the only thing which bothered her was the fear she might be pregnant. It was shaming. Within days she knew she was not and vowed that never again would she be taken off her guard. She gave the news to Charles.

'What a relief for you, my dear,' was his comment.

'Not for you?'

'Oh, yes, for me also.' It was impossible to read anything into his reply.

They made love again before the company packed up and Tessa realised what a tremendous talent for pleasure her body had been granted. Even the memory of Paul seemed to lose its power over her when she was ruled by sexual passion.

Eve had been unusually quiet during the past few days and it worried Tessa.

'You aren't feeling ill again, are you?' she asked.

'No. Thanks,' Eve added belatedly. 'I've got a silly problem. It's hardly a problem, really. It's so idiotic.'

'Do you feel like talking?'

'I don't think you'd understand. Oh, well maybe you might.' Eve gave Tessa a sideways look. 'You're different. I have a distinct feeling that you and Charles Ware—'

'What?'

'Don't snap my head off. That night when you came back so late. You said you'd been to his house. I know his reputation. If he got you on your own somewhere he wouldn't have been content with a few kisses.'

'Nonsense! He's a gentleman who would never take unfair advantage of a woman.'

'Does that mean you were willing?'

Tessa couldn't go on keeping up a front with Eve, especially as she wanted someone with whom to share the discovery of her sensuality. 'Yes, I was willing,' she said.

Eve gasped and for once was held speechless. But not for long. 'You mean you and Charles—? You actually relinquished your precious virginity to a reprobate like him!'

'He's not a reprobate. You're just jealous because you couldn't get him.'

Eve laughed. 'Maybe. What's he like?'

'You know him.'

'I mean as a lover, you dolt.'

'I've no one to compare him with.'

'Don't try to pretend. A woman knows when a man gives her pleasure. Did he—'

Tessa felt herself reddening and the more Eve laughed the hotter she felt. 'All right, it was wonderful,' she cried.

'Good, oh good!' said Eve.

'You were about to tell me something. What's bothering you? I assume it's something to do with a man?'

'Yes. It's David Selby. I like him a lot. He's a stupendous lover. In fact, I've fallen for him rather hard.'

'Is that bad? Oh, he has no money. But do you really care about money? You got rid of Jack and didn't go back to that fellow in the States. Elliot, wasn't it?'

'I know. I've been such a fool. I should have married Jack and taken lovers. He would never have noticed.'

Tessa doubted this, but there was no point in arguing. 'That would be dishonest.'

Eve's brows went up. 'Practically the whole of my life has been dishonest. I've always had to guard my feelings. There's my mother, for instance. When I was little I was desperate for her love, but she had nothing much for me. It all went to my father. And he wanted nothing from me. Nothing at all. So I played his game. I was as cool and distant as he. If I forgot and let my love show even a little he would send me out of the room. I've pretended to care for so many men, but it was all a sham. Now I've been hooked, hoist by my own petard. I've fallen for a man who has nothing but himself to offer.'

'Oh, Eve, don't you think you'd be happy with the right man?'

'Scrimp and scrape, you mean? Have his babies and sit sewing and knitting for them? Dust and clean and cook? I wouldn't know where to begin. Besides—'

'Yes?'

'He hasn't told me he cares about me and now he never will,' Eve said in a voice she couldn't hold steady. 'He made love to me because I made it simple for him.

That's all. He took what I offered in France, too.'

Tessa went to her cousin and put her arms around her. 'He may learn to love you.'

'I don't think so. He saw me as an easy lay. I know – I can tell. He'll wait for some nice innocent little maiden to happen along before he proposes. It's happened to me before, but I've never cared. I want him, Tessa, I want him desperately. Do you know—' she was eager to speak, the words tumbling out ' – he reminds me of Father. He's more friendly, but there are deep reserves in him which sometimes make him seem aloof, but when I showed him how I felt, instead of turning from me in disgust, as Father does, he became vital and alive and passionate. When we make love it's marvellous.'

'And *that* reminds you of your *father*?'

Eve stared at Tessa as if she'd just awakened from a dream. 'Not the sex! For God's sake, Tessa. It's his coolness, the way he keeps his feelings under control. I wanted to pierce his armour, make him lose his self-control, and I succeeded. He proved such a skilful lover that it made me wonder if Father ever unbends? I've certainly never seen him behave affectionately to my mother. I suppose it must be different in private. After all, she had me.'

Tessa said nothing. Eve was pouring out words which had clearly been dammed for years. Was all this connected with her terrible dream which she would never explain?

Eve reached for a cigarette, her fingers unsteady, and Tessa held a light for her. 'I love Father,' said Eve. 'I didn't think I could ever love another man as much, and now I do. Father gives me nothing. He's never given me anything. He's never so much as touched me. Can you imagine what that means?'

Tessa tried. Dad was a simple, uncomplicated man. He wasn't one to show his feelings, but she could recall the days when he carried her on his shoulders, holding her above the heads of the crowd so that she could watch the Whitsuntide procession in Kingswood. He had washed her knees when she had taken a nasty fall. He had accompanied her to the dentist when she had been kept awake with toothache and Mum wasn't well enough to go. Greeting and farewell kisses were the normal procedure in the Morland house. To have a father who had never touched her? No wonder Eve had grown up so – how *had* Eve grown up? The onslaught of information made her feel as if she had never seen her cousin before. She remained silent, afraid to break Eve's concentration. Speaking of her unhappiness might help.

'He's never touched me,' Eve said again. 'Never. And my mother? Oh, she touched me. Sometimes she dressed me herself in silk and satin and velvet and showed me off to her friends. She vetted all my friends and sent me to the best schools. I don't know if I love her or not. She's so unapproachable, especially since I've grown up. What a capacity I have for giving my unwanted love! No one has ever loved me. No one. I've never been able to love anyone properly before and now I've fallen for someone at last and it's hopeless. For the very first time I'm in love and he doesn't want me. Nothing's changed. It never will.'

Eve fell silent again and Tessa put her arms round her cousin. 'I love you, Eve.'

She slowly came out of her trance-like state. 'What?'

'I love you.'

'Do you? No, you couldn't. I've often been unkind to you.'

'I do, Eve. You've let me see your true need. If you never allow anyone to understand you, how do you expect them to care? Why not let David know you love him?'

'You may have something there.' Eve's tone regained its usual flippancy. 'One day I must tell him that I'm nuts about him. With my luck, he'll probably run a mile!'

The short move to Weston Super Mare was accomplished quickly and Tessa took a walk on the well-remembered sands. Sammy came with her.

'Have you heard from your cousins lately?' she asked.

'They wrote. They told me not to visit this year. All Jews are in danger now of assault or worse, even visiting ones.'

'That's dreadful. Couldn't they come here to live?'

'It isn't so simple. The world largely prefers to ignore the plight of my people. There have been a few articles and warnings, but no one wants to fall out with Hitler. My cousins think it will all pass if they can only hang on. They were born in Germany, it has always been their home. They are Germans and it isn't easy to believe that the people who have been your friends and neighbours will suddenly turn on you like mad dogs.'

They paced the sands, collars up against the cool breeze, Tessa's felt hat pulled well down. She shivered, but not with cold.

# Chapter Seventeen

Mum had refused to see the show in Bristol. 'I've never set foot inside the Empire and I never will.' But her lively curiosity would not be denied and she and Dad had travelled on the train to see it in Weston. Afterwards Tessa and Eve took them out to supper.

Mum studied the menu. 'What funny food. I'll have the plaice in batter and chips.'

'I think I'll try fricasée of lamb,' said Dad.

'Foreign stuff!' said Mum. She looked round at the expensive trappings of the hotel with its soft carpets, shaded lights and three-piece orchestra playing softly. 'There seems to be a lot of drinking going on,' she observed.

'Is that all you can see?' asked Eve, amused.

'I can see a lot and most of it bad,' declared Mum. 'Some of the women look as if they're wearing night-dresses.'

'Backless dresses are the fashion,' said Eve.

'Some of them are practically frontless,' argued Mum. 'I wonder they don't catch their death of cold!'

'There's no harm in wearing up-to-date dresses,' said Eve, 'or in people enjoying wine with their meals.'

'Water is much better for you.' Mum sipped some of hers as if to prove her point. 'I suppose you and Tessa drink wine all the time now?'

'Sometimes,' said Eve. 'Mostly we drink cocktails. It's the fashion.'

'Fashion! I don't agree with it,' said Mum. 'Those cocktails are called outlandish names.'

'How do you know?' teased Eve.

'I know.'

Tessa watched and listened, loving her plump little mother with all the subterfuges she employed to gain information. She knew that Mum was quite annoyed with herself because she had enjoyed the show – parts of it, anyway.

'You have to drink a little or people think you're odd,' said Eve.

'Then they're very silly people.' Mum studied the menu for puddings. 'I'll have apple pie and custard for afters.'

Eve had only a single glass of wine, but Lily watched her drink it as if she were pouring poison down her throat. Maybe she wasn't so far wrong. Eve drank rather a lot these days. Since the episode with Charles, Tessa had recognised the weakening power of alcohol. The memory made her hot with different emotions. A measure of regret that she had let her parents and their teaching down; and an onslaught of desire because Charles made her so happy.

Mum didn't easily let go of a subject. 'Do you drink that devil's brew?' she demanded of her daughter.

'Not often,' said Tessa.

'When she does, she really throws herself into it,' said Eve.

Mum stared at her then turned her attention to Tessa. 'You throw yourself into it? Does she mean you drink a lot?'

Eve was quick to intervene with an apology. 'Just a joke, Cousin Lily.'

'I don't think it's funny,' said Mum. She was silent while she tested the pastry. 'Not bad,' she pronounced. 'Nearly as good as home-made.'

Eve laughed. 'Cousin Lily, you're priceless.'

This brought an indulgent laugh from both Lily and Walter.

'What was that lamb stuff like?' asked Mum.

'Quite nice. A sort of stew, but I'd rather have one of your roasts.'

'You could have had a cut off a joint here,' said Eve, 'couldn't he, Tessa?'

'What?' Her attention had been caught by the man who had just walked in.

Eve followed her gaze. 'It's Charles.'

'Who's he?' demanded Mum.

'Charles Ware. A friend,' said Tessa, praying that he wouldn't come over, wondering if she could hide her feelings from Mum who could be disconcertingly sharp. He was beautifully dressed, as always, his dinner jacket faultless, a white flower in the button-hole, his hair expertly cut. He fitted into the scene perfectly, but tonight she saw him through her mother's critical eyes. He was too handsome, too suave, too rich-looking, too everything.

He walked over to their table and bowed slightly. 'Hello, Eve. Tessa. How are you?'

'Well, thank you.' In her determined effort to conceal her excitement the words were abrupt, her voice acerbic. He raised his brows. 'Mum, Dad,' she said, 'I'd like you to meet Charles Ware. Charles, my parents.'

He held out his hand to each in turn and they shook it.

'Won't you join us?' suggested Eve mischievously.

Tessa threw her a furious look which delighted her cousin.

'There's not enough room,' said Mum, barely hiding her suspicion of this smooth stranger.

'The waiter will bring another chair,' said Eve.

Charles said, 'I wouldn't dream of gate-crashing. Are you returning to Bristol tonight, Mrs Morland?'

'No. We're staying at the boarding house we always stay at. The landlady doesn't usually take paying guests in winter, but she took us because we're regulars. We're going back in the morning early. A neighbour's helping out but one of the hens looked sick. I want to see to her myself.'

Tessa caught the flash of amusement in Charles's eyes and wanted to laugh. 'I expect you saw the Kissing Cousins?' he said.

'We did,' said Mum, volunteering no further information.

Much as Tessa loved her parents she could see how they would appear to Charles.

Tessa and Eve walked with Mr and Mrs Morland to their lodging where they said goodnight. 'Be good girls,' said Mum. 'You've chosen a strange life, but as long as you keep faith with the Lord nothing can harm you.'

Tessa kissed her parents. Eve hugged them tight, too tight, and dislodged Lily's sensible brown hat. 'Mind my hat!' said Mum, but she was smiling. 'Don't forget, Eve, my love, that you're always welcome in our house.'

Back at their digs Tessa found a note. 'My dear Tessa,' it read, 'I was delayed and missed the show. I'll be back tomorrow night. Looking forward to our next meeting. Charles.' Not 'love, Charles'. Just a bald statement.

On the following night Eve had a date and Charles was waiting outside the theatre. Tessa stepped wordlessly into his car. He stopped on the deserted promenade overlooking the sea and kissed her. 'Darling, it's good to see you.'

She relaxed in his arms. 'It's nice to see you, Charles.'

'How prim and proper you sound. Not at all like the girl who made love to me. Is this your parents' influence?'

'Possibly.'

'Did your mother warn you against me?'

'Not you in particular. She suspects men in general where her daughters are concerned. She still thinks that performing on a stage is a very dangerous occupation.'

'It can be. For instance, you meet wicked men who seduce you.'

'Very funny.'

'Sorry. Can we go somewhere?'

'Go somewhere?'

'You are being deliberately obtuse. I want to make love. You have a devastating effect on me. Don't you want me?'

'How direct you are! No lover-like pleading for my favours.'

'Will you come with me if I plead?'

'Not necessarily.'

He slid his arms round her and kissed her again, a kiss that became longer as he explored her soft mouth with his tongue. She was breathless when he drew away. 'Now tell me you don't want me.'

'It wouldn't be true.'

'Darling.' He switched on the engine and drove along the promenade, drawing up in the car park of a large hotel.

'Is this where you're staying?' asked Tessa.

'I booked in yesterday – as a married man. I said my wife would be joining me.'

'And will she?' asked Tessa.

'You know the answer.'

'You've got a damned cheek! You certainly took me for granted.'

'Not at all. I simply decided to cover the eventuality of your coming here. If you had not I should have made some excuse.'

Tessa couldn't keep up the air of indignation when her body was clamouring for Charles' love-making. Just the thought of his skill made her tingle. 'Hotels don't like people who arrive with no luggage,' she said.

'They will assume that I have already carried yours in. I brought an extra case.'

'What's in it?'

'A few books.'

Tessa remained seated in the car. 'I've a good mind to return to my digs.'

'I'm yours to command,' said Charles. He leaned back and waited.

Tessa stared at him. 'Wouldn't you be disappointed?'

'Devastated.'

She laughed.

Charles said gently, 'I trust you don't propose that we should spend the night in the car park.'

'Idiot!'

They were shown to their suite with deference. Later, as Tessa climbed from the luxurious bath, she looked at herself naked. Her figure was good, her breasts firm and high, her waist and hips slender, her bottom well-shaped and tucked in.

'Perfection,' said Charles and she realised that he had been watching her. She made no attempt to cover herself. She enjoyed the way his eyes devoured her.

'Sneak! Villain!' she hissed, like a heroine in a melodrama.

He laughed and seized her, holding her half-dried body in his arms, the silk of his dressing gown caressing her skin. 'Come, my love, let's make the most of our time.'

After a few weeks on the road it seemed to Tessa as if she had never done anything but pack and unpack her trunk, wait on draughty stations, and sing. Sometimes she forgot which town she was in. She wrote home every week, her letters glossing over the difficulties.

She came to vibrant life in the theatre. She wanted to talk to someone about this brilliant new sensation, and Charles proved a perfect listener. He had driven to see Tessa a few times and she welcomed him, often simply because he was a sympathetic ear. He sometimes laughed at her enthusiasm, sometimes applauded it, and he didn't necessarily expect to make love to her. At least, mused Tessa, if he did he was a model of control. He probably knew that he had little need to persuade her. He had brought her body gloriously to life and she craved his embraces.

Then his visits grew gradually farther apart and she hadn't seen him for several weeks. If she allowed herself to think about it she was angry, more with herself than with him. She was afraid he had simply used her, tired of her and rejected her, and felt humiliated because she had been an easy, eager conquest. Looking back, she could see how skilfully he played the game of love. Now he was doubtless coaxing some other woman the way he had her, allowing her, like a fish on a line, to believe she controlled all the moves, permitting his catch to run away from him with the tide, drawing her back so skilfully that she believed she came of her own free will. But believing this made no difference to her sexual awakening and its refusal to lie dormant. Sometimes she feared she would end up like Eve, sleeping with any man when the mood took her.

When she had the opportunity she attended a nonconformist chapel, frequently only so that she could tell Mum she had been, although sometimes familiar words and sacred songs brought her peace of mind. In her letters she had to describe the chapels, the preachers and the congregations, tell Mum what hymns had been sung and the text of the sermons so that she could relay the news to her friends.

Through everything, in spite of Charles, she never forgot Paul. Sometimes she heard of him through Eve, at others she read news of him in society columns. The young Mr and Mrs Paul Jefferson were to be seen on all the fashionable occasions and in the best nightspots, and Tessa was able to read descriptions of Andrea's clothes and jewels. She devoured the information.

'You're such an idiot,' Eve told her. 'Fancy hankering after a married man.'

'I'm not,' Tessa denied angrily.

'Well, why are you so interested in him?'

This was one of the questions Tessa frequently asked herself and to which she had no answer. She was also confused by the fact that she loved Paul and yet had enjoyed Charles's love-making. She refused to rise to Eve's bait and her cousin shrugged and returned to her film magazines. Tessa watched her for a moment, marvelling as she always did at the purity of Eve's beauty. In spite of her avowed love for David she allowed some of her dates to make love to her and insisted, brazenly, on relating their performance, giving them marks out of ten. Tessa tried to prevent the flow of talk, but Eve was relentless. Her hunger for men's attention and her need to boast seemed insatiable. More than one of her men had followed the band to the next town, believing that she had fallen for him, vowing his adoration, even proposing marriage.

'Idiots!' snarled Eve. 'Conceited oafs! They think I care for them just because I take pleasure from their bodies.'

'You also take presents,' Tessa reminded her drily.

'Why not? If they want to spend money on me, let them, I say.'

'I'm sure some of them spend more than they can afford.'

'More fool them. The choicer the gift, the more money I can raise on it.'

'Don't you feel anything for any of them?'

'No.'

'Do you still think you are in love with David?'

Eve had flushed and flown into a temper. 'I don't think I'm in love. I *know* I am.'

Tessa stared gravely at her cousin. 'I believe you are. I'm sorry.'

'I don't need your pity! He writes to me sometimes which is more than you can say for your precious Paul.'

It was Tessa's turn to lose her temper and the effort to control herself made her shake. 'Paul is not my precious anything. He never can be. He's married.'

'That little matter need be no handicap. I'm sure if you offered yourself, he would—'

'Shut up! You say you love David yet you're promiscuous.'

'Promiscuous! It that so? *You* can talk. You love Paul, but you've let Charles Ware into your bed more than once. And for all I know, you've had other men, too.'

'I have not, as you so graciously put it, "Had other men".' Tessa dragged a brush through her hair so angrily that she pulled out quite a handful.

'That won't do your hair much good.'

'Leave me alone.'

'OK.' Eve climbed into bed and leaned back wearily. 'What a pair of bloody fools we are. We've fallen for the wrong men.'

Tessa could talk to Eve properly in this mood. She said gently, 'That's true, but I have no hope of Paul, while David might come to love you.'

Eve shook her head. 'No. He's conventional at heart. I shocked him because I was too easy. He tried it on because they all do, don't they, but he didn't expect to succeed. Sometimes he treats me as a casual pick-up and I know he has his eye on several girls who'd make suitable wives. He'll never love me and I know I'll never care for anyone else.'

The band arrived back in London in the spring of 1934, having been on the road for almost six months. Josh had bookings for the entire summer and several dates on the wireless. He had also accepted offers of Christmas shows, even one for pantomime in a small provincial town.

When Eve heard this she was outraged. 'Pantomime! "Cinderella." Is he crazy? What does he expect us to do?'

Tessa said casually, 'I dare say you'll be cast as Cinderella. I see myself as a thigh-slapping prince.'

'I'll be damned if I'll do it!'

'But imagine how pretty you'll look in the ballroom scene.'

'It's degrading! I shall refuse.' Eve paused. 'I suppose I would look good in a crinoline. They usually wear crinolines, don't they?'

Tessa looked up from her book. 'Who?'

'What do you mean, "who?" '

'Who looks good in crinolines?'

'Don't be so annoying! We were talking of "Cinderella".'

'Oh, yes.' Tessa carefully placed a bookmark and shut her book. 'You'd have a white gown sparkling with jewels, and a tiara. Powdered hair, too.'

'Nobody's going to fill my hair with powder!'

'You can wear a wig.'

'Why can't I wear my own hair just as it is?'

'Princesses must have white hair. Or golden.'

'My prince will have to put up with auburn. What about having to dress in rags for the first scenes?'

'They'll make sure you have very becoming rags. Of course, the theatre management may have someone else in mind.'

Eve stared, then gave a reluctant grin. 'You're horrible, Tessa. You're just tormenting me. None of that will happen.'

Consequently, the girls were surprised when Christmas actually found them performing in pantomime and Josh did actually offer them the parts Tessa had predicted. The theatre was small, but it was regular work and Josh never wasted a single opportunity to make his band and the Kissing Cousins known. They had also appeared on the wireless in the prestigious Henry Hall's Guest Night, a real accolade.

'I haven't done any acting,' Tessa said worriedly to Josh. 'I'll make a mess of it.'

'Nonsense! You obviously don't realise the tremendous way you put over your songs. That's acting, isn't it? You appear to feel every emotion, but you don't really, do you?'

'I suppose not, but I should still like a few pointers before I venture on the stage.'

'That can be arranged.'

Eve read the script and said disgustedly, 'What a dismal part. I have to be so sweet and gentle.'

'And I have to be manly and courageous.'

'It's all right for you to laugh. I'm going to tell Josh I want something different.'

'If you're not careful we shall be cast as the Ugly Sisters.'

Eve glared. 'All right. I'll do it if I must, but never again . . .'

'Our wages have gone up again. Josh is a good boss.'

He found them an instructor, an elderly retired actress

who had never been seen, except by her maid, without thick make-up.

'She looks quite disgusting,' said Eve. 'She only shows her wrinkles more with all that powder and paint clogging her pores.'

Tessa liked her and thought she was rather a dear.

Hearing the news Mum wrote: 'I don't know why you couldn't have come to Bristol and acted there. And,' she added confusingly, 'I don't like the idea of you acting. It's not like singing.'

Charles sent an enormous bouquet to each girl on opening night and was at the party Josh threw. 'You were splendid,' he said to Tessa. 'I could have believed you were a man if I hadn't good cause to know different.'

'Is that so?' She tried to control a blush as she accepted a cigarette. 'What a liar you are. The costume is designed to prove I'm a woman. Anyway, I'm surprised you bothered to come at all. It's ages since we met.'

Charles blew a skilful smoke ring. 'Look at that! Sometimes they work, sometimes they don't. Don't think I ever forget you, my love. I've been busy.'

'It's a matter of indifference to me whether you remember me or not.'

'That's all right then.'

'You're infuriating! What have you been doing that's kept you so busy?'

Charles struck an attitude. 'Moved as I am by your solid hard work, I decided to sacrifice the easy life for a career.'

'You? Work? I can't believe it.'

'I assure you,' he said, hand on his heart. 'I've bought a rather run-down antique shop in Bristol. I meant to spend only a little time in it, but found it so absorbing I spend much of my time there now. I've been going to auctions all over the place. The shop is actually picking up.'

'I'm so delighted to hear it. Why didn't you write and explain?'

'Did you really miss me?'

'Mmm, sometimes. Just a little.'

'Was it my scintillating wit you regretted or other things?'

'Everything,' she said firmly. 'I missed everything. Why have you been so secretive about the shop?'

Charles smiled broadly. 'You missed *everything*? Tessa, you're a darling! I wanted to see if I could make a success at something before I told you. Will you come to my room tonight, or shall I visit yours?'

'Neither.' Tessa blew out a stream of blue smoke. 'Sorry, I can't do rings.'

Charles watched her for a moment before he said, 'When can we be alone?'

'Maybe sometime, maybe never.'

'You sound like the title of a song.'

'I suppose it's all this singing. It's had an effect on my conversation.'

He shrugged. 'Why can't we be together tonight?'

'I don't feel like it.' She was lying and he knew it.

He glared at her. 'I think I'll have a word with Josh. He's terrific at business. I've learned a lot from watching him.'

Tessa watched him walk away, cursing herself for a fool. He had given her a good reason for his apparent neglect and she wanted him. Anger boiled inside her, partly directed at herself, but mostly at Charles for taking her for granted.

Eve was having a fling with Lenny Curtis, the new pianist engaged a few months ago, and, as usual during one of her essays into romance, was absorbed by it.

They were all worried about Sammy who had decided he must go to Germany to see what was happening to his cousins.

Josh and Tessa had tried to dissuade him. 'What can you do?' asked Josh. 'You could find yourself arrested. You know how Hitler's treating the Jews. He's ordered everyone to boycott their shops and businesses. You haven't heard from your cousins for a long time.'

Sammy said patiently, 'Reuben is a doctor and Jacob a jeweller, but how can a man make enough to feed his family when he is deprived of work? Reuben has no children but Jacob's are segregated at school and taught that to be Jewish is to be evil. The last letter I had said that his youngest child, just a little girl born late to them, came home from school weeping and saying, "I don't want to be a Jew." Now I've met a friend who has managed to get out and he says that Jacob protested to the school and has been arrested and sent to Sachsenhausen concentration camp as a political prisoner. His wife, Ruth, is distraught. How can I refuse to help her?'

'But how can you help her?' asked Josh. 'Even non-Jewish visitors to the country have been attacked. Remember the case of Barclay Jones Cecil? He tried to protect a lady in his party from insult by some Nazis—'

'And was beaten unconscious for his pains,' finished Sammy. 'The papers here made quite a fuss, but very few bother in Britain about Jews who get beaten – many refuse to believe it happens at all – and in Germany people simply laugh. Do you think I don't know what's happening to my people?'

'Of course not, Sammy,' said Josh.

'We're afraid for you,' said Tessa.

Josh said urgently, 'Germany is a one-party state now. The Nazis are in complete control.'

'Why do you tell me things I already know? Should I leave Ruth and the children to struggle on alone?'

'No,' said Tessa miserably. 'Of course not. But you'll be in such danger and – well, we are very fond of you.'

Sammy smiled, then shrugged. 'And I of you. If I'm going into danger, I am. I've lived a good free life here. I'm no longer young. It's time I did something to show my loyalty to my people.'

They stopped arguing then and everyone wished him God speed. Sammy went to Manchester to kiss his wife goodbye before he left and now hadn't been heard of for months.

When the band had played in Manchester, Tessa and

Josh had visited Sammy's wife in her small, neat house.

Hannah was a plain woman with strongly accentuated features which were transformed to beauty by her welcoming smile when she opened her front door. 'So good of you to come,' she cried. 'Come in, come in. I'll bring refreshments.'

She had insisted on preparing tiny sandwiches and carried them in on a tray covered with a snowy cloth. She poured glasses of wine. 'It's so good of you to visit me when you must be so busy.'

Tessa said, 'Have you heard from Sammy?'

'Not a word. It's as if he's disappeared, and I get no answers to my letters to Ruth.'

'Do you know exactly what he intended to do?' asked Josh.

'He said he was going to visit Jacob and try to arrange his release. He wants to bring him and his wife and children here.'

'That means confronting the Nazis!' said Josh in alarm.

'Yes, I know. I lie awake at nights . . . But I have faith in my Sammy.'

'Have you any news of your other cousin?' asked Josh.

'One letter only from Reuben. He and his wife are trying to disassociate themselves from Jacob's problems and who can blame them? Reuben has work still. Doctors are always needed and they have no children to worry over.' She shook her head as if to chase away her thoughts. 'Tell me how the show is going.'

They left her soon afterwards.

Tessa said sadly to Josh, 'She's so brave. We can only pray he comes back.'

Eve was discontented, a state into which she fell if she hadn't met a satisfactory man for a while. The new pianist's charms were wearing a little thin. 'He's a bore,' she stated. 'And I'm sick of the stage, and especially of pantomime. Let's do something different.'

'Sick of the stage?' Tessa was amazed. 'How can you be? You've only acted for a few weeks. We still have such a lot to learn.'

'We had lessons. Diction . . . as if I needed them!'

'They didn't think a pantomime heroine should sound American,' Tessa pointed out.

'I don't see why not. And it isn't as if I have a strong accent. "Voice control, Miss Brook," ' she mimicked in close resemblance to the teacher engaged by Josh. ' "Profound power of expression, Miss Brook." "Audibility, Miss Brook. Can you be heard from the back row?" Anyone would think we'd been acting Shakespeare, God forbid.'

'It's work,' said Tessa.

'*Pantomime.*'

'We're paid for it, and we're unlikely to get anything else at this time of year.'

'And I loathe having all those dancing kids around,' said Eve, 'racing about, shrieking, half the time totally out of control.'

'Every pantomime has a children's dancing troupe and they're not so bad. They need to let off steam sometimes.'

'Well, I don't like it. Any of it.'

'You're fed up because Josh was angry with you after last night's performance.'

'Stupid man! Just because I forgot my lines.'

'You've said them a hundred times. You couldn't possibly have forgotten.'

'Are you suggesting I messed up on purpose?'

'And you came on stage from the wrong side and the Demon King had his back to you.'

Eve giggled. 'I know. It seemed to take him ages to realise I was behind him. The audience liked it. They laughed.'

'They're not supposed to laugh at the Demon King,' reminded Tessa drily. 'He was furious. Besides, you looked bored and an attitude like that can affect everyone's performance. It was wrong and unfair of you.'

Eve shrugged. 'You talk as if we were in London instead of a tin-pot town.'

'People are entitled to receive value for money wherever they are.'

'You're so damned smug.'

'I am not!' Tessa stopped. If she wasn't careful they would find themselves in the middle of one of their idiotic arguments that often left her drained while appearing not to affect her cousin.

'All right,' said Eve, 'I was wrong. I should have thought of the kids in the audience.'

This was an unexpected concession and Tessa asked, 'Do you want to be a serious actress?'

'No, I damn' well don't! I want to be in a musical play like Elsie Randolph, or better still, Gertrude Lawrence. How wonderful to play opposite Jack Buchanan or Noël Coward. I want to hold an audience in my hand then see them stand to applaud me. I want people to stare at me when I go into a restaurant. What wonderful lives they lead!' She began to sing: ' "Some day I'll find you; Moonlight behind you—" Do you remember when we went to see *Private Lives*?'

Tessa said, 'Of course I do, but stardom like that happens to very few and most stars had to begin in a humble way.'

'I know, I know.' Eve strolled to the window and looked down at the rain-washed street. 'Sunday and absolutely nothing to do. What a ghastly place.'

'You could come to chapel this evening with me.'

'You're such a hypocrite. You only go so you can tell Cousin Lily about it.'

'Not entirely. I enjoy the singing.'

'Do you really believe in God?'

Tessa was startled. No one in her life had ever queried the existence of the Almighty. 'I suppose I do. I like His songs, anyway.'

Eve's humour swung the other way. 'I'll come with you. The songs aren't at all bad.'

The pantomime season came to an end and Josh was

preparing to move to London where they had a spot on radio, followed by another tour.

'Won't we ever stop in one place?' fretted Eve. 'Why can't you get us a permanent spot in a night-club like some of the other bands. Or, better still,' Eve's face lit up, 'in a film. Like Jack Payne.'

'He had to earn his reputation. Our day will come if we work hard. It's a matter of waiting.'

'I'm sick of waiting.'

'You seem to be sick of everything!' snapped Josh. 'You messed up the pantomime more than once, you grumbled incessantly during the run, and you behave like a prima donna constantly.'

Tessa stared at him. It was the first time she had seen him in a temper. He looked tired. It must be a terrible strain for the one who had to find and organise work.

Eve's own astonishment held her silent for a moment. 'I'm not all that bad,' she mumbled.

Josh cooled down. 'I didn't mean to yell. You're good when you try. Maybe you're not strong enough for this kind of life.'

'I am, I am,' protested Eve, and stopped grumbling. At least in public.

Tessa only half listened to her moans as she concentrated on their wireless performance. They were about to leave on the tour when Eve launched her bombshell.

'Leave the band?' said Tessa, aghast. 'Just like that? Let Josh down? Let *me* down? And what for? What do you think you can do without us?'

'Get into films. Why not, Tessa? We've got the looks, the voices and the experience.'

'Are you crazy? Half the girls in Britain are trying to become film stars.'

'I know, it's the same in the States, and some of them break through with far less talent than we have. Oh, do come with me.'

'Even if I believed we had a chance, I wouldn't leave Josh in the lurch. I don't know how you can think of it after he's been so good to us.'

'He criticises me.'

'He criticises anybody who needs it, and so he should.'

'He's never said much to you.'

'I listen to him and learn.'

'Oh, go to hell!' Eve slammed out, leaving Tessa wondering once more why she continued to put up with her cousin's vagaries.

She knew the answer really. She was sure that Eve was desperately unhappy. She had once asked her why she didn't visit her parents and Eve had replied, 'Why should I? I'm not so very fond of Mother and as for Father . . .' She had paused. 'If I don't see him, I can imagine him. He's different when I keep him in my head.'

Bristol was not included on the new tour and a short pause before starting enabled Tessa to visit her family after a lapse of months. She hardly recognised the tall girl who was seated at the kitchen table. 'Susan?'

'Tessa!' Susan jumped up and kissed her. 'You look lovely. And your clothes! London or Paris?'

'London. It's wonderful to see you. Where are the others?'

'Prayer meeting.'

'Joey, too?'

'Joey, too.' Susan giggled. 'He's got religion. Isn't it a scream? Sit down. I'll make some tea.'

Tessa sat down. 'Got religion? *Joey*?'

'You can't believe it, can you? I couldn't at first. I thought he was shamming to get something out of Mum, but he wasn't. Mind you, he's a bit difficult to live with. He's liable to come upstairs at night – I've got your room now, by the way – and ask if I've said my prayers? At first I said no, so he'd say them for me. Out loud.' She warmed the pot, made the tea and produced a plate of home-made biscuits with practised movements. 'So now I just answer the way he wants.'

'I can't wait to see this. And, Susan, you're a woman. When did it happen?'

'I am, aren't I? But Mum still won't let me go out with boys. Honestly, I ask you! In 1935. Anyone would think

386

we were back in Victorian times. My friends laugh at me.'

'Does that worry you?'

'Good lord, no. In any case, I manage to have a few chats to boys. Mum and Dad force a person to be deceitful, don't they? You had to tell fibs to get your own way, didn't you?'

Tessa was speechless. When she had crept out secretly to sing she hadn't really understood why her parents should have been so upset. Nor had she realised how worried they could be about the safety of a much-loved daughter.

'Don't worry,' said Susan. 'Actually I don't bother much about boys at all because I don't mean to get tied down. I want to do something with my life.'

'What sort of something?'

'I haven't decided yet. I might be a fashion model. I've got a job in an exclusive gown shop.'

Tessa opened her mouth to advise her sister that it was no easier to get into modelling than it was to get on the stage, then shut it. All Susan's puppy fat had gone and she had more than beauty – she had presence. Tessa suspected that she would get anything she went after.

She had come prepared to spend the night and took her things to the attic room where Susan pulled out the camp bed. 'I'll have this. You can have the bed,' she said generously. 'No, I won't hear any argument. It's your room, really. I've left your things in the bottom drawer. Mum put sprigs of lavender in.'

Voices downstairs told them that the others were back and Susan called over the banister rail: 'Family! We've got a visitor.'

'Upstairs?' Mum's voice was sharp.

'Yes, upstairs,' carolled Susan, mischievously. 'Why not?'

'Who is it?' That was Dad, sounding authoritative.

'Who do you think Susan would have up here?' cried Tessa. She ran lightly down the stairs and into her mother's welcoming arms.

'Let me get at her,' said Dad, hugging her.

They stood back and she found herself surveyed by Joey. He examined her appearance with eyes that seemed faintly accusing.

'Hello, Joey. Are you pleased to see me, too?'

'I am. I dislike your being away. I wish you'd come home and take a job nearby. We'd meet more often then.'

Tessa decided to disregard his stern words and stepped forward and kissed him. He was unresponsive. 'I see you use make-up off the stage as well as on,' he said.

'Everybody does now,' smiled Tessa, determined not to get riled.

'We'll have cocoa,' said Mum, nervous, turning to an activity over which she had control. She put the steaming cups on the kitchen table. 'Now, let's all sit down. Susan, bring the cake tin. I've got a new recipe for lemon sponge, Tessa. Try a slice.'

Joey seated himself solemnly at the table and sipped his drink. 'Mum lets us read your letters, Tessa,' he said. 'I'm glad you go to chapel, though not often enough.'

'Oh.'

'The devil's always seeking to undermine God's handiwork. Learning His word will help you defeat him. I believe a woman is in particular danger in your chosen profession.'

He made it sound as if she had gone on the streets and Tessa felt like telling him, in a vulgarity she had recently heard, to put his opinions where the monkey put his nuts. She refrained.

'Joey's in great demand as a lay preacher,' said Mum proudly. 'His name is printed in the new list. "Joseph Morland", it says. "Always available to spread the word of the Lord." He's saved ever so many. Even little children come to the altar for him.'

'For God, Mum,' reproved Joey.

'How wonderful,' said Tessa, unable to think of anything more constructive. As Joey explained his work in more detail she studied her mother. Her eyes were alight

388

with pride and satisfaction. At last, all her years of striving and teaching had resulted in one of her lambs being led to God. How she must enjoy hearing her son give forth. He was still only seventeen, but that was not considered too young to take on the task of a man. Indeed, there were boys of fifteen who had already begun their lay ministry.

When Joey had gone to his room, she explained, 'None of those other boys is as good as our Joey, though some have had a better education. They do their best but they're not inspired. If a boy's got the makings of a really good preacher, he gets his inspiration from above and that's all he needs.'

In bed that night Susan got a fit of the giggles. 'Joey says we have to call him Joseph now. Isn't he a scream!'

Tessa said carefully, 'We shouldn't make fun. I'm sure he's doing good work. Have you heard him in the pulpit?'

Susan sighed noisily. 'Have I heard him? He goes on and on, and when you think he must surely have finished he begins on yet another point. Even when he says, "Finally, brethren" you dare not hope for mercy. He can make a final point last for twenty minutes.'

'Do people get bored?'

'Bored! I should say not! They come from far and near. He's called the New Evangelist by a good many. I shouldn't be surprised if he became quite famous. In a way it's the same as you. You'll both be known for your public performances.'

'It's not quite the same,' said Tessa.

'No, I'd rather have your kind of fame. And one day I'm going to be well-known too, as a fashion model. You'll see.'

'I'm not all that well-known.'

'Anyone who goes on the wireless is famous.'

'You can't be a fashion model on the wireless.'

Susan laughed. 'That's true. But you'll see my picture in the magazines. Even *Vogue*, I shouldn't wonder.'

'That's right. Aim for the top.'

389

'I mean to.'

'Is Joey, I mean Joseph, still in the boot factory?'

'Yes. It isn't much of a job, but he says all work is ennobling. I suppose Mum wrote and told you he'd left school?'

'She did, but she said nothing about his becoming an evangelist.'

'I think at first she and Dad thought he was having them on. He's always been such a tease. Now they're fully convinced he's got a vocation.'

'I see. What's your job like, Susan?'

'It's wonderful. We get all the nobs in and I've already begun to model gowns when the clients want to see them worn. My boss, Mrs Endicott, laughs and says I make them believe they'll look the same as me when they wear them.'

'That sounds like exactly the right talent for a fashion queen.'

Susan laughed. 'That's what Mrs Endicott says.' She yawned and soon afterwards her breathing became even. Tessa lay awake for quite a while. She wasn't used to early nights and had been given a lot to think about. While she had been struggling to fulfil her ambition, her little brother and sister had grown up almost unnoticed by her. Lying here in the cosy darkness in her childhood room her mind roamed free and admitted memories she usually denied: memories of Paul and what he meant to her. She could never have him. He was married to Andrea and she had heard recently that she was expecting their second child. Their first, a boy, had been born with difficulty and something was wrong with him. Poor Paul. Poor Andrea, too.

On the following day Tessa took a tram to town and walked up Park Street to visit Susan. She entered the shop which was softly carpeted and illuminated by muted lights. The gowns were well displayed and in the height of taste and fashion.

'May I help you?' The voice was gentle and cultured.

Tessa turned. She was being surveyed by a short

woman with a curvaceous figure. 'I am Miss Morland's sister.'

Before she could say another word, the woman said, 'One of the Kissing Cousins?'

'Do you know me? Oh, of course, Susan will have told you.'

'She did, but once I had heard you I was not surprised at her praise. I make a point now of listening in. You and Miss Brook are so good.'

Tessa smiled. 'Thank you.' It sounded inadequate, but she never quite knew what to say when someone praised her.

'You'll want to see Susan. Such a promising girl. She's being fitted by my dresser. One of our clients needs several ballgowns to take to India – all cotton, of course – and she's coming in today to look at the styles. Why not go on up?' She gestured to the back of the shop.

Tessa climbed a steep stair and found Susan standing patiently on a dais while a small woman with straggly grey hair and glasses perched on the end of her nose, stuck pins in a gown.

'Tessa,' squealed Susan. 'Miss Benson, it's my sister.'

She stood up. 'All right, Susan, say hello to your sister. I'll never get this right unless you keep still.'

'Sorry,' said Tessa. 'Mrs Endicott said I could come up—'

Susan jumped down and hugged her. 'This is Tessa.'

Miss Benson smiled. 'I know, a Kissing Cousin.'

'Oh dear,' said Tessa. 'Does Susan go on and on about me?'

'She is proud of you, but I heard you even before Susan came to work here. I love my wireless and I always listen in when you're singing.'

When Tessa left the shop she felt a glow spreading through her. The audience for radio was unseen and had seemed unreal to her. But it was there. People actually remembered her. Liked her. Was this fame? Maybe the beginning, anyway? If it was, she loved it.

# Chapter Eighteen

Tessa left Mrs Endicott's shop and walked on up the hill until she reached an antique shop which bore the legend 'Charles Ware', and in smaller letters underneath, 'Antiques bought and sold'. She opened the door which activated a set of musical chimes.

An elderly man who was seated in a comfortable chair looked up from behind the counter. He smiled. 'Do you just want to browse?'

'Yes, please.' Tessa wandered around looking at cases of small objects, many of which bore no relationship to one another. Silver spoons were with silver and enamel bracelets; pictures of different sizes and qualities, some framed, some not, were hanging on the walls or leaning against and partially concealing glass-fronted cupboards stuffed with artifacts; a green velvet upholstered chair was upside-down on a similar one in crimson; a few leather-bound books were stacked in a corner; Toby jugs, tankards, silver cups, scent bottles, snuff boxes mingled beneath a couple of large glass domes which should have covered Victorian waxed fruit.

'Frightful, isn't it?'

Tessa whirled round. 'Charles! I didn't know you'd be here.'

'How unflattering. Why should I not be here?' His handsome face was creased in a large smile.

'I don't know.'

'Josh telephoned me the other day. He told me you were coming to Bristol. I hoped to see you.'

'A spy system?'

'Certainly not! He wants me to look out for any antique musical instruments. He intends to build a collection.'

'And he happened to mention my name?'

'No. I asked about you.'

'Oh.' She looked around. 'This is a bit of a mess, isn't it? How have you made it prosper?'

'I'm gradually clearing the dross. Some people enjoy the confusion. They think it's fun when they believe they've unearthed something underpriced.'

'I suppose they do. Does it happen often? You won't make a fortune that way.'

'I know what I'm doing. You should have seen the place when I bought it. I'm gradually bringing it to order. And my assistant here knows his job. Oh, sorry, you two haven't been introduced. Tessa, Mr Albert Harris. Albert, Miss Tessa Morland.'

Mr Harris rose and gave her his hand. 'Happy to make your acquaintance.'

'Albert has worked here since he was a boy.'

'That I have.' He sat down again. 'Man and boy I've looked after this place. My former employer took over a few years ago from his uncle. He didn't have much of a notion about running an antique shop.'

'Hence the conglomeration,' said Charles. 'We are doing our best to tidy it up.'

'Was it worse than this?'

'I'm afraid so,' said Albert. 'He was a nice man but with no ideas of business. It's no wonder the shop went downhill. It was a good day for me when Mr Ware took over.'

Tessa smiled. 'It's rather dusty. Don't you employ a cleaner?'

'Good heavens, no,' cried Charles melodramatically. 'Our customers expect to find some dust. It gives the stuff an even more antiquarian air.'

'Maybe, but you really should polish up that sweet little table and the two inlaid boxes.'

'She's right, Mr Ware,' said Albert. 'She's absolutely right.'

Charles laughed. 'Tessa, can I take you somewhere for a cup of tea? Coffee?'

'I could make some here,' offered Albert.

'And I could do the dusting,' said Tessa.

'Certainly not. Miss Morland is a singer,' he told Albert.

'I know. I've heard you on the radio. You're one of the Kissing Cousins.'

'Did Mr Ware tell you?' asked Tessa.

'I knew before. I always read a stage newspaper, *The Era*,' Albert explained. 'I wanted to be an actor, but times were hard for my family and I had to get a steady job. But I've never lost interest. The theatre is my re-creation, along with the wireless nowadays.'

Charles escorted Tessa to the door, a hand placed tenderly beneath her elbow. The effect was somewhat spoilt when he tripped over a mud scraper which lay on the floor with several iron doorstops and a bronze dog. Tessa laughed.

Outside, he said, 'Fancy mocking me. I might have broken something.'

They turned into a small cafe and he ordered coffee. Tessa said, 'It doesn't matter whether the shop pays or not, does it? You've plenty of money to bail yourself out.'

'That's where you're wrong. Oh, yes, I do have plenty of the necessary, but after buying the shop and contents I decided to allow myself a fixed capital sum, and not a huge one either, and I'm determined to make the place a success without drawing on further money.'

Tessa thanked the waitress with a smile as she set down a pot of coffee. She poured it. 'Why are you doing it?'

'Buying you coffee?'

'Don't be an ass. I meant running a shop.'

'To impress you,' said Charles promptly.

'Nonsense!'

'I mean it. I admire your professionalism. I would like you to admire mine.'

She looked at him, searching his face for a sign of

the mockery she was sure lay behind his words, but he returned her gaze with steady seriousness. 'I believe you mean it.'

'That I admire you?'

'That you want to work at something properly.'

'I do. And I do admire you.'

She sipped her coffee. 'Ouch, that's hot. I can't afford to burn my mouth.'

'I should say not. It's far too kissable.'

'I was thinking of my singing.'

'That too,' he agreed equably.

'You already knew something about antiques, didn't you? There are some beautiful things in your house. I remember them.'

'I hope you remember seeing me there?'

'How could I forget?'

'There are some splendid antiques in the family seat, too. I hope to show you one day.'

'You have a family seat as well?'

'I'm afraid so. It's in Somerset, quite near Bath.'

'Good gracious! Fancy having two so close together.'

'The Bristol house was bought when horses and carriages were used and it took an age to travel between the two cities. Then, when the car arrived, my parents decided to keep them. My mother loved them both, you see.' His voice softened.

'They're no longer living, are they?'

'No, and I miss them. Enough about me. May I take you somewhere nice tonight?'

'Sorry, I'm visiting my family. I haven't seen them for ages and I don't know when I will again.'

'You don't see much of me either.'

'No, but that isn't my fault.'

'Do you miss me?'

'Yes, I do.'

'How much?'

She put the palms of her hands together and drew them apart about six inches. 'That much.'

Charles frowned. 'I suppose you think that's funny.'

'Sure do,' said Tessa in a heavy American accent which made him smile. 'Sorry,' she added in her normal tone.

'If you won't spend a whole evening with me, at least give me a little time. Tonight, perhaps? We could go to my house in the woods.'

'Like Little Red Riding Hood, I suppose, with you playing the wolf?'

'You're determined to mock me!'

'You make it easy.'

He was silent for a while and her thoughts drifted off.

'Should I stop trying, Tessa?'

She wasn't listening. 'Have you seen Paul and Andrea in the Frenchay House?'

Charles said smoothly, 'Yes. I went to dinner there not long ago. Paul seems to be happy with her.'

'Seems to be?'

'As far as someone outside a marriage can tell. She wouldn't suit me with her autocratic ways.'

'How does Paul cope with them?'

'All right, I suppose. He seems easy-going. Perhaps he doesn't have deep feelings.'

'What a thing to say about him! You're wrong. I know you're wrong.'

'How vehement you are.'

'She's expecting a child, isn't she? Do you know when?'

Charles stared at her. 'In about three months.'

'What's wrong with their son?'

'He's slow. That's how they describe it. I saw him only once. He's kept out of sight with his own suite of rooms and two nurses.'

'Slow?'

'He's defective. Mentally.'

'Poor Paul.'

'Poor Andrea. And poor little boy.'

'Of course. Are you angry with me?'

'No. Not angry.'

'What, then?'

'Disappointed.'

'*Disappointed*? Because I ask after an old friend?'

'Because you're hankering after a married man.'

'I am doing no such thing.'

'And because you won't stay longer with me.' He called the waitress and paid the bill. 'I must get back to the shop. Have you got a car somewhere?'

'No, but the trams are perfectly adequate.'

They parted at the antique shop door and Tessa walked down the hill feeling dissatisfied, angry and regretful in turn. Then she forgot Charles as she thought of Paul. He was so near. If only she could think of an excuse to see him . . .

In the morning Dad, Joey and Susan went off to work and Tessa wiped the breakfast dishes while her mother washed up.

'How's Dad managing with his job these days?'

'Well enough. We aren't too badly off with Joseph and Susan bringing home pay packets. I was going to write and tell you that we don't need money from you any more.'

'I want to contribute.'

'No, love. You spend it on something you need, or better still, save it.'

'Is there no chance of Dad getting back to carpentry?'

'Doesn't look like it. Whenever he's been elsewhere for a job in his trade they never ask to see his work, or look at his references. They just see a man who's getting older and sweeps up in a market. Not that there are all that many private building jobs around. Everyone seems to be working on the roads these days. I suppose it's because of the cars. There are so many now and they churn up the roads something awful.'

'Is Dad unhappy?'

Mum smiled at her. 'He's content enough. He never had much ambition and while he's got his chapel he'll be all right. What are you doing today?'

'I haven't made any plans. I thought I could spend some time with you.'

'Good. You can dust the best room. Put a bit of polish on. And I'm baking this morning and it's the Bright Hour this afternoon. You can come to that. Some of the ladies admire your singing.'

'Only some of them?' Tessa laughed. 'Do the others dislike it?'

'Not that I know of,' said Mum. 'If they do they wouldn't tell me. Of course, a few don't have wirelesses.'

'I suppose not.'

'If Joseph had his way we would get rid of ours, and the gramophone, too. He disapproves of worldly goods.'

Tessa handed her mother the damp tea-towel to wash. 'You disapproved of the wireless once, remember?'

'I remember. I've got used to it now. You don't have to listen to rubbish or buy silly records.' She wrung out the tea-towel in her small, strong hands and hung it to dry over the range. 'Bring me the flour and butter, there's a good girl, and crack these eggs into a basin and beat them for me.' As they worked Mum asked, 'How is Eve these days? I wish she'd visit. Didn't you suggest it?'

Tessa hadn't. She liked a break from Eve with her wearing emotional swings. 'She's busy,' she said, giving only a half truth.

'Busy with what? Hasn't she got time off like you? She could have visited her cousin Paul and his wife.' Mum lowered her voice. 'I've heard that their first, a boy, is wrong up here.' She tapped her forehead with a floury finger.

'So I believe.'

'Poor little mite. I wonder what sin they committed to make that happen?'

'Mum! That's a dreadful thing to say.'

Mrs Morland beat her sugar and butter mixture energetically. 'Maybe it is, maybe it isn't. It's what some folk think. Our Joseph for one. Bad blood, he says, and he sends up powerful prayers that we haven't got any from Dad's side.'

Tessa controlled her amusement then stopped whisking as the thought hit her. Paul was her cousin, a blood relative, and Andrea a cousin by marriage. There was nothing to stop her visiting if she chose. And she *did* choose.

'I'll go and see them,' she said.

'That would be kind. You might be able to say a few words of consolation. It must be hard living with such an affliction. Mind you, it's an awful journey on the trams or buses. You have to go to Old Market, then catch one back.'

'I know. Is anyone using the old bicycle?'

'No, it's out in the shed. I insist on Dad's taking a tram to work. He's too old to be climbing all the hills. Joseph's bought a better one for himself so he can cycle to meetings.'

'I'll dust the room first.' Tessa polished Mum's few precious pieces of furniture with loving care. All of it matched, all of it was as immaculate as the day she and Dad had bought it. She pictured them choosing the stuff for their new home together and for a moment envied them their uncomplicated love. On the mantelpiece was a photograph of Edward, Prince of Wales. Mum was proud of the royal family. 'An example to foreigners,' she asserted.

Tessa recalled the repeated reporting in *Vogue* of the prince's constant proximity to an American woman, a Mrs Wallis Simpson. Well, that would blow over. He was destined to be king and she was a divorced woman.

A few drops of oil and a wipe over with a rag rendered the bicycle usable and Tessa climbed on and began to pedal. The distance in miles was not great for a young and healthy woman, the roads were fairly quiet and signs of approaching spring were everywhere. She breathed in the scents of her childhood with deep pleasure.

When she reached Frenchay she dismounted and wheeled the bicycle to the gates of Padding House. They were closed and looked formidable. She peered through the iron-work at the shining windows hung with velvet curtains and the immaculate front door. A man came round from the back pushing a barrowload of young plants. Tessa turned away, reluctant to break the peace of the old house. She stopped. Who was she trying to fool? She hated the idea of meeting Paul and seeing him a husband and father, happy with Andrea.

Something masochistic within her forced her on. She propped the bicycle against the stone wall and pushed open a smaller gate set beside the main one and walked up the drive, her feet scrunching the new pale grey gravel. There was a hollow sound as she banged the knocker and after a moment footsteps approached the front door.

'Hello, Partridge,' she said.

He peered at her 'Miss Morland?' He admitted her. 'I will see if Mrs Jefferson is at home.'

He walked ponderously to a door near the back of the hall and opened it. 'Miss Morland is here to see you,' she heard him announce. 'Are you in, madam?'

Then Paul came hurrying out to greet her. 'Tessa, how splendid to see you. Andrea will be glad, too. She's in here in her own room, resting. Take Miss Morland's coat, Partridge.'

Andrea lay on a day-bed wearing a pale gold cashmere afternoon dress, her legs covered with a red and gold silk shawl. A fire blazed in the grate. By her side was a table on which stood a carafe of fruit juice. She looked ethereally beautiful, reminding Tessa, as if she needed it, that few women could have competed with her in looks for Paul's love and she had money to spare and time to concentrate on them. Her rich brown hair was softly waved, her face, carefully made up, her hands, tipped with pale pink nail polish, were soft and white. Add to that her fortune . . .

'See who's come to visit, darling,' said Paul. 'Tessa.'

His word of endearment sent a sharp pain through Tessa. She had been a fool to come.

Andrea stared at her. 'I'm sorry, I can't remember . . . oh, yes, now I do. You're a distant cousin, aren't you? Do sit down. Shall I ring for refreshments?'

Mum would have just pushed the kettle to the hob automatically and there would have been a plate of biscuits or cakes on the table before the visitor had time to settle into a chair.

Paul said, 'Of course she would like something. Is there anything you want, my dear?'

Andrea sighed. 'No, thank you.' Her eyes went down to her swollen figure and she sighed again.

Tessa caught a glimpse of herself in a mirror. No wonder Partridge had stared. No wonder Andrea scarcely recognised her. Her face was red and shiny, the curls which showed beneath her hat were tangled. And the hat was a small felt one she had grabbed for cycling and had meant to take off when she arrived. She looked a mess. Women like Andrea were unfair competition.

'Are you keeping well?' asked Tessa, in an effort at conversation which Andrea seemed in no hurry to begin.

'Yes, thank you,' she said.

Paul put in, 'She has to rest a lot. Doctor's orders.'

'Damn doctors,' said Andrea. 'Having children is such a bore. Have you any, Tessa?'

'I'm not married.'

'Oh, I see.'

'You heard Partridge announce her as "miss",' said Paul in exasperated tones.

'You're on the stage aren't you, Tessa?' Andrea said languidly. 'You could be using a professional name.'

Tessa said, 'Quite a lot of women do. I suppose I shall when – if – I get married.'

'Anyone on your horizon?' asked Andrea.

'Not at the moment,' said Tessa, wishing even more she hadn't come.

'How's Eve?' asked Paul.

'She's well. She wasn't able to get to Bristol this time.'

'Why not?' Andrea asked.

'I'm not sure. Of course, we have to be careful with our money.'

'She should have plenty of money,' said Andrea. 'Paul got her a good price for her car.'

Paul was watching Tessa and couldn't have failed to

notice her start of surprise. She drank tea, then said she must go. Paul accompanied her down the drive to where she had left her bicycle.

'You didn't know that Eve had sold her car, did you?'

'I've been busy lately. When was the sale?'

'A few days ago. I sent her a cheque.'

'Oh, that explains it. I've been in Bristol.'

'She must have got the money before you left London.'

Disinclined for further talk on the subject, Tessa walked to her bicycle.

Paul followed her. 'You look very well,' he said.

'I'm not at my best.' Tessa removed her hat and combed her fingers through her hair.

'You look beautiful to me.' His vehemence startled her.

'Thank you, cousin.' Somehow she managed to sound flippant.

'You're welcome.' There was a deeply serious note in his voice.

'I really must go. Mum's expecting me.'

'I wish you could stay longer. I should like to hear more about your life. It must be enthralling. We're very quiet here.'

'That's natural. Andrea needs peace and—'

'She does nothing but complain. I can never please her.'

His unhappiness affected Tessa, but she said, 'You shouldn't be talking to me like this. She's your wife.'

'I'm very aware of that.' Paul looked around swiftly, then reached out for her and pulled her clumsily towards him. Instinctively, she resisted, then stayed passive in his arms while he kissed her. She found herself responding. She should stop him. She must.

She put her hands on his chest and pushed. 'Don't! Outside your house with your wife inside. What if someone should see us?'

'Is that what's worrying you? We could meet later. Where do you suggest?'

'Nowhere. How could you ask me?'

She climbed on to the bicycle and rode off as fast as she could pedal, not looking back. All the way home she thought of him, of the desperation in his voice, but he was married and that was that. She tried not to feel glad that he wanted her.

She returned to London the following day to make preparations for the coming tour. As soon as she let herself into the lodging house where she and Eve rented a back room, a door opened and the landlady stood glaring at her.

'So there you are!'

'Yes,' agreed Tessa mildly, 'here I am.'

The woman's anger faded a little. 'I'm sorry, Miss Morland. I thought perhaps you were like your friend and I'd been left in the lurch.'

'What do you mean?'

'Don't say she's done it on you, too? Better look and see if anything's missing!'

'What are you talking about?'

'Your friend. She's gone. I saw her leave in a taxi with a man and the rent's due.'

'All right, so Miss Brook went somewhere. Why should that worry you? She'll be back. We have to leave on tour.'

'I know she's not coming back. She's taken all her things except her big trunk and that's empty.'

'You've been going through our things?'

The woman flushed. 'Well, what would you do? I'm a woman on my own with four kids and I need the rent. It's not the first time this kind of thing's happened. I've found cases left behind stuffed with bricks before now and the tenant flown and no money for me.'

Tessa went upstairs to their room. Her corner was neat, but Eve's was in its usual chaos. She opened her trunk and confirmed that it was empty; she riffled through the things that lay around. They were all garments which Eve had tired of, plus some torn underwear. Then Tessa saw the envelope tucked behind her make-up box on one of the shelves.

Dear Tessa,
I gave you the chance, but you turned me down. I
can't stand the thought of another tour so I'm
going to get a job in films. Sorry and all that, but
you should have come with me when I asked.
Love, Eve.
P.S. Lenny Curtis is with me.
P.P.S. Sorry about the Kissing Cousins.

Tessa went cold. In a moment of pure selfishness Eve
had broken up their act and robbed Josh of a pianist just
as their tour was about to begin.

'Bad news?' enquired the landlady.

'Bad for me. Not for you. I'll pay you all that we owe
you. I'll be leaving in a couple of days myself.'

'Thank you, miss. I'm sorry I went on at you. It's the
worry, you see.'

'I understand. It doesn't matter.'

Tessa sounded so dispirited that the woman asked, 'Is
there something I can do?'

'Nothing, thank you.' Tessa took money from her
purse and handed it over. 'Now I must begin my
packing.'

The woman left, shaking her head, and Tessa sat down
heavily on her bed. She wondered if Eve or Lenny had
told Josh of their intentions? She was very tired, but she
went to a callbox and tried to get hold of Josh. 'He's out,
dear,' said his landlady. 'Said he'd not be back till the
early hours.'

In the morning Josh was rehearsing the instrumental
numbers in an old warehouse. He was playing the piano
and conducting when Tessa appeared. 'Have you seen
Lenny today?' he said.

She shook her head. 'I have to tell you something,
Josh.'

'Take five,' he called, and the band gratefully lit cigarettes. 'You look very serious, Tessa.'

She handed him Eve's note. Angry colour came into
Josh's face and he glared at her. 'That bloody cousin of

405

yours! She's a promiscuous little tart. She not only messes up her own life, she has to meddle in mine.'

'She's unhappy,' said Tessa.

'Not as unhappy as she'd be if I sued her for breach of contract.'

'Josh, you wouldn't!'

'No. Not through any feeling for her, but because she doesn't have any money and I don't have the time to spare. I'm sick of her vagaries. She needn't think I'll ever take her back.'

'She really isn't happy,' Tessa said inadequately.

'Lots of people aren't. They don't take it out on everyone around them.'

'Should I go after her?'

'Have you any idea of how many film studios there are? I thought not. There's Beaconsfield, Gaumont-Gainsborough, and many small ones – ten at Shepherd's Bush alone. We leave tomorrow and open on Monday night. You'd never trace her in time, and I've told you – I don't want her back. She's been a damn' nuisance. And what in hell am I going to do about a pianist?'

'There must be plenty needing work. *The Era* is full of them.'

'And I've got until tomorrow morning to select a few and hold auditions!'

Tessa was silent and Josh said, 'Sorry, it's not your fault. You don't happen to have another kissing cousin, do you?'

'Not that I know of.'

'You've been billed as a pair. You're wanted as a pair.'

'Does that mean you'll look for another act?' Tessa waited in trepidation for his answer.

Josh paced back and forth a few times. 'I could say Eve was ill and we might get away with you as a soloist. You're good enough. But I need a gimmick. Everyone needs a gimmick these days. Kissing Cousins was perfect. Can you think of anything?'

Tessa said hesitantly, 'The only thing I can offer is a

song I wrote. I'm not much good at music, I mean, I can't write it properly, but I've composed a tune and you could enlarge on it. That's if you like the lyric.'

'You've written a song? Tell me more. Could you do it again? Sing it to me.'

'Now? Here?'

'Where else? This is a rehearsal room. Quiet, you fellas! Tessa's going to give us something she wrote herself. Have you brought your music?'

'No. I told you, it's pretty crude. The tune, I mean.'

'Well, you'll have to sing unaccompanied. What's it called?'

' "Remember?" ' Tessa began to sing, her voice weak with nerves, standing there in the large draughty building which swallowed sound and spat it back in tinny echoes. She thought of the first time she had spoken of it, to Paul on that hot, happy day in France, and her nostalgia showed through every note.

> Remember me?
> I'm the girl you left;
> I'm the girl who promised to be true,
> To you.
> Remember me?
> Can you forget the wine-soft kisses in the sun?
> The fun?
> You took away my pride;
> You kissed me and it died
> In sweet surrender.
> Now I count the cost;
> Now I pay the price;
> Of love forever lost.
> Do you remember?

The echoes died away and she stood in the silence feeling foolish and very vulnerable. Then the band began to applaud and cheer and she looked at Josh. He was smiling.

'Great, Tessa! Just great. I'll work on the music. I'm

sure we've got a winner here. You must write more and we'll give you a special place on the bill. We must think of a name for you.'

'Composing Cousin?' suggested the first violin.

He was laughed and jeered at good-humouredly.

'No, that won't do,' said Josh. 'We'll think of something. If any of you gentlemen can come up with a good name for her, one that takes the eye on the billboards, let me know. Now, we'll get on.' He turned to Tessa. 'Don't feel upset over Eve. She's not worth it.'

He might be right. Eve might not be worth worrying over, but Tessa worried all the same. She couldn't get her cousin out of her mind. She hoped that Lenny would be good to her.

A new pianist was found, a man whose band had just folded. 'Lucky for me,' remarked Josh. 'Dennis is better than Lenny.'

By the time they arrived in Birmingham Josh had orchestrated Tessa's simple tune and she was billed as 'Tessa the Songbird' and, in brackets underneath, 'Warbling her very own song'.

The new name had to be stuck over the original billboard, and the theatre manager was indignant. 'I booked the Kissing Cousins. Where are they?'

'I don't blame you for being angry,' said Josh in his most ingratiating tones. 'Eve, the other singer, is ill and we hadn't time to find anyone else.'

'What's wrong with her? You haven't brought something catching to my theatre, have you?'

'No, no,' soothed Josh. 'She's not strong and a chill led to a chest infection. She has to rest for some time to come.'

'Does Tessa really write her own stuff?'

'Absolutely. Wait until you hear her new song. It's going to be premiered here.'

Tessa stepped forward when her name was announced. The audience stared at her, annoyed and muttering because they had paid good money to see both the Kissing Cousins who were on the wireless, but when she began to sing they fell silent and the applause at the end was loud and sincere.

'You've passed the first test,' said Josh.

She wiped the sweat from her palms. 'Thank God.' Then she hurried to the dressing-room to touch up her make-up for her next appearance.

She shared a dressing-room with other girls on the tour, one of whom was the soubrette, Dolly Driver. 'You've been doing great stuff,' she said generously to Tessa.

A dancer looked up from her make-up box. 'Where have you been playing, dear? I've never heard of you.'

'You'll have heard of the Kissing Cousins,' said Dolly. 'She's one of them, and the better in my opinion.'

Tessa was surveyed by several pairs of eyes, some admiring, some envious.

'Where's Miss Brook?' asked Dolly.

'She wasn't well enough to come on the tour,' Tessa said, 'so Josh altered the billing. It's just temporary.'

'Temporary, is it?' asked Dolly. 'I shouldn't bother with that Eve if I were you. You don't need her. That's my humble opinion, for what it's worth.'

'She needs me,' said Tessa. The other girls had lost interest and only Dolly heard.

She said, 'You ought to get away from her. She's the kind who'll always be a burden to someone.'

Tessa changed the subject. 'Have you heard how Cissie Barnes is getting on?'

A listening silence fell. Most touring companies knew Miss Barnes.

'That dumb cow!' said Dolly. 'She got herself pregnant . . .'

'That was clever of her,' shrieked a dancer. 'I thought it took two.'

'. . . and she married the baby's father, her boyfriend,' continued Dolly, ignoring the bawdy humour. 'The one with octopus hands,' she added in an amused whisper to Tessa. 'Actually,' she continued quietly, 'I wonder sometimes if she just let it happen. The baby, I mean. Her act was definitely going off and she couldn't ever seem to be on time. Perhaps she dreaded getting the bird. Though, God knows, it happens to us all.'

Tessa missed Eve far more than she had expected to. She wished she would write, wished she knew where to write to her. The tour proceeded and Tessa composed another song, 'The Pain of Love'.

Josh said one day, 'Both your songs have been sad. Can't you write something happy?'

'I'll try.' Tessa found that the essence of happiness was a more difficult thing to grasp than sorrow.

However, she was able to tell Josh she had written another one which she called, 'The Joy of Love'.

It was added to the repertoire but although it was well received it didn't get the applause of the others. 'Remember?' was a particular favourite. The whole act grew all the time in popularity and there were favourable reviews which brought in the crowds.

They completed the tour and began to pack for London. 'You're a marvel,' said Josh to Tessa. 'I've got offers from all over the place for you.'

'For me on my own?'

'Some,' he said. 'Tessa, I won't hold you back. You should grasp the chance of stardom while you're hot. You can make the top on your own.'

'After all your kindness? No, I'm not going to leave you.'

Tessa was packing. She carefully folded one of her stage frocks, a Schiaparelli-inspired ankle-length gown in heavy blue crêpe, and put the showy costume jewellery into her jewel case.

Josh perched on the edge of her bed and lit a cigarette. 'You're hoping Eve will come back, aren't you? I shan't employ her. Loyalty is all very well but it can be carried too far.'

'I don't agree.'

'Are you being honest with yourself? On your own

410

you know exactly what you're doing.'

He was right but she couldn't just cut Eve out of her heart.

'What do your parents think about it?'

'I haven't told them.' She folded another frock.

He smoked in silence for a while. 'You're crazy, but I can't help admiring you.'

Back in London the radio engagements were more frequent and Tessa began to meet some of the famous people who came in and out of the broadcasting station. There were celebrities who appeared on 'In Town Tonight', stars from the variety shows, musicians from the BBC Symphony Orchestra, and many who were still only voices to the majority, including the newscasters Stuart Hibbard and John Snagge, both in obligatory evening dress for evening broadcasting. She was in demand for solo spots and Josh gave her the freedom to accept engagements.

Eve should be here when so much was going on. Was she enjoying similar success in films? Sometimes Tessa lay awake wondering if she was all right.

She visited Bristol as soon as she could. When she arrived Mum was seated at the kitchen table with a cup of tea, the *Radio Times* opened at the day's page. 'Your name's in here,' were her first words, 'and in the newspaper.'

'I know, Mum. Do you mind?' She bent to kiss her mother.

'Not if it's all respectable like you said. It says here, "Tessa Morland is a star of the London nightclubs." Is that true?'

'They're exaggerating. I do have engagements in restaurants.'

'As long as it isn't nightclubs. Gangsters own nightclubs and a lot of fighting goes on in them. I can't feel really happy about it all, Tessa, I'd still rather you used your gift for God. What a blessing you'd be to Joseph. He could use hymns to emphasise his points. He makes a lot of his points. His sermons last for ages, but not a word is wasted.' She jumped to her feet. 'What am I thinking of, babbling away, when I haven't seen you for months! How are you? You look well. What's happened to Eve? Why do you sing on your own nowadays?'

'She's trying her hand in films.'

'Moving pictures? I don't think I approve of that. She needs someone to keep an eye on her. Here, drink this. Supper's nearly ready and there's plenty for you.' She reached for the biscuit tin, but Tessa waved it away.

'No thanks, Mum, I'm not eating sweet stuff. I have to keep my figure.'

She frowned. 'That's all girls seem to think of nowadays. You're too thin, like Susan. She's nothing but a clothes horse these days.'

Susan returned in time to hear the last remark. She laughed gaily and winked at her sister before kissing her.

The evening meal was lively, Susan relating the funny things that happened in the shop, Tessa picking out the amusing parts of her latest tour and Dad in jocular humour.

'Joseph's going to be late,' Mum explained. 'He's taking a prayer meeting over Hanham way. He's a powerful man for a prayer, is our Joseph, and folks don't seem to mind how long he takes.'

'And sometimes that's very long indeed,' said Susan cheekily.

'Now then, don't make fun of your brother,' said Dad. 'He's doing good work.'

He might be doing good work, but when he arrived home the atmosphere became sombre. Dressed from head to toe in black, he looked like an undertaker. 'Which is all very well,' said Susan later, 'but he's a bootmaker.'

Joseph hung his coat behind the kitchen door and seated himself opposite Tessa while Mum fetched out his plate of sausage and mash from the oven.

'I hope it's not dried up,' she said. 'I covered it with buttered wax paper.'

412

'It doesn't matter if it is,' said Joseph. 'When I'm doing the Lord's work, I take no count of the cost.'

He bent his head to say grace and Susan made a face at Tessa. It was intercepted by Mum who frowned.

Later, in bed that night, Susan said, 'Poor Mum. After all her exhorting us to pay attention to the minister she finally got what she wanted – a fervent worshipper. Now she doesn't know whether to be glad about Joseph, or fed up because he's no fun any more.'

'Is he always so lugubrious?'

'Always. He's been offered a tour of chapels in Devon and Cornwall. I hope he goes. I'm sure Mum does, too, but she feels guilty because she wants him to accept for the wrong reasons.'

Susan was almost asleep when Tessa sat straight up in bed.

'What's up?' asked Susan.

'Nothing. A bit of cramp in my leg. It's better now.' She felt even further from sleep. Paul was first cousin to Eve. He might have her address.

This time she took a taxi to Frenchay, an expense which shocked Mum.

'You must earn a fortune if you can't bother to travel on the trams.'

'I don't have much time,' said Tessa. She wasn't sure if her motive in visiting Paul was entirely selfless. She could have telephoned him.

Her clothes were very different from those she had worn on the last visit. Her coat was dark blue with ruched sleeves and a large grey fur collar, a tiny hat to match and black suede shoes and bag. Her gloves were pale grey. Partridge admitted her with an air of ceremony which did justice to such fine garments and Tessa saw with amusement the exact second he remembered who she was. At the last moment Tessa realised she couldn't ask directly for Paul if Andrea was in.

'I will see if madam is at home,' said Partridge.

As before, Paul greeted her. 'Tessa, my dear girl, it's so long since we met.'

413

His sudden appearance, his warm smile, the whole welcome of his attitude undermined her. She knew now that he was weak, but still she wanted to put up her lips for a kiss. A cousinly kiss couldn't do any harm, could it? He held both her hands for a moment. 'Andrea's resting. She'll be so pleased to see you.'

He threw open the door to the small sitting room. Andrea was reclining as Tessa had seen her before. She held out a languid hand. 'How are you, Tessa? Paul, pour her a glass of sherry. You don't belong to that idiotic Temperance Movement, do you?' She laughed, not waiting for an answer.

Tessa sipped her sherry, a good one, as she would expect.

'Have you heard from Eve lately?' she asked.

'Not a word,' said Andrea. 'By the way, I had a son.'

Tessa coloured. What a ghastly social gaffe! And not only social. It was unkind. She had seen the newspaper announcement and it was unforgivable of her to forget that Andrea had just been through childbirth. 'I did hear,' she said, then stopped, wondering what to say next, afraid in case this child too was not quite right.

'Yes,' said Paul, 'a beautiful son. Over ten pounds birth weight.'

'As I had good cause to know,' said Andrea pettishly. 'There should be a different way to have babies. I certainly don't want any more.'

'You'll forget in time,' said Paul, 'and want another.'

Tessa got the impression that this was a conversation they often held. She wondered if they talked like this in front of everybody. One never knew in these outspoken days.

'It's rotten about Eve's father, isn't it?' said Paul. 'You met him at the funeral, didn't you.'

'Mr Brook? What about him?'

'Such a fine figure of a man to be struck down.'

'I haven't heard anything. What happened?' asked Tessa urgently.

'He was cleaning a gun and it went off accidentally.'

414

'Do you mean he's injured?'

'Yes. Very badly. He's not regained consciousness and until he does no one will know if he'll be in his right mind. His brain is damaged.'

'That's horrible,' said Tessa. 'Horrible.' How had Eve borne such a blow? What would it do to her? 'Has Eve gone home?'

'No,' said Andrea. 'Paul wrote to her care of her last address. She didn't answer. We imagined she had gone home until the letter was returned "Not known".'

'This is terrible! She must be told.'

'I take it you know where she is?' said Paul.

'Not exactly.'

'Have you any idea where she is?' demanded Andrea.

'No, not at the moment. But I'll find her. The theatre world isn't so big.'

'Where is she singing?' asked Paul.

'She's so unreliable,' said Andrea, before Tessa could reply.

Paul said, 'Do find her quickly. Her father is barely alive. He may never come round.'

'She might not think it's worth dashing to the States to see him just lying unconscious,' said Andrea. 'And it might be better if he never regains consciousness if his brain is so badly injured.' Her white fingers picked at the red and gold fringe of the shawl and Tessa remembered that somewhere, presumably in this house, was a boy who was said to be mentally sick.

'When did all this happen?' she asked.

'About a week ago,' said Paul. 'Mother sent me a cablegram and followed it with a letter. I contacted our solicitor, but he doesn't have Eve's address. I also wrote to you. I suppose the letter is waiting for you somewhere.'

Tessa took a sip of wine to moisten her lips. 'Poor Eve. She adores her father.'

'Does she?' Andrea looked as disbelieving as she sounded. 'She has a funny way of showing it. I gather she hasn't been to see him for ages. Now it may be too late.'

'Don't say that, darling . . .'

Andrea interrupted her husband. 'Reliable people leave an address where they can be reached.'

Paul said, 'I'd look for her if I had an inkling where to begin.'

'Your first duty is to me and our child – children,' said Andrea.

'I dare say I'll have a better chance of contacting her,' said Tessa. 'I'll certainly try.'

Paul looked relieved. 'Good.'

Andrea said angrily, 'I don't see why you're both so bothered. She just went away without leaving a forwarding address. I don't think Eve really cares for anyone.'

'She does,' protested Tessa. 'She has to take work where she finds it. She needs the money.'

'What an idiot her father was to risk everything on something as volatile as the Stock Exchange,' said Andrea. 'It's simply another form of gambling.'

'I must go,' said Tessa. 'I'll return to London and set about searching for Eve. Could Partridge call me a taxi?'

'No need,' said Paul. 'I'll give you a lift.'

Andrea frowned and Tessa said, 'That isn't necessary, thank you.'

'You don't have a car of your own?' asked Andrea.

'I've no real need for one at present.'

'You won't have forgotten the driving lessons I gave you?' said Paul, his voice warm.

'Never,' said Tessa with what she realised too late was too much emphasis. She couldn't blame Andrea for her frown.

# Chapter Nineteen

The taxi stopped by the bridge over the River Frome, to allow another car to proceed. Dark water flowed fast and speeded into swirls and eddies. It was very different from the river in summer when Mum and Dad had brought them here for picnics and Tessa had paddled with her knickers over her frock, her bare feet sliding on the smooth stones as she tried to keep her balance. She smiled at the thought, a smile which quickly faded.

She hoped desperately she could find Eve in time, though finding her would only be to deal her a terrible blow. She remembered Eve's recurring nightmare and shuddered. Did she dream of her father's death? She must find her. She remembered her own singing engagements and knew she couldn't let Josh down. Someone who had no particular ties might help. Someone who knew Eve and was compassionate. Charles!

After she had directed the driver to take her to Park Street she was filled with doubts. For one thing, she should have telephoned him first. He might not be in the shop. He could be in any one of his houses or abroad. He might look upon such a request as an imposition which would be doubly resented because he had a poor opinion of Eve.

Mr Harris greeted her with a smile and said, 'Mr Ware is in the back having a bit of lunch.' And Tessa scarcely knew whether to be relieved or apprehensive.

She knocked on the door of the back room and Charles shouted: 'Come in.' When he saw her he jumped to his feet. 'Tessa!' he cried in tones of pure delight which warmed her. 'Sit down. Have you eaten? Would you like something? I haven't much, just bread, butter and cheese. No, that's not enough for you. I'll take you out to lunch.'

He was casually dressed in flannels, a sports shirt and pullover, a cravat knotted about his throat, and looked more handsome than ever.

Tessa smiled, 'I'm lucky to find you here.'

'It wasn't just luck. The antique business is absolutely fascinating. I only leave the shop to attend sales. Did you notice the improvements?'

'I'm afraid I didn't. I'm sorry.'

'It doesn't matter. I'll fetch my hat and coat.'

'No, bread and cheese will be fine and it's so lovely and warm here.'

She sat by a large gas fire which diffused a welcome glow throughout the room, wondering how to broach the subject when he looked upon her visit as a pleasantly unexpected social encounter. She ate a little and they lit cigarettes.

'I hear you're going great in London, Tessa. I always knew you'd be a star. I haven't heard Eve lately. Did Josh fire her?'

'No.'

Charles gave her a searching look. 'What's troubling you? You look worried. Your eyes . . . has someone been upsetting you? Just lead me to 'em.' He held up his fists.

Tessa laughed. 'Don't be so idiotic. It's Eve.'

'I might have known. What happened?'

'She got tired of singing and decided to become a film star.'

Charles threw back his head and gave a shout of laughter. 'She decided, did she? Some hopes. She doesn't have enough talent.'

Tessa sighed. 'You're always so beastly about her. You don't really know her.'

'And you're always so nice about her and you don't really know her either. I doubt if anyone does.'

418

'She needed to do something different.'

'She let you down, didn't she? I suppose she just upped and left. I'd bet a pony that Josh was angry.'

'Yes. She ran off with the pianist. I don't know where she is and I need to find her.'

'Why bother?'

'Because her father is gravely ill and I don't think she knows.'

Charles's merriment died. 'That's bad.'

'Oh, it is,' said Tessa in a rush, 'and I don't know how I can look for her without breaking some engagements. Josh says there are lots of film studios and she could be in any one of them.'

'Or working as a waitress, perhaps. Or worse.'

'What do you mean? Worse?'

'Don't keep flying off the handle! My God, she doesn't deserve a champion like you.'

Time was being wasted and Tessa said, 'Charles, I came to ask for your help. I thought that maybe you . . .' Her voice dwindled. 'I'm being selfish. I should go.'

'You want me to look for Eve?'

'Please.'

He was silent, his fingers tapping the arm of his Windsor chair.

She got up. 'It's too much to ask. I must go. I'll think of something . . .'

'I'll do it.'

'You will? Oh, thank you a thousand times. I can't tell you . . .'

'Once will be enough,' he said drily, 'and I'm doing it for you, remember that.'

'If she cares for anyone in the world it's for her father.'

'Then it's going to be pretty awful having to break the news to her.'

'Oh, of course, you'll be the one who will have to tell her.' Tessa clenched her fists in angry frustration. 'I should do it.'

'If her father is dying it won't much matter who breaks

the news. Nothing will help. And I can be kind.'

Tessa looked at him quickly. 'Yes, I know, but she'll need me. Bring her straight to me.'

'I had already decided to do so.'

'I should have known I could depend on you.'

He smiled ruefully. 'Thanks. What exactly happened to Ralph Brook?'

Tessa explained. As she was leaving Charles asked, 'Have you told Paul?'

'I've seen him. He already knew, but he can't leave Andrea. She's just had a baby.'

Charles looked sceptical and she insisted, 'Honestly, he couldn't leave her. She wouldn't let him go.'

Tessa was so abstracted she almost missed her cue. They were playing at the BBC and Josh was annoyed with her. 'We can't afford to make a mistake on the air. It'll be heard by thousands. There are plenty of other bands ready to step into our place if we lost it.'

'I know. I'm so sorry,' she said.

'You're worried about Eve, aren't you?'

'I can't help it.'

Josh sighed. 'She's lucky to have a friend like you.'

Five days later Charles arrived at Tessa's bed-sit with Eve. Tessa's insides seemed to contract at her cousin's appearance. Her shoulders were bent, her shadowed eyes sunken in a deathly white face. She moved like an automaton.

Tessa went swiftly to her side. 'Eve . . .'

'No,' she said, putting out her hands as if she was blind. 'Don't! Don't touch me . . . Just tell me. Is there any news of my father?'

'I telephoned Paul. Your father is still in the same state. No worse.'

'But no better?'

'No. I'm so sorry.' Charles led Eve to a chair near the gas fire. Tessa made tea and Eve accepted a cup and drank a little. 'I must go to him,' she said.

'Of course, but it's too late to do anything tonight,' said Tessa. 'You need rest.'

'I can't rest.'

Tessa saw Charles to the door and out on to the landing. 'Thank you,' she breathed. 'I shall always be grateful to you.'

'I wonder if I've done you a favour? She's in a bad way. She was existing in a ghastly rented room. I don't think she's been eating properly and she's devastated by the news. I managed to get a few words out of her on the drive. Apparently she sold her car, she couldn't get work, and when the money ran out, Lenny Curtis abandoned her. I believe you, Tessa, she truly does love her father. I'll stay in London for now. Call me at my flat if you need me.' He gave her the number and left.

Tessa persuaded Eve to eat a little and helped her to bed. Eve lay there, staring up at the ceiling, and Tessa wondered if Ralph Brook could possibly look worse than his daughter.

Eve put out her hand. 'Tessa, you're a brick. After the way I treated you.'

'It's all right. All that matters is to get you home as fast as possible.' She stayed by Eve's bed until she was sure her cousin slept then she undressed and curled up on the couch.

In the morning Eve stayed in bed and accepted a piece of buttered toast which she picked at and a cup of coffee. There was a knock on the door. Charles was there.

'I've bought Eve a ticket on the first available berth.'

'Oh, how good of you,' said Tessa.

'I can't pay you,' said Eve quickly. 'But you must let me know what I owe you . . .'

Charles nodded.

'When do we leave?' asked Eve.

'We?' asked Charles.

'Do you mean you booked only for me?' Eve's voice rose hysterically. 'Tessa's coming with me, aren't you?' She clutched her cousin's hand convulsively. 'You must come with me. You must. I can't be alone.'

Tessa caught Charles's eye. She wasn't quite quick enough to hide her dismay.

He sat down and lit a cigarette, lighting one for Eve. 'This is a family matter. Your mother will be looking to you for support. She will think it odd if you bring home a stranger.'

'Tessa isn't a stranger,' cried Eve. 'Mother has met her. Tessa is family and I won't be left alone! Not again. I've been on my own for weeks. It was awful. I can't be alone, not now, I won't!' Her voice rose to a piercing pitch as she repeated over and over, 'I can't, I won't!'

Tessa ached with pity, yet at the same time she nursed a seed of resentment.

'Tessa, for God's sake,' begged Eve, 'don't leave me.'

She said to Charles, 'Can you get another ticket?'

'It's quite late in the year for tourists. There should be room.'

Eve heard. 'Tourists!' she shrieked. 'You haven't booked me into Tourist Class?'

'It was all I could get.'

'Nonsense! There must be a first-class berth. I insist that you change my ticket.'

'How anxious are you to get away?'

'I'm desperate. You know I am.'

'Then you must accept what there is. As it is, you must wait a week.'

Tessa saw him to the door. She said, 'I doubt if Eve can pay you anything. You must let me know what we owe you.'

'Don't worry about money. You've enough on your plate.' He took a step away then turned back. 'I could tell her it was impossible to get a berth for you. Why should you go?'

'I must. I can't let her down.'

Charles said angrily, 'Why do you have to be such a bloody martyr?'

'I'm not a bloody martyr.'

'She wouldn't give up a dinner date for you.'

'I don't know. Perhaps not, but I have to go with her. I wish I could make you understand. She's not at all what you think.'

'You may be throwing your career away.'

'Don't say that. Don't undermine me. Get the ticket for me.'

She wrote at once to her parents telling them what had happened. She received a letter from Mum by return of post.

Dear Tessa,
Please tell Eve we're all very sorry about her dad.
You have to go with her if she needs you, and
from what you said in your letter that seems to be
the case. Please be very careful in America. Don't
forget how lawless it is. Even though Prohibition is
over the gangsters still think of wicked things to
do and they all carry guns.
Love, from Mum

Tessa showed the letter to Eve who smiled for the first time since she had heard of the accident. 'She's a lovely woman. I wish . . .' Her voice trailed off.

Josh was incredulous. 'You're going to throw everything away for *Eve*? I don't believe it. You couldn't be so crazy!'

'I've no choice, can't you see that? She has no one but me.'

'She's plenty of relatives, some here and many more in the States. I know the family. There are aunts, uncles, cousins, not to mention her mother.'

'She doesn't get on with her very well and hasn't seen her other relatives for years.'

'What about you? If you walk out on engagements here you'll never work again. No one will trust you.'

'I can't be the only performer who's had to cope with a crisis in her life, then made a comeback.'

'Even a well-established artiste would have a tough

time. The public forgets quickly and you're only just becoming known.'

'Don't rub it in, Josh. It's bad enough.'

'Tessa, listen to reason. Not one in a million would throw away all you've achieved for someone else's whim.'

'It's more than a whim.'

'Don't try to tell me that Eve feels anything deeply.'

'All right, I won't. I hoped you'd help me. I thought you might tell people that I've had to go to be with a dangerously sick relative. Surely they'd be lenient?'

Josh swore beneath his breath. 'I'll do my best.'

'Thank you. And you'll soon get a singer for the band.'

'Not like you, Tessa the Warbling Songbird.'

'Don't.' Rare tears began to flow down her cheeks.

Josh was appalled. 'Don't cry, Tessa. Sorry, I'm a brute!'

'You're not. You're good and kind and you're right about Eve, I know you are, but I have to go. I can't explain. She's so . . . so . . .'

Josh handed her a large white handkerchief. 'When you return, come straight to me and I'll do my best to get you fixed up with work.'

A week later Tessa and Eve boarded an ocean liner for America. Eve complained constantly. 'It's so small. I'm not used to small boats.'

'It looks big enough to me,' said Tessa, who had been overawed by the hull which towered above her and looked as if it might capsize in the merest wavelet.

When Eve discovered that their berth was to be shared with two other women she went white with fury. 'He's done it on purpose,' she raged. 'He probably thinks it's funny. He must know I've never travelled in such a way as this. I'm used to an outside cabin to myself with plenty of space and service. This is horrible.'

Tessa gave up remonstrating even gently with her. She had made up her mind to put up with her cousin's moods whatever form they took. She needed an outlet from her inner misery. Tessa didn't feel quite so forbearing when she discovered that the two strangers who shared their cabin suffered from sea-sickness. She had been relieved and delighted to discover that she could eat heartily whatever the weather, but the sour smell of the cabin dented her appetite.

'You see?' said Eve triumphantly. 'I was right to be cross. You don't like sharing.'

'The poor things can't help being ill. They must hate it,' said Tessa.

For a day she picked at her meals until her hunger reasserted itself. The food was excellent and she was pleased to see that Eve ate steadily. Now that the first shock had passed, emotion appeared to strengthen her appetite for everything. As the journey progressed she threw herself into the amusements on board in a frenzy of faked enjoyment. It was Tessa who held back, unable to play, her mind dwelling on what she had lost and what lay ahead. She had to appear serene in front of Eve, but every mile that took her from England removed her further from a life in which she had been happy. It was galling to realise that Eve could easily have managed without her. Tessa had pictured her sick and wan, leaning on her for support; the reality was altogether different.

Eve didn't stop grumbling about the accommodation. One of the narrow bunks was occupied by a fellow traveller who had introduced herself as Eunice Clark. She listened in silence for a while as Eve raved on. 'First class is as luxurious as the Ritz, especially on the big boats. I'm sure Charles could have got us on one if he'd really cared. My God, I hope no one in our set is on this voyage and sees me. I'll never hear the last of it. Thank God the journey won't take long and we'll be out of this ghastly cabin.'

This was too much for Miss Clark. She sat up in bed, holding her head which was aching after a spell of sickness. 'Shut up!' she yelled. 'Shut up! You're nothing but a snobby, moaning, miserable cow. I've been looking forward to this trip for a year. It took me that long to save the money and now you're spoiling it for me.'

Eve shrugged. 'I would have thought being sick would have spoiled your holiday.'

'I'm getting better and I'm fed up having to listen to you whining on and on.'

Eve slammed out angrily and Tessa apologised. 'She's on her way to visit her father who isn't expected to live after an accident.'

Miss Clark was crestfallen. 'Oh, I say, I'm sorry. I didn't know. She seems so gay and carefree when she's not grousing about something.'

'It's an act she puts on. She's very unhappy.'

'Are you her sister?'

'Her cousin.'

'Do you live together? I shouldn't think she was easy to live with.'

'We're together a lot of the time because we have a singing act.' The woman's interest was roused and Tessa told her about the Kissing Cousins. Eunice's eyes widened.

'I've heard you on the wireless. You're good.' Later, she apologised to Eve for her outburst. 'I was feeling rotten,' she said, 'but I shouldn't have abused you. It's not the way I usually am.'

Then on the following day Eve returned to the cabin, her face dark, her eyes stormy. 'I've just been approached by the entertainments officer. He said he'd heard that I was half of the Kissing Cousins. When I said it was true he asked if we would perform tonight. I wonder who told him about us? I've said nothing. Did you?'

'I mentioned it to Eunice Clark.'

'Whatever for? The damn' woman must have gone straight out and spread the news. Now they want us to sing at the fancy dress ball. For the *first*-class passengers! Everyone would be bound to recognise me.'

'What time do we go on?' asked Tessa. She felt

pleased at the prospect of singing.

'We don't! I sent him off with a flea in his ear. As if I can sing in public, the way I feel.'

Tessa was instantly contrite. 'No, of course not, darling. I'm sorry, that was dreadfully thoughtless of me.'

The entertainments officer coaxed Tessa. 'I quite understand about Miss Brook, but would you give us a song on your own, Miss Morland? I mean, can you?'

'Can I sing alone? Oh, yes, and I will.'

She had brought only a plain dinner dress with her, but Eunice was about her size and offered her the choice of two dance dresses. Tessa rejected a shiny, rustling, blue taffeta and chose an amber-coloured artificial silk which had been well cut and fell in folds about her. The other, older occupant of the cabin lent her a pale jade green necklace and Tessa wore her own gold earrings. She sang a couple of popular songs and many of the revellers joined in the choruses.

Josh had given her the music for 'Remember?' as well as her other songs. 'Take them with you, Tessa,' he had said. 'You may need them. You can always earn something by singing. They're original and good.'

She had decided to sing her own special song and the band began to play the opening bars. The words took on a new poignancy. She was leaving behind all that she held dear, and that included her career. If she stayed away for long, would anyone remember her? The public was fickle, ready to take any new star into their hearts. Absorbed in the song, it took her a while to realise that the dancers were merely swaying to the music, their eyes fixed on her as they listened. The storm of applause took her aback and she made her bows in a pleasant daze.

She was thanked, and as she reached the ballroom door was approached by a corpulent man who wore a lot of gold jewellery. 'Great, my dear, that was great. Just let me have your name and address and I'll look after you.'

Tessa was used to being importuned by men who offered her a glittering career and wanted her address.

427

She smiled at him, but brushed past him and hurried down the long corridor to her cabin.

That night the women were awakened by Eve's cries of anguish. Tessa knew at once what was happening. She leapt from her bunk, grabbed Eve's shoulders and shook her. 'Wake up! Wake up!'

Eve's eyes stayed closed but she began to moan and struggle, then gave a terrible shriek as her eyes flew open. Eunice put on the light. Eve's eyes were filled with horror. She caught Tessa's hands in a painful grip. 'He's dead. My father's dead.'

'No, no,' Tessa soothed. 'You've been dreaming. It was only a dream.'

Eve flopped back on to her pillows. 'He's dead. I know it,' she moaned.

Neither girl slept again that night.

In the morning Tessa asked to see the first officer who was sympathetic. 'I'll cable Miss Brook's mother. I'll be tactful. I'll just ask how he is and sign it with Miss Brook's name.'

The answer came quickly. 'Ralph died last night.'

Tessa waited until they were alone in the cabin before she broke the terrible news. Eve said tonelessly, 'I know. I told you he was gone. I saw him. In my dream, I saw him. He was – different. It was horrible.'

'Don't try to be brave,' said Tessa. 'Cry. It will ease you.'

'Nothing can do that. I'd cry if I could, but everything's dried up inside me.' She lay on her bunk with her face to the wall.

Eve lay staring upwards, seeing nothing. Two days had passed since the news of her father's death. She stirred restlessly. That fearful dream. If it came again she thought it would kill her. Thank God she'd brought Tessa with her. She didn't ask a lot of questions. That Eunice woman had tried to talk to her, insisting that telling someone about a nightmare sometimes made it go away.

This one never will, she thought. It'll live with me forever. She was perspiring with weakness. She had eaten nothing since she had received the news. Tessa brought her food, but she couldn't go to the trouble of chewing and took only liquids. She had lain awake at night until an exhaustion too deep to resist claimed her and she slid into a doze – and suddenly was back again in the worst nightmare of all. This time, she knew she was dreaming. She tried to wake up but she was paralysed.

She was in bed with her lover. The man she loved best in all the world. He smoothed her breasts, her thighs, he kissed her willing lips. He was going to make love to her and she wanted him to. Part of her mind begged for mercy. In past dreams at this point her lover had always revealed his face and always it had been the same: her father's.

The new dream was far worse. Now she knew she must expect a horror far more hideous, but struggle as she might her limbs refused to move, she couldn't turn her head or even close her eyes. The man lifted his head and she saw it again, the skull, the holes for eyes, the grinning teeth. Her father's.

She had been shaken, hard. 'Tessa,' she moaned, 'Tessa. Help me.'

'It's me, Eunice.'

Eve had struck her hands away. 'Leave me alone.'

Eunice had stood back and stared down at her. 'I'm sorry about your father. I'm sorry you suffer so dreadfully from nightmares. All the same, I wouldn't put up with you the way Tessa does. I'm glad we dock tomorrow. I hope I never see you again.'

'Go to hell,' snarled Eve.

When the New York sky-line came into view Eve stayed in her cabin and Tessa was able to experience without hindrance one of the world's most impressive sights. She had seen pictures of sky-scrapers, the buildings which soared like sculpted towers into the air, but the reality was breathtakingly better than any picture. The Statue of Liberty held her torch aloft as the huge boat was manoeuvred into the dock which was crowded with people. Tessa looked down, wondering which of them was here to meet Eve. She got her cousin to the disembarkation point, their hand luggage carried by a sympathetic steward. Eve trembled uncontrollably. All around them people were embracing, laughing, weeping. Eve's emotion was betrayed only by the persistent shaking of her body. No one had come to meet them.

'Get a taxi,' she said. 'I'll give him directions.'

Rose Brook stood by the side of her husband's coffin and stared down into his face. He had been brought home from the mortuary only yesterday. He appeared unmarked. A shot to the brain was not the cleanest way to die, but the bullet had torn through his ear and exited near the back of his head and enough of his face was left intact for the mortician to work on. It had taken her hours to wash away the blood in the study. She had refused all help.

'Ralph,' she whispered. He looked calm and as handsome as always. Soon the lid would be screwed down and he would be laid to rest in the family vault and no one would ever know what had really happened. The gun was one he had brought home after the war and kept in his desk as a souvenir. Belper and Grace knew that Ralph was in the habit of keeping his revolver clean, he had not given way to the strain of losing his money as so many others had done by ending their lives and it was logical to deduce an accident.

That woman, Irene Martinez, and her brother had actually had the temerity to come to the house. They had been admitted by Belper because the woman had been Ralph's secretary. They were there, Irene explained to Rose, because her brother, Maurice, had asked to be allowed to see Ralph's body, to say a proper farewell. Rose had stood staring at him, her hatred so powerful it had taken on an almost tangible presence.

'He's dead,' said Irene. 'No one can have him now. I cared for him, too, you know. I've been hurt.'

'Leave my house!' Rose, gasping for breath, had only just managed to get the words out.

'If you won't let me see him, then please, allow Maurice . . .'

Rose had turned her blazing eyes on the boy. He was slender, his face more beautiful than his sister's. His eyes were bleak, appealing. He had held out his hands in supplication. 'Just one look,' he had begged in his soft tones. 'He would have wanted me . . .'

'Leave my house!'

The boy was unable to let go. 'Please,' he begged.

Rose stood motionless, outraged by the barbarous insult with which these two were desecrating her place of mourning.

After a long silence, Irene asked, 'Did he leave a message?'

'A message?'

'Was he able to speak before he died?'

'No.'

Maurice said, his words coming out in a soft rush, 'When we saw him last he was very upset, but he wouldn't tell us why. He looked as if he might even weep. We tried to comfort him.'

Rose spoke with deliberate calm. She must at any cost hang on to her fury. If she let go . . . If she said the wrong thing . . . 'You have learned the cause of my husband's death.'

Maurice blundered on, his eyes bright, 'I wondered . . . was it really an accident? He was so unhappy . . .'

'What are you suggesting?'

'Maybe Ralph found his problems too hurtful to bear,' said Irene. 'Maybe he decided to end his life.'

Rose's fury boiled higher within her. She controlled it with an effort of will that made her head ache. She said in low tones, 'How dare you! My husband died by accident. I've a good mind to call the police and have you thrown out.'

'You won't, though,' Irene said angrily. 'Someone might start asking questions. They might discover how miserable he was with you.'

Rose's tumultuous anger crystallised into a cold, still

rage. 'My husband was perfectly happy with me. We had a perfect marriage. Do you think I did not know he was amusing himself with you? We laughed about it many times.'

'I don't believe you,' cried Irene.

'Neither do I,' said Maurice. 'He disliked you. I've a good mind to tell the authorities of our suspicions.'

'Do you think anyone would listen to you?'

'They might.'

Irene had intervened. 'No, darling,' taking her brother's arm, 'you can't do that. Think of his reputation. He's dead. Let him rest in peace.'

Rose had summoned the butler. 'Show Mr and Miss Martinez out,' she had ordered. The pair had gone without further argument. 'If they ever call again, I am out,' Rose had told Belper. She had poured herself a glass of brandy and drunk it, the glass clattering against her teeth. She hated spirits and the powerful fluid made her gasp. She stopped shaking, though the pain in her head persisted.

She sat now in her small drawing room and thought over the events since Ralph's death. It tortured her to remember, but only by facing up to the truth could she hope to exorcise the horror and erect a barrier between herself and the dreadful facts.

No one could ever prove a thing. She had burned the letters he had left. Hers had been a short apology for the distress he would cause. The one to Irene had been kind, almost brotherly, in spite of what they had been to each other. It was the one he had written to Maurice which tormented Rose. She knew its message by heart. It kept returning to her brain.

It won't do, Maurice, my dearest boy. You know the way I feel about you. I can no longer fight my resistance to you. I feel as if my whole being is disintegrating. I am a coward. You must find a better man, one who is not afraid to surrender to such joy and love as you will give. Please, forgive me.

432

The whole house had heard the shot, but she had been first on the scene. Ralph's head lay on his desk and she had instinctively snatched the envelopes up before the spreading pool of blood had reached them, and thrust them into her pocket.

She had a compulsive need to see him in his coffin and walked upstairs to where it lay in his bedroom. She bent and kissed the cold mouth. 'You're mine now. You will always be mine.'

She left him and asked Grace to make sure that Eve's room was ready. She wished her daughter was not coming. She wanted to keep a wide space between herself and others. She had already begun to erect the wall which would conceal the truth from herself, and as time passed she would build it higher and stronger. After the years of humiliation she would have all the dignity of an honourable widowhood. It was a role she looked forward to with all her heart. For days the house had been busy with sympathisers. Some viewed Ralph's body, all left flowers. Their scent filled the rooms. She found it cloying.

She could not get out of asking Paul to find Eve and now she would have to stand by while she looked down at her father. She expected this to be a mere formality. Eve had felt no more for her father than for anyone else.

She was about to go to her bedroom when she heard voices in the hall. Eve and another female. A maid, perhaps? She walked downstairs and her eyes met Tessa's.

Eve watched her mother's progress down the stairs. She waited for some sign that she was welcome. Surely now her mother would want her; surely she would share her grief with her daughter?

'This is a sad occasion,' said her mother. And Eve knew that even from her father's death she was excluded. The thread of hope curled and died.

'Very sad,' she agreed. 'Is he at home? May I see him?'

433

'Of course you may. First you must settle in. What a surprise to see you, Tessa. Eve quite forgot to let me know you would be arriving.'

'She came to give me support,' said Eve.

'That was kind.' Rose's voice and manner made it perfectly clear to Tessa that she was an interloper.

She said quickly, 'I've no wish to intrude, Mrs Brook. I can quite easily book into a hotel.'

'Certainly not. You are a cousin, if a distant one. We have plenty of room. You will stay here as long as Eve stays. Meanwhile, perhaps you had better sit somewhere until a room has been prepared for you.'

Eve was angry. Did she have to make it so obvious that Tessa was expected to stay for only a limited time? 'Tessa can wait with me,' she said, before she followed Belper and a maid upstairs as they carried the luggage to her room.

Eve said to the maid, 'Unpack my things. Later you can see to Miss Tessa's.'

'Yes, miss.'

The servants left and Eve said, 'He'll be in his bedroom. I'm going to see him.'

She reached her father's door and hesitated fearfully, hanging on to her courage. She pushed open the door, entered, and closed it behind her. The room was sickly with the overpowering scent of flowers. She walked slowly to the coffin. With a tremendous effort she looked down at her father. She studied his face for a long time. It was smooth and tranquil, all emotion erased, but she could have traced every line of it from memory: his frowns, his rare smiles, the way his mouth set when he was angry. This face held no expression. Here lay a stranger. But he had always been a stranger to her.

She leaned over him. 'Father,' she whispered. She touched her lips to his forehead, to his cheeks, then to his icy mouth. She felt suddenly faint. She tried to hang on to her swooning senses, but slowly sank to the floor, one hand clinging to the coffin side as she struggled to retain consciousness.

'Eve!' Her mother's voice cracked across the room like the sound of a whip. 'What in hell do you think you are doing? I gave you no permission to enter this room. Get up at once.'

Eve lifted her head and stared at her mother.

Rose took a step back. 'Why do you look at me like that?'

Eve tried to speak, but her mouth was dry, her throat constricted.

'Stop it!' cried Rose. 'Get up.'

The dizziness was passing and Eve rose to her feet, one hand still on the coffin. 'I have as much right to be here as you,' she said. 'I am his daughter. I carry his blood. Something you could never have. I am part of him. What were you?'

'His wife. I was his wife. No woman can get closer to a man than that.'

'I believe there were some who did.'

'You dare to rake up evil rumours in this room, in the presence of one of the finest men who ever lived?'

The two watched each other. Rose walked slowly forward. For a moment Eve thought that the bitter confrontation might somehow have succeeded in breaching the barrier between them. Rose walked to the coffin and struck Eve's hand from it. 'Leave him alone,' she hissed. 'He is mine and always will be.'

Tessa was shown into a pretty bedroom whose predominant colour was pale yellow. When the maid arrived to unpack her case she felt quite embarrassed. The girl was young and nervous and Tessa wanted to reassure her, to help her in her task, but forced herself to behave with Eve's careless acceptance.

There was a knock on the door and Eve came in. 'Come and see Father.'

Tessa glanced at the maid. 'Now?'

'Of course. They'll screw the lid down soon and you won't have a chance.'

The maid looked at Eve. She sounded so casual. Her

435

cousin turned and walked out and Tessa followed.

Ralph looked almost life-like. His hands were clasped over his breast, his face slightly yellower than live human flesh, but colour remained in his lips and cheeks. 'They paint them, you know,' said Eve. 'Morticians paint corpses. And they sew their lips together so that they won't lie with their mouths hanging open.'

She put out her hand and smoothed his glossy hair. 'I've always wanted to do that. Isn't he the handsomest man you ever saw? He never touched me, Tessa,' she continued conversationally, 'never once. Well, not that I remember. Have I ever told you that? Maybe he did when I was a baby. I don't know. Let's go to my room and I'll order something to eat. Dinner won't be for ages and I'm hungry. Funny, isn't it? I haven't felt like food for days, but now I've seen him I'm starving.'

Tessa sat in Eve's room which was light and cheerful, the shelves crowded with books, dolls, toys, all the para- phernalia of childhood. How odd, Tessa thought. As soon as she and Susan and Joseph had outgrown their toys, the ones fit to be used again were passed on to less fortunate children. Tessa remembered Mum darning and patching, finding boot buttons for missing eyes, scrub- bing away the collected grime, until she felt the toy fit for some child to find on Christmas morning.

'Didn't you play with your toys?' she asked.

'What?' Eve looked at the crowded shelves. 'Some- times, but I was always kept so busy taking lessons. Dancing, tennis, skating, riding, golfing, swimming . . . anything you care to name. And everyone gave me dolls. Dolls of all sizes and shapes. Boring, aren't they? I never really got fond of my toys.' She pulled out the top drawer of her dressing-table and riffled through the contents. 'Look at this! Powder, lipsticks, scent, eye make-up. We can use it all. It's good stuff. Better than I can afford now. You can have some if you like.'

'I've got my own,' said Tessa.

'Well, don't then! Do you have to sound so smug?'

'I didn't mean it that way. Our colouring is quite different and I need my own stuff.'

'And I suppose you've been making a lot of money while I was trying to get somewhere in films?'

'More than I used to.'

'I thought so. If you'd come with me I'm sure we'd have become famous as the Kissing Cousins. There are plenty of musical films being produced.'

The maid answered the bell. Eve said, 'It's always you. Where are the other servants?'

'What servants, miss?'

'The housemaids?'

'There's only me and one other, miss, and Mr Belper and Mrs Brook's maid.'

Eve frowned. 'Ridiculous. You've probably got it all wrong.'

'No, miss.'

'What's your name?'

'Nellie, miss. My real name's Eleanor, but your mama – I mean, madam – changed it.'

'I should think so. Miss Tessa and I would like coffee and sandwiches here.'

'Yes, miss.' The girl gave a small bobbing curtsey. She couldn't have been more than fifteen years old and she was nervous.

'You were hard on her,' said Tessa.

'What do you mean?'

'She's still a kid. There's no need to sound so bossy.'

'It's plain to see you were never brought up in a first-class house.'

'Maybe not,' flashed Tessa, 'but I was brought up in a first-class home and that's more than you can say.'

Eve turned her head away and Tessa put her arms round her. 'Sorry, Eve, I'm so sorry. How could I have been so mean to you when your father . . . please forgive me.'

'It's my fault. I'm so edgy.'

'And no wonder.'

# Chapter Twenty

The funeral was well attended. Besides family there were friends, businessmen and dignitaries, golfing partners and church members. Rose and Eve stood together, their faces veiled in black. Later they showed no trace of tears. The reception was held in the house with a buffet and drinks and after the obligatory remarks about how Ralph would be missed and a few solicitous enquiries after their hostess's well-being, the talk veered into different channels. The servants hurried and scurried but found it difficult to keep pace with the demands and Tessa heard a woman say, 'This place has gone down. I remember when they would have had a dozen servants on any occasion.'

'I know,' agreed her female companion. 'I suppose it's a sign of the times. Ralph lost his money in the crash, didn't he?'

'Yes, but she has a fortune of her own.'

'Obviously she intends to be mean with it.'

Tessa burned with anger at the unpleasant remark. One of the women stepped back and bumped into Nellie, the little maid, causing her to drop a tray of savouries. A lobster patty hit the woman and left a smear on her skirt. She shot Nellie a look of angry contempt which flustered the maid still further and, scarlet-faced, she grabbed the skirt and started to rub the mark with a corner of her apron.

'You fool,' cried the woman. 'You're making it worse.'

Rose hurried over. 'Nellie, clear this mess then change

your apron. Quickly! I'm so sorry,' she said to the woman. 'Naturally you must send me the cost of cleaning your skirt. Such a smart costume too.'

'I may have to replace it.'

Rose nodded. 'Of course.'

Tessa bent to help the girl pick up the mess, then took a tray from the long side table and began to circulate.

Eve made her way to her. 'Tessa, for God's sake, put that down. You're a guest. What will people think?'

'What does it matter what they think? We'll be leaving here anyway in a few days to go back to England. They'll never see me again.'

'That's not the point. You've been introduced as my cousin. They'll be shocked.'

'Let them. You can tell them I'm a poor relation.' She expected further argument, but Eve just turned away.

The men were beginning to cluster and talk of money. Of money gained, but chiefly money lost. They rehashed the Wall Street Crash, speculating on what would have happened if the right steps had been taken at the right time, listing the numbers of acquaintances who were existing either at subsistence level or working in menial jobs, or else had died or just disappeared from society.

By helping the maid, Tessa seemed to have rendered herself as invisible as a servant and no one bothered to lower their voice in her presence. As she reached one group she was in time to hear a rotund man say, glancing as he did so in Rose's direction, 'When I heard the news about Brook, I assumed he'd ended it himself.'

'The verdict at the inquest was definite,' said his companion. 'It was an accident. He left no note. That clinched it for me.'

The first man hadn't finished. 'I heard from my valet that Rose was first on the scene. Who knows what evidence there may have been?' He took a savoury from Tessa's tray.

She felt like hurling the contents of it into his face. She realised that someone had been clicking their fingers at her and a voice was calling impatiently, 'Over here, please.' Biting her tongue to keep it still, she continued with her self-imposed task. As she meandered among the guests whose spirits were rising as the decanters of wine and spirits were depleted, she remembered the funeral of a well-loved uncle, one of Mum's brothers. He had never married and Mum had arranged things. Many had gathered in the chapel to 'pay their respects' to him and there hadn't been room for everyone in the small cottage in Kingswood so the men had stood in the garden. To be sure, there had been laughter and chatter and the women especially had waxed gregarious over their glasses of sherry, but nowhere had there been vicious criticism, no picking over of the deceased's bones.

Later, in her room, Eve asked angrily, 'Don't you mind being taken for a servant?'

'What's wrong with being a servant?'

'If you like it so much perhaps you'd better give up singing. I'm sure you could find a job as a skivvy somewhere.' A glance at Eve kept Tessa silent. She was white and exhausted and there were dark rings round her eyes. 'Well,' she goaded, 'what have you to say?'

Tessa said gently, 'I just wanted to help you and Cousin Rose. You told me yourself that her income had fallen. I suppose that's why the servants have had to leave.'

Eve turned away. 'Sorry,' she muttered. 'I'm sorry.'

At the funeral Paul's parents had merged with the other black-clad guests and Eve decided to take Tessa on a round of family visits and insisted she must meet Reginald and Betsy Jefferson properly.

In their house Tessa felt at ease for the first time since leaving England. This was a home where magazines and newspapers were strewn across tables, where there was a comfortable untidiness. A couple of small dogs greeted them noisily then curled up on a couch beside their mistress, on whose lap a grey long-haired cat was purring. Tessa bent to pat the dogs.

'You like dogs?' asked Betsy.

'Very much. We have one at home. He's getting old now.'

'I always say a home's not a home without a dog,' said Reginald in his hearty way.

'Mother wouldn't allow one anywhere near our house,' said Eve. 'She fired a servant once because she smuggled hers in. And he was only little. I wish she hadn't.'

Betsy shot Eve an anxious look. 'You've been having a dreadful time, my dear. I'm so sorry.' Her thin fingers scratched the cat behind its ears, sending it into paroxysms of pleasure.

Eve took out a silver case and inserted a cigarette into a long holder. 'You don't mind if I smoke?'

Betsy half smiled, but Reginald said, 'Sorry, Eve, my dear, but smoke makes your aunt cough and it hurts her. I go to my study for an occasional cigar.'

Eve pulled the cigarette from the holder, threw it into the fire and closed her handbag with a snap.

Betsy looked ill-at-ease. 'You do understand, dear, don't you? I'm still not really well.'

'Your Aunt Betsy has had a bad time of it,' said Reginald.

Eve studied her aunt. 'You're thinner.'

Tessa thought that was probably an understatement. Betsy had the appearance of a woman who had lost weight far too quickly. Her skin sagged in places and her complexion had a yellowish tinge. She said, 'I'm sorry you haven't been well, Mrs Jefferson. I hope you'll soon recover.'

'So do I,' said Eve.

Betsy smiled. 'Thank you, my dears. I'm sure I shall. Did you see a lot of Paul in Bristol, Eve?'

'Not much lately,' she said. 'I moved out when he got married and Tessa and I have been busy.'

'I visited Padding House just after the new baby was born,' said Tessa.

'Did you, my dear?' said Betsy eagerly. 'Did you see the little fellow?'

'I'm afraid not.'

'How did Andrea look? And Paul?'

'She was resting. She looked as pretty as ever. Paul was obviously proud of his family.'

'They send me photographs all the time,' said Betsy, 'but it isn't the same. And I have only one of their first son. I would like to hold my grandchildren.'

When Reginald saw them off in the hall Eve demanded, 'Why don't Paul and Andrea come to visit?'

Reginald dismissed the butler, helping the girls with their coats. He seemed not to have heard Eve's question. 'Your aunt is ill, very ill. I fear she may . . .' He stopped.

Eve said, 'You don't mean that she's in danger of her life?'

'I'm afraid I do. In fact, it's a certainty. Paul must come home soon.'

'Does he know?' asked Tessa.

'I've told him,' said Reginald, 'but course he couldn't leave his wife when she needed him so much. There was a happy outcome this time, wasn't there? The new little fellow is perfectly well, but poor Andrea has been under a dreadful strain. She finds the fact of her first son's – illness – difficult to accept.' He opened the front door. 'My wife loves all small living creatures, perfect or not.'

Eve said impulsively, 'I'm sorry, Uncle Reginald. About Aunt Betsy, I mean. I wish I had given her a bigger kiss. I'll go back and give her another.'

'No!' Reginald's voice was sharp enough to startle Eve.

'Why not? Surely she knows she's going to die.'

Tessa was shocked at the cruelly direct word which Reginald had avoided. He coughed then said, 'She knows, but she doesn't want to be fussed. She'll slip away quietly—' he paused '—the way she's lived.'

'I'll see her again before we leave New York,' said Eve.

As they walked along the street Eve said, 'Andrea could cope if she wanted to. Paul's place is with his mother. What a weak bastard he is.'

'He is not!'

'My God, you're still enamoured! How can you defend him? If your mother was dying, wouldn't you hurry to be with her?'

Tess was silent as the impact of Eve's words struck home. Somehow she had never thought of her parents as mortal. Of course, she knew they were, and preachers emphasised it, talking constantly about heaven and hell and in the midst of life being in death. She suddenly ached with the need to go to Bristol, to see her parents and hug them.

'When are we leaving?' she asked.

'For heaven's sake,' said Eve, 'I only used your mother as an example. You don't have to rush back. I'm sure she and Cousin Walter are all right.'

'I know. When are we leaving?' Tessa repeated.

'Give me a chance, please. I've been away so long and I want to visit my family and friends.'

'Oh. Of course you do. Sorry.'

In spite of being frustrated over time lost with the band, Tessa enjoyed going out with Eve as she waited for her cousin to get over her first grief. Not that she showed grief, though Tessa believed it went deeper than people generally realised. But as the round of visits went on, she began to feel bored. She had little rapport with most of the people she was meeting and their long, formal meals were an ordeal.

One morning when a spring sun shone brightly she said again to Eve, 'When do we leave? When can we go home?'

'Home? Oh, England, you mean. Some time, I guess.'

'I have engagements to fulfil.'

'I thought you said Josh had someone else.'

'On a temporary basis.'

'Is she good?'

'Very.'

'Then why should you return? How do you know he'll employ you again?'

'He will if he can. If not, he'll find me other work.

He's pleased with the songs I wrote.'

'What songs?'

'I forgot you didn't know. I write some of my material now and set it to music then Josh orchestrates it. I sang the first one on board ship at the fancy dress ball.'

'Let me hear.'

'I will.'

'Now!'

'I don't feel like singing. And this house is in mourning. Your mother would hate it.'

'She's gone to visit Aunt Betsy. Sing. You're only making excuses. Come on, you can play the piano as well.'

Tessa played and sang 'Remember?' and Eve listened intently. At the end she said, 'It's not bad. You were singing about Paul, weren't you?' Tessa flushed as Eve continued mockingly, 'Did he really give you – what was it? – "wine-soft kisses in the sun"?'

Tessa tried to laugh. 'You have to allow some poet's licence.'

'So he didn't?'

'Shut up, Eve.'

'He did! And you thought he'd fallen for you. Poor old you. Is your heart broken?'

'No more than yours over David.'

Eve scowled. 'I love David. I make no secret of it. And if you're hankering after Paul I don't know why you can't admit it.'

'He's married with two children. What kind of a woman would I be if I still hankered after him?'

'Any kind of woman,' flashed Eve. 'You can't help where you lose your heart. Hey, that's a great title for a song. Why not use it?'

'We're getting off the point. I should like to know when, or if, you plan to travel to England? If you don't come with me I must go alone.'

'You'd leave me?'

'Why not?'

'Because I need you.'

'But you left me!'

'I was in love, or thought I was. Oh, it's all right for you. You don't need someone the way I do.'

'There are many kinds of need,' said Tessa, annoyed. Tears welled into Eve's eyes and trickled down her face. 'Oh, don't cry,' begged Tessa. 'Please don't cry.'

'I can't bear to lose you. You're the only one who cares about me, who's ever cared about me. When you're with me I'm stronger. Without you I go to pieces. Charles would tell you. When he found me I was in a shocking state. Please, please, don't go anywhere without me. Not ever again.'

Tessa sat on the bed beside her cousin and slid an arm about her waist. 'Eve, you make things very difficult.'

'Say it! You'll never leave me again.'

'I'll stay with you for now, but I'm sorry, that's too big a promise.'

'You must make it. Promise me you won't leave me. Promise! I've no one but you. You care, Tessa, don't you? You helped me when I had that operation. You're kind to me. Even when I don't deserve it, you're kind to me. You're more like a sister than a cousin. I beg of you, don't leave me.' Eve's voice was rising into hysteria.

Tessa sighed. She was so vulnerable. And there was the nightmare. 'Calm down,' she said quietly. 'I'll stay while you need me.'

Eve threw her arms about Tessa's neck and gave her a childish hug. 'You're a great girl. I really do think of you as my sister.'

So the days passed and Tessa was bored and irritated in turn at the waste of time. There were some enjoyable times, visits to the cinema or, better still, the theatre, with cocktails first in the luxurious Madison Room of the Biltmore and supper afterwards in the Ambassador where Pancho and his Orchestra played. In fact there was music everywhere nowadays. Except in Eve's home which was echoingly silent.

'Mother doesn't care for the wireless,' explained Eve. 'She enjoys a quiet life.'

446

Tessa found the house chilling, not in actual fact because it was centrally heated in a thorough way that astonished her, but metaphorically. Each room was permeated by Rose Brook's passionless personality. And this was where Eve had spent her formative years.

Not even Eve dared to defy the convention that insisted on a period of mourning and non-attendance of any big parties. Maybe she didn't want to. In public her face wore a smile; in private the smile died and she had a tormented air. She and Tessa attended 'girls only' functions, a 'shower' for engaged girls or expectant mothers, to which every guest was expected to bring a handsome present. Eve's friends were all from irreproachable backgrounds and if their families were suffering from the slump it wasn't immediately apparent among the younger ones, who talked excitedly of the social season which was approaching when they would be in the right places to meet the right men.

Eve was scathing about the young matrons. 'Already bogged down with husband and babies.'

She was particularly unpleasant to a pale blonde who was in the middle stages of her first pregnancy. 'How's Elliot?' she greeted her at an afternoon tea.

'He's well,' said the girl in a gentle voice.

'I hope he's attentive to you.'

It was no secret that Elliot had once been devoted to Eve and it was she who had broken the connection. The girl flushed. 'He is. Always.'

'So glad,' said Eve carelessly.

'What a droopy female,' she said to Tessa afterwards. 'Elliot was wild to marry me, but I wanted a more interesting life. He's as boring as hell.'

Tessa made non-committal replies to these sort of comments. Sometimes this annoyed Eve who then went to extreme lengths of sarcasm in an effort to goad her. Tessa read the American newspapers and learned that the world Eve and her kind inhabited, even those whose fortunes were depleted, was vividly different from that of the majority of Americans. 'Economic Depression' were the words frequently employed. Men marched here as they did in Britain to draw attention to their plight. Farmers were suffering too.

'What are dirt farmers?' she asked Eve.

'Oh, men who have a small strip of land and some kind of shack to live in.'

'It says here that the topsoil in the farming belt has blown away. There are dust storms and many families have taken to the road.'

'Have they?' said Eve. 'How unpleasant for them, but it won't mean the same to them as it would to us. Their kind are used to roughing it. Listen to this. There are now eighteen thousand one hundred and ninety-two cinemas in America. Imagine that! They must need hundreds of films to fill them all. Think of the opportunities in Hollywood.'

'Maybe one day you'll be in a film,' said Tessa.

'Why "one day". Why not now?'

'Perhaps Josh and his Melody Men will be invited to make a film. We must go back and consolidate our position in the band. There's a lot of interest being shown in them in Britain.'

'Oh, *Britain*,' said Eve. 'Hollywood makes bigger movies than Britain can produce. Everyone in America knows about the stars. Wouldn't it be wonderful if people paid to go to movie-houses to hear us sing? Maybe we could act, as well.'

'We might stand a better chance of being discovered if we went back to Josh. Hollywood is always on the look-out for new talent from any country. Think of Greta Garbo and Marlene Dietrich.'

'Don't forget Maurice Chevalier. He's a singer, too.'

'I doubt if you'd get offered the same parts as him.'

'Don't joke about it. I'm serious,' Eve sighed.

'So am I. Josh could be our passport to fame. We just have to be patient.'

'Patient! I want it now!'

'That seems to be your philosophy about everything.'

'What's wrong with that? We Americans are dynamic, we want things to happen quickly, not like the English, content to plod along hopefully. Look at your father.'

'What about my father?' demanded Tessa.

'He lost his job and seems content to be a sweeper in a market. What kind of work is that?'

'Honest work,' said Tessa.

'My father was honest!'

'Have I said otherwise?'

'Some people are blaming men like Father for the Wall Street Crash.'

'Some people always want to blame others for their folly.'

'You don't blame him?'

'How could I? It seems to me he was a victim just like the others.'

'He was, wasn't he? A victim.'

Tessa let the conversation die then but the following day she tackled Eve again. 'We really must leave here. Your mother wants to be alone with her memories.'

Eve glared at her. 'What about mine?'

'No one can take them away from you.'

'No one can take Mother's away, either, and she's got better ones than me.' Eve's voice was harsh.

Tessa said gently, 'I know that you and your parents didn't always agree—'

'Didn't agree? That's an understatement if ever there was one.'

'—but you must have something nice to look back on?'

'I've nothing. I told you, he never touched me. Never! Memories? All I have are memories of wanting him to love me, wanting a father who cared. He made me feel stupid and ugly.'

Tessa felt inadequate as she always did when Eve spoke this way. She said rather lamely, 'Mum and Dad love you. They'd welcome you. You could have a good life. Store up a few happy memories of your own.'

'Everything I do seems to go wrong.'

'We all make mistakes. We have to go on, trying and failing perhaps, but at least trying and one day we shall succeed. Here, we do nothing but make a round of aimless visits.'

'All right, we will go. To Hollywood! It says in *Photo-*

*play* that 20th Century Fox are casting for *On the Avenue* – that's a musical. Melody Pictures are looking for people for *With Love and Kisses*, and Universal are casting for *Top of the Town*, all musicals. Just think, Tessa, next year we could be in any one of a dozen films.'

'But you've already tried to get into pictures in England and . . .'

'Oh, I know, but Hollywood is different. More go-ahead, more up-to-date, altogether more marvellous. And I don't see why we shouldn't have as good a chance as anyone else. Better. We know we've got a good act.'

Tessa said, 'Not as good yet as some I've seen in films.'

'We can polish it.'

'We'd have to rehearse more than we've done before. Do you know that even Fred Astaire rehearsed every day for nine weeks before he performed a single dance for *Roberta*? And he's a stickler for punctuality.'

'You got that out of *Photoplay*, didn't you? I saw it. I would be punctual always if only I could get into movies. If we didn't get taken on by one studio, we would by another. There are so many. We'll make it, I know we will.'

Tessa said, 'Eve, I must return to Britain.'

'Later,' she said. 'Not just yet.'

Tessa let the argument drop. One morning she got a letter from her mother. She and Mrs Brook were eating alone while Eve stayed in bed. Tessa hated these early morning confrontations. Not that anything much was said, but Rose Brook made her feel uncomfortable.

'Do read your letter,' she said. 'I have my own correspondence.'

Dear Tessa,
    We got your letter all right. I'm glad lots of
people came to the funeral. It's always a comfort
to the bereaved. Give Mrs Brook our deepest
sympathy and Eve as well and tell her we think of
her a lot and mention her name in our family
prayers. Joseph holds them every night now. Poor

Mrs Jefferson. It sounds as if she's very poorly.
You seem to be living a grand life. I think it's time
you came home.

I had a letter from Sammy Jacobs's wife. We've
written a lot since you gave me her address. She
says that she's heard from Sammy at last. He's
been waiting for permission to visit his cousin in
prison and thinks he'll get it soon. It sounds as if
those Nazis do everything they can to upset folk.

Susan is getting on well. They had a fashion
show in Taylor's. One of their girls was ill and
Susan was asked at the last minute. The gown
buyer told me she's got a good future in fashion.
Joseph doesn't like it. He says it's trivial. He's
right, I suppose, but I don't think being a
mannequin is immoral the way he does. He says
she's showing off her body to all and sundry.

I wish you'd stop gallivanting and come home.
Everyone's getting excited about the new king
and his Coronation. It'll be next year, I think. Poor
old King George, going like that. He wasn't old.
Now we've got Edward. He's young and Dad
thinks he'll be good for us because he cares about
the poor. He flew in an aeroplane to London from
Sandringham. No king's ever flown before. When
the old king had his funeral procession the gold
and sapphire cross fell off the coffin into the road
and some say that it was a bad omen.

Joseph thinks that's foolish. He doesn't believe
in omens. Neither do I, of course. Joseph doesn't
approve of the ways of King Edward. The Sunday
after his father died he did some gardening
instead of going to church. Joseph said that was a
dreadful example to set before his people.
Perhaps it was, though your dad says that he feels
near to God in a garden. Some people say that
King Edward wants to marry an American called
Mrs Simpson, but of course he won't. He's a king
and can't marry a divorced woman. He'll look for a

proper princess to make his queen. Everyone sends love.

From your loving Mother

Tessa smiled at the artless messages. Since arriving in the States she had learned a lot about the new King Edward and his love affair and knew that many Americans believed (and hoped) that he wouldn't easily give up Mrs Simpson. Rose was watching her.

'Good news, Tessa?'

'Just an account of the day-to-day activities of my family.'

'How pleasant. Today I shall make a round of visits. I dislike them intensely and always have, and now that I am a widow—' her voice cracked just a little on the word '—I intend gradually to stop them completely. We shall meet at dinner unless you and Eve have a prior engagement?'

'I don't know. Eve tends to spring things on me.'

'You should be firmer with her.' Rose gathered up her correspondence and walked to the door. She turned. 'I am sure that you wish to resume your career. Paul sent his mother several accounts of functions at which you have been heard. You were praised. You should not allow opportunities to slip.'

Tessa thanked Rose, although she felt that the praise was simply a tool to prise her out. It made her uncomfortable. She would have another go at Eve and tell her she absolutely must go home. Then she forgot everything as she thought of Paul's interest in her. It warmed her to know that he still thought about her.

That night Eve woke the whole household with her screams. Tessa raced to her room and tried to wake her. It took a frighteningly long time. By the time Eve had her eyes open and was clinging to Tessa, sobbing hysterically, Mrs Brook was in the room with her maid and other servants were clustered at the door. Rose ordered them away.

'What on earth caused you to make that fearful noise?' she demanded.

Eve was shaking too much to reply. 'She has a recurring nightmare,' said Tessa.

For the first time Tessa saw Rose disconcerted. 'What dream could cause such dreadful agitation?'

'She's not told me.'

'Do you mean this happens often?'

'Not often, but when it does—' Tessa stopped as Eve fell into her arms weeping.

'It was worse again!' she cried.

Rose stood tall in her dark dressing gown, her eyes fixed on her daughter. 'You had better leave her to me, Tessa. I will question her. Grace, you may go.'

'No, she can't leave me,' shrieked Eve. 'Tessa mustn't leave me. Not now. Not ever. I'll go mad without her. I'll die!'

'Such – such immoderate language,' Rose stammered.

'I'll stay with her,' said Tessa.

All Eve's engagements for the following day were cancelled. She spent it wandering round the house, only pausing sometimes to enter her father's study and sit there.

Rose returned in the early evening. 'Where is she?' she asked.

'Lying down. She was tired.'

'Might she not dream again? Shouldn't you be with her?' asked Rose nervously. 'Has she told you her dream yet?'

Tessa shook her head.

'Did you ask her about it?'

'No. I have in the past, but she won't tell anyone.'

'I think she should see a doctor. A psychiatrist might help.'

Tessa knew little about mind doctors, so she said nothing.

When this proposition was put to Eve she erupted into such a storm of anger that Rose was again shaken.

'What has occurred to make her like this?' she asked. 'Last night she sounded less than human, screaming the way she did, quite like an animal in pain. And today she is hysterical, simply because I suggest a treatment which might cure her. Do you know of something in her life to cause her such fear?'

Tessa thought of the times when Eve had confided her worries, her assertions that her parents cared nothing for her, that her father had never so much as touched her. 'I think you should ask Eve yourself,' she said.

'I have and she told me to go away.'

Tessa remained silent.

'You are very self-possessed,' said Rose. 'Have you nothing to tell me?'

'She is upset over her father's death.'

'I find that difficult to credit. She left us as soon as she could and scarcely bothered to write.'

'Some things go too deeply to be written.'

'Is that meant to be a criticism?'

'No.'

There was another silence, then Tessa got up. 'I must change for dinner.'

'Please, wait. Clearly, Eve depends on you. You will be taking her back to England with you?'

'If she'll come. So far, she has resisted the idea.'

'She can't stay here.'

In the face of such monstrous rejection Tessa fell silent again.

'I hope you will keep her with you,' said Rose. 'She seems to depend on you.'

'I would like to do so.'

Rose didn't try to hide her relief. 'When are you planning to go?'

'I would very much like to get the first available berths.'

'Splendid.'

'But Eve wants me to travel to Hollywood with her.'

'Hollywood? Where motion pictures are made? Now what? Has she some notion of becoming a film actor? I have heard that some very odd things go on there. I'm sure it wouldn't be wise for her to go there. For either of you.'

'I dare say much of the gossip is unfounded,' said Tessa.

'There is usually a spark of truth behind gossip.'

'Maybe. I'm hoping Eve will forget the idea.'

'If she insists, does that mean you will allow her to go alone?'

'I have commitments in England.'

'She needs you.'

Tessa looked at Rose for a long time. Her face was perfectly composed, but her eyes showed something. A trace of love for her daughter? Tessa didn't think so. More likely fear that she would be burdened with her.

Rose said, 'If Eve goes to Hollywood on her own there is no telling what mischief may befall her. She appears to have no sense of responsibility to her family or to herself. She might bring scandal down upon us. I abhor scandal.'

So it was a worry about her own possible involvement that moved Rose. Oddly enough, it was this selfish, uncaring attitude which decided Tessa that she must stay with Eve. Even as she made the decision she was angry with herself, angry because of the way her self-centred, often bitchy, cousin could undermine her resolve, but having chosen her course she would have to come to terms with it.


'You'll come with me!' Eve's face was alight with pleasure. 'Tessa, you're a brick, you really are.'

'Thanks. How do we get there?'

'I'll ask Mother for the train fare. You'll love Hollywood, I just know you will. The stars have wonderful lives. They go to parties every night, meet other stars, have lovely houses with swimming pools. Oh, everything they want!'

'Not everyone is a star.'

'No, people without talent are the same everywhere, but audiences like us, you know they do. Haven't you any curiosity at all about Hollywood?'

'Of course I have. Who wouldn't?'

'There you are then.'

Rose willingly gave Eve enough money. She'd give her anything to be rid of her, thought Tessa. It made her feel even more protective towards her cousin. And perhaps something wonderful would happen to them in the film colony? Her naturally optimistic spirits lifted her.

'You should visit your Aunt Betsy before you leave,' Rose said to Eve.

'We've been there once already!'

Tessa reminded her, 'You told your uncle that you'd visit again.'

Eve frowned. 'That was only a polite way of saying goodbye.'

'If you promised to go then you must,' said Rose.

'Oh, all right, if I must.'

'May I come?' asked Tessa. 'I would like to see Mrs Jefferson again.'

On the way to the Jeffersons' house in a taxi, Eve said, 'You don't care if you see my aunt or not. You just want another look at Paul.' When Tessa simply stared from the window she went on, 'He's probably out, anyway. I've heard that he and Andrea don't get on very well and that he spends a lot of time away from her.'

The butler said that Mrs Jefferson was confined to bed and that Mr Paul was sitting with her.

'You had better not come up, Tessa,' said Eve. 'It sounds as if she's having a bad day.'

Tessa sat in the library. Eve had been right and she did want to see Paul. Just a sight of him made her happy. She idly picked up a leather-bound book. *Love Poems*. She opened it. There was a message written on the fly-leaf. 'To my dear Betsy from Reginald. These poems express my love for you better than any words I can find.' A lump came into her throat as she thought of the extent of Reginald's grief. She turned the pages, stopping at a poem by John Donne, and read, 'I am two fools, I know. For loving, and for saying so in whining poetry.' She replaced the book carefully on the library table.

I'm another fool for loving, she thought, and a fool for saying so in my songs.

Eve burst in. 'Aunt Betsy would like to see you.'

Paul was at his mother's side, holding her hand. He looked up and she saw that he suffered for his mother. 'Mother, here's Tessa.'

Betsy smiled. 'So nice to see you. Eve tells me you are going with her to Hollywood. I am so glad.'

Eve gave a false laugh. 'I *can* look after myself, you know.'

'Of course, my dear, but you are so very pretty. You should have a chaperon. Oh dear, that sounds frightfully rude, Tessa. You are pretty, too.'

Paul said teasingly to his mother, 'Enough said, darling.'

Tessa took the hand held out to her. 'You'll forgive me I know,' said Betsy. Her hand was wasted and quivered to the beating of her heart.

The door opened and Mr Jefferson walked in. 'Hello, Uncle,' said Eve.

'Partridge told me you girls were here. I'm glad you could come.'

'You've lost weight, Uncle Reginald.'

He patted his girth. 'I needed to.' He smiled but his eyes were sorrowful.

'It's in sympathy with me,' smiled Betsy. Then a spasm of pain twisted her mouth. 'You must all go now, my dears.' A note of urgency crept into her voice, 'Reginald, please ask the nurse to come back.'

Downstairs, Paul led the way to the drawing room where he poured himself a large whisky. 'It's ghastly to watch the way she suffers,' he said.

'She doesn't let you watch,' said Eve. 'She sent you away.'

'I know. She hates anyone but the nurses and Father to be there when the bad attacks come, but I can't stop thinking about them.'

Andrea came into the room and looked coolly at Eve and Tessa. Motherhood, disappointment over her first-born, the tragedy being enacted upstairs, her marriage whether happy or not, had not affected her looks in any way. 'Your son wants you,' she said to Paul.

'I'll go up. Would you like to see the boys, Eve?'

She looked horrified. 'No, thank you. I don't know what to do or say to kids.'

'How about you, Tessa?'

'I'd love to meet them.'

She followed Paul up the wide, carpeted stairs. He went slowly and when they turned into a corridor, stopped and took both her hands in his. 'Tessa, my dear girl, I truly am glad to see you.'

She was taken aback by his fervour, especially here, especially now, but there was no mistaking the joy in his voice.

'Oh, Paul.'

He pulled her to him and kissed her and her body responded. With all her heart she longed to make love to him.

A door along the corridor opened and a small maid in a white apron and cap appeared and trotted past them to the back staircase.

'Damn,' said Paul. 'We'd better get to the nursery.'

A door opened into a large day room beyond which Tessa could see another room containing two cots. An elderly woman rose to her feet. 'How's Mrs Jefferson, Mr Paul?'

'No better, I'm afraid. Tessa, this is Nanny Brown. She was my nurse and now looks after my boys. She's promised to come to England with us.'

'If he must go, that is,' said Nanny, nodding at Tessa. 'I don't like foreign countries.'

'Be careful,' warned Paul. 'Miss Tessa is English.'

She smiled and looked past the nurse to a small boy who sat on the floor playing with building blocks. He had just erected a tower. He knocked it down accidentally and, with a piercing cry, threw himself down, then sat up and began to build again. Once more the building blocks wobbled and fell before he was prepared and the boy shrieked his rage.

'Now, now, Master Reggie, this won't do,' said the nurse.

The child continued to scream and she picked him up

and carried him through to a third room where they could hear him shrieking and drumming his heels on the floor while Nanny tried patiently to soothe him.

'My elder son,' said Paul bitterly. 'Poor little devil. He'll never get much better than that. Come and see Timothy.'

Paul's second child lay asleep in his cot, one rosy fist curled beneath his cheek. 'He's beautiful,' said Tessa, feeling a sharp pang of hurt at the idea that he might have been her son and Paul's. The racket kicked up by Reggie finally reached the baby who opened his eyes, stirred and looked up. When he saw his father he smiled, showing his few small white teeth.

'Isn't he great, Tessa?'

'He's lovely.'

Timothy gave her a considering stare, then pulled himself upright and held out his arms to her.

'He likes you,' said Paul. 'What excellent taste.'

Tessa held Paul's son close to her heart. She looked into his eyes, so like his father's, then bent and kissed his soft, flushed face.

The nursery maid came in from the day room and spoke in a breathless, hurrying way. 'Excuse me, sir and madam, but it's time for Master Timothy's bath before supper.'

Tessa handed over the baby who greeted the maid with a happy gurgle.

Little Reginald was quiet now and had returned to his building blocks. Tessa helped him to erect a tower that was stable, and laughed when he knocked it down. 'More,' he said. Twice more she obliged, before the nursery maid coaxed him into the bathroom.

Downstairs, Eve was curled in an armchair with a large glass. 'Andrea makes the darlingest cocktails,' she squeaked in a falsetto tone.

Andrea frowned. 'Would you like something to drink, Tessa?'

'A cocktail would be nice. Not too big, though, please.'

Andrea shrugged. 'You make it, Paul. I'm tired.'

Before they left, Reginald Jefferson came downstairs. 'Your mother is asleep,' he said to Paul. 'The nurse assures me she'll not wake up for a good while.' As Partridge was helping Eve on with her coat Reginald handed Tessa an envelope. 'A little gift of money from Eve's aunt,' he whispered. 'Eve needs looking after. It'll help you.' He raised his voice. 'I'll look forward to seeing you two on the silver screen.'

'What was my uncle whispering to you?' asked Eve on the way home.

'Just wishing us a good trip with a nice job at the end of it,' said Tessa, quelling the impulse to tell Eve that she had some money. It would slip through her careless fingers like water.

Tessa found fifty dollars in the envelope and tucked it into her little make-up purse. Rose had handed over money to carry them safely across the USA to the west coast and Eve hurried out to buy tickets. On her return she was elated, her eyes full of mischief. Tessa knew that look and waited apprehensively to hear what had happened. Eve kept her counsel and only grinned when Tessa asked if she had their tickets.

That night, Tessa climbed into bed minutes before her cousin came into her room. 'You'll never guess,' she said triumphantly. 'I suddenly remembered that we can both drive and decided we could use a car and save a lot of the money Mother has given us for expenses. A second-hand model costs almost nothing and gasolene is cheap. We can eat at roadside diners and sleep in inexpensive lodging houses, then if we don't get jobs straight away it won't matter because we'll have time to look around and maybe even have some fun first. In Hollywood, if you're young, female and good-looking you're OK.'

By this time Tessa was sitting bolt upright. 'Eve! Have you told your mother about the car?'

'Of course not, you ninny. She'd probably want some money back. She's a dreadful skinflint these days.'

'You shouldn't deceive her.'

'Oh, here we go again. Good little Tessa and bad old Eve.'

No matter how determined Tessa was to ignore Eve's sarcasm, her cousin could still get under her skin. She wondered what she was doing here. Why she was being so crazy? She wanted to sing, Josh was an excellent boss and her life in England had settled into a happy pattern. She said as calmly as she could, 'Do be sensible, Eve, and get the tickets.'

She looked sulky. 'It's too late. I've already paid for a car.'

'Can't you take it back? Surely the garage wouldn't mind if you explained.'

'Explained what? And the man would never let me return it. I agreed to take it with all its faults.'

'Honestly, Eve, you're the giddy limit! You may have bought the most dreadful rattle-trap. What do you know about the workings of cars? And I thought we had resumed our partnership! How can we ever live and work together if you go behind my back and behave so idiotically? Show some sense.'

'Show some sense? That's all I ever hear from anyone!'

Tessa said drily, 'Is that so? Have you ever stopped to think there may be a good reason for it?'

'No, I haven't. Life is for living, for having fun. God knows, there's been little of it so far this trip.'

'I hardly expected it to be fun.'

Eve said quickly, 'No, of course not. I'm being a bitch, aren't I? And you're a brick. I don't mean to be unpleasant to you. But, oh, Tessa, I need to forget . . . it'll be a swell adventure and we'll see America.'

'I still don't like the idea of deceiving your mother.'

'And you've never deceived yours, have you?'

Tessa sighed. 'This is somewhat different. To set off on our own . . .'

'America isn't the African jungle! We'll come to no harm.'

'. . . in a car which may be dubious, neither of us

knowing the first thing about engines! And it will take us much longer.'

'What of it?'

'I thought you were in a frantic hurry to reach Hollywood?'

'A few weeks here and there won't matter. They're making hundreds of movies. We'll probably be a huge hit as soon as we start.'

'From all I've read lately that's what thousands of girls think.'

'You're such a wet blanket!'

'Because you're so damned mercurial!'

Eve laughed and after a moment, so did Tessa.

'All right,' she conceded, 'I'll come on the great adventure with you. I don't seem to have much choice.'

'You won't tell Mother?'

'No, she's had enough to bear.'

'So have I,' flashed Eve.

'I know.'

'It'll be a long time before I can forget I've lost my father.'

'I'm sure it will.'

'So we're off in our automobile,' cried Eve with one of her lightning changes of mood. 'Off on the grand trek.'

'We'd better take some food with us,' said Tessa, 'and buy more in stores on the way. We can save money by not going to restaurants. Have you much left?'

'Enough,' said Eve airily. 'It's going to be great!'

After Eve had gone, Tessa put on the light. She had almost told her about the fifty dollars, then decided against it. It would be safer with her. It would be a fascinating trip and maybe they would impress some Hollywood impresario and see their faces on screen, so much larger than life. In Eve's movie magazines there were stories of stars discovered working in menial jobs who often needed coaching in speech and movement. She and Eve were experienced in stage work and already had an act.

The next morning she wrote to her parents, to Josh,

and lastly to Charles, telling them of her change of plan. She told Charles she missed him. It was true, she did, and more than she had bargained for. She said she hoped that business was good and she would visit the shop as soon as she returned to Britain.

On the following day Tessa received a letter with a New York postmark.

> Dear Tessa,
>     Can you meet me before you leave? I need someone to talk to. I'll be at the Grand Central Art Galleries, 15, Vanderbilt on Wednesday and again on Thursday. I'll try to get there by ten in the morning and wait for you in the Exhibition Print Room.
>     P.

Paul wanted to see her! Knowing how unwise it was, she still decided to meet him.

The best way to put Eve off was to tell her the truth about her destination. Eve wasn't interested in art unless it came out of Hollywood – though much of that, thought Tessa, could scarcely be called art.

Eve was still in bed and looked up lazily from her magazine. Before Tessa could speak, she said, 'Look, it says in *Variety* that three hundred and fifty Hollywood stars earn more than a hundred thousand dollars a year.'

'Do they really? They don't actually earn it, you know, they just get paid it, and it's immoral when millions can't find work.'

'Get off your soap-box,' said Eve absently. 'What I could do with that kind of money!' Her eyes were shining. She was so caught up in her dreams that she scarcely listened when Tessa told her she was visiting an art gallery.

'Fine, fine. It says here that . . .'

Tessa escaped and arrived early, instructing the taxi to drive round the block again. Then, at five past ten, she walked into the Exhibition Room where a few people were wandering round. Paul stood with his back to her surveying an etching of an early American painting. He heard her quick footsteps and swung round. 'I knew it was you. I'd recognise your step anywhere.'

Tessa was taken aback. 'Would you?'

'It's wonderful to see you on your own.'

'You wanted to talk,' she said, striving to keep her emotions under control. What power he had to stir her! Her reaction to him was increased by his obvious dejection and even more obvious relief that she had come.

'We need to be somewhere less public,' he said.

The gallery had emptied and Tessa smiled. 'Where can we go that is more private than this?'

Paul didn't smile. 'Someone may come in at any moment and there are so many gossips.'

She hesitated, feeling herself to be on the threshold of a situation which could get out of hand. 'We can talk here,' she said.

He was adamant. 'No! Please, Tessa, there's not a soul I can turn to but you.'

In the face of such a bald statement of need she gave in. Their taxi stopped in a residential district and Paul led the way inside an old-fashioned apartment house and into a lift which creaked to the third floor.

'Where are we going?' she asked, keeping her tone light with an effort.

'To a friend's apartment. He's out of town today and lent me his key.'

They entered the apartment which was small and sparsely but comfortably furnished. A pulse beat hard in Tessa's throat. She sat gingerly on the edge of an easy chair and waited.

'Coffee?' asked Paul.

She shook her head. 'You didn't bring me here to drink coffee.'

His face lit up. 'Of course I didn't. You understand perfectly, don't you?' He knelt beside her. 'Darling

Tessa, what a fool I've been.' He slid his arms round her waist. 'I knew from that wonderful time in France that I needed you, wanted you.'

She looked down into his troubled eyes. 'Then why did you marry Andrea?'

'I was flattered, I guess. She's everything a man from my sort of family is supposed to desire in a woman. Beautiful, clever, rich, well connected. I saw her as a perfect wife, a suitable mother for my children. It was easy to persuade myself that I was in love with her. But she's cold, Tessa, so cold. She just accepts my love-making . . .'

Tessa held out her hand. 'Stop right there! I'm not going to discuss Andrea in that way.'

'Not even with me? It's me, Tessa. You loved me in France. You did, didn't you? You wrote a song that told me so. I knew you had me in mind when you sang it. Tessa, I've brought you here to tell you how much I love you. I'm crazy with wanting you. Give yourself to me, just once before you go away. Just this once. I'll never ask again.'

'Give myself to you?'

'Yes, please, please do.'

Her thoughts became chaotic. She had dreamed of such a moment, longed for it. 'What about Andrea?'

'I've told you, she's cold. I don't love her.' He slid his hands up her body until they cupped her breasts. His touch inflamed her. 'Just once, Tessa, and I'll never ask you again.'

'Won't you? Why won't you ask again?'

'My dearest! I might have known you would say that. You're so warm, so passionate. Even those few kisses in France told me that. You want me, don't you? Knowing I can make love to you sometimes will help me endure my marriage.'

'I see.'

'You would, darling. You understand everything about me, don't you? I knew I had to marry well. It was expected of me.'

'But now you're dissatisfied with your bargain?'

'Tessa, don't. You sounded as cold as her and you're not. You're warm. I can feel your heart beating fast. With you I could be truly happy, I know I could.'

'Are you saying you'd leave Andrea for me?'

'Leave Andrea?'

'That's what I said.'

It dawned on Paul that Tessa's response was far from ecstatic. 'You sound so clinical.'

'No, just practical.'

'Of course. And you'll understand that I can't leave her or my son. One doesn't do that sort of thing.'

'Your sons, you mean, don't you?'

'Yes, my sons. I forget about little Reggie. Andrea never mentions him. Anyway, he's in a world of his own. He's happy as long as he has his nanny.'

'Is he?'

Paul's arms tightened round her. 'Darling Tessa. How I love you!'

Tessa looked down at him. He was as attractive as ever, the memory of her long-held love pervaded her being. She wanted him to make love to her. But she pushed his arms away and stood up. 'Am I to take it that you want me as a mistress while you go on living in a respectable marriage?'

Paul got to his feet. He frowned. 'Don't say it like that, it sounds so heartless. And I'm not heartless, you know that.'

'I happen to have principles and one of the chief ones is that I don't sleep with other women's husbands.'

Paul grasped her arms. 'Not even when you love the man?'

Again she shook him off. 'No. And, yes, I do love you. Or thought I did. But now I see you're very different from the man I imagined. I find I don't love the real Paul at all.'

He reddened. 'I never took you for a prude!'

'And I never took you for a cheat.'

Tessa walked a long way before she hailed a taxi. It

wasn't easy to accept the fact that the man of her dreams had feet of clay – and unattractive clay at that.

# *Chapter Twenty-One*

Tessa slept little that night as the scene with Paul played itself over and over in her brain. How long had she been nursing her secret love for him? When had they met? Six, no, seven years ago. Wasted years as far as love went. She plumped up her pillow and tried to sleep. It was her own fault. Paul had behaved towards her as he might towards a girl from his own sphere who would probably have laughed the whole thing off. Yet he professed to love her. In the morning she looked so washed out that even Eve noticed. 'Are you ill?'

'No, just tired.'

'Why? You've usually got lots of energy.'

'Well, I've very little today.'

'Now I think of it, you looked a bit off when you came back yesterday. You did go to the Art Gallery, didn't you?'

'Of course.'

'What made you suddenly decide to do that? And what happened there? Did you meet someone there? Oh, don't tell me you met Paul! Surely goody-goody Tessa hasn't been cavorting with another woman's husband.'

'I won't tell you that because I haven't.'

'I can keep secrets,' said Eve. 'I've kept enough of my own. You met Paul, didn't you?'

Tessa felt much as she did when a dentist probed a tooth. 'I'm going to my room. I've things to do.'

Eve's disbelieving laugh followed her and Tessa strode about her room, anger filling her. Anger at Eve for being so near the truth, at Paul for snatching away her dream, at herself most of all for feeling wounded by the behaviour of a man who was not hers to dream about, around whom she had built a myth. What a fool she had been! And she was about to make a fool of herself again. She was setting off on an adventure with a girl who had proved an expert in messing up her own life. She wished she had never met Dad's family.

The next day only increased Tessa's misgivings. Eve took her to a garage in downtown New York where she was introduced to a man who specialised in selling second-hand cars.

'This is Mr Elmer Stratton, Tessa. Elmer, my cousin, Miss Morland. Elmer guarantees his cars!'

'For how long?' asked Tessa as she looked around at the yard crowded with automobiles in all stages of decrepitude.

'For three months. A man can't do more with an old jalopy, can he?'

'In writing?' asked Tessa.

Mr Stratton looked pained. 'My word's always been good enough. A bit of paper doesn't make a man more honest. You can trust ole Elmer.'

'I see.'

'She's a Chevrolet.' He patted the bonnet. 'A car you can depend on. She'll run for ever. Just keep her fed with gasoline and oil and make sure you've got a spare wheel and you'll never need anything else.'

The car was canary yellow, built like a cabin on wheels. It was a closed model which, Tessa supposed, was something to be grateful for. She climbed inside. The leather seats were badly scuffed and torn in several places. 'What year is it?' she asked.

'1925,' said the man. 'So you see she's still quite young. Ten years is nothing in the life of an automobile like this.'

'There seems to be a lot of straw lying around.'

'A farmer sold her to me. I expect the straw came off his boots.'

'Did the strange smell come off his boots, too?'

Elmer Stratton frowned. He was beginning to dislike this young woman. 'I expect he's carried the odd animal in her. You know what farmers are. He didn't want to sell her, but farmers need dough these days. A couple of girls like yourselves can soon have her spick and span. No need to worry at all, little lady, I assure you. Elmer Stratton never let a client down yet.'

Tessa climbed out. The car had the air of a grande dame come down in the world. A long way down. But she was a gallant old lady and Tessa decided she rather liked her. 'Are you absolutely sure it's roadworthy?'

'Absolutely. You can take her away whenever you like. She's yours already. Paid for all fair and square.'

'Can you keep her here a little longer?' asked Eve. 'We'll be back with our luggage.'

The man winked. 'Don't want your folks to know you're off somewhere?'

'That's right.' Eve gave him one of her more alluring smiles. 'We're going to Hollywood.'

'Hollywood, eh? It's a mighty long way from coast to coast. And you're going on the movies?'

'Yes,' said Eve. 'Look out for us on the screen.'

'I'll do that. Best be careful, though. There's odd things go on out there, so I'm told, though two pretty little ladies like yourselves will be sure to make the big time. Trust old Elmer to know what's what.'

Over the days that followed, Tessa cursed old Elmer. The car was difficult to start and required one of them to swing the starting handle while the other kept her foot flat on the accelerator, and it gobbled gas and oil. They took turns until Eve swore she had strained her arm too painfully to use it so Tessa swung grimly whenever they stopped for food or to use the toilet facilities that grew less adequate every time they left a town and drove further into what Eve called 'the sticks'.

There were many others on the road. Some in big, new vehicles which honked at the slower ones, some bicycling, a large number hiking. Of the hikers Tessa soon learned to distinguish between those who walked for pleasure and those who struggled on through necessity. Sometimes they gave lifts to families.

Eve protested daily. 'They're sure to have lice and bugs. We may catch something.'

Tessa, seeing the pinched features of the children and the white strained faces of their parents, ignored her complaints, even when they proved to be true and they had to strip in a lonely spot near a trickle of a river and wash their clothes and delouse themselves and the car.

'Now will you listen?' demanded Eve angrily as she sat on a warm rock waiting for her frock to dry.

'How can you be so unfeeling? These people are desperate. Remember their stories. Nowhere to live because they can't pay rent, not enough to eat, no work . . .'

'They're just bums!' said Eve. 'Lazy bums who can't be bothered to get jobs.'

They took turns in driving through towns, villages, farmlands, until one scene merged into another in Tessa's mind and at night she was so weary she forgot the name of the last stopover. But she made sure they ate properly and stayed in decent lodgings, disregarding Eve's demands that they drive in shifts through the night.

'It's your fault we're taking so long,' Tessa reminded her. 'We could have been there by now if we'd used the train.'

'All right, don't rub it in.'

'I won't if you don't demand the impossible. We need our rest.'

When her cousin complained of a sore throat Tessa took her to a doctor who examined her. 'Badly inflamed,' he pronounced. 'Some kind of bug you've picked up. Where have you been lately?'

'We're travelling from New York to California,' said Tessa.

'To Hollywood,' croaked Eve.

He shook his head. 'To Hollywood? You and hundreds of others. Well, Miss Brook, you must rest up a while.'

'We can't stop,' Eve rasped. 'We have to get there.'

'What's your rush? I suppose your money is inadequate for such a journey?' The doctor sighed. 'The same old story. It's your decision, but if you were my daughter I'd make you rest. You could end up with a quinsy, a painful condition that would land you in hospital.'

'She'll rest,' said Tessa. She booked them into a small, clean, family-run hotel where they stayed for a week. As Eve recovered she began to grouse. 'I'm better. We're wasting time. They'll be giving the best parts to other actresses.'

'We stay until you're well,' said Tessa and refused to discuss it. She caught the infection in a milder form and it took another couple of days for her to get over it.

Eve grumbled, but paid both the doctor's and the hotel bill from the money her mother had given her. Tessa let her. She meant to hang on to Betsy's money as long as possible. 'Perhaps now you'll stop giving lifts?' Eve said. 'I must have picked up the illness from one of these bums and there's a large part of our precious money gone. We can't afford expense like that.'

Tessa knew she was probably right, but couldn't just pass a family in distress.

As they drove further west they met more and more people who had once been part of a thriving farming community and had now taken to the road in bewildered desperation, seeking a livelihood that was no longer to be found on the land which had dried up.

After what seemed to Tessa like driving through eternity they hit the state of Kansas. There they picked up a family who were dressed in the usual farmer's way, dungarees, shirts, hats and hard shoes. Only the mother wore a skirt, quite long and patched in places. They all carried bundles.

'Need a lift?' asked Tessa.

They climbed in gratefully, sitting on one another's

knees. 'We had a car,' said a boy of about fourteen. 'We don't have her no more, nor a house neither.' He sounded bitter.

'Now then, son,' said the woman. 'Sorry if he's a mite rude, but you can't blame him for bein' upset. Not long ago we had a good house an' land an' the children went to school an' Sunday school. Then the bank failed – the Burlington Bank it was.'

'One day we was makin' a livin',' said the man, 'the next we was paupers barterin' wheat for anythin' we needed. You'd to give a bushel just to get ice cream cones as a treat for the kids an' if you wanted a suit, that's if you had anywheres to go in it, it would cost a hundred an' twenty bushels – that's seven acres. Just about everyone's left. There's no school an' no chapel, an' worst of all, not enough food.'

The woman said, 'The soil's just gone. Wind got up an' blowed it away.'

'We got throwed off our land,' said her husband angrily. 'Been in my family for three generations. Now we're hoboes an' my sons got no inheritance like I had when my pa passed over.'

They asked to be set down in a small town where they had relatives and the girls drove on in silence. After a while Eve said, 'Not all the people on the road are bums.'

The countryside was flat and dull. It looked like a desert and to complete the illusion the heat rose higher and higher until the whole landscape shimmered in the broiling sun. They took off all the clothes they could, but still the sweat ran down their bodies.

'You girls ought to rest up at noon,' said a woman who owned a small store. 'Wait for the sun to go down a bit. It's dangerous to get so over-heated.'

Tessa looked round at the half-empty shelves. The stores at the start of their drive to the west had been well stocked, and permeated by the aromas of apples and spices and dried fruit. Here, everything smelt of dust.

The woman sighed. 'I reckon I'll be closin' any day

now. My customers most all took off. There's no money left in these parts. They're all goin' west to California. I've heard there's work there for farmers, but I don't know if it's true. Seems like someone ought to give them work. Where are you bound for?'

'Hollywood.'

'That your friend?' The woman nodded in the direction of Eve who was sitting under the shop awning fanning herself.

'My cousin.'

'Well, miss, if you're venturin' that way you'd best buy water as well as food. Sorry I got to charge for it but it's scarcer now than hen's teeth an' I got to pay for it.'

Eve was outraged. 'You paid for bottles of water? That's ridiculous!'

'Ridiculous or not, I took the store-keeper's advice. She evidently knew what she was talking about. Besides, I've read about deserts. The thing people need more than anything there is water and this is beginning to look like a desert to me. She also said we should rest in the heat of the day and I agree with her.'

'What nonsense! That's just a waste of time.'

Tessa drove. Repeatedly she had to wipe her damp hands on her skirt, but the sweat trickled out of her and in the end she simply clung to the steering wheel as best she could. Still the heat grew greater. It had sucked the water from lakes and rivers and every drop of moisture from the land. There were sudden whirlwinds and eddies of dust which spattered sharply on the car like rain. To avoid it they closed the windows and the air became suffocatingly hot. They opened the windows and put up with the dust.

Tessa stopped in a place which was once a busy, happy community. Now half the small houses were empty, while others were peopled by men and women who looked like grey ghosts. She bought fruit, more out of compassion than need. 'It's a bit dried up this year,' the farmer's wife said. 'Crops can't get goin' in this weather. Never knowed such heat. It's scary.'

'Storms are scary, too,' said a small girl, clinging to her skirts.

'That's true enough,' said her mother. 'You think they'll never end.'

Tessa drove on and Eve fell asleep, scarves tied round their faces against the dust. They kept going, mile after flat, tedious mile. Sometimes it seemed to Tessa as if she and Eve were the only living beings in a parched world.

Her cousin awoke. 'Where are we? God, the dust. It's in my mouth. It's everywhere.'

The wind had got up and was whining round the car like a hungry beast. Tessa peered through the windscreen. 'What's that? Looks like fog.'

'My God!' shrieked Eve. 'It's water! We're going to drown.'

Tessa stopped and the engine died. A great, high cloud was rolling towards them, the base as black as Indian ink. Birds were flying in front of it in a desperate race to save their lives. 'It isn't water!' cried Tessa. 'It's dust!'

Then she was choked by the cloud. They had thought themselves uncomfortable before, but it had been nothing to the monstrous horror that hit them now. Before they got the windows closed dust had filled their noses and stung their eyes and their mouths were gritty with it. The heat became searing.

'Drive on,' cried Eve. 'We must get through it.'

'I can't drive! I can't see!' yelled Tessa, her nerves snapping in the face of Eve's useless command.

'We'll choke to death. Oh, my God. Tessa, drive, we can't just sit here and die.'

Tessa, unnerved by Eve's terror, climbed out. She felt she was being skinned alive by the sharp dust, but she swung the starting handle. The engine didn't fire. She swung and cursed and swung again and nothing happened. She staggered back to the door and fell into the car.

'The engine's not working,' yelled Eve.

'I know! It won't start!'

'It must. You couldn't have swung hard enough.'

'Shut up, damn you!' cried Tessa. 'If you think you can do better, get out and try.'

'I can't, I can't,' wailed Eve.

'Oh, Eve, please. You're making things worse.' Tessa wiped the dust and sweat from her face and they swilled a little precious water round their mouths. 'We'll have to sit it out.'

'How can we? You heard what that woman said about dust-storms. We might be sitting here for days.'

'We've got food and water. We'll survive.'

Eve clawed at her throat. 'We'll suffocate. I can't breathe.'

'Yes, you can, and you'll only suffocate if you keep opening your mouth and letting it fill with dust. Oh, hell.'

'What now?'

'If anyone drives this way they won't see us. We could be hit.'

Eve moaned. 'One way or another we'll die, I know we will.'

'I don't think so. If we can't see, neither can anyone else.'

'Someone who knows the road could come along.'

'Only an idiot would be going fast in this. In fact, only an idiot would be driving at all.'

'There are plenty of idiots about.'

For once, Eve was making sense. Tessa had another try at swinging the handle.

'It's no good,' she gasped, 'come on, get out. Tie your scarf as tightly as possible round your face.'

'I'm not getting out! Why should I?'

'I can't push the car off the road on my own.' Tessa examined the ground. She had to bend double to do so, the dust whipping against her bare legs and arms like needles; there were no fences and no ditches, nothing to stop its onslaught. She looked round and realised that the car had vanished in the swirling cloud. She yelled and Eve answered until she was guided back, coughing, grinding the dust between her teeth.

'Let's move,' she said.

'One of us has to stay in and steer,' protested Eve.

'There's nothing to bump into.'

'The car might run away. We'll need to brake. Tell you what, Tessa, you push from the back and I'll push from the open door, ready to jump in and brake.'

Tessa pushed and strained and the car began to move. When she decided she was clear of the road she yelled, 'Brake!'

The car continued to run and she raced to the driver's seat. Eve had gone. She leapt in, but before she could apply the brake, there was a jagged sound and a permeating smell of oil. She stopped and ran back to find Eve sitting down, nursing her arm. 'I'm sure it's broken,' she moaned.

'That's terrible. Let me help you into the car.'

'Please, Tessa, get us away from here. I need a doctor.'

'Get in and let me have a look.'

The only sign of damage to Eve's arm was a long scratch. 'Can you move it?' Tessa asked.

It quickly became clear that Eve was suffering from nothing more than a nasty graze. 'For God's sake, Eve! You should have stayed with the car. It ran into something and there's oil leaking. Heaven knows what's happened.'

'Give me some water,' said Eve. 'I need to wash this wound.'

Tessa dabbed the scratch with a clean piece of rag damp with water and antiseptic and applied ointment.

'That's not enough. Do it again.'

'It is enough.'

'The wound might fester.'

'I doubt it.'

'I could get blood poisoning.'

'If we've no water you'll die of thirst.'

Eve sulked and they sat in silence, except for the whining wind. It grew hotter though the sun had been obliterated. 'How long shall we be trapped here?' moaned Eve.

478

'I don't know.'

'You don't seem to care.'

'Save your strength,' said Tessa. 'You'll need it after this. We may have to walk.'

Eve began to weep. 'You're hard and cruel. As hard and cruel as my mother.'

Tessa was too tired to argue, too weary even to feel indignant. 'You're losing moisture,' she said. 'Wipe your tears away.'

She drifted into a doze and dreamt of England, of rivers and streams and reservoirs, of waterfalls and rushing taps. She surfaced to the sound of running water and it took her a moment to remember where she was. But the sound of water was real. She turned to see Eve tipping some over the graze on her arm. She snatched at the bottle. 'Are you crazy?'

Eve clung to the bottle, losing more of the precious fluid, and Tessa lost her temper completely. She slapped her cousin hard across the face so that she loosened her grip on the bottle. Trembling with rage she snatched it away and put in the stopper.

'You bitch!' screamed Eve. At least, she tried to scream, but the dust defeated her. Once again she began to cry. 'I thought you cared about me! Nobody does. Nobody at all.'

'Shut up, Eve! For God's sake, just shut up!'

For two days they waited, the dust an enemy which no one could master. They ate the food Tessa had brought and shared the water. Even the half-dried up fruit was better than nothing. In that time they saw or heard no one, though people could have passed within yards, invisible and soundless in the storm. They scarcely spoke. When Tessa slept she wrapped the water bottles in a cotton skirt which she tied round her shoulders. It increased her suffering from the heat, but it kept the water safe. At last the wind died, though the dust continued to fall, silently, like grey snow. They stumbled out of the car, their hair grey, their mouths, noses and eyes, red-rimmed and sore.

'We should have taken the train,' wept Eve.

479

With an enormous effort Tessa refrained from replying. She tried to start the car, jerking the handle over and over again until her hand was blistered. She opened the bonnet, peering in at the dust-covered engine.

'It's probably completely clogged,' she said. 'And there's a large pool of oil underneath. I wonder if it can be repaired? We'll have to walk until we find help.'

'Walk! Someone is bound to pass by soon,' said Eve. 'People who've been waiting like us for the storm to pass.'

'Maybe they will, maybe not,' said Tessa. 'We can't afford to wait. Our water's very low. Come on, Eve, we need to find a filling station. The men who run them know a lot about cars and they're sure to have something to drink.'

'I'll stay here and look after our cases,' said Eve.

'You will not! I may not even find help and I'm damned if I'm going to trail back miles just to tell you that.'

'Not find help!' Eve said in high, hysterical tones. 'What will we do?'

'I've told you, we walk. Either until we get help or else find alternative transport. Actually, I don't know much about cars but I'm pretty sure that ours can't be repaired. At least, not without a hell of a lot of money.'

'Where will we get the money for transport or repairs? You made me pay for lodgings and a doctor, and I wouldn't have been ill at all if you hadn't picked up those disgusting bums.'

'They weren't bums,' said Tessa wearily.

'What about our things?'

'We must carry them.'

'But I've got three cases!'

'You'll have to pick out what you really need.'

'I can't just abandon my lovely clothes. They cost a lot of money and I shall need them for auditions.'

'You'll have to manage without.' Tessa was so tired, all she really wanted to do was curl up in the car and sleep.

'If we carry everything with us we could sell some of my stuff,' said Eve. 'You could take one of my cases.'

'No. I shall be carrying food and water as well as my case.'

'I can't leave my fur coat.'

'What? You brought a fur coat? Where in hell do you imagine you'll need it? You told me that California was always hot.'

'I bet some share-cropper's wife would like a fur coat and we need money.'

'No one round here *has* any money. Do you fancy offering your coat for seven acres of wheat?'

'You're being horrible to me.'

'I'm being practical.'

'You probably think it's a judgement on me because I bought the car?'

'Eve, for heaven's sake! There could be another storm. Get one bloody case and let's go.'

'How do you know which way?'

Tessa looked at the flat landscape and the road which stretched into the distance to either side in a straight line. Eve unstrapped her cases and, after an irritating period of deliberation, made her selection. She left a case locked in the car and, when they trudged off, was carrying one in each hand. They were leather and monogrammed with her initials and heavy even before they were packed.

The dust still enveloped them. It rose at every step, filling their shoes so that they had to make frequent stops to empty them. In the end they gave up and put up with the intense discomfort. They passed the skeletons of animals which had died where they had fallen, a feast for birds of prey. Tessa carried the remaining water and a few cans of food on her back. Time became meaningless. Their watches had stopped, clogged by dust, and she had no way of telling what distance they had covered or how long they had taken when they saw a lone cabin in the distance.

'Thank God,' said Tessa.

'A dirt farmer's shack!' said Eve.

'They're sure to have water. And maybe a vehicle. Perhaps we're near a town.'

As they got closer the place looked unpromising. No dogs came to bark at them, no children greeted them. Dust lay in heaps around it, parts of the roof had blown away and one of the board steps hung, splintered, lop-sided.

'They're probably staying inside until the dust clears,' said Tessa. 'Remember how one of the women we met said they huddle for hours, sometimes days, even hide under the floors.'

They knocked on the door, but no one answered and they pushed it open. The cabin was empty save for a few sticks of furniture. There was dust everywhere here, too, in piles against the wall, coating everything they touched.

'Is there anyone here?' called Tessa.

There wasn't a sound and Eve said despairingly, 'They've gone.' She dropped her suitcases, sending more dust up to envelop them. She sank down on a chair, her elbows on her knees, her head in her hands.

Tessa felt like joining her. She was so tired she longed to rest. She had a look round. Besides the living room there was a bedroom, across the middle of which hung a curtain. In a small third room she found a brick fireplace and a few utensils. And a pump. She tried the handle, but no life-giving water gushed out. That was probably what had finally driven the family away. There was a bundle of sticks beside the stove, and she lit them with a match from her pocket and poured some water into a dust-scoured battered saucepan. Then she returned to Eve. 'We'll rest here a while. I'll make some coffee and heat up a can of beans.'

'Coffee and beans? I'm sick of beans! We've eaten little else.'

'You should be thankful I bought plenty. They're filling and good for you. And, I might remind you, I carried them here.'

'When I'm rich and famous, I'll never eat beans again.'

'What about coffee?'

'How can you joke at a time like this?'

After they had eaten Eve grew a touch more cheerful. She stood up and stretched. 'Where are the beds?'

'There are a couple of platforms in the other room. I suppose they're beds.'

'Mattresses?'

'I dare say they took them away.'

'God, what a fool I've been! I could have married Elliot Murfitt or even Jack. I'd be rich, with servants, not stuck in this stinking hole with you!'

'Thanks.'

'I didn't mean . . . Oh, you know what I mean.'

'If I hadn't listened to you I'd be back in Britain enjoying professional success.'

Eve was silent for a moment, then said in a small voice, 'I suppose you're wishing me in hell?'

'No. I made my choice and I won't grouse. We'll make Hollywood if we have to walk there.'

'I've been awful to you.'

'You've not been at your best,' said Tessa drily.

'I'm sorry.'

'Thanks. That's something.'

They lay on the board beds, using their clothes to ease the hardness of the wood.

'Do you think we'll get out of this alive?' asked Eve in the darkness.

'I shall do my best to see that we do.'

'I'll try to be good,' said Eve. She sounded like a child.

Tessa almost laughed. She said, 'Go to sleep. Tomorrow's another day.'

Thirst had become a problem that would soon grow serious and Tessa was far less optimistic than she had led Eve to believe. Though she was bone-weary, at first she couldn't sleep. Her mind wandered over all that had gone before. She wondered if she was doomed to die here. If she was, she might as well have had Paul's love to remember. Or rather, his lovemaking. He had never loved her and she was left with an empty feeling, a sense of deprivation. Just before she went to sleep she wondered what Charles would say if he could see her now. He would laugh and think of a way to rescue her. He was resourceful. He was a good lover, too. He always made sure she was happy.

In the morning both girls were stiff, sore and desperately thirsty. Tessa allowed them one cup of water each.

'I need more,' said Eve.

'So do I.'

Eve bent and picked something up. A scarlet ribbon, still tied in a bow. 'Some kid lost it,' she said. To Tessa's surprise, tears filled her eyes. 'I wonder what's happened to the people who lived here?'

'I suppose they're on the road. Like us.'

Eve tried to speak, but only gulped. She smoothed out the ribbon, rolled it carefully and put it in her purse.

Tessa's head went up. 'Listen!'

'There's nothing to listen to.'

'There is. I hear an engine. Someone's driving our way.'


Eve sat beside Tessa on a mattress on top of a rickety truck loaded with everything the share-croppers who had rescued them could carry. The Landons, the whole family, were in or on the truck, father, mother, grandfather, and six children, all looking half-starved. Mrs Landon was expecting another child soon, but had given the girls water and food and added their weight and that of their luggage to the already overburdened vehicle. That night they drove into a tented camp where families who looked identical were resting under canvas, or living in trucks and cars.

The Landons unloaded their passengers and Mr Landon helped the girls down.

'You're welcome to stay with us a spell,' he said. 'You'll have to share our tent or lie outside.'

'We can't crowd you,' said Tessa. 'We'll lie outside.'

They ate small portions of the stew cooked by Mrs Landon on a wood fire and, for once, Eve didn't grouse.

'Time for bed,' said Mrs Landon. She sat on the only chair and her husband helped her to her feet. 'Reckon this baby won't be long in comin'.'

'Has it started, Ma?' asked the eldest girl.

'I think so.'

Eve said, 'Someone fetch a doctor.'

'Lord, we ain't got money for no doctor,' said the girl. 'I've helped Ma before an' I can do it again.'

'That's right,' said Mrs Landon. 'Abby's helped birth three of my babies.'

'I'll take the young uns away,' said the girl. The other children were welcomed by nearby families.

The night was mild and Tessa and Eve were not uncomfortable outside. They slept, to be awakened later by muffled cries. Mr Landon came out of the tent and Tessa got up. 'How is she?'

'She's bad. I've got to get help. She's not ate a decent meal in weeks. Got no strength. Baby's took what little she had. And now this and she's like to die.'

Before Tessa could speak, Eve, who had followed her, said urgently, 'I have some money. Enough to pay for a doctor.'

Mrs Landon groaned and cried out and Eve said, 'Go, quickly. Here, take my purse.'

Tessa was silenced by the first unselfish gesture she had known her cousin make.

'I shouldn't rightly take your money,' said Mr Landon, but even while he made the courteous gesture of reluctance he was climbing into the truck. He drove away as fast as the rickety vehicle would go.

'You did the right thing, Eve,' said Tessa.

She sighed. 'I'm beginning to think I was meant to make this journey. I'm certainly learning a few things.' She sat down on their improvised bed. 'Tessa, I'm ashamed. I thought these people had no feelings, but that man loves his wife and children. He gave us food when there's not even enough for his family and you can see that tortures him. He's only got love to give.'

'I know.'

'Yet my father . . . We had everything money could buy . . . He gave me money and nothing else. Why?'

She lay down and closed her eyes, clearly not wanting an answer. Tessa waited. Mrs Landon gave a muffled scream and she went to the tent. 'Abby, is there anything I can do?'

She poked her head out. 'Nothin' much, unless you understand birthin'. Where's Pa?'

'Gone for a doctor.'

'The Lord be praised. Ma's awful bad. Tessa, could you change the water? Here's the pan. There's a small stream over yonder.'

The stream was sluggish, the water brown. Tessa collected what she could and poured a generous amount of her antiseptic lotion into it. Then she sat listening to Mrs Landon's moans and cries, praying that help would arrive before it was too late.

Abby came out, gasping for air in the oppressive heat. 'She fell asleep. She's too tired to birth this baby. She'll wake in a minute an' it'll begin again.'

'Can I get you anything?'

'I'll take a drink. Cold coffee will do. Listen! I hear an engine.'

'Oh, thank God!'

'There's more than one. If the locals come out tonight it'll surely kill Ma.'

'What do you mean?'

'It's clear you ain't been long on the road. We're hated by most of the folk who still got houses and money. They attack us, sometimes with clubs, and make us move on.' She listened again. 'There's definitely more than one engine.'

Tessa was silent, then Mrs Landon called and Abby slipped back into the tent. To Tessa's infinite relief a single car entered the camp behind the Landons' truck and a young man carrying a bag got out and walked to the tent. He sounded confident and reassuring as he examined the labouring woman. 'You'll soon be all right,' he said gently. 'Breathe on this pad, it'll help the pain. You girl, hold one leg and you, Pa, the other.' He called to Tessa. 'You can administer the ether. Just a few drops on the pad at a time. But first fetch someone to hold her shoulders.' Tessa went outside and several women appeared from the shadows. 'He needs someone to hold her.'

'It'll be forceps,' said one of the women. She followed Tessa into the impossibly overcrowded tent and the temperature rose further. The ether dripped, its fumes filling the air, mingling with the animal-like scent of blood, and Tessa began to feel sick and faint.

The doctor pulled, hard, and Mrs Landon groaned. 'Don't be alarmed,' he said. 'She can't feel a thing. Keep that ether coming.'

It was a nightmare that seemed to Tessa to go on for ever as the doctor waited for contractions then heaved with the forceps, but at last the baby entered the world and, after a few gasps, began to yell. The doctor smiled and Tessa stared at the child, blood-stained, covered with mucus, its face blue after the protracted battle. 'A girl,' said the doctor. 'Put her to the breast as soon as possible. That will help the mother.'

One of the women took the child to clean her and the doctor bent over his patient. Her eyes were huge and staring in her ashen face. 'You have a daughter, my dear,' he said, 'and you must rest up awhile. It's been an ordeal for you.'

Outside the tent he said to Mr Landon, 'Your wife is frail and was too weak to give birth without help. She's lost a lot of blood and needs feeding up, plenty of good liver and red meat, port wine and cocoa, not mixed of course—' His voice trailed off at this feeble attempt at a joke as he realised he had slipped into his usual hearty doctor's role. He looked at the tent, at the attenuated figures and drawn faces of the women who still waited to help. 'Do the best you can. She shouldn't travel for at least two weeks.' He hurried to his car.

As he watched him drive away Mr Landon's face was a mask of despair.

On the following morning most of the trucks and cars moved out in convoy. Mr Landon said, 'You girls get another lift. We have to stay till Ma can be moved.'

'What if the townsfolk come?' asked the eldest boy.

'Surely they'll not molest you when your wife is so ill!' said Eve.

'They don't care. They think we got no feelin's an' I suppose they're worried in case we go after their jobs.' Eve flushed. 'Folk like us will take less wages to feed our families. You been good to us, Eve. I reckon you saved Ma's life.'

A battered car on its way out stopped by the truck and the occupants wished the family well.

'Thank you kindly,' said Mr Landon. 'These girls have been very good to me an' mine. They're goin' west. Could you maybe give them a lift?' He turned to them. 'I wish I could give you somethin' to show my gratitude.'

'It's enough to know we helped,' said Eve. 'Besides, you shared with us.'

Tessa and Eve went to say goodbye to Mrs Landon. Women had searched their possessions for gifts: a tiny hairbrush, a scrap of soap and a couple of soft toys. Eve brought out the red ribbon she had picked up in the shack and laid it on the small pile. She kissed Mrs Landon and the sleeping baby, then left. Tessa knelt by the mattress and held out twenty-five dollars. 'Take this, please.'

Mrs Landon stared. 'I've never seen so much money in one go. But I can't. You girls need it.'

'No. We're young and can work.'

'Work, is it? Pray God you find some. You keep your money, an' God bless you for the thought, but you done enough for us last night. Without that doctor my man might be buryin' me now an' my kids without a ma.'

'You saved us, don't forget.'

'No. Someone would have come along if we hadn't.'

Tessa said no more. Mrs Landon was getting agitated and that was bad for her. She kissed her and the new-born girl and left. But outside she spoke to Mr Landon. 'I tried to give your wife something to show how we appreciate your kindness. She won't take it, but you're the head of the family and you can't refuse.'

He shook his head. 'If Ma said no, then I say no.'

'You heard what the doctor said. She must have good food before she'll be well. Besides, if the townsfolk come, you can show them you're not paupers.'

He stood looking down at the money and swallowed hard. He took it and turned it over and over in his fingers. 'For a while there I thought I must be a fool for offerin' to share our mite with you. Now I see that the Lord's hand was in it an' I never recognised it.'

'I hope you find work,' said Tessa and climbed into the back of the waiting car, settling herself between several little girls on one side and Eve on the other. The roof rack carried bedding, three boys and two suitcases, one a monogrammed leather.

'You've left a case behind,' said Tessa to Eve.

'Yes, I gave it to Abby. Tents can get cold at night especially if you're as ill as Mrs Landon. And there's the baby. They might need a warm cover.'

'Eve! Not your fur coat!'

'Sure, why not? It's hot in California. Everyone knows that. And they can sell the case.'

Tessa's heart swelled with love for her cousin. She turned her head and brushed her lips briefly along Eve's cheek.

'We'll find work,' said Eve, 'I know we will. We could sing our way to Hollywood.'

Tessa laughed. 'And I've got twenty-five dollars. Aunt Betsy gave me money, though you didn't know that when you gave your purse away.'

'No, I saw you give something to Mr Landon.'

'Twenty-five dollars,' said Tessa. 'Half of what Mrs Jefferson gave me.'

'Fancy Aunt Betsy coming up trumps like that. You

were right to give those poor folk half. Perhaps we've got enough to take a bus,' said Eve.

'I don't know. We must keep some in reserve for emergencies.'

'Like food?' enquired Eve.

'Something like that.'

The car drove through the north-west corner of Oklahoma, before reaching New Mexico. They stopped at camps on the way, some well-found, others like slums, harassed constantly by locals who hated these gaunt men and women who reminded them of hunger and poverty and lost employment. They ate sparsely, paying their way, and their funds were getting low when they said goodbye to their new friends who branched off in New Mexico. They began to walk along the dusty road, carrying their cases.

They reached a truck drivers' pull-in. The sign in the window said 'Jed and Trudy's Place'. Both girls were thinner and none too clean, but inside, as they drank coffee and ate a sandwich, men turned to give them the usual appraising stare. There was a piano in the corner, its lid down. Tessa wandered over to it.

'Is it all right if I play?' she asked the proprietor.

He turned to his wife who nodded, her double chins almost meeting her large bosom. 'Go ahead. It's not been touched since our girl got married. But it'll sound OK. We got it tuned in return for a meal. Got to keep it right for when our girl visits.'

Tessa opened the lid and sat on a chair that a friendly truck driver slid over to her. She ran her fingers over the keys.

'That's pretty,' said the man. He was young and good-looking.

'Got a favourite?' asked Tessa.

There was a chorus of suggestions from the others and she laughed. 'One at a time.' She began to play and sing, 'Lovely to look at, delightful to know . . .' Eve came and stood by her side and joined in and the talking and laughing stopped as the men listened.

490

'Say, you're good,' said Trudy.

'Good enough to go on the stage,' said Jed.

'Sure are,' said the young truck driver. 'And pretty enough too.'

'We are on the stage,' said Eve. 'At least, we were. We've been on radio, too. Now we're on our way to Hollywood.'

'Oh, you're sure to do well there. Play and sing some more,' they were urged and they did, enjoying this brief respite.

'That's worth a meal,' said Trudy and fed them well.

'Could we have a bed for the night?' asked Tessa.

Trudy shook her head. 'Sorry, honey. All we've got is one big dormitory for the guys . . .'

'We'll share it,' was yelled in chorus.

Trudy grinned. 'Now, boys, that's no way to talk to ladies.'

'They could have Shirley's room,' said Jed.

Trudy frowned. 'You know we keep that for her.'

'Is there anywhere else we can go?' asked Eve. 'A barn? We're getting used to roughing it.' She was tired and anxious.

Trudy stared at her, then at Tessa. 'What are your folks doin', lettin' you two out on the road?'

'They didn't,' said Eve. 'We started out in a car with money, but we've had problems.'

'Who ain't got problems?' sighed Trudy. 'OK, you can have Shirley's room. If you'll sing for the men you can rest up a while. You look as if you need it.'

Shirley's room was light and chintzy. Her bed had a comfortable mattress and clean sheets. Her pillows were soft. There was a bathroom with hot and cold running water.

Trudy showed them its glories with pride and the girls had no need to pretend enthusiasm. They revelled in the warm water and that night shared Shirley's bed.

'It's funny,' said Eve, 'but I've got kinda used to sleepin' on the cold, hard ground. Don't rightly know if I'll ever rest on this here mattress.'

Tessa laughed. 'I didn't know you were a mimic.'

'To tell you no lie, there's a whole lotta things I only jest found out about myself.'

They slept well. Trudy invited them to stay a little longer. 'The guys like you and so do we. How about it? I'll trade food for songs.'

After four days they felt a great deal better and Eve was growing impatient. Trudy watched her one night as she flirted with the truck drivers and said to Tessa, 'You could have trouble with her in Hollywood. From all I've heard there's plenty of room for goin's-on there. She's too pretty by half, and too . . .' She stopped.

'I know what you mean,' said Tessa. 'She likes men and men like her.'

'You're still miles and miles from the coast. Say, I've taken a fancy to you. How about if I lent you the bus fare and you can pay me back when you strike it rich? I bet you will. You sing as good as anyone I've heard on the wireless or the record machine.'

# Chapter Twenty-Two

People don't change overnight, reflected Tessa, with the possible exception of Paul on the Damascus road and maybe a few of Joseph's converts. During the long bus journey Eve began complaining again. Tessa found it easier to bear, having seen that her cousin retained a spark of humanity that hadn't been entirely extinguished by her up-bringing.

'I wish I had the stuff I left in the car,' Eve said several times. 'There were some of my prettiest frocks and a beautiful nightgown. Pure silk. I wonder how long it will be before I can afford pure silk again?'

Tessa enjoyed the varying scenery but was thankful when at last they were set down in Wilmington. From there they caught another bus which drove them twenty miles through straggling suburbs to Hollywood.

In spite of the warm sun, Eve was quite pale with delight. 'Let's hire a car and look around.'

'We don't have anywhere to live yet,' Tessa reminded her, 'and we can tour the homes of the stars in a department store bus.'

'How do you know that?'

'I saw an advertisement which you would have noticed if you could see anything through your rosy glow.'

Eve grinned. 'It's all so exciting! Don't you feel anything, Tessa?'

'Of course I do. It'll be wonderful to work again.'

'I can hardly think of it as work. Being a film star must be the most marvellous thing in the whole world.'

By nightfall they had rented an apartment for twelve

dollars a week which had everything, including a tiled bath.

'It's ridiculously cheap,' enthused Eve.

'It's pretty good,' said Tessa, 'but our money is low. Tomorrow we'd better look for an agent. We stand little chance here without one.'

Finding an agent presented no problem. They were everywhere a person could hang out a shingle. Getting one to take an interest was something altogether different. By the end of the day they had been refused even an audition by nine of them.

Back at the flat where they ate a modest meal Eve was alternately angry and tearful. 'Fancy, they wouldn't even listen to us! And did you hear that blonde girl screeching? She came out grinning all over her face. She must have got a job. I wonder what she had to do to pay for it? She looked as if she'd do absolutely anything. Sleep with him, I shouldn't wonder.'

'I hope you're not considering that as an option?'

'I don't suppose it'll come to that.' But Eve sounded none too sure.

The second day followed closely the pattern of the first, except that at one point Eve went off on her own while Tessa shopped for food and met an agent she called Wolfie.

'He wants to take me to dinner,' said Eve. 'And when I mentioned you he said he'd bring a friend.'

'Is he nice?' asked Tessa.

'Who cares if he gives us work? We certainly could do with it.'

Wolfie proved to be handsome and smooth, and instinctively Tessa mistrusted him. Eric, the friend, was also very good-looking and preoccupied with himself, making sure that he always presented his best profile. He was looking for juvenile leads, he said.

The girls were taken to a cocktail party in a small Spanish-style apartment which grew louder and louder as the night wore on and people grew drunker. Tessa hated it, but stayed on because Eve was drinking far more than was good for her and was openly embracing Wolfie. Eric had tried several times, without success, to slide his hands inside Tessa's blouse or under her skirt and had finally abandoned her to seek a more compliant girl. Before doing so he gave her a few words of what might be termed advice.

'You're a dumb bitch. You've got to learn the rules of the game if you want to get on in Hollywood.'

'If the rules state that a woman has to permit herself being fumbled by a complete stranger, then I guess I won't get on,' Tessa replied.

The music was constant and she watched the rhythmic contortions of the others. She loved to dance, but that was not in the forefront of the partygoers' minds as they clung together.

A very drunk girl wandered up to her. 'Your face is all shiny, honey. You need some powder.' Without warning she pulled a powder puff from her pocket and enveloped Tessa's face in a violet-scented cloud which made her eyes sting. By the time she had found the bathroom and bathed them, Eve had gone and no one knew or cared where or why. In the end Tessa went home. She couldn't sleep. Eve arrived after two in the morning and Tessa heard her giggling outside, before a car drove off and she stumbled into the hall.

She wobbled her way to Tessa's door. 'Tessa,' she called in a stage whisper. Receiving no reply she muttered, 'Spoilsport. What a rotten, rotten spoilsport.' Then she went to her room where Tessa found her in the morning, asleep on her bed, fully clothed. She watched her for a while. Eve's make-up was smeared, there was mascara on her cheeks and she was pallid, yet she looked as beautiful as on the day they had met at Great-grandmother Brook's funeral.

She opened her eyes, groaned, and closed them again. 'You're already dressed.'

'It's almost noon.'

'Shit! Bring me a coffee, will you? I'm parched.' She sat up in bed and tasted the coffee which was black and strong with plenty of sugar. 'Ugh! It's too damn sweet.'

'Drink it, it's good for you.'

'Can't I have some cream?'

'No. It's better to take it black. Come on, Eve, we must get out and try again.'

She smirked. 'It's all right. We don't need to. Wolfie says he can get work for us.'

Tessa sat on the end of the bed. 'You sang to him?'

'A bit.' She grinned. 'He was more interested in me than my voice, but that doesn't matter.'

'If he can get us both into films only on the strength of your personality, he must be a miracle worker!'

'Don't be horrid! He explained things to me last night.' She held a hand to her head. 'My eyes hurt. Can I have more coffee and a couple of aspirin?' Tessa supplied her and Eve went on, 'In Hollywood it's a case of who you know.'

'That's hardly new.'

'No, but it matters more here than anywhere, Wolfie says.'

'Is his name really Wolfie?'

'It's short for Wolfgang. Wolfgang Golding is his name. His folks came over from Germany. His surname was different then, longer, but they changed it. Well, Wolfie says that Hollywood is so full of people wanting to be stars that Central Casting can take their pick so you have got to get friendly with folk so that you'll be noticed. And before you argue, he says that singers are a dime a dozen.'

'I see. In plain terms what exactly does getting to know people mean?'

'Being friendly.'

'How friendly?'

'You're not going prudish on me again, are you?'

'Did you go to bed with Wolfie?'

'What if I did?'

'If that's the only way to work then I'm heading straight back home.'

'But you'll take a job if I can get you one, won't you?' jeered Eve.

'Not if it means you have to sleep with someone. I think that's degrading yourself.'

'I am *not* degraded.'

'There's no need to shout. I'm entitled to my opinion.'

'And I to mine.'

'Of course. You try your way and I'll try mine.'

'And we'll see who'll come off best,' yelled Eve. She got up and left soon after to meet Wolfie.

Tessa continued the rounds of agents until her feet were sore and her spirits low. Offices were closing down for the night and she was tempted to return to the flat for a cool shower, but once more seeing the word 'Agent' on a door she climbed the inevitable stairs and entered yet another crowded waiting room, where yet another gum-chewing stenographer with long, red nails looked up. 'Yes, honey?'

'I'd like to see Mr O'Neill, please.'

'Can you sing?'

Tessa felt a surge of hope. 'Yes. I can.'

'He's lookin' for a couple.' The girl pressed a button on her desk. 'Lady here says she can sing . . . OK, I'll do just that. He says to go in, honey.'

Almost cringing from the many eyes that glared at her, Tessa entered the agent's office. For a moment he continued writing, then looked up. 'You can sing?'

'Yes.'

'You've sung in public?'

'And on the wireless.'

'Is that so? United Artists want a girl duo. Busby Berkeley it ain't, but a job's a job. Previous couple's out. One of them went down with appendicitis. It's no good sending you along on your own.'

'I've got a partner.'

'Give me a sample of your voice.'

Hope buoyed her up and she sang the first thing that

497

came into her head. 'I'm in the mood for love, simply because I'm near you . . .'

He sat back and listened. 'Swell voice,' he said. 'You just might make the grade in Hollywood. Is your partner as good as you?'

'My cousin, yes. She's a light soprano. We harmonise well together.'

He peered at her. 'I've seen you before. Is your cousin a gorgeous redhead?'

'Yes.'

'I was at the same party as you last night. I left early but not before I saw her go off with Wolfie Golding.' He shook his head. 'A bad move. She must be dumb not to see through him. Well, the spot's for a duo if you want it and can get through the audition. Tell your cousin if I take her on as a client, I get sole rights. I'm not finding work for anyone unless I get my cut. That's business.'

'Of course,' agreed Tessa.

'Be on the lot at six in the morning. My secretary will give you a card. My name's O'Neill. My terms are ten per cent. Good luck.' He resumed his writing.

In the waiting room the stenographer asked, 'Did you get lucky, honey?'

Seeing in the faces around her desperation, envy, hunger, Tessa just nodded, took the card, and hurried away. As she went down the stairs she heard the stenographer's voice again. 'OK, that's it for today. Come back tomorrow. There might be something.'

She returned to the flat with cold meat, tomatoes and bread and wine. She would wait for Eve to celebrate with her. She was too excited to eat yet anyway. Eve came back at eight. 'I've got us a spot,' cried Tessa. 'A singing duo in a film.'

Eve rushed past her into the shower. 'You'll have to fill it on your own. Wolfie's found a part for me. A *speaking* part. I'm going to be a star.' She turned on the shower.

Tessa sat down abruptly, all the wind knocked out of her.

When Eve came out she said, 'Don't look so miserable. It's obvious that it's a lot easier to get work here than we were told. You'll soon get something else. Can I borrow a pair of stockings? I've torn mine. I've got a date with Wolfie. He's giving me dinner in a place where I'll see all the big stars. Eric won't come. He's cheesed off with you.'

'I'll try not to be too disappointed.' Tessa watched her cousin, endeavouring not to blame her. A speaking part, however small, was something every aspiring actor dreamed of.

'Are you sure you can cope? You're not really an actress.'

'It's a chance. I have to take it.'

Tessa returned to the agency the following morning and was waiting when it opened up. She told O'Neill what had happened. He leaned back in his chair. 'I said she was dumb. Wolfie'll promise anything for a good lay. I'm real sorry, honey. I'd like to help you if I could.'

'Does that mean he hasn't got Eve a part at all?'

'He'll have found her something, but what kind of part is the question.'

'What does that mean? Is she in any danger?'

'Say, you really care about that kid, don't you?'

'Yes.'

'Try to get her away from Wolfie Golding. He's poison to women.'

'In what way?'

'I've said enough. Just keep an eye on your cousin.'

'I'll do my best.' Tessa paused. 'Is there anything for me?'

'Sorry, honey.' Tessa, disappointed, turned to leave, but O'Neill called her back. 'Could I take you out to dinner tonight?'

'I don't think so.'

'We're not all like Golding. I said dinner and I do mean dinner.'

She gave him a searching look. He was quite nice-looking if you liked carroty-haired men with a heavyish physique, a blunt nose, and a wide mouth. His eyes were a clear blue.

'OK, honey? I'm no oil painting, but I'm real nice when you get to know me.'

She laughed. 'We have a date.'

'Fine. I'll call for you. I've got your address.'

Tessa visited more agents and always the response was the same. 'Nothing today. Try tomorrow.'

She returned to the apartment. Eve was already there. She had been crying and when she saw Tessa began to cry again. 'That no-good low-down bastard!'

'Wolfie?'

'He sent me to a stand-in job. I'm the same size and colouring as the star and they used me to get the lighting right. I had to just stand until I ached while men yelled at me, then someone threw custard pie in my face. I screamed at them, but they said I'd not get paid if I didn't do as I was told. They were horrible to me. I had half a dozen pies in my face. I've had to wash my hair three times to get the muck out. And I only got a few dollars after going through all that.'

Tessa stared at her. For a moment she felt like slapping Eve hard for her stupid weakness, then she began to laugh. The more she laughed the more Eve cried until her tears dried up and she smiled. 'I was an idiot, wasn't I? If you could have seen me! I should have come with you. Did you get the part?'

'As a singing duo?'

'Yes. I'll come with you for the audition. When is it to be?'

'It was at six this morning.'

'Oh! We've lost the chance?'

'You said it.'

'Oh, God. Let's open the wine. I haven't had a drink since last night. I wish we had somewhere exciting to go. I need a break after today.'

'A. a matter of fact, I have a date. With a man called O'Neill. For dinner. He's an agent.'

'And you were playing holier than thou!'

'He's not looking for sex.'

'That's what they all say until they get you alone. Then, afterwards, they just walk away.'

'Is that what Wolfie did?'

'Yes, the bastard!'

'So you gave in to him?' Eve didn't answer and Tessa said, 'Well, at least he kept his promise to find you a job. You might be offered more work.'

'I don't want stuff like that.' Eve flounced into her bedroom and slammed the door.

O'Neill arrived early when Tessa was in the shower. Eve let him in and when Tessa entered the living room was seated on the arm of an easy chair, swinging her legs in Tessa's sheer, dark stockings and listening to him with rapt attention, her beautiful eyes fixed on his face, her lashes fluttering.

O'Neill seemed unimpressed. He got up when Tessa came in. 'Honey, you look great. See you another time, Eve.' And the two of them left.

Tessa thoroughly enjoyed her outing. She asked her escort his first name. 'Just call me O'Neill. Everybody does.' He was warm, kind and humorous and she basked in his company. She told him of Eve's experience in the film studio and he said, 'Some girls would have made the most of the chance. Now neither of you have got work.'

'No, but we'll keep trying.'

There was a brief silence and O'Neill asked, 'Aren't you going to beg for my help? I'm stuck in the car with you. I can't escape.'

Tessa said, 'If you offer us a job I'll be glad, but I won't take advantage of the situation.'

He sighed. 'I wonder if you're tough enough for Hollywood?'

'I'm tougher than you think. The fact is, I never wanted to come here. My real love is singing direct to the public. On stage or even on the wireless, but the theatre is best – the atmosphere backstage, fellow performers, the extravagant happiness when someone makes a hit, even the misery when someone fails. It's like a grand club where you all know the rules. There's life and laughter and sympathy in the theatre. Oh, I know that you come across unpleasant types, but it's different. It's personal, face to face.' She stopped abruptly. 'Heavens, what a speech! Sorry.'

O'Neill glanced at her. 'That's the most sincere thing I've heard since I came to tinsel-town. You should head straight for home.'

'I can't leave my cousin.'

'You should. She's on course for disaster. I know the type.'

'In that case she needs me more than I realised.'

'She needs you? Like a boa-constrictor needs a victim she needs you!'

'No, you're wrong. You don't know her as I do.'

'All right. I admire you for your loyalty, though I think you're crazy. I promised you dinner and I intend to feed you, but could you wait a while to eat? There's someone I have to see, and visiting their godammed parties is the only way to get hold of some actors.'

'I'm fine.'

O'Neill drove to Beverly Hills and turned into a long, dark drive. They were met by two enormous men in sweaters and caps. 'Chuckers out,' muttered O'Neill. He stuck his head out of the car window. 'Hi.'

'Hi there, O'Neill.'

They stopped in front of a heavy front door and a servant parked the car. When the door opened they were met by a blaze of light.

'Liveried servants,' breathed Tessa.

They were shown into an enormous drawing room full of croupiers and tables. 'Gambling!' she exclaimed. 'My parents would have a fit!'

O'Neill grinned and spoke from the corner of his mouth, gangster-style, 'Don't let anyone hear you say that. We'd be run out.' He was greeted on all sides.

'Hello, O'Neill. Who's the little lady?'

'Tessa Morland, a member of the Kissing Cousins. They sing. They're good.'

Several faces were turned their way; eyes surveyed Tessa, some amused, some hostile.

'Have a drink while you're here,' invited a man in white tie and tails. 'It's on the house.'

'That's kind of him,' said Tessa.

'Don't be fooled,' said O'Neill. 'All drinks are on the house, and eats too. They can afford it while they rake in the gambling money.' He clicked his fingers and a waiter appeared. 'A cocktail for the lady. I won't be long, Tessa. The girl I want is over there.'

The 'girl' was a woman well past her youth. Her face lit up when she saw O'Neill and she talked animatedly. He quickly rejoined Tessa.

'Poor cow. She came to Hollywood years ago straight from a small-town repertory company. I get her a part now and then, but she turns work down because she says it's the wrong kind. She still sees herself as young and gorgeous. I've arranged for her to be at MGM in the morning. I also advised her to go and get some sleep. She won't, of course, but if she doesn't turn up ready to perform this time I really will have to finish with her. I'm the one who gets his arse kicked when actors let me down. No one can afford to be magnanimous in Hollywood. Not if they want to stay alive.'

'What will become of her?'

O'Neill looked at her quizzically. 'You really care? I believe you do. She'll get help from the Motion Picture Relief Fund, though they're run off their feet by the number of applicants. When that gives out she'll either see sense and go back home where she's got relatives or, most likely, skid lower and lower, getting more drunk more often. Then she'll end up in a charity ward or on the streets.'

'It sounds terrible!'

'It is terrible, honey, and every day more hopefuls pour into Hollywood.'

'Just like Eve and I did.'

'That's right, except that you aren't in the general run of girls. You've got a voice and you've also got scruples.

503

Hang on to them, honey.' He called for his car and they drove back to the highway.

'I'd hate to lose you now that we've met,' said O'Neill, 'as a friend as well as a client, but if you believe you can make a living on the stage you should go right back. Let me give you a few figures. Apart from the few hugely successful actors in Hollywood there are about three hundred full-time employees on the acting lots. One casting office alone that I know has seventeen thousand people on its books.'

'How does anyone ever become a star?'

'Sometimes a little talent and a lot of luck. Sometimes a giant talent and a little luck. Eve won't make it. Not without you.'

'Don't be depressing. I'll take care of her.'

'I doubt if she'll let you. Now, we'll eat. I hope you like the place I've chosen.'

'I'm sure I shall.'

She was less sure when O'Neill stopped at a small, dark cottage south of Sunset Boulevard. 'What's this?'

'My place. It's humble but it's home – and don't get the idea that I'm about to stage a seduction scene. I've got dinner all prepared for us.'

He had cooked an enormous pot roast and she sat in the kitchen over a glass of wine and a cigarette while he heated it. It was delicious, followed by fresh fruit which was so plentiful in California, and an excellent cheese.

'That was wonderful,' she said. 'It's very like English cooking.'

'That's because I had an English grandmother. She married Kevin O'Neill and they emigrated to the States. My real friends like simple meals. Some of them will be along soon, so you can stop wondering if I've been about to make a play for you. I'll admit you attract me, but I like a willing woman in my bed.'

Nine of his friends arrived and helped themselves to the simmering pot roast. The men were mainly from England, actors lured to the film colony by the reports of fabulous contracts. They played small parts and in

504

between got jobs as butlers to the successful.

The girls became hash-slingers in the many small cafés, or returned to their former trade. One was a stenographer and two had jobs in beauty parlours. One was a masseuse. She said she had plenty of work and told a few tales of the actors she ministered to which made everyone laugh. Tessa heard about a side of Hollywood that was kept out of the fan magazines. Of an actor making one big movie and ending in such debt that he had taken his life. Of others, younger men, who hung about on the fringe of society, doing anything and everything to make money enough to stay and wait for a break.

The hours passed and more people arrived. Those in funds brought bottles and food. The English voices reminded Tessa of home and she felt homesick.

O'Neill dropped her at the apartment as the sun was coming up and she fell asleep the minute she got into bed.

Eve woke her. 'What time did you get in?'

'Late. Did you have to call me?'

'No. I just felt like it.'

'As unselfish as ever!' Tessa sat up and drank the coffee Eve had brought. 'Did you stay in last night?'

'I did not. I was bored so I called Wolfie.'

'Eve, you didn't!'

'Well, I couldn't very well go out on my own and I don't know anyone else. I'm glad I did. He told me how we can make as much money as we need just making short movies. And when I say short, I mean they take a day or two.'

'It sounds too good to be true.'

'That's what I said, but he explained. Seems there are a lot of small companies who make films only for adults. They're always looking for young guys and gals with decent figures.'

'Adult films? What kind of adult films?'

'Suspicious, as usual! Nothing wrong, Wolfie says, but we'd have to be willing to wear clothes that attract men. I said I'd try. How about you?'

'When you say clothes that attract men . . . ?'

'OK, sexy underwear.'

'I don't like the sound of that at all. I'll ask O'Neill. He's dropping by later.'

'My God, Tessa, I don't see how you'll ever get anywhere in Hollywood when you're so distrustful.'

Eve went to meet Wolfie and when O'Neill arrived, Tessa told him what she had said.

He frowned. 'She's talking about blue movies.'

'Does that mean what I think it means?'

'You have to be willing to appear half or completely naked and simulate sexual behaviour.'

'That's what I was afraid of.'

'Some of them don't even simulate. They go the whole way. There's a huge market for these movies. They're degrading and can have a lastingly bad effect on the actors, women especially.'

'Why women especially?'

'Come down from your high horse. It so happens that I've got a somewhat old-fashioned view of the ladies, probably the result of my dear old gran's moralistic instruction, and I believe that women, however clever and capable they are, need more stability than men in the love department. Taking part in salacious scenes can damage their self-respect.'

'Doesn't it affect men?'

'Men are different and it's no good trying to pretend otherwise. Sex to a man, even when it's great, often even when it's with a woman he loves, is only a part of life. I think women give it much more importance.'

'I don't think Eve believes that sex is significant.'

'From what I've seen of her I don't think she gives it any significance at all. Every man is a notch in her belt.'

'You're wrong, O'Neill. She's like the rest of us, looking for love.'

'Are you looking for love?'

'We were talking about Eve.'

'She may think she is. What she's really looking for is conquest.'

'That's not true! She loves a man in Britain! She was devastated because he isn't interested. She's trying to find someone who cares.'

'That's tough, but if you were disappointed in love would you feel obliged to go to bed with any man who asked you?'

'She doesn't. And I'm different, that's all.'

'You bet your boots you're different. If I didn't think that, I'd have had you by now.'

Tessa stared at him. She had seen him simply as a friend. Now she tried to picture him as a lover and was surprised to realise how attractive she found him.

'Don't look at me like that,' he begged. 'Or I may sweep you on to my horse and gallop with you to my desert tent to have my wicked way with you.'

'Fool!'

'I thought all women fantasised about The Sheikh? But if you don't care for the idea I could take you to my place to seduce you in the simple, time-honoured fashion.' He glanced around. 'Of course I could try here, but Eve might walk in and we wouldn't want to shock her, would we?'

'You couldn't.'

'Couldn't shock Eve?'

'Couldn't seduce me.'

'That's what I thought you'd say. I've got an offer for you. Metro-Goldwyn-Mayer are making a movie called *Rosalie*. They need two thousand extras singing, dancing, or just standing on a sixty-acre stage, would you believe? Nelson Eddy and Eleanor Powell are the stars and Porter has done the score.'

'Oh, thanks, O'Neill.' Tessa smiled. 'Imagine that! Two thousand extras all trying to impress the director with their individual brilliance.'

'You never know. Many have begun in smaller ways.'

Eve scoffed when she heard. 'I don't want that kind of stuff. I've got a star part in one of Wolfie's films.'

'So he's a producer, too?'

'Sure. He knows how to make money and how to give a girl a good time. See this?' She held up her arm which was encircled by a gleaming gold bracelet.

'O'Neill says you'll be asked to take off your clothes. You may even have to pretend to perform sexual acts in front of the camera.'

Eve shrugged. 'It's all acting and it pays well.'

'Won't you be embarrassed?'

'I was at first, but I'll soon get over it.'

'Do you mean you've already begun?'

'Today.'

'Eve, you won't go too far, will you?'

'Always the worrier. You get on with your life and I'll live mine, and we'll see who comes off best.'

Tessa got a job on the MGM musical and found that filming could be amazingly boring. The dialogue writers frequently changed the script so that the actors didn't know their lines, then when rehearsals began it was the turn of the director to rewrite. After that, some of the principal actors had a go until satisfaction was reached by everyone. 'Or maybe,' said O'Neill later, 'no one, especially not the poor devil whose script it was to begin with.'

Everyone had to be on the set by six o'clock which meant being up by five at the latest with no late nights because any weariness showed up on film. In spite of this edict, sometimes they were expected to work until midnight while a scene was shot over and over again, until everyone was sick with frustration.

Sometimes the director only gave way when one of the stars had a fit of screaming hysterics, something which could afflict the men as well as the women. Indifferent food was served at wooden tables. But Tessa kept going. She was getting paid, including overtime and extra on Sundays, and it took care of the rent and filled the icebox, items which Eve failed to remember.

She saw quite a lot of O'Neill who escorted her to parties where she could watch the really big stars and to movie theatres where she saw the completed products and marvelled that something good could come out of such a shambles.

Eve worked much shorter hours, returned with plenty of money and took advantage of every party invitation going. She came back from them in a frenetic state aggravated by drinking, or else stayed out all night. There were times when even she looked haggard and needed to spend ages covering the eye-bags and puffiness with make-up. Apparently blue movie makers were not particularly concerned with faces.

One rare evening, when they were both at home, Tessa said, 'Eve, wouldn't you prefer regular film work?'

'Stand on a stage with two thousand others, do you mean, instead of being the star?'

'Are you a star?'

'You bet I am! I'm in great demand now. Every producer is after me.'

'Any of the big ones, the ones who produce real films?'

'What a bitchy thing to say! You know they're not, but I'm perfectly satisfied with what I'm doing. I'm being paid a lot more than you, Miss Goody Goody.'

Tessa held on to her temper. 'I've never thought myself more good than anyone else. I just couldn't bear to be filmed in that way.'

Eve laughed raucously. 'What a prude! I'm not the only one to take all my clothes off. Some stars do it for publicity pictures.'

'Well, as long as you don't mind being exploited.'

'Of course I mind!' Eve yelled. 'I'd much prefer to be Marlene Dietrich.'

'Stop doing it, then, and give yourself a chance. I thought you wanted to sing.'

'I did! I do! But I want money! I need it. You couldn't be expected to understand that, brought up as you were in a tin-pot house by two tin-pot people. I've been surrounded by luxury all my life and I must have it.'

Tessa felt hurt and indignant at the insult to her parents, but refused to drag them in. 'We all need money,' she said. 'Some more than others. Have you already forgotten what we saw on the road here?'

'No, I haven't, and I made a vow I'd never end up like those poor fools.'

'Did you think Mrs Landon was a poor fool when you gave her your fur coat, or her husband when you handed him your purse?'

'I felt sorry for them,' said Eve grudgingly.

'You aren't as tough as you pretend.' Tessa forestalled her cousin's answer. 'Eve, if we keep our act together and go after decent work we could end up with money and fame. It might take longer. We don't even have to try for films straight away. There are plenty of nightspots and private parties where we could get work and show what we can do.'

'I had enough of that in England. Wolfie doesn't think what I'm doing is ideal, but I'm getting camera experience, I'm learning the tricks of the trade so that when my big chance comes I'll be ready. You've finished with *Rosalie*, haven't you? I've got engagements lined up waiting. What have you got?'

'O'Neill's fixed me up with a stand-in job.'

'A stand-in? You idiot! You know what happened to me.'

'I haven't forgotten. The point is I'll be seen by directors and may get a chance of something better. It all takes time.'

'I don't have time to waste and neither do you. Do you realise that we're considered *old* in Hollywood? There are kids arriving every day, some of them only fifteen. Soon our chance will be lost. I want success and money, and I mean to have them *now*, not when I'm old and my looks have gone.'

Tessa found the job of stand-in tedious. To fill the hours of waiting between scenes many of the women brought along their knitting, or embroidery. Tessa bought some silk and began to make herself a blouse. She almost grew to enjoy the hours of sitting while the filming process swirled around her like water round a rock before they called her. Then an opportunity arrived. Fay Gerald, the star, was asked to sing.

'Sing? Me?' Fay laughed.

'Sure, why not?'

'Darling, I'm so bad my mother told me to keep my voice down at church.'

'Well, just warble a little. We can dub you in the movie.'

'Nix! I don't sing.'

'Well, hum the song. We just need to get the timing right and see if it comes over good.'

'Fay does not sing!' The star stalked off and went into her dressing room. The director pushed his hat back on his head. His hair stood out in spikes. He looked distracted as well he might. Fay's bouts of temper were notorious.

'How about you?' The director nodded to Tessa. 'Can you sing?'

'Yes,' she said, her voice emerging in a screeching falsetto in her excitement.

The director frowned. 'Perhaps we'd better look for someone . . .'

'I can sing,' said Tessa. She broke into the first bars of 'Remember?'.

The director looked surprised. 'Honey, you sure can. And I like the song. I thought I'd heard 'em all, but that's new. Where did you get it?'

'I wrote the lyrics and the melody. The leader of the dance band I was with orchestrated it.'

'A girl with looks, talent and stage experience? You deserve better than this. Right, everybody on set. Lead up to the song, then you – what's your name? Tessa? – can sing. It'll be a lullaby in the finished product. Bring on the cradle!' he yelled. 'It'll have a kid in it when the film is shown, but meanwhile we pretend. You can pretend, can't you, honey? God knows, that's what filming is all about. Rock the cradle and sing your song.'

Tessa had difficulty in controlling her shaking limbs. Singing with Josh was one thing, but this, without music in front of so many people, so totally unexpectedly, was nerve-racking. She had heard the actors' lines so often she knew them by heart and was ready for her cue. Her courage grew as she started to sing and in the end her voice rang out and echoed round the huge set, reminding her of the rehearsal warehouse and Josh. She was paid the finest compliment of all. People stopped what they were doing to listen.

'That was great, honey.' The director grinned. 'A lullaby will be a bit quieter.'

Tessa blushed, but Fay who had come back was generous. 'She should have a real part. She's damn' good.'

'I'm thinking the same,' said the director. 'We could dub you, but if it's OK by you we could have Tessa as a nursemaid and give her the spot.'

The script-writer, the latest to be engaged, said tentatively, 'There isn't a part for a nursemaid.'

'Then go and bloody well write one,' said Fay.

'OK, Tessa,' said the director. 'Take your place. We'll get another stand-in for Miss Gerald and rehearse you tomorrow.'

When Tessa told Eve that she had a talking, singing spot she was furious. 'I don't suppose you bothered to tell them about me?'

'They could hardly use two nursemaids to sing to one child.'

'Did you ask?'

'Of course I didn't. And don't forget that when we had an audition as the Kissing Cousins, you refused to attend.'

Eve flounced off and reappeared in a skin-tight sequinned evening gown and white fur cape. 'I shall be late,' she snapped, 'that's if I bother to come back at all.'

Tessa had sent postcards home, but as soon as she had a permanent address had written to Mum. She had glossed over her experiences on the road and led her mother to believe that Hollywood was a marvellous place with plenty of opportunities.

She re-read Mum's last letter.

512

Dear Tessa,

We all miss you. Joseph is doing better than ever. He can fill the Central Hall now with his sermons. The whole chapel is proud of him, but he says all praise must go to the Lord.

Sammy Jacobs has come back at last. He managed to get into the prison camp to see his cousin, Jacob. He's ill doing forced labour. Sammy thinks he'll die. He brought Ruth and the children back and left them with his wife in Manchester who's taking care of them. He couldn't have done as much, but because the Olympics are on in Germany things are a bit easier. They don't want bad publicity, Sammy said.

We're all shocked by what he's told us. Herr Adolf Hitler took away Jews' citizenship and they've got no rights to anything, not even work. Tessa, Sammy's so thin and white and has a very strange look in his eyes. He said that Herr Hitler wants a war, but surely he must be wrong. Who could want another war after the last lot? Dad didn't say much.

Sammy had a job persuading Ruth to come out of Germany and I must say I can understand her not wanting to leave her husband, but Jacob wanted it for the children's sake. Sammy had to bribe people.

It's a pity our King Edward wasn't as devoted to his duty as Sammy. Fancy abdicating over a divorced woman! Joseph says the new king, his brother George, is a better man. A good Christian with a sweet wife and two lovely daughters.

Susan is second sales in the shop now and quite in demand as a model for dresses and things. She gets asked out by a lot of boys and we let her go sometimes. Dad and me don't really like it, but times are changing and not for the better.

Mr Eden tried to make Germany join a pact that

would make everybody friends, but Herr Hitler
wouldn't. There seems to be trouble everywhere
with fighting going on. Sometimes I think the
world's gone mad. I'm glad you haven't met any
gangsters.

I keep well, thank the Lord, the hens are laying.
Ruff is getting short-sighted. I think one of his
eyes has practically gone blind. Of course, he's old,
but we'll keep him as long as we can.

How's Eve? Is she working? Give her our love
and tell her she's got to visit us when she comes to
England. Why don't you come home? With your
voice you could easily get work here.

Gracie Fields has signed a contract with a talking
picture company. She's going to make three films
for *one hundred and fifty thousand pounds*.
Imagine that.

Tessa, if it looks like war you'll come home,
won't you? Families must stay together in times of
trouble.

Tessa mentioned Mum's fear of war to O'Neill who
looked grave. 'She could be right. Hitler and Mussolini
are crazy for power and land. America won't join in this
time. Once was enough. If Europeans start wars they
should fight the battles.'

'I'm surprised at you! You're European yourself.'

'No. When you take American citizenship you're an
American. Nobody cares where you came from. That's
all behind you.'

Tessa searched the newspapers but little was said
about the possibility of a war in Europe. Most American
newspapers were more interested in the love match of
the abdicated king and Mrs Simpson.

Tessa wrote a simple lullaby for the film, but didn't get
to use it because a friend of the producer had written one
as well. But she kept her small part.

O'Neill was pleased for her. 'How about coming to a
party with me as a celebration?'

'Why not? I don't have to be up early tomorrow.'

The party was held in the Beverly Wilshire Hotel. As Hollywood parties went, it was quite a sedate affair. Tessa saw stars she had only seen on-screen. 'There's Joan Crawford,' she breathed. 'And Norma Shearer and Marlene Dietrich.'

'Close your mouth, honey, or you'll catch flies.'

Tessa laughed. O'Neill proved a light-footed dancer, which surprised her in view of his physique.

'I wanted to be a hoofer,' he said. 'My mother sent me to dancing school and tried hard to push me into films. Casting offices took one look at my bush of ginger hair and my muscly legs, and pointed to the door. Poor Ma, she died still disappointed.'

'Were you disappointed?'

'Not after I found what can happen to people in this town. I'm happier as an agent.'

They joined a prancing line to perform the conga which was followed by a tango, then they sat down, breathless and laughing. Eleanor Powell, who was at the next table, had joined in the dance.

'She's a swell mover,' said O'Neill, 'and very moral. Her mother is in Hollywood with her.'

'She's very thin. If *my* mother saw her she'd feed her up.'

O'Neill laughed. 'I dare say hers tries to. The poor girl gets conflicting advice. On the set the director gives her milk shakes while Mr Mayer has introduced her to saccharine to keep her slim. It must confuse her.'

Miss Powell returned to her seat and stared at her plate. Instead of the squab she had ordered there was a pile of bones. A man watching her from across the table laughed loudly.

'That's Howard Hughes and his idea of a joke,' O'Neill explained.

A paper spitball landed on Tessa's breast. 'Another of Mr Hughes's jokes,' sighed O'Neill. 'A barrel of laughs, isn't he?'

Tessa enjoyed several nights out with O'Neill before the experience began to pall.

'The film colony is like a small village,' she said. 'We

515

keep meeting the same people, listening to the same jokes, eating the same kind of food. And the gossip is vicious. Who's in bed with who, whose spouse is cheating, who's the latest hop-head, who's being dried out in time for the next picture. Drink, drugs and fornication, that's what Hollywood seems to be.'

O'Neill shouted with laughter. 'That's summed up the heavy party-goers. They're not all like that. Far from it. A star who's working on a picture leads a very disciplined life. And, believe it or not, there are some happy marriages.'

'I've not seen them.'

'I'll cancel plans for tonight,' said O'Neill. 'Come to dinner with me, Tessa, and we'll just talk.'

She agreed. She and O'Neill were now firm friends. It was this which caught her off-guard when, after a delicious meal and generous cocktails, he slid his arm about her waist and kissed her gently on the mouth. She hadn't realised until that moment how strictly she had been holding back feelings that had been awakened by Charles. O'Neill's kiss was like a torch to dry wood and desire leapt like a flame. The kiss deepened until O'Neill pulled back and said softly, 'Tessa, are you sure?'

'Don't talk so much. I'm sure.'

He was a skilful lover and she enjoyed his embraces. More than enjoyed them. One experience of love was not nearly enough to dampen the heat in her blood. They made love again and again until both were exhausted and lay side by side, smoking contentedly.

'Honey,' said O'Neill in a voice which was positively awestruck, 'you're the best.'

'The best? How many clients have you bedded?'

'Not so many. You're special.'

'How many have you said that to?'

He tossed his cigarette into the grate and swung his legs to the floor, padding across the room naked.

' "And Esau was an hairy man",' she quoted.

'What? Oh. Yep, I'm as hairy as Esau, all right. I'm going to make coffee.' He went into the kitchen then stuck his head round the door and said, 'I've never told any woman before that she was special.'

And somehow she believed him.

She couldn't resist his love-making. She didn't want to. Her starved body revelled in it. But, oddly enough, she thought of Charles more often and sometimes dreamt of him and then felt guilty, which was ridiculous. She decided to write to him. She made her letter amusing, telling him of the journey to California, making light of their problems. She described the Hollywood scene, with its platoons of young, gorgeous men and women all trying to make it into films. She ended by saying that she hoped his shop was paying dividends.

O'Neill was excellent company and knew all the latest scandals. Tessa listened, feeling she shouldn't, but too fascinated to resist. Mae West, that apparently promiscuous woman, kept her private life separate from her public sex-oriented persona, ignoring all the handsome men and pretty boys who wooed other stars. She liked her men muscular and physical, boxers or body-builders.

'She's got away with more than anybody in films until now,' said O'Neill, 'but the foolish woman dared to make a crack about Marion Davies. Marion's been Randolph Hearst's mistress for years. Everyone knows it but no one dares say it out loud. He's one of the most powerful men in the States. Mae had better watch out or he'll crucify her in his newspapers.'

O'Neill never seemed to tire of the Hollywood scandals which so often bedevilled the stars, or were hushed up so that the general public could watch their screen gods and goddesses, believing them to be pure. The stories began to assume a sameness that bored Tessa.

She said as much to Eve. They had agreed to live their separate lives, neither one criticising the other. 'Don't you get sick of all the humbug in Hollywood, Eve?'

'No, I certainly don't. I find it most interesting.'

Eve spoke without enthusiasm in flat tones and Tessa realised that it was quite a while since she had heard her laugh.

'Eve,' she said impulsively, 'why don't we pack up and go home?'

'I consider I am at home.'

'Oh, yes, I know America is where you were born . . .'

'I mean, I look upon Hollywood as my home. Are you running out of work? I have plenty. I can toss some your way if you need it.'

'No, thanks.'

'Still acting the prude!'

'I'm sorry I spoke. Let's forget it.'

# *Chapter Twenty-Three*

Charles's letter arrived the day after Tessa was engaged for a minor part in *Gold Diggers of 1937*. O'Neill had managed to get her a small solo spot as a night-club singer.

The letter read:

My dear Tessa,

I thought you'd never write, but it was worth waiting for. What experiences you had on the road! What an idiot Eve is!

I saw Josh the other day and he says people still ask when the Kissing Cousins are returning. His new singer is getting married. Another little singer is on the way and it's beginning to show! On the remote chance that you are tired of all the glamour, or not succeeding as you wish – though if you aren't, Hollywood must be blind – you are still sought after here.

The shop is doing nicely, thank you. I've got rid of most of the rubbish and bought good stuff and, no, I haven't dipped into any extra money. I find, to my astonishment, that I can make a comfortable living. However, I do not intend to get rid of my money. Say what you will, a healthy bank balance gives one a strong sense of security.

Paul and his wife are back in Frenchay. I went to dinner there. Everything glittered including the hostess. Literally. Andrea wore a silver sequinned dress and her famous diamonds sparkled from every conceivable place – and perhaps a few inconceivable ones for all I know.

Their sons are well, but only the younger was brought down to the drawing room by their nanny for the guests to admire. No one asked after Master Reginald, except me, and I got a nasty look from Andrea and a hurt one from Paul. He seems to be sliding irrevocably beneath Andrea's thumb. Afterwards I discovered that Reggie wasn't there at all. They've put him in a home. A well-upholstered, well-padded home for rich kids, but a home nonetheless. Perhaps I shouldn't judge. I wonder what I'd do if I ever had a child so handicapped?

I miss you, by the way. I hope you miss me a little. Hurry and make your name and come home to those who wait for you.

Love,
Charles
P.S. I suppose you wouldn't consider marrying me, then I could keep you around all the time?
P.P.S. You'd enjoy the shop and the auctions.

Tessa smiled. He was always ready to joke. She sat with the letter in her hand, remembering, realising that she had for some time ceased to think of Paul. But she had thought so much about him, had dreamed of what might have been, that the loss of her love had left a gap in her life. O'Neill gave her warmth and a sense of being needed as well as sexual fulfilment, but he was no more in love with her than she with him.

She thrust the letter into the small writing desk drawer. She had a job, a real one hundred per cent job in a real one hundred per cent movie, one that would be as popular as the other Gold Digger movies. She would be seen and heard by millions. She would forget about love affairs and all the complications they generated.

When Eve heard that Tessa had gained such a marvellous spot she went white with fury. 'Why you?' she stormed. 'And why as a single singer? Did you ask if they'd take on a duet? Of course you didn't. Because you don't want me.'

Tessa tried to stop the flow, but failed.

'You've probably always thought I was a nuisance. You've just used me when it suited you to get where you wanted to go. We'll see who wins out in the end. I'll make good, then you'll be sorry, and so will everyone else. I . . .'

'Shut up!' yelled Tessa, loudly enough to penetrate even Eve's self-pitying tirade and her cousin fell silent, her mouth open.

'I have *never* used you. It's been the other way round. From the moment you came to my home you've manipulated me, and my family, too. We wouldn't be here but for you. I wouldn't even be in America if you hadn't sworn you needed me. I was stupid enough to let you bully me when I was perfectly content with Josh. I've had enough of your tantrums. Unless you cool off and apologise I shall find an apartment on my own. Then you can pay the rent and buy food for yourself. It'll make a nice change for you.'

Eve's anger died, leaving her shaken. 'Apologise? Why should I?'

'I've just given you reasons enough.' Tessa went to the kitchen and put the kettle on. There was no sound from the living room and when she returned Eve had gone. She felt desperately disappointed. Her bout of temper had relieved the pressure on her, but the demolition of her hopes that she and Eve could resume their cousinly friendship saddened her.

'Damn Hollywood,' she said to O'Neill that evening.

'Damn it as much as you like,' he said, 'but you'll be going places if you can stand the pace. Eve won't. The word is already out that she's unreliable which is a greater sin here than promiscuity.'

'She couldn't be promiscuous if men didn't take advantage of her! And if I hadn't signed a contract I swear I'd go straight back home. This place sickens me.'

'Good job you have signed up for a part then, and I've more work for you. Warner Brothers are happy for you to accept singing jobs in the clubs as long as you're advertised as the "Warner Nightingale". You'll be well paid.'

'Are you serious?'

'Would I joke about money?'

Tessa would have withdrawn her threat to find another apartment, but when she returned that night Eve asked, 'When are you moving out?'

'As soon as you like.' She hesitated. 'I'll stay if you want me to?'

'I thought you'd try to get round me. Well, you can't. I've already told a friend she can share. In fact, she's the second lead in some of my films.'

'Of all the damned cheek! This place is rented in both our names.'

Then Tessa's bedroom door opened and a girl walked into the living room. She was well endowed, almost plump, and her hair was too blonde to be natural.

'Eve, honey, when will she be clearing out? I've nowhere to hang my things. Oh, you're here. Can you empty the wardrobe and drawers, honey?'

'I'll be packed and ready to leave within an hour.'

'And that's an hour too long,' snapped Eve.

Tessa took a taxi to O'Neill's. 'You can stay here,' he said.

'Only for tonight, thanks. I need my own place.'

He didn't argue and she moved into an apartment near Griffith Park.

Tessa was entertaining guests. O'Neill, of course, and a mixed bunch of film people. Her job with the Gold Digger movie had ended and she had played in other films, each time getting successively larger parts. She could be accounted a success, especially as she had sung one of her own songs in a film and was composing another, asked for by a producer.

'You're on the up and up, baby,' O'Neill told her.

Tessa knew she should be pleased. Every aspiring newcomer who arrived in a frenzy of hope and determination would be ecstatic at such progress, but she was dissatisfied. She tried hard to hide this from O'Neill, but he knew her too well to be fooled.

'Keep going,' he kept advising her. 'You'll make it to the big time and then you can order your own life and only take parts that appeal to you. Keep a cool head and stick with me and you'll be fine.'

'What about Eve?'

'You've got to stop nursemaiding her. She wouldn't take a single step to help you out of trouble.'

Tessa saw her cousin occasionally, always surrounded by people, always loudly gay and laughing. Her love affairs were gossiped about, her parties notorious, filled with gate-crashers. More than once the police had raided her apartment in a search for drugs. So far they'd been unsuccessful. Tessa, horribly worried about her, had tried to make up their quarrel.

'I promised your mother I'd take care of you,' she had said.

Eve had stared, then laughed. 'You liar! My mother has never asked a soul to take care of me. In fact, she'd feel much better if I was dead.' She turned aside but Tessa heard the words, 'And so would I.'

She looked so miserable, so vulnerable, that Tessa longed to put her arms round her, but she hadn't been allowed the chance. The plump blonde had been replaced by other flat-mates and the latest came into the living-room. This girl was tall, very dark, with luminous black eyes.

'Eve, darling, aren't you ready yet?' she said.

'Meet Sonia,' said Eve. 'She shares my apartment now and we act together. We've done quite a few films, haven't we, Sonia? Just us. No men.' She looked at Tessa from the corners of her eyes and smiled. 'It seems the boys like to watch two females cavorting on a bed.'

Sonia laughed. Tessa placed one of her printed cards on the table. 'If you need me, Eve, this is where I live.'

One night she attended the private showing of a new film, *Girls in Love*. When it began Tessa caught a glimpse of Sonia, with Eve peering saucily from the background. Both wore lingerie which revealed more than it concealed. Tessa went hot and cold, wondering how to get out of the place. Then her host yelled something and the film was removed while he railed against the low-down bastard who had substituted a blue movie as a joke.

'How can she?' Tessa raged to O'Neill later.

'Why the sudden fury? You knew what she was doing.'

'Knowing wasn't the same as seeing.'

'You really ought to forget your cousin. She never thinks of you.'

'You can't be sure of that.'

When Tessa was woken one morning in the early hours by the insistent ringing of the telephone she heard Sonia's agitated voice. 'For heaven's sake, get over here. I think Eve's gone crazy. She's been screaming. Something about a dream. I can't calm her and the neighbours are threatening to call the cops. She wants you.'

Tessa rode over in a cab. Eve was weeping hysterically and when she saw Tessa, held out her arms. 'Please,' she begged, 'please.'

Tessa nursed her cousin until she stopped shaking. She called to Sonia to bring coffee. She did so, sulkily. Tessa stayed the night.

The next day Sonia was viciously angry. Eve was white-faced, tense and nervous. 'I thought you loved me,' Sonia stormed. 'But you have a dream and send for *her*. After the times you've called her wishy-washy and holier than thou! If you want her, you can have her. I can find plenty of other places to live.'

'Don't leave me,' pleaded Eve. 'Sonia, don't leave me. When I have this dream I go a bit crazy. I called for Tessa from habit. Please stay.'

'If that's what you really want . . .'

'I do. Oh, I do. Tessa understands, don't you?'

\* \* \*

O'Neill brought more good news. 'Paramount want you to audition for a part in *Artists and Models*.'

Tessa was telling friends over a restaurant dinner when she realised that Eve was staring at her from the next table. She got up and went to her. 'I'm glad to see you. Is Sonia here?'

'Yes. I had a hard job persuading her to stay with me. She's still furious with you.'

'I came at her request when you needed me.'

'Oh, yes, rub it in. I can't help having bad dreams.'

'Was it the same one again?'

Eve blurted, 'Yes.' She hurried on, 'So you've landed another good part?'

'Not yet. I'm auditioning for *Artists and Models* in two days' time, though O'Neill thinks it's a cert.'

But Tessa didn't get chosen and O'Neill discovered why. 'Your cousin! What a bitch she is! She deliberately led on a man in casting who's a sucker for a pretty girl. He's given her the part.'

Tessa sat down heavily. She was in O'Neill's house. 'But she knew it was to be mine!'

'Why else do you think she went after it? You shouldn't have told her.' He brought her a drink.

'I feel like giving it all up and going home,' she sighed. 'I have some money saved and I've paid all my debts.' Including, she thought, the one to Trudy, the woman in the café who had so generously given help when it was needed.

O'Neill said, 'You don't give up because of a setback.'

'There's more to it than that. A lot of the time I hate it here. I'll never be able to watch a movie again without wondering about the actors' private lives.'

'There must be just as much mayhem in any theatre in the world?'

'I don't think so. A theatre company usually pulls together. Here, you daren't turn round for fear someone will stick a knife in you.'

'You've known that for some time. I thought you

525

could deal with it. Give yourself a little more time. There'll be other parts, probably better. MGM are casting for *Puttin' on the Ritz*. They've already got Clark Gable.'

'What? I'd certainly like to meet him!'

'Then you'll stay?'

'To meet Clark Gable? No, but I'll give Hollywood another chance. You've done a lot for me. I'd like to make good for you.'

'Swell. The new film is scheduled for showing in 1939.'

'That's two years away!'

'Not quite, honey. It's November already. Haven't you noticed the drop in temperature? The rain?'

'Oh, yes, but I always forget that California has a winter. We call this weather mild in Britain and rain has always been a part of my life. Almost Christmas,' she finished dreamily.

'Don't say you go moony over Christmas?'

'You would if you came from a home like mine. It's the greatest celebration of the year.' She was overcome by a wave of nostalgia. 'It's so long since I saw my family.'

O'Neill said urgently, 'Don't be sad. Soon I'll get you a long contract with one of the big companies, then your worries will be over.'

'Some hopes!'

'You're a pessimist.'

'I'm a realist.'

'More or less the same thing.'

Tessa stared down at the type-written note which had been pushed into her letter box. It was from O'Neill and asked her to come to his house that night for dinner: 'Lots of the guys and girls will be there. I hope you can make it.'

She wondered why he hadn't phoned. He probably had, but she had been out since early morning. The dinner was set for eight o'clock. No need to dress up for his informal evenings so she wore black lounging trousers and a midnight blue velvet jacket.

She climbed out of the cab and opened his front door which was never locked while he was in. There was the sound of voices, though not the usual carefree babble. She glanced at her watch. It wanted fifteen minutes to eight and it was nothing for his guests to arrive hours late.

The living room was dimly lit. Voices were rising from the high-backed sofa which doubled as a bed for impecunious friends. 'O'Neill?' she called.

There was a frantic movement, a soothing whisper, then Eve's head appeared over the back of the sofa. 'Tessa! Fancy meeting you here.'

'Tessa? Eve, get off me!' That was O'Neill's furious voice.

'Darling, how can you speak to me like that?' she chided. 'After what I've just done for you.'

'Move, you . . .'

Tessa wanted to leave, but she was transfixed. Then O'Neill appeared, buttoning his pants. 'Tessa, honey . . .'

His voice broke the spell and she ran out of the front door, into the street. She heard O'Neill yelling after her. She saw a cab and hailed it and arrived back in her apartment bathed in perspiration. It was obvious that Eve had sent her the note.

At six the next morning O'Neill was hammering on her door. She opened it and he walked in. 'I haven't slept all night,' he began.

'Too bad. I slept quite well.'

'Are you sure? You look heavy-eyed to me.'

'If I am it has nothing to do with you. I don't own you. You're free to behave as you please.'

'Quit talking rubbish! I'm a heel and you should tell me so. I know how Eve likes to needle you and now I've helped her.'

'I suppose you've had other women while we've been dating?'

'No, I haven't.'

She gave him a long stare. 'Do you know, I believe you. Does that make me a first-rate sucker?'

'Tessa, please, I can't stand this! Give me a blazing row and have done with it.'

'I don't intend to quarrel. I'm not your keeper. You never promised me a thing.'

'Eve arrived last night unexpectedly. She asked me if I'd take her on, become her agent if she sacked Wolfie. I told her nothing doing. She got angry, then she began to take her clothes off. I protested, but I'm weak, Tessa, and she's beautiful, and I'm not a man who can refuse such a succulent display when it's offered. I just kept on watching her and she kept on undressing with all the skill of a stripper. Laughing at me, taunting me. So I thought, what the hell?'

'I'm not blaming you. Eve is lovely. And you're a man.'

'Why did you turn up out of the blue like that?'

Tessa walked to her writing desk and produced the note.

'Eve's work,' said O'Neill, 'or probably that dyke she's living with. She's vicious, but she's mad about Eve. She'd do anything for her.'

'I'm really sorry it happened, but it's helped me to decide. I'm leaving, O'Neill, and this time no one will talk me out of it.'

'Tessa, don't! Why should you? We've never pretended to be in love, but you're special. You're the first woman I've considered settling down with. I meant to ask you to marry me one day. Will you marry me, Tessa?'

He sounded utterly sincere, but she shook her head. 'It wouldn't do. I appreciate the compliment, but you're not a man to be tied down and you don't really love me any more than I love you. When I marry, I want it to be for life.'

'I can offer you a good marriage. Maybe not romantic, but that stuff is for movies.'

'No, thank you. I just want to go back to a place where I understand the values.'

'You've sworn to leave before today. You know you won't go.'

'This time I will. I've enjoyed my brief acquaintance with Hollywood in a masochistic kind of way, but it isn't for me. I don't belong here.'

'Tessa, don't leave me,' he begged. 'Eve's not the only one who gets lonely.'

'I know. I'm sorry, O'Neill, but if you had a loving family to go home to, would you stay here?'

'I have got a family, but this place is my life. I'm hooked for ever.'

'Well, I'm not.'

'Tessa, think carefully. I believe there's bound to be war in Europe. Adolf Hitler is re-arming as fast as he can. He's only waiting for an excuse and Britain will be drawn into it. Sure to be. You'll be safer here.'

'If you're right, I see it as another, even stronger reason for going home. Families need each other at such times.'

O'Neill nodded slowly. 'I wish I'd met you years ago. I shan't give you up without a struggle.'

But not all O'Neill's reasoning and pleading altered Tessa's mind, any more than the loudly voiced disappointment of the friends she'd made. In the end O'Neill said, 'I give in. Do me one last favour. Spend one more night with me?'

Tessa shook her head. 'No. You've made me happy. In fact, I don't think I would have stuck it so long without you, but when I say goodbye I go.'

'You would have made it to the top, I know you would. You could have been rich and famous.'

'Perhaps. Maybe I'll return one day with Josh.'

'If you do, give me a call,' said O'Neill gloomily.

Tessa wrote to her family and to Charles telling them that she'd be home early next year. She went to call on Eve. Sonia opened the door and scowled.

'It's *her*,' she called.

Eve was curled up on a sofa. She wore a rather grubby wrap and her hair needed a wash. 'I suppose you've come to say something nasty?'

'Why should you suppose anything of the sort?'

'I got the part you wanted.'

'I hope you do well in it.'

Eve sat up. 'You've landed something better?'

'Much better. I'm going home. I wouldn't leave without saying goodbye.'

Eve swung her legs to the floor. 'You can't go!' she cried, alarm ringing in her voice. 'You can't leave me.'

'You don't need her,' said Sonia. 'I can do more for you than she ever could.'

'Shut up! Tessa, please, don't go. I shouldn't have taken the part from you . . .'

'Forget it. My reasons go much deeper than that. Take care of yourself.'

When Tessa left she could still hear Eve's insistent pleading and it rang in her ears for a long time.

She decided to sail from New York so that she could see how Eve's Aunt Betsy was faring. She left her luggage in her hotel and went to the Jeffersons' house. Reginald shook her hand warmly. 'How kind of you to think of us.'

When Tessa asked after his wife he shook his head. 'She's very ill. She begged to come out of the hospital so I have her here. She's nursed round the clock and the doctor visits two or three times daily. I'm afraid it's only a matter of time, and not much of that.' His voice broke as he added, 'And the best I can wish for her is that her suffering won't be prolonged. Oh, Tessa, what it is to watch someone you love die. And in such pain!'

'I'm so dreadfully sorry. I don't want to intrude. I needn't see her. Just tell her I called.'

'I'm sure she would love you to go up. She respects you very much. I'll just check with the nurse.'

Tessa was allotted a couple of minutes. 'You'll find her very much altered,' warned Reginald. 'Her voice is hoarse and her eyes wander. The pain-killing drugs have done that to her.'

Betsy was propped up on pillows and Tessa would not have recognised her. She was bone-thin and yellow-skinned. Her eyes were closed. As Tessa sat by her bed and waited until she opened them, she held out a hand like a claw and spoke in a harsh whisper. 'Good to see you, dear. So kind of you. You look well. How is Eve?'

'Fine. She's fine.'

'Are you here on business?'

'I'm going home.'

'Home? To your family?'

'Yes, I miss them.'

'Eve . . .' Betsy began, stopped, then continued, 'We have to do our best. Paul and Andrea will be here soon. I can't go without saying goodbye to them. I've asked them to bring the boys.'

The nurse stepped forward. 'That's enough, Mrs Jefferson. Please go now, miss.'

Reginald waited to escort Tessa downstairs where he gave her a glass of wine. 'I'm so sorry,' she said, wishing she could think of something more helpful. 'I meant to tell her how much her gift of money helped Eve and me. Should I stay a while and perhaps visit her again?'

'No,' he said sadly. 'It's best to keep her quiet. She's got guts, Tessa, to use a vulgarism. Always had. I'm going to miss her. But I must soldier on. She would. Will you call on Eve's mother?'

Tessa visited Rose Brook. Partridge showed her into the house which seemed to exude an even colder atmosphere. Rose greeted her without enthusiasm. 'Why hasn't Eve accompanied you?'

'She's happy in Hollywood.'

'And you were not?'

'Not very.'

'Did you find it too competitive?'

'That isn't why I left.'

'No? Perhaps it takes more courage than you possess to become successful in America?'

'I shall be glad to see my family.'

'Ah, yes, the family. I remember your parents well.' Rose left no room for doubt as to her opinion of them. Her venom surprised Tessa who had forgotten how acidic she could be. Rose still wore unrelieved black. 'Eve wrote to tell me she has another excellent part in a film. She says she is never short of work.'

'That's true.'

'I must say I'm surprised that you have left her. I understood that you would remain with her?'

Tessa was glad to leave and go to the liner. On board she settled into the tourist cabin she shared with others with a deep sense of relief. Her affection for Eve had taken a serious battering and she viewed the voyage as a breathing space to be enjoyed.


Eve was exasperated.

'What's biting you?' asked Sonia.

'My Aunt Betsy's died. My mother thinks I should go home for the funeral.'

'What rubbish! Why put yourself out for a dead body which is simply going to be dropped in a hole and covered with dirt? I hate all the fuss attached to funerals.'

Eve's mind had been busily working on excuses to avoid going to New York, but Sonia's belligerent attitude annoyed her. It did so more and more lately.

'It's time I went home,' she said. 'I haven't seen my mother for ages.'

'As you've told me many times that your mother is cold and unloving, I can't see why that should bother you.'

'She's still my mother. I don't have any engagements I can't get out of.'

'We were going to settle with Wolfie about our new film. I was looking forward to it. I hate it when you act with men.'

'I've told you over and over, I like men.'

Sonia scowled.

'I think I'll stay in New York for a while. If you don't

want the tenancy of the apartment, I'll give the landlord notice.'

Sonia's dark brows drew even further together. 'I knew it! You're trying to ditch me! Well, you won't succeed. We've got work lined up as a pair.'

'We haven't signed anything. Besides, I'm tired of pretending I'm lesbian.'

'If you had any honesty, you'd admit you are one.'

'I'm not, and I'm sick of faking it. I've had enough of blue movies. I shall ask Wolfie for something different when I get back.'

Sonia laughed. 'Some hopes! You'll never get out of them now you've begun. Too many people have seen your all.'

Sonia's vulgar guffaw annoyed Eve still further. 'I'm not the only woman to have done something risqué to earn money. Other stars have posed in the nude. What about Jean Harlow?'

'They haven't displayed their fannies being entered by a large penis. Or made love on screen with another woman.'

'It was simulation only!'

'Simulation, my arse! What would your dear daddy have said if he could have seen his little Eve?'

'Leave my father out of this!'

'Willingly, if you could.'

'What does that mean?'

'Everything you do, everything you are, has been determined by your father. And as far as I can tell, he didn't give a horse's shit for you.' Eve swayed. 'You're not going to faint on me, are you?'

'No.'

'Eve, don't go! I didn't mean to be bitchy. Fathers can have devastating effects on their kids, especially the girls. Mine was such a bastard he turned me off men forever. What I can't figure out is why you don't hate yours after the way he treated you?'

'You don't have to bring that up. I was drunk when I told you . . .'

'Sure you were, and that's when you tell the truth.'

533

'I'm sick of this conversation. I'm going to pack. I shall take the first train home.'

'OK, do! I can manage without you. There are plenty of girls ready to step into your shoes.'

During the first part of the journey to New York Eve thought of little else but her father. She had pushed all thoughts of him to the back of her mind, especially since Tessa had left, but Aunt Betsy's death had reactivated her sense of loss. She wished with all her heart that Tessa was with her. She was the only one who could dispel the horror when Eve had the dream. Thank God it hadn't come back since the night Sonia had sent for her, but Eve lived in its shadow. If only she had some warning. But she was always plunged into it without mercy and forced to see it through to its horrible end.

Why hadn't she listened to Tessa? Her so-called career in Hollywood was a mess. She should have listened to her cousin. Together, as the Kissing Cousins, they might have made the grade. Would have, she was sure. Now, no one would want her. Not only had she performed in blue movies, she had seen them at parties which catered for such tastes, seen herself, up there on the silver screen, not as she had imagined, the star of some brilliant film, but enacting scenes that made her shake with nerves to watch. People around her had laughed and passed remarks which had made her cringe.

She admitted that she loathed everything about the films: the clothes, the sketchy plots which were merely an excuse that led to sexual excesses, the other actors, the camera men; above all the producers and directors who cared nothing for the feelings of their puppets and demanded and received behaviour fitted to whatever extreme of obscenity was required.

As she drew nearer to New York memories of her childhood and all its miseries and disappointments returned. She tried to drag her mind from them, fearing that they would bring on the dream. Towards the end of the journey she slept only in snatches, afraid to let go.

When she arrived home, her appearance startled Rose.

'Good heavens, what a fright you look!'

'I couldn't sleep on board the train.'

'You slept well as a child when I took you on trips.'

'There weren't many of those.'

'No. You had too full a life to travel often.'

Full of nothing, thought Eve. Riding lessons, ballet classes, special coaching, elocution. The list went on. Nothing worth having. 'When is the funeral?'

'In two days' time. Have you any black things?'

'Yes.'

'Fashionable stuff?'

'Yes. I like black. It suits me. I have several outfits.'

'You appear to have brought enough luggage with you to last for months. How long do you propose to stay?'

'I need not trouble you for long.'

'There is no need to be unpleasant. I merely wish to instruct the servants. You may have to do some things for yourself. I cannot afford the large staff we once had. I never entertain.'

Did her mother need to make it quite so obvious that she was not wanted? 'I've left my apartment,' Eve said, 'so naturally I brought my stuff with me.'

'Why did you stop sharing with Tessa? I was astonished when she turned up here without you. I thought she was fond of you.'

'She is. We quarrelled.'

'I suppose she was jealous of your success?'

'No. She's far more talented than I am.' The observation slid past Eve's guard.

'I doubt that. You should be more positive in your attitude to life, but you have always been defeatist.'

'Is my room ready for me?'

'It is.' Rose rang and the maid appeared. 'Take Miss Eve's luggage to her room.'

'I'll help,' she said. 'I've got used to looking after myse'f.' She picked up a case in each hand and the maid staggered behind with the heavier things.

\* \* \*

The funeral was sombre as one would expect, and harrowing because Reginald could not hide his grief. Paul and Andrea stood on one side of him, Rose and Eve on the other. A reception was held afterwards in the drawing room which Betsy's presence had made so welcoming. Betsy, thought Eve, had been unfashionable, plump and homely. A lot like Tessa's mother, in fact. She remembered the insults about Cousins Walter and Lily which she had flung at Tessa and was ashamed. She must apologise as soon as she could.

Rose's voice cut into her thoughts. 'Eve, your cousin is addressing you.'

'Sorry, Paul.' She smiled wanly. 'I was lost. I'll miss Aunt Betsy.'

'Yes.' He sank into a chair beside her. 'I regret the years I've spent away from her. I wish I had come back sooner. I reached her bedside just in time to say goodbye.' His voice cracked.

'Did you bring the boys?'

'Yes, both of them. Mother wanted to see them. Do you know, I believe she loved Reggie as much as the new baby. Perhaps more.'

'Because he needed love more?'

Paul glanced at Eve with surprise. As well he might, she thought. She seemed to be waking up to some realities. 'I think you're right,' he said. 'I wish Andrea – but neither of us can cope with our son's condition.' He looked around. 'I thought I would find Tessa here.'

'She returned to England.'

'Without you? You had a double act.'

'We did. We split.'

'What a pity. You were excellent together. What are you both doing now?'

'I don't know about Tessa. I'm not doing anything at the moment.'

'Did you find what you were looking for in Hollywood?'

'No.'

'That's a shame.'

536

'The problem is, I don't know exactly what I was looking for.'

'Do any of us?' sighed Paul.

Eve took a good look at him. He had a defeated air nowadays. He was putting on weight and the smile which had so attracted Tessa had become at times almost a grimace. Well, one wouldn't expect happy smiles at his mother's funeral, but Eve gained the impression that he was secretly miserable. She wondered if Tessa would meet up with him again? She could probably take him away from Andrea if she tried.

'I'm going to write to Tessa, care of her parents,' she said, suddenly making up her mind.

'Give her my very good wishes,' said Paul.

Andrea, who had been watching them with increasing irritation, walked towards them. 'Paul, your father needs help. He should not be left to manage everything on his own. He looks ghastly.' Her tone implied that she disapproved of such public displays of grief.

# Chapter Twenty-Four

Eve knew she should leave, but although her nervous discomfort grew with every day she spent in her home, she was lethargic. She had come to a crossroads in her life and didn't know which way to take. America had been her home during childhood, yet she felt drawn to England. She couldn't be certain if this was simply because Tessa and her family were there. And Tessa might not want her. The thought hurt, but she tried to face it. If her British family rejected her it didn't really matter to anyone in the world where she went.

She studied her reflection. Her hair had lost nothing of its burnished auburn beauty, her skin was as white as it had always been, her mouth with its full lower lip as inviting as ever. She could regard her own attractions almost dispassionately. Taking part in blue movies meant that she had needed to make up and dress for whatever fantasy she was about to display and that required unbiased study.

Her eyes looked different, she decided. They were still lustrous, but now their expression was altered. They were the eyes of a woman who had seen too much. 'What can I do?' she asked her reflection. 'Where can I go?'

Rose had asked her for three mornings running if she had finalised her plans for returning to Hollywood. She had tried to pretend it was out of interest but Eve had not been fooled. Her mother wanted the house to herself again.

On the fourth morning she was asked, Eve said, 'I've

been thinking. I'm not returning to Hollywood.'

'Not returning! But I understood you to say you were doing excellently there. You told me you have been offered many parts and you must be making good money judging by your clothes. When Grace was putting your things away she was astonished at their number and quality.'

'Nevertheless, I'm not going back. I have decided to go to England.'

'To England! Why England? Oh, I suppose you wish to join with Tessa again and visit her gross parents?'

'They're not gross.'

'Plump, tubby, fat, vulgar, gross . . . call them what you please.'

Eve looked at her mother's bone-thin figure. Wallis Simpson, who was now married to the former English king, newly created Duke of Windsor, had said that a woman could never be too rich or too thin. She would have approved of Rose's figure though Eve feared it was achieved by sheer lack of interest in eating rather than by design. It was useless to try to describe to Rose how she felt about Eve's parents. She simply wouldn't understand.

When Eve told Grace she was leaving the maid said, 'Oh, Miss Eve, I wish you wouldn't. Your mother needs you.'

'No, she doesn't. She wants me to go.'

'She thinks she does, but if you stayed maybe you could get her to come out of mourning for your father? I don't know what'll become of her.'

'I'm sorry. I must go.'

The night before her departure, Eve went downstairs into the hall and stood outside her father's study. She hadn't been in since his death, though Rose went there often. She pushed open the door, stepped into the room, dimmed by heavy curtains drawn across the windows, and closed it behind her. A desk light shone. She walked over to it and stared at it. Here was where the accident had happened. Here her father's brains had spilled out

540

with his blood. Here was where she had lost any chance she might have had of getting close to him.

She sat in his chair and leaned her arms on his desk, trying to sense his presence, trying to comprehend the reason for her dreams. She had never dared to attempt to analyse them. Were they the result of her need for her father's affection? Or did she in some dark, terrifying corner of her soul crave his caresses as a woman wants a man? No matter how hard she struggled she could come up with no answer. Her head began to ache and she laid it on her arms, tears forcing themselves between her lids and trickling down her face on to the leather-topped desk.

She was never sure afterwards if she had fallen into a doze, but she hadn't heard the door open and was shocked when Rose's voice, violently angry, cut across the room.

'How dare you! How dare you sit in his chair! Even I have not done so and I have the right.'

Eve looked up and Rose cried, 'Tears? Who do you shed them for? Yourself? Your self-pitying, maudlin self? He would have scorned them.'

'As he scorned me?' cried Eve.

'He did no such thing. I doubt if he ever thought of you for more than a moment.'

'That's what I figured.'

Rose had started across the room, but she stopped. 'You sound bitter. If a man cannot care for his daughter, is he to be blamed?'

'Perhaps he would have preferred a son. Is that why he cheated on you? Because you couldn't give him a son?'

'There is no proof that he cheated on me, as you so vulgarly put it. And, no,' Rose's voice was quiet and deadly, 'he did not want a son. He did not want *you*. He wanted no encumbrance in his life.'

'Were you an encumbrance?'

'If you understood anything about marriage you would not ask me such a question.'

'But I'd like to know why you've given everything up

541

to skulk around in semi-darkness, behaving like a grieving widow. I'm not sure there was ever any true love between you.'

Rose had come close to the desk. 'You have dampened his desk with your stupid tears. Leather should not get wet. I shall have to dry it, clean and polish it.'

'Will you do that yourself?'

'Of course. No servant has been allowed in here since the day of his death.'

'The whole room is a shrine.'

'Call it what you will. It's the only place I find any comfort.'

'Do you honestly find comfort in sticks of furniture?'

'You betray how little you cared about him. If you had, you would know that his presence lingers here.'

Eve wanted to hurt her. 'I'm one strike up on you. I have his blood. You were only his wife.'

'A wife comes far closer to a man than his daughter. The very act sacred to marriage ensures that.'

'Did he often make love to you?'

'How dare you ask me such a question! Not even a daughter has the right.'

'This is the nearest we've ever got to talking about anything important. Is it because we're here, in his room? I've tried to reach him, but it's impossible. It was just as impossible when he was alive. I don't think he loved anyone.'

'He cared for me enough to marry me.'

Eve shrugged, deliberately provocative. 'He might have thought he did, but perhaps he was only pretending. You were quite a catch, weren't you, Mother, with your fortune and your impeccable American background? Father wanted a foot in the financial market. That's why he chose you. And you were stupid enough to fall in love with him.'

'Be quiet!'

'I won't! All my life I've been forced into silence. Just this once, only once, Mother, give me a straight answer. Tell me the truth. Wasn't Father a cold, heartless bastard with not a vestige of love for anyone?'

Rose stepped forward until she bent over Eve. Her eyes glittered and her face was twisted. Eve wished she hadn't gone so far but it was too late. Her mother's voice was low, sibilant. 'Why do you think he died?'

The question hung between them.

'He had an accident,' faltered Eve.

'No! He killed himself. He took out his gun, put a bullet in it and shot himself through the head. And do you want to know why he did it? Because he was in love! You see, you're wrong. He *could* love. He discovered he could love. But only when he met a beautiful boy.'

Eve gasped and held out her hands imploringly. 'Stop! Don't!'

'He loved no woman for reasons which he himself could not understand. When he discovered what he really wanted he could not live with himself. So he took the coward's way out.'

Eve stood up and shoved the chair back. 'No! I won't listen! It's lies, all lies. You're just trying to hurt me.'

'Hurt, are you? Poor Eve. She's hurt. How do you think *I* feel?'

'If he'd done what you said, he would have left a note.'

'He did. More than one. I reached him first. When I picked them up it was to prevent their getting soiled. There was a lot of blood. In my distress I forgot them until later, which was fortunate. Mine was a formal affair. The one to his mistress, Irene Martinez – yes, he had a mistress, I think it bolstered his need to believe in his masculinity – her letter was friendly. The one to Maurice, her brother, was very different. It asked for his forgiveness.'

Eve was silent, trembling with shock.

'Of course, Maurice and Irene knew nothing about the notes. They never had that satisfaction. Now I must live with what's left. I do so in the only way I know how.'

Eve looked up at her mother whose face was ugly with her frantic grief. She had an impulse to try to comfort her, but it was impossible to reach her. It always would be. 'Will you leave me here for a few minutes?' she asked.

Rose walked away. At the door she turned. 'Of course, no one must ever know what really happened.' She laughed harshly. 'Imagine that, Eve. You and I will share a secret for the rest of our lives. How frightfully cosy. Don't stay in here long. I will return when you have gone.'

Eve watched her mother leave, feeling half-stunned by the revelation. She thought again of Ralph. He had taken a gun from this drawer, sat in this chair, held the gun to his head, squeezed the trigger. She pictured Rose arriving on the terrible scene, snatching at the letters.

She had only her mother's word that it had all happened that way. If Rose had discovered that Ralph was having an affair with a young man she would have been devastated. She would have done anything to keep the matter quiet. Even murder? Eve considered this possibility. Was it sorrow or guilt which bound her mother to this house, this room?

She stood up and wandered round the room, touching objects that Ralph had collected. A carved sphinx, an alabaster vase, a pair of Wood and Hughes goblets which Rose had given him, an Aaron Willard Clock, another gift from her. It occurred to Eve for the first time that his room was furnished entirely with American artifacts as if he had tried to expunge his Englishness.

She held the heavy curtain aside and looked out at the quiet street. She let the curtain fall and, standing still, surveyed the study, surprised to find herself calm. No bad memories claimed her, no yearning after what might have been. She harboured no secret terrors. She took a deep, long breath and exhaled slowly. Perhaps Rose's spiteful tirade had numbed her? Somehow she didn't think so. Rose had cut the cords which had bound her. The fact that her father had cared nothing for her now held only minor sadness. She had never before questioned the value of his love. Now she did and it had no value at all.

544

She sat again in Ralph's chair, thinking of the way she had sought love in any form she could find, grabbing at its sexual manifestation wherever it was offered. She saw herself with glaring clarity. She had believed herself to be utterly degraded, used by men. Now she understood that she had been the user. She had given her body in excesses meant to wipe out her hunger for Ralph's love. She hadn't succeeded and never would have.

Rose's revelation had given her freedom. She regretted her past, but it belonged to a different woman in a discarded life. She longed to be at home. The thought startled her. Home? That was where Tessa, Lily and Walter were. Where Susan and Joey welcomed her. Even the dog wagged its tail when she appeared and licked her hand.

She walked out of the study without looking back.

'I shall be leaving as soon as I can get a berth,' she told Rose.

Her mother stared at her, her eyes reflecting apprehension.

'Don't worry, I'll never speak of anything that's passed between us today.'

'You've changed. I don't understand.'

'As long as I understand, Mother, that's what matters. Don't worry about me.'

As if she would. Eve felt sorry for Rose who would remain here. She was caught in a bondage which she embraced though it could destroy her. Eve would go to Tessa a new person, someone in her own right, someone with much to learn and space in which to do so. I can start all over again, she thought. A beginner at my age. She laughed aloud.

Rose said goodbye to Eve. 'Write when you have time and tell me how you fare.'

The taxi waited, but Eve stopped and said impulsively, 'Mother, have you ever cared for me?'

'What a foolish question. I am your mother.'

'Yes. You are.'

'You will write?' Rose took a small step back, eager to end this leave-taking.

'Of course. Mother, try to be happy.'

Rose lifted her chin. 'I shall live as best I can, as we all must.' She came to the door, watched Eve get into a cab, saw Grace and Partridge load the luggage, then waved as her daughter was driven off. She returned to the barren sanctuary of her house.

Tessa had sent word that she was coming home and Mum and Dad welcomed her at the station. They had both put on weight and were even more roly-poly than she remembered. She put her arms round each one in turn, hugging and kissing in an excess of pleasure. 'I'm so glad to be back. I've missed you dreadfully.'

'Have you, my love?' said Mum. 'That's nice to hear. When we knew you were a success in Hollywood we thought you'd stay there. More than one of our neighbours has come and told us they've seen you in a film. Quite small parts, they said, but you were good.'

'Do you still not go to the pictures?'

Mum shook her head. 'No, and not even the panto now you're all grown up.' She sighed. 'I miss the days when I had all my children at home, little and depending on me.'

'We've got a surprise for you,' said Dad as they came out on to the station concourse. 'Look. That's our motor car.' Tessa looked at the tiny Austin Seven, as polished and gleaming as the furniture in the best room.

'It's second-hand,' said Dad, 'but everything works. It's grand to be able to drive to work and get back earlier, and petrol doesn't cost much.'

Tessa embraced them again. 'How marvellous! Do you drive, Mum?'

Mrs Morland looked astonished. 'Of course not. Dad does all that. We're lucky because Frank Anderson's got on very well and owns two garages. He does the repairs at cost price, for old times' sake.'

'What old times?' asked Tessa, teasingly.

Mum looked a bit blank. 'Now you come to mention it, I don't really know. He was very sweet on you, and of course his family belongs to our chapel.'

'He's a good chap,' said Dad, settling himself behind the wheel while Mum eased herself into the passenger seat. 'Now that Susan gives us housekeeping and Joseph sends us money, we do very well.'

Mum turned in her seat, a hazardous movement which threatened to shift the gear lever. 'And we don't forget that you've sent us money, my love. It's been much appreciated.'

After the American limousines Tessa found the interior cramped, but she leaned back behind her parents, looking at the backs of their heads – Dad in his bowler, Mum in a discreet brown felt with a very small feather – delighted to be home, watching the familiar scenery, truly happy.

The cottage seemed tiny as she entered the dear little kitchen where a sweet scent of baking seemed to linger. It was no illusion. Susan came hurrying through the door in an apron.

'Tessa!' She flung her arms around her sister. 'Thank goodness you've come home. Don't stay away so long again. I've missed you terribly.'

'She's a grand cook,' said Dad. 'Of course, that's no surprise with the teacher she's had.'

Mum smiled complacently as Susan opened the oven door and took out a tray of pasties. 'I bet you've not tasted a Cornish pasty since you went away,' she said.

Tessa's mouth watered at the memory of crumbling pastry, onions, potatoes and a little meat. Not much. Mum said there shouldn't really be any in a true Cornish pasty, but she thought things didn't taste quite right without it.

Joseph was away so the four of them sat down to their meal and Tessa answered questions as fast as they were fired at her.

'How's Eve?' Mum asked. 'Why didn't she come with you?'

'She likes being in films.'

'Have you fallen out?'

Tessa hesitated. 'I suppose you could say we have.'

'Cousins should stay friends.'

'Quite right,' said Dad, spearing a lump of meat.

'We did work together for quite a time, but she likes a different kind of acting.'

'Oh? What kind?' Mum was frowning.

'I only wanted parts that would help my singing career, but Eve enjoyed the acting more,' dissembled Tessa. 'And we got to know different people. Don't forget, Mum, we were brought up very differently. That must affect us.'

'You're as good as anyone,' snapped Mum, 'and better than many.'

Tessa laughed. 'It wasn't like that. Hollywood is difficult to explain.'

'Did you see any gangsters?' demanded Mum. When Tessa said she hadn't she looked a little disappointed.

'But I saw some of the stars who act as gangsters. James Cagney, Edward G. Robinson, Humphrey Bogart . . .'

'I like him,' said Susan.

'Do you go to the pictures?' asked Tessa.

'Mum says I can. Did you meet Humphrey Bogart?'

'No, unfortunately. Be sure to see him in *The Petrified Forest*. Leslie Howard and Bette Davis are in it too. I saw the preview in Hollywood.'

Susan drew a deep breath. 'Fancy being able to say that so casually! What a glamorous life you've led.'

'Hollywood isn't all glamour,' said Tessa. 'It's wonderful for those who succeed, but dreadful for the many who don't. Have you any thoughts of the stage?'

'No fear! I want my own fashion place, and one day I'll get it. You'll see. But I'm interested in Hollywood. My friends know you were there and ask me questions all the time. They all read the film magazines. Did you meet Clark Gable? Or Errol Flynn? And what about Ronald Coleman? Or Fred Astaire and Ginger Rogers? Is Olivia de Havilland as lovely as she seems on the screen? And—'

'Good gracious!' Mum cried. 'Your sister is scarcely inside the door. Giver her a chance. She's picture mad, Tessa. She'd go twice a week if I let her. It's enough to turn her brain.'

Susan laughed. 'I've still got my brain the right way round, and both feet on the ground. Did you meet any of them, Tessa?'

'I did, or rather I saw them at various places. And, yes, Olivia de Havilland really is beautiful. I'll tell you everything I can in time.'

'Does that mean you'll be staying here?' asked Mum.

'If I may. Until I find a place of my own.'

'If you may, indeed! This is your home.' Mum stood up and began clattering plates as she cleared the table. Susan jumped up to fetch the pudding.

'I know that, Mum, but I'll find a flat. I've got used to having my own place.'

'In London, I suppose?'

'I may need to, though I'll be in Bristol for a while. I've written to Josh through his agent and I'm waiting for a reply. It'll come here, of course.'

'Can you afford a flat?' asked Dad.

'It'll be cheaper for you if you stay at home,' said Mum.

'You can have the bed,' said Susan.

'You could have Joseph's, though we never know when he's going to turn up,' said Mum.

'I'll not put you out and I can afford my own place. I've saved a fair sum of money. Now, tell me what you've all been doing?'

Susan said happily, 'I'm first sales now and resident mannequin for both shops. Did I tell you that Mrs Endicott has opened another place in Bath? It's really very posh. Mrs Endicott says I'm the youngest first sales in Bristol. Will you come to our next show, Tessa? Mrs Endicott hires a couple of girls to help out, but I get the best things to wear.'

Mum shook her head, but smiled indulgently. Times had changed, reflected Tessa, and Mum had changed with them. But not all that much. On Sunday everyone was expected to attend chapel twice during the day, three times for Susan who had been persuaded to teach in afternoon Sunday School.

'She's a good girl,' said Mum after Susan had left. Dad was taking his post-lunch nap and Mum and Tessa sat at the kitchen table, having washed up and made a pot of tea.

Tessa smiled. 'Unlike me?'

'Now then, that's all in the past and forgotten. You were never a bad girl. I think perhaps Dad and me were a bit strict with you. It's often the way with the first one. Times are changing.'

'For the worse?'

Mum sighed. 'I can't tell. Joseph is preaching and saving souls, Susan never does anything without telling Dad and me, and you're a success. I've nothing to grumble about. Except you growing older and not married. Isn't there anyone you like enough to wed?' she ended wistfully.

She looked so sad that Tessa wanted to comfort her. She said, 'There is a man I like a lot.'

'Who is it?'

'Charles Ware. He's older than me, about ten years. But you met him in Weston. Remember?'

'Oh, him. He was very smart.'

'He's more than just his clothes. He has an antique shop now in Park Street.'

'Oh, that Mr Ware. Susan knows him.'

'He wrote to me when I was in the States and asked me to marry him, but it was a joke.'

'A joke! No man would propose unless he meant it.'

Tessa began to wish she hadn't said so much. Now Mum would worry at the subject.

'Not usually, but we've had a jokey kind of relationship.' Tessa was glad she no longer blushed readily or she would certainly have coloured up at the memory of Charles' expert love-making. To take her mother's mind off him, she said, 'You know, Mum, I thought for a long time I was in love with Paul.'

550

'Your cousin?'

'Yes. I was very unhappy when he married Andrea.'

Mum put out her hand and covered Tessa's. 'My poor girl.'

The gesture and words brought a lump to Tessa's throat. 'You're a wonderful mother. I've met the other kind. Eve's mother—' She stopped, but Mum was waiting expectantly. 'I don't think Eve's mother cares tuppence for her. Nor did her father. Eve is such a lost soul.'

'Never say that,' said Mum quickly.

'I didn't mean in the biblical sense. She seems to have no anchor, no guide-lines to tell her the way she should behave.'

'Does that mean she's been living a sinful life?'

'Don't ask me to judge her, Mum. I'm very fond of her. And I know she cares a lot for you and Dad.'

Mum opened her mouth, then closed it and got up to make more tea.

Joseph returned that night. He was very thin and dressed entirely in black. He kissed his elder sister ceremoniously. He did everything ceremoniously, thought Tessa. He moved, ate, drank and talked in a ceremonious way which made her nervous. It made her parents nervous, too.

Susan was the only one who seemed unaffected. 'Been to any good meetings lately?' she asked.

Joseph frowned slightly. 'You know I have. I never go to any other kind. How is your Sunday School class? Proceeding along the right lines, I trust.'

'I do my best,' said Susan, 'but it's difficult for children to think of God when their bottoms are hanging out of their trousers and knickers and their poor feet are blistered from the holes in their shoes.'

Joseph frowned again. 'Unemployment is bad,' he conceded, 'but nothing should interfere with the revelation of God's mercy and love.'

'They might find that easier to believe if someone gave them decent things to wear. Most of the girls dress in their mother's or big sister's cut downs, and some of the women are bad at needlework and make a real hash of the sewing.'

'Perhaps you could do something more constructive than criticise?' said Joseph. 'You are a skilled needlewoman.'

Mum intervened. 'She's teasing you, Joseph. She takes a little evening class in the vestry and teaches anyone who wants to learn how to sew.'

He turned his gaze full upon Susan who bore it with aplomb. 'Teasing is all very well,' he pronounced, 'but plain truth is infinitely better.'

'Did I tell you a lie?' She turned to the others. 'Did I tell him a lie?'

'You lied by implication,' said Joseph.

Tessa wondered mischievously what he would say if she confessed *her* sins.

Dad said, 'That's enough from both of you. Make the cocoa, Mum. It's time we were all in bed.'

Tessa and Susan whispered to one another in the darkness. There were several young men who had made various propositions to Susan, including marriage, but she intended to have a career and money behind her before she settled down.

Tessa lay and thought about Charles. Tomorrow she would go to his shop.


The morning post brought a letter from Josh who professed himself delighted at her return and offered her a job immediately.

'It's in Bristol,' said Tessa excitedly to her mother. 'He's got work lined up for a couple of months then it's off to London for a regular spot on the wireless and engagements in hotels.'

Joseph frowned. 'You still intend to use God's gift to sing corrupting songs?'

'They are not corrupting,' protested Tessa. 'As a matter of fact, I've written some myself. Perfectly harmless ones.'

'Have you?' Susan was fascinated. 'Do sing them to us.'

'Not this early,' said Tessa.

'Come along, Susan, or you'll be late for work,' said Mum. And Susan grabbed her hat, bestowed kisses all round and departed.

Tessa wrote briefly to Josh, posted the letter and walked to Kingswood tram depot. She rode on the top of the trams, enjoying the views of her native city. Arriving in Park Street she looked in at Mrs Endicott's where Susan was engaged in selling an exclusive gown to a customer in fox furs.

'It's simply you, madam,' she was saying. 'As soon as the gown arrived I thought of you. In fact,' she lowered her voice confidentially, 'I refused to allow another lady to see it until you had had the chance. If you don't want it, I'm sure she will.'

Her honeyed tones conveyed no threat, but the customer caught the message. She smiled. 'So kind,' she murmured. 'I'll try it on.'

When Susan had disappeared with the customer Mrs Endicott laughed softly. 'The frock's as good as sold,' she told Tessa. 'Your sister is a marvel. I hope she works for me for a good many more years.'

Miss Benson, the alteration hand, crept from her cubby-hole, her apron stuck with pins, pieces of thread clinging to her woolly jumper. 'I saw you in the pictures, Tessa. You're very good. I don't know how you could bear to leave Hollywood.'

'It was a sudden decision. I'm happy to be home.'

'There's nowhere to beat it,' said Miss Benson.

As Tessa walked on up the steep hill, she admitted to herself that she missed the glamour and excitement of the film world and wondered if she would ever return. She looked into the shops, wandering into one or two, buying nothing. She was killing time because she half dreaded the idea of meeting Charles. By the time she reached his place she had persuaded herself that she hoped he'd be out.

553

He was in. She was ushered to the back room with great ceremony and he looked up from studying a book of artifacts and prices. Mr Harris faded discreetly away as Charles jumped up so suddenly the book slid to the floor.

'Tessa, my—' He swept her into his arms. 'It's great to see you.' He released her without kissing her.

She held up her face. 'No friendly kiss?'

He laughed. 'When I kiss you it'll be more than friendly.'

'Sure of yourself, aren't you?'

'No,' he said, suddenly serious. 'Not at all sure. You never answered my suggestion.'

'Which one was that?'

'You know damn well! Would you like coffee? Wine?'

'Wine? This early? Coffee, please. Do you often drink first thing in the morning?'

'I don't call ten-thirty first thing in the morning. My day starts around seven and often earlier. And I drink in the day only in the way of business. I keep good wines here for my more discerning clients.'

'Is the shop still doing well?'

'It most certainly is.'

Tessa sat on a wide chair with cabriole legs. 'Isn't this a bit expensive for everyday use?' She looked around. 'In fact, the whole room is like a treasure house.'

Charles laughed. 'It is. More than one client has decided to make a purchase after enjoying my hospitality here.'

'You mean, you fill them with heady wine then sell them something they didn't know they wanted?'

He grinned. 'It's all good stuff. What you are sitting on is a Georgian settee for two.' He struck a romantic pose, one hand to his forehead, 'Perhaps one day we may share it together.'

She laughed.

'Your sister often wanders up this way during her lunch hour. She's an excellent saleswoman. Once when I was busy she sold a vase to a lady on my behalf. I gave her commission and she was too good a businesswoman to refuse. She's extremely pretty.'

Tessa was surprised by a pang of jealousy.

'You've nothing to fear, darling. Susan is just a delightful child to me.'

Tessa, feeling rather raw because he had correctly interpreted her thought, said unguardedly, 'Men have married delightful children in the past.'

'Good God! What put such an idea in your head. In any case, I intend to marry you.'

'Then you weren't joking?'

'Absolutely not! Did you think I was?'

'I wasn't sure.'

Charles sat beside her, sliding an arm about her waist, tilting her chin to force her to look him in the face. 'I love you, Tessa. I want you to be my wife.'

She felt breathless. His nearness set her heart racing and filled her body with tormenting desire.

His arm tightened. 'You want me, don't you?'

'Yes, I do. But is that love?'

'Won't you give it a try?'

'Marry you to test my feelings? I can't do that. Marriage is for life. What if I made a mistake?'

'Tessa, I love you. I'd do everything, be anything you want. I'd make you love me.'

'A man who would do everything and be anything I want would be very bad for me. I can get extremely bossy.'

'Don't make light of it, Tessa, please.'

She sighed, turned her face to his and kissed him softly on the mouth. 'I care more for you than for any other man I've met. Won't that do for now?'

'More than for Paul?'

'Much, much more. He was just a silly girl's fancy.'

'He made you suffer.'

'Everyone needs to suffer at least once.'

'Did you meet anyone in Hollywood?'

'By anyone, I take it you mean any special man? Just one. My agent.'

'You fell for him?'

'No.'

'You made love to him?'

'Yes.'

'And he let you go? What a fool.'

'No, he wasn't a fool. Just weak at times.'

'Why? What did he do to make you think that?'

'What makes you think he did anything?'

'A certain something in your voice.'

'That's a good first line for a song.'

'What happened?' Charles asked.

'He was tempted and he fell. I was a very unwilling witness. And that's all I intend to say on the matter.' She extricated herself from his embrace and stood up. 'Josh will be back in Bristol soon and I'm going to work for him again.'

Charles leaned back and lit a cigarette. His upper lip was slightly damp, his hands shook a little. He held out his case to her and she smoked as she wandered restlessly round the room, stopping to peer at a picture or examine an artifact while he watched her.

'Will you go to bed with me, Tessa?' he asked.

She turned and smiled. 'Well, I do like a man with a subtle approach.'

He sprang to his feet, held her tight, stared down into her mocking eyes, and asked in toffee-sweet tones, 'My dearest, darling love, will you grace my couch?'

Laughing she said, 'How can I resist?'

'How about now?'

'Good lord, drinking and fornication before lunch!'

'I don't call our love-making fornication. Will you come home with me? At once? Damn it, I've waited long enough.'

'You've been very patient. All right, I'll come.'

He left the shop to Albert's care and they drove to the house across the suspension bridge.

Their love-making was infinitely sweet, gentle at first, then explosively, marvellously violent as her passion rose to match his. Tessa lay back, sated as she had not been since they were last together. She wanted to tell him how happy he had made her, but in her euphoria was afraid she might say too much. It was tempting to imagine herself married to him, cherished, his love always ready for her. But it wasn't all she wanted. 'You were wonderful,' she said.

'So were you. Can't you see, Tessa, how suited we are?'

'I do see. Sweetheart, don't look downcast. I must have my time of freedom.'

'Marriage to me won't put you in chains.'

She smoothed his face with a gentle touch. 'I know. I trust you, but I can't give my answer yet. I promise one thing, though. From now on, I'll keep you informed of what I'm doing.'

'I'll be content with that for a while. But I shall ask you again.'

'Good. I must let Mum know how persistent you are. She thinks I'm going to be left on the shelf.'

'You're not afraid of that?'

'Sometimes, the shelf, without emotional complications, looks very tempting. That's a joke, Charles.'

'Don't let the joke go on too long, my love. Such jokes have a habit of losing their humour.'

Josh returned and immediately contacted Tessa who was still living at home. The whole family, even Joseph, had wanted her to stay, though her brother's motives were suspect. He still hoped to convert his sister to religious singing. 'To tell you the truth,' he explained earnestly, 'I don't see the necessity even of hymns. Christianity should be all bible study and prayer. The only joy should be in thanksgiving. But if people must sing, let them have holy songs. You could lead people to God with your voice.'

Mum listened and when he had gone out she sighed and said, 'You know, I find our Joseph a bit gloomy at times. I mean to say, you know I devote my life to the chapel, but there's no harm in a bit of a laugh. We always have one at the Bright Hour.'

When Tessa was persuaded to stay with her family for the short time Josh would be in Bristol, Dad smiled and nodded his approval.

Josh greeted her in the cocktail lounge of his hotel. 'You look sensational! I saw you on the screen. What made you decide to give it up? What happened to Eve? Sorry, I shouldn't overwhelm you with questions. Shall we have cocktails? I'll order them and you can tell me about Hollywood.'

They spent a couple of hours chatting about the film colony, about old times and new ones. Josh and his band were very much in demand. 'I haven't had a really first-rate singer since you left. You're all I need to make everything perfect. Have you written any more songs? You have? Good. How do you feel about making a gramophone record?'

'Of my songs?'

'Yes, among others. With my band?'

'Is it really possible?'

'Sure it is. I tell you, Tessa, there's good money to be made in sheet music and records. And it doesn't just stop at one sale. You get royalties. A regular income. Provided you can keep up the supply.'

'I definitely like the sound of that. Fancy having a regular income by doing just one thing.'

'So you'll record with us?'

'You bet I will.'

Josh grinned. 'Picked up a few Americanisms?'

'Sure thing, honey. Josh, don't you ever want to return to the States?'

'I get a yen for my country, yes. I'll visit sometime, but I've no close relatives left. It's people who make a place important to you.'

'People?' repeated Tessa. 'Yes, you're absolutely right. Talking of people, is Sammy still with you?'

Josh looked sombre. 'He is. Sometimes the hustle and bustle seem too much for him, he's not getting any younger, but he's keeping his cousin's family. Heaven knows how they manage in that small house. Soon, though, he'll be getting his first royalties, and when you've made recordings I know our sales will increase.'

'I could help Sammy by singing?'

'Of course. We all work for one another.'

'That's the nicest thing I've heard in years.'

Sammy looked careworn and had aged far too quickly. He kissed Tessa as naturally as if he were her father.

'What happened in Germany?' she asked.

'Horrible things. Terrible things. And it's getting worse. Tessa, Adolf Hitler is making his plans to conquer as many people as he can. In the process he is practising unbelievable cruelty. Not only on Jews but on other races, even on gypsies.'

'Gypsies? Why?'

'He considers them to have tainted blood. According to him, everyone must be ethnically pure. Anyone who isn't an Aryan is deported or arrested. Jews are struggling to make enough to eat, and often are tormented in the streets, while folk just stand around and laugh. Some are tortured for trivial reasons or no reason at all, in private, where their screams can't be heard.'

'Oh, God, that's dreadful!'

'There are other horrors. Forcible sterilisation of non-Aryans, or tramps, or the mentally sick. There is even talk of eradicating those whose brain is retarded.'

'Eradication? Does that mean what I think it means?'

'Yes, people slaughtered like diseased animals. Haven't you read about it? It's no secret. Hitler is too arrogant to care what other countries think.'

'Americans don't pay much attention to European news. I suppose you can't blame them. They don't want to get involved in another war. They know that refugees are coming in and most make them welcome, especially the clever ones, but that's as far as it goes.'

Sammy shook his head. 'There are the other dictators, too, but none so evil as Hitler. I tell you, Tessa, his wickedness is a stain on Germany, and that stain will spread and spread until it takes in the whole of Europe.'

'I've heard a lot of talk of war since I came home.'

'It will happen. It must happen. The world can't stand by and allow millions to be cruelly enslaved.'

Tessa didn't want to believe everything he said. Surely he was being overly pessimistic? 'You had a bad time yourself?'

'I did. So many obstacles were put in my way but I managed to get to my cousin in the end, what's left of him. He's so frail and ill. I was lucky to get his family out, but it was terrible to leave him rotting in that awful camp.'

They were silent for a while, then Sammy asked, 'Where is Eve? Will she be joining the band?'

'I don't think so. She found Hollywood to her liking.'

Tessa went back to performing with Josh and his band. One night she sang at a private dance which went on and on. Afterwards she arrived home in the early hours. She had bought a smart little car and parked it in the lane. She was surprised to see lights in the cottage and ran the rest of the way, fearing to find someone ill. She opened the kitchen door which was unlocked and stepped into the kitchen.

There sat Eve at the kitchen table, Mum opposite in her dressing gown and steel curlers. Both had their hands round steaming cups of cocoa.

'Eve?'

'Tessa! I'm so happy to see you.' Eve flung her arms around her cousin and, to everyone's surprise, burst into tears. 'I got to the station very late and hired a taxi here,' she sobbed. 'I couldn't wait to come home.'

Mum patted her shoulder. 'There, there, Eve, my love.' She said to Tessa, 'Dad doesn't know yet. Nothing wakes him. He'll be ever so glad in the morning.'

Tessa hugged Eve and patted her back like a baby while Mum smiled and tutted.

Eve wiped her eyes. 'What an idiot you must think me. I *am* an idiot. I've done such stupid things. Why didn't you tell me, Tessa?'

'Well, er—'

'No, of course you can't answer. I never wanted your good advice. Hollywood stinks.'

'That's not very nice language,' said Mum, but she was too happy to be cross. 'I don't really understand why you've both left the films, though I'm glad. What's it really like?'

Tessa said, 'I'd need all night to tell you. It's not as glamorous as the magazines make out. Like everywhere else it's what you make of it. Are you going back, Eve?'

'I don't think so, though I didn't really intend to leave. I just meant to go to Aunt Betsy's funeral, then I knew that what I wanted most in the world was to be with you and dear Cousins Walter and Lily and Susan and Joseph. And even old Ruff.' At the sound of his name the dog looked up and Eve scratched the top of his head.

Mum patted her arm. 'You can join Tessa in the singing. She can, can't she?'

'Can we be Kissing Cousins again, Tessa?'

'I'm sure we can.' She dismissed as unworthy the slight pang of regret for her solo career.

'Eve, you must stay here tonight,' said Mum.

'Of course you must. You can have my bed. I'll sleep in the kitchen. I'll be comfortable with plenty of cushions.'

Eve refused the sacrifice and Mum actually made her a bed on the couch in the best room, a privilege never before accorded to a living soul.

'She's a dear little thing, isn't she?' said Mum as she and Tessa tiptoed up the stairs by candlelight.

Tessa smiled. Eve was inches taller than Mum, but she knew exactly what she meant. Eve still possessed an air of fragile vulnerability and now it was overlaid with something else. Tessa wondered if Eve would tell her just what had sent her rushing back to her English relatives.

# Chapter Twenty-Five

Josh decided to record Tessa's new song at once.

'Haven't you used "Remember?" at all while I was away?' she asked.

'No. We've played the music for dancing, but the words are yours. I just kept hoping you'd come back and record it for me. I'm sure it'll sell in thousands. You could end up rich and famous, Tessa. How about that?'

'I like the idea of fame through my own songs, and I'm not exactly averse to money either.'

'Good, though you're not acquisitive, are you?'

'What makes you say that?'

'I've heard you could have gone much further in Hollywood. And then there's Charles.'

Tessa frowned. 'Charles?'

'Don't get mad at me. He was lonely and got pretty tight one night and confided in me. He's nuts about you.'

'And?'

'And he's rich.'

'Yes.'

'He wants to marry you.'

'How charming of you both to talk about me in your cups.'

'It wasn't like that. The poor man had no one to confide in. I just happened to be there.'

'Where are we performing next?'

Josh sighed. 'You *are* mad. I should have kept my big mouth shut. We're on stage at the Princes Theatre. There's a good variety bill.'

'I thought variety was supposed to be dead?'

'It still has a kick, and if there's a war it's bound to come back. Variety is the spice of life, don't forget.'

'Very amusing.' She couldn't stay angry with Josh.

She sang her new song from the stage of the Princes Theatre. It was received with acclaim and a little later she and the band recorded it. They had rehearsed until they were note perfect.

Record sessions were an ordeal. Once the wax recording disc had begun turning no one could afford to make a mistake or they had to do the whole thing again. This cost money and was frowned upon by the record companies. Eve missed a cue one day and was terribly upset. The band was tolerant, though when the trumpeter played a wrong note they called him every name which Tessa had heard and some which were new to her. Still, the records got made and she and Eve became accustomed to seeing their pictures in music shop windows.

Recording her own song made Tessa far more nervous than usual, perhaps because the words exposed her feelings. She breathed deeply to calm herself and sang:

> I'll never fall in love again,
> There's too much sorrow, too much pain
> To bear.
> And so I'll play the coward's part,
> And keep a guard upon my heart,
> Not share
> The idiot gold of loving bliss,
> Or taste the magic of a kiss,
> Not I.
> I'll not lie in the dreaming shade
> Of crazy hopes that always fade
> And die.
> But then you pass my way
> And dark night turns to day
> I fall to dreaming one more time
> That your caresses can be mine
> And love will rule,
> I'm just a fool.

The record was an immediate success and Eve congratulated her cousin. Tessa was now enjoying life as never
before. Eve was so amenable that Tessa was afraid she
was bottling something up which would be released in a
massive explosion of temper. But all she ever manifested
these days was irritation at the things which annoyed
any performer. A dressing-room which had not been
properly cleaned so that their stage gowns picked up
dust, a fractious act which allowed bickering to spill over
back-stage. She was cross with herself for even small
failures in getting a song exactly right.

Tessa had never succeeded in actually disliking her
cousin. Now she loved her with a much stronger love
than before. God only knew what had changed her, but
it had given her a fragility which made everyone want
to protect her. They moved to London and the Kissing
Cousins' career took a leap upwards as they made
records whose popularity was helped hugely by regular
broadcasts.

'The more we play something on the wireless, the
more the sales go up,' Josh enthused.

'It was a good day for me when I met you,' Tessa said.

'And a good day for the boys and me when I met you.
The Kissing Cousins can compete with anybody: Vera
Lynn, Evelyn Dall, Bruce Trent, Peggy Dell, any of
them. They're all wonderful singers, but no better than
mine. Not even the Americans beat you girls.'

'Have you heard them?' asked Eve.

'Only on record. Have you heard them in person?'

'Some of them. Tommy Dorsey's band has Jo Stafford
and a young fellow called Frank Sinatra, very thin but
with a powerful voice. And there's Dick Haymes and
Peggy Lee, Perry Como and Doris Day—'

'Enough,' laughed Josh. 'I'll back you girls against any
one of them.'

When they next visited Bristol, Mum said, 'You can't
move in town without your faces staring at me from

some window or other.' But Tessa suspected that she wasn't altogether displeased, while Susan was ecstatic.

'When anyone learns that I'm your sister and Eve's cousin they treat me like a celebrity. It's very exciting.'

Charles always had time for Tessa. He was a tender lover who studied her happiness and she basked in his love.

'You get more wonderful,' she said after a particularly pleasurable bout of love-making. They were always hungry for each other.

'So do you. One day our whole lives will be lived just for one another.'

The words were enough to make her uneasy. She was content to let things drift on and had hoped he felt the same. 'One day perhaps. I've told you, I'm not ready to settle down. If you meet someone else—' She stopped. She hated the idea.

'I shan't.'

'How can you be so sure?'

'Don't forget I was playing the field before you grew up. There's no doubt at all in my mind who I want.'

Tessa and Eve always stayed with the Morlands on their Bristol visits. Dad had used his skills to make a small extension reached through the best room, an enormous concession in itself because it meant that it must be left unlocked for access. The extra room was just big enough for a bed, a small wardrobe and dressing table. A rag rug waited at the side of the bed to save Eve's feet from the cold linoleum and Mum had made pretty flowered curtains. They presented it to her as her very own place.

Her gratitude brought her close to tears. 'It should really go to Susan or Tessa,' she said. 'Susan's camp bed can't be very comfortable.'

'I could sleep standing up,' said Susan. 'You needn't worry about me.'

'I hope you'll look upon this as your second home, Eve,' said Mum. 'All I want now is for you and our

Tessa to meet good men and settle down as near me as possible. I'd like to see your children in chapel, then I'd really be happy.'

They had been in England for several months before Eve said, 'I've had a letter from my mother. She tells me that Paul's elder son is ill. Uncle Reginald has written, too. He wants me to visit them and find out exactly what's the matter with Reggie. Tessa, will you come with me?'

'Of course.'

'You're not worried, are you, at the idea of seeing Paul? If so—'

'Not in the least,' said Tessa too cheerfully for Eve to doubt her sincerity.

Paul had put on more weight and Andrea had grown thinner. 'They look like Jack Spratt and his wife only the other way round,' whispered Eve.

'Reggie is very poorly,' said Andrea. 'We were told from the first that his condition would deteriorate and he would not live past early boyhood.'

'Poor little soul,' said Eve.

Andrea gave her a resentful look. 'You don't know him.'

'It just seems a shame, that's all.'

'I disagree. My son has no chance of making anything of himself. He is a burden to himself and those about him. Death can be merciful in such cases. Paul agrees with me, don't you?'

He said, 'Andrea's right. She usually is.'

'How was he when you last saw him?' asked Eve.

'Not good. Not good at all,' said Paul.

Tessa hated the whole scene: Paul's lack-lustre agreement with Andrea, their apparent carelessness in relinquishing the life of a child whose only crime was to be born different. It reminded her of what Sammy said about Hitler eradicating the weak and simple. She wanted to leave and not come back here ever again.

'How long ago did you see Reggie?' Eve asked.

'When was it, darling?' Paul asked his wife. 'About a month?'

'Three months,' she said.

'How do you know what his condition is?' demanded Eve.

'We are in constant touch with the home through letters and telephone,' said Andrea, growing angry at Eve's intrusive questioning.

'Could I visit him?' she asked.

Nothing she might have said could have emphasised more the change in her attitude.

Paul and Andrea stared at her as if she had gone crazy. 'Why should you?' asked Andrea. 'He scarcely recognises us. He would not know you. In fact, you could frighten him.'

'Perhaps a visit from Eve would amuse him a little?' said Paul.

'Nonsense!' snapped Andrea. 'I forbid you to go near my son. You could upset him quite disastrously. I won't have him upset.'

To the amazement of Eve and Tessa, her voice broke and she turned her head away.

Eve said quickly, 'I wouldn't wish to distress him, Andrea. Uncle Reginald asked me to enquire after his health.'

'Do you really want to see him?' asked Andrea, turning to look at them. Her face had resumed its customary cold expression, but the mask had cracked briefly and it was enough for Eve.

'If you will give your permission.'

'I'll drive you there,' said Paul.

'It's kind of you, but there's no need for you . . ,'

'I want to drive you,' he said quickly. 'And of course Tessa as well, if she wishes.'

'Thank you. I should like to see Reggie.'

Timothy, the younger son, was brought down and the girls exclaimed suitably over his strength and beauty. It wasn't difficult. He really was a lovely child and obviously intelligent.

Arrangements were made. Outside, sitting in Tessa's car, the two girls looked at one another.

'Would you believe it?' said Eve. 'I thought Andrea was nothing but a cold-hearted bitch, but she seems to care about that poor little soul.'

'I think Paul does, too,' Tessa said.

'That must please you?'

'It does in a way. I must say I'm glad to know I didn't spend so long thinking I was in love with a totally callous man.'

'Will you marry Charles?' Tessa frowned and Eve said quickly, 'Sorry. Didn't mean to pry. Entirely your own business.'

Tessa drove down the lane to the common. She said carefully, 'Did you meet anyone special in Hollywood?'

'No. There's no one I'd have given a cuss for. It's still David with me. I love him.'

'You've been out together since you came back, haven't you?'

'Yes. I believe he likes me. We're friends.' Eve stared from the window. 'Tessa, I'm truly sorry for the way I bitched you up. O'Neill didn't really want me. It was all my fault.'

'It takes two to make love.'

'I know, but I did everything that night but actually rape him.'

'A woman can't rape a man,' pointed out Tessa drily.

'She can when she deliberately drives him crazy.'

'Well, maybe.' Tessa turned to the road that led home. 'I'm glad you spoke up, Eve, but there isn't any need for you to worry. I was furious at the time, but I didn't love O'Neill, nor did he love me. He only thought he did.'

'You might have become a famous film star.'

'And I might not!' She turned into the lane, parked the car and switched off the engine. 'I left America for more than one reason. O'Neill thought Britain would go to war again. Sammy Jacobs is convinced that it's inevitable.'

'He could be biased.'

'Maybe, but it seems to be getting more likely and if anything happens I want to be here with my family.' For a moment she stared up the lane at the cottage. 'You could go home. You are American. No one would blame you.'

Eve said softly, following her gaze, 'As long as Cousins Walter and Lily will have me, I shall think of this as my home. I love them so much. I wish they were my parents.'

Her last impassioned sentence silenced Tessa. They climbed from the car and walked up the lane together.

Paul drove them out into the Somerset countryside to the private home where Reggie stayed. A nurse wheeled him into the visiting room in a large perambulator. Tessa and Eve stared down in pity and horror. His body had not matched the growth of his head. He could only sit up with help and his head lolled. When he was touched he emitted an unearthly scream which fractured the nerves of both girls.

'Poor Andrea,' said Eve. 'I can understand why she can't bear it.'

Paul smoothed his son's head where there were silky strands of hair. When the child screamed he removed his hand hurriedly.

Tessa bent over the pram. 'Reggie,' she said. 'Do you remember me?'

He stared up at her with uncomprehending eyes. His loose mouth opened in a grotesque smile. They left quite soon. Paul sat in the driving seat for a few moments before beginning the journey back. 'You see, don't you, that it would be better if he should go? Andrea and I do care for him, though we are weak when it comes to looking after him.'

The girls couldn't answer. Who were they to judge?

Eve said later to Tessa, 'According to Joseph, Reggie will soon be in the arms of Jesus now, smiling at his grandmother.'

'Don't mock!' chided Tessa.

'I wasn't. Not really. I would like to think it was true.'
When some weeks later they were informed of his death
they felt only relief that he and his family were spared
any more suffering. They wrote separately to his
grandfather.

Most of the world seemed to have erupted into a bloody
battlefield. Japan was destroying the Chinese, Italy's
Mussolini had swept into Ethiopia, using mustard gas on
the defenceless population, Spain was a horror of civil
war, and in England Sir Oswald Mosley and his comic
army of fascist brownshirts were suddenly no longer
amusing. There was rioting in India between Hindus and
Moslems and even in Palestine, Mum noted with fearful
dismay, there was cruel fighting between Jews and
Arabs.

'Just imagine it,' she said, shaking the newspaper in
her agitation, 'the place where our Lord was born and
crucified.' She read fearfully about people being bombed
from aeroplanes. 'How can such things happen?' she
wanted to know. 'Fancy dropping bombs, not knowing
where they'll land. It's dreadful.'

'Britain was bombed in the last war,' reminded Dad.

'I know, but nothing like what they can do now. We
can't possibly go to war! We can't allow an enemy to hurt
people and knock down our lovely cities.'

Dad said soothingly, 'Their aeroplanes will never get
as far as Bristol, love.'

'I hope not, though it'll be terrible for the places
they can reach. Do you really think there'll be a war,
Walter?'

Dad smoked his pipe thoughtfully. 'Hitler has
marched into Czechoslovakia,' he said. 'No one seems
inclined to protest, except Anthony Eden. He's resigned
from the government over our appeasement policy.'

'Germany's not our business,' said Mum.

'Not yet, I suppose, but dictators always want more
and Britain is a country worth having.'

'I know that,' said Mum indignantly.

It was a relief to Tessa to immerse herself in the world of the theatre where there was much talk of an eighteen-year-old ballet dancer called Margot Fonteyn who had triumphed at Sadler's Wells in *Giselle*.

In Germany, in the course of one night, seven thousand Jewish shops were looted and bystanders laughed as youths beat Jews senseless with lead piping.

'You see,' said Dad, to the assembled company round the kitchen table, 'he'll just go on and on. Someone will have to stop him.'

'The Austrians welcomed him,' said Eve.

Later Tessa asked Josh apprehensively, 'Do you think there will be a war?'

'I don't see how we can avoid it.'

Tessa said, 'You could return to the States.'

'I'll stay,' he said. 'Britain's done me proud and I'll not desert her.'

Josh and His Melody Men divided their time between London and Bristol and Tessa and Eve were able to spend more time in the little cottage near Kingswood. Sammy came there to say goodbye. He was retiring at last and going to live with Hannah and their extended family as best they could.

'Hannah and me will have our pensions and I'll take odd jobs in Manchester,' he said. 'There's always someone needs a piano player. I'll get by. Josh says I'm to let him know if I fall into real need. He's a good man.'

'Yes, though I don't suppose you'll ever complain.'

Sammy shrugged. 'I should complain? My cousin may be dying or dead. His wife gets whiter and thinner by the day, in spite of all that my Hannah cooks for her. And I haven't heard from Reuben in an age. He thought he'd placate the Nazis by lying low. He was wrong, of course. Even so-called Aryan children are forbidden to speak to Jewish children. They teach the little ones to hate.'

Prime Minister Chamberlain visited Hitler and

returned flourishing a piece of paper which he said ensured that there would be no war between Britain and Germany. He declared, 'I believe it is peace for our time.' He was hailed as a deliverer by some, as a gullible fool by others.

In spite of all the uncertainty, life remained sweet for Tessa. Her songs kept selling well on record and in sheet music and her income rose accordingly so that she was able to help out generously at home, to buy a better car, and to save money. Her involvement with Charles grew sweeter. Their shared passion was a comfort when she was bothered by Mum's fear of war and Dad's resignation before an uncertain future.

'Susan isn't worried,' said Tessa to Charles as they lay together in the gathering darkness one night. 'She can't visualise what awfulness it could bring.'

'Few people can, I suspect.'

'Can you?'

He climbed out of bed to fetch more cigarettes. Tessa watched him. His body was well proportioned and strong and gave her the most exquisite pleasure. He lit cigarettes for them both.

'Will Eve stay in Britain when war begins?' he asked.

'What do you mean *when*? You mean *if*.'

'I know what I mean.'

Tessa jumped up and began to dress, her movements quick and angry.

'Nothing is gained by not facing the truth,' said Charles. 'I thought you understood that.'

'Chamberlain promised peace.'

'He is an optimist. Hitler has to be stopped. Have you forgotten Sammy and his relatives?'

Tessa sat down on the side of the bed. 'Oh, God, I suppose you're right, but it's unbearable. And the awful thing is I sometimes think of it as an interruption to my career, just as I'm getting famous. That's horribly selfish of me, isn't it?'

Charles laughed softly and stubbed out his cigarette.

She was still in her underwear and he smoothed her long back with expert fingers.

She shook herself pettishly. 'Stop it. Haven't you had enough?'

'I've never had enough of you, my darling.'

Tessa turned to him and kissed his exploring hand. 'I – care a lot for you.'

'You almost said it.'

'Said what?'

'That you love me. You do, you know.'

'I do, in a way.'

Charles didn't persist. He seemed prepared to bide his time. Once more they embraced, their passion seemingly endless.

Afterwards he lay and watched her dressing, his hands behind his head. 'When war breaks out, Tessa, don't be in a hurry to join anything. Entertainers will be needed as much as guns.'

'Do you think so?'

'Would I say it if I didn't?'

He wouldn't. Charles never said a word to her he didn't mean. He was eminently suited to be a husband. Mum and Dad thought so too, once they had got over their original shyness and their slight hostility at his (in their eyes) decadent background.

In February, 1939, free air raid shelters were delivered to London homes. To qualify for one it was necessary for the household income to be below two hundred and fifty pounds and there were plenty that fulfilled that condition. The shelters were ramshackle-looking affairs which had to be sunk partially into the ground and were received by many with raucous amusement.

In March Mr Chamberlain gave a solemn undertaking: if Hitler invaded Poland as he threatened, Britain would go to war. He was cheered by MPs in the House and lauded by many. Minds were turning to the apparent inevitability of conflict and the British championship of the underdog held sway. Mum read the news gloomily. Two million, five hundred thousand children were being evacuated and many arrived in Bristol, a safe area. Conscription of twenty year olds also began.

Eve was drifting along in a kind of daze. She listened to the talk of war, she sang with Tessa, she was punctual and conscientious. Tessa once said she should write to her mother more often and Eve had flown into a brief spate of temper. Tessa had laughed. 'Thank God! I like to catch a glimpse of the old Eve sometimes.'

Eve had laughed with her, but much of the heart had gone out of her. At first her newfound freedom from the dark terrors of her nightmare had been heady, but she wanted love, she needed it. She could no longer take refuge in its physical aspects. When she made love she wanted to be *in* love.

David was never far from her thoughts. He had travelled to Australia again and seldom wrote. Sometimes she heard of him through friends who included Kitty and Rupert Bamford and Tiddles Henley. The craziness of their earlier days had gone. They were all married and waiting apprehensively like everyone else for Hitler's next move. Only Poppy hadn't changed. She, too, was married and led her husband by the nose, as Eve told Tessa later.

Hitler invaded Poland and on a quiet, sunny Sunday morning, Chamberlain announced on the wireless that Britain was at war with Germany.

The Morlands and Eve sat and listened together. Afterwards Walter switched off the wireless. 'So it's come,' he said. He looked infinitely sad.

There were tears in Mum's eyes. 'I can't believe it. Not again. Not so soon after the last one. All our boys, all our men, they'll have to go, just like last time, and lots won't come back . . .' She couldn't continue. She just stared with frightened eyes at the people she loved.

At five o'clock France announced that she, too, was at war.

Germany wasted no time. On that same day a U-boat

575

sank the Glasgow liner, *Athenia*, with the loss of one hundred and twelve lives. Londoners waited fearfully for the bombardment to begin. Nothing happened. As the months passed Mum relaxed. 'They're calling it the phoney war. Maybe it'll all blow over.'

The war proved more of an irritation than a threat. Every light had to be blacked out, car head lamps were painted over leaving only a slit and, with no street lights, walking and driving at night became hazardous. The carrying of gas masks frightened people at first, bringing memories of gas attacks in the Great War, then they were looked upon as a nuisance. Women made covers for the awkward square cases to match their outfits and many used them as receptacles for sandwiches and the like.

In the early days of war all places of amusement were arbitrarily closed down.

Josh didn't lose hope. 'It's a panic measure. They're sure to open them again soon.' He was right and the theatres, cinemas and dance halls were re-opened and Bristolians flocked to them in greater numbers than ever before, as if they needed to take comfort in romance and music and the company of their fellows.

Eve said, 'It looks as if the only casualties we'll get will be from road accidents.'

When Tessa repeated her words to Charles he said, 'Wait and see.'

'You're such a pessimist,' she teased.

They made love and later he said, 'Won't you make an honest man of me now?'

'Don't joke about it!'

'I'm deadly serious. This might be a phoney war at present, but it's going to get a good deal more real.'

'If the war is phoney we can afford to wait. If it's for real it's best not to tie one another down. Marriage should be undertaken in a calmer atmosphere.'

'My God, Tessa, sometimes you sound like a grandmother.'

'I do not! Why?'

'Such caution, such wisdom in one so young.' She laughed. 'There are lots who don't think your way. Couples are overwhelming churches and registry offices.'

'Yes, and I suppose there will be a lot of women having babies which will be an added problem for them. And, of course, some of their men won't return and they'll have to struggle on alone. I wouldn't want to bear a child in wartime.'

'If everyone thinks like you there won't be anyone to replace the dead.'

Tessa shuddered. 'Don't.'

'And have you thought that the men who lose their lives will die happier for knowing they've left a part of themselves behind?'

'I've heard all the arguments.'

'So it's useless to ask you to marry me before I join my regiment?'

'Your regiment? You're not old enough to have been in a regiment.'

'I was an officer cadet at school.'

'You don't have to go. You're too old.'

'I'm only ten years older than you, my girl, and there's plenty of life left in me yet.'

'You give me proof on every possible occasion. If you fight as well as you make love . . .'

'For that bawdy remark you will be punished by a bottle of champagne when we have our farewell romp in bed.'

'Romp in bed?'

'Isn't that what it is to you? If it were anything deeper, you would marry me.'

'Oh! I'm sorry. Give me just a little more time.'

He looked sombre. 'There may not be much time left.'

She put her fingers over his lips. 'Don't say things like that. I can't bear it.'

The British Broadcasting Company's light entertainment, variety, music and drama and religious affairs departments evacuated to Bristol and established themselves in Whiteladies Road, adapting various church halls in Clifton to use as studios.

'It couldn't be better,' said Josh. 'Of course, we'll still take London engagements, but Bristol is sure to be much safer.'

'Are you afraid?' asked Tessa.

'Remembering the terrible pictures in the news reels, Guernica, for instance, the idea of being bombed isn't exactly pleasant.'

Tessa and Josh were enthusiastic studio guests at the first performance of It's That Man Again, or ITMA as it quickly became affectionately known.

'The British are great,' said Josh.

'That's why we're called Great Britain,' Tessa replied.

When not performing, members of the band joined other volunteers, filling sandbags, helping farmers, assisting in the building of shelters which, to their alarm, were now being issued to Bristolians. As Tessa saw girls of all ages and backgrounds joining the women's services, or volunteering as official Land Army workers or fire-fighters, she grew restless.

'I can't just sit around and watch other women doing the important jobs,' she said to Charles.

'Believe me, darling, this phoney war will end and then you'll be needed as never before.'

He was right. More and more men were called to the forces and found themselves away from home, anxious and bored, needing amusement which entertainers were glad to supply. Many were sent to France but there were always more recruits.

Eve heard that David Selby had arrived in England after a hazardous journey through the U-boats which attacked anything which sailed. He attended a small dance at which the Kissing Cousins sang.

'Look, there he is,' said Eve. She gazed at him. 'He hasn't looked this way once. I wish . . . Look at the girl he's dancing with!' She was a beautiful brunette who couldn't have been more than seventeen. 'And look at her frock! A Mainbocher. She must be rich, too. That's the kind of girl he'll marry. A sweet young wealthy innocent.'

'He should speak to us. After all, he does know us.'

'I don't suppose he will, not while he's with her.'

So it surprised Eve when, at the end of the waltz, David left his partner with her friends and came to the stage. 'How are you both?'

'Fine,' said Tessa.

David smiled. 'You certainly sing fine.' He turned to Eve. 'And are you fine, too?'

'Yes, thank you.' She sounded stilted.

'I'm fine.' He smiled. 'We're all fine.' He smiled again and Eve couldn't help returning his smile.

The band played the opening bars of 'In the Still of the Night', a hauntingly lovely number, and David bowed slightly to Eve. 'May I have the pleasure?'

She actually blushed. 'I can't, I have to sing. Besides, you already have a partner.'

'No, she's just a member of my party.'

Tessa gave her a swift jab in the back. 'Don't be an idiot. I'll carry the song.'

Eve climbed down the few steps and was in David's arms. Tessa watched them. Their steps blended perfectly. She put her whole heart into the words. Josh's brows went up when he realised that one of the Kissing Cousins was cavorting instead of performing.

Tessa couldn't keep her eyes off Eve and David. They didn't seem to be talking. Was that a good sign or a bad one? The song ended and he brought Eve back to the stage. Her eyes were shining. Tessa thought it was with happiness, then realised that her cousin's eyes were filled with tears.

On the way home she asked, 'Do you still love David?'

'I do. I don't care that he has no money. I'd live with him anywhere.'

'Then you must love him,' said Tessa.

Eve smiled. 'I suppose I deserve that.'

'Sorry, you don't. That was bitchy of me. I do so want you to be happy.'

'I know you do, darling.'

'He danced with you. That must mean something.'

'He thinks I'm promiscuous.'

'But you're not. Not now. Eve, surely he didn't say so!'

'No. But I was and he knows it. I gave myself to him in France without a second thought. It's not the kind of thing a man forgets.'

Rationing had been introduced at the beginning of 1940 and housewives searched for recipes that would help them still to supply nourishing meals.

Holland and Belgium fell to the Germans, then the most terrible disaster of all hit the British troops when they were driven back across France towards the Channel coast, to a small place called Dunkirk where they lay in sand dunes, waiting, coping with constant assaults and horrific injuries as their compatriots in England banded together, boarding any craft which sailed, to rescue as many men as possible. Over three hundred and thirty-eight thousand were snatched from Dunkirk.

Bristol was told to prepare for refugees and the citizens were amazed when, instead of terrified women and children, they found themselves helping weary British soldiers who left the trains at Temple Meads and Stapleton to be accommodated in barracks or temporary shelters in Eastville Park. They were filthy, hungry and thirsty, their uniforms in tatters, their weapons abandoned. But instead of being greeted as failures, as many of them had feared, they received a hero's welcome. Bristolians got together all the sweets, cigarettes and food they could lay their hands on and donated them to the men, gave them clothes and offered their bathrooms to anyone wishing to wash away the blood and grime of battle.

'You look gorgeous in uniform,' said Tessa.

Charles preened himself ridiculously which made her laugh. 'Do you think I shall turn the heads of the girls?'

There was no doubt at all in Tessa's mind that women

would find him overwhelmingly attractive. And even if they married he might not be impervious to other girls' charms. He had once been ready to play the field.

'You'll turn them all right,' she said.

'Do I detect a note of anxiety?'

'Don't flatter yourself.' Charles looked hurt and she said swiftly, 'I wouldn't want to lose you.'

'Marry me and wear my ring and I swear I'll wear a wedding ring, too, then everyone will know I'm spoken for.'

Tessa didn't laugh. 'You could be sent heaven knows where and I've no idea what will happen to me. There's to be a special entertainments regiment which I shall join. We might not see one another for years.'

Charles put his arms around her and hugged her tight. 'Don't say that.'

'You know it's true. And one of us could easily be killed.'

He held her close and brushed his lips over her hair. 'Belong to me, Tessa, just in case.'

'I do belong to you.'

'Properly. Legally. Give us the right to put one another as next-of-kin on all the damn forms we keep having to sign.'

Tessa was startled. 'Next-of-kin! That's horrible.'

They ended up making love and the question of marriage was shelved once more.

Eve left the theatre after a rehearsal and stopped abruptly. David was waiting at the stage door, holding flowers.

She smiled tremulously at him.

'Hello, Eve.' He handed her the posy. 'Will you have supper with me?'

He was in naval uniform and looked unbearably handsome. 'I should like that very much,' she said.

He seated her in a small open sports car and drove her, wrapped securely in tartan car rugs, to a hotel where he had already booked a table for two.

'Sure of me, weren't you?' she said. She attempted to use her old teasing manner, but the words emerged shakily.

'Not at all.'

'Or did you have another woman in mind if I'd said no?' Why couldn't she stop this stupid badinage?

'No other woman,' said David.

'What would you have done with the second place?'

'It would have remained empty.'

'Wouldn't you have felt just a little embarrassed? The waiters would have guessed you'd been turned down.'

'It matters nothing to me what the waiters think.'

'No, of course not.' She felt as gauche as a bashful school girl. 'Sorry.' Now she was apologising.

'Are you feeling unwell?'

'No, I'm pretty tough. Why?'

'You look tired out.'

'That's not very flattering.'

'I wasn't trying to flatter you.'

'Oh.'

'I think people in general look tired. I find war the most damnably exhausting time I've ever known because it's mostly waiting around for something to happen. Doing nothing is so boring. Thank heaven I shall soon be joining my ship.'

Her heart began to pound. 'Where are you going? The U-boats are everywhere.'

'Hush. Remember, walls have ears.'

'I'll pray for your safe homecoming.'

His eyebrows went up. 'You and prayer?'

'Please, don't make fun of me. I don't know anything about religion really, but I live with my cousins, Tessa and her family, and they've taught me a lot. I do know that if I couldn't pray sometimes I'd go crazy.' She couldn't say any more for the lump in her throat.

David's hand went out to cover hers briefly. 'You've changed since we first met.'

'War has a way of bringing us down to basics, doesn't it?'

582

'Will you be joining one of the women's services, or working on munitions, or maybe the land?'

'Josh says we must wait until we're recruited into an entertainments regiment. He says there will be a great need for us.'

'He's right. It could be as dangerous for you as for a fighting man. You might be sent into war zones. Are you ready for that?'

'I think so.'

'You're an American. No one would blame you if you chose to go home.'

'I prefer to stay in England.'

'Do you?' David smiled. 'You're brave. Quite a few British people have fled to the States.'

'I'll take my chances here.'

They ate the economic meal advised for war-time restaurants, talking in a desultory fashion. Sitting opposite him, glancing at him, noting the way a lock of his hair defied the military cut and tended to fall forward so that he brushed it back impatiently, watching him eat the spartan fare with keen enjoyment, Eve knew that her love for him was too strong to die. She began to wish she hadn't accepted his invitation. How would she bear to be separated from him, not having the right to know if anything happened to him?

After the meal he saw her to the car and they sat there side by side. 'It's a lovely night. I'm sorry I don't have enough petrol to take you for a drive. The rationing is strict.'

'And you obey the rules?'

His hands rested lightly on the steering wheel. 'Don't you?'

'Yes, and I mean to go on obeying them.'

'Good girl.'

He started the engine and they drove to the Morlands' lane. He stopped and looked up at the small cottage. 'I can't imagine you living in such a tiny place. How many are there?'

'Six.'

'Good lord. Where do you sleep?'

'My Cousin Walter has built a delightful extension for me.'

'I say, that's extremely thoughtful of him.'

'Yes. They are wonderful people. They give me friendship and understanding and affection.'

'There's no light anywhere in the cottage. That seems to typify the war.'

'Cousin Walter was a carpenter. He's made boards to fit all the windows. He's joined a demolition squad. If there are air raids he will be rescuing people, pulling down unsafe places and shoring up damaged walls.'

'That could get grisly.'

'But Bristol won't be bombed. Everybody says so. Aeroplanes could never reach this far.'

'They've issued shelters.'

'You think they will get here, don't you?' David didn't answer and Eve said reluctantly, 'I must go in. Cousin Lily often stays awake listening for us.'

'Where's Tessa tonight?'

'With Charles Ware, I expect. He wants to marry her. Oh dear, forget I said that, please. It's none of my business.'

'It's already forgotten. Come along, Eve, I'll walk you to your door.'

When he said goodnight he kissed her lightly. She stood behind the door, listening to his footsteps as they died away.

# Chapter Twenty-Six

When Tessa arrived home late Eve was in her dressing gown sitting by the warm range, drinking tea. 'Did you have a good time?' Eve asked.

'I always do with Charles. Why are you still up?'

'I've been out with David. He was waiting for me. With flowers.'

'Eve, that's lovely. What happened?'

'He took me to dinner and we talked.'

'That's all?'

'That's all.'

'He likes you, doesn't he?'

'Because he took me to dinner? Perhaps. Liking isn't enough.'

Tessa held out her hands to the fire. 'I hate to hear you so downcast.'

'Sorry. It's all my own fault. Oh, Tessa, I've been such a fool.'

Tessa poured herself a cup of tea from the metal pot on the hob. It was strong and dark. 'We all make mistakes. Ugh. This tea is horrible!'

'I'll make some more.' But Eve stayed where she was, slumped in her chair. 'My mistakes have been bigger than most.'

'It wasn't your fault.'

'Maybe not. Not all of it, anyway, but we have to take responsibility for the way we run our lives. I'll never know what I might have been.'

'Do you feel like talking to me about anything?'

'No, thank you. Tessa, you're a dear, but I'll go to bed

and so should you. We've a rehearsal early tomorrow.'

Tessa paused at the kitchen door. 'I want to see you happy, Eve.'

'I know. I wish I had some good news for you, but I won't whine. Whatever happens now, I'll do my best.'

The rehearsal went well, except that Eve lost her place a couple of times.

'Pull yourself together, girl,' yelled Josh. 'We've only booked another fifteen minutes here.'

She pushed all thoughts of David away so successfully that she felt dazed when she met him outside.

'Was the rehearsal tough?' he asked.

'No. Josh is a good boss.'

'Why do you look so . . . ?'

'I was surprised to see you.'

'That's obvious. Can I take you to lunch?'

Eve glanced at the tramway office clock. 'It's only ten-thirty.'

'So it is. Coffee, then?'

They drank coffee and ate ring doughnuts in Forte's café on Park Street, laughing because their fingers got sticky with sugar.

'I haven't done this for years,' said David. 'I'm expecting Nanny to swoop at any moment with a damp flannel.'

They strolled up the hill and made their way to Brandon Hill where they sat and stared out over Bristol.

'She's so lovely,' said David. 'I couldn't bear to think of bombs raining down on her.'

'It won't happen,' said Eve. 'It mustn't.'

'Eve, I have to leave soon. I've been posted.'

'Where?'

'Walls have ears,' he reminded her.

'For God's sake,' she cried passionately, 'tell me. There aren't any walls here and I would never do anything to bring danger on you.'

'I shall be on board a ship protecting convoys of merchant shipping.'

'That's terribly dangerous! The U-boats are everywhere.'

'I must take my chances. Like you, Eve.' Her name sounded sweet on his lips. 'I would like to know that you'll think of me when I'm away.'

'I told you I'd pray for you.'

'Yes, so you did.'

'Is there something more I can do? Just ask. Anything.'

He was silent for a while then said, 'I've never forgotten our love-making.'

'Don't! Oh, don't!'

'Would you prefer me to forget?' She couldn't answer and he said, 'I want to remember.'

'Do you? Why? You've never bothered with me since. I thought . . .'

'Yes?'

She said in low tones, 'I thought you rather despised me for being so easy.'

'I was younger and rather priggish. In those days I saw women as two kinds, pure and virginal or promiscuous.'

'I see.' A tight band seemed to be constricting Eve's chest. She breathed deeply, trying to free herself from pain. She gasped out her words, 'I was driven by . . . I was very unhappy. I thought I could find something . . . I wanted love . . .'

'Stop, Eve, don't torture yourself.'

She looked over the city to the blue hills beyond. Torture herself? She did that merely by sitting here with the man she loved with all her being.

'Eve, will you write to me?' He was anxious.

'You really want me to?'

'Yes. Tell me what's happening to you. I'd like to know how you're getting on.'

'Will you write back?'

'Definitely.'

Again they fell silent and David took Eve's hand and lifted it to his cheek. 'I'm very fond of you.'

He. blood ran hot; tumultuous feelings threatened to overcome her. 'And I of you.'

'More than fond, perhaps?' He slid an arm about her waist. 'We began badly, but I've never forgotten you. I had hoped there was more to you than one could see on the surface. Since meeting you again, I know that there is.'

'David,' she breathed.

He released her hand but only to put his arms round her. Their kiss was softly affectionate. Such gentleness was almost more than her flesh could endure. Did he realise that? More than once she had given him proof of her ardent nature. His kiss deepened. For an instant she held back before her body began to clamour for more. When they broke apart, Eve wondered if she had revealed too much of herself.

'Such an ardent, warm woman,' he murmured. 'I'll think of you every day and night while I'm away. Will you wait for me?'

'Wait for you?'

He smiled. 'Will you be my girl? Will you send me photos to pin over my berth?'

'Oh, yes! I'll deluge you with photos and I'll wait for you for ever.'

'Let's hope it won't be that long.'

He took her home and they embraced again. She watched his car disappear round a bend in the road.

Mrs Morland said to Eve, 'You look pleased with yourself, young lady.'

'I am! Oh, Cousin Lily, such a wonderful thing has happened. David has asked me to wait for him.'

Mum went straight to the point. 'Have you got a ring?'

When Eve shook her head Lily was disappointed. In her view a ring was an absolute necessity to confirm declared honourable intentions. 'No ring?'

'No, but I made my promise.'

'Are you satisfied with that?'

'For the moment.' To force her relationship with David would be like trying to bring a rare plant into flower too soon.

Josh and His Melody Men were appearing for one night in the Princes Theatre.

'Dad and me will be there,' said Mum. 'Josh sent us tickets.'

'I'm sure you'll enjoy the show,' said Tessa.

'I hope there won't be any smutty comedians?'

'Sorry, I can't guarantee anything. We're filling in for a band that couldn't turn up.'

There were smutty jokes. 'Do you think they're still in the audience?' asked Eve.

'I expect so. Mum wants to see us and when she sets her mind on something it's impossible to stop her.'

The band closed the first half and during the interval Mum and Dad came back-stage to the dressing-room.

'We enjoyed the singing, didn't we, Walter?'

'We did,' agreed Dad.

'We thought some of the jokes were not fit for the ears of decent Christians, but that's not your fault.' Mum looked around. 'I've never been in a dressing room before. It's not very big.' Her eyes went to the piles of stick make-up. 'That's the stuff you put on your faces, isn't it? I don't see the need. You're both pretty enough.'

'We'd look washed out under the lights without it,' said Eve.

Mum got up. 'You know your own business best. We're off home now.'

'Did you like our act?' asked Tessa.

'You're lovely singers, both of you. I was very proud.'

'Won't you stay for the second half?' suggested Eve. 'We're on again and there are some great acts. One of them's a belly dancer,' she added mischievously. 'She can twist and turn and . . .'

'No, thank you,' said Mum firmly. Tessa thought Dad looked a little disappointed.

After Walter and Lily had left Eve said, 'They're so sweet. It was a happy day for me when my parents insisted on my being at Great-grandmother Brook's funeral. I wonder if she's looking down on us feeling pleased?'

'I couldn't say,' said Tessa, 'not having known her. What do you think?'

'Paul said she was quite a jolly old girl.'

Then the call boy came round and banged on their door. 'Five minutes, ladies.'

Tessa and Eve had agreed to open the second half, singing while a bevy of long-legged beauties danced. They would sing again with Josh and His Melody Men before the last spot which was reserved for a famous comedian. As they hurried to their places before the curtain rose, Tessa said, 'Perhaps it's just as well Mum and Dad have gone home. He's one of the bluest of blue jokers.'

When they were back in their dressing room at the end of the show the theatre manager knocked and came in. He looked sombre.

Eve said, 'What's up? Has someone run off with the takings?'

'I'm afraid I've got some rather bad news for you, Tessa. There's been an accident.'

Her mind went instantly to Charles and she waited in desperate fear for the next words. 'Your parents have been in a car crash. They're both in the Infirmary.'

Tessa stared at him uncomprehendingly. 'Mum and Dad? They were here.'

'I know. I'm really sorry, Tessa. Damned black-out!'

'Eve—?' said Tessa, numb with shock.

'Get changed quickly and we'll go to the Infirmary. Is there any news about their condition?' she asked the manager.

He shook his head. 'Mrs Morland gave them details of where to contact Tessa so she sounds all right. I don't know about Mr Morland.'

Eve drove the short distance between the Hippodrome and the Bristol Infirmary.

They went straight to casualty to learn that Lily had been taken to a ward with heavy bruising and shock. 'Mr Morland,' said the Sister in charge, 'is in the operating theatre.'

Tessa sat down, white-faced and shaking, and Eve felt sick.

'How bad is he?' asked Tessa.

'He has sustained a head injury. I'm afraid I have to warn you he's very poorly, but the doctors are doing their utmost to help him.'

'Oh, my God!' Her strength drained out of her.

Eve sat beside her and put her arms round her.

'I'll send you some tea,' said the Sister.

At Eve's persuasion, Tessa drank hers without tasting it. Soon afterwards Susan and Joseph arrived.

Joseph said, 'We must pray for Dad.'

Tessa nodded.

The Sister appeared. 'Your mother is asking for you. In the circumstances we can allow you to visit her one at a time for just a few minutes. Don't forget that the rest of the patients are sleeping.'

One by one Tessa, Joseph and Susan crept to Mrs Morland's bedside. Her face was heavily bruised, as were her legs, she said, and she had badly strained her arm. 'Pray for him,' she said to Tessa as she kissed her.

'We have. We will,' Tessa assured her.

'Keep on praying. Where's our Eve?'

'Downstairs,' said Tessa.

'I want to see our Eve,' said Mum.

'Hush now, Mrs Morland,' said the Sister. 'Eve is not your daughter. You need rest and quiet.'

'I want to see Eve,' sobbed Mum, giving way to this lesser emotion. 'She's like a daughter to me.'

Eve was allowed to see her and, like Susan, returned weeping.

The night seemed very long. Tessa wanted a cigarette, but smoking was not permitted and she was afraid to go outside in case her father wanted her. 'If only they hadn't come to see us,' she said. 'Driving in the black-out is awful and they don't really like that kind of show. They just wanted to support us.'

'I know,' said Eve.

For once Joseph didn't pontificate on the sins of theatre life.

The Sister returned. 'Mr Morland's out of the theatre.

He's still very poorly, but the doctors are hopeful. If I were you I should go home. He won't regain consciousness for some time. Are you on the telephone? No? Well, you may call us any time after seven o'clock.'

'What if something – goes wrong before then?' asked Tessa.

'In a case like this we telephone the local police station and they send someone to inform you.'

'That all takes time!' cried Susan.

'I know, but it's the best we can do.' The Sister was harassed. Accidents were increasing daily. She looked at the anxious young faces and went on gently, 'He'll need you to be strong and your poor mother certainly needs your full support. She has no serious injuries but her bruises will take a long time to heal and she'll suffer a lot of pain. I've given her a sleeping draught and she won't wake until the morning. For the next few days you may visit out of hours.'

The girls were stunned by worry and weariness and Joseph took charge. 'We must do as we're told. Let's go home.'

Eve drove. On the way Susan spoke once. 'We've all been worrying about air raids and never given a thought to other kinds of danger. You never think something like this will happen to you, do you?' In the kitchen she stirred the fire which had been banked by Mum, another cause for tears to flow as she put the kettle on.

'I'll get out the biscuit tin,' said Eve automatically.

Tessa reached down the cups and saucers. Joseph fetched the milk and sugar from the pantry.

The four of them sat drinking tea, ignoring the biscuits.

Susan got up. 'I must go to bed. I won't sleep, but I have to go to work tomorrow. Dad wouldn't let anything stop him and I want him to be proud of me when he comes home.'

'He will be,' said Tessa. 'How about you, Eve? I'll fill your hot water bottle. You look cold.'

Joseph said goodnight and went upstairs and Tessa

carried the bottle to Eve's room. She was undressed, her clothes lying on the floor as in the old days, and she was weeping, huge tears rolling silently down her face. 'Tessa, I don't know how to bear it. I've lost one father. I can't bear to lose another.'

Tessa smoothed her hair from her forehead. 'Send him get well thoughts.'

Eve hugged the bottle. 'Of course I will. You shouldn't sit here, Tessa. It's too cold.'

'I don't like to leave you. You look quite ill.'

'I feel it. I'm sorry to be a burden. He's your father, not mine, but he's been so good to me—'

Her tears fell again and Tessa kicked off her shoes, pulled back the covers and climbed into her cousin's bed, putting her arms round her. 'You've suffered too much.'

'I've made you suffer, too.'

'All that's over now.'

Eve said, 'I've dropped my clothes on the floor. I'll pick them up. You're not to touch them.'

'What makes you think I meant to?' Eve managed a smile and Tessa said, 'Actually, I'm rather glad to find you're still less than perfect. There are times when I actually miss the old Eve.'

'You've always followed me round tidying up my messes. Almost always. I got out of the one in Hollywood myself, but that was only because Aunt Betsy died.'

'You love Mum and Dad a lot.'

'I do. Oh, I do, far more than I could ever love my own parents. Dad will get better, won't he, Tessa?'

'Of course. He acts as if he's the quietest man alive, but he's as stubborn as a mule.'

Eve smiled again. She didn't seem to realise she had just called Cousin Walter 'Dad'.

Tessa said, 'You're calmer now. I'll leave you to sleep.'

She kissed Eve who snuggled beneath the bed clothes. 'You'll wake me if you hear anything?'

'I promise.'

Tessa gave the dog some milk. He was old and slow and slept a lot but tonight he was restless, missing his life-time companions. 'They'll be back,' murmured Tessa, scratching his neck.

She locked up, made up the range, turned off the lights and went to bed, but not to sleep. She was trying to come to terms with a truth that had manifested itself. Susan was right. No one expected tragedy to strike them. Now Dad was lying helpless, critically ill, and for the first time she had a powerful sense of her own mortality. How foolish she was, when all her life she had heard the inevitable fact of death thundered at her from pulpits. None of it had made the sense it made now.

And during the long night she had to face another startling fact. When she had heard the word 'accident' it had been Charles who had sprung first to her mind. She knew, without a shadow of doubt, that she loved him with no reservations.

In the morning, Eve slept on and Tessa got breakfast and walked the dog. Bodily, she felt she was a zombie, but her head was spinning from lack of sleep. She had been dressed since five and on the dot of seven was in the nearest phone box calling the Infirmary. She returned to the cottage, able to tell the others that Mum was improving. There was no change in Dad. 'We can all go to the hospital today. Susan, you in your lunch hour. Joseph, perhaps you could manage this morning? Eve and I will take the evening.'

Susan went to work and Joseph departed on a round of sick visits.

She left a note propped on Eve's dressing table and went back to the phone box, vowing that she'd have one installed as soon as possible, war or no war.

Josh answered her ring and expressed his sympathy. 'Take off all the time you want,' he said.

'There's a broadcast tomorrow,' said Tessa. 'We'll be there.'

'Give your mother my warmest wishes and hopes for Mr Morland's quick recovery.'

* * *

Walter Morland remained unconscious for almost a week. Mum was discharged after three days but spent most of her time by his bedside. They had put him in a side ward. Tessa went in three times a day and sat on the other side of her father's bed, talking to him. The doctor assured them that he might be able to hear. When he finally opened his eyes, Lily, Tessa and Eve were there watching together. They waited in desperate anxiety to see if he recognised them. They had been warned that his brain might be irreversibly damaged and his memory gone. He smiled a little. 'You're all here? No, where are Joseph and Susan?'

He closed his eyes and Eve hurried to fetch the Sister who called a doctor to examine him. When next she saw them in the waiting room, she said, 'He's doing fine. A wonderful recovery.' The three women laughed and wept together.


Joseph announced that he had volunteered for the army, requesting that he should be given non-combatant duties. In view of his background this was agreed. Susan signed on with the Civil Nursing Reserve.

'But you've never been a nurse,' said Eve.

'I'm to drive an ambulance.'

'Can you drive?' asked Tessa.

'Of course. I learnt from one of my boy friends. We are doing the right thing, aren't we, Tessa? In my enthusiasm I didn't stop to think. What if Mum needs one of us to help her with Dad?'

'You're doing the right thing,' said Tessa. Fear invaded her as she thought of her young brother and sister making ready to go where the fighting would be thickest. 'I'll stay with Mum as long as I can.'

'So will I,' said Eve.

'When he's well,' said Tessa, 'we shall join ENSA. Basil Dean has already organised lots of shows. It's supposed to recruit only those above the age for national service, but they'll need some tough young ones for entertaining overseas.'

'What makes you think we shall fight overseas?' asked

Joseph. 'We've been driven back from France.'

'Of course we shall,' cried Susan. 'We'll never allow anyone to invade Britain!'

Charles had been attentive but undemanding during the terrible week following the accident. When Dad regained consciousness he and Tessa celebrated with champagne in their usual restaurant.

As they toasted Walter's continuing recovery, Charles said, 'I wonder how soon this will disappear?'

'Champagne? Is it going to?'

'It'll be scarce, possibly impossible to buy. So will everything else that enhances life. Alcohol, tobacco, chocolates, foreign fruit.'

'How frightful,' said Tessa in mock dismay. 'All those exotic necessary things.'

'Mock if you will, woman. How will you feel if you can't have a smoke?'

'I don't know. Ghastly, I suppose. Charles, surely, it won't get that bad?'

'Well, I do have some excellent wines stored in my cellars. No cigarettes, though. Rationing is bound to become more severe and life will get damned uncomfortable.'

'How do you know so much?' she teased.

'I just know. It's been easy enough to read the signs over the past few years. Comedians may make all the fun they like of Hitler, but his war machine is superb, his armies better equipped and better trained than ours, his air power almost invincible, his navy supreme, thanks to the U-boats. It's going to be a devil of a job to beat him.'

'You don't think we'll lose?'

'Of course not. What Britisher could think that?'

'That's a relief.'

Charles said something but Tessa wasn't listening. 'You're not paying attention,' he complained.

She drew a deep breath. 'I love you,' she said with simple directness. 'Will you marry me?' Charles stared at her. 'Darling,' said Tessa tremulously, 'close your mouth.'

'Did my ears deceive me?' he said in his best music hall voice.

'I hope not.'

'You proposed to me?'

'Yes.'

'Well, it is a Leap Year!'

'Certainly is!' Why didn't he touch her? Why didn't he say something serious? Something loving?

'This is far too public a place for such an earth-shaking situation,' he declared, standing up and calling the waiter.

Outside in the inky blackness he said, 'I tipped him far too much. That's what happens when you give me shocks. I could swear you proposed to me.'

Tessa said hesitantly, 'You seem to be taking it as a joke.'

'No damn fear! It's no joke to me. Come here.' He took her in his arms and held her close. 'Sometimes,' he murmured, 'the black-out is a positive advantage.' He kissed her. 'Now say those words again.'

'Which ones?'

'Now *you're* being frivolous.'

'Sorry. I want to marry you. I've been such a fool. A coward, really, afraid to take a step into the future. I love you, Charles, far too much to let you go without first marrying you.'

'My dearest love.' His lips found hers again in a kiss which spread warmth through her body.

'Shall we go to your place?' she whispered.

'Hussy.'

They were married the following week. Joseph pushed Dad in a wheelchair down the aisle by Tessa's side. A friend of Charles' in officer's uniform was best man and Susan and Eve were bridesmaids. Mum did the weeping.

The reception was small, wartime restrictions and Dad's weakness allowed for nothing else, but Tessa hardly noticed. She was happier than she had ever been.

Speeches were made, toasts drunk, then Josh went to the piano in a corner of the small hotel room. 'As a grand finale to these happy proceedings,' he announced,

'Tessa will sing something she's written especially for Charles. There will be no break in her voice because this is a happy one.'

Tessa took her place by the piano, Josh struck the opening chords, and she went into her song, her eyes on Charles.

Every second of every minute of every hour of
    every day,
I'll think of you,
Every day of every week of every month of every year,
I'll long for you,
As lovers do.
No pain, no sadness, no regrets can touch me now.
I love you, dear, as you love me.
We've made our vow.
Like other lovers we must part,
I'll live my dreams within my heart,
And wait for peace, my dear,
And love's release.

There was applause which she scarcely noticed. All she could see was her husband's face expressing the most exquisite pleasure. They left soon afterwards. Charles opened his front door and carried her romantically across the threshold and the first night of their marriage was spent making love with only short intervals for sleep.

Tessa had thought that nothing could surpass her delight in love-making but she had been wrong. Belonging to Charles completely enhanced it.

'I can never get enough of you,' he said.

'I know, my darling. It's going to be so inconvenient. How will we ever find time to work?'

'We'll have to do it in short bursts.'

'Bawdy again. You know I disapprove of bawdiness.'

'I meant work in short bursts, woman.'

They went on making silly, inconsequential jokes, pushing aside the knowledge that their separation could be long and would certainly be hazardous.

Tessa said, 'How will I bear to be apart from you?'

'I know how you feel, but we shall manage as others must.' Charles raised himself on one elbow and his fingers stroked the length of her body. 'You're incredibly beautiful. And talented, clever, amusing, delicious to make love to . . . I never believed I'd get this lucky.'

'I know,' said Tessa, laughing softly, thrusting aside the dark gloom which threatened to intrude upon their final days together.

He shook her gently. 'I must stop these extravagant compliments or I'll make you vain.'

She put her arms around his neck. 'I love you, Charles. More than I believed it possible to love anyone. Promise me we shall be together here, in this house, after the war? Swear that nothing will stop us. Hold me tight and we'll both swear. We'll do our duty in the war, but afterwards nothing and no one will keep us apart.'

'Nothing and no one,' he promised.

# Ragtime Girl

## Elizabeth Warne

### A rags-to-riches saga in the bestselling tradition of *A Woman of Substance*

As a child Laura Blackford was sent to live with her Granma, for her own family, with Mum either pregnant or nursing, could not afford to keep her. For twelve years she has lived with her strict, religious Granma, whose acid tongue is as fierce as the cane she uses to beat obedience into her wilful granddaughter. At seventeen, apprenticed to Gregory's Department Store in Bristol, the highlight of Laura's week is her visit to a neighbour, Edith Morton, to learn the art of millinery.

Laura's world is shattered when, accused of stealing an important customer from Gregory's, she is dismissed – without references. The only job she finds is tobacco stripping. But the dreary, mind-numbing work roughens her hands until she cannot find relief even on her evenings with Edith, for the needles torture her sore hands. She refuses to give in and keeps her mind off the pain by thinking of the wonderful hats she is determined, one day, to create.

At last rebelling against her Granma and fighting impossible odds, Laura stakes everything and opens a hat shop. Though her business is a triumphant success and she finds wealth beyond her dreams, she falls first into an unhappy affair and then into a marriage that exposes herself and her family to public agony and violence before she finds the love she has always craved.

**FICTION/SAGA   0 7472 3396 9**

*More Compelling Fiction from Headline:*

# WILD SILK

## Elizabeth Warne

*The new rags-to-riches saga from the author of*
*RAGTIME GIRL*

Adela Danby is the pampered, unworldly daughter of a
wealthy Bristol family. When she discovers she is
pregnant after the death of her fiancé of pneumonia
caught in the trenches at the end of World War I her
horrified parents offer her a choice: marriage to a man
of their choosing or an operation in a discreet London
clinic. Unhappy and confused, determined not to be rid
of her baby or be sold off to the highest bidder, she runs
away from home and ends up, penniless, in the slums of
Bristol — and a life for which she has never been
prepared.

The only thing that keeps Adela and her baby from
destitution is her skill with the needle and she takes in
repairs and dressmaking commissions from the
surrounding close-knit community. Gradually she makes
friends and is accepted by those around her — though
she can never truly be one of them they admire her
pluck and determination. From humble beginnings with
a market barrow she slowly builds up her business as an
interior designer and rises to success and fortune. But
her desire for emotional fulfilment is not so easily
satisfied, and she is torn between convention and
passion, until she finds love where she least expects it.

'Ms Warne has conjured up a vivid creature in Adela, and
her riches to rags to riches story is enhanced by her gritty
realism that makes her trials and tribulations – and her
successes and passions – all the more believable' *Prima*

Also by Elizabeth Warne from Headline
**RAGTIME GIRL**

**FICTION/SAGA   0 7472 3643 7**

# A selection of bestsellers from Headline

| | | | |
|---|---|---|---|
| THE LADYKILLER | Martina Cole | £5.99 | ☐ |
| JESSICA'S GIRL | Josephine Cox | £5.99 | ☐ |
| NICE GIRLS | Claudia Crawford | £4.99 | ☐ |
| HER HUNGRY HEART | Roberta Latow | £5.99 | ☐ |
| FLOOD WATER | Peter Ling | £4.99 | ☐ |
| THE OTHER MOTHER | Seth Margolis | £4.99 | ☐ |
| ACT OF PASSION | Rosalind Miles | £4.99 | ☐ |
| A NEST OF SINGING BIRDS | Elizabeth Murphy | £5.99 | ☐ |
| THE COCKNEY GIRL | Gilda O'Neill | £4.99 | ☐ |
| FORBIDDEN FEELINGS | Una-Mary Parker | £5.99 | ☐ |
| OUR STREET | Victor Pemberton | £5.99 | ☐ |
| GREEN GROW THE RUSHES | Harriet Smart | £5.99 | ☐ |
| BLUE DRESS GIRL | E V Thompson | £5.99 | ☐ |
| DAYDREAMS | Elizabeth Walker | £5.99 | ☐ |

*All Headline books are available at your local bookshop or newsagent, or can be ordered direct from the publisher. Just tick the titles you want and fill in the form below. Prices and availability subject to change without notice.*

Headline Book Publishing PLC, Cash Sales Department, Bookpoint, 39 Milton Park, Abingdon, OXON, OX14 4TD, UK. If you have a credit card you may order by telephone – 0235 831700.

Please enclose a cheque or postal order made payable to Bookpoint Ltd to the value of the cover price and allow the following for postage and packing:
UK & BFPO: £1.00 for the first book, 50p for the second book and 30p for each additional book ordered up to a maximum charge of £3.00.
OVERSEAS & EIRE: £2.00 for the first book, £1.00 for the second book and 50p for each additional book.

Name ..................................................................................................

Address ..............................................................................................

...........................................................................................................

...........................................................................................................

If you would prefer to pay by credit card, please complete:
Please debit my Visa/Access/Diner's Card/American Express (delete as applicable) card no:

| | | | | | | | | | | | | | | | | | |
|---|---|---|---|---|---|---|---|---|---|---|---|---|---|---|---|---|---|

Signature ...................................................... Expiry Date .........